Praise for
THE RISING TIDE

"The wonderful first volume of a planned trilogy . . . Shaara evokes the agony of desert warfare and the utter chaos of an airborne assault . . . [A] sprawling, masterful opening act."
—*Publishers Weekly* (starred review)

"Mr. Shaara's research is finely woven into his narrative. . . . [He] can certainly bring a scene to life— whether he is inventing it from his own head or transforming a diplomat's memoir. . . . Mr. Shaara provides a nonfiction introduction to *The Rising Tide* that should be required for every middle-school American history class. It is far better in its brief account of the greatest conflict of the twentieth century than most of today's textbooks. . . . Mr. Shaara is apparently giving the people what they want—and what they need."
—*The Wall Street Journal*

"[A] sprawling tale thoroughly researched and told with meticulous detail that includes real-life characters such as Dwight Eisenhower, Omar Bradley, George Patton and the infamous "Desert Fox" of the German Army, Erwin Rommel. All that's missing is the smell of gunpowder."
—MSNBC.com

THE RISING TIDE

THE
RISING TIDE

A NOVEL OF WORLD WAR II

JEFF SHAARA

BALLANTINE BOOKS • NEW YORK

2008 Ballantine Books Premium Mass Market Edition

Published in the United States by Ballantine Books, an imprint of The Random House Publishing Group, a division of Random House, Inc., New York.

BALLANTINE and the colophon are registered trademarks of Random House, Inc.

Originally published in hardcover in the United States by Ballantine Books, an imprint of The Random House Publishing Group, a division of Random House, Inc., in 2006.

This book contains an excerpt from *The Steel Wave* by Jeff Shaara. This excerpt has been set for this edition and may not reflect the final content of the published books.

ISBN 978-0-345-46137-7

Printed in the United States of America

www.ballantinebooks.com

OPM   19 18 17 16 15 14 13 12

To
Colonel Jesse Wiggins
USAF (RET.)

CONTENTS

TO THE READER

When I began to think about writing a series of novels dealing with the Second World War, one obvious question came to mind. What could I possibly add that hasn't already been written about so many times before? I felt I knew much about the history of the war, certainly the high points: Pearl Harbor, D-Day, the Holocaust. I knew who Patton was, and Rommel, Eisenhower, Hitler, Mussolini, and Churchill. I've seen films about fictitious characters with names like Mr. Roberts and Private Ryan, that to some are as familiar as the figures in our high school textbooks. But when I began digging into the research, the diaries and memoirs, the personal lives of the characters I hoped to use in this story, I found out that I didn't know nearly as much as I thought I did. What I also found was a *story*.

None of my books are comprehensive accounts of a historical event, the detailed, blow-by-blow fact upon fact that you'll find in a textbook. My goal is to find a few voices, and to tell their story through their eyes, to put you in the same room with some of the most important and fascinating characters in our history. In this kind of story, there must be a variety of characters, different perspectives, different experiences. I focus not only on the famous, those men who changed history, but also the unknown, whose experiences mirrored the experiences of thousands, or hundreds of thousands, just like them. The events are real, the history is accurate, the conversations are often from recorded memories. But this is a novel by definition because I take you into the characters' minds, using dialogue and action to tell a story, as they might have told it themselves.

The Rising Tide covers the war in North Africa from spring 1942 to its conclusion in 1943, and then, the Allied invasion of Sicily and Italy, through the beginning of 1944. It is the first book of a trilogy that will take you to the end of the war in Europe. I am well aware that as the time line of this book unfolds, an extraordinary drama has been unfolding throughout Western Europe, another in Russia, another on (and beneath) the Atlantic Ocean, and another across the Pacific. Each of those stories has as much drama, sacrifice, and heroism as this one. But those are stories that would not fit here. To those who feel that their own history or that of their ancestors has been ignored, I apologize. The war in the Pacific, certainly, is an epic story that I would one day like to tell.

This story follows several primary characters, including Dwight D. Eisenhower and Erwin Rommel, and two who are far more obscure, a tank gunner, Private Jack Logan, and a paratrooper, Sergeant Jesse Adams. Included also are the voices of several well-known historical figures whose pivotal roles make them essential to the story, including Bernard Montgomery, George Patton, Mark Wayne Clark, and Albert Kesselring. Not all are heroes, not all are "good guys." But they are all important.

One note about the language in this book. Occasionally I receive somewhat hostile letters condemning my use of even mild profanity. This amazes me, since with rare exceptions I do not go beyond the bounds of what any child might hear on prime-time television. I am no prude, but if I chose to make the dialogue in my novels as graphic as it certainly was, it would likely make *me* blush. Some of our most illustrious historical figures were famously profane, but I have always believed that if I cannot tell you their story without bombarding you with stark profanity, then I'm not doing my job. But, four-letter words serve a purpose. They reveal character and they illustrate and emphasize emotions. I am aware, and extremely gratified, that young people read my books, and I do not believe that any boundary has been crossed that makes these stories inappropriate for young readers. And believe me, when you're writing from the point of view of George Patton, or a twenty-year-old paratroop sergeant, a great many boundaries *could* have been crossed. The most profane words in this book are direct quotes, and their inclusion is, I believe, entirely appropriate.

You may disagree with my portrayal of certain historical

figures. This is, after all, my interpretation of who these people were, and how they responded to events around them. However, I take few liberties with characters whose thoughts and actions are well documented. In all of my books, I take pride in historical accuracy. To portray these events and these characters any other way would be a gross disservice to the legacies of these extraordinary men.

Ultimately, this is a story about people not so very different from us, though their experiences are quite different indeed. Some would describe our world today as an endless source of bad news: war and bloodshed, horror and strife, bombings and chaos and civil war. But imagine a world where the ongoing event filling our daily news reports ultimately claims the lives of *fifty million* people. It is not my place to question or pass judgment as to whether the Second World War was, as some have described it, *the last good war,* or whether it should have been fought at all; whether it could have been avoided, whether mistakes were made on all sides, or whether there are lessons we should learn from this human catastrophe . . . these are questions for historians and political scientists. My goal here is to offer you a good story. I hope you find it so.

JEFF SHAARA
October 2006

RESEARCH SOURCES

The question I receive most is what are my sources for the characterizations, dialogue, and historical events in my stories. In this case, I made considerable use of the memoirs, diaries, collections of letters, and assorted documents from the following historical figures, among many others:

Field Marshal Sir Harold Alexander, BEF
Field Marshal Claude Auchinleck, BEF
General of the Army Omar Bradley, USA
Captain Harry Butcher, USNR
Prime Minister Winston Churchill
General Mark W. Clark, USA
Admiral Lord Andrew B. Cunningham, BRN
President Dwight D. Eisenhower
Lieutenant General James M. Gavin, USA
Field Marshal Albert Kesselring, Deutsche
    Wehrmacht
Historian Robert Leckie
Journalist and historian Sir Basil Liddell-Hart
Colonel Hans von Luck, Deutsches Afrika Korps
Field Marshal Bernard Law Montgomery, BEF
Journalist Alan Moorehead
General George S. Patton, USA
Journalist Ernie Pyle
General Matthew Ridgway, USA
Field Marshal Erwin Rommel, Deutsche Wehrmacht
Major Heinz Schmidt, Deutsches Afrika Korps
General Siegfried Westphal, Deutsche Wehrmacht
Lieutenant General William P. Yarborough, USA

In addition, I wish to heartily thank the following, whose generous assistance in providing research material for this book is most appreciated:

Colonel Keith Gibson—Lexington, Virginia
Ms. Phoebe Hunter—Missoula, Montana
Bruce and Linda Novak—Needham, Massachusetts
Ms. Kay Whitlock—Missoula, Montana
The American Armored Foundation Tank Museum—
   Danville, Virginia

LIST OF MAPS

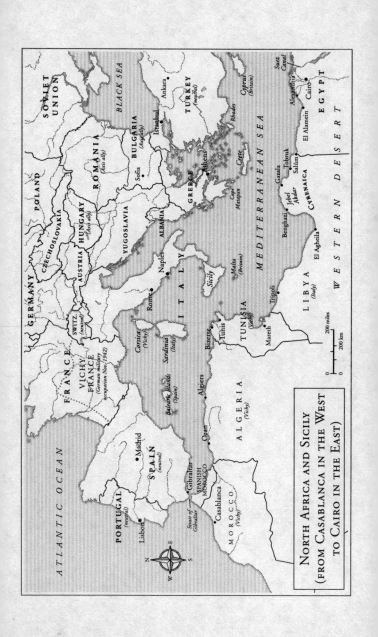

NORTH AFRICA AND SICILY
(FROM CASABLANCA IN THE WEST
TO CAIRO IN THE EAST)

THE RISING TIDE

INTRODUCTION

In war, it is axiomatic that the victors of the last war fight the new one with the tactics of the old. Having won, the victor is content with what won for him; but the vanquished wants to know why he lost.

HISTORIAN ROBERT LECKIE

The Second World War begins with the conclusion of the First. On June 28, 1919, Germany is forced to sign the Treaty of Versailles, which officially ends what would come to be known as the First World War. The terms of the treaty are dictated primarily by the two dominant allies, France and England, who seek to punish Germany economically and geographically. The Allies believe that their hard line will prevent a weakened Germany from ever again threatening the peace. What the Allies do not predict is that by nearly destroying the German economy, the treaty insures just the opposite. Within a few years, loud voices of German nationalism rise up, men who would inspire their people by appealing to fear and revenge. The most effective is Adolf Hitler. In the early 1920s Hitler is considered a fringe-element radical by the German politicians in power, but his message appeals to German citizens suffering under a massive economic depression. Hitler's following builds throughout the 1920s, and his political opponents lack his skill at oratory and his lack of conscience for brutalizing his enemies. Hitler's political organization becomes a deadly tool for his ambitions, and anyone opposing him is subject to a level of violence that shocks and intimidates voices of reason.

Hitler's Nazi Party secures sufficient public support so that in January 1933 the aging German president, Paul von Hindenburg, has no choice but to appoint Hitler as chancellor, hoping that Hitler will create a coalition government. Instead, Hitler dissolves the Reichstag, Germany's governing body, and in March 1933 declares himself dictator. By now, no one is strong enough to oppose him.

Throughout the 1930s, Hitler stages a saber-rattling campaign that alarms his European neighbors. One aspect of the Treaty of Versailles that Hitler uses to great advantage is a clause that strips away German territory, ceding it to neighboring countries, including Poland, Czechoslovakia, and France. But those territories are still primarily occupied by ethnic Germans, who welcome Hitler's calls that they should once again become part of Germany. In March 1936, German troops occupy the demilitarized zone along France's border, former German territory known as the Rhineland. Though Germany's military leaders are apprehensive, the French do virtually nothing in protest. Hitler learns his first lesson about the Allies' unwillingness to enter into an armed confrontation. It is a lesson he will take to heart.

In 1938, Hitler annexes Austria, which falls willingly into his grasp. His next goal, which he announces with great fanfare, is to "rescue" ethnic Germans who inhabit a slice of Czechoslovakia known as the Sudetenland. Finally, European governments protest. British prime minister Neville Chamberlain goes to Munich to meet with Hitler and returns home triumphantly waving the documents Hitler has signed, documents that promise that if the Allies simply allow the Sudetenland to fall into German hands, Hitler will make no further territorial demands. Europe breathes a collective sigh of relief, despite the fact that the Czech government has no say in the matter, and no recourse. To other European leaders, it is simply the price of peace.

On August 23, 1939, Hitler signs a nonaggression pact with the Soviet Union, which allows him to act without fear of Russian reprisal. His next move comes on September 1, 1939. German troops, aircraft, and tanks surge across the Polish border, sweeping away the grossly inferior Polish army. In little more than three weeks, Poland is crushed. (Barely noticed is that Russian troops have made an invasion of their own and occupy roughly half of Poland as well—one key term of the nonaggression agreement Hitler had made with Joseph Stalin.)

Western Europe reacts with outrage, and by September 3, 1939, both Britain and France declare war on Germany. But it is a diplomatic gesture that carries no real weight. Though France possesses what is thought to be the most powerful military in Europe, the French seem unwilling to actually commit arms to a struggle against Germany. Memories of the Great War are still too vivid. Much of the land along the French-German border is still a wasteland.

While Hitler cements his hold over the German government, the German military is rarely involved in Hitler's frequent public demonstrations of patriotic fervor. The Treaty of Versailles is specific that Germany is to maintain a minimal army and navy, but among the veterans of the Great War, officers begin to emerge who understand that the backbone of Germany's proud military heritage is still intact. Far below the radar of official Europe, the German army retrains and reequips itself. Though German officers are taught that they did not truly lose the Great War, they are aware that mistakes were made. The tactics must be different in the future. As Hitler shouts into microphones all over Germany, the army discreetly goes about its business. Distrustful of the West, Stalin allows German tank and aircraft units to undergo training deep inside Russian territory, far from the eyes of Western diplomats.

Technology becomes as important as manpower, and enormous energy goes into the design of modern tanks, aircraft, and submarines. When Hitler single-handedly abolishes the Treaty of Versailles, the German army, the Wehrmacht, and the air force, the Luftwaffe, are given a free hand to add to their men and machines, so that they once again become a powerful force.

During the invasion of Poland, Hitler is astonished at his army's efficiency, at their skill in crushing an enemy by what he learns is blitzkrieg tactics. Those tactics had first been used in the Great War, German commanders ordering shock troops forward in a hard strike with lightning speed, launched along a narrow front. In 1918, the tactic could not be sustained by the meager technology that supported it. In 1939, Hitler sees for himself that all that has changed.

For several months after the invasion of Poland, both Germany and its professed enemies seem to take a breath, shocked perhaps by the reality that what Hitler has begun might again erupt into another human catastrophe of a kind that no one believed could ever happen again. Though the British deploy their Expeditionary Force in Belgium and northern France from September 1939 until May 1940, there is no fighting in that region at all.

The French work feverishly to complete their Maginot Line, which they believe is an impregnable defensive wall along their German border. Diplomatic efforts continue, ministers from all sides beginning to believe that Hitler's aggressiveness can be halted. There is considerable unhappiness with Hitler within Germany as well, and the British receive discreet feelers from German officials who suggest that many German army officers would cooperate with efforts to remove Hitler altogether. Nothing results but talk.

The next six months allow the world to breathe easier, and in capitals all over Europe life returns to a kind of normal, journalists referring to the ongoing state of war as a "Phony War."

Throughout the calm, Hitler's propaganda ministry, under the master manipulator Paul Joseph Goebbels, fuels a passion for war in the German people, inflaming their fear of communists and foreigners, convincing them that all of Europe is preparing to invade their homeland. According to Goebbels, the brutality imposed on Germany in 1919 will be repeated. Though many Germans have no taste for another war, the propaganda is successful and secures widespread support for Hitler and his policies. After a long winter of anxious planning and maneuver by both sides, the Phony War ends. Hitler strikes first.

In April 1940, German troops embark on what becomes a race with the British to occupy the neutral country of Norway, strategically important to both sides due to its proximity to so many of the sea-lanes that feed northern Europe. Though the British claim that their intention to occupy Norway's ports has the blessing of the Norwegian people and their king, the Germans make no such pretext. To the dismay of the British navy, the Germans win the race, occupying Denmark along the way. The fall of Norway is the final straw for the British people and their parliament, who have heard too much of Neville Chamberlain's continuing calls for appeasement, for peaceful diplomatic solutions to Hitler's aggressiveness. Chamberlain is swept out of power, and the new British prime minister is Winston Churchill.

On May 10, 1940, Hitler's military attacks Holland and Belgium, two countries that had astonishingly refused to go along with Britain and France in their official declarations of war against Germany. As Belgian and Dutch officials put hope in their diplomatic efforts, Hitler simply ignores their neutrality. German troops quickly overrun both countries, making effective use of paratroopers and glider aircraft for the first time. In a matter of days, the Low Countries fall. But to Hitler's military strategists, the primary enemy and most dangerous adversary remains France, still thought to have far superior forces in both men and arms. Any attack against the Maginot Line would surely produce disastrous numbers of casualties, too reminiscent of the slaughter of the Great War. To the north of the Maginot Line are the dense thickets of the Ardennes Forest, thought impassable, especially by German armor. But the Ardennes has carefully been studied by German commanders, and as German troops sweep across Holland and Belgium, an enormous force of German tanks suddenly swarms into the forest, which proves not so impassable after all. In only days, German tanks roll across the Meuse River, bypassing the Maginot Line almost entirely. The lightning strike allows the German panzers to slice a wide gap between French and British defenses. With German tanks rolling rapidly past their flanks, the British have no choice but to retreat. As the Germans continue their pressure, nearly all of the British forces, and other Allied troops, are backed up against the English Channel. Their only avenue of escape is a single French seaport called Dunkirk.

Throughout the first few days of June 1940, the British make every effort to hold off continuing assaults by German aircraft, though many of their troops are helplessly exposed on open beaches. To the dismay of German tank commanders, Hitler has ordered them not to attack the massed British troops. For reasons known only to Hitler, he is skeptical of his generals' reports of overwhelming victory and refuses to believe that his army has been so successful against forces he knows outnumber his own. In addition, Hitler is convinced by his overbearing and boisterous air commander, Hermann Göring, that the Luftwaffe alone can destroy the British on the beaches at Dunkirk before they can make good their escape. For days, Luftwaffe fighters and bombers harass the British, but cannot compel any British commander to surrender. Instead, as frustrated German troops look on, a thousand British seacraft, from warships to fishing boats, ferry desperate Allied soldiers away from the beach and transport them across the English Channel. Nearly a third of a million British, French, and Belgian troops are saved.

With most of the British gone from the fight in Western Europe, the Germans turn their attention to the French, who are braced to defend their own country, as they had done in 1914. But this time, German tactics and battlefield skills far outstrip what the French bring to the fight. On June 14, 1940, after less than three weeks of fighting, German troops march triumphantly into Paris.

Hitler now installs a puppet government in France, known as Vichy, headed by Henri Pétain, one of France's most popular and decorated heroes from the First World War. Pétain is feeble and easily manipulated and believes that by going along with Hitler's wishes, France can be spared a brutal conquest. In return for Pétain's cooperation, Hitler agrees not to invade southern France. For Hitler, this is no sacrifice at all. He has conquered Paris, something no German leader has been able to do since the Franco-Prussian War.

With Western Europe firmly under Hitler's thumb, the German strategists turn their attentions elsewhere. One key challenge to maintaining control over such an enormous military force is supply. The Germans begin to look beyond Europe, where vast natural resources may yet be exploited. To the dismay of many professional soldiers in Hitler's command, Hitler has cultivated a friendship with the bombastic Italian dictator, Benito Mussolini, which is formalized into an alliance in September 1938. Mussolini also signs the Anti-Comintern Pact, an agreement first drawn up in 1936 between Japan and Germany, which pledges mutual assistance should either be attacked by Russia. The pact is a thinly disguised treaty that insures that neither Japan nor Germany will act against the other's best interests.

Mussolini's ambitions have taken him to East and North Africa, and since the mid-1930s Italian armies have attempted to subjugate lands from Tunisia to Ethiopia. But the Italian war machine does not compare to that of the Germans, and in Africa, Mussolini is dealt major setbacks by the British. Though the German strategists would much rather focus on capturing the British-held oil fields of the Middle East, Hitler agrees to supply German troops to assist Mussolini in what the Italian dictator believes is his personal destiny, to conquer Africa as part of a glorious new Roman Empire. But Hitler has his own distractions. With Western Europe secure, the German military reorganizes its commanders and begins to look forward. But Hitler stuns them all with his own plans, insisting on a devastating attack on Russia. Though the Russians are ostensibly German allies, Hitler cannot be swayed from his dream of subduing such an enormous foe, especially with the virtually unlimited natural and human resources the Russians possess. There are two other motives for Hitler as well. For one, he feels a searing hatred for Joseph Stalin, which hardens into a personal vendetta that has no basis in sound military practice. The second motive is Hitler's loathing of the Russian people, whom he considers subhuman. It is an all-consuming philosophy that has already spread its bleak hand across Germany and the countries that have fallen under the German bootheel.

For years, part of Hitler's appeal to the German people has been in his boisterous insistence that they are unique and racially superior, that the German bloodline should prevail over all others. With so much German territory lost by the Treaty of Versailles, it is easy for Hitler to convince his nation of the need for more *Lebensraum,* or living space, allowing the pure bloodlines of Aryan Germany to flourish and prosper across Europe. To make room for his version of the Chosen People, Hitler has already begun ordering the forced relocation of sizable numbers of immigrants and Jews from their homes in Germany, Poland,

Czechoslovakia, and other countries, including France. These uprooted people are being transported into enormous camps, where they are often told they will only remain until new homes can be found for them. But few are allowed to leave, and instead, enormous numbers of men, women, and children are led into gas chambers, where they are simply exterminated.

In the first two years of the war, knowledge of the camps is confined mostly to the Gestapo, Hitler's secret police. Many close to Hitler's inner circle choose to ignore the rumors of what is happening to the Jews. Others accept Hitler's philosophy without qualm. Most of the professional soldiers, whose duties keep them far out in the field, have little or no idea what is taking place in the concentration camps.

On June 22, 1941, a force totaling more than 186 German divisions, nearly two and a half million men, crosses the frontier into Russia. Hitler's dream of conquering the enormous country will occupy most of his attention for many months to come.

As Germany's might spreads eastward, in North Africa a far smaller force has been deployed. They are mostly mobile and armored forces, many of the same men who had launched the stunningly successful attack across France and Belgium. Now, they will be asked to drive the British away from the places held dear by Mussolini, and if possible to secure all of North Africa. Compared to the enormous army surging across the plains of Russia, the two panzer divisions that land at the Libyan port city of Tripoli are barely a token force, not nearly the juggernaut Mussolini has hoped for. But Mussolini will take what he can get. The panzers are led by the man whose name has already gained him a considerable reputation in the German high command. His name is Erwin Rommel.

In the years following the Great War, the American government is as divided as its people. As had been the case in 1914, many Americans are enormously reluctant to get involved in the rest of the world's problems. In the 1920s, isolationist sentiment returns with even more vigor.

When Franklin Delano Roosevelt assumes the presidency in 1933, the nation has suffered through three years of a Great Depression, and Roosevelt's New Deal policies are designed to put the American economy back on its feet. His policies succeed, and throughout the 1930s Americans begin to emerge from their economic gloom. American newspapers trumpet the turmoil around the globe, the civil war in Spain, Mussolini's conquests in Africa, Japan's aggressions against China. As Hitler's land-grab in Europe evolves into full-scale war, American celebrities such as Charles Lindbergh warn the nation that any alliance the United States makes with Hitler's enemies will only result in America's destruction. Roosevelt does not agree.

America's relationship with Great Britain is based on more than economic alliance, and Roosevelt believes that the American people are enormously pro-British. After Britain's near catastrophe at Dunkirk, Roosevelt responds with several aid packages, including military supplies and ships, loaned to Britain on terms that clearly demonstrate where America's allegiance lies. In March 1941, the Lend-Lease Act formalizes this alliance. Roosevelt's enemies, including Lindbergh, are outraged.

On December 7, 1941, that outrage is silenced. The Japanese launch a devastating surprise attack on the American naval fleet at Pearl Harbor, Hawaii. As Roosevelt conveys the news to a shocked American public, the isolationists and pacifists are suddenly ignored. Within days, America is at war.

Immediately, American military leaders discover that two decades of antimilitary sentiment have reduced the American armed forces to a pitiful state. From aircraft to tanks, rifles to fighting men, the armed forces are woefully underequipped to confront an enemy that possesses the most modern tools of war. General John Dill, the senior British officer stationed in Washington, notes, "Their armed forces are more unready for this war than it is possible to imagine. The whole organization belongs to the days of George Washington." Thus begins a crash program involving every industrial resource the United States can muster. Within weeks, factories dedicated to appliances and modern conveniences are converted to the manufacture of munitions. Automobile makers begin producing tanks. The aid to Britain continues, but in Washington, the American military begins to divide its priorities, some believing that America should first confront Japan, others, Europe. A wrestling match for resources ensues. The difficult balance is maintained with a skilled hand by the chief of staff, George C. Marshall, who is convinced that if Britain falls, America will be isolated, squeezed hard between two great military powers. Marshall convinces Roosevelt that Hitler must be defeated first if there is to be any hope that the British can devote their own resources to helping fight the Japanese.

As American troop strength rises, and volunteers fill the training centers, the American officer corps undergoes convulsions of its own. Marshall's unenviable job is to find the right men for jobs no one has trained for. Command in the Pacific is given to the former chief of staff Douglas MacArthur, whose experience in the field has come mostly in the Philippines. Though the British are also confronting Japanese threats against their colonies in Singapore and India, there is no united front, and MacArthur takes command over a vast area in the central and western Pacific that is primarily an American affair. In Europe, Marshall's choice of commander is less clear-cut. With no Allied forces actually fighting on the European continent, America's first role must be to support an invasion, to stand beside the British, seeking the means to crack Hitler's stranglehold. The Americans strongly favor an invasion across the English Channel, directly into France. The British disagree vehemently, and Winston Churchill pushes for regaining control of the Mediterranean Sea. Churchill believes that if Germany prevails in North Africa, the threat to the Suez Canal and the oil fields of the Middle East cannot be overcome. Churchill's plan is to strike first at German and Italian interests in North Africa. Since early 1941, British forces have been engaging Erwin Rommel in a seesaw duel across the Libyan desert. Churchill convinces the Americans that if the Germans are swept clear of North Africa, all of southern Europe, especially Italy, would become vulnerable to an Allied attack. Though Marshall and Roosevelt continue to push for a cross-Channel invasion, Churchill prevails. All that is required is a commander, one man to lead the combined forces of America and Britain. Though the British have experience against Hitler's armies, Churchill understands that American resources are essential to success. To that end, the American people must feel that their military is standing side by side with Britain, not one step behind them. Therefore, the commander of the overall campaign should be an American. Though many in the British military are quietly convinced he will be but a figurehead, George Marshall chooses the man he believes to be the most dogged and clearheaded administrator in the American command: Dwight D. Eisenhower.

DWIGHT DAVID EISENHOWER

Born 1890, in Denison, Texas, one of seven sons (only six survive to adulthood) of hardworking, devout parents. He is originally named David Dwight, but reverses his names after he graduates high school. Eisenhower spends most of his early years in Abilene, Kansas, learns the conservative values of American life from the small-town experiences of a world cut off from the buoyant temptations of the "Gay Nineties."

He is an exceptional athlete and is sensitive about his family's humble position in the community. Handy with his fists, he quickly establishes that he will tolerate none of the high-handed snootiness of the town's more aristocratic boys.

In 1911, Eisenhower applies to the Naval Academy at Annapolis, Maryland, and as an afterthought, and to increase his chances for acceptance, adds an application to West Point as well. He has no plans for a military career, believing only that the service academies will offer him a first-class college education, which otherwise his parents could simply not afford. To his disappointment, his age makes him too old for acceptance at Annapolis, but he is accepted by West Point. At twenty-one, Eisenhower is the oldest member of his class. His journey east is his first trip away from his close-knit family.

He graduates in 1915, sixty-first in his class, leaving behind a reputation for prowess on the football field far more than in the classroom. He cannot know at the time that of the 164 members of his graduating class, fifty-nine will rise to the rank of general, the most of any class produced by West Point. Included among these will be his friend Omar Bradley.

In late 1915, he is sent to San Antonio, Texas, where he meets Mamie Geneva Doud, who bears an uncanny resemblance to actress Lillian Gish, and whom Eisenhower describes as "the most beautiful woman I have ever seen." In July 1916, they are married. In September 1917, Mamie gives birth to Doud Dwight Eisenhower, but the baby's life is cut short by scarlet fever, and Eisenhower's first son dies in January 1921, at age three. It is a tragedy he will rarely speak about. In August 1922, Mamie gives birth again, to another boy, whom they name John.

Throughout the Great War, Eisenhower remains stateside, training tank crews, and he serves as commander of a tank brigade at Gettysburg, Pennsylvania. He meets and becomes friends with the army's tank-school commander, George Patton.

With the conclusion of the war, Eisenhower accepts a role in the downsized army, serves as General Fox Connor's chief of staff in Panama, with the rank of major, a rank he will hold for more than fifteen years. Connor had served closely with American commander John "Black Jack" Pershing and is one of the army's most outstanding minds. He educates Eisenhower in literature and the arts, broadening the young man's perspectives, and gives Eisenhower the opportunity to hone his skills at military planning and organization.

In 1924, Connor suggests that Eisenhower enter the Army's Command and General Staff College at Fort Leavenworth. After a two-year study, Eisenhower surprises himself more than anyone else by graduating first, out of a class of 275 officers.

In 1927, Eisenhower serves as aide to retired general Pershing, as part of the American Battlefield Monuments Commission. Pershing influences him, as had Fox Connor, and encourages him to read and study the tactics and strategies of the bloody fields of the Great War.

In 1933, Eisenhower accepts a staff position with then Chief of Staff Douglas MacArthur. He serves in a continuing role on MacArthur's staff in the Philippines and remains there until 1940. The two men are oil and water, but Eisenhower performs his duties with complete professionalism, though he genuinely dislikes MacArthur. However, Eisenhower respects MacArthur's experience, and long before Pearl Harbor, MacArthur tells him that another large-scale war is a certainty, a prediction that Eisenhower takes seriously.

In February 1940, he is stationed at Fort Ord, California,

named executive officer of the Fifteenth Infantry regiment. He begins to speak of his fears, warning all who listen that the United States is simply not prepared for a war he feels is inevitable. To the officers around him, he becomes known as Alarmist Ike.

In September 1941, Eisenhower is promoted to brigadier general, and when news comes of Pearl Harbor, Eisenhower is called to Washington, where he is named to command the general staff's War Plans Division. Now under the direct eye of Chief of Staff George Marshall, Eisenhower finds himself critiquing MacArthur's strategies in the Pacific, which he does without prejudice, though he often finds fault with MacArthur's planning. Marshall is impressed. In March 1942, Eisenhower receives a promotion to major general. His friendship with Marshall continues to grow, the two men seeing eye to eye on most of the critical matters erupting around them.

On April 8, 1942, Marshall flies to London, where he meets with Churchill and the British chiefs of staff. Their discussion covers every aspect of the coming campaigns against Hitler's army, and for the first time, the chiefs discuss which officer will be chosen to lead the Allied command. On June 15, 1942, Eisenhower receives the final word from Marshall. The command is his.

ERWIN ROMMEL

Born 1891, in Heidenheim, Germany, the son of a schoolmaster, the middle child of five. His childhood is spent in the hills and woods of his Bavarian home, and he quickly discovers that he has little aptitude for studies, which of course does not please his father. One teacher remarks, "If he ever produces a dictation without a mistake, we will hire a band and go off for a day in the country." Always preferring athletics, by his teen years Rommel becomes an exceptional skier and has a fascination with flying machines. Though the Rommel family has no military tradition, he begins to see himself as a soldier, and in 1910, to his father's enormous disappointment, Rommel joins the army.

In 1911, while attending the German War Academy in Danzig,

East Prussia, Rommel meets Lucy Maria Mollin, a moderately aristocratic girl who sweeps him completely off his feet. A year later, Rommel concludes his officer training and is assigned to an infantry regiment as a second lieutenant, training new recruits. Loyal always to Lucy, Rommel does not participate in the rowdy temptations offered to young officers, rarely drinks, and never smokes. He is considered an uninteresting bore by his fellow officers. His superiors interpret that differently and note the young man has the right material to become a proper officer.

In August 1914, Rommel marches to war with his regiment. Immediately, the men under him recognize something unusual in their lieutenant, a fearless devotion to the fight, a sharp mind that reacts decisively under fire. Brave to the point of recklessness, Rommel's reputation grows. By January 1915, he is twice awarded the Iron Cross, for heroism and leadership under fire. But as the fighting along the Western Front settles into a stalemate, Rommel chafes at the inactivity. Promoted to first lieutenant, he welcomes a new assignment, joins a mountain battalion, and is sent to Romania, and then the mountains along the Italian border. In November 1916, during one brief furlough, he returns to Danzig and marries Lucy.

He continues to excel in combat through the mountainous terrain of northern Italy, and in October 1917 his unit is assigned to assist Austrian forces in a struggle with the Italians near the city of Caporetto. Rommel leads two companies in an audacious attack against Italian defenses, and gathering additional troops along the front lines, he scales a formidable mountain fortification and captures nearly ten thousand Italian soldiers. He is thus awarded Germany's highest military honor, the Pour le Mérite (known also as the Blue Max).

After the Great War ends, Rommel, now a captain, continues in the downsized German army. In 1921, he is assigned to Stuttgart, commanding a regiment of infantry, a post he holds for eight years. There, in 1928, his only child is born, a son he names Manfred.

In 1929, Rommel is assigned as an instructor to the army's Infantry School at Dresden. Unhappy with most of the texts and manuals he must use, he begins to write his own, though the book will not be published until 1937.

In the early 1930s, as high-ranking German officers begin to cement their plans for rebuilding the German military, Rommel's name is often mentioned. Though he never participates in such closed-door meetings, he is highly respected, regarded as the kind of officer the army must have. In 1933, he is promoted to major and is assigned to command a mountain battalion at Goslar, in central Germany. Here he becomes known as a no-nonsense drill instructor who drives his men relentlessly. Few can object, however, since Rommel drives himself with the same level of physical intensity.

Rommel is shocked by Hitler's rise to power, has paid little attention to the political wrangling of postwar Germany. When Hitler names himself dictator of Germany, Rommel is disgusted by the brutish tactics of Hitler's henchmen. To his wife, Rommel remarks that the Nazis "seem to be a set of scallywags." But Hitler begins to intrigue him, seems to Rommel to be an idealist, a man with the energy to rescue Germany from the clutches of its enemies, especially communism. Rommel comes to believe that Hitler is precisely what Germany needs: a man who can reunite the German people and reclaim Germany's lost pride.

As Hitler cements his power over the highest-ranking military officers, Rommel feels the pressure to become a member of the Nazi Party. But he still regards politics as unbefitting a soldier and does not join. Regardless of their discomfort with many of Hitler's ideas, the military appreciate that Hitler is allowing them a free hand to modernize and reequip. Thus even those who object to Hitler's aggressiveness against Czechoslovakia and Austria keep their criticisms behind closed doors. Compared to the chaos of the 1920s, Hitler has given Germany's officers a powerful structure within which they can ply their trade.

In February 1937, Rommel is assigned to command the Hitler Youth, a new organization that seeks to educate German boys in the art of war. But Rommel recognizes the group for what it quickly becomes: a nest of bullies and spoiled misfits. Rommel finds the job utterly distasteful, remarks that he did not join the army just to train "little Napoléons." A year later, he is given command of the War Academy at Wiener Neustadt, near

Vienna, Austria. Once again he captures the attention of Joseph Goebbels, who has arranged for Rommel's textbook, titled *Infantry Attacks,* to be published. For this, Rommel will feel a debt toward Goebbels for the rest of his life.

In August 1939, Rommel is promoted to major general, and he witnesses the invasion of Poland from Hitler's headquarters. Ignoring the brutality inflicted on the Polish people, Rommel absorbs the lessons of the German attack, which plays into his own military instincts: strike hard and fast, with overwhelming power. He is especially drawn to the brutal success of the German armor, the panzers. He realizes with perfect certainty that his place is at the vanguard of a massive column of powerful tanks.

During and after the invasion of Poland, Rommel is assigned to command Hitler's personal security force, essentially becoming Hitler's bodyguard. During this time, Hitler forms an attachment to Rommel that will influence both men. But Rommel chafes at such a command, despises the staff officers who flock around Hitler, referring to them as "so many pitiful birds." When Hitler offers Rommel a command in the field, Rommel does not hesitate, and Hitler grants his particular request, command of the Seventh Panzer Division. Within weeks, Rommel begins preparing for the order from Hitler that will unleash the German army westward.

In May 1940, Rommel's Seventh Armor bursts through the frontier south of Liège, Belgium, and he is the first German commander to cross the Meuse River. Driving the enemy before him, he nearly drives too far and is almost crushed by British tanks, who are surprised to find themselves on the German flank. But Rommel's audacity rescues him, and continuing his push westward, he arrives at the coast near Dunkirk, only to be told that Hitler has ordered a halt.

After the British escape at Dunkirk, a disgusted Rommel goes on the attack once more and captures several French towns, crushing pockets of French and British opposition as he goes. On June 12, 1940, he captures the coastal town of Saint-Valéry, France, along with twelve thousand British and French prisoners. Two days after the Germans march into Paris, Rommel captures the city of Cherbourg and receives the surrender of thirty thousand French soldiers.

In the overall campaign that results in Hitler's conquest of Western Europe, Rommel's command captures nearly a hundred thousand prisoners, three hundred artillery pieces, and more than four hundred tanks. His own division suffers casualties of less than three thousand men, with a loss of forty-two tanks. Though Rommel's star rises considerably, he receives his first taste of the jealousy and backbiting from other officers that will haunt his career. Hitler is not swayed by talk from Rommel's superiors, who insist that Rommel is too brash for high command.

Though Hitler soon becomes obsessed with his dreams of conquering Russia, he cannot completely ignore his own staff officers, who suggest that Mussolini is unstable. Hitler is convinced that if the Italians continue to suffer setbacks against the British in North Africa, Mussolini might simply drop out of the war. Hitler calls upon Rommel, and against the advice of many of his senior staff, Hitler offers Rommel command of what will become the Deutsches Afrika Korps.

On February 12, 1941, Rommel arrives in Tripoli, in western Libya.

Almost immediately, Rommel changes the landscape of the war in North Africa, and the British are sent reeling back toward Egypt. But Rommel receives neither the resources nor the cooperation of his Italian superiors, and the British begin to fight back. Throughout the rest of 1941, the campaign swings in both directions, momentum changing hands, Rommel's audacity and superior tactics balanced by his inability to match the British in numbers and avenues of supply. Regardless of Rommel's shortcomings, including his tendency to separate himself from his own headquarters, his successes overshadow his mistakes. The legend of the "Desert Fox" begins to grow, and even the British share Hitler's high regard for Rommel and his tactics. To the British parliament, Winston Churchill remarks that Rommel is "a very daring and skillful opponent . . . a great general."

On December 8, 1941, Rommel learns that the Japanese have bombed Pearl Harbor. He knows that America's entry into the war will help the British immeasurably. As word reaches him of German setbacks in Russia, Rommel realizes that Hitler's vast dreams may not be attainable. Rommel begins to understand: unless he can destroy the British who confront him and conquer North Africa, Germany cannot win the war.

PART ONE

The bravest are surely those who have the clearest vision of what is before them, glory and danger alike, and yet notwithstanding, go out and meet it.

THUCYDIDES

I would rather be the hammer than the anvil.

ERWIN ROMMEL

1. THE DESERT RAT

They huddled in the chill, encased in hard steel, waiting, energized by rumors. Behind them, to the east, the black horizon was visible, silhouetted by the first glow of sunrise. The wireless radio was chattering, the voices of nervous officers far behind the line, the men in tents, who pored over maps, unsure, powerless to do anything about an enemy who might be anywhere at all.

They had climbed into the tank at the first sign of daylight, each of the four men finding his place, their commander perched higher than the rest, settling into his seat just beneath the hatch of the turret. It was still too dark in the west, and the narrow view through the prism of the periscope was too confining, and so he stood, his head and shoulders outside the hatch. The long, thin barrel of the two-pound cannon was just below him, pointing westward, where the enemy was thought to be. He stared until his eyes watered, tried to see the horizon. But it would not be there, not yet, not until the sun had given them enough light to distinguish dull, flat ground from the empty sky.

The air was sharp and cold, but that would not last. Once the sun rose, the heat would come again, and the infantry, a mass of men waiting far behind their armor wall, would seek whatever shelter they had, waking the insects and the scorpions and the snakes. The tank was as good a shelter as a man had in the desert, but there was a price for shade. The thick steel made a perfect oven, and the men would man their posts and glance instinctively toward the hatches, hoping for the faintest wisp of a breeze. He blinked, wiped his eyes with a dirty hand, annoyed at the crackling intrusion from the wireless.

"Turn that off!"

"Sir, can't do that, you know. Orders. The captain . . ."

He ignored the young man's protest, stared out again. The sun would quickly rise, nothing to block the light, no mountains, no trees, no rolling terrain. In a few short minutes he could see flecks of detail, an uneven field pockmarked by small rocks. There was a shadow, right in front of him, beneath the barrel of the two-pounder. It was his, of course, the low, hulking form of the tank. It makes us a target, he thought. But, then, the Germans are in the west, will have to attack straight into the rising sun. We'll be able to see them first, certainly. Stupid tactic. But what isn't stupid out here? Sitting in a fat tin can, armed with a two-pound popgun, hoping like hell we see him before he sees us.

There was a loud squawk from the wireless.

"Dammit, at least turn that thing down!"

"Sir, I think it's Captain Digby. He's upset about something."

Digby. He stared at the horizon, clear, distinct, thought of the officer who sat sucking on that idiotic pipe. His tank smells like a Turkish whorehouse. And he's upset. Good. Bloody fool. Carries fat rolls of maps so he can find his way. In a place with no landmarks, no signposts. Stuffs the damned maps into his ammo holders, and so, he runs out of ammo. Begs the rest of us for help. Just look at the sun, Captain. All the signpost you need.

The radio squawked again, and he heard the voice now. Yep. Digby.

"Rec report . . . enemy in motion . . . zzzzzzzzz . . . two hundred . . . zzzzzzzz." The wireless seemed to go dead, and he looked to the north, could see the British tanks in a ragged line. The crews had climbed into their vehicles, and most of the tank commanders were standing up, searching for something across the vast emptiness. He still looked to the north, thought, yep, there's Digby. The sixth tank over. Brew yourself a cup of tea, Captain. There's nothing out here but us Rats.

He glanced down through the hatch, could see little, the tank dark. He knew each man well, more experienced than most, but so very young. They were better than the tank they pushed, the

A9. She was fast, maybe faster than anything the Germans had, could maneuver easily over the rocky ground, spin around like a top. In training they had been told that the two-pounder was an effective antitank weapon, firing a solid-steel projectile, supposed to pierce anything the enemy had. It had certainly worked against the Italians, who had come at them with machines that were worn-out in 1918. The armor battles had been one-sided affairs, British tanks and artillery decimating the primitive weapons of their enemy. He remembered the first Italian tanks that had actually put up a good fight, something called an M13. But even that machine was small, and far too light, padded by a sad pile of sandbags around the turret. He could see it in his mind, the direct hit on an M13 that made it seem like an exploding sack of flour. And no one inside survived, ever. Bloody awful, that one. Target practice. Brave men sent to die in broken-down toys.

But then the Germans came, and they brought the real thing, heavier, faster tanks, bigger guns, and suddenly the A9 crews were no longer as fond of their machines. There was something else the Germans had, a particular genius for weaponry. They had an eighty-eight millimeter antiaircraft cannon, long barrel, that threw a shell high enough to churn any pilot's guts. But the Germans figured out that lowering the barrel and pointing it horizontally made for an antitank weapon like no other. Most of the larger artillery on both sides was like the basic howitzers, firing their shells in an arc. You could hear them coming and might even have a brief second to prepare for impact, time enough perhaps to dive into a slit trench. But the long barrel of the eighty-eight blew a shell right through you in a straight line. No high-screaming wail, no warning. And there wasn't a single British machine that the eighty-eight wouldn't blow to pieces.

He lowered himself into the hatch, tried to see the wireless operator, Batchelor, the man who doubled as the gun loader.

"Batch. Did Digby say anything else?"

"I'm trying to raise him, sir. He said something about the rec, then I lost him."

He pulled himself up, stared out again, mulled over the word: *rec.* Reconnaissance. Hell of a job, flitting all over the place in light armored cars. They run right up to the Jerries, see what's what, then run like hell to get away. Nothing but machine guns for protection. Ballsy chaps, those fellows.

Below the gun barrel in front of him, a small hatch opened, and a head emerged. It was the driver, Simmons.

"It's warming up a bit, sir."

Simmons was the youngest man in the crew, with bad skin and an unfortunate natural odor that even soap could not seem to cure. But there was no soap here, barely enough water to keep a man alive, and so Simmons had become just one more tank crewman who had to be accepted by his own, regardless of whatever unpleasant personal traits he might bring to the confined space. By now, they all smelled bad enough to offend anyone but themselves. Like Captain Digby's pipe smoke, it had become a part of each tank's personality.

"I say, sir. What's that?"

Simmons was pointing out to the left of the barrel, eleven o'clock, and he stared with the young man, could see the cloud rising up, dark, obliterating the horizon. Simmons said, "A dust storm. Big one. Bloody hell."

The young man disappeared into the tank, the hatch pulled down over his narrow compartment. The cloud seemed to spread out to the south, farther left, swirling darkness, sunlight reflected in small flecks. The radio squawked again, a chaos of voices, and now he could see new motion, a vehicle emerging from the storm, then two more, their dust trails billowing out behind them as they roared toward the line of tanks. His heart jumped, and he raised his binoculars, saw that they were armored cars, their own, the rec boys. He glanced toward the north, toward Digby's command tank, looking for the colored flag that would tell them to start the powerful engines. But Digby's wire antenna held nothing but the command flag, no other sign yet.

He glanced down into the tank, said, "Hands off triggers. Those are ours."

It was an unnecessary order, the big gun not yet loaded, the machine guns still waiting for the belts of ammo that would feed them. The armored cars rolled past the line of tanks, did not stop. He said aloud, to no one in particular, "Jeez. They're moving like hell."

He calmed now, ignored the new sounds from the wireless, thought, guess those chaps don't like eating that dust storm any more than we do. He looked out toward the dark cloud again, no more than a mile away, rolling closer. He let out a breath. Sure. Why not start the day with another one of these damned storms? By all means let's eat dirt for breakfast. He began to move, lowering himself into the tank, then he stopped, frozen by a new sound. He looked again toward the great swirling cloud, ugly and familiar, the dull roar of wind and fine grit, a dozen tornadoes winding around themselves. But there were other sounds now, familiar as well. Tracks. Steel on rock. Engines. He froze, stared at the sounds, felt a light breeze in his face. That's not a dust storm, you bloody idiot. That's armor. Making their own damned storm.

"Jerries!"

Close by, he heard engines turning over, great belches of black smoke spitting from the other tanks in the formation. He looked that way, saw men disappearing into their tanks, hatches closing. He did not wait for the order from Digby, dropped down to his hard leather seat, pulled the hatch shut, shouted, "Fire 'er up!"

The driver responded, the tank pulsing, a deafening roar that drowned out the ongoing noise from the wireless. He leaned forward, searched through the periscope, felt for his machine gun, shouted again:

"Load 'em! Guns ready!"

The men moved with tight precision, each one doing his job. He looked down, saw the gunner, Moxley, right below and in front of him. He slid forward, put his knees right against the young man's back. It was the position they had repeated many times, and Moxley never protested, the discomfort of the pressure giving them both leverage as the tank rolled and tossed them about. He reached down, tapped the gunner on the shoulder.

"Wait for my order. Patience. Use the sights. How many rounds?"

"A hundred twenty."

"They'll go quick. Don't want to run out. Not in the mood to be a sitting duck, Private."

"Me either, sir."

"Loader!"

"Sir!"

"My Vickers ready?"

"Fit to fire, sir!"

His fingers wrapped around the trigger, and he squeezed, testing, the machine gun coming to life, a brief burst of fire. It was the signal to Simmons to do the same, the driver blessed with two of the Vickers machine guns up front. Simmons let loose a short burst. Well, all right then. We're ready for you, Jerry. He was breathing heavily, the exhaust swirling around them, and he focused through the periscope, the dust cloud rolling closer.

"Where the hell are they?"

He punched the button on the crude intercom, wanted to give Simmons the order to move forward. No, wait. Show a little patience yourself. We don't know what's out there, not yet. Find a target. He spoke into the intercom now, the only way they could hear him through the roar of the engine.

"Gunner. Anything?"

"Nothing yet. Just dust."

He stared as they all stared, the fine sand blowing thin clouds against the glass of the periscope, blinding, his eyes watering. He pulled his goggles off the hook beside him, slid them over his head. He hated the goggles, the lenses scratched, blurred, but they kept his eyes dry. He caught a flash of movement, above the dust cloud, coming at them, fast, now right above them. He heard the scream as it passed by and he hunched his shoulders, instinct, shouted, "109s!"

More planes roared past, barely a hundred feet above them, and he tried to ignore them, thought, no sightseeing, you bloody fool. You know what a Messerschmitt looks like. And, we haven't been blown to hell, so they're not coming for us. The supply dumps or the support trucks, most likely. Strafe the infantry. Poor bastards. He thought of the antiaircraft gunners, far back, dug into patches of camel thorn brush, lucky to get a brief burst of fire at the low-flying planes. Shoot straight, boys. Knock a few Jerries out of their seats. He stared into the dust cloud again, scanned from side to side. He could still hear the Messerschmitts ripping past, thought, a good-sized flock. If there's that many 109s, there's something coming with them. Come on, where the hell are you?

And now he saw them.

On both sides tanks erupted from the dust, rolled right past, the air punched by dull sounds, streaks of white light. He turned in his seat.

"Port! Ninety to port. Move it!"

The tank lurched forward, then spun, pivoting to the left. The dust cloud was everywhere, churned into thick, gray fog by the movement of the big machines. The tank rumbled blindly forward over a carpet of small rocks, and there was a bright flash, a sharp streak of light, thunder on the right side. He jumped in his seat, searched the dust frantically. You missed me! Hah! The gunner spun the turret, and he saw the tank now, black crosses on the sand-yellow armor. The German turret was moving as well, the big gun trying to follow his movement. He shouted to Moxley:

"Ten o'clock! A hundred yards!"

The turret kept moving, painfully slowly, and he watched the barrel of the two-pounder slide into position.

Moxley said, "Got him, sir!"

"Fire when ready!"

The words still hung in the air as the tank rocked from the recoil of the big gun. He fought to see through the smoke and dust, saw the crosses again, said, "Again!"

The two-pounder fired again, and Moxley let out a sound.

"Hit him! Hit him!"

"Fire again!"

They worked in perfect unison, the loader feeding the shells into the breech of the gun, the spent shells ejected automatically into the canvas bag that draped below. He coughed, the cordite smell filling the cabin, and still saw the crosses right in front of him.

"Stop! Watch him!"

They jerked to a halt, and he could see smoke coming from the German tank, waited for the movement, saw it now, the hatch coming open. A thick plume of black smoke poured up from inside the tank, and the men appeared, scrambling out, escaping the burning hulk. His hand gripped the trigger of the machine gun, and he watched four men drop to the ground, staggering, wounded, blinded by the smoke and the shattering blast that had ripped into them. He pulled the trigger, sprayed the machine-gun fire back and forth, all four men going down quickly. He paused, took another breath, fought through the stink of gunpowder, saw movement beyond, more tanks, streaks of light. The fight was all around them, tanks and armored cars, perfect confusion, enemies only yards apart, seeking a target in the dust, firing point-blank.

"Move! Ninety degrees starboard! Forward!"

He searched for another target, all four men rising to the battle, all a part of the chaos, a desperate dance of men and machine.

They were a part of the British Seventh Armored Division, and from their earliest days in the fight in North Africa, they had been known as the Desert Rats. They took the name from the greater Egyptian jerboa, a strange and awkward rodent that bore an uncanny resemblance to a tiny kangaroo. The jerboa had made its appearance at every supply depot, every place where man brought something edible to this inhospitable place. They seemed to hate the sunlight and avoided the heat, which seemed more than a little odd for a creature who made his home in the desert. It was a trait the jerboa shared with the men of the British Seventh Armored.

The tank commander's name was Clyde Atkins, and at twenty-eight he was among the oldest of the noncoms who ran the tanks. Most of the big machines were run by sergeants, men who were inappropriately called "sir" by their crews. No one seemed to care about the breach of protocol. To the Desert Rats, being in charge of a tank earned a man the right to be called sir. There were officers of course, at the head of each squadron, men like the despised Digby, who commanded groups of six or eight of the big machines. But driving a tank in battle was a young man's game, quick reflexes and a hardiness required to work in conditions that no amount of training could accurately duplicate. In the chaos of a fight in the desert, each tank fought its own war.

Though the Italians had fared well against the first British troops they'd confronted, when the Seventh arrived, the tide had turned. The British had marveled at the gallant men in obscenely outdated vehicles, whose bravery and amazing willingness to die had not slowed the British from sweeping them entirely across Libya. The power of the British tanks was a shocking surprise to the unfortunate Italians, who had been told their own tanks would crush any foe. And no matter how gallant they had been, their commanders had seemed utterly worthless, something the British had observed from their very first confrontations. The lack of respect the British felt for the Italian commanders extended all the way up the chain of command to Mussolini himself. The British quickly understood that the Italian armies were being sacrificed by an arrogantly stupid man whom the men began to call a "small-bore dictator," a stooge for Hitler. Even now the Italian prisoners brought the stories, how Mussolini had assured them that their conquest of North Africa was only the first chapter in the birth of a new Roman Empire. But the prisoners Atkins had seen cared nothing at all for some glorious legacy and seemed to care little for Mussolini himself. Their officers were a different story. They had marched into the British camps protesting all the way, outraged at being captured, insulted by defeat, oblivious to the catastrophic ineptness that had killed so many of their own good men.

The Seventh Armored had been a major part of the push that had driven the Italians halfway across Libya. Near Benghazi, the Desert Rats had emerged from their tanks with the glow of victory, many speaking of a quick end to the entire war.

Then, Rommel arrived.

The Desert Rats knew little of the new German commander, but in the battles that followed, they learned that he had brought the most modern guns and armor in any theater of the war. The Italians who had survived were now alongside an ally who had known only victory, who had crushed the French, and the British themselves. Sergeant Atkins and the other tank commanders soon understood that their cherished two-pounder was seriously outgunned. If the A9 was to succeed, it had to be at close range and to the side, firing into the thinner, weaker flank of the German armor. Otherwise, it would take a lucky shot beneath the turret to have any effect at all. To many, the bigger guns on the German tanks, combined with the eighty-eights lurking behind their armor, made Rommel seem virtually unstoppable.

The Seventh had suffered as badly as any, but worse for their morale, they had lost their beloved commander. General Jock Campbell had brought fire to the Seventh Armored, but Campbell was dead, not from combat, but by the cruel joke of an auto accident, his car overturning on a dismal stretch of desert road. Campbell had inspired not only his men, but the British high command, and convinced them to understand the value of the massed, carefully coordinated armor strike, the same kind of tactic Hitler's army had used in France. The Seventh took pride that they were recognized as the very force that would lead this kind of strike, what were now called "Jock columns." Though the Germans might have the better machines, Campbell had given his Desert Rats the confidence that no army had better men.

Darkness brought the fighting to an end.

They huddled beside the tank, beneath a thin canvas shelter they had unrolled from the rear of the turret. The canvas partially covered the tank itself, an attempt at camouflage, hiding both men and machine. They were filthy and exhausted and slowly fumbled with their ration tins, the first food any of them had eaten all day. Simmons had poured a cup of gasoline into a small, round hole in the dirt, the fire surrounded by a circle of rocks, just wide enough to support a pot of water. At least they would have tea.

No one spoke. Atkins scanned the edges of the canvas tent, reached out and pulled one side away from the tread of the tank. He was careful, no light could leak, nothing to give any gunner a place to aim. Somewhere, on all sides of them, men were doing as they were doing, finding time for food, sleep perhaps, a little tea. The Germans were there too, in all directions, two armies lost in the same span of desert, scattered tanks and armored vehicles, some in small clusters, others alone, all of them knowing that in the darkness, just *out there,* the enemy was close.

The tank was still warm, but the air was already cool, would get colder, and the men had wrapped themselves in ragged sheepskin coats, pulled from hidden nooks inside the tank.

The routine at the day's end was to gather the tank squads into camps, canvas sheets draping the tanks, which were parked in uneven rows. In this part of the desert, the British had made good use of any cover they could find, patches of camel thorn that would add to the camouflage of the vehicles. If the Germans sent a patrol to poke around, either side might fire starlight flares, the black desert suddenly bursting with light, tanks silhouetted for a brief moment, enough time for an artillery observer to guide a well-placed shell. But with the profiles of the tanks blending into the brush, there was not enough time for the enemy scouts to choose a target. That was the routine. But today, nothing had been routine. The fights had swept over the entire front, all the way north to the great escarpment that separated the sea from this flat table of desert. And the British had taken the heavier blow, Rommel's massive surge of armor flowing right through and around the British units. Confusion and fiery destruction had sent many of the British tanks back, panicked drivers blindly seeking the safety of the artillery support to the rear. But many could not get that far, were cut off, chopped to pieces by Rommel's rapid advance. It was the German's great genius, avoiding the head-on confrontation, sweeping the flank of the British armor. The tactic was obvious to the men in the tanks, and yet somehow the British command was all too often caught off guard by Rommel's rapid circular attacks. Today, the blow had been terrifyingly precise, and all across the British position, tank squadrons had been obliterated, some of the wrecked machines visible even now, scattered across the desert, small specks of flame.

Atkins waited for Simmons to pour the boiling water, stared at the cup in his hands, holding the last of his special hoard of tea. He knew that somewhere to the east, the food and water wagons were waiting, anxious men wondering if the tank squads they served had survived the day. Yes, we're alive, he thought. No bloody idea where we are, or what's between us and all that hot food. And water. And gasoline.

"How much petrol we have left?"

Simmons looked at him, said, "An hour. Maybe a quarter more. Not enough to play around."

"How many shells?"

Moxley was holding his tin cup as well, staring at the small, dimming fire. "Maybe . . . twenty-five. Thirty."

Atkins nodded, and Batchelor, his loader said, "Four boxes for the Vickers."

Four boxes. Enough machine-gun fire for what? Maybe an hour of fighting? Then what? Did that bloody Rommel get to our ammo dumps today too? He stirred the water in his cup, knew they were looking to him, would measure their own despair by his response. He nodded, tried to seem as positive as he could.

"That's enough. Ought to get us out of this mess. We've got at least a half dozen tanks to our south. We can team up at first light, drive east."

He knew they would understand the word: *east*. Retreat. No, more than retreat. Get the hell out of here. He thought of the big tents, the men with the maps. Hell, you don't know where we are any more than we do. But you sure better know what kind of whack we took today.

Simmons pushed dirt into his fire hole, killing the last flicker of light. They sat in total darkness, each man's eyes trying to find some glimpse, something to adjust to.

Simmons said, "Sir, we took a good licking, eh?"

"It wasn't pretty."

"I saw Captain Digby brew up. Looked like he got hit by an eighty-eight."

"You don't know that."

Simmons was silent for a moment. "I saw him brew up, sir. Nobody got out."

Brew up.

Atkins sipped at his tea. Damned strange description of it. He had seen the explosion as well, but there was no time to think about it, beyond the glimpse of Digby's command flag. Never liked that chap. But . . . not what I had in mind.

There was a burst of firing, a machine gun, and Atkins pulled back the canvas, saw streaks of tracers arcing toward the north. Now another, a sharp streak of white light, then red, the response. Damned fools. Shooting at ghosts. Just as likely to kill your own.

"Sit tight, chaps. A lot of itchy fingers. Maybe wounded, just shooting to show how pissed they are. No targets until morning."

Simmons said, "You think they went after Tobruk again, sir?"

"Hell if I know. That's forty miles from here. I think. Rommel pushed around the south of us. He might have pushed north too. Tobruk's not our problem."

There was a long silent moment, and Atkins pushed at the canvas again, tossed it back, the cold air rolling over them. No one protested, the men simply huddling up tighter, tugging at their coats. He slid out from beneath the heavy cloth, could make out the dark shapes of tanks, trucks in the distance, faint silhouettes in the light of a low crescent moon. There were still fires, smaller now, distant, but most of the burned hulks were cold and silent. He looked up, stared at the vast open sky, a million flickering lights, the night perfect and clear. He watched the stars for a long minute, felt the chill inside his coat. He realized now how truly tired he was, how every part of him ached. He looked back into the dark canvas cave, thought, you better get some sleep. Tomorrow, if we're lucky, we can get the hell out of here, regroup, wait for those damned generals to figure out what we're supposed to do next. But we weren't lucky today. Today, Rommel kicked us in the ass.

2. ROMMEL

He had been out front again, his command truck careening in and around the storm of dust and debris. The panzer divisions had staggered the British throughout most of the fight, but it was far from decided.

Rommel's command vehicle was a British "Mammoth," a huge, lumbering hulk captured in one of the many fights the preceding year. He rode up on top, high above anyone else, sat on the hard metal with his feet hanging down through an open hatch. The driver knew to push the fat truck right into the dust, that Rommel would not be satisfied until he could see it for himself, tank against tank, and if that meant he must direct the fight from the front lines, then that's where he would go.

The truck was a communication center, alive with crew and equipment designed to maintain some control of the battle around him. But the radios only brought confusion, coded messages that might require long wasted minutes to translate, or worse, voices speaking "in the clear," using no code at all, panicked men whose reports were a waste of time, since the enemy could hear them as well. His decisions were based on what he saw, not what he heard, and he would not rely on some bloodied tank officer to guide a fight from the blind hole of one tank. With so many tanks and armored gun carriers swirling around each other, a man whose survival depended on perfect control of one gun had better things to do.

Rommel had heard all the discreet complaining from his staff, well-tempered urgings that he should stay put, keep away from the worst of the bloody fighting. They knew not to push him too hard, and he tolerated the pressure from his senior staff, the men he respected, like Westphal, a good loyal officer who did his job. Now, in the midst of a full-scale tank battle, the staff's job was to coordinate things from the rear, keep the supplies moving forward, fueling and feeding this marvelous army.

The two heavy-armor divisions of the Afrika Korps were only a part of the total force he commanded, which included other German infantry and motorized units whose mobility and firepower had usually overmatched the British. In the field, he also commanded the Italians, both armor and infantry, men who had seen too much of defeat. But he tried to show respect for the Italians, knew that a fighting man should not be judged by his uniform, but by how he met the enemy. His respect for the frontline Italian soldiers had inspired them, this hard-bitten German who expected them to fight. The Italians responded, offering more tribute to Rommel than they ever had to their own officers. But the officers continued to listen to their paper commanders, the men appointed by Rome, who had been told that they outranked Rommel, or a delusion greater still, that Rommel would actually obey them. He knew his place in the chain of command, understood obedience as well as any good soldier. But he had seen too much of the Italians' petty grandstanding, pompous authority exercised by worthless officers who knew nothing of strategy and tactics. The Italians were embarrassed, humiliated, chose not to understand why Mussolini had allowed the Germans to come into North Africa. For all Rommel knew, even Mussolini was humiliated, though no one would ever detect a hint of that from the man's absurd declarations.

At first, he'd actually liked Mussolini, the man the Italians called Il Duce. Rommel had been attracted by the man's aggressive charm, and more, by Mussolini's ability to make good his own boasts. It was the luxury of being a dictator. No matter how bombastic his pronouncements, he would suggest only those strategies he had the absolute power to carry out. That way, he could maintain an aura of flawlessness. But Rommel had soon learned that Germany's ally was anything but flawless. Il Duce would do anything to save face, whether it made sense on the battlefield or not.

Even before Rommel had come to Africa, Hitler's overwhelming success in northern Europe had put Mussolini in the background. It was a form of humiliation that the Italian dictator would simply not accept. And so, he would make a glorious show of his own. In late 1940, Mussolini made the astonishing decision to invade Greece, without consulting Hitler at all. It was clear to all that Il Duce was attempting his own blitzkrieg, a lightning strike to conquer an inferior foe, more to impress Hitler than to accomplish anything of strategic value. But Mussolini's grand scheme backfired dramatically. Greece was no outclassed weakling. The Italian invaders were severely bloodied and sent reeling back. The message to the Germans was clear. Despite all of Mussolini's rousing oratory, his army might not be as inspired as their leader had promised. It was a lesson not lost on Rommel. Mussolini's ambitions for North Africa had little to do with the reality of what was required there, especially in confronting a British army that was constantly reinforcing and improving its equipment. Despite the exhortations from Rome, the Italian supply service did little to actually help their cause. The navy seemed far more interested in preserving their ships for posterity than risking them by hauling essential cargo across the Mediterranean. Rommel had struggled not only to secure an adequate number of troops and armor, but the food and fuel essential to maintaining his army in the field. Promises poured over him from Rome, and every day, fewer ships arrived to fulfill them. All the while, Mussolini spoke loudly of his valiant campaign to secure Africa for the new Roman Empire.

Rommel passed the burning wreckage of a British scout car, ignored the black shapes that still sat upright behind the shattered windshield. His tanks had mostly moved away, pushing northward, in rapid pursuit of a disordered British retreat. He coughed from the smoke, adjusted his goggles, shouted into the Mammoth, "Forward! Follow the dust. We must not lose contact."

The Mammoth continued to move, picking up speed, bouncing over rocks, swerving slightly to avoid black debris. He gripped the hatchway with one gloved hand, raised the binoculars with the other, but there was nothing to see, the smoke and dust blocking any sign of the fight. He could still hear the thumps of the artillery, knew from the sound it was the good work of the eighty-eights. But there were not as many now, the artillery fire beginning to slow.

"Stop! Stop now!"

The Mammoth crawled to a stop, and he scanned the dusty horizon. Still nothing to see. He lowered the binoculars, clasped his hands tightly around them, could hear scattered fights in all directions, even behind him, something he was used to now. But the sounds were too infrequent, too spread out.

"Send word to Crüwell. I want him in the air. If his tanks aren't firing, he's lost contact. He must find the enemy before they escape!"

The radio operator went to work, and Rommel still scanned to the north. Yes, General, get in your airplane and find them. That's why we do not sit in tents.

Ludwig Crüwell, the commander of the panzer divisions, was a man Rommel had come to rely on. The man had a quick mind and agreed with Rommel that leadership should not be exercised from behind. Most of the senior commanders had their own small planes, Rommel included. It was usually a Storch, a narrow two-seater that could land and take off on nearly any short stretch of flat ground, and the desert here was nothing but flat ground. Crüwell had adapted well to Rommel's habit of seeing a fight from the air, though unlike Rommel, Crüwell used a pilot. Rommel had learned long ago that a pilot was one more man, one more *detail* to keep track of. The most efficient way of getting around in a plane was to fly yourself.

"Sir, General Crüwell acknowledges your order. He will scout the enemy immediately."

Rommel stared ahead, thought, I should not have had to tell him. When your guns grow quiet, General, you have either killed all your enemy, or he has left you. I do not believe the British have allowed themselves to be obliterated.

The dust was drifting past him still, driven by a light, hot breeze. He spat dust, pulled his scarf up over his mouth, searched for some movement, some sign of his armor. Or anyone else's. He was feeling the familiar frustration, the blindness. Where have they gone? He turned, looked more to the east, thought of the British. You're out there, still. You didn't just simply run away like so many gazelles. And I am not yet finished with you.

The air above him ripped with a high scream, the sound fading, the shell landing far to the west. He laughed, said aloud, "So, you read my mind, eh? You don't care for my little insult?"

Another shell streaked overhead, and he could see the thin, white line, the trail of the shell fading quickly. Big one, he thought. Shooting at nothing. A protest of their own fear. Now another shell came from behind, the streak more red, the scream passing over in the opposite direction, quickly fading away. He waited, heard a small burst of thunder to the east. He smiled now, looked up again, waited for the next one. It came seconds later, followed by two more. The shells were arcing straight over him, and he ignored the nervous voices in the Mammoth, had heard all of that before, concern that they should move, get Rommel out of harm's way. Why? They aren't shooting at us. We're in the perfect place, right between them. A duel, and we're the audience. He felt strangely excited, thought not of the guns, not of the men who worked them. He thought instead of the observers, far out in front somewhere, maybe close by, right here, around us hidden in some low pile of rocks. Here is the chess game, the *fun,* waiting, watching for your enemy to make some mistake, an enemy gunner carelessly revealing his position. He imagined himself deep in some thorny brush, peering over rocks. Yes, there, the flash, the brief plume of smoke. I *see* you, fool. He leaned back slightly, put his hands behind him, the gloves protecting him from the searing heat of the Mammoth's rooftop, smiled. So, now you know where they are, and so, you make the call to the battery. The power is yours, guided by your hand. First one shell, to judge the range, then, adjust, nearer, farther, to one side or the other. And for the enemy there is no escape. He knows what he has done, knows that he has made a deadly error, and in seconds it will kill him, his gun, his entire crew. And the observer . . . he will see it happen. It is a perfect moment.

He waited for more, a minute, then two. But the guns were silent and he looked back toward the west, to where his artillery would be, knew it was done. This one belongs to us. The final shot of the duel. Yes, good work. Whoever you are, I would shake your hand.

The Mammoth slowed, dust billowing from below, bathing the small sea of tents in a choking fog. Rommel was down quickly, saw officers gathering, was surprised to see Kesselring.

"Field Marshal, I did not expect to see you. I came for General Crüwell's report."

"Come, let us walk."

Albert Kesselring's primary responsibility was the Luftwaffe, the German air forces that patrolled throughout the Mediterranean. He answered to Hermann Göring, who controlled all of Hitler's air forces. But Kesselring outranked Rommel and was in nominal command of the entire southern theater of the war, and so, Rommel's decisions were subject to Kesselring's approval. Rommel did not particularly like the man, and he suspected that the feeling was mutual, but from necessity they had formed a good working relationship. Kesselring was far more of a diplomat and so could deal far more gently and effectively with the Italians both in Rome and in North Africa, who continued to believe they were running the show. Rommel's constant screaming for supplies had made him an unwelcome voice in Rome, and increasingly, in Berlin. Kesselring was highly regarded by Hitler and could soften the indiscreet blows made by Rommel against "chairborne" generals and inept staff officers.

The two men walked away from the dusty tents, and Rommel, feeling impatient, said, "I don't need to hear bad news just now. Do you not hear the fight?"

Kesselring stopped, and Rommel knew he couldn't prevent the man from telling him of yet another calamity in Rome, some new reason why gasoline could not be sent.

Kesselring said, "I will inconvenience you anyway. General Crüwell has been shot down. Word was received here that his Storch took fire, and that he landed among the British. We do not know if he is dead, and certainly, there is hope he may only be captured."

"How long ago?"

"Within the hour. I received word back at my headquarters and flew up here as quickly as possible. We tried . . ." Kesselring stopped, and Rommel knew what was coming. "We did not know where you were. Colonel Westphal said you were somewhere at the front."

"I am here now. Do we know the enemy's position?"

A low roll of thunder erupted in the east, beyond the flat ground. Both men turned, and Kesselring said, "From what I can tell, the enemy is holding on to several key positions. We have taken a heavy toll on his armor, but he is not defeated. What do you intend to do?"

Rommel looked at the man, the genial face, the man's bald head hidden by the distinctive white-crowned hat of the Luftwaffe. The shape of the man's mouth made him appear to be smiling, though Kesselring was usually quite serious, was certainly serious now. Rommel pointed toward the sounds of the firing.

"I intend to find out why we do not hear more of that."

He saw words forming, Kesselring preparing the same tired protest. But Kesselring let it go, stepped back, made a short bow.

"Go. Do not let me stand in your way. This is your fight. I should notify Berlin about General Crüwell."

"Might it wait a moment? I need you to do something more important. Come."

Rommel led Kesselring toward the largest tent, Crüwell's staff gathering. He focused on the small table, maps spread out, papers overlapping. Rommel studied one, looked out, listened, the low rumbles coming again. He looked at Kesselring, said, "With Crüwell absent, the ranking officer in this sector is Italian. I would prefer . . . the panzers require a German to lead them. I need you to take over this position, take command of this wing of the attack. Coordinate the tank battalions. Find where the enemy is holding strong and push the fight around those positions."

There was a low hum in the tent, staff officers suddenly uncomfortable with Rommel's request. Rommel ignored them, saw surprise on Kesselring's face.

"Albert, this battle is yet to be decided. I cannot manage this entire affair, you have told me that yourself many times. General Crüwell's absence puts us at a disadvantage. I require a senior officer to take command in this sector. As we speak, the enemy is either running or regrouping his armor. It is just as likely that he is severely wounded and must be extinguished."

Kesselring scanned the faces around them, said, "Very well, General, I am in your charge. I understand my, um . . . orders. May I ask where I might find you?"

Rommel moved quickly to the Mammoth, the engine belching smoke, the crew loading up before him.

"I shall know where I am to be when I arrive there. I must see to the supply line for this front. Without fuel trucks, we will make no fight at all, and right now, it is likely that the enemy still has forces between our supply depots and where we now stand. In any event, the priority along *this* line is to find the enemy and engage him wherever he may be."

Rommel climbed up, resumed his perch on top of the Mammoth, the truck slowly turning away, a cloud of dust rising, engulfing Kesselring and the men who watched him go.

The supply trucks found their way through, helped by Rommel himself, who led the convoy to the desperately exhausted tank crews. The British had pulled farther into their defenses, and Rommel could sense the indecision, the pause, while the British command tried to organize. It had become the particular trait of this enemy that no matter how severe the crisis, they would weigh and evaluate, discuss and debate. It was a grotesquely inefficient way to run an army, especially in the middle of a fight. Regardless of fuel and supply and the number of tanks, Rommel was convinced that the mind of the British commander was his enemy's greatest weakness.

The Mammoth dropped down into a wide, shallow riverbed, what the Arabs called a wadi. He ordered a halt, could see smoke now, rising streaks of fire. Kesselring was doing his job, on the ground, and with the Luftwaffe as well. Dive bombers were dropping out of the sky, targeting British positions with pinpoint precision. He loved the sound of the Stukas, the pure terrifying scream as the gull-wing planes dove straight at their targets. The planes had sirens mounted on the wings, someone's delicious idea to terrorize their victims, letting them know that when they heard that awful sound, death was at hand, right now, right in your face.

He stood on the roof of the Mammoth, heard the radio chatter rising up to him, faces glancing up. He could see what they saw, out on the far side of the wadi: German tanks withdrawing, pulling back toward him. Armored trucks and half-tracks were darting among them, all moving toward the wide riverbed. Trails had been marked, the best places to cross, and the tanks began to move together, pushing down through the thick, sandy banks, across quickly, then up the near side. Rommel raised his binoculars, watched the horizon, the telltale dust rising, the pursuit from an enemy who believed the Germans were in full retreat. He smiled. Yes, he thought, come to my party.

From behind him, other vehicles moved forward, and quickly the wadi itself was filling with a river of trucks, gun carriers easing down into the dry sand, turning, positioning their cannon. Rommel loved the eighty-eights, the best weapon he had, the long barrels now placed just above the lip of the riverbank, pointing out toward the enemy, the enemy who had been baited, lured into believing that the Germans had withdrawn.

The dust cloud in front of him began to take shape, tanks appearing, more of the rapid armored cars, machine-gun carriers, spoiling for a fight, convinced the Germans were on the run. He stared, picked out the larger machines, a different shape, the short, fat cannon set to one side. They were the new Grants, the American-made tanks, said to be the equal of anything the Germans had. Well, we shall see about that. His heart was racing, and he gauged the distance, a mile perhaps, no need to wait much longer. The orders rolled through the gun crews, and the wadi erupted into bursts of fire and thunderous roars. All along the riverbank, the eighty-eights spit their deadly fire toward the enemy. Rommel stared through the binoculars, could see the first impacts, bursts of black smoke, sheets of fire. The dust of the enemy had turned to smoke, the British column coming apart, the formation dissolving, men and their machines scrambling to escape the ambush. Some began to return fire, and the ground on both sides of the wadi erupted into dirt and loose rock. But the shells had no targets, were poorly directed by British gunners who now knew what their enemy had done.

From their low perches, the concealed eighty-eights continued to launch deadly fire at the disintegrating British battalion. Rommel looked down into the faces watching him, waiting for his order.

"Send them in! Straight forward, and flank to the right! All speed!"

From behind him came a new sound, the German tanks returning, plunging into the wadi, then up, moving quickly toward the dense fog of black smoke. The panzers were moving into attack formations, some sweeping toward the right flank of the British line, others driving straight into the dust and smoke. With their own machines blocking their line of fire, the gun crews in the wadi began to gather up, the trucks moving to attach their guns. The fight roared all across the open ground in front of them, German and British tanks engulfed in deadly chaos. But the shock was complete, the enemy routed. Rommel knew it without seeing what was happening in front of him. He sat down, shouted the order to advance, and the big machine kicked into motion, drove up and over the soft riverbank. Behind him, the eighty-eights were moving as well, the gunners preparing to follow their tanks. No, we do not rush straight into your guns. We invite you instead to rush straight into ours.

The maneuver had been perfected all across North Africa, the tanks baiting and drawing the enemy forward, while the big guns lay in wait. The eighty-eights would do their work and the tanks would surge forward again, mopping up. They would repeat the tactic over and over, Rommel's simple game of leap-frog.

The names of the villages and oases were like so many of those spread all over this part of the massive continent: Sidi Muftah, Bir el Hamat, Acroma, El Adem. Often villages weren't villages at all, but a hut or some ragged tents perched around a deep hole in the dirt, a place where blessed water could be found, sometimes a cluster of trees separating the precious well from the desolation that surrounded it. It had been the same all across Libya, meaningless names, barely visible landmarks a tank driver would ignore as he rolled past. There was no stopping to fill canteens, no marveling at the odd bits of ancient architecture, the occasional Roman ruin. This land was now only a battleground, a stage for hundreds of tanks and troop carriers, mobile machine guns and half-tracks. The infantry was here too, swarms of men suffering through the fog of dust that was their only protection, seeking an enemy who was mobile, or armored, or simply dug into slit trenches in the hard ground.

In the north Rommel had placed the Italians, infantry and mobile troop carriers, armored cars and their outdated tanks, pushing eastward along the coastal road, to pressure the British flank, drawing precious British strength from the fight in the center. There, and in the south, Kesselring, Rommel, and the German armor pressed and prodded, taking every advantage of the indecisive tactics of the British. But it was not a one-sided fight, no simple victory. For days, the British held tightly to what they called the Gazala Line, a stout defensive position that ran from the sea in the north, far down along a string of mine-fields, outposts, and fortified "boxes." From the first day of the attack, Rommel had pierced and flanked the line, but still, the British held to their strong points, and so, as days passed, both sides were used up, the sea of dust and rock littered with growing numbers of machines, and the bodies of the men who drove them.

In the center of the line, the fight came from every direction, perfect confusion, large battles and small duels, tanks fighting tanks, infantry caught in between. The place would soon appear on the British maps. They would call it The Cauldron. After a long desperate week, both sides were losing energy and equipment, but Rommel's tenacity prevailed. The British positions began to collapse, and gradually the machines that could still move pushed eastward to make their escape. Though Rommel had won the day, his own panzer divisions were a shadow of themselves, hundreds of wrecked and charred vehicles spread among the carcasses of the British. But no one on either side doubted that this time, the fight belonged to Rommel. By withdrawing from the Gazala Line, the British had pulled their protection away from a garrison penned up inside a strong defensive ring on the coast. The city and its valuable port had long held Rommel's attention. It was called Tobruk.

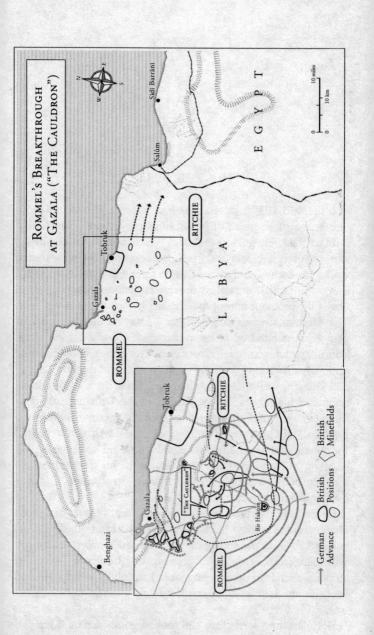

ROMMEL'S BREAKTHROUGH
AT GAZALA ("THE CAULDRON")

E G Y P T

Sidi Barrâni

Salûm

RITCHIE

Tobruk

Gazala

ROMMEL

L I B Y A

Benghazi

N
W   E
S

10 miles
10 km
0

Tobruk

RITCHIE

"THE CAULDRON"

Gazala

Bir Hakeim

ROMMEL

German Advance
British Positions
British Minefields

3. ROMMEL

In the mid-1930s, the Italians had come to Tobruk, to carve out one more piece of Mussolini's playground. The Italian military had recognized the city's value and its vulnerability, and so, the engineers had ringed the entire area with trench works, tank traps, and minefields. When the Italians were swept away, the British improved those fortifications, making good use of the precious harbor to help supply their army in the field. The Germans' main supply lines came through the port of Tripoli, nine hundred miles to the west. For that reason alone Tobruk, which was much closer to the front lines, could become an invaluable supply hub for German men and matériel. Rommel knew as well that if Tobruk remained a British stronghold, no matter his success on the battlefield, the British would continue to have a major presence in the area, a permanent thorn in his side. With his success at the Cauldron, the British were ripe for pursuit, but any major push eastward would leave the British garrison at Tobruk in his rear, allowing the troops there to threaten both his supplies and his flank. To Rommel that was simply unacceptable.

He had been in the same position the year before, one more chapter of the seesaw battles that had rolled in both directions across Libya. In the spring of 1941, he had focused on Tobruk with dangerous arrogance, believing that his forces were unstoppable, and that the enemy would simply give way. He had been wrong then, and the result was his greatest failure of the war.

His plan the year before had looked good on paper, but fell apart almost immediately. First, the Italians had failed to supply him with accurate maps of the fortifications they themselves had constructed, and Rommel could only guess what kinds of obstructions lay in the path of his tanks. But then, his attacks were uncoordinated, and supply problems immediately plagued both the German and Italian forces. Bad intelligence and poor coordination would usually doom any attack, but Rommel was confronted by yet another surprise, the tenacity of the enemy troops, who stoutly manned their fortifications, not as eager to quit as Rommel had believed.

Every veteran of the Great War knew of the Anzacs, the men of the Australia and New Zealand Army Corps, men who had stood tall throughout that horrible war, who had fought with a fierceness that had made them legends. Twenty-five years later, at Tobruk, Rommel was facing some of those same men, and their sons as well. The fortifications that surrounded the city had been occupied by the Australian Ninth Division, under the command of Major General Sir Leslie Morshead, and the Australians would not yield. The result was a long, fruitless siege that produced losses Rommel could not afford. The British had taken advantage and, late in 1941, had pushed Rommel back across Libya.

But that was then. This time, there would be no failure. This time there were accurate maps, and officers in the field who knew what they were expected to do. And the British high command had made a significant mistake. The Australians were no longer in Tobruk. Their replacements were South Africans, under the command of General Hendrik Klopper. The South Africans were certainly respected, and Klopper was a reasonably capable commander. But no one believed they had the backbone of Morshead's Australians.

At dawn on June 20, Kesselring's bombers opened the attack, and within two hours, Rommel began the kind of assault he had wanted to launch the year before. Rather than a diluted general advance all along the thirty-mile front, Rommel bluffed an attack in one sector of the line, then pounded his armor against unprepared defenses in an area where the South Africans had almost no armor. German engineers quickly opened pathways across the once treacherous antitank ditches, and using the same blitzkrieg tactics that had overwhelmed Poland and Western Europe, Rommel's tanks went forward in tight punching blows, ripping breakthroughs in the South African defenses. Once through the gaps, the German tanks fanned out behind the enemy, surrounding and engulfing them. In twenty-four hours, it was over.

JUNE 22, 1942

He had briefly stayed in Tobruk, allowing himself the luxury of a bed. The staff had been scattered and busy, coordinating with the rear services for the handling of prisoners, and the cataloging and distribution of the amazing haul of goods they had captured in the city. Klopper had surrendered nearly thirty-five thousand men, and the German success had come so quickly that the South Africans had had no time to destroy their precious supplies. Besides the critical fuel, food, and ammunition, the Germans had captured nearly two thousand vehicles of all kinds, including thirty undamaged British tanks.

Rommel had met with Klopper, a brief, formal ceremony, the South African concerned about the treatment of his men. It was never an issue with Rommel, there would be no mistreatment of prisoners, ever, but he did not spend any more time than required in the presence of the enemy commander. There was nothing to be gained by humiliation, and Klopper would certainly not reveal any British plans. Besides, Rommel knew that his own intelligence people probably knew more about British intentions than the one senior officer they had left behind in Tobruk.

He had decided to make a quick tour of the city, was being driven in a new command vehicle, an actual staff car, typical for senior officers, but unusual for Rommel himself. The Mammoth had been left behind for now, but the staff knew to have it prepared and ready, that this brief rest was no vacation.

They were near the small harbor, and he ordered the car to halt, climbed out, would see what ships the British had left behind, what Kesselring's bombs had destroyed. It was always a price for the capture of a port, enemy vessels either sunk or scuttled by their crews, always blocking the channels, making the job more difficult for the engineers to clear passage for the supply ships of the port's new owners. He walked close to the concrete of a shattered pier, stepped over debris, could see more of the same all around him. If there had been beauty here, there was none now. The streets were hardly streets at all, narrow passages that wound past gaping bomb craters, the wreckage and destruction not just from Kesselring's bombers, but from Rommel's own siege the year before, long, drawn-out artillery duels that had converted most of this seaport city into complete ruin.

He knew his army was worn-out, so many weeks of constant motion, the hard fight that had finally given them victory. The cost was high, men and tanks, the figures alarming. He was down to fewer than two hundred serviceable tanks, and even with the precious gasoline captured at Tobruk, they were dangerously low on fuel.

He stared into the harbor, watched work crews on small barges, cranes straining to move sunken debris. We can make good use of this place, he thought. It is not so big as Tripoli, but it is one more port that is ours and not theirs. Perhaps now Rome can be persuaded to send us some supply ships.

"Sir!"

A second staff car pulled up alongside his own, and he recognized the big man, oversize in any vehicle he rode in. It was Berndt, the man pouring himself out of his cramped seat.

Berndt moved toward him, all smiles, and Rommel said, "You have returned, Alfred. How was Berlin?"

Berndt stopped, made his formal salute, always the good show for the men.

"Berlin is celebrating, Herr General. You have brightened the light in every staff room. The Führer has never been in a better mood. Your name is spoken with great respect! And, I come with a very special message." Berndt seemed to prepare himself, puffing out his chest a bit more than usual. "General Rommel, it is my honor to communicate to you the Führer's personal congratulations for your magnificent victory. I have been instructed to notify you that the Führer has promoted you to the rank of field marshal. The appropriate certification will arrive shortly. Allow me to be the first, sir."

Berndt took a step back, saluted, said, "Field Marshal Rommel."

Rommel didn't know what to say, Berndt seeming to expect a speech.

"That is quite . . . wonderful. Yes, I am deeply appreciative."

There was an explosion out past the pier, the engineers blasting through some obstruction in the waterway. Rommel turned that way instinctively, watched as smoke drifted past the men working hard at their task. Yes, he thought, promotion is good. Lucy will be proud. I should write to her tonight, though surely she has heard of this already. In Berlin, success is not kept secret.

Berndt was fidgeting, moved up beside him now, seemed mystified by Rommel's lack of response.

"Does this not call for a celebration, sir?"

Rommel nodded slowly. "Yes, I suppose so. It will be good for the men. They should know that someone beyond this dreadful place is paying attention to us."

Alfred Berndt was a Gestapo officer, sent to Africa by Hitler's propaganda master, Dr. Joseph Goebbels. Berndt was not a spy, precisely, though Rommel understood that the man's job was to serve as a direct conduit between his command and Hitler's inner circle. There had been nervousness by some of Rommel's staff that Berndt must be handled discreetly. He had arrived in Libya with a bit too much noise, seemed to have an inflated notion of his own value. It was an annoyance Rommel had been quick to correct, and the man had actually fit in quite well, had become accepted by the staff as just one more man with a job to do. If there was one lingering absurdity, it was that Berndt was, technically, only a lieutenant. It was a poor attempt to hide the man's influence, a decision made by someone in Berlin who no doubt believed Berndt would draw less scrutiny as a junior officer. Rommel was certainly not fooled, had quickly learned that the big, overbearing man did not come to Africa to be ignored. But he had come to trust Berndt's intentions, believed that anything the man reported to Berlin would be accurate and fair. It was perfectly reasonable that Hitler and his staff would want to know precisely what was happening in Africa, and at the same time, by reporting to Goebbels, Berndt would pass along the kind of information that the propaganda ministry would find useful. Whether those news reports were accurate was not Rommel's problem. He knew that he had no control over anything Goebbels put into the newspapers, or any control over how Rommel himself would be presented to the German people. Regardless of the discomfort Rommel had given many of Hitler's "chairborne" officers, right now he was certainly being trumpeted throughout Germany as a great hero, the man of the hour. For the moment at least, his harshest critics would have to keep silent.

ROMMEL'S HEADQUARTERS, NEAR TOBRUK— JUNE 22, 1942

The celebration was hardly a party at all, a few of his staff toasting him from a single bottle of whiskey they had secured from some unspecified stash in Tobruk. Rommel had actually allowed himself to take a drink, a rare occurrence in the desert. He accompanied his glass of whiskey with a tin of South African pineapple. It was all the luxury the evening required.

The celebration concluded, the men drifting back to their work. He moved out into the open, the air cooling, no breeze, the daylight nearly gone. There was activity in the distance, trucks and armored cars, the first of the night patrols moving out, heading east, toward the enemy. It was a constant routine, scouting, probing, the enemy doing the same. The patrols would often confront each other, short fights that shattered the darkness with lightning streaks of tracer fire. But more often, the patrols would pass right by each other, avoiding the fight. Combat was an inconvenient distraction to the scouts, something to keep them from doing their jobs. Each was patrolling the desert with one goal, seeking information of some movement of the enemy, whether anyone was shifting position, gathering strength. Before dawn, they would scamper back through the cleared pathways in their own minefields, reporting back to their commanders whether the enemy was threatening to launch some dawn attack.

Rommel watched them pull away, thought, there will be no

attack now, not by us, and certainly not by them. We are both used up, bloodied, worn into uselessness. The men . . . no, the men are fine. They can rest now, gain strength. It is the machines that suffer, the power drained from this army by the loss of so much steel. He looked to the west, toward the far distant ports of Tripoli and Benghazi, old habit now. He had grown weary of sending the urgent messages for supplies, but he sent them still. The requests followed the chain of command, went usually through Kesselring, then up the mythical ladder of authority to Comando Supremo in Rome. And there, he thought, my urgent requests go into some box, shoved underneath someone's feet, to use as a footstool.

He heard the sound of an airplane motor, slow, nothing like the hard screams of the Messerschmitts. He saw a Storch, floating downward like a small black bird, bouncing once, slowing, rolling to a stop. Ground crews moved quickly, ropes tied to the landing gear, anchoring the plane against some sudden windstorm that would easily flip it over. The door of the plane opened, and an officer stepped down, followed by the pilot, and the ground crews saluted stiffly. It was Kesselring.

Rommel stayed put, waited for Kesselring to approach. It was a small show, purposeful, discreet disrespect. *No matter your rank, this is my ground, and my army.* If you wish to see me, you will come to *me.* If Kesselring even noticed, he showed no hint of annoyance. There was annoyance enough in Kesselring's visits as it was, for both of them. If he was there at all, it was usually because something bad had happened.

"Good evening, Erwin."

"Field Marshal."

Kesselring laughed, surprising Rommel. "Oh, I stand corrected. Good evening, *Field Marshal.*"

Rommel was suddenly embarrassed, had crossed a line, even for him. "No, sir, I did not . . . I was not correcting you. I was referring to you. I meant it as a greeting."

Kesselring still laughed, put his hand on Rommel's shoulder, a rare gesture of familiarity.

"Humility. A rare trait in the Afrika Korps. Don't bother yourself about it, Erwin. I made a poor joke. But, it seems you have already been informed about your promotion. I had hoped to be the first to bring the news, but then, that was not to be expected."

"Lieutenant Berndt has returned from Berlin. He brought word."

"Berndt. Yes, your public relations wizard. The man thrives on good news, does he not? And if there is no good news, he will provide his own."

"He does his job."

"Quite well too. He has the Führer's ear, you know. That gives you an enormous advantage, should you wish to avoid my nagging and make your grievances known only to Berlin."

Rommel felt cautious, was disarmed by Kesselring's high spirits.

"I assure you, I have not done so."

"I know, Erwin. I have the Führer's ear too. May we take a walk?"

Rommel said nothing, followed, and Kesselring said, "General Bastico is concerned about your intentions. He is concerned about a great deal more, actually. He is not the least bit amused that you now outrank him. I have been told that Mussolini will promote him quickly, to maintain his paper authority over you. They are so very sensitive about such meaningless matters."

"General Bastico is not a combat officer. *Bombastico*. That's what the staff calls him."

"Your staff would not use such a term if you did not allow it."

"I allow it. I agree with it. Loud voices do not make soldiers. I have invited him to visit here, to inspect . . . whatever he feels he must inspect. Most of the time, he simply refuses to come, some excuse about his schedule. I know better. He does not enjoy treading anywhere near the front."

"You cannot simply dismiss him. He is the commander in chief of the Italian forces here. Rome speaks through him."

Rommel ignored the scolding, said, "I would prefer to talk about the future. You know what our next move should be. The enemy is badly damaged. He will seek safe haven, build a powerful defensive line. We must strike him before that happens. I intend to drive him hard. Cairo is within ten days' grasp."

Kesselring looked toward him. "I have received a cable from

Rome. Comando Supremo desires that you not advance east of the Capuzzo-Sollum line. They feel there is enormous risk."

"Of course there is enormous risk. This is war. Do you agree with them? I should simply sit here?"

"Comando Supremo understands the difficulties involved in supplying this army. There is no prediction when Tobruk can be made useful. The Italians are very concerned your supplies will not be adequate if you continue to extend your supply line."

Kesselring stopped, and even in the dim light Rommel could see pain on the man's face, the frustration of having to convey such an absurd message. Rommel felt his anger rising, would not just let it go.

"If they are so concerned about the adequacy of my supplies, then why don't they send more supplies? They would instead prefer that we sit in one place, so that we don't use up any more gasoline and food than we have to. We could all have stayed in Germany, and supply would not be a problem at all!"

His voice had risen, and Kesselring was looking at him, silent, tired eyes. Yes, Rommel thought, he knows. This is not his fight, not an argument I can make with him. Kesselring moved out to the edge of the palms, glanced up at the stars.

"Erwin, if we are to deal with the Italians, we must understand what they want. This war belongs to Mussolini. The rest of them, no matter how much obedience they lather on him, no matter their professed loyalty . . . the senior officers have no passion for this fight. Every one of them is looking past this war, every one far more concerned whether or not he will have a seat of power in whatever follows. The more gasoline they ship down here, the less they will have for their own automobiles in Rome."

Kesselring was silent now, turned again toward the night sky.

Rommel said slowly, "The British are defeated. All they require is a push, and they will hand us Cairo, and with it, the Suez. Should we inform the Führer that it is best if we ignore this opportunity because our ally is afraid I will use up too much gasoline? What would you have me do?"

Kesselring thought a moment, looked at him now, said, "You know how I feel. I have always believed our priority must be capturing Malta. How do you expect to march into Egypt when the British have a great fat tiger sitting in your rear, swatting away your supply ships?"

Malta. It was the unchanging refrain from Kesselring. The island sat exactly astride the shipping lanes that came from Italy, housed British planes and a naval presence that hammered any supply convoys that ventured toward Rommel's desperately needy army. The Luftwaffe had bombed the island into ruin, months of siege that had accomplished no more than most such sieges accomplished, no more than what Hitler had accomplished by bombing London.

Rommel stared up through the tops of the palms, the stars blanketing the sky, the chill harder now. He looked toward the tents, scanned the empty, open ground, satisfied that no one was close enough to hear. He leaned closer to Kesselring, said, "There will be no invasion. The Führer's staff will not annoy him with such a minor nuisance as Malta, not while he has both his eyes and both his hands on Russia. He will not be distracted."

"What do you know of Russia?"

Rommel was surprised by the question. "I know what Berndt tells me, what he chooses to bring from Berlin. All is well, we are winning a great victory over Stalin's worthless army. When I was last there, I heard the same thing about Libya. Months ago they announced that I would soon push the British into the Suez Canal. So, they also speak of Russia. Perhaps we should leave the soldiers home and fight this war with publicists. We would certainly win."

There was no humor in his words, and Kesselring glanced past him, searching for eavesdroppers, then said in a low voice, "Enough. I will not hear any more." Kesselring paused. "We are stepchildren, you and me. We have had the opportunity here to strike an enormous blow, to cripple the British, to drive past Egypt, to sweep into the oil fields. We could have linked an army with our forces in the Caucasus, driven into Stalingrad from two sides."

Rommel heard emotion in Kesselring's voice, said, "We can not dream, Albert. We can perform. There is a job in front of us, right here, right now. Egypt is ours, if we make it ours."

"But we cannot ignore Malta. I must insist to the Führer."

"And when he ignores you?"

"It is plainly simple strategy. You cannot attack an enemy who holds a strong position in your rear. Why do they not see that?" Kesselring's voice had grown louder, and he caught himself, whispered, "Jodl and Keitel both should tell him. Halder should tell him. Surely *they* understand how a war must be fought. They have all read the lessons of Frederick the Great. Even the Führer knows those lessons. But there are no Fredericks in Germany now. No von Moltkes, no von Hindenburgs. The Führer is concerned with nothing but Russia. The Italians are trained for display, for parades. That leaves . . . *you*."

Rommel did not miss Kesselring's point, thought, of course, he did not say *us*. No, if there is failure here, it is my failure. No matter what happens in Africa, *he* will live to fight another day.

Rommel said, "I have already discussed a plan of attack with my staff. You can study it tonight if you wish."

Kesselring shook his head. "I object to it already. It is not sound unless we subdue the enemy at Malta. For their own reasons, the Italians will object to it as well."

"Allow me to suggest how you might deal with the Italians. May I request that you inform Comando Supremo that we would be honored if Il Duce himself will ride with us as we *liberate* Cairo. Suggest that he might be viewed as the new pharaoh."

Kesselring made a small laugh. "Yes, that might prove effective."

The next day, cables passed over the Mediterranean in both directions. The final cable came from Mussolini, encouraging Rommel to press forward his attack. And Mussolini had accepted the invitation as well. Il Duce agreed to fly to Libya to await Rommel's glorious conquest of Egypt. When he arrived, Rommel's aides saw that there were two aircraft in Il Duce's caravan. One was for Mussolini himself, with his attendant staff. The second plane brought his mount, an enormous white stallion that Mussolini would ride triumphantly into the Egyptian capital, the man who had conquered Africa.

*   *   *

To the east, the British scrambled to organize their ragged battalions, preparing for Rommel's inevitable assault. It began on June 26, with the same tactic Rommel had used before, sweeping around the flanks of the British, who continued to look for the enemy in their front. When the British attempted counterattacks, they threw their tank units in piecemeal, only to be ground up by the German panzers, and Rommel's treasured eighty-eights. In three days, the port of Mersa Matruh was in German hands, the British pulling farther east in tumbling confusion. But the British had two advantages. As they pulled back deeper into Egypt, they moved ever closer to their supply depots, while Rommel once more only lengthened his fragile lifelines. The second advantage was the land itself. Between Rommel and Cairo, the hard, flat desert grew far more narrow, a passageway barely forty miles wide, cut through with ridges and rocky hills. The sea bounded the north, and to the south, the hard, rocky ground fell away to a desolate sea of soft sand, the Qattara Depression, a place no tank could hope to cross. The British squeezed themselves between these two impenetrable barriers, while Rommel pursued as best he could. He understood that even in victory, the sacrifice had been far too great. As his army gathered up to face the ever-strengthening British defenses, Rommel's mighty Afrika Korps had exactly twelve undamaged tanks.

Though Rommel had driven within sixty-five miles of Alexandria, the first great Egyptian prize, he was forced to order his exhausted army to pause. The British responded by launching a counterattack that accomplished little more than adding to the casualty and prisoner lists on both sides. Neither side was, for now, in any position to do much damage to the other.

In any army, failure leads to change, and the British commander in chief, Sir Claude Auchinleck, now removed the British Eighth Army's field commander, General Neil Ritchie. But, as the man in overall command of the theater, Auchinleck himself was just as responsible for the fate of his army. On August 4, with activity along the front lines relatively quiet, Prime Minister Winston Churchill flew to Cairo and removed Auchinleck, replacing him with General Sir Harold Alexander. But the

British still required a man to take charge in the field, to reinvig-
orate the Eighth Army. Under pressure from Churchill, the
British high command gave the job to General William
"Strafer" Gott. Two days later, Gott was killed when his plane
was shot to pieces by a German Messerschmitt. It was one more
blow the British could not afford. From London, one other
name had emerged, that of a somewhat disagreeable officer who
had proven himself a thorn in the side of the high command and
who took a no-nonsense approach to tactics and combat. Soon
after Gott's death, even the reluctant Churchill agreed that he
might be the man to handle this crucial assignment.

4. MONTGOMERY

B ernard Montgomery had never liked Auchinleck, had no reason to like him now. The man seemed to take his time, droning on, what seemed to be an unending speech. Montgomery was already impatient, had endured impatience every day of his life. But now, in the stuffy confines of Auchinleck's headquarters, he suddenly felt like bursting into blind action, tossing furniture through the walls, and possibly Auchinleck with it.

It wouldn't do, of course. The man was still his superior officer. But that particular indignity would plague Montgomery for only two more days. Auchinleck's successor, Harold Alexander, was a man Montgomery greatly admired, who would never try to educate an educated man. But Montgomery first had to endure Auchinleck's parting instructions, the carefully laid out strategies and positioning of the Eighth Army that Montgomery would inherit. Montgomery had no interest at all in any of Auchinleck's plans. He wondered if Auchinleck was enjoying this final moment. Yes, quite a moment in the sun for him. Too bad there has been no sunshine in this place, not ever.

Auchinleck was pointing to a map, going over details of the troop positions. Montgomery ignored the maps, let Auchinleck's words drift past him. He studied the man's face, worn and blistered from the many months of life in the desert. Auchinleck was only three years his senior, but seemed older, and Montgomery found that entirely appropriate. Certainly, he thought, his time is past.

Auchinleck paused, and Montgomery couldn't avoid the

sadness in Auchinleck's face. He felt himself pulled in, watched as the man backed his chair away from the desk.

"It is imperative that you do what you must to preserve this army, General. No matter what Rommel tries to accomplish here, you must not allow the Eighth Army to be destroyed. Failure is always a possibility. Egypt may be lost, or the Suez. But those are merely points on a map, and those failures can be reversed, in time. But if this *army* is not preserved, we cannot fight another day."

Montgomery did not respond, and Auchinleck stood, the signal that the meeting was over. Montgomery stood as well, his escape only seconds away. I was at Dunkirk, you bloody jackass. I know all there is to know about preserving an army. He made a short crisp bow, said, "Sir."

Montgomery was already moving toward the door, and he jerked it open and walked out. The sun blinded him for a few seconds, and he put the wide hat on his head, the distinctive Australian slouch hat, the left side of the brim pinned above his ear. Montgomery admired the Australians, had no objection at all if he looked like one of them. I should like to meet those chaps, he thought. The New Zealanders as well. Make it a priority. Quite likely they are not so infected with Auchinleck's sense of doom. Go home, old man. This is my army now.

He walked past a row of shops, moved with long strides, a one-man march. He had expected more people to be milling about, usually the case around an army in the field. But the atmosphere of Cairo was different, quiet, tense, and distinctly unpleasant. It was no secret that the locals now saw the British as merely temporary occupants. With every sunrise there was a great deal of uneasy talk that Rommel's tanks would likely come roaring and clattering into their streets. A good many British citizens, most of the Jews, and even some of the long-settled Italians, had simply vanished, escaping by boat or air. Well, why not? he thought. Our commander in chief has confused his personal defeat with the defeat of this army. We shall see what we can do about that.

He saw an open door, a woman appearing, wrapped in a white robe. His eyes met hers for a brief moment, and he felt a jolt of embarrassment, saw the robe part just slightly, one bronze leg suddenly appearing. He scowled, turned away, changed direction, moved across the street. He quickened his pace, thought, *fleshpot.* This entire country is one bloody fleshpot. Good for the men, I suppose. They do seem to need their horizontal refreshment. Should talk to the doctors though, make sure everyone is checked out. Can't have this army brought down by something as idiotic as venereal disease.

He saw the truck now, the driver eating some strange piece of fruit. Montgomery had sent the man to the quartermaster depot, to replace the heavy clothing Montgomery had worn on the flight from England. Already, he was sweating, chafing from the annoyance of the heat.

The man stiffened, saluted, said, "Sir. I have a kit for you, sir. Lightweight khaki all around."

"Very good, Sergeant. Then by all means, it's time to go to the desert, wouldn't you say? Right. On with it."

He climbed into the sand-colored truck, glanced at the machine gun that perched up over the windshield. The truck rolled forward, and he reached for the gun, gripped the hard steel, felt the grit of the dust smeared into the film of oil. He thought of Auchinleck, all the man's papers and maps. If your *plans* were so spiffy, we'd be in Tripoli now, not Cairo. No, sir. Burn all of that. Every scrap.

As they moved toward the outskirts of the city, they passed soldiers, lean, hard men with burnt faces. Some had no shirts, wore hats instead of helmets, watched him pass by without smiles, no cheers, no sign of any parade-ground formality. Veterans, he thought. An army of good men. They deserve a good leader, someone with *binge,* someone who believes they can win. By damned, they've got one now.

The new commander sent rapid shock waves through the Eighth Army. Alexander had given Montgomery the authority to eliminate the "deadwood," anyone who did not seem to be prepared or fit for the job Montgomery expected him to do. Some of those were already gone, men whose caustic relationship with Montgomery went back years before the war. They had been a part of the Eighth's command headquarters, who had served either Auchinleck or the Eighth's former commander Neil Ritchie, the man who seemed to collapse under the strain of confronting Rommel. Few of those men had any illusions they would work well with Montgomery. Line officers had been axed as well, some unexpectedly, men who spoke more of Rommel than of their own plans for defeating him. It was precisely the sort of attitude Montgomery would not tolerate, what he saw as Auchinleck's overemphasis on lines of retreat. Montgomery believed that he had been given one primary task: defeat the enemy. Anyone who seemed comfortable with Auchinleck's tentativeness had no place in his army. While some of the veterans accepted his personnel changes with stoic silence, others grumbled, questioning whether this man knew anything about fighting in the desert or was simply a strutting martinet who, once he was confronted by the tactical brilliance of Rommel, would fall on his face like so many before him. Unfortunately, if Montgomery failed, he would no doubt take a good part of the Eighth Army with him.

BURG-EL-ARAB, EGYPT—AUGUST 19, 1942

The ground was hard and hot, and in every direction men were moving with slow, weary steps. But the village of white concrete and date palms offered the headquarters staff a blessed difference from the fry-pan misery of the desert. Here, no matter the oppressive sun, the men could enjoy the enormous luxury of a place to bathe, to wash away the crusty grime of the desert. Montgomery encouraged it, knew that the body needed replenishment the same as the mind. Each day, the men could enjoy a long moment in the relatively cool waters of the Mediterranean Sea.

He had stayed close to his headquarters, had received word that Alexander was bringing him a visitor. He always looked forward to Alexander's visits, knew that his chief would allow him to lead the briefings and strategy sessions without the annoying need some commanders had to interject their own views. Alexander had seemed eager to give Montgomery a free hand. But not everyone in London was altogether comfortable with Montgomery assuming command in such a vulnerable theater of the war. He had not heard more than the occasional hint of grumbling, but today, he might hear a great deal more. The visitor was Winston Churchill.

*   *   *

Montgomery's explanations of strategy had been formal and precise, and he was surprised that Churchill had not offered much feedback of his own. They met first in Montgomery's map truck, a stifling hulk, but the one place where he could show both Alexander and Churchill what he was preparing to do. From there, they would go to the field, Churchill insisting on a tour that would take him close to the men who would do the fighting. They had made a point of visiting the New Zealanders and Australians in particular, had passed through the lines of ragged men, who found the energy to offer Churchill a rousing welcome. Montgomery had seen some of that enthusiasm for his own visits, but not like this, and certainly not from the officers. Even Montgomery was impressed.

They returned to the village, and the staff officers were already seeing to the details of the evening meal. But for the moment, dinner could wait. With the blistering sun still high, Churchill had his own ideas.

They left the hard gravel street, strolled toward the glistening blue of the water, the image of perfect coolness, soft whispers that rolled up onto the stony sand. Montgomery and Alexander followed close behind Churchill, flanking him as he moved with short, precise steps toward the water. The two officers were wrapped only in towels, but Churchill stood out quite differently, the short, rotund man chomping heartily on a cigar, wearing only his pith helmet and his shirt. Montgomery kept his eyes focused on the water.

Churchill stopped, stared down the beach. No more than a hundred yards away, the shallow water was alive with a mass of men, the glassy calm broken by their obvious enthusiasm. The closest men were in full uniform, guards, keeping the soldiers at a respectful distance from their commanders. But beyond, as far down the beach as Montgomery could see, the men were clearly enjoying the same experience that the prime minister was about to share.

Churchill pointed with the cigar, said, "I say, Alex, you said we had no requisition for bathing trunks. Yet those men have clearly been issued white trunks of their own. Did you mean . . . only the officers should do without?"

Alexander laughed, looked at Montgomery, who smiled himself, the first good smile he had enjoyed all day.

Montgomery said, "Mr. Prime Minister, those men are not in fact wearing bathing trunks. The white is . . . um . . . their skin, sir. What would normally be covered by their shorts."

Churchill plugged the cigar into his mouth, made a short laugh.

"Ah, yes. I see. Quite a suntan these lads have, eh? Understandable. Believe I shall join them."

Churchill removed the shirt, was wearing only the pith helmet now. He moved into the water, and the two officers followed, all three settling into a waist-deep coolness. Churchill submerged to his chin, only his head and round hat above the water like some fat mushroom.

"Splendid. Truly splendid. Washes it all away. Tell me, Monty. I've seen so much today, good men, good preparations. But can you truly say you are prepared? For months now, Rommel has had everything to his advantage. His tactics have been unmatched. From what I see, he has stumbled only when he has exhausted his supplies, when his tanks simply can't go. But they have gone quite well lately. He is a great general, no doubt of that. The Fox, they call him. The Desert Fox. Once the fight begins, there is no doubt he will unmask some new tactic, something you must be prepared for. He has one goal now, to capture Cairo. There are those who consider that a foregone conclusion."

Montgomery glanced at Alexander, no smiles now. "I do not consider that to be a foregone conclusion at all. Not at all."

"Ah, but when he has been the most successful, it is because Rommel has found the means to slip past us, swallow us up on the flank. No one has yet found the solution to that dilemma."

Churchill was not looking at him, seemed to focus his stare out to sea. Montgomery was feeling annoyed now, thought, did you not hear any of what was said today? Did you not see my plans for yourself? Did you not pay attention to any of it? He saw a hard look on Alexander's face, the silent order: *Speak wisely.* Churchill still looked toward the far horizon, showed no sign that he was waiting for a response.

Montgomery tried to calm himself, said, "Sir, Rommel has succeeded thus far because he has confronted an army that persists in making desperate mistakes. Those mistakes were made by my predecessor and will not be repeated."

Alexander interrupted him, a stab at diplomacy. "Sir, as you saw today, General Montgomery has designed a formidable defense, whose very design encourages Rommel to do exactly what he has done before. It is our hope that Rommel moves around our flank. Instead of vulnerability, he will find a strong force dug in, and waiting for him. Am I right, Monty?"

"More than right. Mr. Prime Minister, if I may illustrate. I was authorized to remove those officers who could not seem to break with our poor traditions here. General Renton, of the Seventh Armor, a good man, certainly. But this week, when I first met with him, his sole question was whether I would let him loose at Rommel. What he no doubt believed was enthusiasm for the good fight was precisely the tactic that Rommel would hope to see: British tanks, leading the fray, charging headlong into Rommel's guns. That is precisely why Renton is no longer in command."

Churchill looked at him now, said, "Wingy Renton? You replaced him?"

"Sir, I am quite sure Rommel would delight in Wingy Renton charging his tanks straight into the barrels of those damned eighty-eights. I would much prefer that Rommel grind himself into *our* lines. Let him come to *us*. We are in a bottleneck here, and there is only one likely course for Rommel to follow. He will not assault us head-on, and he cannot make an effective assault here, against the sea. We are far too strong, and he certainly knows that. If he comes, it will be to the south, the one place where he would feel we are vulnerable. Only . . . we are not vulnerable at all. We are waiting for him."

Montgomery was truly angry now, had not thought his decisions would be held up to such doubt. He saw concern on Alexander's face, but he could not stop the words.

"And the artillery. Until now, we have scattered our big guns in every part of the field, using them in small, useless packets. No longer. I have massed them into one body, to focus on one primary point of attack. The armor should be used the same way, with emphasis not just on their mobility, but on their firepower. A tank is a mobile cannon, but it is still a cannon. I have no intention of throwing tanks away piecemeal, like we have done so many times before."

Churchill turned slowly, the short stub of the cigar clamped in his mouth, his eyes peering at Montgomery from under the brim of the ridiculous hat.

"I know."

Montgomery was confused. "Sir?"

Alexander laughed now, and Churchill smiled.

"I said, I know. I saw it all today, Monty. Just wanted to hear you say it. Napoléon wanted generals who were lucky. I would rather have generals who were prepared, who understood their enemy. Claude Auchinleck was a good man, no matter how you feel about him. He failed because he put the wrong people in the wrong place. Whether he was unlucky or not, I don't know. But he wasn't prepared for what Rommel gave him. It broke my heart to remove him, but I had no choice. He had played his last card."

Montgomery said nothing, had never considered luck to play any part in what he did.

Churchill stared out to sea again, said, "Gentlemen, failure is more expensive in London than it is here. I must answer to the parliament and to the people, people who don't know beans about war. But they know humiliation, and we've had quite enough of that." Churchill tossed the spent cigar into the water. "I was in Washington, in a meeting with Roosevelt, when word came that we had lost Tobruk. Nothing like being humiliated right in front of your most critical ally. It was as bad as Singapore, hearing how the Japanese kicked us straight in the privates. Defeat I can take. But not disgrace. England won't stand for it. I won't stand for it. We need a victory, Monty. You have far more armor than the Eighth Army has had before. That should inspire you to take a chance here and there."

Montgomery said, "There is no gamble here, sir. This is not some bloody game of politics, where the loudest voice, the hottest rhetoric, wins the day. I have the tanks and the artillery and I bloody well have the ground. If Rommel does not attack us, then in six weeks' time, I am prepared to attack him."

Churchill looked toward Alexander, said, "Six weeks? It will require six weeks? I had hoped . . . sooner."

Alexander said nothing, and Montgomery said, "We must be prepared, sir. Only then."

Churchill turned slowly in the water, searching the shoreline.

Alexander said, "Is everything all right, Prime Minister?"

"Quite. No bystanders lurking hereabouts. Tell me, Monty, how much has Alex told you about Torch?"

Alexander said, "I've not discussed the details with anyone in my command, sir. Premature, I'd say. A good many things to be worked out yet."

Churchill grunted. "That's the Americans for you. Strong-minded lot. You bloody well have to lead them on a damned leash. But, without them, we'd be in a serious pickle. Roosevelt is a friend to England, and the one man who can provide the means for us to win this war. I suppose that gives him the right to have his people decide where that war is going to be fought. It's been a devil of an effort, but I finally got them to stop looking across the English Channel. Every damned one of them, Marshall on down, wants to invade the French coast. I can imagine every general in their army wants to go back to that bloody cemetery in Paris just so he can say something about Lafayette again: 'Lafayette we are here.' That's all some of them remember from the first big war. They do so like their slogans."

"I believe they're holding out on us, sir."

Montgomery's words settled on the water like a dull slap. Alexander looked at him, frowned, shook his head, a silent no.

Montgomery was surprised by the reaction, and Churchill said, "What the hell are you talking about, Monty?"

"The Grant tanks, sir. I was told they'd be delivering four hundred new tanks. I counted a hundred sixty. No mystery there. They're hoarding them, keeping their best armor for themselves. Leaving me to fight Rommel with outdated equipment."

Churchill stared at him for a long moment, his eyes closing into tight slits.

Alexander said, "General Montgomery is aware, sir, that the Americans have been extremely helpful."

"Damned right they have. You say they've delivered a hundred sixty Grants?"

"Yes, sir."

"Sounds to me like a bloody load of armor. You used any of them yet?"

"They're being placed into position, assigned to the appropriate commands even now, sir."

"Then before you bellyache, General Montgomery, perhaps you should find out if a hundred sixty new American tanks might win you a battle. So you think they're holding back a few, eh?"

Montgomery ignored the scowl on Alexander's face, said, "I believe they should provide what they said they would provide."

"Torch, General. Look past your own command. You've got Rommel sitting right in front of you. I can think of no more intelligent a plan than to send another army right up his backside. That army will be American, mostly. And, despite your objections, it might be fitting if they provide some armor for their own people."

Montgomery had heard the first details of what they now called Operation Torch, the first large-scale assault by American forces in the European theater. He held tightly to his words now, watched as Churchill turned away, the man working his jaw, attacking a cigar that wasn't there. Alexander seemed to relax, but Montgomery refused to feel chastised, spoke to Churchill in his mind: We don't need another army on this continent. Send the damned Yanks to France, let them find out what Jerry can do to them. I've got Rommel right where I want him, and damned if I'm going to let some Yank who's never led a rubbish detail grab this victory.

Churchill removed his pith helmet, splashed water on his head, then stood up, stared out to the open sea. "Any U-boats around here?"

Alexander said, "Highly unlikely, sir. The air force keeps a close eye on the coast. Destroyers are patrolling regularly."

Churchill looked down at his own vast expanse of chalky skin, put a fat hand on his stomach.

"Hmph. Too bad. I'd like to see a periscope pop up right out there, let him get a look at this. Might scare him worse than any damned destroyer."

5. ROMMEL

Dearest Lu,
The situation is changing daily to my advantage. . . .

He hated lying to her.

He set the paper aside, had no energy to complete the letter. *What do I tell her? She knows that what she hears from the propaganda ministry is just that: propaganda. Should I simply add to that?*

Westphal was outside the tent, restocking the Mammoth. Rommel stood, stretched, probed the dull ache in his side, felt the slight dizziness, the same sensation now every time he stood up. He tried to ignore it, was suddenly hungry, unusual, called out, "Colonel. Have you a tin of sardines there?"

Westphal appeared at the tent. "Certainly, sir. Just one? We have a whole crate of them."

"Just one."

Westphal disappeared, and Rommel went to the low, hard cot, sat, his knees groaning. He probed the pain again, too familiar now, draining his energy, the pain that usually took his appetite away. *This is not good,* he thought. *Not good at all. What is it about this place that requires so much of a man's body? The war alone is not sufficient to break down an army. This desert must take its toll as well.*

He looked at the short legs of the cot, each one immersed in a small can of oily water. The cans were a barrier, a trap for the astounding variety of wingless pests that would attack while he slept. He stared at the variety of dro thought, my own personal minefield. And just as ineffective. Now . . . this. He stretched his side, could not escape the ache. What other beast has invaded me?

He had suffered from jaundice the year before, something the doctors blamed on the food, a diet so inappropriate for the heat and dryness of the desert. He thought of the doctor, Horster, the man's gloomy diagnosis, the harsh recommendation that Rommel should return to Germany, recover from the jaundice. He knew that Horster had sent that same recommendation to Germany, the strong hint that Rommel might not be fit to command. Kesselring had come again, was in camp frequently now. Yes, he's watching me, they are all watching me. Stay here awhile, all of you. Find out for yourself what the desert does to a man. There are plagues out here no man can stand up to, caused by . . . what? Just look at the creatures that are spawned here. He struggled to take a deep breath, looked again at the odd mix of bugs in the water cans. If not you, then what? He had no idea what kind of creature caused the diseases that were attacking his army, whether it was a creature at all. No man seemed immune, the torture of sun and dust and dryness ripping sores in the skin, and then, when a man's outsides were weakened, the insides would be attacked, all manner of ailments spreading to the gut, or worse, like the jaundice that had swelled Rommel's liver. I've been nineteen months in the desert, he thought. Horster claims no officer over forty has equaled that record, like I should be given some Olympic medal. It is no accomplishment, Doctor, it is duty.

His batman, Gunther, was there now, holding the tin of sardines and a small fork.

"Sir. Colonel Westphal instructed me to bring this."

Rommel took the sardines, the smell of the oil turning his stomach. He shook his head, handed the tin back to Gunther, said, "No now, Herbert. I've changed my mind. Eat them yourself. Waste them."

"Sir? I can fix you something else."

"Get the Storch aloft. Search out the British de-_____ man at the top, there will be uncertainty, _____ Montgomery anxious to put his own

stamp on his army. I should see what they're up to. You care to
join me?"

It was a standing joke between them, as much as Rommel
would joke with anyone.

"Is that an order, sir?"

Gunther's expression never changed, a testament to his loyalty, but Rommel knew the young man was terrified of the tiny
airplane.

Rommel smiled. "Tell Colonel Westphal to have my plane
prepared. I shall go aloft."

Gunther was quickly gone, and Rommel forced himself to
stand, blinked at the dry crust in his eyes, wiped his face with a
dirty handkerchief. He took another deep breath, a futile effort
to clear the staleness from his lungs. He heard Westphal's voice,
the man suddenly appearing at the tent.

"Sir, Corporal Gunther tells me you wish to take the Storch. I
must insist not, sir."

"You what?"

"Sir, the enemy fighters have been out in considerable force.
Our pilots are not able to control the airspace."

"Nonsense."

"Marshal Kesselring has been very precise, sir. The Luftwaffe cannot guarantee your safety."

Rommel wanted to protest, but he could not deny that Westphal was right. For weeks now the Spitfires and Hurricanes had
dominated the skies, more evidence of Kesselring's failure to
convince the Italians to send more fuel. But he knew it was
more than a lack of gasoline. The Messerschmitts had become
outnumbered by a wide margin, the flow of British aircraft increasing at a rate the Germans could not hope to match. He
could see Kesselring in his mind, the man that some called
Smiling Al. But there is nothing to smile about now. Even his
spirits have come to earth. Kesselring must beg Göring for aircraft, and still Göring ignores him. Why send Messerschmitts to
Africa when there is so much glory to be had conquering Russia? No, Berlin doesn't listen to Kesselring any more than Rome
does, and none of them listens to me.

"Sir, I must insist you remain on the ground. We cannot allow
anything to happen to you—"

Rommel held up a hand. "What did Kesselring tell you?"

"He was very plain, sir. He said . . ."

Westphal paused, and Rommel smiled again, said, "He said, 'Rommel won't obey me anyway,' or something close to that."

Westphal smiled as well. "That's approximately correct, sir."

"Did Marshal Kesselring order me to sit in my tent?"

Westphal seemed unsure if Rommel was teasing him or not. "I don't believe so."

"Relax, Colonel. I'll leave the flying to the Messerschmitts, if Berlin decides to send us a few. You have any problem with me *driving* to the front? Or am I too fragile to see anything for myself?"

"Would you prefer the Volkswagen or the Mammoth, sir?"

"The Volkswagen will suffice. You remain here. Have five armored cars follow well behind, scattered formation, in case I run into something unexpected. Tell them to keep behind me. I've eaten enough dust for one day." He stepped outside, blinked at the sunlight, saw Gunther close by, finishing the sardines.

"Let's go, Corporal. If you won't fly with me, you can ride."

Rommel moved toward the auto park, saw Westphal beside the open-topped automobile. The Volkswagen carried no mounted machine gun, but the driver, and now Gunther, both carried sidearms. Rommel had no interest in getting into a firefight with anyone. His armored-car escorts were a different matter, each with a heavy machine gun, and a crew whose sole job was to keep watch on the horizon, to swarm forward and protect Rommel should the enemy suddenly appear.

The engines of all the vehicles were running now, and Rommel saw Westphal speaking to one of the armored-car drivers. He smiled to himself, thought, don't worry, Colonel, I'm not going to run off and leave anyone behind.

Westphal was coming toward him, said, "Sir, which direction are you traveling? In the event—"

"Southeast. I want to see this Qattara Depression. I can't believe it's as impassable as I've heard."

Rommel ordered his driver to halt, glanced back as the armored trucks behind him stopped as well. A few yards in front of him, the hard, rocky floor of the desert fell away abruptly, a sheer drop of more than a hundred feet.

He stepped out of the auto, said, "Remain here."

Rommel stepped across the hard ground toward the edge of the precipice. The desert spread out before him in a golden sea of sandy hills, waves of tall dunes, dropping away into deep swales darkened by shadows. He moved along the edge of the hard ground, saw a shallow cut leading down to a gentle slope in the face of the rocky cliff. There were tracks, some kind of hoofprints, a camel perhaps, and he followed the trail, saw that the beast had walked down into the vast sand plain, the tracks changing to dimples in the sand, and then, the tracks were completely gone, absorbed by the endless landscape. He eased his way down the slope, used the rocks as steps. He had moved out away from the shadows, felt the heat rising up to meet him, a hot breath of stifling air. He put a hand over his mouth, pulled the goggles down over his eyes; he was in the sand now, his boots sinking into the hot softness, ankle deep. The breeze stopped, and he raised the goggles, looked out toward the vast mountains of sand, the surfaces scored by the wind, wisps of dust clouds in the distance, rippled by the glassy shimmer of heat and breeze. Stillness and movement, he thought, like an ocean. But there is a difference, one distinct difference. In all the vastness, the heat, the gentle sprays of sand, he could hear only one sound, the sound of his own breathing. There was no other sound at all.

He smiled.

How far does it go? he thought. He had seen the maps, sketchy details, tens of miles, certainly. And then, to the south and west, the greatest sand sea of them all, the Sahara. This is just a small piece, a child of an enormous mother. And here we choose to fight a war. The arrogance of that, that any of us believe we will *occupy* this place. We do not occupy the desert, any more than a ship occupies the ocean. How many conquerors have swept through here with the same arrogance? The Romans certainly, and how many others? But we believe we are superior, that with our modern machines we can make war anywhere. And all the while, the desert watches us and waits for us to pass, and if we don't pass, if we remain too long, the desert will consume us. Like it is consuming me.

The smile was gone now, and he turned, saw figures silhouetted along the precipice above him. All right, enough of this. He pulled his boots from the sand, struggled toward the rocks. We may have brought war to the desert, but not to *this* piece of desert. I'm not sending any tanks into this.

AUGUST 30, 1942

Rommel had rebuilt his *Panzerarmee* to a strength of more than four hundred fifty tanks, but over half of those were the inferior Italian machines. Across from him, he could only guess, the scouts bringing him reports that the British faced him with as many as seven hundred tanks, including a hundred or more of the Grants, the new American machine that carried a seventy-five millimeter gun, nearly as strong as anything in Rommel's army. He did not dwell on numbers, held tightly to the belief that no matter what kind of man Montgomery was, the British were still the British, and they would fight as they had fought before. Numbers mattered little if the enemy launched his tanks at you in small clusters. And whether Montgomery planned to launch them at all, Rommel knew that trading casualties with the British had become an unacceptable option. Every day the British were pouring supplies and reinforcements through the Suez Canal, and with Rommel's army sprawled across the desert, far from their dwindling supplies, suffering from the neglect and the unwillingness of the quartermasters in Berlin and Rome, time was clearly not on their side. There was only one way for Rommel to have his victory in North Africa. He had to press forward.

The plan was simple: The British were spread out over the ridges and hillsides from the coast at El Alamein, southward into the desert. Rommel had one good option, to sweep around and past the British position, then turn north, slicing across their rear. If the German armor could reach the seacoast, the British would be cut off from their supply lines. Montgomery would learn as the others had learned before him. Armor meant mobility and armor meant power, and Rommel understood both far better than his opponents.

It was called the Battle of Alam Halfa Ridge, and Rommel

did as he had always done, using the tactic that had almost always worked. August 30, he shoved armor and infantry in a noisy threat to the British right and center. But then, in the darkness, he slipped the armor down to the south and, in the moonlight, pushed them eastward.

Almost immediately, the plan disintegrated, an unmapped British minefield causing the first major delay. Then, the ground below the British flank proved much softer than expected, which slowed the tanks and caused them to consume more fuel than they could afford. Rommel was forced to shorten the routes of the armor and send them northward much sooner than he had planned. This ran the German tanks straight into the strongest part of Montgomery's position: Alam Halfa Ridge. Instead of counterattacking Rommel's tanks, the British held fast to their good ground, and British artillery and the guns of their armor began to punch gaping holes in Rommel's strength. By nightfall on August 31, Rommel was forced to halt the attack.

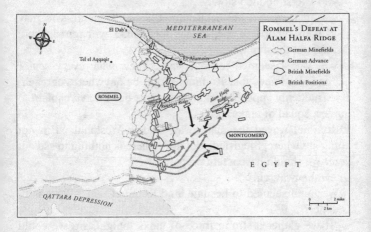

SOUTH OF ALAM HALFA RIDGE—AUGUST 31, 1942

"There is no fuel, sir! We are halted!"

The man's voice cut through him like a hot razor, and Rommel fought the instinct to shout.

"General von Vaerst, you will exercise restraint in my presence."

Von Vaerst now commanded the Afrika Korps, and Rommel saw the anguish on the man's face, the same twisting pain that was cutting through Rommel's gut. They stood in the open, the armored cars gathered in an uneven row beside them, silent, the drivers conserving their gasoline.

Von Vaerst stared down toward his feet, said, "Sir, we are merely dueling the British guns. They are dug in on the high ridges. If we remain in place, at dawn we will simply provide the enemy with targets. And we have no fuel to resume the flank attack!"

"Return to your command, General. The British will not just sit on those ridges. By morning, Montgomery will believe he has opportunity, and he will order his tanks out of their holes and send them forward. They will attack us as they have always done, and then we will have them! Be sure your men have ammunition. We will be the ones seeking targets."

Von Vaerst nodded slowly.

Westphal moved beside Rommel, said, "General, you may send your reports to me, at this location. I will remain here throughout the night."

Von Vaerst seemed to understand, knew what every senior commander knew, that Rommel might be anywhere, unreachable, suddenly appearing alongside some bewildered captain to guide a squad of tanks.

Rommel waved the man away, said to Westphal, "I'm not going anywhere, Siegfried. Not now. There is nothing to see out here. We should have a tent prepared."

"Right away, sir."

Westphal seemed to hesitate, and Rommel said, "What is it, Colonel?"

"If we gather a strong force of tanks tonight, sir, we could send them into the enemy position on a narrow front."

Rommel raised the goggles, blinked through the blowing dust.

"He will come, Siegfried. They have always come. We will wait for them."

*   *   *

Rommel stared east, saw the first gray glow. He could hear the rumble of artillery, most of it British, the sky streaked with white light. He looked toward the west, expecting to see more of the same, but the German guns were firing only sporadically, a single tracer streaking toward the enemy hills.

The reports had reached him throughout the night, and none of the news was good. The British controlled the skies, and throughout the day their bombers had obliterated enormous numbers of German guns. In front of him, his armor waited for the opportunity he still believed would come, some sign that Montgomery had ordered his tanks to move forward, to meet Rommel's waiting gunners head-on.

The horizon was lighter now, and he climbed up into the armored car, surprising the crew. There was no sign of Westphal, but he knew the man was dealing with the flood of messages, managing a staff engulfed in the business of war. Fuel had been promised, word that the Italians were sending five thousand tons of precious gasoline, some of it coming by air, another promise from Kesselring. But no word had come, no reports of fuel arriving anywhere along the front. Now it is day, and it will begin again, and we can barely move at all.

The anger was too familiar, and he slapped the armor plate in front of him, the windshield that supported the machine gun.

"Drive!"

The crew obeyed, Rommel continuing to stand, the goggles now over his eyes, the entire line of armored cars moving into the gray dawn.

SOUTH OF ALAM HALFA RIDGE—SEPTEMBER 1, 1942

There had been one attack by his armor, the Fifteenth Panzers driving a short, quick stab into a mass of British armor along the ridge itself, inflicting heavy losses. But with the full daylight, Rommel could see that Montgomery still held tightly to the good ground.

Nothing had changed. It cut him like a dull sword, ripping into his gut, draining him of the energy he needed, the strength to hold back the sickness, to keep his men in the fight. The big gun roared into life, another hard blast that knocked him to one side. He stared at the hill, thought of Montgomery. Where are you? Why do you not come? The fight is here, *we* are here! His ears were a fog of ringing, but he heard shouts, turned, saw men running, felt a hand on his arm, a hard grip. He saw the faces looking up, saw it himself, a formation of silver planes, coming straight at him, no more than fifty feet above the ground. The hand released his arm, and Rommel saw men dropping down into narrow slit trenches. The planes were right above him, a rush of sound, and Rommel dove into an opening, hit hard, the wind leaving him. The ground came alive around him, a thundering blast, shaking him, bouncing him hard, punching the air from his lungs. He fought to breathe, dirt falling on him, holding him down, and then there were hands, pulling him. No, let me lie here! He was up in the sunlight again, the air thick with dust, hands holding him upright, faces, shouting at him, meaningless words. He saw fire now, a truck, more trucks, black smoke, and now the voices came.

"Sir!"

"Sir! Are you all right?"

He felt his chest, put one hand on his face, looked down, no blood.

"I'm all right! See to the men! The wounded!"

The smoke was choking him, swirling blackness, heat on his face, and he moved away, looked for clean air, a place where he could see. The air began to clear and he saw the cannon in pieces, bodies of men scattered around it. Two of the armored trucks were in flames, more bodies, men tending to anyone who was still alive. He looked up, clear blue sky, heard the sound again, the roar of engines, another formation of planes. They were farther away, and he could see it all, a flock of silver birds, bull's-eye circles on the bodies, slight tilt of the wings, catching the sun, the sweep of the bombers as they dipped toward their targets. The bombs tumbled out, a brief glimpse, black sticks, and suddenly the ground beneath them burst into fire, blasts of earth and steel and men. He turned away, had seen enough of this, his men splayed out in the open ground like so many cattle for the slaughter. If they had fuel at all, they might have enough to withdraw, to pull back behind their minefields. He stared at the wide ridge, less than a mile away, thought again of Montgomery. You bastard. You would deny me the fight I had to have, the fight that would end this, that would give me Cairo and the Suez and all of Africa.

By September 4, the Germans had pulled back to their defensive positions. As Rommel strengthened his minefields and added to his observation posts, in the ocean to the north the precious tankers began to flow from Italy, driven by the relentless pressure from Kesselring, and from Rommel himself. Rommel could only wait, knowing that for the first time, he could not force the attack, could not attack the enemy's vulnerabilities. Worse, his own vulnerabilities were growing, and the pressure from the doctors and from Kesselring finally overwhelmed his ability to deny the sickness. On September 23, Rommel flew to Rome, a quick stop before he would travel to Berlin. Once in Germany, his first priority would be to see Hitler, and then, his duty satisfied, he would settle into a hospital, to treat the sickness in his body and renew his energy for the fight he still hoped to wage. Whether Montgomery would give him time to recover and return to Africa was beyond Rommel's control.

Far to the west, far beyond the two armies at El Alamein, rumors began to stir, wisps of information and intelligence reports that focused more and more on the Americans.

6. EISENHOWER

LONDON
JULY 1942

The meetings had been incessant, both social and contentious. After so much talk, he had learned to despise conferences, all those high-brass affairs with such stiff formalities, ideas flowing out like cigar smoke, drifting in the stale air until swept away by someone's new thought, new theory, new plan. The disagreements over strategy had erupted long before, the desperation of a battle-worn Britain confronted by the brash enthusiasm of the overeager Americans. On both sides of the Atlantic, the goal was the same, defeat the enemy, but who that enemy was, how to defeat him, and where the first great stroke should fall were questions no one could agree on.

When Eisenhower had arrived in June, the British had offered him a home in the Claridge Hotel, the finest in London. His suite had been a sprawl of rooms adorned with gilded wallpaper, palatially high ceilings, all the trappings the British seemed to feel would suit the new American commander. Eisenhower was as uncomfortable as he was appreciative, and immediately he sought less ostentatious quarters. Now, his home was a three-room suite in the Dorchester Hotel, a modest choice that amused the British. After all, he was American, a product of the rustic, backwoods quaintness that some knew as Kansas. To many in the British high command, it was likely that Eisenhower simply didn't know any better.

His appointment had come from the American chief of staff, George Marshall, and like all such appointments, Eisenhower's name had dredged up voices of dissent in Washington, the same kinds of voices that had echoed around "Black Jack" Pershing in 1917. The nation faced the same sort of crisis then, an ever-expanding war, with America's military caught woefully unprepared. Like Eisenhower, Pershing had been elevated to command when the city was full of senior officers, each man insisting he was right for the job. Eisenhower's critics were a bit more muted than the men who'd attacked Pershing. Many of them seemed to be aware that the world had grown more complicated since 1917, that this war would require the kind of mind that could wrap itself around the enormous challenges in building a military in Europe that could challenge the terrifying might of Adolf Hitler. If the tall hats in Washington didn't know Eisenhower, they had no choice but to trust the judgment of George Marshall, a judgment seconded by Franklin Roosevelt. Outside of the planning and administrative offices of the War Department, few had even heard of Eisenhower.

" 'We must be in action by the end of this year.' "

Marshall put the paper down, said, "That is the essence of the president's cable. I am in agreement with him, though my reasoning is somewhat different. He has political realities to contend with. The president has a sharp eye on the elections this November. I will not go into detail on what this could mean for him. His term, as you know, extends for two more years. But it has much to do with the makeup of the Congress, and so forth. The president's concern is that if we do not show the rest of the world that we can strike back at the enemy in a meaningful way, the voters might interpret that as weakness. President Roosevelt will not accept anything from us that hints of weakness."

Most eyes were on Marshall, but not all, and Eisenhower glanced around the room, saw a dull glaze on many of the faces. Marshall had been in Britain for ten days now, and along with Roosevelt's aide Harry Hopkins had spent every one of those days in intense meetings with British and American war planners, officials, military and civilian, hammering out the details of a plan agreeable to both sides that could make the best use of American resources and British experience. The disagreements were many, and the frustration high. Eisenhower pondered the words from Roosevelt. It's the closest thing to an order that man can send us, he thought. Roosevelt may not be here, but he knows how this sort of thing goes. Talk. More talk. Much more talk.

The room was full, chairs packed tightly, nearly seventy military officers in attendance. The uniforms were mixed, most of the men either British or American, a few from the British Commonwealth, Canada and Australia. A man began to speak, a British naval officer, one face in a sea of uniforms. Eisenhower tried to listen, but his mind was drifting as well. Now others spoke up, every man with his point of view.

The arguments centered on two distinctly different goals. The Americans, led by both Roosevelt and Marshall, had advocated the invasion of the French coast, a hard strike directly into Hitler's Europe. The proposal had amazed the British, who had already waged their own disastrous fight in France, and who seemed far more eager to launch the next major campaign in a theater where Hitler wasn't simply waiting for them. The British were already committed in North Africa. Winston Churchill and most of his senior commanders were very clear that if Rommel could be defeated, pushed out of North Africa altogether, the way would be clear for Allied domination of the Mediterranean. With the added strength of the Americans, all of southern Europe could be vulnerable to assault, what Churchill called the "soft underbelly" of Hitler's European Fortress. Eisenhower knew that Marshall still clung tightly to the cross-Channel attack. But America could not mount any kind of effective invasion on its own. The army was too green, too untested, and the commanders had virtually no field experience leading troops into combat. It was essential that the British and the Americans work side by side and unite their efforts.

One other factor was pushing the decision toward the British plan. A beleaguered Russia was facing catastrophic defeat by Hitler's army, a defeat that would unleash German troops to swarm into the Middle East, as well as all of Europe. In Moscow, Stalin vigorously demanded that the Allies stop talking and take action, opening up a second front that would deflect some of Hitler's troop strength. Marshall had to concede that a powerful invasion on the French coast could not become reality for more than a year. Stalin could not wait. After days of debate, the British would simply not go along with Marshall's proposed strategy. Marshall was forced to concede and agree with the British. If there was to be a campaign at all in 1942, it would have to be made in North Africa.

The meeting was exhausting itself, and Eisenhower could feel the voices growing weak, a chorus of mumbles, the entire room seeming to empty of air. Marshall stood, and Eisenhower saw the British chief of staff stand as well. Field Marshal Sir Alan Brooke was the one man who seemed able to influence and even contradict the wishes of Winston Churchill. Here, he was recognized as the most influential British officer in the room. Brooke was near sixty, slightly younger than Marshall, a lean, sparelooking man. Both men commanded the respect of their officers, and the room was suddenly deathly silent.

Brooke said, "Gentlemen, I do not believe further discussion will change our goal. It is essential that North Africa be targeted prior to the beginning of the rainy season there, which means, the assault should be launched within four months' time. Since General Marshall and I have determined this course, the most urgent matter now before us is how that assault will take place, where that assault will take place, and who will mount it. Those discussions are for a later time. If General Marshall will concur . . ." All eyes focused expectantly on Marshall, who made a sharp nod. "Very well, this meeting is concluded."

Eisenhower stood, felt the entire room exhaling its final breath. He felt a hand on his arm, heard a low voice.

"If they painted this place when we got here, it's dry now."

Eisenhower was too weary to smile, looked at the tall man beside him, the thin frame topped by a long face, a nose like a sharp beak. The man rarely made jokes, but he was far more impatient than Eisenhower and would just as likely have announced his ill humor to the entire room.

Mark Wayne Clark had been the first man chosen by Eisenhower to accompany him to London, and Marshall had immediately approved the man to be Eisenhower's second-in-command. Clark had been two years behind Eisenhower at West Point, and even then the men had formed a friendship that was only handicapped by the separate paths their army careers had followed. When both had returned to Washington, the friendship had returned as well. Once Eisenhower began to establish himself as a force in Marshall's headquarters, he quickly developed an instinct for those officers who could handle the extraordinary tasks of training, organization, and administration, the very tasks that Eisenhower had now been handed. When Eisenhower left for London, Clark left with him.

There were voices around them, the room full of impatient men forced to wait for another long moment as the most senior officers filed from the room. Eisenhower was surprised to see Marshall looking at him, no smile, no emotion at all, just a silent stare.

Eisenhower began to move that way, and Clark was beside him now, standing a head taller than many of the men around them, saying, "Sleep would be good. An hour, maybe. Seems we've finished here."

Eisenhower began to move along with the flow, said to Clark, and to no one at all, "Nothing is finished. It's only just begun."

CLARIDGE HOTEL, LONDON—JULY 26, 1942

Marshall stared out past him, seemed lost for a moment, said, "Stubborn chaps. Dig their heels in with more gusto than my wife, Katherine."

Eisenhower said nothing, saw Marshall drift away, thoughts that reached far beyond the lavish room. He knew the place Marshall had gone, could see it in the man's face, the mention of his wife giving him a brief glimpse of home. Already, it was a moment Eisenhower knew well.

Marshall focused on him again, said, "The president understood them. I think he has a pretty stout relationship with Churchill. In the end, it came down to whether or not we could carry out our own campaign, alone. FDR was testing me, though God knows why he feels he must do that. 'Sure, George, stick to your guns, if you think you can go it alone.' Well, no, we're not going anywhere alone, not yet. Admiral King's not convinced we should do anything here at all, still thinks it's a mistake not to push Japan. Try telling Doug MacArthur how he *should* have pushed Japan." Marshall stopped, sat back in the thick cushion of his chair. "You know what's in front of us, Ike? What we have to do here? The full coordination of air, sea, and land. Never been done before. A good many of these officers around here don't believe it can be done now. Pessimists on both sides. If it wasn't for Churchill, I'm not sure how the Brits would even be in this thing, not after Dunkirk, Singapore, Tobruk. But they're not licked, not yet, and they have the one thing we don't have: battlefield experience. I cannot order our people to march into a fight I don't believe we can win, and without the Brits . . . we can't win. So. We'll do it their way."

There was something instinctive about Marshall, silent authority, none of the big talk or the showmanship of men like MacArthur. Eisenhower had served with both, had learned a great deal by simply observing. MacArthur believed in the force of his own personality, as though he could *will* his men to victory, inspire them just by ordering them to win. As revered as

MacArthur was, a special darling of the newspapers, the American forces in the Pacific were a long way from winning anything. The disaster in the Philippines had snuffed out whatever optimism had followed MacArthur, the absurd notion that once our boys got into a fair fight, the Japanese would simply fold. After a vicious fight on the Bataan peninsula, and then, the last-gasp defense at the fortress at Corregidor, the Japanese had captured seventy thousand American and Filipino soldiers. Before the final collapse, MacArthur had escaped to Australia, inspiring some claims that it was a victory after all, that the man himself was worth as much to the American army as five corps of fighting men. Caesar would return. But as much respect as MacArthur inspired, Marshall and many others in the War Department believed that they would need more than the image of a Caesar to defeat either the Japanese or the Germans.

Marshall was looking at Eisenhower now. "You know how the Brits feel about you, Ike. You've impressed them every step of the way. I wonder how many of them expected us to ride in here like a flock of idiotic cowboys, shooting up the place? There's a good bit of that kind of thinking, you know. We're still colonials to some of them. The great unwashed, Daddy Warbucks with lots of money and no class. Some of them forget what Pershing did here, what it took to whip the kaiser. It's up to us to show them again. Well, no, not us. *You.*"

Eisenhower was hanging on Marshall's every word now, was surprised, said, "Me? Why—"

"You command the American forces in Europe. Until now. The British have agreed . . . well, Mr. Churchill has agreed with me, and with the president. We're agreed that we will unite both armies into one Allied strike force, including both navies and air forces. This is more than simply a partnership effort. It is a *combined* effort, one army, one mission. And, one commander. Actually, it was about the only topic we didn't have to argue about. You're in command, Ike. Torch. All of it."

Eisenhower stood, felt a cold turn in his chest. "Thank you, sir. I had thought Lord Mountbatten . . ."

"Yes, well, Louie Mountbatten is certainly qualified. But he spoke out for *you.* He's one of your strongest supporters. And there were a good many more. Accept it, Ike. This fight needs a

man at the top who knows how to *manage* an army. You're the
best man for this job, Ike."

"Thank you, sir."

"I'm heading back to Washington pretty quick, and I'll push
the formal paperwork through channels. But you've got the job,
Ike. This whole operation has to be drawn up from scratch. And,
you've got less than four months to bring it off."

EISENHOWER'S HEADQUARTERS, THE DORCHESTER HOTEL—AUGUST 9, 1942

He had barely slept, routine now, most of his staff putting in as
many hours as their commander. In front of him, papers spread
across the desk, with more papers on the conference table, on
the floor, all of it merely the sharpened tip of a monstrous ice-
berg. There was no avoiding the plague of conferences, continuing arguments over various theories, a swirling storm of words
and documents, all flowing in his direction. But there was no argument over the mission, only how to bring it about.

He fought through the cold coffee, set the cup aside, stared
blankly at the wall. For two weeks he had forced himself to see
past the personalities, focus only on the plans, the maps, some
strategy that would put the troops ashore in North Africa where
they might actually accomplish their mission. There would be
casualties of course. There were always casualties in a plan like
this. Eisenhower had spent most of his career viewing troop
counts as merely figures on paper, had never marched through
the horror of what his orders could do to the men who carried
them out. He leaned back in his chair, stared at the dull plaster
on the ceiling. So, you had better give the right orders, decide
on the right plan. Because if it doesn't work, the mistake will be
yours. Your responsibility. And no time to cry about it. You
asked for this. You worked for it, dreamed it would happen, and
now, here you are. Don't muck it up.

"Sir?"

He saw Butcher leaning in.

"What is it, Harry?"

"General Clark's here, sir."

Eisenhower called out, "Come on in, Wayne."

Butcher turned away, and Clark moved up beside him, both men in the doorway. Butcher said something to Clark, kept his voice low enough that Eisenhower couldn't hear him. Clark's frown turned quickly to a self-conscious smile. Butcher was gone, and Clark stepped into the office, moved papers from a chair, sat. There was silence for a moment, Clark suppressing the smile. Eisenhower was used to this, knew that Harry Butcher could always be relied on for some inappropriate comment, something raw and indiscreet. He had known Butcher for more than fifteen years, their paths crossing in Washington more in social circles than either man's specific job. Butcher was a naval reserve officer, the only blue uniform in Eisenhower's sea of khaki, referred to himself now as "Ike's naval aide," which implied that he had some influence on the relationship between Eisenhower and the navy brass. But Eisenhower knew that Butcher was on his staff only because Eisenhower had asked for him.

"You going to share the joke?"

"Nope."

"Just as well." Eisenhower let out a long breath, felt a dull ache in his shoulders, long days settling across his back like some great barbell. "I need to talk to you about the French."

Now Clark let out the breath. "De Gaulle?"

"Oh, hell no. We'll talk about de Gaulle only when we have to. I'm much more concerned with the larger picture. Torch. The Brits believe that no matter where we land, the French will fight us. There are different opinions on the matter. Some say that, depending on where we go ashore, we'll be welcomed as liberators. If the Free French are running the show, whoever's in charge will put up American flags as soon as our ships come into view. They'll start shooting their Vichy collaborators as quick as they can line 'em up. Others say the Vichy leadership has more influence than we think, that their troops will follow Vichy's orders. You heard anything more? What do you think?"

Clark seemed overwhelmed by the question. "You're asking me if I am willing to predict whether our landing will be a stroll on the beach, or a bloody massacre. I'd say, we should be prepared for the worst. If they shoot at us, shoot back."

"That's the point. We can only shoot at them if they shoot first."

"Ike, the Nazis are running that show, make no mistake about that. The French can claim to be neutral or hostile, or our best friends. But the Krauts aren't going to just sit by and allow us to put an army in Rommel's backyard. Algeria, Tunisia, French Morocco. Doesn't matter. The French will weigh the cost of fighting us against fighting the Nazis. We want to come ashore, the Nazis are already there."

There was commotion in the outer office, one loud voice.

Eisenhower nodded that way, said, "Well, if the French are going to make a fight of it, we've got the right man to lead the way."

Clark looked toward the door, seemed to recognize the voice as well, said, "Can't argue that one, Ike."

There was motion at the doorway, heavy boots on the wood floor. The man burst into the room, slammed his bootheels together, made a crisp salute, said, "So, Ike, when do we kill some Krauts?"

Eisenhower stood. "Wayne, I believe you know George Patton?"

Patton unrolled a coil of paper, and Eisenhower saw the magazine, the tattered cover of *Life*.

"Right here, Ike. Yep, here it is. Impressive photo of our gallant leader, with his name clearly spelled out: 'D. D. Eisenberger.' "

Eisenhower had seen the photo, had hoped no one else would remember. But of course, he thought, George Patton would never forget anything like this. At least they got the initials right.

Patton sat, pointed a hard finger toward Eisenhower, said to Clark, "I outranked him, you know. His whole damned career. Hell, couple years ago, when I was taking command of the armored division, I tried to get Ike assigned to be my chief of staff. A plum job, that one. You'd have done a good job too, Ike. Hell, I guess somebody made you a better offer."

Clark laughed, said, "I guess General Marshall pulled rank on you, George."

"Hmm. Yep. Marshall. He's concerned, you know."

Patton's mood had abruptly shifted, and Eisenhower saw the hard, familiar glare. Patton had been chosen to be the senior American commander for Operation Torch, would lead one of the three prongs of the invasion, the westernmost landings at Casablanca. But Patton had no real reason to be here now, in London. His part of the assault would come directly from the east coast of the United States, a naval armada that would carry the Casablanca force across the Atlantic.

Eisenhower said, "What's going on, George? Marshall's got problems with Torch?"

"Yep. That's the real reason I'm here. Sent me to look things over, report to him on my conclusion. Hell, there's nothing for me to see in London. Damned ugliest women. Fattest ankles I've ever seen."

Eisenhower thought, Patton would be the world's worst spy. Marshall wouldn't send George here just to eavesdrop on us. Of course he's concerned. Anyone who looks at these plans should be concerned.

"We're working on every detail, George. But there is one enormous uncertainty. The French. Lots of opinions on what they'll do, no one knows for sure."

Patton sniffed. "I can handle the French. We get a battleship to drop a few sixteen-inchers into downtown Casablanca, they'll come around. If that doesn't work, I'll charm them. You ever know a Kraut to charm anybody? I'll have Casablanca in my pocket in two days' time."

It was the tonic Eisenhower needed. But he saw the scowl, Patton's bluster changing again.

Patton said, "What about the other two landings, Ike?"

"Fredendall and Ryder will command. You know the plan."

"Yeah, I know the plan. But what about the damned Brits? They going to wait for us to go in first? You know what the French will do if they see British uniforms on those damned beaches. All hell will break loose."

The British had acknowledged the problem from the start. Any landing that hoped to find a cooperative French reception had to be led by American soldiers, with American officers in command. This kind of annoyance had plagued the Allies throughout the First World War, and now, the centuries of animosity between Britain and France could boil over into a major conflict in North Africa.

"The Brits will wait for us, George. Once we've secured our bases on the Mediterranean, the Brits will move overland and occupy Tunisia."

Clark said, "Rommel won't know what hit him. He'll be squeezed like a grape."

Eisenhower watched Patton's reaction, saw a flicker of disgust. He wasn't sure how Patton felt about Clark, and Eisenhower had no time and no patience for personality clashes. No, he thought, George doesn't make friends.

Patton stared at Eisenhower for a moment, said, "We do the work, and the Brits grab the victory, that it? Or, will the damned Krauts grab it first? You think we can coordinate three major amphibious assaults, quiet the damned French, then bring the British in, equipment and all, and send them marching into Tunisia? And all the while, the Krauts are just gonna sit and watch? There's a fight to be had, Ike. Rommel, or someone else. They'll pour reinforcements into Tunisia, and if the British don't get there in God's own hurry, the Krauts will be waiting for 'em, begging those limey bastards to march right up to those Kraut tanks."

Eisenhower felt his gut tighten, saw Clark twist slightly in his chair, thought, dammit, George, I don't need to hear that kind of talk. Patton seemed oblivious to his insult of the British.

Eisenhower said, "You're right on one count. This is a complicated operation. It won't succeed without cooperation. The British understand that clearly, and it's up to all of us to make it work."

Patton shook his head. "Fifty-fifty, Ike. The landings, no real problems there I can see. Tunisia, different story."

Eisenhower looked at Clark again, could see that the man shared his gloom, had not expected pessimism from Patton.

Eisenhower said, "Those might be the best odds we can get. But if we don't do this—"

"We'll do it, Ike. That's what I'll tell Marshall. We'll do it, or we'll die trying."

7. EISENHOWER

" It's the election, Ike. A bunch of congressmen are afraid that if we fall on our face here, they'll have to give out bad news to their voters. I hate politics."

Eisenhower nodded at Clark's words, looked at him through a thick fog in his eyes. "That's Marshall's problem. My orders haven't changed."

Clark pointed to the copy of the letter that covered one corner of Eisenhower's desk. "I don't know, Ike. Doesn't seem like the chief of staff is bearing up well. The pressure on him must be overwhelming."

Eisenhower stared at the paper, Marshall's words a blur. But the shock was still in him, the sting of Marshall's sudden doubts about the entire operation.

There is unanimity of opinion that the proposed operation appears hazardous to the extent of less than a fifty percent chance of success.

Unanimity. Everyone. Eisenhower had read the letter too many times already, said, "You think he'll call it off?"

Clark shook his head. "How can he, Ike? After all this? Everything . . . the planning, the personnel."

"He can if he chooses to, Wayne. Or Churchill, or the president. Hell, if it was up to the navy, there never would have been a plan at all. The Brits think they'll lose half their fleet just getting everybody into position. Admiral King . . . good God, Wayne. The American chief of naval operations sits in Washington and launches his dispatches toward two major theaters of war, telling everyone that everything we're doing is wrong. When he was here, he kept insisting we focus on the Pacific. By the time he went home, he seemed convinced that Torch was the right plan. But now that he can bellyache out of earshot of the British, he's telling Marshall it's all a mistake. How'd you like to be Admiral Ingersoll, commanding the whole Atlantic fleet, working your tail off to prepare for this assault, only to hear that your chief in Washington thinks the whole idea is suicidal? We'd be well served if some of these people were simply shot."

Clark stared at him, and Eisenhower regretted the words, thought, thank God I can trust him. But this is no good. I need to take a walk, maybe go somewhere, into the country. He called out, "Harry!"

Butcher appeared at the door.

"Round up the damned car."

"Where we off to, Chief?"

Eisenhower sat back in his chair, had no explanation to offer. "Just get the car."

Clark said, "Ike, the navy's coming around. No matter what Admiral King is saying in Washington, and no matter how much moaning the British are doing here, they're all coming together. The air people are all in line, all pushing for the plan. Jimmy Doolittle's like a kid with a new toy, since he was told he'll be flying cover for Patton's landing. The British air people, Tedder, the whole lot . . . and that'll spread, Ike. As the pieces come together, everyone will fall in line. Even the navy. Both navies. Until anybody says differently, it's still your show. And it's a good plan."

Eisenhower saw a hopeful smile on Clark's face, felt the man's friendship, his effort to pull away the dark curtain.

"I just need a breath or two, Wayne."

Butcher was back now, stood at the door. "Car's ready to go, Chief. Uh, before you go, there's a message just arrived from the French. From de Gaulle."

The name sent a dull blade into Eisenhower's chest. He closed his eyes for a brief moment. "And?"

"His people are still pretty itchy to know what the plans are. I think they're a little upset."

Eisenhower closed his eyes again, could see the face of Charles de Gaulle, the man's perfect sneer etched in his mind. Their first meeting had been an unpleasant and snippy affair, de Gaulle insisting in flatly arrogant terms that Marshall see him before the American chief of staff returned to the States. De Gaulle had been a midlevel governmental minister and a brigadier general, commanding French armor, when the Germans swept through France. Rather than surrender along with most of the French army, de Gaulle had escaped to England and had immediately proclaimed himself head of a Free French State. The one-man pronouncement had in fact inspired some of his countrymen, and a resistance underground of sorts had begun to spread through the German-occupied territory. Most of France regarded de Gaulle as an opportunist, a lonely voice in a wilderness of propaganda, and he was blithely dismissed by the Vichy government as an outcast rebel. But de Gaulle would not be ignored and found a voice in various British newspapers. Soon he had insisted on more than patriotism from his French followers, and more than simple respect from his British hosts. He had made it known that he expected to be regarded as a head of state, and that as such, he was entitled to know exactly what the Allies planned to do to recover his country. To Marshall he had demanded to know the details of whatever second-front operation was in the works. Whether de Gaulle had actually heard of Operation Torch was something no one could be certain of. Regardless of what de Gaulle might have heard, whether through rumors or leaks in security, Eisenhower had no intention of telling him anything.

Butcher said, "Chief, de Gaulle's people are requesting you schedule a meeting with one of his representatives. I doubt he'll see you himself."

Eisenhower tried to ignore the words, forced himself to leave the desk. He moved past Clark, fought through the fog, put a hand on Butcher's shoulder, said, "You drive."

"So, Harry, you think I should be out there inspecting the troops? More parades?"

Butcher laughed. "You're the chief. Inspect anybody you want to."

"The Brits expect that, you know. Damnedest ritual, a general strutting through his men, showing off his medals, making sure everybody knows how high his promotions have gone, how important he is. If he thinks about it, he pretends to make sure his men are in tip-top shape. How the hell you going to know if a soldier's any good by how he buttons his shirt?"

"Patton would disagree with you."

Eisenhower smiled, nodded. "Yep. Never saw a man more obsessed with a crisp salute. For him, it works. Discipline, can't argue with that. Despite what Georgie may try to tell his men, he's not perfect."

Butcher glanced at him, steered the car past a slow-moving tractor, an unusual sight on the paved road. Gasoline restrictions had made driving anywhere a luxury for British civilians. Eisenhower was lost for a moment, looked into the face of the farmer, an old man, ignoring the staff car as it swerved past him. The whole world is moving past that old man, and likely he doesn't care one bit. He's seen this before, probably done his part already.

"So, you going to tell me?"

Butcher brought him back into focus, and Eisenhower said, "About Patton? Awhile back, war games, down in Louisiana. Lots of Washington brass, everybody watching, pretty impressive. Georgie commanded the Second Armor. He won the day. Pulled a pretty neat trick, got into the enemy camp, took the prize. The official observers said that what he did was impossible, turned the whole event up on its ear. Nobody could figure out how he did it."

Butcher was waiting for more, and Eisenhower stared ahead, braced himself against a shallow pothole in the road.

"Well? How did he do it?"

Eisenhower stared ahead, smiled. "He cheated. Took his armor across country outside the designated boundaries. He'd made a deal with private gasoline stations along the country roads, paid for the gas with his own money, so I was told. Planned it all out in advance."

"He cheated?"

The smile faded, the rhythm of the car pulling him toward a nap. He turned toward Butcher. "He *won*."

Butcher laughed, and suddenly Eisenhower didn't share the humor. "It was funny at the time, I guess. I got my first star just after that. He already was a major general. Now, I have to look at him in a different way. He'll do whatever we need him to do, I know that. But he doesn't like orders. Might not be the best man for following a plan. Improvisation is good, essential in combat. But he's only one part of something far more complicated than any of us have tried to do before."

"Forgive me, Chief, but that's what people like Patton are for. No matter what anyone says in Washington, no matter how much bitching and doubt falls on Marshall or Churchill or FDR, it's the men in the landing craft and the assault craft who matter, the men who fire the big guns. If they do their job, then you'll have done yours. Sir."

Eisenhower looked at Butcher, nodded slowly. "Thank you, Harry."

They rode for another mile, past small farms set deep into thick, green fields. The fog was gone now, the energy returning, and Eisenhower pointed to an intersection ahead. "Turn us around. Too much to do."

Butcher slowed the car, swung wide, made a U-turn, hammered the accelerator, speeding them back to the office. Eisenhower felt the energy of the car, realized how slowly Butcher had been driving. He knew it was calculated, that once Eisenhower had cleared the fog in his brain, he would want to be back to the work *now*. The farms blew past and already they were moving into the outskirts of the city.

He stared ahead. "Make sure Wayne comes to breakfast tomorrow. Be sure Churchill's people put us on his calendar when he gets back from Africa. I want to send a reply to Marshall, plenty of details, logistics, supply, troop, air, and naval numbers, to reassure him. Patton's leaving for the States next week; I want him prepared to give Marshall a full report on progress, not griping. Arrange a meeting with the British Home Office, Mr. Mack, I believe. He has his finger on the French problem."

"Sir, Mack, yes, sir. He dealing with de Gaulle now, Chief?"

"De Gaulle? I have no idea. I'm talking about the real French problem, those fellows in Africa who may or may not decide to blow us to hell."

AUGUST 21, 1942

By the morning of August 21, Eisenhower was given the official report from Lord Louis Mountbatten, the dashing young British commodore who now ranked among the most influential of the British chiefs of staff. The report confirmed the raid at Dieppe had been a complete disaster.

The raid on the French port city had been planned primarily by the British, mostly Mountbatten himself, aimed at capturing a moderate French target, holding the beach and the port long enough to convince both the British and their beleaguered allies on the European continent that an amphibious assault could succeed in putting a sizable force into place, long enough to allow the possibility of major reinforcements over water. Dieppe was not intended to be any permanent prize, only a demonstration that Hitler's Atlantic Wall could be punctured. Of the six thousand men who participated in the raid, most were Canadian, supplemented by British and a small, symbolic contingent of American commandos. What the careful planning could not account for was the German defense, a stout barrier tailor-made for defending against this kind of amphibious attack. The reports were dismal. Half the men who took part in the raid were either killed or captured. As tragic as the raid had been, Eisenhower grasped a subtlety in the British dispatches, a tinge of meaning that the horrified public would never receive. The raid on Dieppe was proof that Hitler would not simply stand by and allow any French port to be so easily assaulted. It was annoyingly clear to Eisenhower that the inclusion of the small force of Americans, who fared as badly as their British and Canadian comrades, would generate the kinds of headlines in the States that no one in the War Department wanted. Men had died, American men, attacking a French port against a formidable defense that would not simply crumble away. After Dieppe, the voices who had continued to speak out against the North African campaign were virtually silenced. If Operation

Torch wasn't popular, Dieppe had provided a convincing message that Torch might have a better chance of success than another assault against the French coast, an assault that would slam straight into Hitler's stoutest defenses.

The invitation came from Churchill, dinner at his official residence. Eisenhower had endured these kinds of dinners before, drawn-out, tedious affairs. With the prime minister just returning from Africa and Russia, he would be certain to dominate his audience with all the various details of his travels, some of it military, much simply Churchill himself, basking in the attention. At least Eisenhower would have one valuable reinforcement: Wayne Clark accompanied him.

They were ushered into the dining room, and Eisenhower saw no one else in the room. Clark was beside him, and Eisenhower said, "Appears we're early."

Clark checked his watch. "Nope, don't think so."

There was a burst of noise out beyond the dining room, and Churchill was there now, padded heavily in, said, "Welcome! Sit! Appetite?"

Eisenhower caught the familiar smell of the cigar, the permanent fixture implanted into Churchill's mouth. The man wore a large smock, shuffled himself to his chair on fat slippers.

Clark moved toward the back of Churchill's chair, polite instinct, and Churchill said, "I can manage, General. Sit down, both of you. Good to be home, you know. No matter where I go, no matter how much hospitality my generals or anyone else gives me, there's nothing to compare with one's own hearth, eh?"

Eisenhower could see that Churchill's mood was far more cheerful than his own.

Churchill was looking at him, said, "Bad day, General? You miss high tea? Don't pay much attention to that myself. Tea's for dowagers and diplomats. Much prefer *high whiskey*."

Eisenhower said nothing, glanced at Clark. Marshall's gloomy cable had been discussed at a hastily called meeting, an American affair, with no one else in attendance. It wasn't a conscious choice on Eisenhower's part to exclude anyone—it had just come about that way. Churchill pulled at the cigar, smoke drifting around his round face, his expression unchanging. Eisenhower thought, he knows, of course. Somehow, he always knows.

"Sir, there is concern, still, in Washington."

Churchill slapped his hands on the hardwood table, seemed prepared with a response.

"Here's what I think, General. Torch offers the greatest opportunity in the history of England. It is the one thing that is going to win the war. President Roosevelt feels the same way. We're both ready to help you in any way we can. The most important thing, of course, is that we have no battle with the French."

Eisenhower absorbed Churchill's enthusiasm, felt his own dark mood rising slightly.

Clark seemed to pulse beside him, straightened tall in his chair, said, "Mr. Prime Minister, we have been subjected to so many different plans, so many strategies, changes of sentiment, changes of mind . . . what we need, sir, is for someone with the necessary power to make some decisions. We're in the middle of day-to-day changes. We must have had ten sets of plans. We're dizzy from so many changes, so many differences of opinion as to what will work and what will not . . . or whether there will even be an Operation Torch or not!"

Clark's voice had grown louder, the tall man leaning forward in his chair, arms on the table. Eisenhower put a hand up, but he could see that Clark's temper was still building, the words continuing to flow.

"Sir, we'd like only to get one definite set of plans, one strategy, so we can go to work on it!"

Churchill pushed his chair back, stood, began to pace slowly, and Eisenhower looked at Clark, saw the expression of a tired man who knows he has said too much. The room was silent for a long moment, Churchill still moving, trailed by cigar smoke. He stared down, moved from wall to wall, back again, never looked at them.

"Joe Stalin has his hands full, you know. Serious difficulties. His army was doing a fair bit holding the Jerries away, but the week after I left, we learned that the Jerries have opened a new attack to the south, against Stalingrad. It could be bad, very bad. But we won't hear anything about it from Uncle Joe. He keeps secrets, thinks we're not clever enough to know what he's up against, or how he's handling it. Damnedest thing about the Soviets. They insist they're our allies, and they expect us to do everything in our power to help them. But try to get a straight answer from any of them, Stalin in particular. 'So, Joe, how many tanks do you have outside Moscow?' He just offers you more vodka, says something about how the Jerries aren't as tough as they're cracked up to be, and so, why don't we attack in France? Every question I asked him came right back to me. 'Why don't the English attack? When are the Americans going to help?' I had to admit to him that we just weren't strong enough. I didn't care for that, not one bit. He didn't either. And he's right to give us hell for it. Jerry's already kicked in his front door, and if they nail the Soviets in a coffin, we're next. That's why we must strike soon, and we must strike where it can make a difference, grab Hitler's attention." Churchill turned, rubbed his back against a corner of a tall bookcase, scratching. "Something I picked up in Egypt. Nasty little buggers." Churchill moved back to the table, tapped his cigar on the edge of an ashtray. He looked at Eisenhower now, pointed the cigar at him.

"Torch, gentlemen. I told Stalin about our plan. He didn't care for it at first, said, no, go to France first. I told him, why stick your head in the alligator's mouth, when you can go to the Mediterranean and rip his soft underbelly? After a while . . ." Churchill paused, smiled. "After several more bottles had been uncorked, Uncle Joe thought that might be a pretty good idea. So, that's the message here, General. *It's a pretty good idea.* I think so, Stalin thinks so, and I will damned well make sure everyone else thinks so, including your president." He looked at Clark. "That what you wanted to hear, General?"

Clark's mouth was open slightly, and Eisenhower said, "What Wayne is asking for . . . what I want from you, from the chiefs of staff, is simply a green light. The president has insisted that American troops be on the ground *somewhere* over here by the end of the year. We have been working on a plan that will accomplish that in the best way possible. We're just frustrated by . . . roadblocks."

Churchill pulled the cigar from his mouth again, looked at it. "Bloody awful mess at Dieppe, eh? Roosevelt got that message loud and clear. The only place your troops can make a good landing is North Africa. I'll tell him that. Again. You'll get your *green light*."

Churchill sat now, called out, "We'll have the soup!"

Waiters filed quickly into the room, bowls of steaming broth placed in front of each man. Eisenhower felt dizzy from Churchill's energy, began to understand now that this was the one man who might actually control this entire affair. The president will listen to him, he thought. I can swap papers with Washington for all time, continue this absurd transatlantic essay contest, but in the end, it may all come down to the power of this man's personality, his will. Roosevelt will listen to him, and Marshall will listen to Roosevelt. And we finally, *finally* can make this happen.

He looked over at Clark, who was stirring the soup, testing its heat. Across the table, noises erupted, Churchill leaning his face low, bathed in the steam, loud slurping noises as the spoon made the short journey from the bowl to his mouth.

He looked up suddenly, soup on his chin, said, "Fine soup, ain't it? Just make sure you find a way to keep the French out of the damned fight."

On October 19, Wayne Clark flew to the British base at Gibraltar and rendezvoused with a British submarine, which transported him to the Algerian coast. The mission was secretive and exceptionally dangerous, Clark landing in the middle of the night on a desolate stretch of beach. The meeting was the result of the good efforts of Robert Murphy, the chief American diplomat in North Africa. But Murphy had one other role as well. He was a spy. For many weeks, he had sent clandestine reports to Washington, reports that were forwarded to Eisenhower. Murphy kept a close eye on French politicians and various French generals and provided Eisenhower with valuable intelligence. Unfortunately, with so much confusion and uncertainty in the French high command, Murphy could not be certain just what might happen when the Americans made their landings. No French general would confide in a simple diplomat. At Murphy's insistence, Clark would attend a meeting himself and, as Eisenhower's second-in-command, would presumably inspire the French to offer some firm commitment as to their intentions.

In a remote house overlooking the deserted beach, Clark met with General Charles Mast, who commanded French forces throughout Algeria. The meeting was cordial and constructive, the French offering information on troop and artillery positions, Mast insisting he was a friend to the Allies. Mast of course expected Clark to provide details of any imminent invasion, something Clark simply could not do. But Clark returned to London with Mast's assurances that the bulk of the French army would welcome the Americans. It was certainly cause for optimism, though Eisenhower knew that conflict was likely among Mast's peers, that the French political and military landscape was still a minefield. Once the Allied ships appeared on their horizon, the French field officers and their commanders would face the reality of an armed invasion. How they responded might have little to do with the friendly handshakes one general had offered to Wayne Clark.

After so many months of planning and replanning, of advice and counsel, argument and delay, Operation Torch was finally in motion. The attack would be made in three major amphibious prongs. The westernmost assault was commanded by Patton and would move into the African coast at and around Casablanca. Patton's men had boarded their ships in American ports and would make the journey without any land stop, would sail directly to their destination. Patton commanded thirty-four thousand troops, combined with a naval armada and air force support that he felt was sufficient to suppress any resistance he might face. The other two prongs would be launched inside the relatively tranquil waters of the Mediterranean, against the northern coast of Algeria. The central prong was to be launched at the Algerian port of Oran, thirty-nine thousand American troops under the command of Major General Lloyd Fredendall.

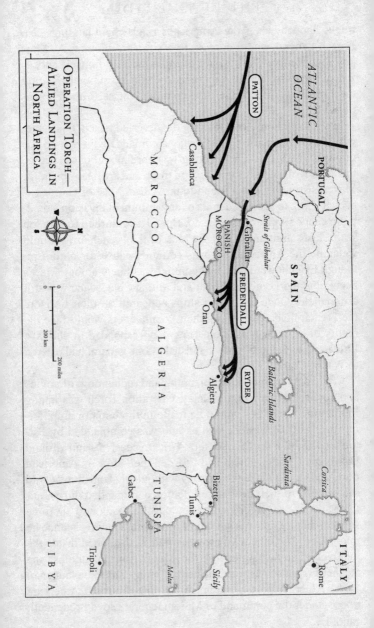

The eastern prong, at Algiers itself, would be led by another American, Major General Charles Ryder, who would command ten thousand American and twenty-three thousand British troops. The Americans were to lead the attack, reflecting the ever-present need to give the French the mythical impression that the British weren't there at all. Once ashore at Algiers, the British would then fall under the command of their own General Sir Kenneth Anderson, who, once the land base was secure, would immediately push the British troops eastward toward Tunisia.

Clark's report to Eisenhower on his mission to Africa had been reassuring in every detail except one. Mast was only a division commander, who had no authority beyond the boundaries of Algeria. While Mast seemed to be a willing ally, Robert Murphy had taken the precaution of going beyond Mast, to find a French general who might have authority over the entire theater. Murphy had found the means to contact Henri Giraud, one of the grand old men of the French military, who had been captured by the Germans in 1940. Giraud had escaped and was in hiding, and though he had been somewhat vocal in his support of the Vichy government, the Germans considered him a dangerous fugitive. Giraud had begun to assist French agents in their efforts against the Nazi occupation, which would naturally enough seem to make him an ally of Charles de Gaulle. But Giraud and de Gaulle were rivals, neither man interested in sharing the spotlight. In the French chain of command, Giraud far outranked de Gaulle, and Eisenhower had to trust Murphy's hunch that Giraud had both the authority and the willingness to take charge of French forces in North Africa and contradict the orders from Vichy. If Giraud accepted the role, and if Murphy's hunch was right, it might prevent a bloodbath on the beaches. At every port, the French were manning strong shore batteries, heavy guns that could devastate a large-scale landing. Each port was bristling with French artillery and infantry as well, the various airfields all filled with French fighters. But Eisenhower could not blindly share Murphy's optimism about General Giraud. Even if Giraud was willing to offer complete cooperation, and even if he ordered all the French forces to lay down their arms, Eisenhower still had an unanswerable question: Would anyone actually listen to Giraud?

"Word received from Norfolk, sir. The task force is under way."

Eisenhower said nothing, looked at Clark, who glanced down, closed his eyes for a brief moment. Eisenhower would not ask, thought, we pray in our own ways. None of my business. He looked up at the map pinned to the wall beside him, said, "Weather is the enemy now."

Clark looked at the map as well. "U-boats."

Eisenhower shook his head. "Not likely. The fleet might be a tempting target, but the destroyer escorts will be on the ball. No navy man wants to see an army transport get hit on his watch. Not with Patton out there to blow fire up their shorts."

Eisenhower was relieved, in spite of himself. He knew that with Patton pushing his people in Norfolk, Virginia, there would be no delays getting the men onto the ships. With that fleet already at sea, the transports in England were preparing as well, the troops who would make the journey southward already loading their gear. The chiefs of staff of both armies had been briefed, and both Churchill and Roosevelt had been informed of the schedule. The landing was to be November 8. If Berlin knew that, there was nothing that anyone could do about it.

One great variable was still to be decided: How would the Germans respond? They were, after all, the ultimate target of the operation. Far to the east of the landing zones, Erwin Rommel's beleaguered armor and infantry still faced the British on the pinch of the hourglass below the village of El Alamein. For many weeks now there had been a lull there, time for the Germans to spread their minefields and dig a stout defensive position into the hard dirt of the desert. Beyond that, the Germans had few options, could only wait for what might happen next. Their armor could make no decisive move on its own, the fuel reserves barely able to sustain a day's operation. If any offensive was to be made, it would have to be made by their opponent. But Montgomery had taken his time, infuriating Churchill, and testing the patience of his commander, Harold Alexander. Alexander knew that the ultimate goal of Operation Torch was to hit Rommel from behind, squeeze the Germans between Montgomery's Eighth Army and the combined forces of Eisenhower's command. But still, Montgomery took his time, would not be rushed by anyone, not even Churchill. There would be no attack on Rommel's forces until he was fully prepared.

The lull had been a blessing and a curse, the British using the time to rebuild and refit, to add to their ever-growing superiority of numbers. For the Germans, the lull should have allowed them to strengthen their supply lines, to stock their fuel and ammunition dumps. Despite so many promises from the Italians, the *Panzerarmee* had received little of the vital necessities for waging a mobile war. Much of the fuel that had been dispatched from Italy had been sent to the bottom of the sea, Italian freighters and tanker ships easy targets for British bombers and torpedo planes. The Germans and Italians who stood fast in the desert had no choice but to allow Montgomery the next move. Worse for the Germans, they could not even draw inspiration from the man who had brought them the victories that had pushed the British so close to their home base in Egypt. Rommel's illness had kept him away for more than a month, and so Montgomery's delay had been a precious gift to his adversary, allowing Rommel time to recuperate. Whether Rommel would even return to the fight was a question no one on either side could answer.

Regardless of Montgomery's reasons for delay, Operation Torch was rolling into motion. With so much at stake, even Eisenhower had begun to wonder if Montgomery intended to participate.

8. ROMMEL

It had been three weeks, but the doctors said it would take him far longer to fully regain his health. In Egypt, he had left behind careful instructions for the continuing defense of his army, to guard against the inevitable offensive that Montgomery must surely launch. From every report he received, it was obvious that the British were continuing to prepare for a new operation, were preparing massive supply dumps and pipelines to fuel an ever-expanding army, an army that the German and Italian forces might not be able to contain. Rommel knew that Montgomery's offensive, whenever it came, would most likely succeed.

Rommel's army was now in the hands of General Georg Stumme, a reasonably capable field commander, who had gained considerable experience in the early days of the Russian campaign. Stumme did not look the part of the lean and hungry panzer officer, was severely overweight, and had suffered a variety of ailments. Rommel had been concerned at the man's appearance, was concerned as well that Stumme seemed to believe that his assignment was permanent. Regardless of what Stumme might have been told in Berlin, Rommel had been specific in his instructions. Stumme was expected to follow Rommel's orders for troop positioning and defense, and if events turned particularly dangerous, Rommel fully expected to be back. Westphal's letters came far more often than Stumme's, and at the very least, Rommel was getting an accurate picture of how his increasingly ragged army was being used.

Throughout his stay at Semmering, his only other source of

information had been the newspapers. He already knew to ignore most of what he saw there, the daily dose of pleasantries that were spoon-fed the German people. Lately, the papers seemed more interested in trumpeting the various triumphs from the other theaters of the war, the Japanese conquests of Asia, the obliteration of British and American forces in the Pacific. But the greatest headlines were reserved for the Russian campaign. The papers blared the loudest for Friedrich Paulus, who commanded the great German wave that was sure to engulf Stalingrad. The news from Paulus's army was presented with the same flare for dramatics that Rommel had once seen spouting from Libya, dutifully reported by men like Berndt. It was their job, after all, to feed Goebbels's propaganda machine, the machine that would then feed the German people. The reports from Russia claimed that Paulus was certain to crush the last major resistance from Stalin's vastly inferior forces, opening the way for Hitler's armies to sweep unmolested into the rich oil fields and breadbaskets of the Caucasus and the Middle East. Before Rommel left Africa, Kesselring had given him a sketchy report, blunt, but hopeful, a delicate optimism that there might be a measure of truth to what Hitler's propaganda machine was reporting. Paulus could indeed crush the Russian defenses around Stalingrad, a victory so significant that Joseph Stalin would be pressured to accept peace, Hitler's peace. Rommel accepted that Kesselring could be right after all. Both men knew that the Führer's energy was directed far more toward Russia than it had ever been to North Africa.

On Rommel's journey northward, he had stopped first in Rome, had been met with accolades and bright flourishes from Mussolini. The talk was the same, promises of vast fleets of tankers and cargo ships, the Italians seemingly more convinced than ever that some monumental success was only days away. Rommel had gritted his teeth through the speeches, the back-slapping congratulations that met him at Comando Supremo. He had become accustomed to the strange blindness of the Italian military, but what he saw in Rome had been far worse. The city itself, vast throngs of civilians, seemed oblivious to any crisis, rolling through their daily lives as though no war even existed. It was a marked contrast to what Rommel knew was happening in Germany, where the cities endured constant Allied bombardment, food and fuel shortages beginning to creep through the countryside. But Rome showed no signs of shortages or deprivation at all. As much as Rommel despised the incompetence and inept leadership that tormented his command, he could not help feeling an odd respect for Mussolini. The man had an amazing ability to wield a unique kind of power, not with the boot or the gun, but with the minds of his subjects. Mussolini had told the perfect lie, had convinced the Italian people that everything was going their way, and they had believed him. If there was a war at all, it was for the good, would insure Italian peace and prosperity for generations. Mussolini's ridiculous ambition for a new Roman Empire had actually been achieved in the man himself, in how the Italian people accepted, even celebrated, his self-proclaimed grandeur. To Rommel, Italy felt like a dream, some bizarre fantasy. And then, he had gone to see Hitler.

The Führer showed him respect, was pleased at Rommel's *progress*. Clearly, Hitler was still attached to Goebbels's portrait of Rommel the Great Hero. The setback at Alam Halfa was merely a minor delay in the grand scheme, Hitler and his staff convinced more than ever that the British were destined to collapse in front of the vast power of Rommel's tanks, tanks that Rommel knew simply didn't exist. Promises were made, renewed efforts at supplying the *Panzerarmee* by sea, an enormous navy of new flat-bottomed cargo ships, impossible to torpedo, and heavily armed against any British threat from the air. Rommel had endured the outpouring of glorified optimism, had felt too weak and too sick to object to any of it. If there was one perfect symbol of Hitler's amazing visions of the war, it came from Hermann Göring, the German air commander. Rommel had been plain and direct that British air superiority had entirely changed the African campaign, and that if the British continued to dominate the sky, there could only be one dismal outcome. But Göring had loudly dismissed Rommel's report, had insisted that the Luftwaffe was far superior and would soon sweep the British away. To Rommel's grinding distress, he could see that Hitler leaned heavily on Göring's boastfulness. As he left Hitler's lair, Rommel tried to hold to the promises, tried to believe that what the Führer had told him might be true. But that dream had faded as well, the blissful air of victory confined only to the staff rooms and quarters of the men who had glued themselves to Hitler's unreal dreams. Beyond the walls of Hitler's headquarters, Rommel felt the depression returning, rammed into him by his illness, and by the truth of what was happening to his men. He carried that with him to the hospital at Semmering, had begun his rest and recuperation under a dark cloud. Despite the attention of the doctors, despite three weeks of pampering relaxation, the cloud stayed with him. He stared out toward the tranquil beauty of the Alps but saw only Africa, could not escape from the visions of his men, good soldiers who squatted in hard, rocky dryness, who manned the ragged tanks and worn-out artillery, who could only wait for the inevitable at El Alamein.

The lunch had been enjoyable, one of the first meals that seemed to agree with his tender stomach. It was a good sign, and Rommel leaned back against the pillow, probed his abdomen with his fingers, touched the sore places, particularly the right side. A bolt of pain shot through him, a surprise, and he groaned, said aloud, "Damn! Not again! What must I do?"

He saw them coming, the nurses responding quickly. It was the luxury of being the *Great Rommel* that every one of the staff would rush to him when he called. His liver problems were still acute, the doctors as frustrated as he was, and they all knew that should something disastrous happen to him, the first inquiries would come from the Gestapo.

The nurses had begun to gather, then stood back, made way for the doctor, a short, stocky man named Besser.

"Your liver again?"

"Yes, dammit." Rommel paused. "Doctor, you must understand. I came here believing I would find rest and rejuvenation. It has been three weeks, and I am not much better than when I arrived. Three weeks, added to a year."

Besser said, "Sir, this sort of ailment requires time. You should remain here for two months, perhaps longer."

"I do not have two months, Doctor."

"Sir!"

Rommel looked toward the woman's voice, the nurse coming toward him in quick, precise steps.

Besser said, "Yes, what is it?"

"Excuse me, Doctor. Field Marshal Rommel has a telephone call. They say it is very urgent, sir."

Rommel felt the pain again, the dull ache as he sat up. He looked at the soft face of the nurse, thought, she's afraid. Good God, what do they think I'm going to do to them?

Besser helped him to his feet, and the nurse moved close, put a soft hand beneath his arm, said in a low urgent voice, "Sir, it's the Führer's headquarters! It is General Keitel himself!"

Rommel felt his stomach reacting to the name. His lunch was turning over inside him, and he shuffled in slow steps toward the door. There were more nurses, and he saw the small office, the place where the telephone waited, knew Keitel's reedy voice, the field marshal whose ability was to function perfectly as Hitler's office boy. Rommel stared down at the earpiece, tried to calm himself. There is only one reason he would call me, he thought. It has begun.

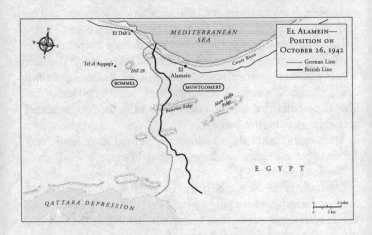

The second call came from Hitler, several hours after the first news from Keitel. Hitler had asked the same question Keitel had: Are you well enough to return to command? Rommel was surprised that Hitler himself seemed genuinely concerned, that should Rommel feel unfit, there would be no order. But the urgency was clear, and Rommel would never have refused. He was going back to Africa.

The first sign of Montgomery's attack had come from the British artillery, wave upon wave of shelling that poured over the German and Italian positions, followed by massive night and early-morning bombing from unstoppable swarms of British bombers. The combined assaults had blown great gaps in the defensive line, some Italian units simply melting away, conceding the ground to whatever Montgomery was sending toward them. Rommel knew that Hitler's headquarters would not know what was really happening, not yet, not until it was over, when the reports were written, the numbers tallied. But the first report from Keitel was less about facts and figures than the one piece of news that Rommel found hard to fathom. Somewhere in the midst of the British attack, Rommel's temporary replacement had disappeared. Keitel had used the appropriate word of course: missing. This one detail gave Rommel the worst agony, kept him awake throughout the endless night. When the *Panzerarmee* most needed the strength of a leader, Georg Stumme, the man whose critical job was to coordinate the defense, had simply vanished.

NEAR TEL EL AQQAQIR, EGYPT—OCTOBER 25, 1942

The plane had taken him directly to Rome, where he had been given the details that had been relayed from El Alamein. He knew not to depend on the reports of the fighting itself, that desert war was fluid, situations changing constantly. For that, he would see it for himself. But far worse was the confirmation that came from the supply officers. No matter how much effort had been put into transporting fuel to Rommel's army, the British bombers and torpedo planes had continued to find their mark. Much of the available gasoline meant for his armor was being sent to the bottom of the Mediterranean.

When he reached the airfield at Qasada, he made the last leg of the flight himself, in the Storch, his own small plane. He stayed low, skimmed the smooth surface of the desert, had ignored anything that might be flying high above him. The Storch was small enough that it would be ignored as well, no squadron of British fighters caring much about a single slow-moving spotter plane this far in the German rear.

The smoke drew him to the landing site, the sky smeared with black and gray, but he did not scout anything, had no interest now in observing the movement of his panzers. With the sun a deep red in the west, he brought the plane in slow, touched down. As he pulled himself stiffly out of the plane, the first man he saw was Westphal.

"General Stumme is dead, sir. We found his body this afternoon. There were no wounds. He apparently . . . fell out of his command vehicle. His heart stopped, possibly."

Rommel kept moving, saw the other officers gathering outside the tents. Westphal followed him closely, said, "Sir. I'm not sure what else we could have done."

The words punched Rommel, and he stopped, spun around, had never heard that kind of hesitation from the young man before. Westphal seemed to flinch, and Rommel stared hard into his eyes.

"Done about *what,* Colonel? What did you not do?"

Westphal glanced past him, and Rommel knew the others were listening. Rommel had no patience, the agony in his gut rolling over like bricks of ice. He knew there would be fault somewhere, someone on the line, someone in these tents panicking because of Stumme, because the army had become headless.

"What happened, Colonel?"

"Sir, the British gave us every indication they were massing for an assault to the southern flank. Our scout planes located fuel depots there and we easily spotted an enormous number of vehicles parked under camouflage. Large numbers of troops were seen marching to the south. For weeks they had been constructing a pipeline, which the observers believed to be a fuel line. Every indication was that the enemy was intending to attack us in that direction."

Rommel closed his eyes, thought of Montgomery. "And, instead, the enemy struck to the north."

"Yes, sir."

Rommel was beginning to see it in his mind, tried to imagine a grand plan, something he might do himself. He had wondered about Montgomery's delay, why the British had allowed the *Panzerarmee* to dig in, why there was so much time to repair the tanks. Now it made sense. Montgomery is . . . Rommel mulled the word . . . *meticulous.*

He turned, looked at the others, said, "If you *easily* located vehicles parked under camouflage, is it not possible that the enemy intended you to locate them? After all that has happened here, do you not believe the British are proficient in the use of camouflage? Do you not recall what we accomplished in Tripoli? When I arrived here, we had almost no armor! We constructed wooden tanks, covered Volkswagens in cloth and wood, so the British observers would believe we had strength, when we had almost none! It gave us the advantage! Now, you have given it back to them. You have been seduced by the same strategy."

His energy was gone, drained by the frustration. He looked at Westphal, scanned the faces of the others, burned and dirty, all watching him.

"You don't even know what I'm talking about. You weren't in Tripoli then. None of you."

He moved slowly toward the tents, ignored the darkness, smelled food, sickening, tightening his throat. No, they do not remember what it took to come this far, all that we did. It has been, after all, twenty months. A lifetime ago. Thousand of lifetimes. He thought of Stumme, the fat man swallowed by the desert, a commander who'd accomplished nothing. Rommel knew Westphal was behind him, would always be there. He wanted to say something to the young man, felt bad for scolding him. But dammit, they should have known. They should have been out there, probing, scouting, testing the lines, finding the strength. How could Stumme, how could any of them have allowed the enemy to fool us so badly?

"What do we know of the enemy's movements, Colonel?"

The question was answered by the sound of a vehicle, voices, and outside the tent there was a quick flash of lantern light, a single loud voice.

"Is he here?"

Westphal moved quickly, said, "He is here, this way, yes, sir!"

Rommel knew the voice, the hard energy. It was Ritter von Thoma, the most recent addition to Rommel's army. Von Thoma had been there barely a month, had taken command of the Afrika Korps, the armored divisions, had answered only to Stumme. Now, he would answer to Rommel.

He burst into the tent, a flashlight flickering briefly, searching the darkness. Rommel blinked from the light, noticed a chair to one side, sat heavily. Von Thoma was a tall, angular man, nearly Rommel's age, who knew as much about tanks as any man in the German army. Rommel had liked him immediately. He was so much like Rommel himself, with one difference: he had only been in the desert for a short time, and so, he was still healthy.

"Sit down, General."

Von Thoma obliged, leaned close to Rommel, said, "We are holding the line in the north. Some of the Italians have given way, but overall, the infantry has held as well as we could have hoped. The enemy has attempted to drive forward in the darkness, with some success. But the night can be an ally, and we have stopped him. For the most part. Our armor is causing heavy damage to the enemy, the antitank screen is very effective."

He stopped abruptly, and Rommel waited for more, had not yet heard anything he didn't already know.

Von Thoma glanced behind him, and Rommel said, "Speak your mind, General."

"There is one significant breakthrough. The enemy has captured Hill 28. The Fifteenth Panzers have lost a great deal of strength. Reinforcements are essential."

Rommel stared into darkness, thought, I must have *maps*.

"Colonel, arrange light in here. General, do you have . . ."

He saw the roll of paper now, von Thoma holding it toward him. Rommel took the map, moved to a small table, and the light was there, two aides holding flashlights. He unrolled the paper, saw the lines, a mess of scribbles, circles, numbers. He waited for von Thoma to begin, heard a new sound, distant and low. Suddenly there was a shout from Westphal, and the flashlights went dark. Rommel stared into blindness, could hear it plainly, the roar growing louder, the heavy rumble of bombers. The bombs came now, thundering in the distance, flashes lighting the walls of the tent. He felt the quiver in the ground beneath him, heard men scrambling to the trenches, shouts, Westphal grabbing his arm. Von Thoma pulled him as well, and Rommel followed, moving quickly outside the tent. The flashes sprayed out to the north, and he stopped, fascinated, could see the streaks of antiaircraft fire surging upward, could hear the bombers moving away.

"How can they do this? It is dark, for God's sake."

Westphal was still close to him, said, "Every night now, sir. It never stops."

NOVEMBER 2, 1942

He had ordered the bulk of his armor to reinforce the breakthrough along the northern flank, to strike back at the massive British thrust. Montgomery's advance was checked, Rommel's antitank guns punching great holes in the British armor, the desert littered with blackened hulks of tanks and trucks and the men who drove them. Rommel's counter had seemed to work, and true to form, the British commander seemed to grow cautious. The British advance halted, and Rommel could only assume that Montgomery had paused, baffled by Rommel's hard defense. But then word filtered through the lines, and from pilots as well, those brave enough to fly into the skies so utterly dominated by British aircraft. Behind the first line of the British position, more than eight hundred tanks and heavy armored cars sat unused, not yet committed to the fight. Rommel knew that once Montgomery made his next move, Rommel had no force that would be strong enough to hold the enemy away.

For nearly a week the fight had spread across the minefields and infantry defenses on both sides, the British taking more than a two-mile bite out of the ground once held by Rommel's men. As the fight wound down, Montgomery now controlled hills and defensive positions that Rommel's troops had been forced to concede. Rommel had no choice but to order the rest of the German armor to concentrate toward the northern flank, to add strength to a counterattack that might drive the British back or, at best, cause Montgomery to delay even further.

Rommel's only ally now was time, the time needed to transport precious fuel and ammunition ships to feed the needs of his army. Kesselring had responded to the crisis by sending some supplies by air, cargo planes that somehow survived the gauntlet of British fighters that controlled the air lanes over the Mediterranean. But the big ships continued to go down, and with them sank any hope that Rommel's tanks could go on the offensive.

To the south, along the minefields and infantry positions that stretched toward the Qattara Depression, the German and Italian lines had virtually been stripped of any defensive strength. That part of the line was manned only by Italian and German infantry, light armored trucks, and outdated Italian tanks. Once Rommel had ordered his panzer units northward, the tank commanders knew, as did Rommel himself, that there was simply not enough fuel to send them back again. If Montgomery shifted his attack southward, there would be nothing to hold him back.

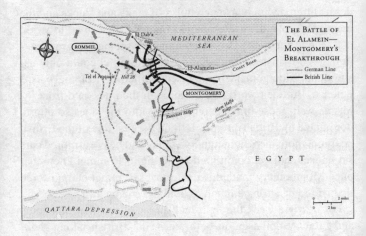

Montgomery had not held still for long, the renewed thrust pounding straight into the tanks and heavy guns that Rommel had hoped would drive the British back. No matter how much British armor was destroyed, there was more to replace it.

WEST OF HILL 28, SOUTHWEST OF EL ALAMEIN—
NOVEMBER 3, 1942

Rommel had driven along the coast road, had found a small hill,
a perch that allowed him to see across toward the British position, the lines that had once been his, where now the enemy continued to gather its vastly superior strength. Von Thoma had
joined him, Westphal keeping close to the command trucks,
where the radios continued to chatter, urgent calls, reports, the
audible chaos of the battle that was consuming more and more
of the German position. All out in front of him, the smoke rolled
forward, obliterating the hills to the east, black clouds that
hugged the ground, unending, a carpet of fire and destruction
that extended beyond the horizon to the south. Rommel scanned
the skies, said, "No bombers. Just . . . artillery, ground forces."

Von Thoma scanned through his binoculars as well, said,
"The bombers will return. Very soon. It has been this way every
day. Their artillery begins, and then the planes come. When it
began, Stumme would not order our guns to return fire. We did
not have the ammunition reserves. We have less now." Von
Thoma paused, and Rommel thought, he will not simply stand
here and watch this, not for long. The enemy is coming, and he
will face them . . . out there.

Von Thoma lowered his glasses, said, "We cannot hold this
line, sir. No matter how much destruction we inflict on them,
the enemy has no shortage of will."

Rommel lowered the glasses, fought through a chill in his
chest and arms. "The enemy has no shortage of anything."

Von Thoma turned away. "I must know . . . forgive me, sir. I
must get to the radio."

Rommel said nothing, raised the glasses again, could see
swarms of vehicles emerging from the smoke, German vehicles, regrouping, making a stand. The smoke covered them
again, and Rommel judged the distance, one mile, perhaps a
mile and a quarter.

The words came to him, rising up from a dark place in his
mind.

We are being crushed by the enemy's weight. . . . We are facing very difficult days, perhaps the most difficult that a man can undergo. The dead are lucky. It's over for them.

He had written the words to Lucy, one of so many letters he regretted now, words that were too honest. Mail was the one cargo that seemed to get through, as though the British allowed it on purpose, hoping word of what was happening at El Alamein would reach every corner of Germany. He lowered his head, thought, do I not tell her? There are so many lies, but I cannot lie to her, not to *her.* She would know something of this, surely. And if she does not, if the newspapers continue to lie, then I will tell her the truth. There is a time for propaganda, to inspire the people by exaggeration of our glorious exploits. But there is no glory here, not anymore, nothing to exaggerate except our destruction. And that is not exaggerated at all. It is real, and it is happening right out there, right in front of me.

He glanced back toward the trucks, saw von Thoma talking into a radio, the man animated, furious, waving his arms. Rommel turned again, raised the glasses, saw only smoke now, heard a steady rumble, sharp thumps, and low rolls of thunder. There was nothing else to see, the sounds telling him what he already knew, the battle rolling forward, coming toward him.

He could not fight it, could not hold the black mood away. It was too real, the failures, the mistakes, the brutally horrible incompetence that had strangled his army. No matter the latest attempts to airlift the precious fuel, restock the ammunition supplies, no aircraft could hope to bring anything to compare to what the big ships carried. And even the aircraft will not get through, not for long. Just the letters. He tapped his pocket, felt the folded paper, had kept the note he had just received that morning. It came from Rome, from Comando Supremo.

Il Duce conveys to you his deepest appreciation of the successful counterattack led personally by you. Il Duce also conveys to you his complete confidence that the battle now in progress will be brought to a successful conclusion under your command.

The letter had been too ridiculous to inspire anger. He didn't know why he had held on to it, why he hadn't simply ripped it to small bits, tossed it into the dirt. So, Il Duce, this is how the world appears to you. We are not yet obliterated, so we must be winning.

Westphal had climbed the hill behind him, said, "Sir! We have received word. Both the Twenty-first and the Fifteenth are taking heavy losses. The Afrika Korps has fewer than forty effective tanks, sir. Colonel Greiss reports that the enemy is massing two hundred tanks to his front. Colonel Fassel confirms this."

Von Thoma climbed the hill again, said, "What would you have me do, sir?"

Rommel avoided the man's sad gaze, raised the binoculars again, stared out toward the fight. The smoke had spread far below him, a surge of activity pushing west. He could feel von Thoma's energy, thought, no need to say anything, General. I see it. Another breakthrough. Closer in front of him there were flashes of light, a carpet of explosions, the sound reaching him in a few seconds. Now he saw the men, a ragged line, moving toward him, followed by more, troops pouring out of the smoke behind them, a slow tide, surging toward the coast road. He watched them for a moment, could see they were running, thought, the Italians. They cannot hold the line. We have nothing to give them.

Above him, the familiar sounds returned, and he looked to the sky, more specks, like flocks of geese in perfect V formation. The flocks began to break up, the planes swooping low, flickers of light dancing on the wings. The bombs came now, blasts among the running men, burying the Italians under clouds of dust and fire. Rommel lowered the binoculars, knew what was happening, what would happen to anyone so exposed. The roads to the west had already begun to fill with vehicles, ambulances, and small trucks, but mostly just men, the infantry, many of the shattered Italian units swarming into the roads, seeking safety away from the steel tracks of the enemy. To the south, he had already ordered the helpless infantry to pull back, would not just sacrifice men for no good reason. But the planes will find them as well, he thought. Rommel felt a hand on his shoulder, Westphal, the man's voice urgent.

"Sir! We must leave here!"

Rommel lowered the glasses. "Yes, Colonel. It is time to leave. It is time for all of us to leave."

He looked at von Thoma, saw the man nod slowly. He understands, of course.

"General, order your armor to pull back. We cannot fight on this ground."

Westphal said, "Sir! Retreat?"

Rommel looked at him, felt the stirring, the fire growing inside of him.

"It is time, Colonel. We are a mobile army, and if we are to survive, we must be mobile again. Order the infantry commanders to withdraw in good order, if possible. The artillery should withdraw as rapidly as possible. They are our best line of defense. Everyone should attempt to reach the line we have established below Fuka."

Westphal stared at him, said nothing.

Von Thoma said, "Sir, if we withdraw the artillery, the enemy will be able to maintain close pursuit. We must put up a rearguard screen. If not . . . it could be a slaughter, sir."

"Obey my orders, General. Send word to every senior commander. Do you understand?"

Von Thoma saluted him, moved away down the hill, toward the command vehicles, toward the radios.

Rommel looked at Westphal, said, "Montgomery will not pursue. There is surprise in retreat as well as attack. When he realizes we have disengaged, he will assess and analyze. That is still our great advantage."

NEAR EL DABA, EGYPT—NOVEMBER 3, 1942

The battle at El Alamein had been lost. But the *Panzerarmee* could survive, and there was still a strong defense to be made, if somehow the flow of ammunition and fuel could continue. There were good places for defensive fighting all across Libya, the obstacles that Rommel had once breached against Wavell and Auchinleck, strong positions that would hold Montgomery at bay until some decision was made in Berlin, a decision about what Rommel was expected to do next. Salvaging what remained of the *Panzerarmee* was Rommel's priority, and if Hitler agreed, the tanks and heavy equipment could be withdrawn to the seaports. There, the Luftwaffe could make a strong showing, protecting the ships that could pull Rommel's forces out of Africa altogether, forces that would still be able to make a good fight where the Führer might need them. Once Montgomery realized how complete his victory had been, he would come again. The only question was, when?

Rommel had made his way westward, along roadways choked with a desperate wave of humanity. Throughout the day, the British had held fast to their new breakthrough, no signs yet of a major pursuit. Rommel had to believe that Montgomery was simply reveling in the victory, or even better, the British commander was completely unaware the victory had been handed to him.

The command car rolled out into the desert, passing a crippled truck, its crew abandoning the vehicle, making their way on foot, joining the vast throng of retreating soldiers. The car lurched and bounced, Rommel holding tightly to the side, could see an oasis, a cluster of palm trees. He knew the landmark, knew they were only a few miles from the line where the army could make its next stand. It would be a temporary defense, putting the remaining eighty-eights and the heavy tanks in position to screen the rest of the army as it made its escape. If Montgomery followed at all, he would first have to absorb a horrific pounding from Rommel's guns. Rommel guessed that the British soldiers were as exhausted as the Germans and the Italians. Confronting Rommel's defensive screen might give Montgomery's troops the excuse to stop.

He knew from the maps and landmarks that he was still ten miles east of the village of El Daba. There were ridges here, dry wadis where the eighty-eights had begun to dig in. The car rolled down through a trail in the wadi, then up the other side, and he saw another cluster of palms, pointed, the driver obeying. They reached the oasis, and the car rolled to a stop. Rommel saw tents being raised, officers shouting instructions to work crews, who were shirtless and sweating. He stepped out of the car, moved toward them, and they saw him now, the work stopping, the men giving him a cheer.

He held up a hand, a silent gesture, thank you, pointed to the worn canvas, said, "Do not stop work. This is the new headquarters, at least for now."

More cars stopped, and he watched as his staff officers scrambled to work, men with radios, moving quickly to string an antenna into one of the palms. More trucks were gathering, and beyond, he could see the makeshift airstrip, a row of cargo planes, blessed fuel, a meager supply that had somehow found him. He saw staff officers carrying bundles of maps from the car. Good, very good, he thought. We'll be in operation here very quickly.

"Sir!" Westphal was coming toward him now, held a paper in his hand. "A wireless message, from Berlin, sir!"

Rommel took the paper, began to read, felt a cold tumble in his stomach.

> . . . In the situation in which you find yourself, there can be no other thought but to stand fast, yield not a yard of ground, and throw every gun and every man into the battle. . . . As to your troops, you can show them no other road than that to victory or death.
>
> Adolf Hitler

The paper fell away from his hand, settled to the hot ground at his feet. He stared toward the roadway, his eyes not focusing on the parade of exhausted, beaten men.

Westphal said, "Is it new orders, sir?"

Rommel could not look at him, turned away, stared out toward the vast, empty desert. He had ignored the sickness for as long as he could, the pains in his side, the tightness in his throat. He had drawn strength from the power of his army, a power that even now, beaten and bloodied, could still make the good fight, if they were only given the time, precious time to gather and refit and resupply. He felt himself drained of strength, as drained as his army, could see only the face of Hitler, the man's utter detachment, his inability to see an unpleasant truth. And now, you would order us to fight and die and sacrifice this army, sacrifice the men who are *devoted* to you . . . for what?

"Sir? What does it mean?"

"It means, Colonel . . ." He stopped, held on to the words inside him, could not betray what he had held on to for so long. But it is there, he thought, lying at my feet, the simple order on a piece of paper, the order from a man who lives only in his dreams, who believes only in the fantastic and the glorious, and ignores the truth. No, that is not right. He does not *ignore*. He simply does not hear at all. To Hitler, none of this is . . . *real*.

"It means, Colonel, that the Führer is insane."

NOVEMBER 4, 1942

He had sent Lieutenant Berndt in the first available plane to report to Hitler's high command, to explain exactly what was happening to the *Panzerarmee*. Rommel had not been polite, had stopped worrying about the boisterous Gestapo officer. It had always been known that Berndt had Hitler's ear, and so, Berndt would go directly to the Führer, would be told exactly what Rommel needed him to know. The report would be brief and direct: if the *Panzerarmee* stands its ground, in no more than a few days it will be exterminated.

"They have never done this before. Never. There was advice and complaining, but never did anyone, not even the Führer, tell me how to move my army."

Kesselring nodded, rubbed his chin. He had only been on the ground for a few minutes, had seemed as surprised as Rommel by the extraordinary order from Hitler.

"Albert, I have obeyed him. I have halted the army. We are able to stand here now only because Montgomery is confused, as I knew he would be. But he is coming, and when he comes, any of us who remain here will be swallowed up. There will be no *Panzerarmee,* no Afrika Korps."

Kesselring looked past him, toward the other officers, the men who stood silently, said slowly, "This is not an order you should obey. The Führer has made an error, does not have the proper information. You say Berndt is on his way there?"

Rommel nodded. "He should arrive in a few hours. If he is not shot down."

"I will contact the Führer myself and explain the situation. He can be made to understand. He must. If this army is destroyed, all of North Africa will be lost. The Führer will understand that it cannot be so."

Rommel turned away, did not want to hear Kesselring's optimism. It seemed mindless, idiotic now. He looked toward Westphal, said, "We have one chance for survival. We must move west, to the Fuka line, regroup, and then move west again. If we fight a strong retreating action, we can hold the British away. But there must be *speed*."

There was silence for a long moment, and Kesselring said, "I would have had you withdraw much sooner. You should not have made a stand at El Alamein."

Rommel stared at him. Are you trying to be fatherly? He felt the explosion coming, knew it should not happen, not with the others there. But the words came out in a rush, no strength left to hold them back.

"You would tell me how to command my army? You would tell me *now* what I should have done? You would give me advice that no one can follow?" He was shouting, and his voice began to crack, waver. He began to shake, his throat tightening. His fists were clenched, and he pulled his arms up to his chest, pulling at himself, trying to hold the anger inside. Kesselring stepped back, and Rommel suddenly realized, he is afraid of me. Yes, damn you! You should be afraid of me! They all should.

Westphal had moved up beside him, and Kesselring spoke softly, the words directed toward Westphal.

"I will send word to the Führer. I will explain. It will be on my authority. Have the commanders make immediate preparation to withdraw to the positions designated to them before the halt. Speed is essential. Maintain a strong defensive rear guard. Where is General von Thoma? How many tanks are operational?"

A voice came from behind Rommel. "Sir, General von Thoma was taken by the enemy. We do not know if he is alive."

Kesselring was wide-eyed, said, "My God. We must learn if he was captured."

Rommel forced out the words: "He will survive. He is a fighter."

Another voice behind Rommel said, "We have only thirty-five tanks in operation, sir."

"Thirty . . . five? That is all?"

Rommel looked at Kesselring again, saw the face of a man who was trying to assume command, to gain control of a situation where no control could be had. Rommel straightened himself, the chill gone, and he flexed his fingers, worked air into his lungs.

"This is still my army."

Kesselring looked past him, seemed to test the statement, measure the reaction of the others. Rommel did not look behind him, thought, they are loyal to me still. They will still fight for me.

Kesselring nodded to him now, said, "Yes. I agree. I will tell the Führer that. But you must not allow the enemy to confront or ensnare you. Every piece of equipment has value. You must now fight a poor man's war."

Rommel looked hard at Kesselring, weighed his words, said, "I have *always* fought a poor man's war. If I could have fought any other way, we would be in Cairo now." He felt his strength returning, the sickness releasing him. He turned, looked at the others, saw the confidence, hard faces of men who had survived the worst the enemy could give them. And we will survive now, he thought. All we need is time. And one good commander to show them the way.

On November 5, word came from Hitler's headquarters. Influenced by both Berndt and Kesselring, Hitler had changed his mind, had now approved the decision that Rommel should withdraw his army. When the word reached Rommel, the *Panzerarmee* was already out of harm's way. Montgomery had delayed once more, had allowed Rommel all the head start he would need.

Though the British had won a decisive victory at El Alamein, Montgomery could not complete the task, could not deliver the final blow. The fight with Rommel had taken an enormous toll on the fighting strength of the British troops and their machines. When Montgomery finally gave chase, the men who pushed across the desert knew that by allowing Rommel to escape, it only meant that there would yet be another fight, that no matter how many tanks they had, how superior the British were in numbers, they would still have to risk another costly and dangerous duel with the *Panzerarmee,* and the man who led them.

9. EISENHOWER

F ive planes were in the formation, each one carrying ten officers or aides, dividing the headquarters staff so that if any one plane was shot down, someone might survive who could still command the operation. There had been fog, a blessing of course, since no German fighter was likely to find the heavy bombers, and despite the nervous fingers of the gunners who stared into the gray darkness, the trip had been as uneventful as anyone could hope. Eisenhower flew in the *Red Gremlin,* the same plane that had carried Clark to Gibraltar, the first leg of Clark's secret mission to Africa. The pilot was the same as well, Major Paul Tibbets. The decision to leave London, to make the flight despite the inclement weather, had been Eisenhower's. The decision about just how to get there safely belonged to Tibbets, who now had a reputation as one of the finest pilots in the U.S. air force.

After a steep descent, they landed abruptly, and Eisenhower could see now why the airfield was such a challenge. The runway was surprisingly short and was flanked by dense rows of British Spitfires. The fighters had been assembled for one purpose, would serve as the screen for the invasion fleets, hoping to hold back the enemy planes that would certainly try to interfere in the landings along the North African coast. Whether those planes would be German or French, even Eisenhower had no idea.

Eisenhower was met by the royal governor, General Sir Frank Mason-MacFarlane, and the staff would be housed in MacFarlane's home, a gracious gesture from their British host. But there was little time for social pleasantries, something the governor seemed to recognize. Immediately, Eisenhower was escorted to his new headquarters, down a corridor nearly a half mile deep into solid rock. It was a formidable fortress, a place that had for centuries guarded British interests in the Mediterranean, but Eisenhower could see now that this extraordinary landmark was far more than a great lump. The British staffers led him down long, damp corridors that had been carved right into the rock. The Rock of Gibraltar was in fact an enormous office building.

The room, lit by one bare lightbulb, was barely eight feet square. There were two desks, two chairs, and Eisenhower sat in one, watched as the piles of folders, maps, and documents were hauled in by the aides. Clark had the other desk and stood by the narrow door, directing the flow, the aides unloading their haul, then moving quickly out. Clark shifted a box behind his desk, laughed, said, "Well, this is cozy. I'll do you the favor of taking a bath once in a while."

Eisenhower tried to smile, felt the chair hard against his back, the tightness in his chest gripping him, stiff and uncomfortable. It had been this way for nearly a week now, the same feeling of anxious helplessness that had engulfed him once the final orders had been given. It was all in motion, 120,000 men, planes, tanks, artillery, all of it rolling across the seas, two great arms extending slowly toward Africa. He imagined it as some beast, claws extended, one arm to the west, Patton, in the open ocean, driving slowly toward Casablanca. The other was shorter, sliding through the Strait of Gibraltar, and once there, opening into two fists, each one punching its target, like a boxer unleashing a hard left hook. But the punches were three days away, and the targets themselves were hidden in doubt, obscured by the absurd political fog of the French. Through it all Eisenhower could only wait, sitting in a tiny office, deep inside a wet, cold rock.

"Ike?"

He looked up at Clark, the tall, thin man leaning across his desk, focused. "What?"

"I thought you'd want to get word back to England. The courier says there're some pretty jumpy folks in London, wondering if we got here okay."

Eisenhower realized there was another man in the room, short, standing behind Clark. "The Brits didn't send word?"

Clark shook his head. "Apparently not. I'm guessing the prime minister is doing a dance all over the walls of Ten Downing Street. We should let them know we landed."

"Yes, of course. Send word. Send it twice. We're giving them enough to worry about already."

Clark gave the instructions, ordered the aide away, moved to his desk, sat, said, "You see all that gasoline?"

"The governor told me about it. Didn't go looking for it."

"Holy mackerel, Ike, they've got gas cans stuck in every crack on this rock. The British say they're holding a million gallons at least, every bit of it in four-gallon tin cans. With the two hundred Spitfires sitting in the open out there, you know that the Krauts are gonna send a few bombers overhead. The governor says the Germans have observers draped all over that barbed-wire fence, watching everything that goes on here. One bomb hits that gas . . . this whole rock might turn into a Fourth of July celebration."

Eisenhower scratched his head, worked the stiffness out of his back. "Where else they supposed to store it, Wayne? This is the only friendly spot on the whole damned European continent."

"Well, ships, for one. The governor was hoping we could get a tanker in here, keep the stuff offshore."

"You don't think a tanker would be a target?"

"*We* wouldn't be on that tanker, sir."

Eisenhower heard a soft plop, saw a small splatter on his desk. He looked up, the drip gathering on the rock above him, another plopping on the floor beside him. He felt a chill, could see a watery sheen on the entire ceiling above him, smears of crusty color, from whatever minerals made up the rock.

"Hard to imagine this place would ever catch fire. Forget

about it. We have too many other things to sweat about. We heard from the sub?"

"I'll check on it. Radio room down the hall."

Clark left the room, and Eisenhower could see activity outside, more of the bare lightbulbs, the wetness, men hustling through the rock corridor, boxes, papers, all the business of war. He looked at the papers on his desk, began to sort through the pile, stopped, thought of Giraud. How much of this depends on you? And where the hell are you?

Henri Giraud was supposedly en route to Gibraltar, after a haze of messages and requests had jammed the airways in both directions. According to the diplomat Murphy, Giraud had seemed completely receptive to the role the Allies needed him to play, Giraud suggesting that he be taken directly to Algiers. But neither Giraud nor any of the French commanders had yet been informed of the specific details of Torch, did not yet know the timetable for the landings, had no idea that the invasion fleets were already in motion. Rather than put Giraud right into the middle of a combat zone, it made far more sense to bring the Frenchman to Gibraltar, to meet directly with Eisenhower, to clear up any doubts about the French general's loyalties, and what he could do to prevent a bloody fight at the landing zones. The plan called for him to slip away from his hiding place in Lyon, to a designated site along the beach, where a submarine would be waiting. Once away from the French coast, he would be picked up by a seaplane for the final leg of the trip to Gibraltar. The submarine was the *Seraph,* the same craft that had transported Clark to the Algerian beach. But true to form, the Frenchman would not accept any transport by a British ship. It was the old ugliness rearing its head, French resentment against the British. There seemed to be no ignoring the centuries of rivalry and animosity between the two countries. The British had opened the latest wound after the fall of France, when Admiral Darlan, who was becoming Pétain's number two man in the Vichy government, would not agree to allow the French fleet to escape the umbrella of German control. The French navy was the fourth largest in the world, and should those ships sail alongside the Germans, the British would certainly lose whatever dominance they had on water. With Darlan refusing to

release that part of the fleet anchored in French ports in North
Africa, the British had no choice but to treat those warships as
hostile. In July 1940, the French ships anchored in Oran, Algeria, refused British ultimatums and chose to fight. It was a significant mistake. The British navy responded by sinking several
major craft, which not only cost the Germans eventual use of
the ships, but was of course an embarrassment to the French ad-
miralty. Regardless of British logic in their approach to the
problem, it was just one more thorn in their relationship with the
French, a thorn that was now digging into Eisenhower's planning. Giraud had demanded that he be transported in an American submarine, despite there being no American subs available
anywhere near the Mediterranean. So the *Seraph* would become
American, with an American skipper, just long enough to bring
Giraud to safety.

GIBRALTAR—NOVEMBER 6, 1942

A dozen aides were scattered throughout the vast cavern, voices
low, all noise subdued by the dense rock around them.

Butcher was there now, and Eisenhower asked, "Have we
heard from George? What about the weather in the Atlantic?"

"Latest reports don't change the forecast. Still calling for
rough seas."

"Keep me posted. Less than forty-eight hours. I want to know
what those beaches are like."

"Aye, sir."

Butcher moved away, and Eisenhower stared again at the
map, British staffers using long sticks to adjust the position of
the blue ships, the fleets, edging them closer to their goals. He
scanned the map, his eyes resting on Spain. He thought of Patton, couldn't help a smile. The surf conditions near Casablanca
were notoriously difficult, rough seas that would make any
landing a challenge. There had been concern that the landing
might be canceled, Patton's troops forced to shift to another
zone, perhaps linking up with one of the other groups inside the
Mediterranean. Patton's response had been no surprise: *If we
can't land in West Africa, we'll find someplace else. How about*

Spain? Leave it to Georgie to start a whole new war. He'd win it too.

"Sir, the press are in the briefing room. Commander Butcher has given them a briefing, but they're asking to speak to you."

Eisenhower turned to the aide, who made a smart, unnecessary salute.

"Fine. I'll be right there."

He usually did well with the newspapermen and radio reporters, had actually built a friendship with Edward R. Murrow. It was an essential part of his job, one reason why Eisenhower could function outside of the public eye so effectively. And it was a mutually beneficial relationship. If the reporters wanted to know what was going on, for the most part Eisenhower would tell them. In return, it was clearly understood that they had to exercise extraordinary discretion in what information they passed on to the public.

He saw two Americans and two Brits waiting at the door of the briefing room, the only reporters allowed to make the trip. They made a path for him, and he moved through a cloud of cigarette smoke, scanned the familiar faces, moved to one end of the small room.

Butcher appeared in the doorway now, and Eisenhower looked toward him, said, "Commander Butcher has briefed you, I understand?"

There were nods.

"Quite."

"Yes, sir."

"Good. I don't have much to add. The timetable has not changed. Weather could still be a factor in the Atlantic. I understand that you all brought a considerable amount of winter clothing."

They smiled with him, and Wes Gallagher, of the Associated Press, said, "Still looking for the glaciers, sir. Can't seem to find any fjords either."

"Sorry. Couldn't be helped. We had to indicate at every opportunity that we were going to Norway. It was simply too important to mention anything else."

Gallagher said, "I'd donate my heavy woolens to the Red Cross hereabouts, but they don't seem interested."

Another man, Cunningham, from the United Press, said, "Sir, if no one else has done so, allow me to be the first to congratulate you."

Eisenhower glanced at Butcher, saw a smile, said, "What do you mean?"

"We got word that MacArthur, Ohio, has changed its name to Eisenhower."

Butcher laughed, the others joining in, and Eisenhower held up a hand, quieting them.

"If that's true . . . well, I'm certain that before this is over, they'll change it back. You all know full well that I'm not as, um, *juicy* as General MacArthur."

They grew silent now, and he said, "You know your jobs, gentlemen. The public needs to know the facts, and I'm all for that, as long as nothing gets out that helps the enemy. There has been a great deal of planning for this operation that was extremely sensitive, and so, we had to hold back telling you things. I know you want to win this war as quickly as we do, and you can all assist by doing the right kind of job here. We'll be as open with you as we feel we can, so don't spy on us. Be assured that if anyone here violates the faith we've placed in you, if I can catch you, I'll shoot you. Good day, gentlemen."

He moved out through the small room, was past Butcher, who beamed a smile, said in a low voice, "Nicely done, sir."

Eisenhower didn't smile, turned toward his office, said, "I meant it."

"Sir, it's Admiral Cunningham."

Eisenhower stood, and Butcher stood aside, stiff and formal, making way for the older man to enter the office. Cunningham stepped in slowly, leaned on a cane. He clamped his hat firmly under one arm, the dark blue uniform having a formalizing effect on Butcher that made Eisenhower smile. Yep, Harry's still a navy man.

Andrew Browne Cunningham was one of Britain's most effective fighting sailors. He had scored impressive victories over the Italian navy early in the war, which had allowed the British to maintain naval control of the Mediterranean. He was several years older than Eisenhower, carried himself with that distinctly

British stiffness, but bore no resemblance to those officers who strutted and preened far more than they actually fought. The admiral had been named overall naval commander of the Allied forces in the Mediterranean and North Africa and, as such, was the highest-ranking naval officer under Eisenhower's command. It was a fortunate choice, since Eisenhower had taken an immediate liking to the man.

Cunningham held his pose, said, "General, I understand from your staff that you have not yet been informed of our latest triumph. Thus it is my honor to bring you some exceptionally positive news. May I do so?"

Eisenhower pointed to Clark's chair. "Please, sit down, Admiral. Good news should be delivered from a comfortable position. If you have bad news, stay standing. That way you can get away quicker. Keeps me from killing the messenger."

Cunningham smiled, took the advice, pulled Clark's chair around, sat, one hand on his cane, his hat still under his arm.

"Reports have come in from Harold Alexander, in Cairo. We've given Rommel a heavy licking at El Alamein. Twenty thousand prisoners, and we destroyed maybe four hundred tanks, a good bit of artillery too. It took Monty a while to get going, but once he did, it was a masterstroke. Bloody as hell, as I hear it, but victory, nonetheless."

"Thank God. Thank God." Eisenhower paused, let out a long breath. "What's Rommel's situation now?"

"Full retreat, so we hear. Monty's following up. Could make your job a damned sight easier, you know."

"I'd rest a little easier if Rommel was in the bag."

"Give Monty a chance. Needs a bit of prodding now and then, but he'll handle it. I suspect this will take some pressure off Tunisia. The Jerries might be inclined to pull out before you even get there."

"Not sure I agree with you. If Rommel escapes Montgomery, he'll be moving west, straight for Tunisia. He might be whipped, and he might have lost most of his armor, but I can't assume Hitler will abandon him. And, he's still Rommel. I had hoped Monty might eliminate him altogether. Seems we may end up fighting his front instead of his rear."

Cunningham seemed to concede the point. "At least, if you're in front of him, Monty will be behind him. Same principle applies. Rommel will be pinched."

Eisenhower thought, it can't be that easy.

Cunningham moved on. "On the local front, one more bit of news. Intelligence reports the Jerries are preparing to give us a good wallop at Sicily. We'll have our distress call on the air tonight. Ice the cake, so to speak."

It was Cunningham's perfect contribution to the subterfuge of the operation. Eisenhower had to assume that German U-boats had located the invasion fleets, and so, the Allied vessels and radio operators throughout the Mediterranean had leaked various messages that the invasion was in fact heading for Sicily. So far, the fleets had reported no major losses, the U-boats staying clear of the heavy screen of destroyer escorts that ringed them. Only one ship in the Mediterranean had taken a torpedo hit, disabling her, but no lives had been lost. Now, Cunningham was preparing for a ship to be sent toward Sicily as a decoy, a ship that would fill the air with frantic distress calls as the time for the landings drew close. The theory was that German bombers could be persuaded to take a look, might patrol the Sicilian coast with a heightened urgency, keeping them away from North Africa for precious hours.

GIBRALTAR—NOVEMBER 7, 1942

Despite anxious hours, and garbled radio messages, Giraud's journey had been completed without major problems, beyond the Frenchman's near drowning as he was hauled aboard the submarine.

Giraud was taller than Eisenhower had expected, wore rumpled clothes that showed the effects of the saltwater soaking. He carried himself erect, seemed unaware that his face was brushed with a thick shadow of unshaved beard, framing the sad droop of what seemed to have once been a proud handlebar mustache.

The secretive journey had been the latest chapter in what Eisenhower could only assume to be the man's difficult and frightened existence. Giraud's escape from a German prison camp had made him something of a legend in France, and a seriously wanted man to the Gestapo. Somehow, he had evaded capture, and from everything Murphy had said, Giraud held tightly to the notion that his time had come, that he was now willing to give everything to an Allied victory. Eisenhower was prepared to offer the man a great deal of authority over the French civil and military forces in North Africa, a friendly administrator in a land where friends might be at a premium. All he required of Giraud now was that he agree to endorse a broadcast, made prominently in his name, addressing the military commanders along the African coast who were about to be confronted by a major invasion force. If Giraud carried the influence and authority that both he and Murphy insisted he did, the landings might happily be uneventful.

Giraud stood alongside Jerauld Wright, the American navy man who had played the role of alleged captain of the *Seraph*, successfully convincing Giraud that an American was indeed in command. Wright made the introductions, and Eisenhower shook the fragile hand of the man who seemed an unlikely bearer of the power that could decide so much of the outcome of Operation Torch. Eisenhower motioned to the door, a silent command to Wright, who seemed to understand completely that his part of this strange mission was at an end.

Wright made a short bow toward Giraud, said, "I leave you now, General. May God go with us all."

Wright left the small room, was replaced by Colonel Julius Holmes, who was there to serve as Eisenhower's interpreter. Behind him, Clark closed the door, flicking a switch that illuminated a red bulb outside the office, its meaning clear: *No one enters*.

The men all sat and Giraud stared past Eisenhower, seemed already to be impatient with a meeting that had not yet begun. Eisenhower began to talk, emptied his mind of details, revealed the facts and timetable of Torch, of everything that was already in motion. Giraud did not react, sat motionless, allowed his eyes to drift to Eisenhower's face. Eisenhower stopped, had used up everything he had expected to say, waited, and Giraud seemed to come alive.

The man straightened his back, sat upright, said, "Now, let's get it clear as to my part. As I understand it, when I land in

North Africa, I am to assume command of all Allied forces and become the supreme Allied commander in North Africa."

Eisenhower felt his mouth opening, heard a short grunt from Clark. Giraud seemed satisfied, as though he had answered his own inquiry. Eisenhower had no words, stared at the Frenchman, who tilted his head slightly, waiting for confirmation. Eisenhower looked at Holmes, the interpreter obviously surprised, the man nodding nervously to Eisenhower, yes, the words were accurate. He looked again at Giraud, tried to think of a response, thought suddenly of Murphy. What kind of promises did you make, what did you tell this man? Is this how you got him to come here? Promise him the entire damned world, you amateur diplomat son of a bitch? He fought against the fury, held it hard inside him, tried to smile again, his fists clenched beneath the edge of the desk.

"There must be some misunderstanding."

"I think not, General. It is perfectly clear to me. My duty is in North Africa, and Giraud will do his duty. As well, I should also take command of a force that will immediately invade southern France. Once the Nazis learn of our attack on North Africa, they will certainly respond by occupying the remaining French territory now held in control by the Vichy government. I fear if we do not act quickly, the Nazis will bring further destruction to my country. We shall prevent this."

Eisenhower looked at Clark, who stared at the Frenchman with disbelief. After a long moment, Eisenhower said, "There *is* a misunderstanding."

Giraud seemed to stiffen further, growing even taller in the chair. "I understand my role perfectly well, General. If there is any misunderstanding, it must be coming from you."

The meeting dragged on for three tedious hours, Giraud maintaining perfect stubbornness. An invitation had come from Governor Mason-MacFarlane for Giraud to enjoy a dinner with his official British host. It was a marvelous opportunity for adjournment that Eisenhower leapt on, if for no other reason than to empty his office of this astoundingly disagreeable Frenchman.

* * *

Both men sat back in their chairs, stared at the wall for a long moment. Eisenhower looked at Clark, said, "Are you quite certain that General Mast understood you?"

"Absolutely. Ike, I didn't promise Mast anything. I'm certain of that. It has to be Murphy."

Eisenhower shook his head, worked himself up out of the chair, tried to ease the cramps out of his shoulders. "We can assume that. It's possible, certainly. But I can't believe that Murphy is that stupid. He knew he couldn't make promises about command authority."

Clark stayed in the chair, rubbed a hand on the back of his neck. "You know how those people talk, the politics, all that diplomatic greasiness. Half the time I have no idea what they're saying anyway. Jesus, Ike, Giraud refers to himself in the third person." Clark paused. "So, what do we do now?"

Eisenhower moved to the open door, stared into the dull light of the corridor. "Mast did this. It has to be Mast. He insisted to you that he could bring Giraud to Africa, and if he hadn't delivered, his honor would have been compromised. You know how those people are. Honor, all about honor. Never mind that their country is in Hitler's back pocket, that their great damned hero Marshal Pétain is no more than Hitler's shoeshine boy. This whole damned plan, Wayne, all of it, is designed toward one goal: kick Hitler's ass. Eventually, that means we have to move into France, somehow, some way. *Liberate* them! And in the meantime, we have to ally ourselves with petty autocrats. No, not *ally*. *Depend*. We *need* them, for God's sake."

"They know that, Ike. That's why Giraud thinks he can pull this stunt, that we have to give him command. He needs a lesson in muscle. Influence doesn't come from an inflated sense of honor, it comes from guns."

"Dammit, Wayne, we're under the gun here. I'm not a politician and I need to act like one. I have to tread lightly with him."

Clark sat back in the chair, looked up toward the ceiling. "Treading lightly won't get us anywhere, Ike."

Eisenhower thought a moment. "I should emphasize what we're offering him. Civil and military control over French forces, over the local governments. That's a big damned plum for a man who has spent a year afraid to show his face, wondering if the next knock on his door is a man with a machine gun." Eisenhower paused, saw Clark looking at the paper on his desk, the letter that Giraud had to sign, the entire reason he was there in the first place.

"Dammit, Wayne, we *need* him."

Clark held the paper up. "You know, if he doesn't sign this . . . well, we can broadcast it anyway. Who's to know?"

"That would be dangerous, Wayne. There could be hell to pay in Washington, it could put the president's butt in a sling, could wreck any chance of an alliance with the French. It's politics, Wayne. There are rules about things like that, and I'd have to take the consequences for it. Marshall wouldn't approve of that, for certain. We're not supposed to monkey around with all this political crap."

"But we are. We're right in the middle of it. France is, what? Three countries now? Loyalty to Vichy, loyalty to de Gaulle, loyalty to Giraud. Every popgun commander in North Africa controls his own little army, Ike. Okay, so we need him. But if he doesn't go along with us, if he doesn't take charge like we need him to, there's gonna be hell to pay right here."

Eisenhower put a hand on Clark's shoulder. "We need to keep our tempers in check."

"For how long, Ike? Our boys will start hitting their landings in less than eight hours."

Eisenhower looked at his watch, knew Giraud had been gone nearly an hour. "The governor will get him back here pretty quick. We just have to do what we can to convince him to sign this order."

Giraud's stubbornness had not mellowed with British hospitality. Eisenhower tried again, spoke for long minutes at a time, reason and logic, long lectures about political and military reality. As Holmes translated, Eisenhower was already moving ahead, impatient for Holmes to complete the words. As the time ticked past, Eisenhower felt himself losing control. The man's stubbornness was absolute, Giraud simply repeating what he insisted to be his only condition for going along with the plan. Eisenhower was beginning to feel hatred for the Frenchman, recalling all the memories of the schoolboy aristocrats, the sons of rich fathers, parading their superiority. Now it wasn't about money or the importance of a family's name, it was just one man who refused to relax his grip on his own importance, who was pushing Eisenhower further into a despair that was heightened by the ticking clock, the movement of so many ships that carried the men whose lives might depend on this one annoying man agreeing to sign a piece of paper.

He was nearly hoarse, was close to simply killing this Frenchman, who had become nothing more than a tall strutting rooster. There was silence for a moment, and Eisenhower fought for the strength to look once more at Giraud, was surprised to see a flicker of weariness, the man's age and his rough journey to Gibraltar showing itself in frayed edges around the man's arrogant pronouncements. But little had changed, and Eisenhower knew his own fuse had been lit, was growing shorter.

He turned toward Clark, said, "General, please make an attempt here. I've run out of words."

Clark sat up, seemed to energize, stared at Giraud, and said, "We would like the honorable general to know that the time of his usefulness to the Americans, and for the restoration of the glory that was once France, is *now*."

Giraud seemed unaffected by Clark's energy, shook his head. "But what would the French people think of me? What about Giraud? What about the family of Giraud?"

Clark said, "It shouldn't make much difference whether *Giraud* is governor of North Africa, or general of all the armies. We have made all the preparations. We have completed the planning, and we are the ones who will liberate North Africa from the Nazis. We are fully prepared to give you command of all French troops in North Africa, once we have made successful landings. We simply cannot give you any higher military authority."

Giraud turned away, sniffed, "Then I shall return to France."

Clark leaned forward, and Eisenhower saw a strange smile on his face.

"How are you going back?"

"By the same route I came here."

Clark laughed, and Eisenhower could see Giraud's expression change, that even he understood what Clark was about to say.

"Nope. No, you won't. That was a one-way submarine."

Giraud seemed to quiver. Clark was like a lean, lanky beast, his jaw clamping down on the neck of a much-sought-after prey.

Giraud said, "Perhaps I shall wait, then, to see if you are truly intending to liberate the French people. We will not allow ourselves to be advantaged by conquerors."

It was pure ploy, a gambit that Eisenhower could see right through. He will delay, see how the chips fall, then decide whether he will ride our wagon. There is no time for that.

Clark seemed to follow his thoughts, said to Holmes, the interpreter, "I have nothing else to say to General Giraud directly." Clark glanced at Eisenhower, who gave a short nod. "Tell the general that if he does not go along with us and put his signature to this order, he's going to be out in the snow on the seat of his pants."

GIBRALTAR—NOVEMBER 8, 1942, 2:38 A.M.

Giraud was gone, had still not signed the paper, and Eisenhower had wired the annoying details of the meeting to Washington.

Cots had been brought into the tiny office, filling what space was left, and Clark and he lay side by side, each man seeking some kind of sleep, some way to sweep away the sour taste of the meeting with the Frenchman. Eisenhower's mind had grabbed at hope, that if only one of the landings was moderately successful, Algiers, perhaps, the Americans making quick work of occupying the city, then Giraud would agree to authorize the broadcast. Lives could still be saved, French commanders persuaded not to strike back at the invaders. Surely he knows that I will not turn over this entire theater of the war to his authority. It was his bargaining chip. It had to be.

Eisenhower turned over on his side, the stiffness in his shoulders tormenting him. He could not erase the image of the tall, hollow-cheeked old man. He did not blink, he thought, did not waver. What kind of horse trader would be so inflexible? They *are* a different breed, those people. Giraud is far more concerned with how he will be regarded by the history books than by how many men will die for his arrogance. How do you believe you are holding on to honor when you sit by and allow a disaster to happen?

He turned on his back again, angry at himself now. It is not a disaster. It will not *be* a disaster. Patton, Ryder, Fredendall, Cunningham, Doolittle . . . and Clark. How many *Girauds* would it take to fill any of their shoes? Have faith, General.

The door opened slowly, a crack of light splitting the room. He heard the whisper, Butcher.

"Sir?"

Eisenhower sat up, Clark as well.

Butcher said, "Word received, sir. The Eastern Task Force. First report from General Ryder indicates the landing has been successful on three beaches at Algiers. We're ashore, sir."

Eisenhower slid to the end of the cot, Butcher extending a hand, helping him to his feet. Clark was up as well.

Eisenhower gripped Butcher's shoulders. "Are you certain, Harry?"

"Definitely, sir."

Eisenhower felt the wall cracking inside him, so many months of work, the planning, the arguments, the politics. None of it mattered now. There was only one thought, and it filled him, rolled through his mind like a great boulder, crushing the fears, the annoying thoughts of men like Henri Giraud. For nearly a year America could only fight one war, MacArthur's struggles in the Pacific, American Marines and sailors locked in a deadly game with the Japanese. No longer. Now the Germans will know what we can do, what kind of fight we can make. Now, it is not just a world war. It is America's world war.

PART TWO

We must remember that we are no longer alone. We are in the midst of a great company. Three-quarters of the human race are now moving with us. The whole future of mankind may depend upon our action and upon our conduct. So far we have not failed. We shall not fail now.

WINSTON CHURCHILL

You name them. I'll shoot them.

GEORGE PATTON (TO EISENHOWER)

PART TWO

10. LOGAN

He had fought seasickness all his life, fought it now, stared into misty darkness, tried to distract the turmoil in his stomach by searching for silhouettes of the other ships. The bow of the ship rose again, and he braced himself, the movement too familiar now, the soft wallowing as the transport rolled over the swell, his gut rolling with it. In the darkness, he saw a small shadow, a glimpse of a break in the horizon. Destroyer, maybe? No, too small. Another of the landing craft, same size as this one. Full of miserable tank crews. He gripped the rail, tried to invent a new prayer, one of dozens now, another distraction, said in a low whisper:

"Please, O Lord, giveth me calm insides, forever and I will always . . ."

Always what? The words drifted away. He tried to see the ship again, searched in the darkness. He had never been religious, thought, does God know that? Yeah, probably does. *Get to the end of the line, Logan. I'll get to you after the True Believers. If I have time.* You know, God, I wouldn't ask You if it didn't matter.

He realized the ship had slowed, unmistakable, the swells softer, less motion. There was activity behind him, and he turned, saw a brief glimpse of a flashlight, a hatch in the bulkhead opening, the light gone quickly. Voices began now, and he thought of Captain Gregg, and Hutchinson. Yeah, I know. You'll be looking for me. Hell, I'm not lost, I'm just up here on top, trying to get my guts to behave.

The others were mostly below, the tank crews bunking in

tight quarters that were no more than net hammocks slung from stout overhead plumbing. The smells had surprised him, oil and paint. There had been little sleep for those with tender stomachs, and so new smells came as well, sickness and cigarettes, the stale air of too many men huddled into too small a space. Logan had stayed mostly on deck, kept himself inconspicuous, out of the way of the officers and the British sailors, who seemed always in motion. He had grown used to the dampness, the hard, windy chill, went belowdecks only in the daytime, when the crews were assembled, lectured, schooled in what they might expect when they finally launched their tanks on the beach.

The ship was a Maracaibo class "landing ship, tank," *LST* for short, had been converted from a shallow-draft oil tanker, originally designed to float on the relatively shallow waters of Lake Maracaibo in Venezuela. The massive oil tanks had been replaced by a layer of decking, planks coated in asphalt, a floating parking lot that could fit eighteen tanks. She was nearly four hundred feet in length, even with her nose chopped off, the bow of the ship now a flat steel plate, an inch thick. It was the "door," the passageway that would lower like the tongue of a drawbridge. Attached to the steel panel was a hinged extension that would unfold, lengthening the platform, creating a driving surface nearly a hundred feet long, long enough, it was hoped, for tanks to move from the LST itself onto some dry surface. The ship's draft was shallow enough that in theory torpedoes would simply pass underneath, and once the ship had reached its landing zone, she could push close enough that the tanks, trucks, or jeeps could drive from ship to shore without drowning their crews. Logan learned quickly that shallow-draft ships had one distinct disadvantage, something the British sailors seemed delighted to bring to his attention. With so little of the hull below water, the ships were unstable in rough seas, tossing side to side in even the gentlest swells. It was an observation Logan had made his first hour at sea.

They had embarked from the Clyde, in Scotland, one part of the fleet that grew into a vast armada as they sailed beyond the coasts of England. Around Logan, the rumors had flowed far faster than the rolling sea, and he had tried to distract the torment in his gut by focusing on the astounding variety of claims as to where exactly they were going. Every rumor seemed to originate only from the most reliable source, every man claiming to pass along what had come from the mouth of only the most senior officer. Norway was a popular favorite, as well as France. Some were convinced with total certainty that they were in fact going back home. But Logan knew his stars, had spent too many hot nights on the perfect beaches near his home. The fleet was sailing south, and even the most stubborn had to admit that Norway might not be the destination after all. There was one unmistakable clue: none of them had been issued winter clothing. Those who clung to the idea of a landing on the French coast had to concede that such a journey would take hours, and not days. The talk turned to the Mediterranean, and again, the rumors flowed, word of landings at most points between Gibraltar and Palestine. Logan had kept his own thoughts quiet, silently agreed with those who believed they were heading straight for Rommel.

All along the trip southward, there had been briefings and drills, and Logan had no doubt that the exercises had been more about passing the time than honing their skills. Every crew knew their own tank, knew the sounds and smells, the feel of the steel tread on all types of terrain. But then, one briefing had changed the entire mood of the ship. It was the orders, specific assignments, maps, official and direct, passed through to the officers who would lead each tank squad. And there was news as well, reports from a place called El Alamein, a magnificent British victory, Rommel's army in shambles. The reports had raised new rumors of course, but one had been put to rest. Their target was not Rommel after all, at least not yet.

Logan had hung on the captain's every word, the others sitting in a small semicircle as the officer read them their orders. They were part of the Center Task Force, would land to the west of the Algerian city of Oran. The landing zone was designated as Beach X, a small bay, scooped out of the African coast alongside a point of land known as Cap Figalo. The landings at Oran would be a pincer, three prongs, combining infantry and armor. One attack would be aimed at the wharves of the city itself, a quick grab to prevent the French, or anyone else, from scuttling whatever ships were berthed there, possibly clogging the harbor with wreckage. The others would involve more infantry and armor, a rapid deployment across open beaches into short hills. The question in every man's mind was answered before any of them could voice it. The officers had no idea if anyone was going to be above or behind the beaches shooting at them.

As the ship drew closer to the landing zone, the chatter became intense, low voices, the men revealing fears, curiosity, some speaking too loudly, shows of bravado that masked little of what they fought against inside themselves. Still Logan was mostly quiet, fought the churning in his stomach, magnified now by the raw excitement—when this ship finally came to a halt, he would climb aboard the tank, plant himself in the gunner's seat, and begin the search for his first target.

Other men were moving toward the rail, and he could feel them, electric energy, men too nervous to sleep. Many were leaning out, trying to see toward the bow, some glimpse of the land that was surely close, brief comments from the ship's crew that the landing was virtually on schedule. Along the rail, no one spoke, each man deep in his own mind, memories, images private to each one, prayers certainly, letters already written, envelopes marked: *In the event I don't return* . . .

He heard a rumble, stared out toward a flash of light on the horizon. Men pointed, and more flashes came, the sounds reaching them, soft thumps. More men began to gather behind him, questions, and there was a voice, older, the deep, crusty growl of Captain Gregg.

"That's Oran. They've hit the port."

Logan stared in silence, felt the churn in his gut again, different now. Men were tight along the rail, alongside him, low voices.

"I thought they wasn't gonna fight back."

"Looks like a fight to me."

"Back up, boys." It was the captain again, Gregg, making his way to the rail. "Get below, prepare to disembark. You've got your instructions. You don't need to be sightseeing up here."

They began to move away, nervous chatter growing, men stumbling into each other in the dark. Logan waited, saw the short, thick shadow of the captain standing at the rail, staring

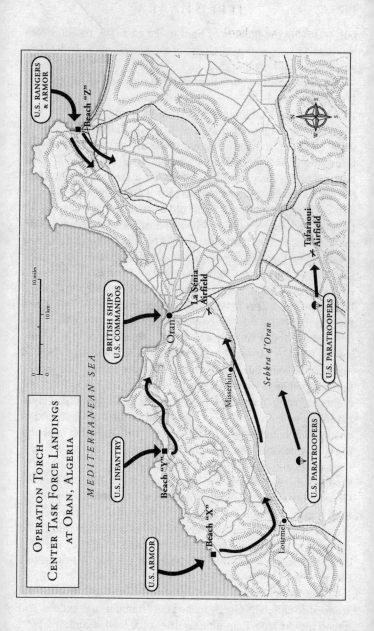

OPERATION TORCH—
CENTER TASK FORCE LANDINGS
AT ORAN, ALGERIA

U.S. RANGERS & ARMOR

Beach "Z"

MEDITERRANEAN SEA

BRITISH SHIPS
U.S. COMMANDOS

Oran

La Sénia Airfield

Tafaraoui Airfield

U.S. INFANTRY

Beach "Y"

U.S. PARATROOPERS

Misserhin

Sebkra d'Oran

U.S. ARMOR

Beach "X"

Lourmel

U.S. PARATROOPERS

out, watching the flickers of light to the east. The rumbles continued, and Logan moved closer to the stocky man, said, "How soon till we roll off this ship, sir?"

"Not long. You know where you're supposed to be, soldier? It's not up here, is it?"

"No, sir. I'm a tank gunner. Private Jack Logan."

The captain ignored him, and Logan suddenly felt like an idiot. Yeah, of course, he wants to be my pal. He had always liked Gregg, had noticed him immediately on the grounds of the tank school, a man who drew attention by the way he walked, the orders he gave. Logan had no idea if Gregg had ever been in combat, though he didn't seem old enough to have been in the Great War. The captain was just one of those men who commanded respect, a hard man who knew his job, none of the meaningless fury that some of the officers spewed out at their men. If you gave him no crap, he gave you none as well. Logan had wondered what the man would be like outside the army, if he was married, kids maybe, destined to follow their father into the service. When they'd first reached England, Logan had wondered if he would actually serve under the man, or if he would see no familiar officers at all, the tank crews scattered. He had heard the officers complaining, and so, more rumors had grown, that the battalion would be reorganized, units shifted from one command to another. But Gregg was still there, would still command the squadron of M-3 Lights, and no matter what kind of enemy they faced, no matter all the talk from the others, jabbering about combat, the unknown, the fear, the stupid bravado, Logan had convinced himself that if there was one man in the First Armored Division who simply had no fear, it was Captain Gregg. It was the one lesson he repeated to himself, that if the men simply did what the captain told them to do, there would be no screwups, no one would have to feel afraid of anything. The captain knows what the hell he's doing, and if we stick our M-3 close to his, we'll get the job done and get out of this in one piece.

Logan felt a jolt under his feet, a hard vibration, the ship now stopped completely. Gregg leaned out, stared into darkness, and a man moved past them quickly, his voice low, urgent.

"H hour minus two. Crew, man the plank!"

The voice was British, with the crisp efficiency of the sailors that had impressed Logan as well.

Gregg backed away from the rail, said, "Let's get moving, Private."

The captain led the way, and Logan followed, the two men moving toward the steps down to the main deck. Logan followed the stocky man down, reached the bottom, pitch-darkness, his eyes seeking shapes, the columns of tanks waiting for them. He hesitated, could tell that Gregg was still in front of him, and he waited for the man to move forward, to clear the way. The captain dropped to one knee, and Logan was surprised, thought, he's praying, I guess. Never thought he would have needed that. Move on, let him be. Then the captain bent over, face close to the deck, and threw up.

After Pearl Harbor, the lines had wound around the Federal Building in St. Petersburg for more than a block, young men tossing aside thoughts of school and girls and jobs, for a chance to join the army. The posters had been colorful and direct, designed to inspire patriotism, a call to the brave, but the brave didn't need posters to inspire them. There was glory in a soldier's life, or so Logan had been told, stories from the older men, his best friend's father, his own uncles. They spoke of heroes, Sergeant York, Eddie Rickenbacker, of whipping the Hun, marching into Germany to toss Kaiser Bill into a cesspool. But Logan had surprised his friends, had enlisted months before the Japanese attack, when so many still believed the country had no business joining anyone else's war.

The army was always in his future, the path opened for him before he was born. Those who had joined up before him had seemed inspired by a kind of patriotism Logan couldn't fathom, so much lust for glory, boys hoping to become men by mimicking Hollywood, Gary Cooper, Clark Gable. Logan had his own hero. His father had been a pilot in the Great War, had flown the absurdly fragile biplanes, had flown once too often, and so, he was still in France, buried in some piece of ground alongside a thousand comrades, some place Logan had never seen. His mother had told him as much as she could, but it was nothing a boy wanted to hear, a widow's loss, the pain and loneliness.

There were no artifacts, no uniforms, none of his father's legacy except a handful of unmarked photographs. His mother had kept them carefully matted into wooden frames, the usual poses: his father in a uniform; another; a group of men, his father's squad perhaps, boyish smiles. But Logan's favorite photo was the smallest, no more than three inches tall, his father standing beside a two-winged Nieuport, one hand up on the machine gun, the other a fist, raised like a fighter's, a playful frown. His mother didn't care for that one, and so, it became his.

The Great Depression had not hit them as hard as it had the cities up north, and even if a man couldn't find a job with a good wage, he could provide for his family, netting fish, trading for vegetables and fruit from farms that spread out east of Tampa Bay. Logan's uncle Henry had been the great teacher, had taken the boy out in a wide, flat-bottomed boat, fishing, while the boy stared down into crystal water, watching the trout and mackerel, or the heart-punching glimpse of the big sharks. When Logan was old enough to handle a fishing pole, his uncle revealed the closely guarded secrets, would carve a short stub of a stick to look like a minnow, wrap it in colored ribbon, one handmade hook dangling from the tail. The stick would float, Henry twitching it across the surface of the rippling water, irresistible to the predators below. The watery explosions were a pure delight to Logan, inspiring the boy to learn, and by the time he was ten, the bucket of fish they took home would just as likely have been his. There were other lessons as well, closer to shore, his uncle easing the boat silently past clusters of tangled mangroves, edging into shallow coves, looking for the vast, swirling schools of mullet. They were an easy target for a man like Henry, who had skills with a net that Logan could never match.

The family gatherings were mostly on Sundays, on the wide, breezy beach, the older men carting beer and smoked fish, the women carrying bowls of potato salad and cabbage slaw. Immediately, the small children would scamper away, mothers handling the inevitable crises as tender, bare feet collided with the occasional sandspur. With the beer flowing, the men would tell the stories, but to Logan, they seemed to be more like Hollywood than Hollywood itself. The men would lower their voices, drawing the younger boys in close, would roll out the bawdy stories, risqué jokes, tales of indiscreet French girls and too much wine. It was an annoying mystery to him that the veterans seemed so focused on stories about parties and drunken adventures, as though there had never been a war at all. But Logan had seen the photographs, the film clips, smoke and barbed wire and biplanes swooping out of the sky. In 1918 there had been *combat,* the dead and dying, outrageous weapons, a horror that swept away ten million men. He wanted a glimpse, some notion of what that was like, and so he pushed them, kept asking the hard questions, began to wonder if any of these men had been there at all, if their stories were more from stateside barrooms than any battlefield in France. He knew from his mother that Uncle Henry had been captured, had at least come face-to-face with Germans.

Even as a teen Logan had a deep curiosity about combat, not what Errol Flynn showed him, but the truth, what the sounds were, the smells, and the hardest question of all, what it was like to kill a man. Logan had rehearsed the questions, then waited for the right moment, a quiet time on the bay when the fishing was slow. His uncle Henry had made a point of avoiding Logan's specific questions about the war, the fighting, never revealed any more than the others, instead told the same tired tales about adventures in Paris. This time, Logan insisted, probed his uncle for answers, experiences. He pushed him hard, too hard, and his uncle had exploded at him, had seemed to come apart, shouting at him to mind his own affairs. Logan was shocked at his uncle's response, the man refusing to speak to him for many days. But soon, Henry had rejoined the others at the beach, had returned to entertain the high school boys, regaling them with more of the same harmless adventures. Logan tried to understand, wondered if Henry was embarrassed, ashamed that he had been captured, or perhaps there were memories that Henry had sealed away, secrets that were best left alone.

When Logan enlisted, he had tried to become a pilot, but his unwilling stomach betrayed him, and so, he had taken one piece of wisdom from all the tales he'd heard of the Great War. The veterans had spoken of the brutally absurd marches, comical tirades about endless roads, marches to nowhere that destroyed the feet. Logan absorbed that lesson with perfect clarity. If he was going to be a soldier, he would find some way to avoid the infantry. If he couldn't fly, he would ride.

The First Armored Division reached Northern Ireland in May of 1942, the tank crews training there for nearly five months, exercises that repeated many of the same drills and maneuvers Logan had endured at Fort Knox. Northern Ireland didn't seem that different from Kentucky, enormous fields of green, patches of forest, but the rains were worse, and so the men had to learn to deal with mud, a great deal of mud. He had learned about tanks by training in the M-2, a machine considered obsolete now. With the astounding success of Hitler's blitz across Europe, the American army had seemed to wake up to the brutal necessity of tanks, as though generals in Washington had completely forgotten their usefulness in the First World War. With the tank battles rolling across North Africa, the urgency for better armor had increased even more, and factories in the States began to churn out hundreds of machines that might at least compete on the battlefield with the exceptional German armor. Most of the heavier American tanks had been sent to the British, but once the American First Armored Division had been mobilized for England, their own tanks had gotten better as well. The M-2 was replaced by the M-3 Light tank, what the British called the Stuart. It was a strange salute from the British, that they would label the American machines with the names of famous American generals, particularly Civil War generals. "Jeb" Stuart had been the Confederacy's finest cavalry commander, and so Logan had accepted the logic that this new, fast tank was the closest thing the Allies had to a fast armored horse. Another enormous improvement in the M-3 Light had special appeal to a man trained in the handling of rolling artillery. The M-2 had been armed only with machine guns. The M-3 Light had machine guns as well, but now, a real piece of artillery was attached, the turret mounted with a 37 mm cannon.

The Americans had produced a larger weapon as well, the M-3 Medium tank, carrying a 75 mm cannon. Logan had heard enough talk from the tank commanders to know they were proud that the larger M-3s had been sent to the British, were in use now against Rommel, to respond to the power of the German armor. The British referred to the M-3 Mediums as Grants. Logan hadn't spent much time studying the Civil War, but it made sense to him. The tank with the bigger gun should be named after the man who'd won the war.

LANDING BEACH X, CAP FIGALO, ALGERIA—
NOVEMBER 8, 1942

The infantry had gone ashore first, squads of reconnaissance soldiers, fanning out through darkened houses that lay scattered along the beach. Behind them went more infantry, mortar carriers, and machine-gun crews. But for the tanks and heavy trucks, the gaping mouths of the LSTs had not provided easy passage to the beach. Hidden sandbars had nudged the ships to a halt more than three hundred yards from shore. The work had then fallen to the engineers, transport vessels hauling pontoons forward, the engineers working feverishly to hammer together a makeshift bridge. The bridge was only one delay. As the troops rolled ashore, one of the landing craft caught fire, nothing more sinister than mechanical failure. The men on board had safely escaped, but the flames from burning oil had provided an unmistakable beacon for miles in any direction. Any hope that the landings could remain a secret were erased.

By seven in the morning the last of the tank squadrons had rolled ashore, the machines pushing quickly across soft sands. Beyond the beach, the ground rose, a low, rocky escarpment that lined the coast far out in both directions. The reconnaissance battalions had already moved inland, had marked their way along several trails, cut into the crevasses of the escarpment. The trails were wide enough for the Stuarts to pass through, allowing them to climb the rise. The maps showed a single road, leading away from the beach, and the scouts had found that as well, a narrow strip of hard gravel. As the jeeps and light trucks came ashore, the infantry began to push off the beach, a tight column of anxious riflemen, engineers, and gunners, every man wondering when the shooting would start. Far out in the deeper water, British naval warships stood broadside to the shore, the big guns aimed toward the heights, nervous

gunners waiting for the orders to fire the first salvo. To all of
them the orders were specific and brief and had been passed
down from officer to crewman, the same order that the tank
commanders had been given, passed from General Oliver to
Colonel Todd to Captain Gregg, and finally, to the crews of
every tank, and every man with a rifle. The wording varied, but
the message was clear: *Do not fire upon any person unless that
person first fires upon you.* But out in front of the tank columns,
the infantry had advanced unopposed, had not found a confrontation, had found almost no one at all.

Logan sat in his perch, could see faint daylight through the
magnification of the gunsight. The hatch above him was open,
Hutchinson sitting up behind him, head and shoulders exposed.
With no enemy yet in front of them, it was the best position for
the tank commander to see the terrain, to spot whatever might
be waiting for them. Logan shivered, had not stopped shivering
since he had climbed down into the tank. Disembarking the
LST had seemed to take endless frustrating hours, but once the
tank was in motion, the impatience was gone, erased by the hard
roar of the engine, the M-3s moving quickly to reach the
heights, to find the road, to find out just what was *out there.*
Logan moved his foot lightly over the pedal that fired the cannon, stared out now through the rectangular glass lens of his
periscope. No one spoke, all eyes focused forward, watching for
any movement, some flash of light, a flare, the streak of artillery
fire, any sign the infantry had finally found a fight.

Nothing.

The intercom crackled now, startling him, the sound cutting
him through his earphones.

"Easy, screwballs. Eyes sharp."

It was Hutchinson, beside him, a needless order from a man
Logan knew was probably more nervous than the other three
men in his command. Brinkley Hutchinson was four years
younger than Logan, had earned sergeant's stripes as quickly as
any man in the tank school. He was a Kentuckian, had come to
the army from near Lexington, some of the loudmouths in the
company claiming that his rise in rank had come only because
he lived close to the base, indiscreetly joking that his mother

must be *friends* with the base commander. Logan had arrived there the same week as Hutchinson, heard it every day, a relentless drill sergeant singling the unfortunate man out for his strangely aristocratic name. If the sergeant saw Hutchinson as a target for his sadistic playfulness, the others soon learned that *Brinkley* hated his name even more than he hated the drill sergeant.

Early in their training, Logan had made friends with the young man, had learned immediately that Hutchinson preferred to keep his privileged upbringing a secret. Hutchinson had none of the aristocrat's snottiness, had not come into the army looking for a rich boy's advantages. Logan knew that Hutchinson had earned his sergeant's stripes only because he was one of the best tank commanders in the company. Logan was certain that in time the aristocratic young man would end up an officer on his own.

Hutchinson commanded Logan's tank now, fitting well with Captain Gregg's idea of how an armored squad should be run. To the left, in front of Logan, the driver, Skip Parnell, steered the tank along the narrow ribbon of road, and beside Parnell was the front machine-gunner and assistant driver, Pete Baxter. They were the lead tank in the column, a decision made by the captain. Behind them, nine more tanks spread out in a single, snaking line, half the tank force that had come ashore at Beach X. The rest of the battalion would hold back at the edge of the escarpment, allowing a gap to form in the advance, waiting for the order from the battalion commander, Lieutenant Colonel John Todd, to move out along the same route. It was a precaution against dive bombers; if enemy planes suddenly appeared overhead, the entire column wouldn't become one fat target. But so far, there had been no sign of planes at all, no telltale antiaircraft fire from the infantry ahead of them.

The infantry was to move quickly to their first objective, a village called Lourmel, a crossroads, where the primary rail line in this part of Algeria extended east and west, connecting Oran to the border crossings that led into Morocco. At Lourmel, the column would turn eastward, on what was supposed to be a primary highway. That route would lead them toward the crucial airfield at La Sénia, one of two major airfields where the French maintained fighter wings. Whether or not the French had any intention of making a fight, capturing and occupying the airfields was a priority. Both La Sénia and the second field at Tafaraoui could be used by incoming German fighters and bombers, should the French call for reinforcements in counterattacking the Allied invaders. If the French welcomed the Americans as friends, the airstrips would allow British and American transports to begin the enormous job of supplying the men in the field. Tafaraoui was the objective of the easternmost pincer, another heavy column of armor and infantry that was to have come ashore east of Oran, a place designated Beach Z. Only when the armor and infantry forces had established secure bases across Algeria could the next part of the operation begin: the rapid push toward Tunisia, to occupy the primary seaports that had served as the crucial back door to Rommel's army.

The M-3 had a top speed of just over thirty-five miles per hour, and Logan knew the rhythm of the engine, the familiar whine, the vibrations, knew through the rumble below him that Parnell was following orders, the tank moving only about twenty-five, a precaution to ensure that the column would stay close together. The gray sky above him had grown lighter still, the sun just breaking above the hills to the east, rising directly over the city of Oran, what the maps said was forty miles away. The tank crews knew nothing of the fighting there, no word of how or why there was a fight at all, no word either if the landings at Beach Z had been as uneventful as at Beach X, which, up until now, resembled a training exercise. But the action at the city itself had been serious, heavy artillery, either from British warships or French shore batteries, or both, and Logan had tried to hold on to the images, those curious thumps and flashes of light, the first sign of any real combat he had ever seen. But the dawn had swept it away, his attention focused only on the stretch of road that lay right in front of him, ribbons of tracks from the jeeps and small trucks of the infantry, still advancing far out in front of his gunsights.

They had driven along the smooth roadway for several minutes, Logan's nervousness fading, the tension in all of them giving way to curiosity. Away from the beach, the ground settled into low, rolling waves of rock and scrub brush. Logan's view was more limited than that of the other three, but even he could see across the vast stretches of open ground that spread out along both sides of the narrow road. It was no place to hide an army, no suitable spot for any kind of ambush. He heard a crackle in his earphones, the voice of Parnell.

"Hey, Hutch, this looks like home. You sure we're in Africa?"

"Pay attention, Skip. We're a long damned way from Texas."

Skip Parnell had grown up in the rugged scrub country west of San Antonio, was no older than Hutchinson. Logan could only see the young man's back, knew that Parnell was peering ahead through the driver's hatch, a flap of steel that opened forward, giving the driver a clear view in front of the tank. The rugged ground spread out in endless gray waves, the road still only a faint, pale ribbon, and Logan thought of their first objective, the details on the map he had been ordered to memorize, Lourmel. Who the hell would build a town out here? He glanced at Parnell's back again, could hear the man's drawl in his head, stories of deer hunting and rattlesnakes. Well, somebody had a reason to build Uvalde, Texas, so I guess the damned Arabs can build a place out here. I'm guessing we'll know it when we see it. This road's gotta end somewhere.

The earphone spoke, Parnell again.

"Hey, Hutch, I thought there were Frenchies out here. How we supposed to know if they're friendly if there ain't nobody home? You absolutely sure we're in Africa? Leave it to the damned limeys to send us ashore in godforsaken anywhere, and Colonel Todd not to admit that we're just plain lost."

The sprawl of words was familiar, the Texan never allowing silence to pass for long. Even through the hard roar of the tank engine, Parnell seemed uncomfortable if no one was talking. Hutchinson responded with his usual reaction to Parnell's gripes.

"Shut up, Skip. Drive the damned tank."

They had come more than five miles, no sign of an enemy, no sign of anything but scrub and rock. Logan hadn't expected this, not after so many days of gut-twisting tension. Every tank crew had been lectured on what kind of fight might be in front of them. They were certainly prepared, loud boasts of confidence, the officers and instructors believing they had the right training and the right equipment. But Logan knew from the low talk, all those prayers and letters home. Every man had wondered if the officers or anyone else could really know what was going to happen, if they would advance their tank straight into some kind of hell. But now, moving deeper into what was supposed to be hostile ground, there was still no enemy, no artillery fire, no greeting at all. And so, the tension had begun to give way to the usual comical bellyaching between Parnell and Hutchinson, exactly as it had been for so many months of training. Logan leaned down slightly, glanced at the back of the man sitting close in front of him. Through it all, Baxter had stayed silent, the fourth man in the crew so quiet he might not have been there at all. He was another man barely twenty, the first soldier to emerge from a family of Indiana farmers. Baxter was small, barely tall enough to qualify for the army, but had made it through training as well as any of the others. His size was an obvious advantage to a man whose seat was forward in the compact hull of the M3.

"You keep your mouth shut about Colonel Todd."

"Well, hell, Hutch, he's an officer. Ain't seen an officer yet who wouldn't rather be sitting back in some liquor hole, stroking some sweetie. Even Captain Gregg . . ."

Logan smiled, had heard it before, knew that Parnell was pumping Hutchinson for a reaction, would push far enough to get the usual explosion. He waited for it, but the earphones were silent, and suddenly Hutch's hand was on his shoulder, a hard grip. Parnell spoke, a single word.

"Hello."

They had crested a low hill, and Logan saw it now, a dark shape, rolling into the road in front of them. The wireless spoke, orders from behind them, from Gregg, and Hutchinson responded into his microphone. Then the earphones crackled again.

"Driver, halt! Captain says let's give him a chance to withdraw."

The tank slowed, then jerked to a stop, and Logan felt the hand on his shoulder again, said, "I got him in the sights, Hutch."

"He's not one of us. French uniforms. Where the hell did he

come from? The infantry must have run right past him, probably hidden in some hole."

They were less than two hundred yards from the truck, and Logan watched through his gunsight, the truck moving slowly, turning toward them, halting as well, in the middle of the road. Hutchinson's voice came again.

"Looks like a fifty caliber. No other vehicles."

No one spoke, the training in each of them. The intercom belonged to the commander now, and there would be no chatter. Logan put his right hand on the turret wheel, turned it slightly, the hydraulics centering the gunsight just above the hood of the truck. He could see heads, three men, frantic movement, rifles propped up on the windshield, aiming toward . . . him. Hutchinson's voice again:

"Easy. Let's see what they're gonna do. We can't fire—"

There were flashes from the truck, the tank suddenly rattled with hard pings, small punches, Hutchinson shouting, "Ahh, damn! Hatches closed! Bastards!"

Hutchinson dropped down close behind Logan now, the hatch above him still gaped open. Hutchinson said, "Son of a bitch! Is he crazy?"

There was a pause, the heavy machine gun on the truck silent, the only sound the low idle of the tank engine. Logan heard the wireless, Hutchinson adjusting his own headset, talking into the microphone, more orders from behind them. Logan felt the hand again, another grip on his shoulder, the voice in his earphones.

"Orders. Gunner . . . *fire.*"

Logan leaned forward, his shoulders settling against the curved rests, his heel pressed hard on the trigger pedal. He stared at the truck, could see the men, rifles still pointing at him, a wisp of smoke trailing from the big machine gun. He felt a chill, his heart racing, one word ripping through his brain: *stupid . . . stupid . . .*

He pressed his toe forward and the gun erupted, the recoil of the gun jolting him back. The truck erupted in a flash of fire, black smoke, seemed to come apart, the doors falling away, metal in the air . . . men. Logan stared into the sight, frozen, felt quick motion below him, Baxter feeding another shell into the gun. Baxter spoke now, the earphones bursting into Logan's head:

"Loaded. Ready!"

"Hold your fire!"

Logan responded to Hutchinson's order, raised his foot away from the pedal, realized he was shaking, the cold all through him. Hutchinson stood up behind him, peered above the hatch, and the wireless spoke again, Hutchinson relaying the order.

"Driver, advance. Let's take a look, Skip."

The tank rolled forward, the smell of exhaust rolling around them. Logan kept his eye at the sight, a voice in his head, the lessons, watch for movement, watch the fifty cal, someone could still be at the gun. But there was no gun at all now. The truck was on fire, the smoke spilling out to one side, caught by the low breeze.

"Driver, halt." The tank stopped again, Hutchinson's voice. "Man those thirties. Could be more around here. Keep an eye out."

Logan put a hand on the trigger of the machine gun, mounted alongside the cannon, felt for another gun on his right side. The M-3 had five thirty-caliber machine guns, guns that were cursed all through training, the guns that took up precious space inside the hull of the tank. There was silence now, no one cursing anything. He heard Hutchinson speak, outside the tank, realized another tank had moved up alongside. The talk continued, voices, his earphones blocking the words. He shifted to the periscope, saw men in front of him now, walking out past the tank, Gregg, two others. They moved around the truck, away from the flow of smoke, Gregg holding a pistol, the others carrying small carbines, stared at the remains of the truck for a long moment. Gregg moved back toward the tanks again, out of Logan's sight, more voices, Hutchinson talking, and the earphones coming alive.

"The captain says, good shooting, Jack. He's cursing the infantry a blue streak. They should have rooted out these guys. They were Frenchies. Hey, Jack, you got our first kill."

More orders came through the wireless, the command to advance, to continue along the road, seeking targets, seeking the enemy or the town or the airfield. Logan closed his eyes, sat back in his seat, felt the sway of the tank, the rumble beneath his feet, the power. He could still smell the smoke from the cannon fire, the remnants of gunpowder, blending with the exhaust and the dust, coating the insides of the tank, coating his skin, filling his lungs. He had wondered about this moment, what it would feel like, all those questions that his uncle would not answer. At Fort Knox, there had been so much talk about killing the enemy, so much of the training focused on taking the *thought* out of it, seeing the enemy as the *enemy* and not as a man. Or a truck full of men. He had wanted to climb out of the tank, to see for himself, to see what Gregg saw, what the thirty-seven had done to those men. It was my responsibility, dammit. He scolded himself, no, it's not your responsibility, not for this, not for any of it. What if those bastards had had a seventy-five, or a German eighty-eight. I wouldn't be sitting here having this little chat with myself. We'd be blown to hell, more pieces than that damned truck. *That damned truck.* The image wouldn't leave, and he felt angry, thought of the three men, the one in command, the one who'd ordered a fifty-caliber machine gun to fire at this great steel machine. A stupid, moronic mistake. My first kill, and I killed a truck full of idiots.

He opened his eyes now, felt the cool, dusty air swirling through the tank, focused on the periscope. There was silence in the earphones, no more of the chatter, no more playful insults from Parnell, no more Fort Knox and no more Ireland, no more drills and lessons. The training was over.

11. LOGAN

The infantry had found a fight, but the enemy was scattered, the confrontations mostly brief, one-sided affairs, no sign of any organized resistance by the French. Lourmel was already in American hands, and those few snipers daring to make a stand had been killed, captured, or had simply disappeared. Like the landing zones behind them, the village and the roads out in both directions were quickly secured, guarded by heavily armed checkpoints, protected by mortar crews and infantry manning antiaircraft guns.

The tanks had pushed on, moving east along a snaking ribbon of asphalt that paralleled a vast open sea of dried mud. The maps called it Sebkra D'Oran, Logan assuming the translation to be something about a lake, that perhaps once each year, or once in several years, the place actually held water. Now, it was a flat, smooth plain of gray-white sand. The armor had tested the surface, the tanks faring well enough, but the infantry had learned that what seemed to be dry, hard ground would give way, swallowing a man's boots above his ankles, a well-disguised layer of gluelike clay below the dry crust. It was yet one more oddity in this very odd place.

As the tanks, jeeps, and foot soldiers passed through the villages and small settlements, they had an audience, Arabs who stood aside as they passed, dark, weathered men in filthy robes, often perched on the backs of scrawny burros or foul-smelling camels. Behind them walked their women, faces hidden, black eyes darting toward the huge machines. The Arabs seemed completely uninterested in the war, no flag-waving, no sign at all that they considered the Americans to be liberators. During their training, the tank crews had been lectured that the "natives" disliked the French, hated the Italians, and presumably had little use for the Germans. All of this was thought to be of benefit to the Americans, that the Arabs would gratefully open their doors. What Logan had seen convinced him that the Arabs were simply bystanders, would probably remain that way. This war was no different from other wars fought all across North Africa for centuries, fights between tribes or kings or armies far removed from the lives of the people over whose land they fought. The Arabs seemed to know that no matter the size of the tanks that rolled past them, no victor, no king, no army, ever held on to this land long enough to affect anything the Arabs had to do to survive. The Americans discovered quickly that in the twentieth century, survival seemed to mean commerce, and if the Arabs acknowledged the Americans at all, it was by offering to conduct business, trade. The soldiers found that here even paper money would buy eggs and chickens and goats, and a variety of goods, from carpets to jewelry. But the officers realized that the most valuable asset the Arabs might have was information, troop positions of the enemy. Never mind that the loyalty the Allies purchased was only good until someone else, perhaps in another uniform, made a better offer.

With the Americans pushing inland, radio dispatches, updated reports, had come from the HMS *Largs,* General Fredendall's command ship, sent through the outposts at the beach, driven forward or transmitted to the senior officers who led their troops and armor closer to Oran. The landings on Beach Z, to the east of Oran, had been successful as well, U.S. army rangers there subduing a coastal battery, other small fights breaking out with French troops. The tank and troop columns were in motion there as well, pushing south and west, sweeping aside most of the French resistance, as they pressed to their own objective of the Tafaraoui Airfield. Closer to Oran, French defenses were more organized, and if hope remained that the French would lay down their arms and recognize the Americans as friends, that optimism was crushed in the harbor at Oran itself. As the armored and infantry troops approached the beaches beyond the city, two small British ships, the *Walney* and the *Hartland,* entered the harbor itself. They carried a force of some five hundred men, whose mission was to capture and secure the wharves, preventing the French from scuttling their own vessels, thus keeping the entrance to the harbor unobstructed. Before the two ships could put their troops ashore, French searchlights illuminated the vessels, and in the tight confines of the harbor, shell fire from the French shore batteries rained havoc on both ships. With no room to maneuver, and no escape route, the confrontation became an Allied disaster. Nearly 90 percent of the British crews and their American cargo were either killed, wounded, or captured. While both wings of the pincer movement pressed forward their envelopment of the city, the French made it clear that in the city itself, there would be a fight.

With Lourmel secured, the column had been reorganized, eighteen tanks now accompanied by infantry, engineers, and tank-destroying artillery. Most of the column made good use of the paved road, the tanks fanning out into patches of flatland, seeking out any resistance, any place where French troops might attempt an ambush.

Hutchinson's crew still led the way, Captain Gregg bringing up the rear of the squad, three Stuarts sent to probe a smaller road that dipped close to the great, dry lakebed. The trail wound through desolate scrub, the tanks rumbling up and over short, choppy hills, past narrow cuts and ravines. Hutchinson was above the turret again, his head and shoulders exposed, better to search the small nooks as they passed. Behind him, the other M-3s kept their distance, a gap of fifty to a hundred yards, more precaution. The other commanders stood tall as well, suffering through the dust from Hutchinson's steel treads.

Logan peered through the gunsight, then scanned with his periscope, anything to gain a wider field of vision. He rotated the turret slightly, the barrel of the thirty-seven sweeping past nothing, just empty land, bare hills. Closer to the main road, they had seen signs of scattered fighting, pillars of smoke, streaks of fire from artillery batteries miles away, no idea if the guns were friendly, or if somewhere in this desolate place a garrison of Frenchmen had decided to make a stand.

"Planes!"

The word punched him, and Logan looked up, peered into the only sky he could see, through the open hatch above his head.

Hutchinson said, "Driver, halt! Let's see what they're going to do. If they come this way, try to use the thirties. Gunner, check your elevation. They come in low, you might have a shot."

The intercom came alive again, Parnell. "I see 'em, Hutch. Three of 'em, looks like fighters. Doing some dipsy-doodle moves. Jesus, they're shooting at something!"

Logan felt blind, wanted to stand, see something more interesting than dry hills through a dusty periscope.

Hutchinson scanned through binoculars, said, "They're French. Going after something out there. Along the edge of this lake."

Logan was frustrated, said nothing, knew it wasn't the gunner's place to become a sightseer.

Parnell said, "They're going in low. Jesus, shooting like hell at something. Damn! Hope it ain't our boys."

Logan felt helpless, said, "Who the hell else would it be? We're the only ones out here. They're either shooting at us, or their own people."

Hutchinson said, "They're leaving. Finished what they came to do, I guess. Maybe we ought to see if somebody needs help." He spoke now into the wireless, passing the word to the other tanks, then once more into the intercom. "Let's move, driver."

The tank lurched forward, and Logan whipped the turret to one side.

Hutchinson's voice: "Easy, gunner. You trying to throw me out of this thing?"

Logan didn't answer, stared through the periscope, could see an open sea in front of him, the dry lakebed spread out to the horizon.

Hutchinson said, "Holy Jesus! There they are. C-47s. What the hell?"

Logan could see them as well. A quarter mile out from the rocky hills, a cluster of aircraft seemed tossed about, no order.

At least one of them was wrecked, smoking. Around them, men scrambled like so many ants.

Parnell said, "There's people hurt out there, Hutch. We gotta give 'em a hand."

Hutchinson said nothing, and Logan glanced up, saw Hutchinson staring to one side, then heard in the intercom, "Target! Driver, halt!"

Logan turned the periscope as far as he could twist his body, could see a single man, standing in the scrub, another rising up beside him. More appeared now, men easing slowly up a sharp rise, coming toward them from nearly every direction. Logan's hand went to the machine gun, and he eased the turret to one side, found the men in his gunsight, counted a dozen. But the helmets were unmistakable, and he pulled his hand from the machine gun, focused on one, a dirty face, toothy smile, the man holding a Thompson submachine gun, raising it over his head.

Logan said, "Hey Hutch. They're ours."

"Yep. Driver, shut 'er down. But these guys aren't infantry. Let me check with Captain Gregg, see what we should do. I could use a whiz break."

The tank was suddenly silent, and Hutchinson spoke into the wireless, the two tanks behind them moving up close, their engines shutting down as well. Hutchinson climbed out through the hatch, stood on the hull of the tank, and Logan eased up out of his seat, stood, stretched his stiff legs, his head above the hatch for the first time in hours. He watched the soldiers climb up the rise, most of them carrying submachine guns, not the standard-issue rifle for American foot soldiers. Their uniforms weren't standard-issue either: baggy pants legs stuffed into tall boots, pockets sagging with bulky gear, each man seeming to carry a backpack on each thigh. Logan understood now, had heard talk of these men in England, *Airborne,* some kind of mystique around them, rumors that they were simply lunatics, their unit a haven for the army's misfits and psychopaths. One of the men stepped closer, limping, helped by a medic. Logan saw blood on his face, his shirt open over a mass of white bandages.

Hutchinson said, "You're in pretty bad shape, soldier. Can we help?"

Captain Gregg had climbed down from his own tank, stood beside Hutchinson. The wounded man seemed to gather himself, pushed the medic away, fought to stand on his own, said, "Lieutenant Colonel Edson Raff, 509th Parachute Infantry regiment. I guess it's a damned good idea to put white stars on American tanks. If we hadn't seen that, we would have dropped a bag of grenades down your hatch."

The 509th had been designated to be the first American airborne unit to deploy into combat by parachute. The paratroopers had come directly from England, a massive squadron of C-47 transport planes. But like so many plans drawn out so carefully on paper, plans that called for the 509th to make their drops close to the key airfields at La Sénia and Tafaraoui, strong winds and poor visibility had scattered their planes all along the North African coast. Instead of reaching their drop zones, most of the inexperienced pilots became lost in the darkness, landmarks obscured by a thick layer of cloud cover. Worse, a signal was supposed to be sent from a carefully positioned British ship, a radio beacon to guide the planes toward their drop zones. For reasons no one understood, the radios on the C-47s had remained silent. The beacon had never been received.

When the drops were actually made, the paratroopers had no way of knowing if they were anywhere near their targets, and in fact the C-47s had scattered the battalion from points near Tafaraoui to as far away as Spanish Morocco. As had happened at Oran harbor, the French welcomed the paratroopers and their aircraft with artillery and rifle fire. Several of the C-47s had taken advantage of the slick flatness of the dry lakebed of the Sebkra d'Oran by landing there, in an effort to reload their human cargo, to transport them closer to their intended drop zones. But once the sun came up, French fighter planes swarmed above the unarmed and ponderous C-47s and either shot them out of the sky or followed them down to another landing, where the French gunners took no mercy. Colonel Raff and those who could find some means of reaching their targets overland had no choice but to follow their compasses. Though some of the scattered paratroopers found motorized transport, many were still on the march, slogging their way through the clay of the lakebed, grimly intent on reaching their target at Tafaraoui.

"Gotta be a tough son of a bitch, that colonel . . . what? Raff?"

Logan ignored Parnell, focused on the desolation along the lakebed, knew Hutchinson would respond.

"He was torn up pretty bad. The medic said he was hurt when he landed in the rocks, said they had a jeep for him. I wouldn't want to be the one to try to stop him from going anyplace. Looked like a tough guy. All of them."

Parnell said, "Nuts. That's what they are. Nuts. Jump out of airplanes, hope like hell some oversized bloomer keeps you alive. Give me a damned tank. You still awake back there, Logan? We might need that gun of yours. Just 'cause you got our first kill don't mean you can take a holiday."

Logan didn't smile, said, "Shut up and drive."

They moved back toward the main road, the three tanks rolling off a rocky mound, crushing a trail through more of the thorny brush. The road was crowded with men and jeeps, and Hutchinson stayed up, outside the hatch, was talking to someone, the wireless squawking, Hutchinson ducking back inside, speaking into the microphone.

"Driver, move past these men. Captain says we're to join up with the other tanks farther ahead. They're holding up for some reason. Might be the enemy."

They moved past shouting men, rifles in the air, men who knew the value of armor. They pushed along the roadbed for more than a mile, and Logan could see dust clouds in front of them, more tanks, the machines spread out in a wide fan, sweeping eastward.

The intercom crackled, Hutchinson's voice: "There's smoke. Stay awake. Something's happening up front of us."

Logan shifted the turret, scanned the horizon, the road splitting two low hills, tanks and heavy trucks out on both sides. He saw the smoke as well, closer now, a black column rising from a truck. He sat upright, grabbed the sight, realized . . . Hutchinson's words:

"That's one of ours. They hit a gun carrier."

Logan could see that the truck was split open, the frame visible under thick, billowing smoke. The doors had blown free, one tossed aside, wedged into the dirt, standing upright. Logan saw it now: the white star.

Men had gathered near the truck, one body lying close, too close to the heat, the medics helpless. Logan thought, nobody's gonna live through that. Parnell drove the tank past the burning wreck, but there was no way to avoid the smoke. He kept to the road, pushed the tank through the black cloud, and Logan braced himself for the smell, held his breath, but the smoke drove into him, the hard stench of burning oil, and worse, a stink he didn't want to identify. The tank rolled forward, and he emptied his lungs, the stench still trapped inside him.

Logan blinked hard, focused toward the periscope, the intercom quiet. He eased the turret to one side, scanned the low hills, and suddenly the tank jumped, a hard, thunderous lurch, smoke, dirt clouding the periscope, the tank leaning to one side, then settling back with a hard, crunching drop. His helmet had been jolted to one side, the intercom crackling, Hutchinson shouting above him:

"Ahh, damn! Button up! Hatches closed!"

Logan grabbed at the crooked helmet, pulled it hard onto his head. The tank was still moving, Parnell holding it steady, still on the road.

Hutchinson said, "Incoming fire! Turn left, thirty degrees! Some of our boys are behind those hills. They're taking fire! Gunner, ready!"

There was smoke in every direction, thick clouds of dirt, and Logan spun the turret to the left, saw the tanks, more smoke, shells bursting in the hills just above the armor. Hutchinson was down beside him now, the intercom alive with Parnell's cursing.

Hutchinson said, "Shut up! Anybody hurt?"

"No."

"No."

"Okay here."

Hutchinson was leaning against Logan's shoulder, peering forward through the observation port, said, "That was close, boys. I guess the French can't shoot that good."

Parnell said, "It was good enough for me. Damned thing hit

ten feet from the left tread, right in front of me. Mighta knocked out a tooth or two."

Logan watched Hutchinson, thought, easy Hutch, we're alive.

Hutchinson said, "Driver, left, move in behind that cluster of rocks. There's one M-3 thirty yards on our left flank. Another farther out. Infantry coming up behind us. The enemy . . . not sure yet."

Hutchinson spoke into the wireless microphone, words Logan couldn't hear.

"The damned radio's not working! Coulda knocked the antenna off."

Logan was surprised to see Hutchinson rise up, the hatch opening, dust and daylight pouring into the tank. No, not a good idea, Hutch.

Hutchinson shouted, talking to someone Logan couldn't see, more shouts, Hutchinson dropping back down. The intercom spoke again, Hutchinson's voice.

"There's French artillery out in front of us. A thousand yards, behind the next row of rocky hills. Might be a whole battery, or just a couple guns. The seventy-fives are coming up behind us. Colonel Todd is here somewhere, says nobody can talk to command. It's not just us. Bad radio contact."

No one responded, and Logan moved the turret again, thought, *a thousand yards*. He put his hand on the breech of the thirty-seven. I could hit a target . . . maybe. It would have to be dead-on, kill the gun crew. But then what? This isn't enough gun to take out anything really heavy. And we can't just charge out into the open. We'd be roasted.

There was a hard thump to one side, one of the tanks firing. The response came quickly, shells whistling over them, sharp thunder beneath them, the tank rocking, smoke, a shower of dirt and rocks raining on the tank. Hutchinson again:

"Dammit! We're not in good cover here! We need those seventy-fives!"

Logan swung the turret to the right, searching for any sign of a target, caught a glimpse of movement, moved to the periscope, saw a truck moving past, stopping a few yards away.

Parnell shouted, "Yee hah! The cavalry's here!"

Logan stared, knew the seventy-fives, the largest mobile guns the unit had, mounted in heavy armored trucks. He watched the barrel of the heavier gun, adjusting, elevating, thought of the gunner. Who? That crackpot Jenkins? Maybe Sweeney, the guy who can't hit a garbage can at ten yards. Let it be Fowler, somebody who shoots straight.

All eyes were on the seventy-five beside them, and now the eruption came, the hard punch of the gun, a stream of smoke.

Hutchinson stared forward with the binoculars, a long few seconds, then said, "He got something. Again, hit 'em again, keep firing!"

Logan glanced into the gunsight, saw a small gray cloud, heard the seventy-five fire again, waited for the impact, another long second, another burst in the hills. More of the armored trucks were pulling up, a chorus of thunder, the seventy-fives raining their shells into whatever enemy stood in their way. The wireless spoke to Hutchinson again, and the order came into the intercom.

"Driver, advance! Get past these rocks, make hard for that smoke. Full out, Skip!"

The tank kicked into motion, and Logan braced himself, the tank rocking with the uneven ground.

"Gunner, make ready. Targets ahead!"

Logan glanced at Baxter, the man holding a shell in his hands, another already in the thirty-seven, a sharp nod from the quiet young man. The tank rolled forward, more tanks on either side. The seventy-fives continued their fire on the enemy positions, French crews and their guns obliterated by the accuracy of the artillery. Logan stared out through the periscope, felt the cool wind swirling down through the open hatch, the tank running at top speed, the hills in front of them close. He could see men in the rocks, some scrambling up the hill, some firing rifles, a toothless enemy, and he felt the rage, the cold steel in his chest, put his hand on the machine gun, and pulled the trigger.

Though the French continued to put obstacles in their paths, the French defenses were not coordinated, no large-scale deployment of troops, artillery, or air support. As the first day of Operation Torch concluded, the pincer movement around Oran drew tighter. By midday, the airfield at Tafaraoui had been captured and secured, and though the French still struck at the invaders, the American noose continued to tighten. From General Fredendall's command ship, word had been sent back to Gibraltar, the anxiously awaited "okay" for British cargo and fighter planes there to begin their own missions, bringing in the supplies and reinforcements that would turn Tafaraoui into an Allied base.

La Sénia was now more of a priority than ever, since the French could still launch air strikes that could reach American troop and armor positions in mere minutes. With darkness finally closing in on the first day of the operation, the First Armored Division's tank crews still followed their maps, gathering strength, the officers pulling the squads together, fueling and resupplying the tanks for the next day's fight.

12. CLARK

GIBRALTAR—
NOVEMBER 8, 1942

"Giraud has changed his mind."

Clark stood, blinked, tried to focus on Eisenhower's face, the commander leaning against the open doorway. It was good news, but Eisenhower was not smiling.

Clark said, "When?"

"Right after we concluded the meeting. I saw you slip out. Don't worry about it. We need every break from this mess we can get. The last report from Oran did it. Just as I thought, we give him just enough details to convince him we haven't fabricated this whole operation. He didn't believe Algiers had fallen so quickly, that we had the airfield there, until he heard French radio bellyaching about it."

Clark was still annoyed at the obnoxious Frenchman. "So, he

was surprised that we took Algiers so quickly? *Surprised?* That means he anticipated resistance there. That's why—"

"It was all a game, Wayne. He wouldn't play ball because he thought we'd get our asses kicked." Eisenhower seemed to collapse into his chair. "Now, he's on our team. Fully committed to our cause. As though we should never have doubted him. Jackass."

Clark knew what was coming, what his own role in the operation would be now. "When do you want me to leave?"

"Tomorrow. Giraud is going to Algiers first thing in the morning. Insists on a French plane, French pilot, wants to make his grand entrance into Algiers so he can write in his memoirs what it was like the day he won the war. Surprised he hasn't asked for a planeload of brass bands. You'll be right behind him. General Ryder will be expecting you. I'm preparing an order that you will present to Giraud on Algerian soil. He's in command of the French military and is now governor of the place. But he answers to me, and until I establish my own headquarters there, he answers to you. Once you arrive, you bring our headquarters with you. Make damned sure he understands that. No grand pronouncements, no parades, no orders to anyone without your approval. You're in charge, Wayne. Don't take any crap from Giraud or anybody else."

Clark tried to feel the energy behind Eisenhower's orders, the authority he would carry to Africa, some enthusiasm that the annoying Frenchman might finally contribute something useful to the operation. But there had been almost no sleep for nearly two days, and the only news that could inspire him at all was word that Oran had been captured, or that Patton's Western Task Force had secured Casablanca.

Eisenhower leaned back in his chair, said nothing, his mind focused on some other business at hand. Clark knew that he was anxious about Patton. The only word from Casablanca had come by circuitous routes, Allied intelligence picking up sketchy broadcasts from French military outposts, reports of losses of artillery batteries along the coast, confrontations with American tanks and infantry at several outlying villages. The news was encouraging, broad hints of panic among the French, calls for retreat and regrouping. But no one at Gibraltar could feel comfortable while their only news came from a disorganized enemy. Patton's landing had been scheduled to begin at four thirty that morning, and the navy had reported that, surprisingly, the typically rough seas along the West African coast had calmed. But then, there had been only silence. As the hours passed, Eisenhower had grown increasingly anxious, the entire staff aware that if anyone would crow about the results of a good fight, it would be George Patton. By late afternoon, reports had begun to filter in, passed along by wireless from British naval ships. The fights were difficult, stiff French resistance from naval and land forces, but the landings had successfully been made, the noose closing in on Casablanca as it had around Oran. Patton's silence had been caused by a bad radio on board his command ship, nothing more. Clark had smiled at that, knew that once Patton realized his broadcasts had dissolved only into static, the faulty radio and its operator would likely be tossed into the sea.

With the various Algerian airfields secured, the Spitfires waiting at the compact airfield at Gibraltar could finally offer support, squadrons of fighters swarming toward various trouble spots. By vacating the tarmacs, the fighters had made room for bombers, for a limited number of B-17s waiting in London, which could only make the trip southward if they had some place to park.

Clark had stayed closely in touch with Admiral Cunningham, the British naval commander keeping tight rein on unpredictable confrontations with French warships that had emerged from various harbors along the African coast. The British were also keeping a vigilant eye on any naval force that might suddenly appear from Italy. While Clark focused more on what was actually happening on the ground, Eisenhower himself had continued to deal with the potential danger from political fronts, particularly Spain, for any word that the dictator Franco was reacting to news of the invasion of North Africa with some kind of blusterous outrage, political noise that could justify bringing Hitler's troops into his country, troops whose first goal might be Gibraltar.

And now, there was Giraud.

Clark looked at his watch, thought, it's dark outside. You'd never know it in here. There was commotion in the corridor, Butcher's jovial face at the door.

"Skipper, we got a cable from London. General Brooke has sent confirmation that the Chiefs of Staff believe it is now an appropriate time to give news of the operation to Monsieur de Gaulle. I'd love to be there for that one. Sir."

Eisenhower nodded, said to Clark, "Giraud hates de Gaulle. Says he had too much of an ego. Pot calling the kettle black, I'd say."

Butcher said, "There's more, sir. Reports picked up from Vichy say that Admiral Darlan is in Algiers, directing the defense."

Eisenhower sat up straight, seemed to come awake. "Darlan's in Algiers?"

Clark was surprised by Eisenhower's reaction. "It's all bull, Ike. There's no defense to direct. What else did they say, Harry? They throwing us back into the sea? It's just propaganda, Ike."

Eisenhower stood, seemed energized now. "It's more than that, Wayne. Harry, get a cable out to General Ryder, and to Murphy. Find Darlan. Vichy's number two man could be a hell of a plum, if we can grab him. Wayne, get down there first thing in the morning. Find Major Tibbets, use the *Red Gremlin*. First things first. We'll give Giraud time to strut around, have his show. The first priority is to get the shooting stopped. Like it or not, we could use the French beside us, and not in our gunsights. As soon as we can get command and communication posts established, once the bases are secure, and the supplies are flowing, the Brits can start moving toward Tunis." Eisenhower stopped, smiled. "Darlan's just the icing on the cake."

ALGIERS, ALGERIA—NOVEMBER 9, 1942

The weather had closed in on Gibraltar, and though Giraud's flight had managed to slip out under the dense cloud cover, Clark's flight had delayed. Finally, after hours of boiling impatience, Clark had boarded the plane, the B-17 skimming across the Mediterranean surrounded by a flock of Spitfires, a protective escort against an enemy who did not appear. By the time the *Red Gremlin* touched down at Maison Blanche airfield, Clark's curiosity had grown as fierce as his lack of patience. If Giraud had accomplished his mission, the fighting might already be over.

Major General Charles "Doc" Ryder was in command of the Eastern Task Force, the man responsible for leading the assault that had produced the quickest success thus far, the capture of Algiers. Ryder had graduated West Point the same year as Eisenhower, had earned his second general's star only that June, after taking command of the Thirty-fourth Infantry Division. Ryder understood that once Algiers was secure, his command would be handed over to British general Kenneth Anderson, who would then lead the push toward Tunisia. It was one of those necessary cosmetic touches, American generals leading the assaults, convincing the French that Torch was an American operation. Ryder not only accepted his temporary command, he had been one of Eisenhower's most valued aides, helping to plan this part of the overall assault. Until Anderson assumed command, Ryder was the most senior Allied soldier in Algiers, the man to whom any French officials would have to report. Clark knew that Ryder was an excellent soldier and, like most fighting generals, had little patience for politicians.

Clark slapped him on the arm, and Ryder said, "Damned glad you're here, Wayne. No time for this bull. I got French politicians crawling on me like ants."

"Ike says it's in my hands until he gets down here." Clark put a hand down to his side, tapped at an imaginary holster. "I'm guessing they'll fall into line. Giraud thinks I'm a lunatic anyway. We're all a bunch of cowboys to these people. Shoot first, diplomacy later."

"Giraud? So, you haven't heard?"

Clark saw the annoyance on Ryder's face. "Heard what?"

"Well, as soon as he stepped off his plane here, he started telling me how he was the commander in chief of the French army and had control over all civilian activities. I knew that Ike had given him all sorts of authority, so, I put him in front of a radio transmitter, and he makes these announcements, telling the French garrisons to cease fire, that we're all on the same side. Sounded pretty good to me."

"That's what he was supposed to do."

"Except, nobody paid any attention to him. Nobody. I don't know who this guy thought he was, but every French official I talked to said he had no authority here, and they had no intention of following his orders. Didn't really matter anyway, at least not around Algiers. The shooting's over. But pretty quick he skedaddled out of here. My people say he's hiding out, that he's got some friends who put him up in some villa near here. I'm not sure he's in any danger, unless somebody tries to *ignore* him to death."

Clark's staff had arrived on a second B-17, the *Boomerang,* and Clark had set up a makeshift headquarters at the Hotel St. George in Algiers. The only sounds of a fight came from German bombers, small waves of Junkers, making the trip from bases in Sicily, most of them less concerned with dropping bombs than making firsthand observations of just what was happening in Algiers. If there was confusion and uncertainty among German commanders across the Mediterranean, it only emphasized the value of a plan Clark had proposed weeks ago, while he was still in London. The Germans maintained offices in Casablanca, Oran, and Algiers, staffed by officers whose credentials stated they were part of the German Armistice Commission. It was a poor disguise for men whose duties included close observation of French officials, making sure no one was plotting anything that might upset German and Vichy control. It was one wolf watching the other. When Clark received intelligence reports on the activities of these Germans, he was convinced that, as the Torch landings were rolling ashore, assassination squads should be prepared to target the Germans. At the very least, it might delay word of what was happening on the beaches from reaching Berlin. At best, it could disrupt enemy communication and supply coordination all through this theater of the war. But the idea was dismissed in London, described as too uncivilized. Clark had been astounded that killing rear-echelon officers was considered an affront to the rules of war, the same rules that Hitler had tossed out the window in 1939. Whether or not the plan would have accomplished its goal, Clark could only wonder at the German bombers flying high overhead, if they were observing for themselves or simply confirming reports sent from carefully hidden German agents all through the battle zones.

With his staff in place, the office began to function, updated reports relayed back to Gibraltar. The dispatches had continued to flow in, passed on to Eisenhower, word mostly of the ongoing fights around both Casablanca and Oran. With the comic absurdity of Giraud pushed out of his mind, Clark now confronted the same challenge Giraud was supposed to have prevented. Those French commanders who had sided with the Americans were facing challenges of their own, some of them arrested by their own officers, or senior commanders in overlapping commands. No matter the continuing firefights that ringed two of the three primary targets, Clark's first priority now was to find a French official who was actually in charge of something, who could give the order to the men in the field that might actually be obeyed. The man's name kept rolling through Clark's brain, *Darlan,* the man no one trusted, the man whose loyalties were said to rest squarely on the Vichy shoulders of Marshal Henri Pétain in Paris. One of the first visitors to Clark's headquarters had been Robert Murphy. The diplomat brought word that not only was Pétain's most trusted deputy actually in Algiers, but that Murphy had been in contact with him. With Eisenhower's second-in-command now on French African soil, Admiral Jean Darlan sent word through Murphy that he wanted to talk.

ALGIERS—NOVEMBER 10, 1942

They met in a small room off the lobby of the Hotel St. George, and on Clark's orders the hotel entryways were now guarded by a platoon of American soldiers. The French had reacted nervously to the presence of so many rifles, but assurances had been passed from Clark, through Murphy, that it was simply for the protective custody of Admiral Darlan. Clark wondered if anyone confused that bit of nonsense with the reality. Regardless of what happened at the meeting, afterward no one was going anywhere without Clark's permission.

Darlan was a surprise, bore no resemblance to the tall, lean arrogance of either Giraud or de Gaulle. He was in fact quite short, fidgeted nervously, constantly swiping at beads of sweat on his bald head. He stared up at Clark with watery blue eyes, a soft frown on a round, pudgy face, seemed to flinch at Clark's every move.

The room was too small for the number of officials who filled it, French officers from every branch of their military, along with civilian ministers whose names Clark had already forgotten. Clark had his own people as well, Murphy, who had arranged the meeting, who seemed as nervous as Darlan, others, including Colonel Holmes, the interpreter.

Clark had moved behind a small table, stood a head taller than any other man in the room. Darlan had placed himself in front of the others, a show of authority the French officers and civilians had clearly accepted. Clark knew that Murphy had already presented paperwork to the Frenchman, details of an armistice, a carefully worded arrangement designed to stop the fighting. The document offered assurances that the French were considered to be allies of both the Americans and the British and were welcomed as a capable partner in the fight yet to be waged to push the Germans out of Africa. Clark looked squarely at Darlan, who seemed to lean backward under the American's glare.

"We have work to do to meet the common enemy. Are you ready to sign the terms of the armistice? It will cover all French Africa. It is essential that we stop this waste of time and blood."

Darlan looked away, seemed to struggle with words. "I have sent your terms to Vichy. There will be no reply until the Council of Ministers meets this afternoon."

Vichy. Clark clenched his fists, looked at Murphy, who shook his head, some kind of helpless apology. Clark thought, dammit, you're the diplomat! What are we supposed to do now? Wait for some meeting in France that might not even take place? He leaned forward, closer to Darlan, who flinched yet again.

"I do not propose to wait for any word from Vichy."

"General Clark, I want to see hostilities stopped as soon as possible. But I have been given strict orders by Marshal Pétain to enter into no negotiations until his instructions are received. My associates and I do understand that further hostilities are fruitless. But I can only obey the orders of Pétain."

Clark stood up straight, folded his arms across his chest. "Then I will end these negotiations and deal with someone who can act. You have thirty minutes to decide."

It was a toothless demand. He held his pose, thought, who else can I talk to? Darlan knows there is no one who has more authority here. Clark glanced at Murphy again, saw wide eyes, stared hard at the diplomat, a silent order, *say nothing*.

Darlan seemed gripped in hand-wringing anguish and, after a long moment, said, "I urged acceptance of your terms. I am confident that Pétain will agree. We must allow them time to consider the matter."

"We cannot stand here while government ministers debate. If you will not issue instructions for the cessation of hostilities, I will go to General Giraud. He will sign the terms and the necessary orders."

Clark knew he had gone too far. Darlan looked at him, the milky eyes closing into slits. He shook his head. "I am certain that the troops will not obey General Giraud. This can only mean the loss of more time, and there will be more fighting."

Clark looked at Murphy again, the man seeming to stagger from the glare. What now? Dammit, I am no good at this! There was a low murmur from the men behind Darlan, and Clark felt vulnerable, as though his authority was slipping away. He rolled his hand into a fist, leaned forward again, struck down hard at the table. The men jumped, surprised, and Darlan took a step back, the fear returning to his face. Clark let the words come now, as he had with Giraud, no diplomacy, no tact.

"If the admiral is so sure of the decision from Vichy, why can't you issue the cease-fire order now?"

"I can't assume such responsibility—"

"Your delay means that more Frenchmen, more Americans, and more Britons will die. I presume you know that Oran is nearly in our hands. All Frenchmen and all Americans have the same interests at heart, and here we are fighting among ourselves, wasting time. I know that the admiral wants to stop the fighting between our troops. We will get your signature on the order for the cessation of hostilities right now, or you will bear the cost of a new responsibility. We have a hundred fifty thousand troops on the ground in North Africa, and right now, they are killing Frenchmen. And yet, we have the means of equipping those same French soldiers, bringing them into our fight, our common struggle, and making North Africa a base from which we can launch operations into France itself. How anybody who holds honor and loyalty to France in such high personal regard . . . how anyone like that can fail to join us in an operation that can mean the liberation of France . . . is beyond my understanding."

Darlan seemed ready to cry, and Clark pounded the table again, tried to ignore the pain in his hand.

Darlan sagged. "I cannot act, General, until I receive authority from Pétain."

"By the time that authority arrives here, if it ever arrives here, we might not need the armistice. Talk to your generals. Ask them how much longer they wish to watch their men die. Ask them how much longer Oran can hold out. How many French ships have been sunk? How many cannon destroyed?"

Darlan wiped his brow again, said in a low voice, "Perhaps you will allow me to discuss this with my staff. I ask five minutes."

Clark moved back into the crowded room, all talk growing silent. He resumed his position behind the table, Darlan standing across from him.

Darlan put a piece of paper in front of Clark. "If you will sign this document, General, this will confirm that the Americans have not accepted our refusal to declare an immediate armistice."

Clark fought through the jumbled meaning of Darlan's words, looked at Murphy, who said, "May I examine this, sir?"

"Damned right."

Murphy picked up the paper, read, looked at Clark. "Admiral Darlan is stating that further battle is futile, and that since Marshal Pétain would certainly agree that the loss of French North Africa would be a catastrophe to French honor and national interests, Admiral Darlan proposes that hostilities cease, and that French forces here assume a posture of complete neutrality."

Clark saw a slight smile on Murphy's face, felt a hard weight pressing down on him, the dreariness of trying to comprehend the twists and turns of diplomatic posturing. Murphy handed him the paper, said nothing, would reveal no sign of acceptance to Darlan. Clark saw no satisfaction on Darlan's soft face, just the same tearful passivity. He saw through it now, realized that Darlan was far more clever than Giraud. There was no pomposity in the man, just the ingratiating humility, the perfect walk down the tightrope. Of course, he thought, how else do you survive dealing with Nazis? Clark pondered the word on the paper, *neutrality*. He wanted to ask Murphy about that, but the questions could wait for later. At worst, it means that French soldiers can choose for themselves which way they want to go. It's a convenient way for Darlan to pass any responsibility to his subordinates, and so, Darlan cannot be labeled a traitor. It doesn't matter, not now. The mission here is to get the shooting to stop.

Clark leaned forward again, said to Darlan, "I want a clear and specific order to all French naval, air, and ground forces to cease hostilities immediately. All units will be returned to their bases, where they will stand down. I want it in your handwriting, signed by you."

Darlan nodded. "And what will you do with General Giraud?"

Clark was surprised by the question, saw Murphy lower his head. Of course, Clark thought: a diplomat's nightmare. We're dealing with two kingpins. It is the final question, the issue that has far more weight with these people than whether their troops are dying in the field. Whose cream rises to the top?

"It is of the utmost importance that you and General Giraud reach a working agreement. The Allied governments have granted General Giraud the position as commander in chief of the French forces here, as well as civilian authority."

"The army is with me. They will not obey him."

"Then, Admiral, you must see that they do."

In response to Darlan's request that Marshal Pétain authorize the signing of the armistice documents, Pétain instead issued an order relieving Admiral Darlan of his command. The chaos of French politics quickly spread through the headquarters of the various French commands across North Africa, some officers obeying Darlan's cease-fire order, others responding more to

Pétain, keeping their troops in the field, opposing the steady advance of the Americans. Clark could do little, yet the question nagged at him, as he knew it would frustrate Eisenhower: How could any Frenchman, especially an old war hero like Henri Pétain, collaborate so completely with German interests? Clark had no doubts that in Pétain's office, his order to remove Darlan had been dictated by men in black uniforms, Hitler's watchdogs, who manipulated the old man's fragile strings.

Clark understood that this was a political snake pit that might only be solved when the last firefight had grown silent.

13. LOGAN

T he enemy planes had taken off long before dawn, and the radios had buzzed with warnings about bomb runs, the men staying close to their guns, staring into darkness toward an enemy no one could have seen. But the French planes did not attack, and if the men in the tanks did not understand, the commanders did. With Tafaraoui securely in American hands, La Sénia would be next, and many of the French pilots had made a wise decision. Once the sun came up, the American armor and artillery would most certainly capture or destroy any French aircraft still on the ground. To prevent their destruction, the pilots simply took their planes and left. But not all. As the First Armored Division pushed steadily toward the airfield, French resistance crumbled. The Americans captured sixty remaining planes, and more than a hundred fifty prisoners.

"Not much of an airport."

Logan ignored Parnell, was surprised that Hutchinson did as

well. The tank column rolled out into flat, open ground, passed bomb craters, drifting clouds of smoke. There were low block buildings, white walls lining a gray tarmac, several trucks, one of them a shattered black wreck. Troops were there as well, clusters of MPs, larger groups of French soldiers, hatless, grimy men, most simply sitting on the hard ground.

The wireless had continued to pour out messages, instructions, Hutchinson spending as much time talking to officers as he did his own crew. The orders came again, and Hutchinson responded, then said, "Driver, forty degrees left. Move to that row of low hills."

The tank swiveled, Parnell's voice in Logan's ear: "Fine with me, Hutch. We don't need to be sitting out here like ducks on a pond. I guess all them Frenchies are mighty glad to see us."

Logan said nothing, thought, is that why they were shooting at us?

The tanks spread out in formation, most pointing north, and Logan could see the other machines out on both sides, turrets making slow circles, gunners testing their fields of view. The hills were no different here than they had been near the beach, rocky, sliced by small cuts and ravines, speckled with dull gray brush. Parnell rolled the tank into a narrow cut, good cover. Hutchinson said, "Keep it right here, Skip. Shut her down. We'll wait for orders, see what the colonel wants us to do next."

The tank clattered into silence, the echo still in Logan's ears, welcome heat rolling forward from the engine behind him. The air through the hatch was chilly and damp, a soft breeze, stirring the thin crust of dried mud that coated every surface. During the night there had been a storm of sleet and icy rain, blowing a hard chill through narrow passages in the heavy steel of the tank, a storm that might have kept the rest of the French fighter planes from escaping capture. But the storm had subsided, and whether or not it had cost the Americans a larger prize at La Sénia, the tank crews were grateful. Inside the shelter of the tank, no one expected to be wiping cold mist out of their eyes.

Parnell broke the silence, typical.

"We gotta just sit here, or they gonna let us take a little walk?"

Hutchinson seemed to ignore him, stood high, peered out, then sat again, spoke into the wireless. Logan watched him, knew Hutchinson's look, careful, no misunderstanding what the voice was ordering him to do.

Hutchinson spoke into the intercom now. "Okay, we get a break. Everybody out. Yeah, take your damned walk, Skip. Don't need you pissing in my tank. Colonel Todd says we're to wait here, let the rest of the units gather up."

Hutchinson climbed up and out of the tank, and Logan followed quickly. The air was cool and damp, a thick gray overhead, the horizons clouded by a dark haze. Logan jumped down from the hull of the tank, his boots splashing mud, the other two out now as well, Parnell down beside him, scampering off quickly toward a low bush.

Hutchinson stood at the front of the tank, watched Parnell's haste. "Man's got a bladder like a girl. Should rig him some kind of tube, let him pee right out the front of the tank."

Logan smiled, but there was no humor in Hutchinson's dirty face, the man pulling off his goggles, clean white rings around his eyes. The fourth man, Baxter, was down beside them now, said nothing.

Logan tapped the quiet man on the shoulder. "How you doing, Pete?"

Baxter shrugged. "Thought we'd smack into it this morning. The French just ran off, I guess."

"Don't count on it, soldier."

The voice came from beyond the tank, the familiar growl of the captain. Logan saw the dusty uniform, the same raccoon eyes as Hutchinson. He stiffened, the old reflex.

Gregg said, "We'll be here for a little while. According to Colonel Todd, Colonel Robinett is out that way, pushing toward us. There's another column coming up from the south, Colonel Waters's group. Once we're in place, we've got one place left to go." He pointed to the north. "Oran's about five miles that way. The First Infantry's perched out to the west, ready to move in and take the place. Be kinda nice if the armor could save them some trouble. Those boys have a pretty high notion of how good they are. Wouldn't hurt us if we moved in there first. Show the infantry that we can kick some ass too."

The First Infantry. The *Big Red One*. Logan felt comfort in that,

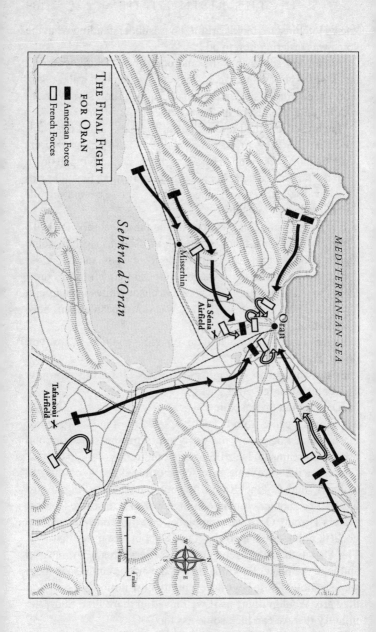

THE FINAL FIGHT
FOR ORAN

■ American Forces
□ French Forces

Sebkra d'Oran

MEDITERRANEAN SEA

Oran

Misserhin

La Sénia
Airfield

Tafaraoui
Airfield

0   1 km
0   4 miles

the army's best foot soldiers heading toward the same target. So, we're going to have a race? Didn't know this was a contest.

Parnell was back now, said, "Hey, Captain, you figure there's some good-looking women in Oran? I ain't seen a looker yet out here in this scrub country. Arab women won't even let you have a peek."

Parnell was the only man in the company who could make the captain laugh, something that had impressed Logan.

Gregg was smiling. "Easy, cowboy. We've got a job to do first."

"Beggin' your pardon, sir, but don't seem like these Frenchies care enough to stop us from doin' it."

Gregg wasn't smiling now. "I said, don't count on that. They shot the hell out of our boys in the harbor. According to Colonel Todd, they've given us a pretty good fight down south. Waters ran into a column of armor from the French Foreign Legion. Hell of a fight. We had to call in some Spitfires, a few British bombers to soften those fellows up."

Logan said, "Foreign Legion? I thought they'd be on our side."

"Hell, Private, I thought this whole place would be on our side. Every damned rumor we hear turns out to be wrong. Instead of a welcome mat, we get shot at. Then, we get ready for a heavy fight, and they back off. Foreign Legion. Hell, the only thing I know about those fellows is what I saw at the movies. Gary damned Cooper. Why they'd fight alongside the Nazis is a mystery—"

The air was ripped by a sharp scream, the blast coming behind them, out in the open ground. There were more shells now, falling farther to the side, out away from the tanks.

Gregg darted away, shouted, "Mount up!"

Logan ducked low, waiting for the next blast, leaned close to the heavy steel of the tank treads. He waited for Parnell and Baxter, who scampered up onto the hull, then up and over through the hatch. More shells came, farther out, the ground shaking beneath him, and Hutchinson slapped him on the back, said, "Go!"

Logan climbed up, paused, saw a row of explosions farther out, hard blasts punching the muddy ground, harmless, no damage to anything but the scrub. Hutchinson was up beside him, and Logan said, "They can't be shooting at us. Even the French can aim better than that."

Hutchinson stared out with him, the blasts moving away still, the air still ripped above them, but no impacts anywhere close. Hutchinson said, "Looks like they're not shooting at anything. Just . . . shooting. Big ones too, maybe one fifties."

Logan swung his legs into the open hatch, looked toward the other tanks, saw men peering out of their hatches, the captain, faces turned toward the rising clouds of dust.

Hutchinson said, "Hell of a waste of ammunition."

"I bet it's just a show, Hutch. They're ticked off, and they know they gotta pull back to Oran, so they'll make like it's a big artillery attack. Lighten their load. Make it easier for them if they don't have to haul their shells."

Hutchinson pushed him down through the hatch. "Mount up, gunner. Nobody's made you a general yet."

The enemy artillery batteries had been silenced, good work from the increasing swarm of American forces, the armored cars and gun carriers that pressed forward, either capturing or destroying the French guns. With the final wall of French resistance crumbling, two columns of American armor were ordered to push northward directly into the city of Oran. They advanced on a parallel course, Colonel Todd's tankers moving parallel to another column led by Lieutenant Colonel John Waters.

The palm trees stood tall over low-slung buildings, white walls topped with ornate iron railings. Captain Gregg took the lead now, kept the squad of tanks at a slow pace, the hatches closed, *buttoned up,* no one's head exposed. They turned down a narrow street, the doorways and windows close enough to hide snipers, or worse, an enemy who might toss a grenade right into an open turret.

Logan ignored the gunsight, nothing to see here, no targets except thick stone walls, glimpses of brown brush behind arching entryways. He peered through the periscope, felt the familiar churning in his gut, cold and uncomfortable, growing worse, the tension coming more from the tight spaces they rolled through than from the enemy who might be anywhere at all. The wireless was silent, every tank commander inside his own fortress, no one seeking instructions beyond what Gregg had already told them: *Stay close, stay behind me.* They were third in line, and Parnell kept them fifty yards behind the man in front, who was fifty yards behind Gregg. Logan leaned down, looked at Parnell's back, soaked with sweat, the Texan silent, staring through a slit in his hatch cover, keeping the tank precisely where it needed to be. The air in the tank was growing warmer, thick with the smell of the men, and something new now, houseguests, the first occupants of the city to offer their own particular greeting. The tank was now full of flies.

Logan watched them enter through every crease and slit in the hard steel, thought, what's drawing them? Our smell? The metal? One by one, dozen by dozen, the flies made their way inside, then darted about, seeking some landing place, gathering in a growing swarm on men and equipment. He forced himself not to watch them, swatted them away from his eyes. Damn you. What have we got in here you can't get out there? I'm guessing this city's got plenty of things for you to paw through.

He looked again through the periscope, saw sunlight, the street opening wide, the close walls falling away behind them. He felt the pressure lift off him, heard Hutchinson in the intercom.

"Glad to be out of that tight squeeze. At least we can see something."

No one responded and Logan smiled, thought, you can't be a tanker and have claustrophobia. But I'd rather be out in that open scrub brush. At least if somebody's gonna shoot at us, we can shoot back.

The wireless crackled now, and Hutchinson spoke into the microphone, then said, "Straight ahead, driver. Follow the wider streets. I guess the captain's not too keen on those narrow alleys either."

Logan knew not to ask, but the questions rose inside his head, and he looked toward Hutchinson. "Hey, Hutch. They tell you where we're going? Is this Oran yet?"

Hutchinson looked at him, nodded, waved a hand. "Looks like a city to me. Ritzy downtown Oran. Or maybe uptown. No signposts I saw. All I know is we're moving east. Captain tells me anything else, I'll let you know."

There was a sharp ping above him, and Logan flinched.

Hutchinson said, "I'll be damned. Somebody shot at us. Sniper. These damned Frenchmen may be the dumbest soldiers in the world."

Logan glanced over to him, said, "Just keep your head inside. For all we know, the Arabs are shooting at us too. Might even be a few Krauts around here." He paused. "I do like a tank."

The wireless spoke again, Hutchinson responding, and he said through the intercom, "Driver, halt."

The tank jerked to a stop, Logan leaning hard against the shoulder braces of the thirty-seven.

"Jesus, Skip, no need to slam on the damned brakes."

"He said halt. I halted."

Hutchinson pushed the hatch open, the sunlight flooding in, stirring the flies. He stood, and Logan looked through the periscope again, saw uniforms, men coming forward. There were voices outside, Hutchinson's, and more. Hutchinson leaned in, shouted, "Shut 'er down, Skip!"

The tank was silent now, and Hutchinson climbed up and out, then leaned his head back inside the tank. "Looks like we're home, boys. Somebody sent a welcoming committee."

Logan was curious, heard laughter, stood, his head outside the hatch. He pulled off his helmet, saw Gregg, other officers, men gathering behind them, *infantry*. They wore the shoulder patch, unmistakable, the simple red numeral 1. The men moved closer, gathered around the tanks, rifles on shoulders, lean and young, dirty faces, smiles breaking out as they felt the steel of the big machines.

Hutchinson was down, close to the captain, called back to Logan, "Hey, Jack. Say hello to the Big Red One."

The officers moved away in a group, and behind him, Logan heard the last of the tank engines shutting down. The wide streets were still filling with soldiers, and there were hand-shakes, more officers, Captain Gregg talking to a colonel. Hutchinson came back to the tank, stood in front, spoke to the open hatches down front, to Baxter and Parnell.

"Come on out. Looks like we'll be here for a while." He

moved around to the side, toward Logan, slapped the tank hull, said, "We're damned lucky, Jack. The First was about to open up with their artillery, blow hell out of the city. They were expecting to fight their way in. Good thing we didn't run out of gas a mile back, we'd have been caught up in a real mess. They didn't know we were here."

Logan climbed out of the hatch, stood high on the tank hull, saw a jeep coming from the east, more trucks, heard tanks coming up from behind, more men emerging. He saw familiar officers, Colonel Waters, Colonel Todd. The two men came forward quickly, were greeted by the infantry officers, more handshakes, quick words, serious. Logan saw another jeep now, coming up behind the infantrymen, another officer, older, the man stepping out, standing tall, thin, wiry, the walk of an athlete. He came closer to the tank, and Logan saw the man's shoulder, *two stars*.

Hutchinson saw him too, said, "You know who that is?"

"Gotta be Terry Allen."

The man who commanded the First Infantry Division moved toward Colonel Waters, who faced him, a sharp salute. The soldiers around them were nearly silent, very aware of Allen's presence.

Waters said, "General, may I offer you the city of Oran?"

Allen put his hands on his hips, shook his head. "I suppose we'll take it. Guess you boys saved us some trouble."

There was commotion to one side, shouts, a rush of color. Logan saw the infantry reacting, rifles coming down. But he could see now, it was civilians, women, men in suits, emerging from barricaded doors. One man was older than the others, carried the tricolor, the French flag, waved it over his head. The man spoke in a torrent of French, the soldiers eyeing him carefully, the man moving closer to the tanks. Soldiers began laughing, calling out to him, rude jokes, then silence, as their commander pushed past them, made his way toward the old man through the parting sea of soldiers. But the Frenchman ignored the general, ran straight at the tank. Logan reached down, felt for the grip of his pistol, but the old man stopped, tossed the flag, draped it across the hull of the tank. The man was sobbing, fell to his knees, his hands up on a wheel of the tank.

"Vive l'Amérique! Vive les Américaines!"

Other civilians were shouting out, calling to the soldiers, their courage growing, men and women old and young stepping into the crowd of soldiers, the soldiers responding, hugs and handshakes. Logan watched the old man, red-faced, more tears, Captain Gregg beside him, leaning low. The man stood, Gregg helping him, Hutchinson there as well. The man seemed to compose himself, more French words, then made a deep bow, moved away into the growing celebration.

Parnell and Baxter had climbed out of the tank, Parnell sitting on the turret, and he said, "That looked like a full-out surrender to me. Damn, this is better'n anything I ever seen. All we gotta do now is find some Krauts." He slapped Logan's back. "Hey, Jack, give me just one chance at a shot. Just one. I'll show you how to aim that gun. This has been a chicken shoot so far. If the *enemy* can't do no better than this, we'll be going home by Christmas."

Gregg looked up at Parnell, no smile, the man staring hard at the Texan. There was no humor in his eyes. Logan wanted to say something, could feel the grim toughness in the captain, realized the stupidity of Parnell's words. The Texan was oblivious, was calling out to the crowd of soldiers, something about kissing the girls. Logan watched as Gregg moved away, the captain returning toward his own tank. The words kept coming from Parnell, a flow of insults and jokes about the enemy, how simple this was, this victory, this glorious display of perfect might, the unstoppable power that would simply drive the Germans right out of the war.

With the three primary targets of Operation Torch resting firmly in the hands of the Allies, attention turned toward the ongoing turmoil in the French high command. Regardless of whose authority carried weight with French soldiers and civilians, the absurd haggling and bickering had already caused costly delays that had kept the next phase of the plan from moving forward as quickly as Eisenhower had hoped. There was more to the French chaos than control of the ports in Algeria and Morocco. Tunisia was occupied by French troops as well, commanders who might still be loyal to Vichy, or men whose fear of the Germans might subdue their willingness to join the Allied fight.

While the Americans in Casablanca and Oran celebrated their victory, in Algiers, the British were scrambling to put their men into motion, the first wave of the march eastward that would bring Tunisia into Allied hands. Whether the French in Tunisia would obey Darlan's neutrality order, or whether they would actually fight the Allies, was another nagging question Eisenhower could not answer. But the longer it took Anderson's troops to occupy the precious Tunisian airfields and ports, the longer the door remained open for Hitler's generals to pour in men and equipment, adding considerable power to the garrisons and defensive positions that guarded Tunisia's western border. Both sides understood that the ports and airfields in Tunisia were the final lifeline and the last refuge for Rommel's army, where the supply ships and cargo planes could sustain what remained of the *Panzerarmee,* an army that was drawing closer day by day.

14. ROMMEL

TOBRUK, LIBYA
NOVEMBER 13, 1942

The fires blanketed the skyline, mounds of supplies and ammunition, torched by the German engineers, the final defiant gesture, a clear message to the enemy that nothing useful would be left behind. Just to the east, along the coast road, and southward, units of armored trucks, heavy machine guns, and small-bore artillery faced east, the final line in the sand. With them were more of the engineers, men skilled in the most vicious tools of war, the well-hidden mines and booby traps, deadly obstacles that could hold up a column, delay a line of British men and their machines at some perfect location for a carefully planned ambush. From the first hours of the retreat, the rear guard had been strong enough and dangerous enough to discourage the lead units of Montgomery's advancing troops from pressing too close, the British as exhausted as the Germans, no one seeking another fight so soon after the bloodying they had both suffered at El Alamein.

Rommel had raced all through his retreating army, placing officers in key points along the roads, trying to break up the logjams in the narrow cuts and valleys, trucks and panicked drivers clogging the narrow defiles, perfect targets for British bombers. From the German and Italians who had survived to join the withdrawal, Rommel squeezed order from the panic. The chaotic retreat became an organized march, and by the time the *Panzerarmee* crossed again into Libya, over the familiar ground of so many good fights, Mersa Matruh, Sidi Barrani, Halfaya Pass, Rommel knew that no matter what Montgomery tried to throw forward, no matter how hard the British pushed, at least some part of the *Panzerarmee* had been preserved.

Rommel had kept them mostly on the good roads that ran close to the sea, away from the confusion of the massive minefields and scattered wreckage of past battles. When the British had finally begun their pursuit, Montgomery had done just what Rommel had expected. The British sent column after column deep into the desert, fast-moving armored trucks on a course parallel to Rommel's retreat. When the British believed they were far enough beyond Rommel's main body, they would sweep northward, driving hard to the sea coast, to cut off the German escape. Rommel himself had perfected the tactic, which relied on speed and surprise. But Rommel knew enough of Montgomery by now, knew that there would be caution and planning, and so, by the time the British accomplished their sweeping left hooks, they reached the coast road to find that the Germans had already passed, were already farther to the west, one more escape. It was Rommel's only satisfaction, a glimpse into what had once been. Even in defeat, Rommel could anticipate and outmaneuver the superior forces that pursued him.

He had allowed himself a pause at Tobruk, could not simply pass by the city that had cost him so much to capture. Now, it would be abandoned, and he watched the fires along the harbor consuming what the men could not carry. Close by, on the main

road, the columns moved past him in the darkness, trucks tow-
ing trucks, small armored cars packed full of anxious men, men
not so afraid of the enemy to the east, but the enemy right beneath them, the truck itself, a mechanical beast grown fragile,
dying perhaps, adding to the dark and silent hulks that littered
the entire route of the withdrawal. The precious supplies of fuel
were doled out now in liters, enough to carry the vehicles a few
more miles, keep them just out of reach of the British. What fuel
they had came from the Luftwaffe, the cargo planes hauling in
some two hundred tons of gasoline per day, barely a fifth of
what they had once received. If fuel was available, the trucks
and the men they carried would try to reach the safety of new
defensive positions at Mersa el Brega, the next line he had
drawn on the map. If the fuel ran out, if the cargo planes did not
arrive, there was nothing Rommel could do to prevent another
piece of his army from falling away, foot soldiers who could
only wait to be swallowed up by the advance of the enemy. He
would not order them to fight to the last, would not insist on
Hitler's ridiculous command that they die rather than submit. It
was an emotion in him that no armchair general could feel. The
Panzerarmee was not simply some mindless obedient servant, a
soulless machine. It was a part of Rommel himself, as much as
he was a part of each of them. He felt it even for the Italians,
many of those who'd stood fast against Montgomery's overwhelming force, who'd fought back against odds they should
never have had to face. Along every mile, as the trucks broke
down, the fuel tanks drained, more of the men were left behind,
with no other means to escape their enemy but the exhausting
march. The British wave would reach them soon enough, slicing
away another piece of Rommel's army. Every day, he felt the
sharp pain in his heart, knew that no one in Berlin, no one in
Rome, would ever know the tragedy of it, would ever know
what it felt like to lose your precious army to an enemy you
should have destroyed.

  He had watched the few remaining tanks and the surviving
pieces of heavy artillery escape, knew that even now, as his men
pulled away from Tobruk, to the west, the teeth of the *Panzerarmee* were preparing to give Montgomery another good fight.
He drew energy from that, held tight to the image of the eighty-

eights and the Mark IVs digging into a good defensive position, then turning their sights to the east, waiting for the British to come into range. No matter how strong Montgomery was, if there was another fight, the cost would be high, perhaps high enough to cause Montgomery to delay once more. And while the British command pondered how to confront the new position, Rommel would pull them away again, to another line on the map.

He sat on his command truck, Westphal beside him. They were just west of Tobruk, and he stared at the fires, the silhouettes of the wrecked buildings, tried to ignore the exhaustion, thought of Lucy, another letter, words forming in his mind.

The end will not be long . . . the army is in no way to blame. It has fought magnificently. . . .

Thank God I have you, he thought. Who else will hear the truth? You might not understand, but there will be time for explanations later. We will sit in the garden and talk of this and wonder what I could have done differently, what villains I have had to confront.

The artillery thundered, flickers of light. He thought of his officers, the men who stood high with binoculars, who fired the star shells, lighting up the ground where the cautious enemy crept toward them. Do not be foolish, do not waste ammunition. They are not coming, not tonight. He thought of Montgomery again, felt no hatred, had never hated the British, never shared in the loud boasting he heard in the camps, all the talk every soldier knows. No, it is not about being a better man, more courageous, there is nothing here of our certain superiority over some mongrel race. The British are not so different from us. Out here, we are all good men, we all show courage, we all know our duty. Victory comes from the strategy, the plan, the tools we are given.

He knew little about Montgomery, had ignored the propaganda, the reports brought by Berndt that always seemed to describe enemy commanders as illiterate buffoons. There had been incompetence certainly, British commanders early in the campaign who did not understand Rommel, who were incapable of predicting surprise. So, Montgomery, how would you have fared here a year ago? No matter what your newspapers say about you, I will never know if you are any better than Wavell or Ritchie or Auchinleck. You were lucky, certainly. They handed you an enormous weapon, an experienced army, bloodied field officers who understand as much about this desert as any German. And they gave you tanks and trucks and airplanes. But it was not your planning, your perfect strategy, that drove us away. It was the tools. It was power. And now, those men you send after us, they are like hunters chasing a wounded lion. You may order them to pursue, and they will make a good show of it. But they know not to come too close. They know, even if their *great commander* does not, that we can still rip your heart out with our claws.

He turned, looked toward the west, black darkness, thought, so much more land, so many miles. And then, another army. Another challenge.

The news of the Allied invasion had reached him in a makeshift headquarters, brought from wireless reports that drifted out of Algeria and Tunisia. The invasion had not surprised him, rumors filtering through North Africa for many weeks, reports of ship traffic, some word that Eisenhower might be in Gibraltar. It was inevitable that the Americans would come, but they would not be confident of success, would have learned something from the foolishness of the raid at Dieppe. So, if they needed to test themselves, they would strike where there would be little chance of catastrophe. What better target than the French?

Rommel had done his fighting in France already, had pushed his tanks over and through armies that seemed powerless to stop anyone. Yes, the Americans would remember that as well. And so, they would join this fight by assaulting an inferior enemy, gain confidence against Frenchmen. It took them three days to silence the guns at Oran, three days to secure their first victory. Take pride in your success, Herr Eisenhower. But there is still a fight to be had.

MERSA EL BREGA, LIBYA—NOVEMBER 23, 1942

It had rained for nearly a week, the flat, hard ground along the roadways softening to deep mud, the wadis filling with dark water, sudden winding floods that swept away the tents and the careless men who stayed in the low cover for too long. Along the coast roads, the Germans continued their retreat, the Libyan desert behind them now. Closer to Benghazi, the land changed, the flat, hard dirt and rock giving way to the steep hills and lush green of the Djebel Akhdar. It was farm country, olive orchards and grain fields, white-walled towns where Mussolini had once sent his people to carve a new piece of Italy from land where Arabs still tended their flocks of goats. The Italians were mostly gone now, the Arabs staking their claim once more, ransacking and looting the towns and farmhouses. What the Arabs did not claim, the armies did, olive groves and orchards ripped and flattened by two years of war. Rommel did not halt the withdrawal around Benghazi, would not try to hold the hillside passes and narrow defiles. His army could not make a stand until they were strengthened, or until they reached a position where Montgomery's caution would make them safe. Rommel moved his men southward, following the coast below Benghazi, destroying supplies and ammunition dumps as they went. South of the city, the roads turned west again, a great sweeping curve of coastline that led to Mersa el Brega and El Agheila, two anchors of a defensive line Rommel had used before, a line that would allow his army to dig in, to rest. To the west was the major port of Tripoli, and if only once the supply officers in Rome would do their jobs, could somehow push cargo ships through the British screen, Rommel's army might again be made strong.

Rommel had sent Berndt to see Hitler once more, hoping to convince the High Command that he should be allowed to pursue a strategy that would create some benefit from his retreat. There was nothing to be gained by holding Libya now, no chance that the weakened and greatly outnumbered *Panzerarmee* could strike at the British again in the open desert. Rommel knew that even a cautious Montgomery would not stay away for long, would endure enormous pressure from London to continue to attack. The line at Mersa el Brega was stout, but it was not impenetrable, and Rommel believed that the only wise strategy was to abandon Libya altogether and pull his army into the narrow valleys and sharp mountainous defenses of Tunisia. With the Allied thrust coming from the west, Tunisia

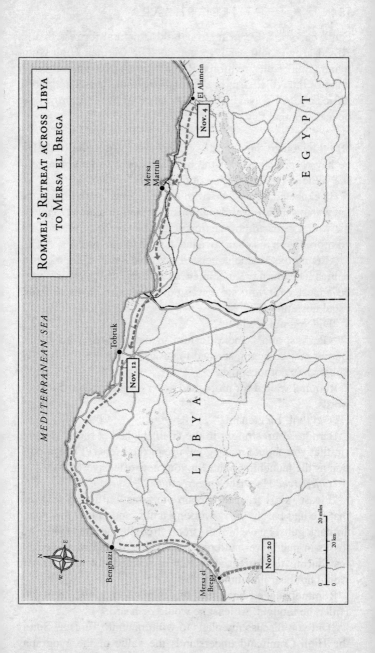

ROMMEL'S RETREAT ACROSS LIBYA
TO MERSA EL BREGA

MEDITERRANEAN SEA

EGYPT

LIBYA

El Alamein

Nov. 4

Mersa
Matruh

Tobruk

Nov. 12

Benghazi

Mersa el
Brega

Nov. 20

20 miles
20 km

could become a German stronghold, a natural fortress that no Allied army could easily penetrate. The German High Command could either reinforce Rommel and strike hard at either wing of the Allied armies or withdraw from Tunisia and North Africa altogether, saving what remained of the *Panzerarmee* to be used another day.

"So, Lieutenant, how did the Führer receive my proposal? Did he have a preference for the offensive, or does he continue to see value in the destruction of this army?"

He expected a response from Berndt, some spark of outrage, knew that sarcasm was dangerous. But Berndt seemed to ignore his words, showed no reaction at all. The big man seemed uncomfortable in his chair, twisted, turned to one side.

After a quiet moment, he said, "My back is causing me difficulties. The journey was somewhat tedious." He paused. "I must be honest with you, sir. I was not received with the Führer's usual hospitality."

"Did you not see him?"

"Oh, yes, and I spoke to him in detail about your plans." Berndt paused again, seemed to struggle with the words. "The Führer was not receptive."

Rommel waited for more, had never seen Berndt at a loss for words.

"Get to it, Lieutenant."

Berndt sat up straight in the chair, looked at him. "He said, sir, that you should make good use of the Mersa el Brega position as the launching point for your new offensive."

"*Offensive?* He wishes me to attack?"

"Please, sir, I tried to explain our situation here. I told him that we had barely thirty working tanks, and only a few dozen antitank guns. I gave him the troop strength, repeated to him our losses in manpower suffered at El Alamein, and what we have lost during the retreat. The Führer seemed not to listen. He would not hear the numbers."

Rommel sagged back into the chair. Berndt was adored by Hitler, he thought. At least he would be heard.

"Did you discuss my plans to withdraw into Tunisia? Surely the High Command understands the value of the geography there. We can hold off any attack. If he will not reinforce me, has he no interest in seeing this army survive at all?"

His voice had risen, and Westphal appeared, standing in the entrance of the tent. Westphal had his usual frown, the caution Rommel was used to. Rommel waved him in, tried to calm himself, said, "Sit down, Colonel. Lieutenant Berndt is no longer so disturbed by my outbursts. It seems Lieutenant Berndt has endured his own . . . how should I describe it, Lieutenant? How did you enjoy the Führer's blindness?"

Westphal said, "Sir . . ."

"Quiet, Colonel. It's all right. Tell him, Lieutenant."

Berndt shifted again in the chair, did not look at Westphal, said, "My mission did not go well, Colonel. I failed to convince the Führer of the seriousness of our situation here. I am to blame. The Führer had many issues before him, many important concerns. The situation in Russia—"

"Never mind, Lieutenant. You are not required to make excuses for our Führer. What of my plans for Tunisia?"

Berndt looked down again. "The Führer was very specific on that point, sir. He said . . . he emphasized that he had every confidence in your command. But you should leave Tunisia out of your calculations."

Rommel felt the air leave him, forced himself to stand. Westphal moved up close to the table, concerned, and Rommel held him away. He moved slowly toward the entrance of the tent, stared out, saw sharp flickers of light in the darkness, flashlights held low, men in motion, an army doing its work. He clenched his fists, wanted to scream something, anything, words, some sound, deflate the anger that blossomed inside him. He had no fear of Berndt now, no fear of Kesselring, of Mussolini. But now, for the first time, Hitler frightened him. It was not for the reasons Westphal cautioned him about, not because there was danger of punishment, some sanction that could fall on Rommel for the indiscreet word, for failing to obey the orders. The fear was that he was being ignored. I can still win here, he thought. If they would just give me the tools. Have I not proven that?

He looked at Westphal, said, "Colonel, send another message to Field Marshal Kesselring. Request in the strongest terms that we should meet. There must be someone in this army who still cares what I have to say."

ARCO DEI FILENI, LIBYA—NOVEMBER 24, 1942

Kesselring had kept himself out of Rommel's path for most of the great retreat from El Alamein, and Rommel knew enough of the perceptions of the German High Command to understand that Kesselring might be putting distance between himself and any attachment to Rommel's failure. But Kesselring was still his commander, regardless of what the Italians might believe, and Rommel knew that no matter how difficult his relationship with Kesselring had become, the Italians would work with the man, cooperate with his requests, far more than they would listen to anything from Rommel. Kesselring responded as Rommel had hoped, agreed immediately to a meeting. Rommel did not expect the Italians to come as well.

Ugo Cavallero was Mussolini's favorite officer, the chief of Comando Supremo, an accomplished industrialist before the war who now had the responsibility for merging German and Italian interests throughout the Mediterranean theater. He was in his sixties, a short, arrogant man, with a talent for pleasing any audience with the perfect promise. Too often, that audience had been German supply officers, or Rommel himself. By his position in the hierarchy of the North African theater, Cavallero was superior in rank to both Rommel and Kesselring. Rommel usually just ignored him.

Cavallero had brought Marshal Bastico to the meeting, the same "Bombastico" Rommel knew too well, the man whose ambitions were squarely focused on achieving a notable place in Italian history books, ambitions that had rarely been accompanied by an ability to lead his troops to a victory in the field.

"Il Duce is enormously proud of our fighting divisions, and how they kept the enemy at bay. He is recommending that you forward a list of those officers who should be decorated. This will do much for morale throughout the army."

Cavallero sat back, satisfied at his pronouncement. Bastico was nodding in agreement, and Rommel saw no emotion on

Kesselring's face. Cavallero was looking at Rommel, waiting patiently for him to concur.

Rommel said, "Morale cannot be won by tossing medals around the camps of officers. Those soldiers who still wear the uniform of Il Duce know who their heroes are. They also know what they are facing."

Cavallero smiled, looked at Kesselring, then at Rommel again. "Quite so. They are facing an enemy who has stretched himself to the breaking point. They are facing the opportunity to turn temporary misfortune into victory. What plan of attack do you propose?"

Rommel scanned their faces in the dull light, Kesselring avoiding his eyes. He took a long, slow breath, the only sound in the dusty hollow of the room, glanced toward the darkness outside, a glimmer of stars through the open stone window.

"I do not propose we attack anyone in the condition we are now in. Perhaps, Marshal Cavallero, you have not had the opportunity to consult your staff. I have issued reports continuously as to our needs and our losses. The army we have now in place consists of a force that could only be described as one weak division. We have lost most of our heavy artillery. We have no more than two dozen heavy tanks, and forty of the lighter Italian machines that, as you know, have not endured well in combat. The Italian infantry has no armament that can compare to what they will face. The British can flank this position at will, and so we must regard this line as only a temporary defense. General Montgomery will probe us, explore his options, and when he is prepared, he will do as I would do. He will find a way to drive us out of this defense. The only reason we are able to maintain our position along the Mersa el Brega line is that Montgomery has, for the moment, ceased his pursuit."

He paused, let the words sink in, saw Cavallero shake his head.

"Marshal Rommel, I am disturbed by your conclusions. Il Duce's army is quite prepared to accept any battle the enemy should bring. I cannot allow you to insult the courage of my soldiers."

"I do nothing of the sort. The Italian soldier, when properly supplied and properly led, is a match for any opponent. But there is no armor and no artillery to give him. Our best hope for the salvation of this army is to withdraw to the hills in Tunisia. I have made careful study of the maps, and I believe the lines at Mareth or Gabès are strong positions. We could hold the British at bay for some time. We must of course rely on Comando Supremo to deliver supplies and armament. Only then can we hope to attack anyone." Rommel looked at Kesselring now, the man staring down, still avoiding him.

Cavallero said, "That is outrageous, a plan for defeat, not honorable victory! Mareth . . . that is far to the west of Tripoli! You propose that we simply abandon such a great city, such a jewel in Il Duce's crown? He will not hear of such a thing, and neither will I! Italian honor is at stake here, even if yours has been debased by your mistakes!" Cavallero's voice cut through the night, and he leaned close, stared at Rommel. "Marshal Rommel, the Italian people will not hear of any plan that calls for the surrender of our territory in Libya, territory that has been gained only by the sweat of our labor. Tripoli is a symbol of all we have accomplished here. You know yourself that all across Libya this army has traveled past the ancient ruins of an empire that we all believe must surely live again. You cannot suggest that this army simply hand it over to our enemy. Even the soldiers will not allow that. They will not obey your orders to abandon the glory of Rome."

Rommel thought, they have obeyed those orders pretty well up to now. He felt the exhaustion, realized he was powerless against their stubbornness. That's what this is, he thought. Two thousand years of lost glory, a stubborn fight to capture a dream. I am serving under men who live in a world of make-believe.

Kesselring looked up now, said, "Any withdrawal of the *Panzerarmee* toward Tunisia will have dangerous consequences for our air bases west of this position, and in Tunisia itself. The British will be able to launch fighter attacks against our airfields, which we cannot prevent. Only by holding the enemy this far to the east can we keep our fields secure."

Rommel looked at his hands, rubbed his fingers together slowly. Airfields. Of course, Kesselring's precious Luftwaffe. Never mind the loss of the rest of this army. Rommel looked at Kesselring, said slowly, "What of the Americans, the British troops massing in Algeria? How long do you think it will require those forces to move into Tunisia? What will become of your airfields then?"

"It has been made clear to you that Tunisia is not your concern." Kesselring stood. "I assure you, gentlemen, we have taken appropriate steps to insure that no enemy forces shall set foot past the mountains that guard Tunisia's borders with Algeria. Even now, several regiments of German infantry and a battalion of engineers have arrived in Tunis, supported by more than a hundred of our most modern tanks and artillery. We will continue to add to these numbers as rapidly as the supplies can be transported to Tunis and the port at Bizerte. Should the enemy press forward from the west, they shall confront the power of our newest machines, most specifically the Tiger tanks."

Kesselring leaned closer to Cavallero, his enthusiasm pouring over the Italians. Kesselring crossed his arms against his chest, ignored Rommel, said, "Tiger tanks, gentlemen. No such power has yet been put onto steel tracks. The Tiger carries an eighty-eight-millimeter cannon and can absorb any punishment the Allies can offer. In a short time, Tunisia shall become a fortress, impenetrable, a deadly trap for the arrogance of the Americans and their British servants."

Rommel stood, saw the familiar grin on Kesselring's face, said, "How will you supply this fortress?"

"Those arrangements have already been undertaken. The Führer and Reichsmarschall Göring are strongly behind this strategy. The Luftwaffe is employing an all-out effort to transport every kind of equipment to strengthen our forces there. The mountains will provide much natural protection, and—"

Rommel glared at Kesselring. "All-out effort? Where are these supplies coming from? Where do we have soldiers to send to Tunisia?"

Kesselring motioned to Rommel's chair. "Please sit down. The Führer has directed that resources be diverted from our efforts against the Russians. He recognizes, as do we all, the value of Tunisia. It is the closest point to Sicily and can control the narrow straits between here and the Italian mainland."

Rommel felt sickness coming, the anger stirring, Kesselring's voice drifting over him.

"By building such a powerful bastion in North Africa, we can keep the Allied forces divided and then destroy them piecemeal. The Führer has considerable confidence that we can maintain our presence in North Africa no matter what the Allies try to accomplish. But the creation of such a fortress will require some time, which is why it is imperative that Marshal Rommel hold this line at Mersa el Brega. Montgomery's troops must be kept isolated until we are fully prepared to drive them away."

Rommel began to shiver, felt sweat on his forehead, clamped his arms tightly to his body, fought the sickness, ignored the talk, the boisterous good cheer that suddenly filled the dark room. Kesselring was speaking to Cavallero now, numbers, more words of encouragement, empty promises flowing from both men like the watery sickness Rommel held tightly inside. After long seconds, the shivering passed, and he loosened the hard grip in his fingers, relaxed his arms. Cavallero was standing, moving around the room, his hands waving in gestures of enthusiasm, Kesselring responding, laughter now.

Rommel watched them through the fog in his mind, said, "Why could you not have made this *all-out* effort months ago?"

His words were faint, the sound barely audible, drowned out by the enthusiasm of the men around him, the men who were planning the next campaign, who spoke eagerly of their great victory to come.

15. ROMMEL

It was one more Roman ruin, a grand archway that stood now on the boundary between the two halves of Libya, the dividing line between Cyrenaica and Tripolitania. They were simply names on a map, and Rommel had grown weary of maps.

He had plotted the best course for his men to follow, the best ground where the stand could still be made. The line ran from the seacoast to the north, across good rolling ground, to the great salt and sand marshes inland, a narrow passageway where even a battered army could make a strong defensive show. The line had originally been plotted by the French, a network of dugouts and blockhouses, making good use of tumbling, rocky terrain. The German engineers had told Rommel that improvements were needed, the French works too feeble to hold back modern artillery, and so Rommel had made the plan, knew that once his army could be pulled into position there, Montgomery would grow cautious once more, would scout and probe, would learn that armor could not flank the position, that the soft sands and marshes were an effective wall, just as the Qattara Depression had been at El Alamein. If Montgomery was to accomplish anything at the Mareth line, it would require weeks of planning, weeks of delay that could be the salvation of the *Panzerarmee.*

For now, Rommel still held fast at Mersa el Brega, followed the orders handed him by Kesselring, a sad echo of the wishes of armchair generals in Rome. A majority of his infantry was Italian now, so many of his foot soldiers following the commands of men like Bastico. The Germans had left too much of themselves at El Alamein, had lost more on the march westward. For two days, Rommel had waited for some hint that his plans had pierced the absurd optimism that Kesselring had poured over the Italians. The dream had exhausted Rommel, a useless fantasy that good strategy would somehow find an ear among men who found far more pleasure toasting imaginary victories in their grand villas in Rome.

He stared up at the arch, knew little of the history, only the name, the Arco dei Fileni. It was yet another symbol of a glorious empire that had collapsed into the dust of this desolate place. What armies have you seen? he thought. How many generals have passed beneath you, expecting their accomplishments to stand like this, a monument to history? How many of them considered destroying you, replacing you with their own archway, their own trophy? And where are they now? He scanned the village, saw movement along every small alleyway, soldiers and staff officers performing some duty. The village provided him his first solid roof in months of desert fighting, a headquarters in an actual house, a bed that gave him the extraordinary luxury of a night's sleep. It was the kind of comfort that he had hoped to find in Cairo. Now, he would settle for what he could find along the retreat, a brief rest in a place none of his officers believed they could hold for long.

He felt a pang of hunger, unusual, caught the smell of meat from somewhere in the village, a wisp of gray smoke rising behind a white block house. He moved that way, glanced toward his driver, who stood ready beside the truck. Rommel held up his hand, *stay here,* moved toward the smoke. He rounded the building, saw a cluster of six men, German soldiers, squatting close to a fire. They stood abruptly, at stiff attention, and he moved closer to their makeshift stove.

"What is this?"

"Gazelle, sir."

"Which one of you shot it?"

One man raised his hand. "Sergeant Haller, sir."

"Range?"

The man seemed surprised at the question. "Three hundred meters, sir. I stepped it off."

Rommel nodded, still stared at the meat, small bubbles of grease oozing, crackling into the fire, flies darting through the heat.

"Fine shooting, Sergeant. I have hunted the gazelle here. Some time ago now. More than a year. It is a challenge . . . unless of course one has a machine gun. They do wander into the minefields occasionally."

One of the others spoke, still at hard attention. "We offer this to the field marshal as our gift, sir. Would you honor us by taking our dinner for yourself?"

"No, I will not. You killed it, it belongs to you. Perhaps a small piece, though . . ."

The man was down quickly, a quick slice with a bayonet, the slab of steaming meat dropped onto a tin plate. The man stood stiffly again, handed the plate to Rommel.

"Thank you for sharing this, Field Marshal."

Rommel couldn't smile, looked at the faces, the eyes glancing at him, then away. They were hard men, thin and haggard, their uniforms ripped and worn through. Rommel made a short bow, said, "Enjoy your feast. But eat it quickly. Every insect in Libya will come to your smoke."

He turned, moved away, held the plate in front of his face, breathed in the steam. Behind him, the sergeant said, *"Heil Hitler!"*

Rommel stopped, heard the others repeat the words, the familiar salute. He looked down at the slab of meat, felt the chill returning, the hole in his gut closing up. He spun slowly around, moved toward them, ignored their surprise, handed the plate to one of the men.

"Thank you. But this is yours. The Führer rewards courage . . . and loyalty."

He wanted to say more, but his caution held him back. It was no time for loose talk, for any show of anger. He moved away from them again, their silence behind him, thought, no matter what this fight has done to me, these men are not defeated. It is still up to me to put them into a good fight.

He turned past the stone building, moved toward the truck, heard another truck in the distance, a cloud of dust, saw Westphal standing tall, waving toward him. Another man was riding low, the familiar hat of the Italian officers. Bastico. Rommel stepped forward slowly, said nothing, saw Bastico watching him with grim discomfort.

Bastico said, "Marshal Rommel, it is good to see you again. May we retire to your headquarters? I have orders for you."

Bastico seemed nervous, paced the room, his hands clamped behind him. Rommel pointed toward the door, the order to Westphal to leave, the young man exiting, the door pulled tightly shut.

Rommel was impatient now. "There is no need for diplomacy. What am I expected to do? Have they at least considered my plans?"

Bastico stopped, took a long breath. "I do not wish to argue this with you, Herr Rommel. The orders I carry are explicit. Il Duce himself conveys to you his most serious desire that you hold this line at Mersa el Brega at all costs. You are not to retreat unless ordered to do so. Marshal Kesselring will be contacting you on a separate matter, to discuss sending some of your forces westward to strengthen our fortifications at Tripoli."

Rommel sat down, rested his arms on the wooden table, tapped firmly with his fingertips. His mind raced with replies, the urge to laugh in this man's face, or better, to throw a bayonet into the man's chest. Yes, you know how idiotic this is too. You just don't have the courage to say so.

"I suppose Il Duce also desires that I plan a renewed attack against the British."

Bastico looked at him wide-eyed, seemed relieved that Rommel had said the words first. "Yes! That is correct! I have been assured that the Luftwaffe will add considerable air support to any plan you propose."

Rommel sat back in the chair. "Have you not heard those promises before?"

Bastico stiffened again. "I do not question the orders from Comando Supremo."

"No, I am quite certain you do not. Am I being promised any more support? A division of fresh troops? Tiger tanks? Or is all that being preserved for our great fortress in Tunisia?"

"I do not respect your attitude toward our superiors, Herr Rommel. There is one more order that I must convey to you. Marshal Cavallero has decreed that should this position become untenable, should the Mersa el Brega line be overrun by an overwhelming attack by our enemies, no one is authorized to issue any order to retreat . . . except me. That authority is mine alone, and I assure you, Herr Rommel, I do not intend to exercise that authority."

"Then I assume I will find you on the front lines, so that you may decide for yourself when the enemy is overwhelming us. Excuse me, Marshal Bastico."

He moved past the man, pulled the door open, ignored the staff officers outside, Westphal, waiting for some instructions. The sunlight blinded him and he stared ahead at the emptiness on the horizon, the vast open lands to the south. He felt like walking, seeing the desert again, but more, taking a straight, unstoppable course through the rocky hills, then down into the great sand seas, leaving the men like Bastico behind him.

But not the army. I cannot leave the army to men like that, to officers who cannot learn anything from the butchering of so many good men. For so long, I have found a way to ignore the ridiculous orders, the deadly mistakes made by officers who are simply worthless bureaucrats, governing the war from comfortable chairs. It is those men who advise Hitler, but Hitler does not always listen, and so, when their advice displeases him, the strategies and decisions come from the Führer alone. But even the Führer cannot force the inept and incompetent to perform their duty. Even if he accepted our condition here, even if he could be made to understand what it will take to *win* here . . . no, that is a dream from which I have already awakened. I cannot even speculate how different it might have been here. My superiors issue the orders and I am to obey them. And their stupidity has cost us a magnificent army. Since El Alamein, I have understood that Hitler does not care to hear from anyone who does not simply hand him victories. But even the Führer is not infallible. And if I am to remain a soldier, I cannot disobey the Führer.

Westphal was there now, said, "Sir, Marshal Bastico has asked for his vehicle. Is there anything else you wish to discuss with him?"

Rommel looked at the younger man, put a hand on his shoulder, felt the man's strength, the power of his loyalty.

"I have nothing further to say to Field Marshal Bastico. I want you to issue orders to the nearest airfield, to whatever officer Kesselring has placed in charge of the transport planes."

"Are you traveling somewhere, sir?"

"Quite so, Colonel. I'm going to see the Führer."

RASTENBURG, GERMANY—NOVEMBER 28, 1942

They met with him in a small office, devoid of maps, of any signs of the war. He knew not to waste his energy on these men, Keitel, Jodl, Schmundt, the very officers who despised him for his accomplishments. They still smiled at him, spoke in genial pleasantries. But he knew that when he left, the knives would come out, as they had always come out, the small men in over-size uniforms doing all they could to counter the image Goebbels had created for Rommel, the image that had found so much favor with the German people. Rommel understood the game now, knew that he was simply a tool, that his name and the image of his weather-beaten face, standing high on a mighty tank, were something to inspire the people. Goebbels's broadcasts still spoke of triumph in North Africa, a poor mask for the truth that seeped across the borders to the south. And so, the men whose hands were never soiled, who never led troops, who never saw the enemy, kept to their offices and plotted the ways to bring this hero to his knees.

He sat quietly, staring out at gray skies and bare tree limbs.

"Sir, the Führer wishes to see you. You will come immediately."

He rose slowly, pushed through the stiffness, the small pains so much a part of him now. The officer led him through another office, pulled open a door, revealing a large, square room, officers standing on either end of long map table, and between them, in a gray uniform, Adolf Hitler.

No one spoke, Hitler staring at the map, pointing.

"Here. Paulus should hold here. He will hold here. There will be a breakthrough along this line within a week." Hitler looked up at Rommel, no smile, no sign of recognition. "Stalingrad will fall before the New Year."

Rommel stepped forward slowly, stood at attention across the map table from Hitler, waited, knew there was nothing yet he could say. Hitler studied the maps again, then stood back, raised his eyes, studied him.

"Are you well, Field Marshal?"

"Quite so, my Führer."

"So then, what are you doing *here*?"

"I wish to report on conditions in North Africa, on the position of our troops, and what I believe to be the correct course of action. I believe you are not being provided with completely accurate information, and I wish to correct that, if you will allow."

There was silence in the room, and Hitler said, "Continue."

Rommel glanced down, the maps of Russia, red circles, scribbled lines. "May I ask . . . if there is a map of our position in Libya?"

Hitler glanced to the side. "Retrieve the map for the field marshal."

Men moved quickly, rolls of paper appearing, the maps spreading out, facing Hitler. Rommel saw no red circles, no marks of any kind. He leaned close, searched for the names, the borders, his weak eyes straining. Hitler reached down, put a hand on the map, spun it around.

"Do you require maps to give your report, Marshal Rommel? I would think you would know your own theater of activity."

There was ice in Hitler's voice, and Rommel straightened. "I do not require maps, sir. It should suffice . . . I wish to report that I do not believe adequate supplies of men and equipment are reaching the *Panzerarmee*. I do not believe a defensive posture in Tunisia can survive for long if pressed by two separate Allied armies. I do not believe the shipping situation will improve, and we have already strained our supply lines past their breaking point. We can neither fuel nor equip the *Panzerarmee*, and both are required to restore us to fighting strength. I do not anticipate those supply situations to change. Thus, I believe that the only sound strategy is to withdraw the *Panzerarmee* into Tunisia, where we can hold off the enemy for sufficient time to allow . . . the evacuation of the remains of that army into France or Italy. We must have no illusion about what can be accomplished with the resources we can provide for. If the *Panzerarmee* remains in North Africa, it will be destroyed."

He stopped, heard no other sound, no one breathing. The

words had come out in a flood of indiscreet honesty, and he braced himself, knew it was an enormous risk.

Hitler squinted at him. "You would evacuate our stronghold in North Africa? You would surrender all that we have gained? Why? *So that you might escape the unpleasantness of war?*"

Hitler's voice was booming, and he slapped the table, leaned toward Rommel, shouted, "Cowards! You run away from an inferior enemy! You abandon your equipment and then cry that you need more! Destroyed? You were given command of the finest army in the world, and you destroyed it yourself! I am surrounded by incompetent commanders, by men who hide from duty, who find every excuse for failure! You dare to march into my sanctuary and parade yourself as a leader of your army? You should be broken down to sergeant, sent to face your enemy with a rifle in your hand! That will show you what kind of courage it takes to be a soldier!"

Hitler seemed to tire, turned away, and Rommel glanced at the others, saw nods, every man in the room scowling toward him, repeating Hitler's tirade in perfect silent mimicry. Rommel felt the burning in his skin, held the anger, tried to calm himself. He spoke slowly, in a soft voice.

"I wish to report that of the fifteen thousand men of the Afrika Korps under my command, nearly two-thirds do not possess adequate weapons. The artillery we lost both during the fighting at El Alamein, and along the retreat westward—"

Hitler spun toward him, pointed a finger toward him, shouted again. "Yes! You see? Cowards! Your men toss their weapons to the roadside in the face of the enemy! I have heard such stories! Who do you blame for this? The Luftwaffe? The Italian navy? I have instructed all of our supply departments to provide for you, and still you speak of failure and loss. I have promised you every advantage, the best artillery, the finest armor, I have given you the best fighting soldiers in the world! And you tell me that they have thrown down their weapons?"

Rommel felt something inside him break, the caution weakened by so much sickness, so much anxiety.

"That is not the case, my Führer. It is not possible for anyone in this room to know what our situation is in North Africa. No one here has faced the British in battle, no one has seen our planes swept from the sky. No one has witnessed a thousand artillery pieces raining fire on our positions. We survived our defeats and our withdrawal not because anyone provided us fuel and supplies, but because the courage of the German soldier held us together. I do not wish to see this valiant army swept away, wasted by the ineptness of our allies, or the unwillingness of your commanders to provide for us. Surely you do not wish it as well. There is still much to be gained in North Africa if we are given the means. But those means have never been given to us. With all respect . . . there is no cowardice in the *Panzerarmee*."

Hitler seemed to calm, slid the map off the table, focused again on the map of Russia.

"There is nothing to be gained by abandoning North Africa. I will not betray our Italian allies by handing their territory to the enemy. You will hold the Mersa el Brega line, to allow time for our bridgehead in Tunisia to be complete. If there is difficulty with supplies . . ." Hitler looked at Rommel now, nodded. "Yes, excellent idea. You shall accompany Reichsmarschall Göring to Rome. If there is a problem with supplies, the *Reichsmarschall* shall carry my direct authority to solve those problems. He has been seeking such a trip. This will be pleasing to him. Come."

Hitler moved out from the table, put an arm across Rommel's shoulders. They moved out of the large room, through the small office, reached the dark corridor, and Hitler stopped, turned toward him.

"You are suffering great strain from this campaign. It is difficult, I know that. We are fighting many enemies, you and I, enemies beyond our borders, and enemies close to home. All will be well. In time every threat to the Reich will be eradicated. Even now . . ." Hitler stopped, patted Rommel's back. "Tunisia shall be an impregnable fortress, and the British cannot sustain their attacks. Their people grow weary of this, they do not have the stomach for death."

Rommel had seen this before, the stark anger suddenly gone, replaced by this odd warmth.

"But what of the Americans? Can Tunisia withstand pressure from two fronts? In front of my army, the British grow stronger every day. In Algeria, the Americans—"

Hitler laughed, slapped Rommel's arm. "The Americans are incapable of making war. I would have thought you understood that. They are a mongrel race, who whine and preen like rich babies. They make sewing machines and paper clips, while, in our factories, we make machines of war. There is no need to fear anyone, Field Marshal, certainly not the Americans. It is not our enemies who can sustain this war, who have the means and the heart for victory. It is *us*."

MUNICH, GERMANY—NOVEMBER 29, 1942

The hotel was small, the rooms dark and cold, none of that in his thoughts. He saw only her, the smile, the sad face of a woman who has lost her husband to the war.

"But I have returned."

"For a while."

"It is all I have right now. I'm not supposed to be here at all. The Führer went to some lengths to remind me of that."

She held out her hand, and he took it, pulled her close, wrapped both arms tightly around her shoulders. She relaxed against him.

"I did not forget our wedding anniversary. Two days ago. I wrote you a letter." He held her away, reached into a pocket, pulled out a folded paper. "See?"

She laughed, took the paper. "I truly look forward to your letters, Erwin. All of them. I wish you could tell me of things that were pleasant. I thought, when you first left for Tripoli . . . I should like to visit Africa someday."

The smiles were gone, and he pulled her gently by the hand, led her to the bed.

"When this is over, I will never go back there. It has cost me too much, too many graves of men I knew. A grave for me as well."

She made a sound, and he looked at her, shook his head.

"No, I didn't mean . . . I have no desire . . . oh, damn. I have spoken too often these days, too many indiscreet words. I find myself in trouble with everyone who has any authority over me: Kesselring, the Italians, Hitler. Now . . . you."

"It is good you know who your superiors are." She laughed. "Do we really have to travel with that horrible man?"

"Göring? Yes, I'm afraid. That's the only condition I could arrange for you to visit. We will travel with the *Reichsmarschall* as his guest. His private train is supposed to be something quite spectacular. It fits the man, I suppose. Larger-than-life. Certainly larger than this war."

He sat on the bed beside her and she said, "What do you mean?"

"Hermann Göring has his eye firmly planted on the future, a world with one man at the top."

"Hitler."

He shook his head. "No. Göring. Hitler adores him, I believe, but Göring shares no one's dreams, holds loyalty to the Führer because it suits his purposes. He sees opportunity in this war, nothing more. If I were Hitler, I would not trust him, I would notice how Göring decorates himself, the large, fat man with the large, fat medals. He has more medals than Mussolini. That train, all the opulence, and for what? Why does the head of the Luftwaffe need a train at all?"

"I have heard things."

He saw a frown, leaned close. "What sort of things?"

Lucy lowered her voice. "Göring is looting the museums, stealing artwork, rare antiques. When he comes to anyone's town, the jewelry must be hidden. If he sees something that strikes his eye, he simply takes it. Including . . . women."

Rommel looked down, knew that Lucy's intuitions about rumors were most always accurate.

"I am not surprised. That would certainly explain the train, those railcars. Power and money both. That makes him more formidable than Hitler. The Führer fights for his own view of the world, for what Germany must do to protect herself. He cares little for . . . *booty*."

She was silent, and he thought of the train ride, Göring expected to accompany him to see Mussolini, Cavallero, the rest of them. Kesselring will be there, certainly, he thought. This could be my last chance, the final opportunity I will have to convince the Italians. If they agree with Hitler and insist on remaining in North Africa, I must be allowed to withdraw from Libya, give up Tripoli, and rebuild the army in Tunisia. If they do not agree, then for me, this war is over. Surely Berndt will help. He is persuasive, knows how to talk to the Italians. I most certainly do not.

"I have heard other things, Erwin." Her words were soft, low, brought him back to the small room. "Everywhere I have been there is talk that something has happened to the Jews."

"The Jews? What do you mean?"

"They are being taken away, Erwin. In the square, Mr. Wiesel, the jeweler, his entire family, suddenly gone. Mrs. Blum and her sister . . . I have heard too many stories, the same thing in every town, all the Jewish merchants are suddenly gone, their shops boarded up. The synagogues have been shut up as well and some of them have been burned to the ground."

He had heard some stories of the Jews being relocated, had paid little attention to something that seemed so far removed from the war. "Yes, I have heard something about a relocation program, that settlements are being created, moving the Jews to their own communities where they will be safe."

She stared at him with black eyes, a hard glare that cut off his words. "*Safe? From what?* Erwin, do not be naïve. I have heard talk of railcars filled with people who are being taken to concentration camps. People are talking about it everywhere. No one dares to speak out, or even to inquire, because they fear the Gestapo."

"Lu, that's ridiculous. What they're seeing are railcars filled with prisoners of war. We have captured thousands of enemy troops. If there are prison camps, it's for the foreign soldiers. We have no enemies within our own borders."

"I wish I could believe you, Erwin. But there are too many others who say something very different. It is not foreigners, it is German citizens who are being taken away from their homes. People are simply disappearing."

He suddenly recalled the words. "The Führer did say something about . . . 'enemies close to home.' But the Jews? What threat are they?"

"I suppose, my husband, you should ask that of your Führer."

*   *   *

In early December, Rommel accomplished his mission, finally persuading both Göring and the Italians that western Libya could no longer be held. The tip of his sword was the keen political persuasion of Lieutenant Berndt, who danced the perfect tune between German military interests and Italian pride. The ultimate plum for Mussolini was the assurance that the loss of Libya would be offset by the conquest of French-held Tunisia, land the Germans would graciously allow the Italians to claim as their own colony. For most of the discussions, Rommel remained silent, fully aware that no one valued his opinions, and that his own sharp impatience would likely alienate everyone involved.

Rommel understood that Mussolini's need to save honor by holding the valuable port of Tripoli had to be balanced in other ways, ways that could be digested by the increasingly unhappy Italians who gave Il Duce his power. The argument became simple. Defending Tripoli against Montgomery's overwhelming forces would result in the near certain death or capture of Rommel's remaining Italian infantry, some twenty-five thousand men. Preserving those men would have a far greater emotional impact on the Italian people than the flutter of an Italian flag over a port city few of them had ever seen.

Through it all, Montgomery advanced, meticulous, cautious, until finally, in early December, he was ready to press his attack. At the first sign of the British flanking move against the line at Mersa el Brega, Rommel put his own troops in motion and began the rapid withdrawal to the defensive line of his own choosing, the stout barrier at Mareth. Once more, Montgomery could only follow.

As Rommel secured his position in the south, in northern Tunisia, German reinforcements continued to pour in, heavy artillery and the newest armor, men and machines gathering along the steep hills, pushing outposts westward into the passes of the Atlas Mountains. Farther west, Eisenhower's forces were on the march, British paratroopers and commandos leading the way. But the delays caused by so much confusion in the French hierarchy had been costly to the Allies. As the Allied armies moved toward their ultimate objective, gathering the strength and momentum they would need to drive the enemy out of Tunisia, that enemy was growing stronger day by day.

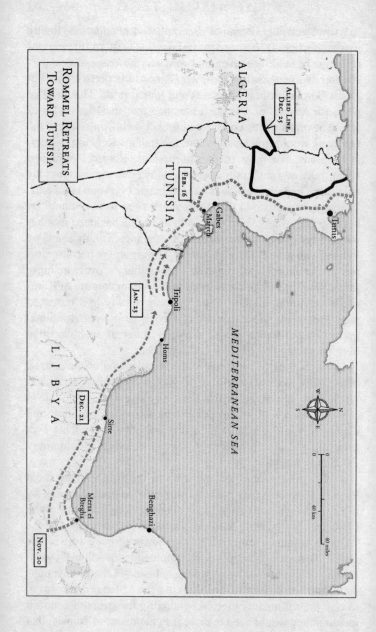

ROMMEL RETREATS
TOWARD TUNISIA

ALGERIA

ALLIED LINE,
DEC. 25

TUNISIA

FEB. 16

Gabes
March

Tunis

JAN. 23

Tripoli

Homs

L I B Y A

DEC. 21

Sirte

MEDITERRANEAN SEA

Mersa el
Brega

Benghazi

NOV. 20

N

W   E

S

0

40 km

40 miles

Göring and Kesselring had engineered command changes in Tunisia that stripped away most of Rommel's authority, placing a veteran of the Russian campaigns, General Hans Juergen von Arnim, in command of the overall Tunisian theater. Though Rommel had now to answer to von Arnim, he still commanded his *Panzerarmee*. Despite their disgust for Rommel's insubordination and unorthodox methods, the German High Command had to agree with Rommel's instincts, could not ignore the new opportunity that Rommel forced them to see. The only effective way to confront the Allied armies was piecemeal, one at a time. With Montgomery held at bay east of the Mareth line, Rommel turned his attentions to the north and west. To the north, a strong British column under General Kenneth Anderson was advancing parallel to the sea, pressing closer to the strongholds manned by a well-prepared body of German troops and artillery. Farther to the south, the Allies advanced as well, the southern wing of Eisenhower's army, a combination of French and American troops. The Americans marched with confidence, fresh from their overwhelming victories in Morocco and Algeria. It was a confidence Rommel was counting on.

16. EISENHOWER

ALGIERS
DECEMBER 1942

His headquarters had been established at the St. George Hotel, what had once been a luxurious suite of three rooms. There had always been some form of luxury in Algiers, a land prized by Phoenicians and Romans, Spaniards and Barbary pirates. For more than a century, the luxury in Algiers had had a French touch, trade and recreation strengthening the city's allure for French businessmen and wealthy vacationers. But the war had brought shortages, the energy of the city drained by Vichy uncertainty, leaving a tenuous back door to Nazi and Italian ambitions to the east. And, just as quickly, the Allies brought change again, the city suddenly bursting with American and British fighting men and all those who supported an army.

Eisenhower had moved his headquarters here on November 23, the entire staff happy to be free of the damp caves of Gibraltar. But Algiers was yet no safe haven, and despite the effort to secure the city as a major hub of command and supply activity, the antiaircraft batteries were inadequate. And so, the bombers came, nightly raids that rattled the windows and sent the populace into terrified hiding. To Eisenhower, the raids were far more than a frightening annoyance. It was a symbol that despite all the talk of victory, a war was still being fought in Algeria. Any thoughts of a simple and rapid conquest of Tunisia were being blown to rubble.

The carefully worded agreement with Admiral Darlan had brought an immediate consequence Eisenhower had not predicted. All across England and America, newspapers began to hammer away with outrage, pouring out editorials that blasted Eisenhower for dealing with "the Nazi devil." If the civilian population back home had known anything of Darlan at all, it was only through his association with Pétain and Vichy, a clearly defined role as Nazi collaborator. Now, the newspapers painted a portrait of a hapless Eisenhower standing beside him. But the critics could not sway their civilian leaders. Eisenhower had gone to enormous lengths to explain the Darlan arrangement to both Churchill and Roosevelt, and though both men had publicly responded with "caution," privately they issued Eisenhower strong letters of support for his judgment. Those who mattered seemed to understand that in the field, political matters are never as simple as they appear from thousands of miles away.

The Darlan deal was certainly not perfect, and problems persisted among various parts of the North African population, French or not. The Vichy French officials had made no secret of their disregard for the Jewish populations in the region, and various civic laws discriminated against Jews in the management of their own affairs, as well as in their various freedoms. But now, French leaders, including Darlan himself, were facing pressure from British and American government officials to liberalize their laws, so that there would be little resemblance to the German ways of doing things. Though many of the local French officials responded to Darlan, some did not, some holding tightly to an unshakable loyalty to Marshal Pétain. It seemed not to matter that their towns were now encampments for Allied soldiers. From Casablanca to Algiers, Darlan's subordinates made indiscreet noise that the only way to actually control the civilian population was to put the muscle of the American military behind the command of the civilian governments. To Eisenhower that meant an army of occupation, something no one had planned for. Despite the swirl of controversy around Darlan and the wildly differing levels of loyalty from those beneath him, Eisenhower had neither the manpower, the inclination, nor the orders to even consider creating a military government in North Africa.

"I don't understand the French."

Murphy nodded, rubbed his chin, pondered the words. "Well, sir, it's like this. The French want to be seen in the best light. They want history to hold them in the highest esteem, want to salute their heroes as the men who profoundly affected history. They want to win the wars, and if they can't actually do that, they at least want to be listed on the winning side."

Eisenhower waited for more, but the diplomat seemed unconvinced by his own explanation.

"So, you don't understand them either. Tell me, Robert, when was the last time they won a war?"

"Yes, sir, I know my history. At least, it seems we can depend on them to help us win this one."

Eisenhower stared out the window, rain falling in hard sheets, the streets below crowded with dark green vehicles, clusters of European cars, donkey carts, an unending stream of men pulling small wagons filled with . . . something. With what? Whatever they're carrying, it's wet. He shivered, turned toward the small fireplace. It was his single greatest luxury in a hotel that had once offered a great deal more.

"I'm cold all the damned time. Where the hell my staff finds this wood is a mystery. No way anything in this whole country will burn." He held up his hands to catch the warmth, studied the charred firewood. "Furniture, probably."

He looked at Murphy again. "I hope you're right. We need them to fight. We need them to help control the Arabs in Tunisia. Hell, it's their land, you'd think they'd be happy to fight for it."

"Who, sir? The French or the Arabs?"

"I'm talking about the French. Well, hell, I guess I could be talking about the Arabs too. But the Arabs don't seem to care whether or not they *own* anything. They'll take whatever you have to give them, or whatever they can steal, but then, they don't seem to care who's in charge. Maybe we're just fooling ourselves. Maybe they're in charge after all. They'll make friends with whoever wins this war."

Murphy still rubbed his chin. "Just as the French will."

"I'm awfully tired of hearing how the French made a half-assed effort against us, and now that they're on our side, we can probably expect them to do the same against the Krauts. They fought like hell while they had the chance."

"They'll still fight, sir. They're motivated, enthusiastic about getting the Germans out of Tunisia. Admiral Darlan assures me that they will do the job. They're already organizing in Oran, putting their people into the field. So I've been told."

Eisenhower studied Murphy's face, thought, you have no idea what you're talking about, do you? He couldn't be angry with Murphy, knew the man was making his best effort in a role where a diplomat's efforts now meant very little.

For the most part the French military was responding as Eisenhower had hoped, organizing and mobilizing units to march eastward, to join in with the beleaguered French forces already in Tunisia. Those troops had manned outposts that had seen no fighting at all, had grown complacent, confident that the war might avoid them altogether. Suddenly, they had been confronted with waves of German transport planes, heavy guns and tanks, and massive numbers of German soldiers. Many of the French commanders there were pro-Vichy, but the Germans pushed them aside as though they were of no consequence. The Germans were now in control of Tunisia, and in both Algeria and Tunisia, the French officers seemed to understand what many of their civilian officials did not: political chest beating is a poor defense against tanks and artillery. No matter how confused their senior officers seemed to be, how shaky their loyalty to whatever regime happened to be convenient, the French soldiers seemed far more inclined to fight alongside the Allies. No one in a French uniform had much affection for the Germans, especially now. Hitler had responded to news of the Allied invasion of North Africa by tossing out his agreement with Pétain's Vichy government, the agreement that called for the southern half of France to remain free of Nazi occupation. In November, the Germans trampled the meaningless boundary between occupied France to the north and the Vichy-controlled territory that stretched to the French Riviera, pushing armies of occupation all the way to the seaports on the Mediterranean. Anyone who held to the illusion that Vichy was somehow free of direct Nazi control reacted with outrage, as though the fragile and increasingly senile Marshal Henri Pétain had ever really had any influence with Adolf Hitler.

Eisenhower knew the reality. Even had the French tried to keep the Germans out of Tunisia, their troops there were only a skeleton force, equipped with none of the heavy armament necessary to keep the Germans from grabbing every major port, airfield, and defensive position in that country. Worse, should the Germans make a strong move westward, no French unit in place along the mountain ranges could hope to hold them back. The only way to counter German superiority was to strike first, before the Germans were fully prepared.

But then, Eisenhower learned something new about North Africa. The planners of Operation Torch had been aware that December brought the rainy season. But the planners had never seen just what the rain would do to the roads, and worse, what would happen to the hard-packed dirt runways and tarmacs of the Algerian airfields. Allied aircraft were a key part of the strategy that called for punching holes in the German artillery defenses, as well as keeping German dive-bombers out of the air. As the rains intensified, so too did the mud, especially on the flat ground that housed the Allied airfields. In Tunisia, the key German-held airfields had paved runways and hard graveled roadways, and German airpower was backed up by the fields in Sicily and Sardinia. In Algeria, the runways and taxiways began to grow soft, and as precious days passed, the Allied pilots watched helplessly as their planes simply sank into deepening mud.

"They're coming out of Sicily as well, all night long. We can send a few fighters at them, carrier-based mostly, but at night, well, we simply can't shoot what we cannot see."

Eisenhower glanced at Doolittle, who kept silent, had nothing to add that would make Eisenhower feel any less angry. Eisenhower waited for Tedder to say more, but the man stared ahead, waited for what they all expected to be an explosion.

He had enormous respect for Arthur Tedder, Britain's air commander. Tedder was expected by all to become Eisenhower's senior deputy for the combined air forces, a position Admiral Cunningham had filled with the naval arm. The inclusion of British senior officers was a logical plan, giving Eisenhower key aides that would give the army a truly "allied" flavor. It didn't hurt that Eisenhower was confident they were the best men for the job. Jimmy Doolittle was Tedder's subordinate, head of the American Twelfth Air Force, and was already a certified American war hero. Colonel Doolittle had received a Medal of Honor and a promotion to brigadier general after his extraordinary raid over several Japanese cities, including Tokyo, early in 1942. The raid was far more symbolic than any kind of strategic victory, inspiring a much needed morale boost in America, and shaming the Japanese commanders who'd allowed a force of sixteen B-25 bombers to reach the Japanese homeland. Now, Doolittle had accepted his role as subordinate to Air Marshal Tedder, a role that at the moment was an advantage. Eisenhower's wrath would be directed past him, right toward Tedder.

Eisenhower composed himself, had read the reports, the same complaints coming from the ground and sea forces, the utter lack of cooperation between them. But that would wait for now. Eisenhower had received one more report, a piece of paper he held in his hand. He stared at it, said, "Marshal Tedder, would you please explain to me the new technology your planes are supposed to be equipped with? Something about *night radar*?"

Tedder cleared his throat, still stared straight ahead. "Yes, well, quite so. A new form of radar, said to be a true marvel at locating enemy aircraft at night. Quite remarkable achievement for our engineers."

"So, apparently it doesn't work? It says here we are still unable to track or shoot down enemy planes at night. Doesn't sound like much of a *marvel* to me."

Tedder's expression did not change. "It has come to my attention, sir, that someone down the chain of command has decided that this new technology is so valuable that risking its use in combat might cause a serious problem for us. If, for example, one of our planes, so equipped, was to be shot down, the instrument could fall into enemy hands."

"Are you telling me that this instrument is so valuable, we dare not use it? Should we simply place it in a museum?"

"I assure you, sir, the person who made this regrettable decision has been advised to correct his stance on the matter. I am quite aware that it does us little good to invent all manner of superior machines if we are too afraid to use them in combat. Much like keeping your horse in the barn and walking to town, so the horse doesn't get used up. Is that an appropriate analogy, sir?"

Eisenhower realized that Tedder was presuming him to be a cowboy.

"Close enough. I'm glad you took care of the matter." He felt himself calming, could not stay angry for long, had to accept that if Tedder said the problem was solved, it was solved. "I must conclude this meeting. Admiral Cunningham is due here, and after that, it's time to appoint General Clark to his new command." Eisenhower looked at both men, saw the confidence, crisp salutes.

"Hang on. Before you leave . . ." He thought a moment. "Keep up the good work, gentlemen. I need every good officer I can find. I can't speak for your people back home, Marshal, but General Doolittle is very aware that in America, people are wondering what's taking us so damned long. The newspapers fuel this damned impatience, this idiotic notion that all we have to do to take hold of a place like this is shoot up a few people, then gather all the French, the Arabs, and the Jews, sit them down in their own congress, set up an election, and that's it. War over. Have a damned parade down Main Street."

Tedder seemed to loosen, his shoulders sagging. He leaned forward, put his hand on the back of a chair, smiled. "The advantage of rank, sir, is that you can cure the blind stupidity in your own command. You find it, you simply order it away, send someone home, replace an imbecile with someone who can do the job. I often regret that we cannot so easily replace the civilians."

Doolittle chuckled, and Eisenhower smiled, said, "But they can sure as hell replace us. Part of this job is tap-dancing around political minefields. Sometimes I think I should reassign myself. Put myself in charge of an infantry battalion and go find a bullet battle. Be much damned simpler. Now, get out of here. Too many meetings already today, and more to come."

Doolittle hesitated, allowing Tedder to leave before him, the room empty now.

There were soft sounds from the fireplace, and Eisenhower looked toward the window, the day ending, dark gray clouds hovering low over the city. One more day, he thought, one more problem, one more tantrum. It wasn't really a tantrum, of course. He didn't scream at them, kept the anger and the frustration inside mostly, and by now, every aide, every officer who stood face-to-face with Eisenhower, knew that a dressing-down was likely to be tense and subdued, none of the brash profanity of a man like Patton, or the hot sarcasm from Clark. Eisenhower had practiced holding his words, staying calm. He had read much about Robert E. Lee, a haggard man facing crisis after crisis with aplomb and dignity. Eisenhower rarely felt dignified, that trait of the aristocrat, but the job he was now doing required control, both of men and his own emotions. Getting everybody mad at you is no way to run an army, he thought. But there is always something, some little stream of stupidity flowing through everything we do. Even the best officers cannot dictate perfection to the men beneath them, and we must delegate, give responsibility to the men trained to handle it. And sometimes they screw up. But if they do it right, well, then, dammit, they deserve a pat on the back.

It was a sore point with Eisenhower now, a scolding Marshall had sent him. The newspapers seemed willing to jump on any glimpse of Eisenhower's failures, and Marshall had responded to some editorial that claimed that Eisenhower wasn't truly in charge, showed weakness as a leader because his subordinates were allowed to take credit for their accomplishments. Marshall's admonition instructed Eisenhower to take more credit for himself, to speak out to the reporters, so they would know how strong a commander he truly was. Marshall should know better, Eisenhower thought, allowing himself to be pressured by some damned columnist. I don't really believe that Tedder or Alexander or Cunningham or Clark would appreciate it if I marched up to the front of every briefing and announced how damned brilliant I am. Let's get the job done, then worry later who gets the damned prizes.

He opened a drawer, looked at the letter, the promotion that had become official for Clark. Three stars. Lieutenant general. Yep, that's a prize. There'll be a bunch more stars flung around this office before this is over with. If we win.

ALGIERS—DECEMBER 10, 1942

It was Patton, in full glory.

"They talk too damned much. Always have. Roundtable discussions about what the hell they should do next. Some of those tall-brass boys should be handed a rifle and sent out into the damned mud."

There was silence, the others glancing down, uncomfortable with Patton's words. Eisenhower slid his fork slowly onto the white china surface, spread the film of gravy, then dropped the fork with a clatter, pushed his plate away.

"As you know, gentlemen, General Patton has sought, and I have granted, permission for him to tour General Anderson's position. I asked General Patton to give me a report on conditions there, to see if we could push a little harder in our objectives."

"We've lost the race, Ike. There's no other way to put it."

"Thank you, George. Yes, I agree that the enemy has made serious work of blocking our advance. General Anderson has engaged the enemy at several points near the seacoast, without success."

"Dammit, Ike, the Brits . . . they seem to favor holding low ground, leaving the high ground to the enemy. They set up defensive positions in front of rivers instead of behind them. They don't support their tanks with armored infantry. The communication lines are a mess, no one talking to anyone . . . except over a damned cup of tea."

Patton scanned the room now, focused on the British officers. "No offense intended."

Eisenhower let out a long breath. "Did you offer these observations to General Anderson?"

"Damned right. He agreed with me. Said they'd discuss it. *Discuss* it. He mentioned that Wayne suggested the British stop using American units as gap-pluggers. He agreed with that too. More discussions to follow, no doubt."

Eisenhower grabbed the opportunity to turn the talk toward Clark. "What of it, Wayne?"

Clark leaned forward, had been enduring Patton's outrage with silent stoicism. "General Anderson says that as we send more American units to the front, he expects them to become a separate command, under an American commander. He was most cooperative about that."

Patton slapped a heavy hand on the table. "Well, good, then, dammit. Time we showed our allies what we can do. And not against the damned French."

Clark continued, "As we all know, General Anderson had scheduled a major advance against German positions to begin this week. But weather has delayed that. He believes our push can begin on December twenty-fourth."

Eisenhower scanned the faces, then looked at Clark. "Do you?"

Clark shrugged, an unusual response, and Eisenhower saw weariness, Clark glancing toward Patton as though he expected some comment.

Patton said, "Never happen, Ike. It's a mess up there. We need our people in place, with all the armor we can give them. We have too damned many people sitting on their butts in Casablanca, when they could be up there lending a hand."

Eisenhower pushed at his plate again, thought, not now, George. This isn't the time.

"Thank you for dining with me, gentlemen. I appreciate your reports. We all know what has to happen here, and I expect each of you to tackle your objectives. If you will excuse me, I have work to do. George, you mind staying awhile?"

The others stood, and Eisenhower could feel relief in the air, the usual response when Patton had rolled over them with the energy designed to blister someone.

Clark stood beside Eisenhower, said, "Should I stay?"

"Not right now. Give me a while. I'll call you if something comes up."

Patton sat back in his chair, pulled out a cigar, rolled it between his fingers. Eisenhower waited for the last man to leave.

The two men were alone now, and Eisenhower caught the aroma of Patton's cigar, the blue smoke rolling out across the table. Eisenhower stood, moved toward the fireplace, the villa's only bit of luxury.

"Olive wood, I think. Hard as hell, burns okay. Smells good too."

"What is it, Ike? Orders?"

Eisenhower suspected that Patton had been unhappy about Clark's new assignment, had been just indiscreet enough that Eisenhower knew Patton was pressing for the job himself. Clark was now commander of the new Fifth Army, a force building from units now in North Africa, as well as the increasing number of troops arriving from the States. The Fifth would not be involved in the fight for Tunisia, would spend their time and energies in training for future operations, which might include an eventual invasion of the European mainland. In the meantime, they would provide security in the area around Spanish Morocco, in the event the Germans suddenly pushed troops down through Spain.

Patton seemed to be reading him, and Eisenhower said, "The Fifth needed an administrator, George. Someone to organize, to train. Wayne's the best we have at that sort of thing."

"If you say so."

"I wish . . . when you decide to launch an artillery barrage on our allies, you do it outside of their company."

"Don't know what you mean."

"The hell you don't. Dammit, George, it does no good to attack the British, when my every effort is spent in trying to work alongside them. Anderson is doing a decent job out there, given what he has to work with. He knows what kind of shape his army is in, and he knows that he needs us to strengthen his flank. It's not politics, it's tactics. And I don't need you letting everyone know how unhappy you are with my decisions."

Patton seemed genuinely confused. "What the hell are you talking about? I never—"

"Your men are sitting on their butts in Casablanca because until we had this French mess sorted out, that's where I wanted them to sit. Your man Noguès over there, he's a loose cannon. I don't trust him. Even Darlan doesn't trust him."

"Yep. He's a crook, for certain. Don't think he's a Nazi though. He respects power, will go with whoever the winner seems to be. Took him a little while to understand that our tank barrels were pointing right up his keister."

"Which is why I kept you in Casablanca. We can't invade the place, then say, 'Oh, well, thank you, now we're off on our next job. You boys be good now.' "

Patton chuckled, nodded. "I was just letting off steam, Ike. You know how much I hate sitting in one spot. There's fighting to be had, and it's east of here. I just want to get in before it's over."

"It's a long way from over, George. I'm creating a Second Corps, with infantry, and the First Armored Division. They'll move as quickly as conditions allow and take up position on Anderson's right. Whether we can have them in line by Christmas Eve—"

"We won't. It'll take more than good weather to push all those supplies out there. Give me the word, and I'll have those trucks moving as quick as they'll go. We'll burn up some gearboxes—"

"It's not your command, George."

Patton froze, the cigar between his fingers, his hand shaking slightly. "What do you mean?"

"The Second Corps will be commanded by Lloyd Fredendall. Next to you, he's the best man for the job."

Patton seemed to sputter, stood up, tossed the cigar into the fire. He spun around, stared hard at Eisenhower.

"Next to me?"

"George, this war won't stop when we're done in Tunisia. The Joint Chiefs are pushing me to look ahead, start work on the next operation. We're talking about Sicily first. Then Italy, maybe. The French keep screaming at us to invade southern France, but that's not in the cards. George, I need you to get involved in planning for an invasion of Sicily. Once the Germans are pushed out of North Africa, we have to move quickly."

"Sicily? When? What kind of timetable?"

"Summer. Six months. We put Torch together quicker than that, so I'm giving you more time than you probably need. Alexander will be in command of the ground troops, you'll head up our part of the operation."

Patton seemed stunned, put his hand into a pocket, seemed to search for something, another cigar, but the hand came out empty.

"Ike, I had hoped to get into this damned fight quicker than that. I can make a hell of a lot of difference in Tunisia."

"We have those pieces in place, George. Once the weather gives us a break, we'll be ready to give the Krauts a pretty good pounding. With Monty on the far side, the enemy's caught in a vise. No matter how strong the Krauts make Tunisia, they can't hold out forever. And if somehow they keep us out of there, we still have to look for the next plan. We won't win the whole war in Tunisia, but we won't lose it either."

"Six months. Jesus, Ike."

"I don't want to hear it, George, you've got plenty of work to do. And, by the way, I know you're itching for something else too, so I'll scratch it. You're getting your third star. That make you feel better?"

Patton nodded, stared down toward Eisenhower's feet. "Thanks, Ike."

He could see that Patton was crushed, that even with the promotion, Patton was more subdued than he had ever before seen him. He had nothing else to say to Patton, had thought the promotion would be tonic enough, thought, dammit, he already knows he's the best we've got. He doesn't have to hear it from me every time he gets the mopes. Patton looked at him now, seemed to pull himself together.

"Anything else, Ike?"

"You think I should go up front, see Anderson myself?"

Patton stiffened, and Eisenhower saw a flicker of fire in the man's eyes.

"You want to lead these people, Ike, you better get the hell out of this cozy mansion and see what they're doing. Their damned headquarters is a hundred miles from the front lines. That's ninety-five miles too far. Fredendall? You better kick him in the ass a few times before you send him up there. Man seems half-asleep every time I talk to him. The paratroopers, Raff's bunch. Give them some medals. They're out there with a bunch of French hoboes holding the Krauts off the entire southern flank. Better yet, give them some tanks. And real tanks too, not those pissy little Stuarts. For chrissakes, Ike, stop giving all our Shermans to the Brits. Let our boys have a chance at some real firepower . . ."

Patton rambled on, and Eisenhower moved toward the fire, stared down, smiled, let the flow of hot words fill the room.

SOUK EL KHEMIS, WESTERN TUNISIA—
DECEMBER 23, 1942

They traveled in a four-vehicle caravan, Eisenhower's armored Cadillac and one large Packard, led by a machine-gun-bearing jeep, one more following behind. The roads were a slick mire, the rain never ending, the men in the jeep suffering from the misery of the weather, as well as the burden of responsibility for protecting the Allied commander in chief. The threat was from above, the constant danger from German aircraft. It was one great disadvantage of the routes that led to the Tunisian front. There was only one usable railway line, and few roads, so that any Luftwaffe commander could guide his planes to the same places they had bombed before, and could expect to find targets again.

They passed by camps, scattered tents, disguised by brush

piles, pitched under shattered donkey carts, dug into muddy hillsides. There were farmhouses as well, many of them destroyed, those still standing a certain target for the dive-bombers, a death trap for anyone who sought a little dry comfort. They passed men and equipment as well, grumbling sergeants and military policemen, who battled with words and tempers, fighting to keep the flow of supplies and men moving forward. There were tanks as well, the M-3 Stuarts mostly, machines that made the generals nervous, reports having come frequently from Montgomery's army that German tanks could roll right through the fire from the Stuart's small cannon. But on the road into Tunisia, the tanks Eisenhower passed by were American, part of the First Armored Division's Combat Team B, men who had come ashore at Oran, who had punched the French resistance away, who'd swept the city clear for the infantry. The tank drivers kept their machines out to the side of the road, so their steel treads wouldn't obliterate the roadbeds altogether. They drove instead alongside the caravan, churning the deep mud, tossing back high wakes of brown spray. Eisenhower watched them as he passed, men who smiled, who stood tall in the tank turrets and saluted, word passing by wireless radio that someone *big* was moving up with them. He waved, wondered if they knew anything of the enemy they were going after, if they questioned the power of these machines that carried them once more toward the war.

"I have analyzed our situation to great extent. I have ordered various rehearsals of our proposed advance by experimenting with different types of machinery, trucks, tanks, armored vehicles of every kind we have at hand. I tested them all to see which ones were best suited to the conditions in which we find ourselves. They were consistent in one key regard. None of them worked."

Kenneth Anderson was a rugged, compact man, thick chested, with a face that never broke a smile. He seemed perfectly at home in the sea of mud. Eisenhower had not expected so much gloom from the man, waited for some sign that Anderson's plan still included an attack on the enemy.

Anderson continued, "I have spoken to many of the local farm people around here, French mostly. They say the rainy season extends into February. I had thought that wouldn't hold us back, but then . . . it is damned well going to hold us back. Unless you can have the American armor brought forward at a more rapid pace, and unless I can begin to receive double the supply caravans now reaching this area, double the ordnance, double the petrol, I am convinced that no attack should begin for at least six weeks."

Eisenhower paced the small room, the headquarters of the British Fifth Corps. There were radios to one side, a cluster of men gathered in what seemed to be a large closet. Noise spilled from the room, a sudden burst of swearing coming across the communication line. Anderson moved that way, pulled the door closed, said, "My apologies, sir. I try to maintain some decorum on the communication lines, but too many of these men have fought the greater part of their war against the sludge at their feet. I suspect they'll feel better when they face a human enemy. Assuming, of course, you believe the Huns are human."

It was Anderson's notion of a joke, no one laughing.

Eisenhower stood with his hands on his hips, said, "Don't waste your efforts trying to keep your men from being pissed off. Hell, everybody's pissed off. I'm pissed off. I expected a fight up here, I expected to be in Tunis by now."

Anderson seemed to bristle. "Sir, we have done all that was possible."

Eisenhower held his hand up. "Never mind. I'm not attacking you, General. My *decorum* is suffering too." He moved toward one wall, stared at a large map of Tunisia. "I had hoped that by now your people would be closing in on the ports, keeping the Germans pinched against the seashore. The enemy in front of you is still concentrated in the mountain passes and defensive positions close to the sea, right?"

"Mostly, yes."

"Rommel's people are still in the south, at Mareth, right?"

"Quite."

"That leaves a hefty gap between them. We need to cut those roads, keep them split apart. I had hoped that by now, we could be pushing an American armored column to the sea, to cut the German supply lines to Rommel, cut the whole damned country in half. I want a spear driven right through Tunisia, aimed . . .

here. These coastal towns, Sousse or Sfax. Maybe Gabès. Do we know how well positioned Rommel is in that area?"

"Not completely. Monty has only reported that there is no enemy directly in his front."

"I've seen Monty's reports. It would be convenient to our purposes if General Montgomery pressed Rommel a little harder, keeping a clear eye on what kind of shape Rommel's in, where he's digging in. Make sense to you?"

"Quite, sir."

There was sarcasm even in Anderson's response. It was Anderson's way, an air of superiority that Eisenhower had already experienced. He had no energy for anyone's snottiness, not now, not after so much disappointment, not after so much good planning had come apart in the rain. He stared at the map.

"Your people need to continue to strengthen their positions and support the French to your right flank."

"Unfortunately, sir, the French require more than our support. They seem game enough, but should the Hun direct his attack into their portion of the line, there isn't much the French can do to stop it."

"My plan, General, has always been to support them with American units. It makes sense politically, since you and I both know that the French have some . . . discomfort taking orders from you. One more thing. Up until now, we've been piece-mealing our troops among the British units, which, until we got organized, couldn't be helped. Speed was the priority, and putting fighting men on the line took precedence over everything else. But we have to move past that now, create an organized front, and I think coordination is best served by separating the units, putting American soldiers into American commands, giving them their own part of the line."

"I quite agree, sir."

Eisenhower was surprised that Anderson had no objection, had expected the man to fight for every soldier he could add to his section of the line.

"Well, good. Glad to hear it. General Fredendall will command the American Second Corps."

"Yes, sir. I have made his acquaintance."

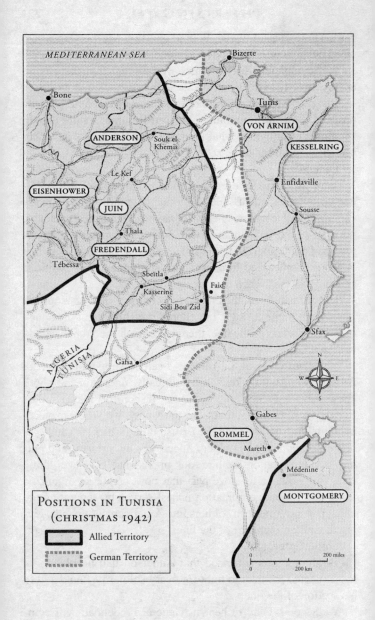

POSITIONS IN TUNISIA
(CHRISTMAS 1942)

▭ Allied Territory

▦ German Territory

Eisenhower stared at the map again. "I can't stomach a six-week delay, General. Is there any way you can push your people forward slowly, shelling positions to their front as they go? Infantry could move with some stealth in these conditions, and once enemy positions are captured, armor can come up to hold the place. Then, do it again, like a damned game of leapfrog."

"I quite agree, sir. It would have to be methodical, but it could be done. But unless the French to our right move with us, our flank would be exposed. We could open ourselves up to some vulnerability there."

"Yes, I know. We can't just ignore the weakness there. Well, the whole damned First Armored Division is headed up here. We can position them where we can make good use of the French and not just order them into a meat grinder." Eisenhower turned, saw Butcher sitting in a corner, the man's raincoat glistening in the dull light.

"Let's mount up, Harry. I want to get to the French position, have a talk with General Juin. Wake up the drivers." Eisenhower looked toward Anderson again. "How do you get along with Juin?"

"Splendidly, sir. Decent sort of chap. His men, however, won't obey British orders."

"That's why we're getting our people up here as quick as we can. They'll listen to Fredendall."

"What of Giraud, sir?"

The name stuck in Eisenhower's gut like a cold, dull knife. "He's in overall command of the French troops throughout North Africa. He answers to Darlan, and I'm told that the French soldiers actually respect him. Most of them, anyway."

Anderson seemed surprised by Eisenhower's show of diplomacy. "I'm told, sir, that your headquarters received a rather touchy demand from him only this week. I don't wish to intrude where my authority does not extend—"

"Giraud sent me a note, insisted he be given command of the entire military operation in Tunisia. Have you received any *orders* from him?"

"Certainly not."

"And you won't. It's just his way. He has to crow like a rooster, make sure we haven't forgotten him, make a grand show once in a while to let his people know he's putting France first. I've learned to put up with him, because I *have* to." Eisenhower turned toward the door, saw Butcher standing in the opening, staring out into a blowing swirl of rain. "General Anderson, with God's help, we'll win this thing. But before we pray for anything else, let's pray for some good weather."

FRENCH HEADQUARTERS, TUNISIA—
DECEMBER 24, 1942

"There is a call for you, General Eisenhower."

Eisenhower was surprised, looked at Juin, who stood, backed away from the table, made a short bow. "Right this way, General. Please use the telephone in my room. I shall allow you privacy."

Eisenhower followed, saw the telephone, the French general ordering people away. He waited for the door to close, picked up the receiver, heard the voice of Clark.

"What is it, Wayne?"

The words filled him, another piece of the absurd puzzle, a black comedy that never seemed to end. He put the phone down, moved out through the doorway, saw Juin, Butcher behind him, several French aides. They watched him silently, and he looked at Butcher, knew the man was reading him, knew that something important had happened.

"You okay, Skipper?"

Eisenhower felt himself wanting to laugh, fought it, reached a hand out toward Juin, the man responding with a soft grasp.

Eisenhower said, "I am terribly sorry to report to you, General, that according to General Clark, Admiral Darlan has been shot. Reports suggest strongly that he is dead."

Juin released his hand, moved to a chair, sat, the other Frenchmen staring in silence, strangely emotionless. Eisenhower wanted to say something consoling, but there were no tears, the men pondering the news with uncharacteristic silence.

Butcher said, "What does this mean, sir? What do we do now?"

Eisenhower shrugged his shoulders. "It means that right now, we go back to Algiers."

*   *   *

The death of Darlan had come by the hand of an assassin, a young Frenchman named Bonnier de La Chapelle, who claimed to be a staunch supporter of Charles de Gaulle. Power now fell to Henri Giraud, the next man in the chain of French authority. Within twenty-four hours of Darlan's death, Giraud authorized the young man's execution. Eisenhower was surprised that despite all his demands and displays of bravado, Giraud accepted the authority with some reluctance. The morass of civilian affairs was apparently no more appealing to him than it was to Eisenhower. But Giraud accepted the role that events had thrust upon him. Much of the authority that he had so angrily demanded at Gibraltar was now his.

Eisenhower could not help but feel the anxiety that Darlan's death might cause, pro-Vichy officials rising up in noisy protest, disrupting the already tenuous civil order in the far-flung territories across North Africa. But the business of the army went on, the French accepting Giraud's expanded authority with barely a ripple, the civilian officials seemingly too occupied with protecting their own positions to be concerned with who was at the top. Ultimately, Eisenhower realized that no matter the twisted confusion that seemed a normal part of French political life, considering the grief and turmoil that had fallen on his head, and across the entire Allied command for their cordial dealings with Darlan, in the long run, Bonnier de La Chapelle might have done the Allies an enormous favor.

The Allied forces continued their snail-like organization, Anderson sparring with German dive-bombers and artillery attacks, the Americans pushing forward to the south, organizing alongside the French, under Lloyd Fredendall's command. Despite the sluggish Allied progress, Anderson's forces attempted to drive the Germans back toward the key objectives of Bizerte and Tunis. In seesaw battles that accomplished little, villages changed hands, crossroads were contested, but in the end, the only clear victor was the mud.

Though progress continued to be made, Eisenhower could not avoid one cost of the pressures he endured every hour of every day. Once back in Algiers, after dutifully speaking at

Darlan's funeral, Eisenhower was defeated by a foe he was too worn-out to avoid. He came down with the flu.

The vast mountains of details, problems, and controversies had driven Eisenhower to a sickbed. But his illness allowed for no relief. The details flowed through and past him still, the mundane and the routine suddenly eclipsed by a piece of news no one in headquarters had expected. In the midst of the chaotic planning, the insufferable weather, the energetic buildup of the enemy in front of them, word came that a summit meeting of the Allied leaders was to take place in mid-January, less than three weeks away. The meetings were customary, but this time the setting was not. Rather than gather their aides and officials in London or Washington, Winston Churchill and Franklin Delano Roosevelt had decided to come to North Africa.

17. LOGAN

NEAR SOUK EL KHEMIS, TUNISIA
CHRISTMAS 1942

"I think I got trench foot."

Logan was in no mood for Parnell's complaining. "You ever actually been in a trench?"

Parnell examined the crust of mud on his boots. "Well, no. Not here anyway."

"And, trench foot is all about feet, not boots. I'm betting your feet are all pearly pink. But don't show me."

Parnell scraped at the mud, seemed to ignore Logan's logic. "Boots are ruined. Shoulda left 'em in the tank and gone barefoot. Hell, back home, it rains like this, which ain't often, nobody wears shoes."

"Don't give me that. Where you come from, nobody wears shoes at all."

Parnell puffed up now, pointed to Logan. "Shows how much you know. You go steppin' on a prickly pear, or a damned scorpion, you'll wear shoes every day, including Sunday."

Logan leaned back against a fat rock, pulled at his jacket, tried to hold away the wet chill. They sat beneath a canvas shelter, tin plates between them, what was left of a dinner of C rations. To one side, Baxter was poking the black skeleton of a barely flickering fire, smoke drifting past him, out through an opening above his head. He dropped his tool, a thin stick, said, "Too wet. Nothing gonna burn."

Logan looked at him, saw frowning frustration, thought, that's the first thing he's said all day. Maybe all week. They sat in rare silence, Parnell occupied again with chipping mud off his boots. Logan looked up, stared at the darkening canvas, thought of his blanket, rolled up in the storage bin of the tank. The tanks were parked in staggered rows a hundred yards away, camouflaged by an uneven carpet of netting and canvas. Around them, men had built shelters, dug holes into whatever dry place they could find, anyplace uphill from the flowing mud. He hadn't been to the tank since that morning, a routine firing of the engine, the oil and fuel trucks coming through to service as many of the machines as they could. The service had been done mostly at night, but over the past few days the rains had grown heavy again, thick gray skies darkening to black, the skies free of bombers, so that work could be completed during the day. Obviously, the weather had finally become too much for the Germans. The daily bombing runs had stopped, a blessed relief to the antiaircraft gunners, who could actually spend their shifts under some kind of shelter.

Parnell pounded his foot on a rock, dislodging a chunk of hard mud from his heel. "I'd sure like a cup of coffee."

Logan reached down, tossed him the small can from the remains of the C rations. "Here. You can have mine."

Parnell looked at the can, made a sour face. "Can't drink this stuff. Whoever heard of coffee you don't have to cook? I'm not so sure this is coffee anyway. I heard talk it's more like ground-up animals and stuff."

"I've heard you're an idiot. So give it back. You'll wish you had this stuff when we're out in the field somewhere. Mix it up right in your canteen."

Parnell tossed the can back to Logan. "Nasty stuff. I'd rather drink mud. Right now, I want coffee, the real thing. How 'bout you, Pete? I'll buy, you go get it, Jack."

Baxter ignored him, stared at the failure of a campfire, seemed lost in thought. Logan tossed the can of instant coffee into the pile of tin plates, alongside the empty cans, some kind of meat and bean stew. He felt a rumbling in his stomach, thought, he's right, dammit. Powdered coffee. Leave it to the army. I'll never tell him that though. We ever run out of ammo, I'll just shoot that stuff at the enemy. Logan shivered, was truly missing his blanket now, said, "I'm not filling my boots full of water for a damned cup of coffee. My feet are cold enough now. You want it, get it yourself."

Parnell grunted. "They need waitresses out here. They'd make some pretty good tips about now."

Baxter seemed to wake up, pulled himself to his feet, his hands pushing up against the low canvas ceiling.

"I'll go. Gotta hit the latrine anyway."

Parnell slapped Baxter's leg as he moved past him. "Good boy. Bring a whole damned pot if they'll let you."

There were heavy footsteps, the edge of the canvas tossed back, a spray of mud and rainwater. It was Hutchinson, the man ducking in quickly, stepping right onto Baxter's futile campfire.

"Damn! This is some fun!"

Logan shielded himself from the chilly waterfall that seemed to roll off the man. "What you find out?"

Hutchinson shook himself, rubbed his hands together. "No campfire? What the hell?"

Baxter moved past him. "Nothing will burn. I'm getting coffee."

Hutchinson sat, pulled off his jacket. "Not for me. Had ten cups. Headquarters had the biggest pot I ever saw. That's why I'm shaking. That, or this wonderful *A-rab* winter."

Baxter ducked out, was gone now, and Logan said again, "What you find out?"

Hutchinson shook the water from his jacket. "No go. There are some Shermans coming up, but we're not getting them, not yet anyway. They're parceling them out between our boys and the Brits. Just not enough of them to go around."

Parnell rubbed his back against a rock. "Well, hell, you might figure the limeys will get first crack. I knew I shoulda said something to Ike: 'Hey, we're Americans, you know. You're shipping brand-new tanks over here just to give 'em to somebody else.' Ain't right."

Hutchinson wiped mud from his hands. "Yeah, *Buffalo Bill,* that's what you should have done. The Old Man comes up here to see how we're doing, and you'd just turn the tank right into his path, stop him cold. I'd like to watch you chew out General Eisenhower. I'm sure that would have changed everything." Hutchinson shifted his weight, tried to find a comfortable place to lean, the rocks jutting out in mostly sharp angles. "The captain made a good case for us. Told the brass that our damned thirty-sevens are no more than popguns. The Shermans have seventy-fives, which according to the brass is about the only thing we got that can stand up to the Krauts. But for now, we gotta make do." Hutchinson looked at Logan. "Make every shot count. Hit 'em in the treads, or, better yet, we try to flank them, put a shell into their ass end."

Logan stared at the ground. "Ridiculous. They send us into a fight with a gun that can't kill anybody."

"I don't want to hear that crap. You're a good shot, so . . . make good shots. There's nothing a Stuart can't do. We can outmaneuver and outrun anything the Krauts have."

Logan let the words fill his brain, wouldn't say them out loud. *Outrun.* That may be a good thing.

Hutchinson was still looking at him. "There's something else. Colonel Todd was killed. Artillery shell hit him when he was outside his tank."

Logan sat up straight. "Where?"

"With the French, up near Pont du Fahs."

Parnell said, "Where the hell is that?"

Hutchinson spit a spray of water toward Parnell's feet. "Does it matter?"

"No, I guess not. Damned shame."

"General Ward's supposed to be up here tonight. The whole

damned division is heading out this way. Lots of talk about what's coming."

The canvas rolled back again, Baxter breathing heavily, shouting, "Out here! They need some help!"

He was gone again, and Hutchinson scrambled to his feet, Logan as well, the two men moving out into thick, wet air. Men were gathering near the road, a jeep turned up on its side, half-buried in a narrow ditch. Others were down in the muck, pulling at the driver, the man screaming, someone else shouting, "Medic! Get a medic!"

Hutchinson jumped down into the ditch, Logan following, mud and water up over his knees, the men pushing against the jeep.

"It's stuck! Push again!"

They worked in unison now, the jeep rocking, more screams from the driver, the men at Logan's feet yelling, "Got him! He's free!"

They pulled the man up and out of the ditch, medics there now, the man's screams calming to a soft whimper. The jeep suddenly gave way, the mud loosening, the jeep rolling upright. A heavy wave of mud and water washed over Logan, and he tried to pull himself out of the ditch, felt a hand under his arm, a hard pull. He wiped the sludge from his eyes, saw Hutchinson staring down at the injured driver, soft words on Hutchinson's lips.

"Oh, dear God."

Logan wiped at his face, fought to see, the medics close beside him, the driver still making soft, shivering noises, medics talking in low, hushed voices. Logan saw now, the man's leg was gone, cut off at the knee, blood flowing into the mud, a black stream oozing into the ditch. The man began to shake, a low sound from his throat, a single note, then a choking cough, a soft rattle. Then he was silent. The medics still worked, a white cloth turned filthy wrapping the stump of a leg. Logan ignored the rain, the dirty water in his boots, soaking his pants and shirt. He stared at the man's bloody pants leg, felt sick, weak in the knees, but Hutchinson still held him, no one speaking.

A man moved close beside Logan, older, an officer, said, "He's done for. Let him be."

A medic looked up, and Logan saw tears, red eyes, the man still working the bandage.

The officer said, "Let him be, soldier. Get a stretcher. You boys jump down there. We need to find his leg. It has to be in that mudhole, right there. A man oughta be buried with all his parts."

Logan stared down at the silent face of the driver, the dead man's mouth open, soft rain wetting his face.

The rains had grown lighter, glimpses of sunlight through broken clouds. The mud was there still, filling the roadways, the ditches, trapping more jeeps and more trucks, spraying filth on any man who tried to walk near the roadways. The First Armored was growing stronger every day, new tanks and half-tracks making their way on the one fragile rail line, machines assembled and fueled and oiled at the gathering points, where the crews would mount up, driving them to the east.

Logan rolled the canvas cloth into a fat roll, Parnell on the other side, Baxter waiting to help them hoist the heavy cloth into the metal chest on the stern of the tank. Hutchinson was up in the turret, testing the hand crank, moving the gun barrel in a slow, wide arc. No one spoke, each man holding his thoughts, what might happen now, what a change in the weather might bring. Orders had cut through the rumors that in a few days there would be a new advance, and the rumors had grown louder that the armor was going hard for the seacoast, to drive a wedge into the German position. Logan had ignored the talk, tried to take himself somewhere else, someplace where the sun shone brightly, where a man could walk on a silent stretch of beach and not be afraid of anything. The fantasy was foolish, the dreamy thoughts broken by the face of the young jeep driver, the missing leg, by the men who knelt in the thick ooze to put their hands on the missing piece of the dead soldier. But the nightmares came more from the face of the medic, a young man with soft red eyes, crying for a man he could not save. Medics don't cry, he thought. Medics are cold and precise and do their job without emotion. He carried the image everywhere he went now, a medic reacting with grief, a man trained for a job he was not yet prepared to do.

Baxter tightened the last cord around the canvas, and Hutchinson climbed up out of the turret, stood high above them, waiting for them to climb aboard. They had no orders to confront the enemy today, would simply move forward, establishing a new tank park, a new camp, making room for the units coming up from behind. One by one they jumped up on the tank hull, Parnell and Baxter dropping down inside the turret, moving forward, opening their hatches. Logan was up as well, stopped, stared down into the turret, to his seat at the breech of the gun.

"Go on, Jack. Mount up."

Logan gripped the hatchway with both hands, took a breath, glanced up, across the rows of tanks, half-tracks, and armored trucks moving into line. He watched as the oil trucks moved away, could see muddy piles of C-ration cans, slit trenches, and deep ruts across the rocky, open ground. He ignored Hutchinson, repeated a thought that had rolled through his mind many times before. One little tank, a tiny piece of power in a vast machine, an entire army rolling into place, generals making their next *great plan.* Hutchinson put a hand on Logan's shoulder.

"You okay?"

Logan looked into Hutchinson's eyes, saw the medic again, fought against the thought, the nightmare that had come to him every night since the jeep driver had died. Are we ready for this? Do we know what will happen when we face a *real* enemy?

He blinked, tried to clear away the image, swung a leg over the side of the hatchway, said, "Yep. I'm fine. Let's go find some Krauts."

18. EISENHOWER

The site was crawling with security people, civilians and soldiers, the Secret Service and British security mingling uncomfortably with uniformed guards. The meetings were taking place on Patton's turf, and so Patton was in charge of security, a comforting thought to everyone in attendance. As far as anyone in the Allied camp could determine, the arrival of both Churchill and Roosevelt was still a secret, in North Africa as well as back home. But the assassination of Admiral Darlan had reminded everyone that threats could come from unlikely and unexpected sources.

Eisenhower had arrived in late morning, a harrowing trip on a B-17 that lost an engine en route, the crew and their passengers donning parachutes in the event the plane failed altogether. Eisenhower had not made a jump before, but he could not remain clamped into his tight seat, and so he had stayed close to the waist gunner, both men eyeing the misery of the terrain below them. As black oil streamed from the failed engine, Eisenhower had caught the distinctive sound of another engine failing, a loud crack, a second prop twirling uselessly. But the plane still flew, and when Casablanca finally appeared, the roar of the two remaining engines could not disguise the audible sighs of relief, especially from Harry Butcher.

"I'd just as soon not do that again, if it's all right with you, Skipper."

Eisenhower climbed into the car. "I'm with you there, Harry. And, frankly, I'd rather not do the rest of this either."

They sat in silence, more cars pulling up close behind, the ever-present jeeps lining up on both ends of the short caravan, machine guns pointing up and out. It would be a short trip, Eisenhower knowing full well that Patton would greet them at the airport's entrance, would give them a proper escort that might even include heavy armor. At the least, Patton would have his gunners eyeing the sky.

Eisenhower knew that Casablanca could be vulnerable to German bombing raids, long-range planes at high altitude, virtually unstoppable unless you knew they were coming, and unstoppable completely if they came after dark. The Germans were fearless about night flying, something that the Americans had yet to master. It was a source of friction between men like Spaatz and Doolittle, and their British counterparts, Tedder in particular. The British had engaged in night bombing runs over Germany's larger cities for some time now, striking deep into Hitler's industrial centers. But the Americans had spent most of their training in daylight, and so their bombing raids were daylight as well, squadrons of B-17s absorbing horrific losses from German fighters and antiaircraft fire. It was one more detail, one more controversy Eisenhower had to listen to, one more difference in philosophy between allies who were still struggling to find common ground in every aspect of the war.

"You think we can keep to your plan, Skipper? Actually leave here tomorrow?"

"I'm counting on it. These meetings are much more about the participants than what's really happening here. Stalin was invited, you know. Said he couldn't make it. Got his hands full knocking hell out of the Krauts at Stalingrad. That could be huge, you know. Hitler hasn't taken a beating like that, could take a lot of starch out of his entire military. I'd like to meet Stalin someday, see what he's like."

Butcher stared out, and Eisenhower saw men riding donkeys, women draped in long, cream-colored smocks, walking behind.

Butcher said, "Shoots hell out of everything I was taught as a kid."

"What do you mean?"

"Joseph and Mary going to Bethlehem."

Eisenhower was puzzled, waited for the joke. "What the hell are you talking about?"

Butcher still watched the Arabs, wasn't smiling. "Well, you know, all those images of Joseph and Mary. There was one hanging in my church when I was a kid, more just like it in those Sunday-school books. They're riding into Bethlehem, Joseph pulling the mule or the ox or whatever it was, Mary riding up on top. Very sweet, you know, the couple searching for the place to stay, 'no room at the inn,' all of that."

"We're a hell of a long way from Bethlehem."

"Not really, Skipper. Same kind of place, same people. But one thing's for sure. No man here walks while his wife rides on the donkey. If anyone rides, it's the man, every time. Makes me wonder if Joseph made Mary eat dust, pregnant or not. You'd think maybe later on, Jesus would have had something to say about that."

Eisenhower saw that Butcher was serious. "Keep that observation to yourself, Commander. I have enough gripes to contend with as it is. We didn't come here to start another Crusade."

"Come in, General! Finally have some time alone. Excellent. Been looking forward to this for a while now!"

Eisenhower heard the door close behind him, Roosevelt sitting beside a fireplace, a blanket over his legs. Roosevelt turned the wheelchair slightly, pointed to a chair. "Sit! Get comfortable. No rank here, Ike. Let's just have a chat."

Eisenhower felt the energy from Roosevelt's smile, the man's enthusiasm filling the room, sweeping away Eisenhower's exhaustion.

Roosevelt rolled himself closer to the chair, motioned again for Eisenhower to sit. "Fine dinner, eh? These people have gone too far. Magnificent hospitality. It's to be expected of course. We've shown them some muscle. They respect that, you know. Always have, all throughout history. A lot of 'eye for an eye' hereabouts. The biggest gun gets the girl. All of that."

Eisenhower sat, felt himself sinking into soft leather, the aching stiffness in his shoulders welcoming the comfort. He twisted slightly, eased the pressure on his back, realized that Roosevelt was watching his every move.

"Relax, General. You've earned it. Drink? They have some truly fine sherry here, or perhaps something with more of a punch?"

"No thank you, sir. There was a good deal to drink at dinner."

"My critics will give me the devil about this when I get back home, you know. They'll accuse me of taking a vacation in the middle of a war. The press won't mind it too much. A president has to lead, and what better place than to come out here where the action is? Churchill will handle it better than I will, tell them all to go to hell. Of course, he's been here before. I'll speak to the people directly, tell them what a bang-up job our boys are doing here, how well they're being led. I had to see it, you know. Had to. You can't be commander in chief and rely on written reports. Enormous responsibility to our boys, sending them over here. I had better know what we're doing firsthand. Churchill feels the same way. He likes to put his hand in a little deep, though. I know better. *You're* the army. I'm just the figurehead."

Eisenhower was overwhelmed, Roosevelt's flow of words pushing him deep into the chair. He saw a smile, the president beaming at him.

"Forgive me for saying so, sir, but you seem to be in exceptionally fine spirits."

"I am! I don't realize how important it is for me to get out of Washington until I do it. Like crawling out of a cave, escaping a dungeon filled with jabbering crows. Forgive *me,* General, but this is quite the adventure! This is what makes being president worthwhile. History is being made *here,* books will be written about what happens *here*! Just coming here, all that secrecy, all the intrigue . . . cloak-and-dagger stuff. How does it feel, General? What must it be like to be the victor, sweeping into the enemy's strongholds, knowing your army has conquered its foe? A man needs to wear a uniform to feel the impact of that. No politician can know."

Eisenhower was concerned now. "Sir, I do not feel we are conquerors. Certainly the French would not appreciate that description. They have a great deal of sensitivity on that subject. We must consider them our allies."

Roosevelt nodded. "Yes, yes. I understand. I get somewhat . . . enthusiastic about this. I would not insult the French. What do you think of Giraud, or de Gaulle? Can we work with these people?"

"We already have, to some degree. Giraud, certainly."

Roosevelt waited for more, smiled now. "Nothing to say about de Gaulle, eh? All right then, be discreet if you must. I can't stand the man. He's like the ruffian at an elegant dinner. Everyone tries to ignore him, but he bullies his way into every corner of the room. He'll end up in charge too. I just know it."

"The army seems to prefer Giraud now."

"De Gaulle doesn't care about the French army, General. He wants the country. He wants to be head of state. From what I've heard of Giraud, he's perfectly happy commanding the French military. It's the compromise those people will need. Giraud keeps his place, de Gaulle takes over in Paris. And, I'll have to be so damned polite to him. Galling." Roosevelt winked. "Good pun, eh? Now I know where it comes from."

Eisenhower shifted in his chair. "Sir, I'm concerned that we not lose our grasp of the present. Paris is not in our plans right now. There is a considerable challenge in front of us in Tunisia. We have not fared as well as I had hoped. Our planning was not always perfect, we could not allow for every contingency. But there is much to discuss—"

"Yes, yes. You're right of course. Understand, Ike, I leave those details to you and to General Marshall. You may have that conversation with him, contingencies and whatnot. I have to look beyond, to what will follow. Nations will be created, new governments. Look back at the first Great War. The entire map of Europe changed. My job is to deal with those kinds of changes, help them along in the proper direction. I have no doubt that your goals will be met, and I must say, General, your burden would be less heavy if you were not so pessimistic. I had hoped you would still be enthusiastic about our strategy for a cross-channel invasion. Is not Paris still your ultimate goal?"

"Well, yes, certainly."

"Then don't lose focus on that! These operations here are the first strokes, testing the water, putting our people into battle to harden them. Our factories are working at full tilt, our people are entirely behind our efforts here. But success will come not just by strength alone. Success will come because history

demands it. I will not entertain the notion that Adolf Hitler's vision of the world can ever prevail, that one evil man can erase
thousands of years of the evolution of civilized society. You do
what you must do, General. Your campaigns for the new year
might indeed be difficult. But you will prevail. *We* will prevail.
It cannot be any other way!"

He had managed to escape the Casablanca conferences as he
had planned, after only one day. But the meetings had become
far more than an exercise for the benefit of politicians. Eisenhower had spent considerable time with Harold Alexander, the
British commander who ruled over Montgomery's army, who
held tightly to the territory that had been taken away from Rommel. Alexander was now to become the overall commander of
all ground troops in the Mediterranean theater, which would include not only Montgomery's Eighth Army, but of course, Anderson, Patton, and Clark as well. In addition, the planning for
the invasion of Sicily was taking shape, projections of a summer
campaign there based on the assumption that the fight in Tunisia
would be won. Alexander would command the ground troops
that would go into Sicily, two primary wings, one British and
one American. At the headquarters of the combined chiefs
of staff in London, the maps were being drawn, the numbers
worked out for that operation, the planners from both countries
hammering out broad details. No matter how much energy was
directed toward a future operation, Eisenhower had no choice
but to stay in the present and look squarely at the map of
Tunisia.

ALGIERS—JANUARY 23, 1943

Marshall stared at the map, pointed to the red line that stretched
across the southern part of Tunisia.

"You've ordered the change?"

"Yep."

"Alexander pretty certain? We thought Rommel might do an
about-face, hit back at Montgomery pretty hard. Didn't think
he'd give up Tripoli without more of a fight."

Eisenhower waited, and Marshall turned to face him.

Eisenhower said, "Tripoli doesn't matter to Rommel. He cares first about his tanks. He's not going to risk his strength fighting for a place he can't hope to keep. I hoped he would have dragged his feet a bit more. I truly thought we would have the time to cut Tunisia in half." He thought of Marshall's question now. "There was no choice but to kill the original plan. Rommel is dug in south of Gabès, and he's too close to Sfax for us to consider a quick push across. We could be caught in the open, cut to pieces. I've ordered Anderson to put Fredendall in a defensive posture for now."

Marshall sat, thought a moment. "You comfortable with Fredendall?"

Eisenhower moved to the map, stared at the network of lines, numbers, Fredendall's position.

"Good man. Handled himself well at Oran." He smiled. "Patton wanted that job, of course. Not sure he would have been the man."

"Hell, Ike, Patton wants every job. Yours, mine. He'd take over the navy if someone told him to." Marshall paused. "You need to keep a rein on him. We're going to need him on the battlefield before this is over. I hear too much grumbling from his people, grapevine stuff. He's a world-champion bellyacher if you give him the room. We can't afford to be pissing off the Brits. How's he handling things in Casablanca?"

Eisenhower turned, shrugged. "Pretty damned good job. I give him credit for not pounding his victory into the faces of the French. Shows them respect, gives them their due. You're right though. He's chomping at the bit."

"How's he handling the command structure? He get along with Alexander?"

Eisenhower smiled, but the humor faded quickly. The command structure throughout the entire Mediterranean had been formalized, had been the one direct benefit to him from the Casablanca conference. As far as he could guess, it was the real reason Marshall had come to see him in Algiers. Eisenhower was now formally in command of the entire theater, assisted by three top deputies, all of them British. Alongside Alexander, Arthur Tedder headed up the combined air forces, and Andrew Cunningham controlled the navies. A fourth part of the command,

the French, seemed content to serve under Giraud, who also accepted his role as Eisenhower's subordinate. The grumbling
Marshall referred to had come from lower-echelon officers,
Americans mostly, who saw the British domination of the command structure as some sort of insult, making a British show out
of an effort that might become mostly American. Eisenhower
had done all he could to stifle that kind of griping, but Marshall
was right. The man most capable of beating a barrel with complaints was George Patton.

Eisenhower said, "Patton will get along with anybody I tell
him to. He knows how to follow orders."

"Good. This is a hell of a thing, Ike. Two countries, one army.
Hell, three countries, if you count the French. Far as I know, nobody's ever done this before. So, how are *you* handling it?"

Eisenhower walked toward the tall window, stared out, chose
his words.

"Good men, every one of them. Couldn't have picked anyone
better myself. They show me proper respect, no one parading
his medals. So far, I don't see any real problems."

Marshall stood, moved to the window beside him. "Except
what?"

Eisenhower was embarrassed now, had hoped he wasn't so
transparent. But Marshall had known him for too many years,
and Eisenhower felt suddenly as if he were under the gaze of a
stern parent.

"Well, I wasn't going to mention this. Figured it would work
out in time."

"What?"

"I was wondering if there were any plans to promote me to
full general. Since I still only have three stars, every senior
commander who answers to me . . . outranks me."

Marshall laughed. "See? You should be making more noise.
You might have had your fourth star by now. Don't worry about
it. The Brits don't care. Things will straighten out with that soon
enough."

Marshall moved away from the window, sat again, and Eisenhower stared out toward the hillside, olive trees and white villas.
Wonder if I'll ever come back here? Bring Mamie, an actual vacation. Seems like a damned pleasant place, when there's not a

war on. Marshall cleared his throat, and Eisenhower turned, saw the older man staring into his hands.

Marshall seemed to hesitate, then said, "You're being mighty careful, Ike. Monty was driving Rommel pretty hard. Everything I heard told me that Rommel was beating a hard retreat. You think so much caution is called for?"

It was a dangerous question, and Eisenhower studied Marshall's face, stern, unyielding, no hint of a smile.

"To Montgomery, sure, it's a retreat. He drove Rommel right into our shaky defenses. Rommel seems to be digging in, but who the hell knows what he'll do next? We've observed columns of reinforcements beefing up his position at Mareth, new tanks, guns. And, besides Rommel, the enemy is far stronger in the north than we thought he would be. The French have shown time and again that they can't hold the center. Our armor is having to spread itself thin to give them enough support so they don't let the enemy cut us in two. The Germans must know how weak we are there. In the south, Fredendall is pulling people into line as quickly as we can send them up there, doing what he can to block every pass, defend against any route Rommel might decide to use. We can't assume that he's going to simply stay put. He is still Rommel. It would have been damned convenient if Monty had actually *caught* him instead of pushing him right at us." Eisenhower stopped, realized his voice had risen, felt the sudden silence, thought of the ears in the offices outside. "I'm doing the best I know how, George. But, no matter how good something looks on paper, if we jump too soon, it could all fall apart."

"You can't plan for every variable, Ike."

"Oh, we didn't. We most certainly didn't. Like the mud. We didn't plan for mud, and it stopped us as effectively as ten German divisions. Forgive me, George, but I don't agree with you. I had damned well better plan for any variable that could stand in our way."

Marshall frowned, rubbed his hand across his forehead. "Some newspaper, I forget which one. Some columnist ran a piece on you, said that 'mud is a silly alibi.' His exact words."

Eisenhower closed his eyes, thought, give him to me, just a

week. Let me see what kind of alibi . . . he stopped himself. Dammit, this is no good.

"I can't worry about reporters."

"No, you can't. Newspapers are a great place for cowards and malcontents to have their say. You start paying attention to all of that . . . well, the point is, you know what's happening out there in front of the guns. No one in Washington can speak to that, no one can really speak out for you and know what he's talking about. You know how I feel about you being back here, so far from the lines. It's giving some people the wrong impression, that you're not really in charge. You need to put yourself out front for the damned photographers, get yourself some headlines."

"Like MacArthur."

"Say what you want to about Doug's style, but no one has any doubts who's running our campaign in the Pacific. Frankly, there are some doubts about you. Not from the Brits. They're behind you completely. It's our own people, damned congressmen, some of the president's own advisers."

Eisenhower thought of Roosevelt, the man's raw enthusiasm. "I didn't hear any of that from Roosevelt. He surprised me, actually. Pretty enthusiastic about the job we're doing here."

"He said that? Well, of course. You were in private. But he's not saying that in Washington, Ike. It's just the reality. I'm surprised sometimes how naïve you are. It takes thunder to grab people's attention. MacArthur's good at that, doesn't give his critics any room to move, drowns 'em out. You're too quiet, Ike. Right now, a lot of people are just standing back, letting you put your neck in the noose, waiting to see if you hang yourself. Not much I can do about that. Hell, not even the president can change that. Our job is to come up with some kind of plan and then give you the men and equipment to make it work. But don't think anyone in Washington is going to stake their career on you, or on what's happening over here. Everybody is *cautiously optimistic.* Privately, the president supports you wholeheartedly, but he can't just jump in with you publicly. It's the way the game is played." Marshall paused. "Just do your damned job. If you make good decisions, if you *win* this thing, everybody will toss medals at you. But if you lose, if you can't kick the Germans out of Tunisia, then there will be no Sicily, no invasion of France. If it all falls to pieces, don't expect the president to put an arm around your shoulder."

Time and again, Kenneth Anderson's efforts to drive the Germans back toward the Tunisian coast had been thwarted, first by the Germans themselves, and then by the dismal weather and the inability to push supplies and manpower forward quickly enough. The Germans continued to hold fast to their stout defensive positions on the good ground, continued to harass and poke holes in the vulnerable French positions, continued to build their forces in the north. In the south, the reinforcements continued to strengthen Rommel, his deep lines at Mareth, causing Montgomery to pause once more. Eisenhower had no choice but to call off any plans of attack that might expose vulnerable points in the Allied position. There was simply no point in driving men into the teeth of the German defenses until the Allied forces were strong enough to make a difference.

Though Eisenhower's chain of command now technically included Montgomery, there was little chance that Eisenhower or anyone else was going to affect the way Montgomery pursued his foe. With Montgomery content to gather his troops in strong lines opposite Rommel's defenses, Rommel was once again being given the extraordinary gift of time, enough time to realize that the Germans might have an opportunity no one had seriously considered, an opportunity to punch a devastating hole in the Allied plans for Tunisia.

19. ROMMEL

Westphal was hesitating, and Rommel kept the smile to himself, knew the young man was fighting to hold back the embarrassment of emotion.

"You should go, Colonel. Your men are waiting for you."

Westphal stiffened, gathered himself. "Yes, sir. I have delayed long enough. There is work to be done."

Rommel let the smile out, held out a hand. Westphal seemed surprised, took it, and Rommel felt the roughness, the hard grip of a man so much like himself, stubborn and tired. But Westphal had the energy of youth, and in an army where so many were gone, where senior commanders had fallen away, captured, wounded, or just used up by the desert, the *Panzerarmee* needed every good commander it could find. Westphal was set to command the 164th Division, infantry and light armor, and for the first time in many months, Rommel's headquarters would not be graced by the young man's tireless efficiency.

Rommel released the hand. "You will have an advantage now, Siegfried. Your enemies will only be in front of you. I must still deal with those who defeat us from behind."

Westphal stood back, snapped his boots together, made a crisp salute, then held his arm out, the palm flat to the ground. "Heil Hitler."

Rommel nodded, said nothing, and Westphal turned, moved to his truck, climbed aboard, and was gone. Rommel turned, saw the other staff officers keeping their distance, motioned to the short man, Bayerlein, the senior officer in the group. The command was silent, expected, and Rommel moved toward the tents, thought of the maps. Bayerlein followed, was close behind him, and Rommel thought, yes, Westphal is correct. There is work to do.

Fritz Bayerlein had been in Africa almost as long as Rommel, had served Rommel in several important roles. Not much older than Westphal, he was a short, stocky bulldog, whose experience already included command in the field. Bayerlein had taken over the Afrika Korps after Ritter von Thoma had been captured at El Alamein. For some time now, he had been Rommel's acting chief of staff, his senior aide, more experienced than Westphal certainly, a better soldier perhaps. But Rommel knew that no one else in the army would ever be as loyal.

They drove west, through a narrow pass, making their way through German artillery positions, formations of heavy armor perched beside the road like so many fat, sleeping beasts. Rommel felt the energy now, the strength, the first time in months he felt stronger than his enemy. There was strength in his army as well, but not just in the machines. It had never really been in the tanks and guns. It came from the men, and those men drew their strength from him. He could feel it as they saluted him, surprised cheers as the truck rolled by them. Many of these men were veterans, had made the fourteen-hundred mile retreat. Now they were rested, had rebuilt and resupplied through a mostly quiet January, had dug in at the dilapidated French line at Mareth, his frustrated engineers working feverishly to improve what the French had left behind, works that were no match at all for the modern tools of war. But Montgomery had done what Rommel expected him to do. The British had made that long march as well, were farther now from their supply base, had worn out their machines and their soldiers, and so, Montgomery would not attack, not for a while, not until he was ready. And every day Rommel's army grew stronger.

The truck moved into a flat plain, a high, rocky ridge behind them, the road winding slightly, a dull gray snake in the low brush, leading them to another ridge, where more German guns protected the pass. He stared out to the north, more ridges, tall rocks, difficult ground, good only for infantry, or artillery observers. The rocks seemed empty, and Rommel leaned forward, said to Bayerlein, "We must have people up there! Take advantage of the heights. The enemy puts any artillery observers up there, it could be a problem."

"I'll see to it, sir."

"Who is in command here?"

"General Belowius, sir."

Rommel nodded, thought, the engineer. Another general pulled from where he is wanted to where he is needed. "Yes, good. He will know how to use the ground."

They began to climb, the road rising into another narrow pass, tanks blocking the way. Rommel stood, said to the driver, "Shut it down. I will walk."

The men stood beside their tanks, some eating, cooking over small fires in the dirt. They stood upright as they saw him, surprise, young faces Rommel had never seen. Replacements, he thought. Untested. Or, they come from Russia, used up by the winter and a fight we cannot win. Here . . . they may still find the way.

He saw a rocky trail, stepped carefully, made his way higher, up to the crest of the sharp ridge. Bayerlein followed, and another man, carrying a machine gun, two more, men with maps and field glasses. He pushed himself over a sharp rock, dropped down, felt a sharp punch in his side, made a sound, his eyes blurring, light-headed, dizzy, his hand reaching for the rock . . .

"Sir!"

"Get some water up here! Now!"

He stared up into faces, focused on Bayerlein, another man with a small tin cup, water spilling onto Rommel's face.

Bayerlein said, "Give me that! Back away, all of you! Where's that medic?"

The water was warm, and Rommel fought the urge to gulp it, felt himself choking. Bayerlein removed the cup, said quietly, "Slow. Just a little."

He could feel the rocks under his back now, sharp, stabbing pain in his side, still felt dizzy. "What happened?"

Bayerlein leaned low, whispered, "You fainted again, sir. Don't worry, the medic will bring you something."

Rommel put his elbows on the ground, pushed himself up. "Bring me *what*? There is no cure for this!"

He pulled his legs in, curled his knees under him, tried to stand, Bayerlein holding him by the arm, a strong grip.

"Easy, sir. No hurry."

"I'm all right! Just slipped on the rocks. Let's move up a little higher. I want to see those passes across this valley." He pulled his arm away from Bayerlein's grip, said in a low voice, "I slipped on the rocks. Isn't that what you saw?"

Bayerlein looked down. "Yes."

"Thank you, Fritz."

He tested the ground beneath him, his legs strong again, the pain in his side still a dull ache. He moved up the trail, steadied himself against the big rocks, thought, how much more . . . how many times? Where will I get the strength?

Despite the wisdom and the strategic necessity of abandoning Libya, loud voices in Italy had called for a scapegoat, and Rommel knew that his name was at the top. When word came finally from Comando Supremo, it came not as an order, but as a suggestion that because of the continuing problems with his health, Rommel should be replaced by an Italian commander, General Giovanni Messe. It was one more pretense the Italians embraced, the reorganization of the Tunisian armies under Italian command, the army now to be titled the German-Italian Panzer Army. But Rome would not press Rommel on a deadline for relinquishing his command, and Rommel was in no hurry to do so. Berndt had gone to see Hitler yet again, had returned with word of the Führer's unqualified support for Rommel's position, a surprise to no one but Rommel himself. It was one more act in a strange drama in Berlin, the Führer's behavior turning with the wind, moods governed by inaccurate reports, either good or bad, whatever bits of information those around Hitler dared to pass along.

Kesselring was still in command of the German forces throughout Tunisia and had made no push for Rommel to stand aside. Regardless of whom the Italians sent to replace him, Rommel still had plans for a new campaign. General Messe would just have to wait.

If Rommel was to remain, then someone else had to absorb Mussolini's public wrath for the failure to hold Tripoli. It was no surprise to Rommel when word came that Bastico had resigned. As much as Rommel despised "Bombastico," he recognized that the man cared deeply for his soldiers and had fought through and survived the same kinds of difficulties that had plagued Rommel. But someone had to absorb the blame for the loss of Italian prestige, and Bastico was the clear choice. Honor had been served.

The Germans were not immune to the absurdities that infected the Italian high command. Though Kesselring ruled in Tunisia, General von Arnim had already shown that he had no intention of merging his forces with Rommel's, or even joining Rommel in a united strategy. Von Arnim had unbridled ambition, and Rommel had to assume that someone, perhaps even Hitler himself, had given von Arnim quiet assurances that Tunisia would ultimately be his own command, free from anyone's interference, especially Rommel's. Despite von Arnim's reluctance to hear any plan Rommel proposed, Kesselring knew that the only way to success in Tunisia was for the two headstrong commanders to combine their talents, and their strengths. With Montgomery quiet in front of the Mareth line, and the Allied armies spread precariously along western Tunisia, Rommel knew he had a singular opportunity. In the north, von Arnim had already gained the better measure of the British and had bloodied the French, causing the Allies to regroup and rethink their offensive strategy. But farther south, von Arnim's left flank faced the Americans. It took no genius to predict that the Americans might be planning a drive down into Rommel's position at Mareth, cutting behind him, or striking his western flank. If Montgomery launched his own assault, Rommel's army would be ground up between the two forces, with little chance of escape. Rommel knew he could not launch any kind of organized attack against Montgomery, not yet. If there was opportunity, it lay in the west, against the still-gathering Americans, whose only real test under fire had come against the vague French resistance on the North African coast. With maps in hand, Rommel examined his position, the passes and narrow gaps that cut through the mountain ranges. On the far side, the Americans had armor, but the tanks and heavy guns were spread out along various intersections, guarding too many places with too few machines. It was the mark of an uncertain commander, addressing what *might be* instead of what *was*. Rommel knew nothing of Fredendall, knew only that beyond the American position, the roads spread in fragile spiderwebs, joined by key intersections. The air observers had made their reports, information that was no surprise to Rommel. Behind the American tanks lay precious supplies, great fuel dumps, truck parks, and ammunition stores. If the Americans could be struck hard and fast, they would break, and if they broke completely, they would be forced back behind those key intersections. With the supplies and those key places on the maps falling into Rommel's hands, the Allies might have no choice but to withdraw from Tunisia altogether. Then, Algeria would be vulnerable, and with confusion and uncertainty in the minds of the Allied commanders, Rommel's army could drive hard toward Algiers. It was audacious and fanciful, but it inspired Rommel, gave him a way to push aside the sickness, to feel some flicker of the old fire, a fire he could still give to his men.

RENOUK, TUNISIA—FEBRUARY 9, 1943

Kesselring shifted the maps on the table, seemed to move slowly for a reason. Rommel watched him, von Arnim across the table staring away. They had spoken in friendly greetings, protocol, the performance Kesselring would expect. But Rommel could clearly see that von Arnim would rather be anywhere else than here.

Kesselring stood back from the table, said, "Before we begin . . . I will assume you have both heard something of Stalingrad."

Von Arnim said, "Unfortunate rumors."

"The news is certainly unfortunate, but it is not rumor. The Führer has made a public announcement to the German people. Paulus's army has been defeated. Surviving German units are in full retreat, but many of them are not expected to escape the Russian army. No final word has been received from many of the senior field commanders, but we know that most are surrounded by Russian troops. Field Marshal Paulus is in Russian hands, as are the remnants of the Sixth Army, some ninety thousand German soldiers."

Von Arnim sat up straight. "*Field Marshal* Paulus?"

"Yes. The Führer promoted him just prior to the surrender."

Von Arnim crossed his arms in front of him, made a short grunting sound.

Rommel said, "I assume Paulus was your friend. I regret his capture."

It was as much diplomacy as Rommel could muster, and von Arnim seemed surprised. "I would not say he was my friend. I served under him. He was a good commander. He should not have been assigned to such a disaster. It sickens me that he will be remembered for failure. The Führer's staff is already spreading word of his incompetence. I know better. The army knows better. He was sacrificed for a useless dream."

Kesselring stood above both of them. "There will be no talk of that here. We may mourn Marshal Paulus in our own way, in private. It is not our place to criticize the strategy of the High Command. We could very well have prevailed in Russia, if not for circumstances we could not anticipate."

Rommel looked up at Kesselring, thought, does he believe that? What circumstances? Winter? The Russian army?

Von Arnim said, "It is a lesson for us all. We must avoid such circumstances here. Our strategy must be sound, without recklessness."

Von Arnim seemed to avoid looking at him, and Rommel fought the urge to respond to the undisguised message. Rommel's mind was beginning to boil with words. What you would call recklessness, General, I call victory. He took a long breath.

"Our goal must be to drive deep into the American rear, either cut them off from escape or drive them back a considerable distance. In either event, the British will have to respond by withdrawing, or lose their flank."

Kesselring stood back, seemed content to let his commanders explain their points of view.

Von Arnim said, "The British will not withdraw unless pressed to do so. Any attack toward the west will leave our columns vulnerable to counterattack from the north. The British will not go away quietly."

Rommel ran his finger along a black line on the map. "Here. If we drive the Americans straight back toward Tébessa, we will have an opportunity to capture their primary airfields, as well as their main supply depots."

Von Arnim leaned close. "The British will not allow that. They will attack you on the march."

Rommel felt rising anger again, fought to hold it in. "They will not simply ignore the forces that will remain in front of them. You can make an attack of your own, prevent them from leaving their current position. Or, join the attack, General. We can effect a pincer movement, from both your position and mine. The key to our success is *speed*." Rommel looked up at Kesselring now. "*Speed!* The Americans must be hit before they are prepared, and if we drive them back with speed, we will put the British flank at a serious disadvantage. There will be no attack from the British because they will be isolated. Their only response will be to withdraw."

Von Arnim sat back now, ignored the maps. "I agree that the Americans can be driven back, but then, the plan must be for our forces to turn to the north, to hit the British before they can withdraw, before they can form their own counterattack."

Kesselring seemed to weigh both ideas, stared at the map. "I tend to agree with Marshal Rommel. If we drive the Americans rapidly, we can predict that the British will put emphasis on protecting their ally. Eisenhower is an American. He will not allow the British to rescue his own people. The loss of pride would cost him his command. He will first preserve his own army. They must position reserves in such a way to respond to an assault, but the Allies will launch no counterattack because Eisenhower has never faced a situation like this. He does not know what to expect."

Rommel had not thought of Eisenhower, had focused most of his attention on Fredendall, the man's inexperience, what seemed to be the poor positioning of his armor. But now, Kesselring had made his case even more strongly. Von Arnim grunted again.

Kesselring said, "General, you will send the Tenth Armor along this path . . . here. Rommel will command the southern wing of the attack. Together you will strike a narrow front around this village . . . Sidi Bou Zid. I would anticipate that you will have few difficulties pushing past the American defenses.

Marshal Rommel will be in overall command of the assault."
Kesselring looked at Rommel now. "How soon can this attack
be prepared?"

"As soon as General von Arnim puts the Tenth into motion on
the northern road. The rest of the assault will be in motion before then." Von Arnim seemed to flinch from the insult, and
Rommel ignored him. "It would be most helpful if we received
a number of the Tiger tanks on the southern flank for this assault."

Kesselring tapped the table with his fingers, a familiar show
of energy. "Yes. By all means. General Arnim, you will make
arrangements. You have . . . how many of the Tigers in your pos-
session?"

"Sixty, sir."

Rommel was surprised, had no idea von Arnim had received
so many of the new machines.

Kesselring said, "Half of those should add considerably to the
power of your assault, wouldn't you agree?"

Thirty Tiger tanks. If I had been given those at El Alamein . . .
"Yes, that would be most helpful."

Kesselring moved the map, slid another out from beneath.
"What of Montgomery?"

Rommel leaned close again, pointed to the space east of the
Mareth line. "He is gathering his men into position here. They
are moving with no hurry. Our position there can be flanked on
the right, but only with considerable effort. Montgomery might
not be aware of that."

"But he will be."

Rommel leaned back, looked at Kesselring. "Oh, certainly, he
will become aware of his options, and the vulnerability of our
Mareth position. But he will not act until he is comfortable.
That will take him some time."

"You will maintain a strong defense at Mareth, yes, in the
event you are mistaken?"

"Certainly. General Messe is in command there, which
should please the Italians."

Kesselring crossed his arms against his chest, smiled. "Much
can be accomplished here. The Führer needs a victory, something to brighten his spirits." He looked hard at Rommel now.

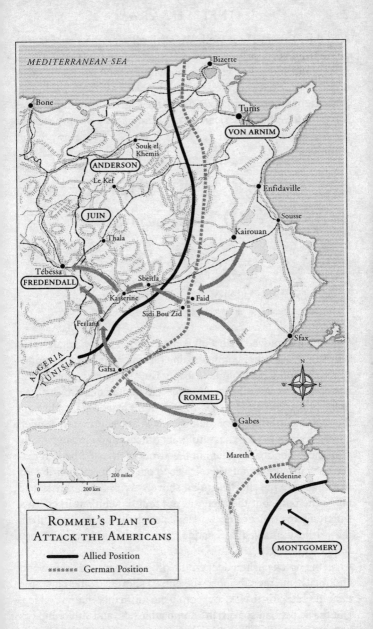

MEDITERRANEAN SEA

Bizerte

Bone

Tunis

VON ARNIM

Souk el
Khemis

ANDERSON

Le Kef

Enfidaville

JUIN

Sousse

Thala

Kairouan

Tébessa

FREDENDALL

Sbeïtla

Kasserine

Faïd

Sidi Bou Zid

Ferïana

Sfax

ALGERIA
TUNISIA

Gafsa

ROMMEL

N
W   E
S

Gabes

Mareth

Médenine

0   200 miles
0   200 km

MONTGOMERY

ROMMEL'S PLAN TO
ATTACK THE AMERICANS

——— Allied Position
••••••• German Position

"Do this, Erwin. Do it well. We shall all reap the rewards that come from success."

Rommel looked at von Arnim, who seemed to ignore them both.

"If General von Arnim sends me the Tigers, we will have the force to drive the Americans away. And, if they do not escape, we will annihilate them."

20. LOGAN

NEAR SIDI BOU ZID, TUNISIA
FEBRUARY 14, 1943

They had moved their tanks into position near a small, dirty village, another comical name on a map, another meaningless hole in the desolate landscape. But the canvas shelters did not come out, the officers ordering the men instead to dig foxholes or narrow slit trenches. As the night had come, so too did the volume of their grumbling, low curses growing louder, anonymous in the darkness, tolerant officers agreeing discreetly with their men that soldiers in the armored division had no reason to work like infantry, no cause to put blisters on their hands working with the short-handled shovels. With the darkness had come the cold, but the men did not feel the chill, worked late, satisfying the officers, holes deep enough to protect a man from the artillery attack that headquarters said could come at any time.

As the holes pushed deeper, the officers approved their work, and finally the men dropped the cursed shovels, settled low into their private fortresses, expecting no difficulty finding sleep. But the sweat had soaked the combat jackets, and shivering, exhausted men stirred and kicked at the ground, stuffing hands deep into pockets, some abandoning their dirt beds and moving

instead to their tanks, grabbing canvas, oilcloth, anything to
help against the hard chill. Around them, the officers kept in
motion, word spreading of orders, precautionary lectures from
above, rumors that Ike himself had been at General Ward's
command post. Throughout the night, patrols had been sent
eastward, heavily armed trucks probing the mountain passes,
holding back just shy of the unpredictable minefields, laid by
American engineers who had not yet perfected their task.
Guards were posted against infiltrators, against anyone who
might move close to them in the darkness. There had been
guards before, the annoying work of detecting the glue-fingered
Arabs, but this time the men were sent forward, and Logan had
watched them go, advancing well beyond the perimeter of the
tanks, shivering privates led by growling sergeants. The lookouts moved as quickly as the darkness would allow, jeep drivers
plowing their way along the rutted roadway. They stopped
where the scouts had marked the road, men with low flashlights
halting them near the bases of high, rocky hills. Now they
would walk, stumbling their way through cuts in the hard
ground. They climbed as far as the rocks allowed, the sergeants
obeying the order to position their men with a plain view of the
larger hills beyond. No matter their weariness, the exhaustion of
a long day's work, no one had to fight to stay awake. This time,
the word from headquarters carried a different kind of urgency,
had silenced the gripes, keeping the lookouts alert, the spotting
scopes and radios in position, the men shivering in dark anxiety,
staring at distant shadows, dark shapes on the horizon, praying
for daylight.

Each man tried to picture it in his mind, what might lie beyond their observation posts, what the enemy might bring.
Many had seen the German armor, mostly from great distances,
brief fights and holding actions to shore up the French, who had
been battered back from the mountain passes. But the French
were away to the north, the ground out in both directions now
manned by Americans, armor and infantry, and this time, the
threat lay out past the vast plain, what the scouts called the *billiard table,* low cactus and thorn bush, a wide valley that led to
the row of sharp, rocky hills. The word had been passed from
headquarters to the battalion commanders, to the captains and

lieutenants who led the tank squads. The Germans were right
out there.

Logan clamped his eyes shut, pulled his knees into his chest,
flexed his toes. There was no warmth in the dirt beneath him,
the cold stiffness in his back and legs complete and agonizing.
He sat up, wrapped his arms around his ribs, pulled hard,
clamped his arms tight, holding himself in a futile attempt to
find warmth. No stars were above him, the darkness thick and
heavy, a light breeze tossing dust and sand into his foxhole. The
mud had dried out, the rain holding off for several blessed days,
the soft ground hardening, a thin layer of sand drifting over the
surface. With the dry weather the tank crews had tended to their
machines, the repair and maintenance crews servicing the
tanks, rooting out the wetness, oiling the engines, greasing the
squeal out of the treads. The ammunition trucks had come as
well, the Stuarts now fully armed, eight thousand rounds for the
machine guns, a hundred five rounds for the thirty-seven. For
the first time, they carried high-explosive shells, replacing most
of the solid shot they had been issued at Oran. Some had said it
had been an idiotic mistake, the solid shot more of a practice
round than what they were supposed to take into combat. Logan
couldn't accept that, that the army would send men and tanks
into battle without the right ammunition. But the loud talkers,
the usual big mouths, had plenty to say about it, the officers finally shutting them up, everyone agreeing that no matter what
stupidity might have plagued the supply units, here, now, they
had plenty of firepower.

There was other talk as well, more griping about the tanks.
Though his crew still drove the Stuart, others had finally been
switched to the larger M-4 Shermans. There were complaints of
course, but Logan had grown too accustomed to the thirty-
seven, still believed that the accuracy of the man at the trigger
meant a lot more than the size of the gun. He had only fired the
Sherman's seventy-five in training, thought of the men who
rode them now, who bragged that they were the division's new
elite. Yeah, fine, he thought. The seventy-five packs a heavier
punch, but I can damned well put a shell into any target up to
five hundred yards, and even farther if the conditions are good.

I made the battalion's first kill, after all, something even the big brass knows about. Put a target in my sights, and we'll see what that thirty-seven can do.

He hugged his sides again, stared into blackness, felt the grit scraping his face. The wind was louder now, a hissing rush over the ground above him. He heard a voice, knew the sound. Parnell. Of course, no way that damned Texan can sit still for long. But he's not climbing in here. This is a one-man hole.

The voice was louder, and he heard his name.

"Jack, where the hell you at?"

Logan stood, chest high in the narrow hole, the wind surprising him, a blast of sand in his face. He put a hand over his mouth, caught a glimpse of a black shape, said, "Here!"

Parnell moved close, knelt down. "Something's up. The supply and maintenance trucks are gone. Pulled out about an hour ago, no headlights. I can't find Hutch."

"Why aren't you in your damned foxhole? You keep running around, you're gonna fall on top of somebody, break your damned neck."

Parnell ignored him. "The trucks are gone, Jack! Nobody out here but the tanks and gun carriers. I'm bettin' it means trouble."

There was a shout to one side, and Logan was relieved to hear Hutchinson.

"Get in your damned hole, Skip! Krauts start throwing shells at us, I don't want my driver scattered to bits. The captain hears you, he'll rip you a new—"

"Hutch! You hear me? The trucks are gone, sent to the rear! I heard some officers talking about it."

Logan ducked down, escaping the wind and Parnell's agitation, thought, you should have been in the infantry. Too much energy to sit in one place. No wonder you love Texas. Lots of room to run around. The wind grew louder, a strange, low roar, sand swirling down into the foxhole. He covered his eyes, thought, good God, what the hell is happening? He curled into a tight ball again, pulled his jacket up over his ears, no sound of Parnell now, no sound of anything but the wind.

It came out of the south, a low, soft rumble that crept through the cactus thickets and thorny brush like some great fat, rolling

monster. The Arabs were used to it, called it the *khamsin*, a part
of life in this dismal land. But the Americans had not felt it too
often, had rarely heard the awful whine, the hellish sounds that
rolled up out of the great desert far to the south. As the tank
crews huddled low in their cover, the odd sounds brought curiosity, and they reacted, daring to peer out, to stand above their
cover. It was a mistake, made worse by the darkness, sand cutting their skin, ripping at their eyes, every breath a choking
gasp, ears scraped by the scouring claws, hats and helmets torn
away. Anyone caught outside of a trench fought to stand, to
move to any kind of shelter, some slithering under the tanks,
hands covering their faces, shirts and jackets pulled high, covering their heads, futile efforts against the grinding waves of
sand. Others scrambled up into the tanks themselves, slamming
hatches. But even the machines gave little protection, tanks and
armored trucks betrayed by small openings, slits and seams that
the wind and sand could slip through. In short minutes, the
storm had engulfed them all, drowning every man in a vast fog
of grit and blind misery.

The wind had calmed, the sand inside his clothes punishing
every movement. He had actually slept, curled up tightly, paid
for that now, tried to unfold his knees, his arms, sharp, aching
pain in his elbows and ankles. He knew not to wipe at his eyes,
his hands filthy, struggled to stand, felt the chill again, put a
hand up on the hard ground, pulled himself up. Voices were all
around him, the tank crews rising, as he was, officers moving
among them. He stood upright, felt a gentle swirl of wind,
shook his jacket, freeing the sand, brushed hard at his sleeve,
then used it to wipe his face, gently probing around his eyes. He
saw movement, a gray shadow, Hutchinson.

"You up, Jack? Let's go, we gotta mount up."

Logan blew out a sharp breath, cleared sand from his ears,
tried to spit, no moisture in his mouth.

"What time is it?"

Hutchinson handed him a canteen. "Almost five. Here. All
I've got. There's more in the tank. Let's move. I'll get the
others."

Logan drank, felt grit in the water, didn't care, washed the crust from his eyes. Men were climbing up out of their shelters, an army rising from the earth, all moving toward the dark shapes of the tanks. He hooked the canteen to his belt, hoisted himself up to the flat ground, sand running down his legs, filling his boots. He tried to ignore it, followed the others toward the tanks, men already climbing up, dark shapes standing tall, catching the first gray light of the dawn. He couldn't see faces, but knew which tank was his, knew Hutchinson would be standing up by the turret before any of the others, waiting for Baxter and Parnell to drop into position first. A low hum surrounded him, soft voices, mixed with the breeze, no loud calls, no one bellyaching about the sandstorm. He heard thunder, saw men halting, standing still, and he stopped with them, listened. There was a low rumble, and he thought the wind was rising again, but then there were different sounds, punches and thumps, *artillery,* and now, the hard voice of Captain Gregg.

"Let's go!"

The voice shocked him, jarred him awake, the men reacting, the captain moving past them. Logan could tell that Gregg was carrying a submachine gun, unusual, and the captain moved quickly toward his own tank, one of the Shermans, hopped up, then quickly dropped down into the turret. The engines began to fire up, loud coughs, hard roars, the smell of exhaust rolling over him. Hutchinson leaned out, held his hand low, and Logan took it, pulled himself up, and with a quick swing of his legs was down in the turret.

He grabbed the helmet, adjusted the earphones, Hutchinson dropping down beside him. Logan's stomach churned with the rumble beneath him, and he felt his pockets, found a chocolate bar, ripped away the paper, stuffed it whole into his mouth. He glanced toward Hutchinson, the young man looking back at him, making a fist, punching it forward, his voice in the earphones.

"You boys wanted to see some Krauts. Looks like we're about to. Captain's orders are to stay close beside him. Columns in parallel formation. The battalion's heading out across the open, then moving to some rough ground close to those big hills. We should find some good cover there, then we'll wait for the Krauts to pop through that pass."

Hutchinson's voice was tense, and Logan leaned down, looked at Parnell's back, expected some comment about shooting prairie dogs, or some other idiocy. But Parnell was silent, waited, as they all did, for the order to come through the wireless, Gregg's order to move out.

Logan shifted in his seat, put his foot on the thirty-seven's trigger pedal, and Hutchinson's voice came over the intercom again.

"Load every gun. Put one in the chamber. We're looking for targets right off the bat."

Baxter responded, pushed a shell into the cannon, the thirty-seven now loaded. Each man then pulled a belt of brass cartridges from a steel box beneath him, and Logan pulled the bolt back on the thirty-caliber, fed the belt of shells into the side of the chamber. He released the bolt, the reassuring sound of metal on metal, his machine gun now loaded as well. Hutchinson's voice came again.

"Any problems? I don't want to hear them. Driver, forward. Keep close to the captain. Let's go find some Kraut bastards."

The tank lurched forward, pressing Logan back into his seat, his gut jumping and rolling with the steel treads. They moved quickly across the short hills, through rock beds, over low thickets of brush. To one side was the main road, hard-packed gravel that snaked toward a gap in the hills to the east, toward some place called Faïd. He stared out through the periscope, faint daylight, the brush sweeping past them, tanks out on both sides. He began to feel the thrill now, a child's excitement, riding the great wonderful toy, like the first day they had ridden the old M-2 at Fort Knox. He had laughed then, bouncing and tumbling across Kentucky grasslands. But there was no laughing now, and he tried to hide from the fear, wrapped his hand on the trigger of the machine gun, dug his heel in hard on the pedal. It was always different when the thirty-seven was loaded, a shell in the chamber, strong, dangerous. Targets? All right, by damned, let's find some targets.

They moved through clouds of dust, sand blowing through the slits around the hatches, and Logan felt a sudden punch of dread, no, not another sandstorm. But then the smell came, sharp and familiar. It wasn't sand at all. It was smoke. Hutchinson's voice was in his ear.

"Opening the hatch. Can't see a damned thing. Shellfire out in front of us. Drivers stay buttoned up. Keep pushing, Skip. "

The hatch opened above Logan, Hutchinson standing, the smells pouring into the tank, choking blackness, the tank suddenly jumping, a hard landing, Parnell's voice:

"Hooee! Close one! We're driving right into a damned attack!"

"Steady, driver. Keep an eye on the captain. We're looking for some cuts in the ground, a wadi or something. Should get us down out of trouble."

Logan stared ahead through the periscope, saw nothing, clouds of dust, gray dawn, brush, more rocks. He looked to the side, the other tanks rolling in formation still, no one firing. All right, where the hell are the targets? He saw a flash of light, a shell hitting close beside a tank on the right, another just beyond. The shellfire was coming in hard and deadly, hitting all around them, the smell curling his face, artillery fire from an enemy they still couldn't see.

"Keep pushing, Skip! Looks like a crest of a hill in front of us. I think we need to go past that."

Logan stared forward again, the tank lurching to the side, punching his shoulder. He felt a chill of sweat in his clothes, sweat in his palms, rubbed at the grease on the cold steel of the machine gun. The tank climbed the rise, and he could see the rocky hills now, much closer, the tank still rolling forward, downhill, the road still there, leading toward the gap between the hills. Hutchinson grabbed the radio microphone, but dropped it, then shouted, deafening in Logan's ears.

"Stop! Halt!"

The smoke cleared, drifted away behind them, a pause in the artillery fire, the tanks all rolling to a stop. Logan tried to turn the periscope to the side, could glimpse the tanks in good formation, no one straggling, no holes, thought, good, we're okay. He looked ahead, could see the gap in the hills clearly, clusters of brush, black rocks. His eyes locked on the rocks, many, many rocks, and they were moving now. He jumped in his seat, felt ice in his chest, and Hutchinson's voice came again.

"Holy Christ."

They sat frozen for a long second, and now Parnell said, "Hey, Hutch. This whole damned valley is full of tanks. And I don't think they're ours."

Hutchinson said nothing, and Logan glanced up at him, thought, we gotta get closer. Too far. And we can't just sit here. He wanted to ask the question, wondered if Hutchinson knew himself. But then the answer came, tanks on both sides firing, launching shells.

Hutchinson shouted into his ear, "Fire! Fire at will! Pick your targets!"

Logan stared through the gunsight, his hands shaking, turned the turret slightly, saw a dozen tanks at one time, all in motion, some spreading out, rolling to the side, some coming straight toward him. He focused on one, his mind racing, the lessons, his brain making the calculation, *a thousand yards, at least.* The range was still too far, and he stared hard, cursed silently, thought, closer, damn you, come closer! The smoke came again, the tanks firing all around him, gunners not as patient.

The ground jumped and Hutchinson said, "Driver advance. Stay close to the captain. Head for the—"

There was a hard jolt, the tank tilting, then falling level again. Logan rocked hard against the tank hull, felt the pain, a sharp punch in his shoulder. The tank jerked forward, Parnell guiding it down toward a narrow cut in the brush, more blasts of fire, smoke filling the tank. The tank moved back up a small rise, and Logan leaned into the shoulder braces, stared into the gunsight, steadied himself, found a target, one tank, a low, square turret, realized now, it was larger than anything he had ever seen. The tank's turret was moving, the gun long and fat, swinging past, a burst of smoke, the open ground swept by black fog. His heel settled hard on the pedal, his brain racing, *four hundred yards,* the ground rocking beneath them, a sudden flash to one side, a spray of metal hitting the tank. He tried to stay focused, couldn't help it, glanced to the side, stared at black steel, blind, could hear thunder from incoming fire, a hard, shattering scream. He spun the turret, had to see, caught the black smoke, fire, a tank close to them in pieces, tread lying flat, the turret tossed to one side, the white star . . .

Parnell halted the tank, the turret just above a low line of brush. Logan pulled the turret back toward the German tanks, focused his eye in the gunsight, the one German tank still coming, closer still. No time, he thought. Shoot him . . . shoot the bastard! He pressed his foot forward, the thirty-seven punching back, a fresh smell of gunpowder. He pressed his shoulders hard into the braces, blinked hard into the sight, thought, come on! Bust him! He saw the streak of fire, a trail that followed his sight line. The shell punched straight into the black tank, a quick yellow blast. He waited for more, the smoke, the glorious flash of fire, the tank erupting in flames. But there was nothing, no change, and he thought, damn! I missed him! He glanced down at Baxter, the next shell already loaded. Logan aimed again, the tank square in the sight, his foot punching the pedal again. He ignored the recoil of the gun, followed the streak of light, saw a flash of fire, the shell impacting the turret, a burst of gray smoke.

Parnell shouted into his ears now, surprising him. "You got him, Jack! Keep shooting! Damn, they're everywhere! There's gotta be a hundred of 'em!"

He kept his eye in the sight, began to move the turret, searching, but then the smoke cleared, and he saw the tank again, rolling forward, still coming, moving straight toward them. He leaned back, stared at Baxter, who had already loaded the gun, held another shell in his hands, waiting, and Logan said, "It bounced right off him! What the hell?"

In the hatchway, Hutchinson still said nothing, the air around them ripping with fire and smoke, and Logan leaned forward again, stared into the gunsight, thought, three hundred yards . . . closer than that. Too damned close. He punched the foot pedal again, but there was no sign of the shell's trail, the German tank hidden in bursts of smoke, blasts of fire throwing dirt and rock into the Stuart, rubble hitting Logan, dirt falling around him. He looked up, Hutchinson still outside the turret, and he shouted, "Hutch, get down! Close the hatch!"

Hutchinson didn't respond, seemed to rock back in the open hatchway, and Logan saw the spreading stain, the man's pants wet and black, and Logan shouted again, "Hutch! Get down!"

He reached up, pulled Hutchinson's belt, felt the wetness,

blood on his hands, tried to stand, to grab . . . and he saw now the man's head hanging to the side, a deep, ragged hole punched in his chest. The blood was spreading, the dust and dirt clinging to the hot stickiness on Logan's hands. There was a voice in his ears, meaningless words from Parnell, and he stared up at Hutchinson's face, the man's eyes open, staring at nothing, Logan's own voice, soft, empty words:

"Hutch . . . get down . . ."

They had withdrawn back to the west of Sidi Bou Zid, gathering what remained of the American armor, a defensive formation along a key roadway, intersected by the same road that led toward the mountains. The tanks that could still move had escaped the disaster, were guided into place by unknown officers. Behind them, artillery pieces rolled as well, heavy armored trucks coming out of the east, bringing remnants of infantry, those men who had not been trapped on the high ground, the observers and foot soldiers who held on to islands of rock in a sea of German armor.

Parnell had driven the tank without anyone telling him what to do, had watched as Logan had watched, as the tanks around them shattered into flaming wrecks, outgunned and outranged by the heavy German machines that rolled toward them. The radios had gone out quickly, the microphone dangling uselessly beside Hutchinson's body, no one on the other end of the line, no one to give any orders. It became a hard race for survival, and the Texan had the instinct, drove them along the same route that had taken them into the fight. For a while, the German armor seemed to pursue, trying to swing around them, cut off the retreat. But the Stuart was still quick and maneuverable, and Parnell drove the tank with perfect skill. Logan had pulled the turret around to face the rear, had fired the thirty-seven in blind anger, useless, little chance of actually destroying anything. But there was one good reason to point the gun to the rear. Logan knew that the front of the turret was the thickest part, the heaviest armor, and if he couldn't take out the Germans with the thirty-seven, at least they would retreat with their strongest armor facing the enemy.

By the time they reached the intersection just east of Sbeïtla,

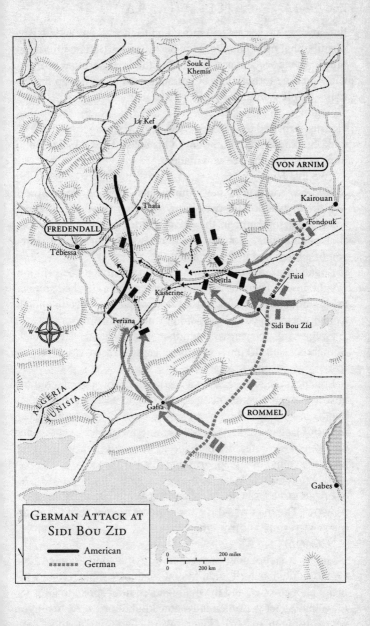

SOUK EL
KHEMIS

LE KEF

VON ARNIM

KAIROUAN

THALA

FONDOUK

FREDENDALL

TÉBESSA

SBEITLA

FAID

KASSERINE

SIDI BOU ZID

FERIANA

ALGERIA
TUNISIA

GAFSA

ROMMEL

GABES

GERMAN ATTACK AT
SIDI BOU ZID

——— American
≡≡≡≡≡ German

0   200 miles
0   200 km

the division's reserves had moved up to meet them, a defensive position that might not hold the enemy away. By late afternoon, the Germans seemed content to hold the valley around Sidi Bou Zid, and they turned their attention toward mopping up the virtually helpless infantry.

He was surprised to see Gregg, the captain sitting low beside his tank, his knees pulled up tight to his chest. Gregg looked up at him, said, "Glad to see you made it."

"We lost Hutch."

"I know. You'll get a new commander. Probably do it myself. My driver was killed, two of my guys were wounded. Some small shell fell right in the driver's lap. Russell, that damned fool. Sightseeing. Nobody would have been hurt if that stupid son of a bitch had just buttoned up."

Logan tried to pull his mind away from Gregg's description, fought now to keep the image of Hutchinson away, had stopped asking himself why Hutchinson had stayed up above the hatch. Logan started to back away, didn't want a conversation.

Gregg said, "Never expected that. They beat us to the punch. Somebody said Rommel was there, leading them. Could be. We lost . . . we lost most everybody."

Logan wanted to escape, was carrying his own grief, couldn't absorb the captain's sadness, didn't want to hear how badly they had been shot up. Hutchinson was gone, and for now it was all the grief Logan could handle. His mind fought for excuses, and he thought of coffee, tried to speak, his words cut off from behind, the sound of a jeep, grinding to a hard stop.

"Captain Gregg!"

Logan turned, saw the jeep, another behind it, an officer stepping out. The man was dirty, his uniform ragged, torn pants, the man's jeep smoking from the engine.

"Captain!"

Gregg was up now, moved toward the man, saluted, and Logan saluted as well, didn't know what else to do. He saw the insignia, a colonel, and the man ignored him, spoke to Gregg.

"Captain, get your men into some kind of order. At first light, we're hitting them hard. General Ward is bringing up more anti-tank companies, field artillery, and armored infantry, anything we can put into line. The enemy is reported to be holding fast around Sidi Bou Zid. We're going to counterattack with everything that can shoot. The infantry's still pinned down out there on the hills. It's up to us to save their ass."

Gregg glanced at Logan. "We lost a lot of people, Colonel."

"So did the enemy, Captain! And they'll lose more tomorrow. Take charge here, or I'll find someone else to do the job!"

Gregg seemed to stiffen, and Logan saw the familiar sight, the man's thick chest, the hard glare.

"I'll handle these men, sir. We'll be ready."

The colonel moved back to the jeep, climbed in, the driver jerking at the gearshift. The jeep paused for a long moment, lurched forward, more black smoke, began to move away. Gregg saluted again, the jeep already past him, dust and sand from both jeeps blowing in a low cloud past the row of tanks, seven machines, what had once been forty.

21. LOGAN

NEAR SBEÏTLA, TUNISIA
FEBRUARY 14, 1943, LATE NIGHT

They camped in an olive grove, men finding sleep anyplace they could, some still inside their tanks. Logan found no sleep at all, leaned up against the gnarled trunk of an ancient olive tree, watched as trucks and armored vehicles rolled past. They had been coming up all night long, spreading out on the primary roads, moving toward what he could only guess were jumping-off points designated on maps that hung on walls in the command posts far behind them.

He reached for the canteen, empty, was suddenly furious, wanted to toss it away, fling it into the night. He gripped it hard in his hand, tried to crush it with his fingers. He looked at the

faint reflection in the dull tin, remembered the foxhole, the
sandstorm, Hutchinson offering him the sandy water. Logan
stuffed the canteen back into the canvas holder on his belt.

"You want some coffee?"

The voice surprised him, Logan suddenly aware that he was
not alone in the world, or even in the olive grove.

"Who's there?"

The man came close, and Logan saw the coffee cup, held
close to him, the voice again, Baxter.

"Here. Half a cup left. They were getting ready to pour it out.
Some food truck back there a ways. Jackass sergeant figured he
wasn't wanting any, so why should anybody else have it."

Logan took the cup, barely warm, and he drank, ignored the
bitterness.

Baxter said, "The rain's coming back in the next day or so.
Maybe. Heard somebody, some officer, talking to somebody
else. We been lucky, he says. *Good fighting weather.* I didn't
stick around, afraid I might have broken somebody's jaw, some
lamebrained lieutenant colonel. What the hell was good about
today?"

Logan finished the coffee, handed Baxter the cup, said nothing.

Baxter sat, faced him. "More Shermans supposed to be here
by morning. Be damned sight better than the Stuart, I guess.
Parnell oughta be happy. The Sherman's slower, but a whole lot
of horsepower compared to the Stuart. Be nice to load something heavier than the thirty-seven."

The image had stayed with Logan, the streaking trail from the
shell of the thirty-seven, the impact of the high-explosive round,
a burst of fire against the turret of the German tank with all the
impact of a fiery snowball. Logan laid his head back against the
rough tree bark, said, "Gregg came by again, hour or so ago. His
crew got pretty shot up. We'll be with him now. We'll be the
lead tank. Again."

"So, Skip'll get to drive his Sherman, and you get to shoot the
seventy-five."

"Yep."

They sat for a long moment, the silence broken by another
column of trucks, the clattering steel of a half-track.

Baxter lay flat on the ground, seemed to stretch his back. "Hard to remember what he looked like."

Logan turned toward Baxter, the man's face hidden by the darkness, knew he could only be talking about Hutchinson.

"Not me. I'll never forget him. His blood's still under my fingernails." Logan paused, felt anger again, the same anger he had felt since the tank had drawn away from the fight. "Damned fool. He rode us into battle like some kid at a county fair, eyes full of the wonder of it all. Forgot how to be a soldier. So, he got himself killed for being stupid."

Baxter sat up again, seemed to look around, searching the darkness. "You know damned well he was the best tank commander in the regiment. There was a whole lot more stupid going on today than what happened to Hutch. There's more than the usual bitching, you can hear it everywhere. Even General Ward's not smelling too rosy."

Logan closed his eyes, desperate for sleep. "Fine. The best tank commander in the regiment got killed because he wouldn't keep his head down. Yeah, bitching about it's not gonna change anything. It's not my job to worry about who's making decisions back there."

"No, we'll leave that to Skip. Here he comes."

Logan saw the shadow, heavy boots punching the ground between the olive trees. Parnell stopped, searched the darkness for a moment, said, "Jack! Pete! Where the hell you at?"

The shout split the silence, and curses rolled out of the grove, sleeping men responding to the rude intrusion.

Baxter said, "Over here, Skip. Shut up before somebody shoots you."

Parnell dropped down heavily, leaned close, his voice in a low, conspiratorial whisper. "We lost a bunch of officers today. There's hell to pay at HQ. Fredendall and Ward are having at each other like two bobcats in a burlap bag. If we don't kick some ass tomorrow, word is, the big brass is done for. Word is, Ike will send a bunch of 'em home."

Baxter lay back down. "Whose word? Yours?"

"Fine. Ignore good intelligence. I picked it up from somebody who was hanging close to Colonel Stack. There's some pissed-off people at Division, lots of finger-pointing. We got our butts tossed in a hog trough today. What we shoulda done . . ."

Parnell's voice was digging into Logan, probing the angry place, annoyance growing into fury, rising up like a long, low, thundering wave, a bolt of lightning in his brain. He lunged forward, grabbed Parnell's throat, rolled him backward.

"Shut up! *Shut up! What the hell do you know?*"

The Texan made a hard choking sound, and Logan kept squeezing, his eyes clamped shut, his fury surging into his hands, fingers digging hard into the man's throat. He ignored the pulling on his shoulders, his mind erasing the loud voices around him.

"Hey!"

"Stop it!"

"Get off him!"

He kept his grip tight on Parnell's throat, the man writhing, twisting frantically beneath him, Logan's eyes still closed, blind to the man's wide-eyed terror. Hands gripped his arms now, pulling him back, and he felt a jab of steel punched against his temple.

"Let him go or I'll blow your brains out!"

Logan froze, his hands loosening, hanging in the air. Parnell fell back, limp, choking, coughing violently, and Logan felt the hard steel pushing against him, felt himself pulled back to his knees, hard fingers still gripping his arms. The steel stayed against his head, and now the voice of Gregg:

"I'll kill you. I'll kill you dead."

Low voices came through the darkness.

"It's okay, Captain."

"Captain . . . it's over."

Gregg stepped back, slid the pistol into his belt, stood over Logan for a long silent moment. "Get hold of yourself, soldier. You hear me?"

Logan stayed on his knees, felt himself shaking, fear, sadness, fought the urge to cry. He watched as the others helped Parnell to his feet. He felt the guilt now, the sadness overwhelming, was suddenly sorry for Parnell, just a loudmouthed Texan, so completely helpless . . . like Hutchinson.

"I'm sorry. Lost my head, Captain. Won't happen again."

Gregg said something, moved away, the others scattering as well. They were alone again, and Parnell sat slowly, kept his distance from Logan. Logan watched him, felt drained, weak, rubbed his temple, where Gregg had pressed the .45. He would have killed me, he thought. He would have. What the hell's the matter with us?

He watched Parnell, the man still gasping for air. "I'm sorry, Skip. You okay?"

Parnell took a raspy breath. "What'd I say, Jack? Didn't mean to rile you."

Baxter said, "It was nothing you said, Skip." He leaned close to Logan, put a hand on his shoulder. "Jack's just mad, is all. The captain's mad. We're all mad. Best we save it for the morning."

The American commanders had drawn the obvious conclusion that, since the enemy had not continued their pursuit of the battered American armor, the enemy's immediate goal would be the mopping up of the American infantry, hundreds of men stranded high up on the *djebels,* the islands of tall rock in the wide valleys now firmly controlled by German armor and increasing numbers of infantry. In the Allied command centers, what Parnell had heard was finger-pointing, the passing of blame, evolving into urgency, to stop whatever thrust the Germans intended to make. West of Sidi Bou Zid, the good roads led straight to key supply dumps and airfields, critical positions spaced far apart, causing the American defenses to be stretched thin, protecting the different routes the Germans might strike. To counter their vulnerability, the Americans intended to push hard toward recapturing the area around Sidi Bou Zid, hoping to rescue the infantry, as well as to drive the German armor back through the mountain passes to the east.

At dawn, the armor rolled forward again, this time in a different formation, a more narrow column, the pointed shape of a V. The tanks led the way, followed closely by antitank guns, half-tracks, armored trucks heavy with fresh troops. The land between Sbeïtla and Sidi Bou Zid was more cut up than the billiard table flatness they had experienced farther east, steep-sided wadis that ran thick with muddy water, soft boggy holes that could trap anyone trying to cross. The tight formations allowed the tanks to approach the uneven ground on a narrow front, saving them time as they moved toward the roughest ground, where the scouts and engineers had found the good crossings. If they moved quickly, they could cover the ten miles toward Sidi Bou Zid and surprise the enemy forces, the enemy who might still be reveling in their complete victory from the day before.

The Sherman was larger, a crew of five, the fifth man serving as loader for the seventy-five. His name was Hapner, a familiar face from the battalion, the only man from Gregg's crew who had not been wounded. There had been no conversation, no time that morning for anything but a quick handshake, a brief polite greeting, silent acknowledgment that they shared the searing sadness, the loss of a friend.

Logan had little time to enjoy the luxury of the larger tank, focused mostly on the gunsight, not so different from what he was accustomed to in the Stuart. He had watched Baxter, the man settling himself forward in the hull, running his hands over the heavy seventy-five-millimeter shells, stacked in every nook of the hull. Baxter had looked back at him, tapping the shells, a silent nod, both men feeling that, finally, they might have something to say about the German armor.

The tank rocked in a slower rhythm, and Logan could feel the weight, a thicker, more massive machine, none of the quick, sharp bounce of the Stuart. Above him, perched on the turret, was a fifty-caliber machine gun, one more bit of power the Stuart didn't have. He fingered his own machine gun, a thirty that pointed out through the turret, parallel to the big gun, peered out through the periscope, the Sherman's scope rotating more freely than the Stuart's, giving him more visibility, a clearer field of fire. He ran his hand over the ammunition belt, the guns all loaded, as they had been the morning before. He tried not to remember yesterday, but the images wouldn't leave him, too many hours spent in the tight spaces in the Stuart. He felt utterly foolish now for ever believing that they had been so powerful, rolling into battle with so much pride in their machine. He was angry and embarrassed at himself for his moronic glee at the adventure of it all, eager to fire his popgun at an enemy who understood what *power* really meant.

As they climbed up into the tank, he had tried to avoid Captain Gregg, and Gregg had seemed to do the same with him. The captain was behind him, up in the turret, as Hutchinson had been, guiding Parnell through difficult ground, leading the formation of tanks forward to find targets. Gregg had said nothing about the night before, his explosive response to the fight, not really a fight at all. After a short hour of sleep, they had gathered to find the coffee and cold rations, and there had been none of the excitement, no big talkers from the morning before. Even Parnell had been quiet, no chatter, nothing at all. Logan still felt the guilt of that, that he had really hurt the man, the big mouth who was only annoying, and certainly harmless. But he realized now, there was nothing harmless about Captain Gregg. Logan could not forget the feel of the .45 pushed against his temple, the cold steel in the man's words, *I'll kill you dead.* Officers didn't do that sort of thing, but that was a rule that came from above, from books, some vague code of conduct. Logan had always seen Gregg as the perfect soldier, the broad-chested portrait of the brave warrior on the recruiting poster, the man with no fear, inspiring his men to conquer any foe. Logan glanced to one side, saw the man's boot, the khaki pants, did not look up to the open turret. What happens now? He's probably embarrassed too, knows he crossed the line. Hell, I'm not going to say anything about it, not to anybody. If he'd have killed me . . . well, I guess someone would have done something about that. He bent low, looked at Parnell's back. And if I'd have killed *you.* Jesus, they'd probably hang me.

Logan stared out through the periscope now, saw a low thicket of brush, tall rocks beyond, the near ground falling away. Gregg's voice came, the first words the man had said in long minutes.

"Driver, follow that trail to the left. The maps show a crossing. Slow it down."

Parnell responded, "Yes, sir."

Logan expected more, well, no, not now. No jabbering to the captain. We're not a damned cozy little family anymore.

The tank slowed to a crawl, and Gregg said, "Move down.

Follow those tracks. The others will follow." He spoke into the radio, and Logan tried to see behind them, knew better than to turn the turret without the captain expecting it. The tank eased into soft sand, the wadi no more than fifty yards wide, a shallow bank on the far side. Parnell guided the tank to the incline, gunned the engine, the tank now lurching up, flattening out on hard ground again.

They pushed through the brush, and Gregg shouted into the intercom, "Krauts! Button up!"

Parnell and Baxter shut their hatches, and Logan expected Gregg to drop down close behind him, but the main hatch stayed open, and Logan stared up, felt a cold chill cutting through him. Outside the turret the fifty-caliber began to fire, and Logan thought, what the hell? He stared ahead, searched the flat ground for targets, saw nothing. The fifty fired again, hard chatter right above him, and Logan searched frantically, still nothing. What the hell is he shooting at? The tank jumped now, dust blowing past, the fifty firing again, flickers and flashes of light, the muzzle fire from more machine guns, more fifties firing from behind them. There were heavy thumps, clouds of sand, and he saw now, black shapes, moving fast, just above the ground, disappearing quickly to one side. *Bombers.*

There was silence now, the big machine gun quiet.

Gregg said, "Junkers. Six of them. They missed everybody. Driver, advance. They'll be back."

The tank rolled away from the wadi, and Logan wanted to see Gregg's face, but the captain was back behind him, awkward position. He knew Gregg was searching the horizon, one hand up on the fifty-caliber. It was a look fresh in Logan's mind, the hardness in the captain coming back, none of the sentimentality from the first big fight. The intercom spoke in his ear.

"I hope you're a better shot than I am, private. Had a damned plane square in my sights and shot right over him."

Logan looked up, saw Gregg leaning over him, a quick nod. "Find me a target, sir. We'll see what this seventy-five can do."

They rolled on for several minutes, Logan searching still, the others doing the same. He heard chatter from the radio, then the intercom.

"Eyes sharp! Observers report a formation of enemy tanks to our front and right!"

After a pause, Gregg said, "There they are! Driver, twenty degrees right. Slow down, let the formation get into position. They're a good way off, maybe fifteen hundred yards. They don't appear to be moving. Button up. Let's keep going."

Gregg dropped down, the hatch closing, and Logan couldn't help feeling relief. He eased the periscope around, could see the other tanks now, moving out on either side, putting distance between them. He leaned forward, stared through the gunsight, felt the churning again, made two hard fists, tried to squeeze the shaking from his hands.

Gregg slapped him on the back, surprising him. "Find us a target, Private. The seventy-five can't bust through the front armor of those big boys. Look for a flank shot. Or shoot low, take out the treads."

Gregg's voice was calm, words coming slowly. Logan flexed his fingers, stared through the sight, could see the enemy tanks now, some in motion, spreading out as well. He expected to see the smoke, signs of firing, but there was nothing yet, the tanks out to the side feeling their way slowly forward, the enemy doing the same. Parnell spoke now, one of the few times Logan had heard his voice since they'd climbed into the tank.

"Sir, flat, open ground ahead. Cover beyond, then some rocks, maybe two hundred yards farther."

"Kick it a little, driver. Get across the open quick. You get to those rocks, let's stop, have a look. I'll tell the formation to halt in cover, whatever they can find. We need to keep an eye out for planes."

Logan stared through the sight, searched for a cannon barrel, signs of a turret pointing to the side, the vulnerable target. But the tanks were still facing him.

Gregg said, "Driver halt. That's far enough. I'm having a look. Something's strange. There's too few of them."

The hatch opened, and Gregg stood, binoculars up. "They're pulling back. They know we're too many. Driver, advance. Let's drive it hard. It's only a few scouts, maybe. We've caught these bastards with their pants down!"

Parnell pushed them forward, the tank now clear of the rocks, and Logan saw the smoke, the first bursts of fire from the German tanks. He waited for it, the blasts falling short, clouds of dirt and rock a hundred yards in front of them. He held the turret steady, and Parnell seemed to read him, driving the tank in a straight line, keeping a mound of thick brush between the Sherman and the enemy.

The gunsight settled on one tank, and Logan said aloud, "Eight hundred . . . keep moving, Skip. I need to catch one turning."

Parnell said nothing, the tank pushing forward, the brush now all around, a shallow ditch appearing, the tank settling low, a good position.

Gregg read him as well. "Halt, driver. Good spot. Let's have another look. You're close enough, gunner. Find us a target. Fire when ready."

Gregg pushed the hatch open again, stood, Logan bathed in the cool, misty air, a light fog drifting across the open ground. He heard a sharp punch, a tank to one side firing, then another. He focused on the German tank in his sight, the machine rocking, climbing a low rise, the turret swinging, the long barrel of the gun pointing out to the left, the voice in Logan's head, *now.*

He punched the foot pedal and the big gun thundered, the tank rocking back. He strained to see, the trail of the shell winding straight toward the enemy, a flash of fire, the captain's shout in his ear:

"Short! Twenty . . . thirty yards!"

Logan knew not to wait for Hapner, the man moving quickly, another shell, and he adjusted the turret, a touch of the gun's elevation. He punched the trigger again, another hard blast, long seconds, a flash of fire, Gregg:

"Contact! Low, on the treads!"

Logan didn't need the captain's report, could see it for himself, saw movement on the tank itself, men emerging. Gregg said, "They're bailing out! Find another target!"

Logan moved the turret, saw another machine rolling down into a low depression, hidden, only the turret visible. There was a flash, the enemy gun firing, more flashes now, hard thumps all around, smoke rolling past, clouding his view. Dammit, where are you? He eased the turret to the side, searched again, rocks, motion, another tank, no, it's an armored truck, a big gun. The smoke rolled across again, but he could see that the ground was alive with movement, the Sherman rocking again, the sound of the fifty-caliber above him, Gregg's voice:

"Planes! Don't worry about me! Keep firing, gunner!"

Logan punched the trigger again, too quickly, the shell ripping past the flank of the big truck. He cursed himself, caught movement from the loader, Hapner, Gregg's voice in the intercom.

"Tanks to the flank! Both flanks! Gunner, swing to the left. Targets approaching!"

Logan cranked the turret, swung the gunsight around, searched, tanks close by, white stars, firing, bathed in smoke, one on fire.

"Where? I only see ours!"

Gregg shouted again. "Driver! Reverse! Get clear of the brush! Prepare to maneuver ninety degrees north!"

Logan felt desperate confusion, thought, where? Why? The targets are in front of us. He said aloud, "Captain! Where are we going?"

The tank jerked backward, Logan's head knocking hard into the gunsight. Dammit! What's happening?

Gregg shouted again. "Enemy tanks to the rear!"

Parnell responded, "Dammit, Captain, which way do I go?"

There was a huge blast, and Gregg dropped down hard, the hatch still open, his helmet off, and he pounded Logan's shoulder, shouted close to his ear, "Fire at will! Anything you can see! We're hemmed in! Enemy tanks on all sides! Driver!"

Parnell ignored him, deafened by the blast, Gregg's intercom useless now. The tank spun to one side, lurched forward, and Logan shouted at Gregg, "Sir! The hatch!"

Gregg stood, pulled the hatch down, steadied himself on Logan's shoulder, leaned close to his ear. "Fire on the move! We might have to shoot our way out of here!"

The tank rocked forward, and Logan's head smacked hard into the gunsight again, his helmet in his face now. He tried to steady himself, pulled at the helmet, saw Gregg bleeding from the nose. Gregg shouted something into the radio microphone, his voice drowned out by more firing, close by, more blasts from shellfire. Logan held tightly to the gunsight, no targets now, just smoke, the tank rocking hard, Parnell pushing it through rough ground, spinning to one side, back again, zigzag movement, the instinct of good training. Logan looked through the periscope, fire, wreckage, men running, more smoke, a spray of dirt and steel. There was a hard punch, the sound of steel against steel, and the tank rose up sideways, fell back down, thick smoke boiling up inside. He heard a scream, the engine suddenly quiet, shouts, Gregg up again, the hatch open.

"Out! Now!"

Logan tried to stand, his lungs burning, blind, the tank thick with smoke, the captain's voice again:

"Get out!"

He felt a hand on his shoulder, pulling his jacket, and he rose up, tried to stand, his hands reaching up for the opening, heat now, coming from below, black smoke blinding him. He climbed, felt for the hatchway, screaming all around him, and he felt Gregg lifting him out, the two men tumbling off the tank, hard landing, no air in his chest. He tried to breathe, fought to see, his eyes burning, choking fire in his lungs, fire on the tank, smoke boiling from the hatches. He tried to shout, *Get them out,* but nothing came, no words, choking tightness in his throat. He lay flat on the soft dirt, saw Gregg back up on the tank, leaning into the hatch, more screams, a burst of fire, searing heat rolling over him. Logan pushed with his legs, rolled over, away from the tank, thorny brush beneath him, his clothes ripped, blood on his hands. He found his breath again, tried to stand, was on his knees now, looked at the tank, boiling fire, Gregg tumbling off the hull, another shape falling with him, smoking black, collapsing on the ground. Logan moved closer, the heat too much, driving him away, Gregg lying flat, moving, trying to crawl. Logan pulled his jacket over his head, rushed forward, grabbed Gregg's hand, pulled hard, burnt skin, the hand slipping away, *breaking,* Logan tumbling backward, another burst of fire, the tank consumed now, gasoline and gunpowder, the bodies of men.

"Are you alive?"

Logan felt the jacket sliding down, opening his face to the cool air. He tried to open his eyes, saw shadowy shapes.

"Ah, so you are."

He fought to see, the shapes growing clearer, men, standing over him. He took a breath, the cool air ripping the soreness in his throat, said, "Water."

The man bent low. "Oh, not now. Sorry."

He felt hands lifting him, his legs under him now, burning soreness in his feet. He blinked, could see more clearly, several trucks, black crosses, the smoldering wreck of the tank. The fire was in his throat now, and he said again, a question this time, "Water?"

The man said something, authoritative, an order, words Logan couldn't understand. Then the man spoke to him again. "Prisoners will receive care in due time. Water too."

Logan saw the man's face now, the khaki hat, the uniform. *German.*

"You are a fortunate man. But you will march now."

They were gathered into long columns, some with wounds, others pulled from their tanks at gunpoint, the men caught in the trap laid for them by the German panzers. Logan was led to a line of men, guarded by German soldiers, men with bayonets. The column was led by a small truck, followed by one armored car, a heavy machine gun perched above, trained on the Americans who could no longer make any kind of fight. They marched toward the rocky passes, the same place where Logan had seen his first German tank, where the shell from the thirty-seven had proved no match for the power of the far bigger machines.

He tried to see where they were going, but there was no strength, the thirst overpowering, his throat clamped shut, lungs still seared by fire. His steps were slow and automatic, like the men around him, driving themselves with what little remained of the energy they had brought to the fight. His thoughts drifted, fire and screams, smoke, the captain. He wondered if they were with him, somewhere, up ahead, far behind. Or if they were not. He had seen no one come out except the captain, and that one . . . body. He tried to clear his mind, thought, the others might have survived, escaping through the hatch, unseen in the fireball. Logan tried to hold that in his brain, said it aloud, *"They could have escaped."*

He tried to see it, Parnell and Baxter making it back to safety, uninjured, telling the story of what had happened. Logan had no idea what had hit the tank, a bomb, a shell from a German tank, artillery. What did it matter, after all? What did any of it matter? He pushed one foot in front of the other, aching soreness in his feet, squinted toward the hills ahead. He tried to count the men in the column, but his mind wouldn't see anymore, his brain not working beyond the simple footsteps. He struggled to ask questions, simple thoughts, where are we going? Are they going to shoot us? Maybe just put us behind some wire. And then what? Will they let us go? Send us home? He thought of the tank again, the marvelous machine, the men in his crew, good men, more, *friends*. Will I see them . . . ? In front of him, a man fell, blood on the man's pants, a German pulling him off the road, a pistol in the German's hand. Logan would not look, closed his eyes, one foot moving in front of the other.

The prisoners were marched away from the battleground, across the wide expanse that spread out in all directions, tank crews and artillerymen joined by columns of infantry, the men who had been trapped in the djebels, the rocky, high ground, unable to fight their way to safety. Behind them, what remained of the American counterattack streamed westward in a desperate escape, men abandoning their broken machines, some retreating with no order, little more than a panicked mob. Those who reached the American defenses were helped by those who still manned the passes, ambulances and medics, shocked officers and desperately nervous troops, who now eyed the German advance with a growing sense of hopelessness, the wave of fear creeping through the ranks that they had stumbled into a hell they could not withstand, that they had finally come face-to-face with the man named Rommel.

In the command posts, the senior officers tried to gather information, tried to communicate with anyone who might still be an organized force, to rally any hope that somewhere around Sidi Bou Zid, somewhere east of Sbeïtla, there was enough organized resistance that the Germans might still be driven back. Scattered fights still raged, smoke and fire dotting the ground, men with rifles and antitank guns making a last effort to stand

tall in the face of German armor. But the commanders knew
how utterly complete the disaster had been, and so they began to
draw new lines, searching the maps for the best route of escape,
pulling the men and their machines back to a new defensive position, a place that might still keep the German wave from
rolling completely through western Tunisia. The last stout ridge
of rocky hills was called the Western Dorsale, the last place
where Rommel's army might still be contained. The American
commanders held out hope that the passes could be held, the
roads that led to the key towns of Tébessa and Thala, beyond a
small village close to the primary pass, named for that gap in
the hills. It was the place that would give its name to this entire
campaign. The commanders and the soldiers who made their retreat through the place would always remember the name. It was
Kasserine Pass.

22. EISENHOWER

DJEBEL KOUIF, NEAR TÉBESSA, TUNISIA
FEBRUARY 15, 1943

For several days the intelligence reports had strongly suggested that the German attack would come much farther
north, near the far left flank of the American position, the junc-
tion with the beleaguered French, through the pass at Fondouk.
Anderson had engineered his defensive strategy accordingly,
had ordered Fredendall to push units of the Second Corps closer
to the French, to strengthen the area certain to be targeted by the
inevitable German assault. Fredendall had obeyed without argument, had accepted wholeheartedly the validity of the intelligence. As a result, the Second Corps' armor had been spread
out in small packets, with a sizable force sent to strengthen the
northern flank. Every indication had been that the Germans

were still coming through the pass at Fondouk. Eisenhower had listened to the reports as well, had wanted to believe that Anderson was well-informed, that the intelligence was reliable. But the maps had alarmed Eisenhower, and Fredendall's complacency alarmed him more, the man believing that armor and infantry in isolated pockets spread along distant roadways and mountain passes was sufficient to keep the Germans at bay. Fredendall relied on the accuracy of the intelligence, that with the German thrust sure to come to the north, the weakened units at the center of the American position would have little to be concerned about.

Eisenhower knew that the American forces had yet to be seriously tested in battle. To ease his discomfort, he had traveled east from his headquarters at Algiers, to see for himself the various frontline positions. He had visited Fredendall first, had then traveled farther forward to see the First Armored Division's commander, Orlando Ward. Fredendall was the picture of loud confidence, a man with definite opinions about everything, his faith in the disposition of his troops unshaken. Ward had seemed strangely resigned, accepting Fredendall's orders with mild protest, but obeying them just the same. It was unusual for Ward, especially because Eisenhower knew that Ward did not enjoy anyone else telling him how to arrange his tanks. Word had already filtered back to Eisenhower's headquarters in Algiers of a simmering feud between Fredendall and Ward, sharp words exchanged, calmed only by Fredendall's rank and authority. Ward was, after all, the good soldier. He would do what he was told.

Both Anderson and Fredendall insisted that any German attack in the American middle would likely be a feint, a demonstration to take American attention off the real threat at Fondouk. Despite those assurances, Eisenhower had recognized the dangerous flaws in Fredendall's deployment and, by nightfall on February 13, had issued his own orders to correct the dangerously scattered armor and troop positions. But before Eisenhower's orders could be carried out, the Germans had struck. And it was not at Fondouk, but farther south, where the intelligence reports had claimed no danger existed. Even as the Germans drove hard into the American armor and infantry at

Sidi Bou Zid, both Anderson and his intelligence officers continued to insist it was only a feint. By midday, with the American position in shambles, everyone finally realized that the
intelligence had been disastrously wrong.

When the German spearhead punched through the passes east
of Sidi Bou Zid, Eisenhower had been close enough to hear the
thunder. As the first waves of confused and panicked troops
flowed through the positions around him, Eisenhower had
obeyed the anxious protests of the officers, the men who knew
this was no place for the Allied commander to be. With the
American defenses collapsing behind him, Eisenhower's jeep
had made a rapid journey back to Fredendall's headquarters, the
command center of the entire American position.

The road wound up a steep canyon, lined by fat rocks, studded
with an uneven covering of tall, thin pine trees. Eisenhower
steadied himself in the rear seat of the jeep, the driver far more
calm than he had been only an hour before. In the front seat
beside the young sergeant was Lucian Truscott, a fiery, no-
nonsense two-star, who had made the trip with Eisenhower
through the frontline positions. Truscott had come ashore north
of Casablanca, a part of Patton's Operation Torch Western Task
Force. Eisenhower had known Truscott before the war, had observed him since, a man who could easily be a hard-charging
disciplinarian, the kind of senior officer the green American
units desperately required. After the successful completion of
Torch, Eisenhower had chosen Truscott to be his field aide in
Tunisia, the commanding general's eyes and ears among the
men charged with confronting the Germans. One of Truscott's
first reports had been tinged with carefully guarded annoyance,
an observation that Fredendall's headquarters seemed to be designed to be permanent, as though Fredendall expected to be in
one spot for quite a while. Eisenhower had gone forward immediately, had confirmed that Truscott was right. Fredendall was
expending a great deal of energy creating a command post that
seemed better suited to withstand an old-fashioned siege. It was
Eisenhower's first hint that the Second Corps might have a
problem with its command.

Eisenhower stared at the rocks, the road, the vast blanket of heavy cover that guarded the entrance to Fredendall's command center. Beyond the fortresslike formidability of the ground, Eisenhower understood now that there was another serious problem with Fredendall's decision. As the push into Tunisia had progressed, the maps of this part of the country had been brought up-to-date. When Fredendall's position was first marked, Eisenhower had thought the aides had simply made a mistake, or that the maps themselves were in error. But Eisenhower had made the trip himself now, not just to see Fredendall, but beyond, to the frontline positions, to observe the various officers whose men pushed into the positions Fredendall had assigned them. Caught by the stunning surprise of the German attack, Eisenhower had been forced to retreat in a mad dash, and so the location of Fredendall's headquarters had become more than simply a blue ink spot on a map. Now, Eisenhower had endured the long miles on muddy roads, too many miles, had felt too much of the misery of the jeep's rock-hard tires, had slipped into too many ditches, making way for long caravans of trucks, the Red Ball Express, American vehicles pushing hard toward the front. He knew now that the maps were not wrong, and along every mile his anger grew, a blossoming fury at Fredendall for finding himself this exaggerated safe haven against what Fredendall must have thought was the imminent threat from German bombers and strafing Messerschmitts. Lloyd Fredendall had put the Second Corps headquarters in a natural fortress that was *eighty miles* from the disastrous fighting at Sidi Bou Zid.

The jeep rolled to a stop, the road ending at a thicket of dense pine trees. Officers were there, surprised men who studied Eisenhower even as they raised their automatic salutes. He waited for Truscott to climb out, then stepped onto the muddy white ground, saw a familiar staff officer, Colonel Akers, Fredendall's aide, the man rushing forward with a hasty salute.

"Sir! Welcome back! If I may lead you. Just follow me this way. I believe you're familiar with the trail. Notice the white tape on the pine straw, leading through those trees."

Eisenhower said nothing, held a tight grip on his anger, had no reason to attack Akers for his helpfulness. They began to walk, and Eisenhower heard the hard, low roar of a diesel engine, stopped, saw a bulldozer emerging from a wide trail in the trees. The machine carried a wide steel bucket, which hung heavily in front, weighed down by fat, white boulders. Eisenhower watched as the dozer spun to one side, the bucket spilling forward, dumping the rock into a narrow ravine. The machine backed away, turned, disappeared quickly up the trail, and Eisenhower's mind began to fill with questions. Fredendall's aide waited patiently, and Eisenhower followed him again, moved along the soft mat of pine straw, climbed toward a clearing. Eisenhower could see men in motion everywhere, the sound of more heavy equipment, men with shovels and pickaxes. There were officers, a cluster of three men huddled over a small wooden table, thick with paper, drawings. *Engineers.* He ignored the aide, moved that way, said, "What is happening here?"

They turned to him, snapped upright, saluted, and one man said, "Sir, General Fredendall has ordered us to make further improvements to the security of his command center, to protect the headquarters against even the strongest enemy bombardment. We are making use of existing caves and other deep crevasses in the rock walls along the deepest parts of the canyon, extending corridors and shelter space far back into the rocks."

Eisenhower stepped closer, couldn't hide the menace in his expression. The man seemed surprised, and Eisenhower said, "You are telling me that the engineers are putting their energy to fortifying a corps headquarters? Are you aware what is happening east of here? What *has* happened? Why aren't your people out there, where they can assist the troops fighting the enemy? We require minefields, fortified defenses. Those damned bulldozers need to be sent east, and quickly!"

He tried to hold his voice down, but the fury was complete, the three officers backing away, eyes wide.

Another man spoke, a captain, clean uniform, clean-shaven, the voice of a boy. "Sir, the combat companies have their own engineers for that sort of work. We are assigned here by General Fredendall's orders, to fortify and strengthen—"

"That's enough, Captain." Eisenhower tried to calm himself, knew they were not to blame. He had enormous respect for the engineers, knew they were good men, well-trained, certainly understood their orders. "All right. Go about your work. Move your damned rocks and dig your holes. But be prepared for *new* orders."

Eisenhower spun away, moved again toward the strips of white tape, the pathway through the pines, the long trail that would take him to the man who was comfortably safe in his impregnable headquarters.

The climb through the pines had drained him of anger, the desperate situation at the front seeping into his thoughts. This is no time for an ass-ripping, he thought. I need Fredendall and Ward, all of them, I need them doing their jobs. I can either jump down their throats, or I can find out just what the hell's going on. Before I start tossing people out windows, it's probably better if I act like a damned diplomat. I hate diplomats.

"Sir! This way!"

Eisenhower followed Akers across a clearing, the village square of the remote settlement, occupied mostly by Arabs who had long worked the various mines in the area. The streets were muddy, hardly streets at all, rutted alleyways that disappeared into dark canyons. Akers led him to the far side of the square, to a lone block structure, what had been a schoolhouse, one of the larger buildings in the dismal village.

The inside was dark and damp, the floor swept clean, the thick walls adding a chill to the room. There were rooms beyond, passageways dug right into the rock, aides in motion, radio operators, several telephones. He saw Fredendall, sitting next to a corporal, the corps commander gripping the man's telephone receiver, the corporal pulled close by the tangle of wires. Fredendall slammed his fist onto the table in front of him, shouted in the receiver, "Hell no! Get those people on the road! I don't care what I told you this morning! I'll have your ass for lunch, *you understand me*?"

He tossed the phone receiver down on the table, pointed a finger at the corporal, who flinched, said, "Damn you to hell! You will tell those people that I won't listen to this nonsense! I expect . . . oh." He saw Eisenhower now, stood, seemed suddenly nervous, self-conscious, rubbed his palms on his shirt. Older than Eisenhower, he was short and stocky, red-faced, known by everyone who served with him as a short-tempered man of many words and a mountain of opinions. From early in the war, Fredendall had been one of George Marshall's favorites, and Marshall's selection for command of the Center Task Force for Operation Torch had not been questioned. Fredendall had done the job, had impressed Eisenhower with his handling of the capture of Oran. Despite his rough edges, Eisenhower had believed that Fredendall would continue to lead his corps with hard-driving discipline and strong command of his tactical situation. Eisenhower watched as Fredendall seemed to compose himself, thought, so why in hell are you eighty miles from your front lines?

"Ike! Ah, good. Welcome back. We're pulling together on this one, pulling together. I've finally been able to convince Anderson of the seriousness of our situation, and he's sending help from the north. That's the problem with the Brits, you know. The man just wouldn't listen. Tried to tell him days ago we might have a problem. He's agreed to release the rest of the First Armor from Fondouk, Robinett's boys, send them down here where they belong! We'll toss the Hun back in no time!"

"I need more than optimism, General. What do we hear from the command posts?"

Fredendall seemed to deflate, hesitated. "Damn them, Ike. Bad communication lines. Can't get reports back from the regimentals. Company commanders ignoring my calls. There'll be hell to pay when this is over. I'll take care of it. No need to worry you with details. But quite a few colonels will be put behind desks for this."

"Who? Which colonels?"

"Well, Drake, Waters. Hightower too. And not just colonels. A few one-stars too. McQuillen for certain. I send out instructions, expecting them to tell me what the hell's going on, and I get nothing but static. As fast as I send orders, I hear how they can't be carried out."

Maybe if you were closer to the fighting . . . "Lloyd, I'm not interested in who you intend to call on the carpet. I want to know who's in charge up there, and who's putting our people where they need to be. Have you spoken to General Ward?"

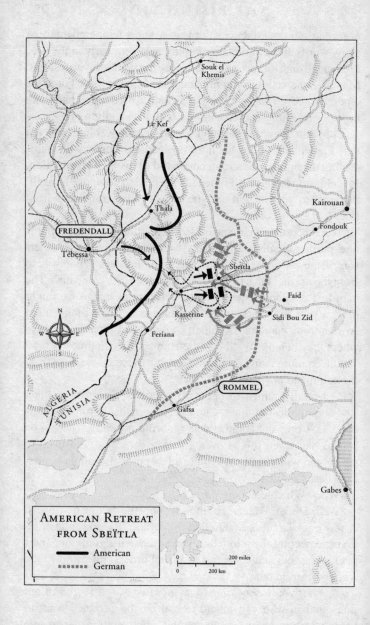

Souk el
Khemis

Le Kef

Kairouan

Thala

Fondouk

FREDENDALL

Tébessa

Sbeïtla

Faid

Kasserine

Sidi Bou Zid

Feriana

ROMMEL

ALGERIA

TUNISIA

Gafsa

Gabes

AMERICAN RETREAT
FROM SBEÏTLA

━━━━ American

••••••• German

N

W   E

S

0   200 miles

0   200 km

Fredendall sniffed, "Ward. There's another one, Ike. That man has no business . . . well, let's just say that once this is over, I intend on filing a report, and it won't be perfume and roses."

Once this is over. "This is a long way from over, Lloyd. What are you doing about defense? Where's the best place to draw up? Who's putting our people into line?"

Fredendall moved to the map, pointed. "General Anderson believes we should fortify here. Kasserine Pass, Sbeïtla, and Feriana. I quite agree. On the far right flank, we're pulling away from Gafsa. Turns out, it can't be held, spreads us too thin. I ordered the engineers to place minefields where they could hold the enemy up in the narrowest confines." Fredendall turned toward Eisenhower. "We need to pull completely back to the Western Dorsale, Ike. I tried to tell them to keep pushing, that Rommel couldn't have the strength they kept reporting he did. But no one would listen, so now, our boys have been shoved back. There's a lot of disorder, no one taking charge up there. We have no choice now but to make a stand along the western approaches to the mountain passes." He turned to the map again, pointed to the road just west of Kasserine Pass. "I don't think the Huns will keep coming. They're stretching their supply lines too thin. But if they do, and we can pull the armor and artillery just west of . . . here, the Huns can be bottled up in the pass. That should hold them for a good pounding. We need air and heavy artillery in support, but I can't make that happen myself, Ike. I need you to order Anderson to throw his weight down this way, I need the air boys to do their piece. I tell you, Rommel's extending his supply lines as it is, and he's vulnerable to a heavy counterattack."

Eisenhower tried to ignore Fredendall's attempt to toss away his own responsibility. He stared at the map, thought, at least he's taking some positive steps.

"I'll send the air, and Anderson will know exactly what I want him to do. You sure it's Rommel out there?"

Fredendall seemed surprised at the question. "Who else would it be? Um, of course, sir. It must be. That kind of rapid advance, busting in on us that quick. I tried to tell them—"

Eisenhower held up his hand. "We don't need to discuss what's already done. I want to know what we're going to do tonight, what we're going to do tomorrow. If Rommel's leading those people, they're not going to stop and give us time to get ready. I agree that you should pull everyone back to the mountains, gather up as much strength as you can. I'll contact Morocco, order units from Patton's forces to head east. We need artillery and tanks, and some damned good troops on those hills. I want those passes blocked!"

Eisenhower turned, saw a young lieutenant emerging from the radio room.

"Excuse me, sirs. Sorry to interrupt. General Fredendall, a call has come in from General McQuillen, passed through General Ward. All indications are that the armored positions have completely given way. There is a general retreat still in progress, much of it unorganized. There continues to be no word from Colonel Waters or Colonel Drake. General Ward expresses his optimism, sir, but it is believed that Colonel Waters has been either killed or captured."

Fredendall slammed his fist against the map, began to shout, empty curses. Eisenhower turned away, ignored the show, felt uncomfortable, thought, get control of yourself, General. Your men need to see their commander *in command.* He looked again toward the aide, who stood stoically, enduring Fredendall's tirade. Eisenhower thought of Drake. Colonel Tom Drake. It had been only days before, Eisenhower's first visit to the front lines here, one pleasant task among many tedious ones. Eisenhower had pinned a medal on Drake's chest, the Distinguished Service Cross. God help you, Colonel. He thought of the other man, the second name, *Waters.* The aide glanced at him now, a silent frown, and Eisenhower turned away again, thought, you know, of course. You all know. It's the only reason you would bring that news while I'm still here. No one should pass that along but me. He shook his head. Yep, you'll have to hear it directly from me, George.

Lieutenant Colonel John Waters was George Patton's son-in-law.

He looked again at Fredendall, the man staring at the map, silent now, his useless display of anger exhausted.

"Lloyd, do you understand what will happen if Rommel pushes past the Western Dorsale? He'll have an open shot at our primary supply bases, our airstrips. We'll have no choice but to pull back into Algeria." Fredendall turned to him, and Eisenhower looked hard at the man, searched for the fire, some sign that he was up to the task. "We're in trouble here, Lloyd. But I don't want to hear bitching about it. If we fail here, all our plans stop. It could take years before we're ready to put our people in Europe. Do you understand that? If we can't stop the Germans here, if we show Hitler we're too weak to drive him out of Africa, who knows what he might try to do?"

Eisenhower pulled himself away from the thoughts, the images, couldn't accept that the planning, the grand strategies, might all dissolve in this dismal stretch of scrub and rocky hills in central Tunisia.

"If we don't stop them here, Lloyd, we may not stop them at all."

23. ROMMEL

NEAR GAFSA, TUNISIA
FEBRUARY 17, 1943

They cheered him, a sound he had not heard in many weeks. He rode tall in the small truck, allowed himself a smile, waved at them as he passed, tank drivers and artillerymen feeling the same joy he felt. It was Gazala again, and Tobruk, Mersa Matruh, and Sollum, glorious memories of the great conquests coming back to life inside him, erasing the sickness, the weakness. For the first time since before Alamein, there was a victorious spirit in his army again, a shattered enemy fleeing his guns. He passed by the wire fences, makeshift prison camps filling with dirty, beaten men, men who stared downward in shock and shame. He rarely spoke to prisoners, but these men were different, new faces, an army he had not seen before. They were Americans. There was no time for casual talk, and so he saluted them in his own way, a quiet stare, thought, now you understand what it means to stand up to Rommel. Now you know what a war truly is.

He had never accepted the racial disregard Hitler had for the Americans, what the Führer had called a nation of mongrels. Rommel dismissed the Americans now for other reasons, for what they had shown him on the battlefield, their carelessness, poor planning, bad execution, being unprepared and underequipped, daring to stand face-to-face with the finest soldiers in the world. And now, many of them were dead and wounded, and many more stood in disgraced silence behind barbed wire.

Out in front of him, the fighting had grown quiet, his men mopping up, gathering the prisoners, cleaning out pockets of resistance. He had been surprised by the evacuation at Gafsa, the town a valuable gateway to the crucial Allied air and supply bases at Tébessa. But Gafsa had fallen without a fight, the Americans pulling away quickly, and the Arabs there had come out with cheers of their own, surprising him again, saluting the Germans, saluting the Führer. As he paused to speak to his officers, he learned why. The Americans had left in great haste, had done the expedient thing by destroying their ammunition dump there. But their haste had been costly and stupid, no warning given to anyone close by, and so, more than thirty Arabs had died in their own homes, buried by the rubble from the massive explosions.

He had no feelings of hate or even hostility for the Americans, thought of them simply as the enemy, like the British. But there was a difference. He respected the British fighting man, who seemed to know the value of his own history. Even the lowliest private seemed to carry some piece of his king's empire, some awareness that he was a part of something that had once been grand and glorious. But the Americans came with swagger and arrogance, and Rommel had seen nothing to justify it. He felt no respect for that, had enjoyed the shocked stares from the prisoners for that reason alone. Where is your arrogance now? How is it to have your perfect confidence crushed beneath the steel of my armor? You are not much higher in God's eyes than the Arabs. Well, no, that is not quite fair.

The Arabs had filled the roadways around Gafsa, and he had passed long lines of men hauling wagons of loot, what they had scrounged from the abandoned American camps. He knew that many of his officers traded with the Arab merchants, found a way to buy eggs and meat. But he had no respect for scavengers, saw the Arabs as the worst kind of soldiers, if they were soldiers at all. Wounded men from all sides had often been stripped bare, their clothes and boots stolen even while they died. It was better to have the Arabs as an ally certainly, mainly for intelligence, eyes that saw everything, allegiance that could be bought. He despised what the Arabs seemed to represent, thought of them as people who only *took,* vultures who waited on the fringes of the war to grab what they could, as though without the great armies the Arabs would have no way to survive at all. It was not logical, and he knew it. Despite how it appeared, these strange, dirty people had survived wars and kings and foreign settlers for thousands of years, and, he thought, they will certainly survive this. And a thousand years from now, they will still be grappling for scraps of booty, abandoned knapsacks and someone else's broken war machines.

"We must push on. Hard and fast! I will not hear of delay!"

The staff officers scattered, each man carrying Rommel's orders, each one on his way toward the front. He looked up, the thick, misty rain washing his face, and he felt the cool for a long moment, felt for the pains in his side, his throat, thought, good, very good. Thank you. I am blessed with good health at the important time. I must push on as well.

He had been furious with Heinz Ziegler, who'd directed the Twenty-first Panzer Division's operations at Sidi Bou Zid. Ziegler had let the momentum slip away, had seemed content to report victory, allowing his men to pursue small pockets of American infantry, scattered tanks and guns that were still making a fight. The delay had allowed the Americans to pull back toward Sbeïtla, protecting the valuable Kasserine Pass, one route that would lead directly to the major American base at Tébessa.

There were other delays as well, the uncertainty and hesitation of untested field commanders who had risen through the ranks, elevated too quickly to positions of authority by the loss of so many men at the hands of the British, men who were dead or captured. The new commanders had not seen Rommel in action, or if they had, they had not understood the need for driving the spear deep into the wounded prey. His frustration was made worse by the control exercised by von Arnim. Ziegler had been

Rommel's man, his subordinate, but at Sidi Bou Zid, Rommel had no authority. That assault had belonged to von Arnim.

The initial attacks against the American position had not been under Rommel's command at all, despite Kesselring's assurances that this was Rommel's operation. It was the single knife blade that cut into Rommel's spirit, the vagueness of Kesselring's orders, the man's infuriating need to keep everyone *happy*. Rommel knew that von Arnim had come to Tunisia carrying the Führer's promise that he would soon be in overall command, and that everyone, especially the Italians, believed Rommel's days in North Africa were numbered. The relationship between Rommel and von Arnim was no more now than an insipid rivalry, made worse by Kesselring's unbridled enthusiasm for Rommel's plan of attack, a plan that von Arnim was forced to cooperate with, a plan that, should it succeed, von Arnim could claim no credit for. Rommel had grown accustomed to the temperamental fragility of rival commanders, had endured two years of that with the Italians. In every case, Rommel had responded by simply doing his job, a job that had, usually, resulted in success. It was the most gratifying response he could make to those men who jockeyed for accolades, who sought the favor of Rome, and now, Berlin. It had been his silent lecture to each of them: Do you expect glory? Then, you will have to perform and you will have to achieve results. And so far, even with the loss at El Alamein, no one in North Africa had performed as well as Rommel.

But Rommel had come to understand the political machinery that had risen against him. There were simply too many voices in Hitler's ear, too much grumbling in Italy about the losses no one in Rome accepted as their own responsibility. He had in fact already been replaced on paper, his Italian successor, Messe, organizing the defenses at Mareth against the gathering threat from Montgomery. And yet, Rommel was still in Africa, still creating plans of attack, plans that were being carried out by men who still worshipped his name, attacks carried out against an enemy that still feared him.

He was certain that the army's victory at Sidi Bou Zid had given him another chance to lay out more of his strategies to a superior officer who was willing to listen. But Kesselring's enthusiasm had made Rommel uncomfortable, signs that Kesselring harbored a strange new fantasy. The man had responded with giddy optimism that Rommel's strategy would prevail, but then there was more, Kesselring confiding to Rommel privately that overall command of the Tunisian theater would soon fall on Rommel himself. As much as Rommel depended on Kesselring's support, he knew it was either delusion or double-talk and duplicity, a backslapping piece of sentimentality. Kesselring seemed caught up in some kind of nostalgia for what used to be, and what, in his mind anyway, should be again. Even Rommel didn't believe the fantastic dream that he would rise from the ashes of El Alamein to reconquer North Africa. There was already too much talk in Berlin, too many wheels spinning past him, too much acceptance of von Arnim's authority.

Once Rommel's plan had been approved, and the wheels of the great attack had gone into motion, Kesselring had returned to Rome, and Rommel learned immediately that von Arnim knew nothing of Kesselring's fantasy and didn't have any intention of handing Rommel any of his own authority. Though it was a piece of Rommel's old Afrika Korps who had driven through the pass at Faïd, who had crushed the Americans around Sidi Bou Zid, those men answered now to von Arnim. It was quickly apparent that von Arnim would push his troops only so far in any fight that would cause Rommel's star to rise in Berlin. And so, with the Americans in a chaotic, scrambling retreat, von Arnim had ignored Rommel's pleas to press forward the attack.

NEAR FERIANA, TUNISIA—FEBRUARY 18, 1943

"General von Arnim is most insistent, sir. He does not consider an attack against Tébessa to be as valuable as a thrust northward, toward Le Kef. He feels his panzer units should be kept united to ward off the inevitable counterattack by the British."

Rommel studied the aide, the man stoic, unflinching. "Does General von Arnim have some evidence that the British are preparing for an attack?"

"The observation planes have mostly been grounded by the weather, Field Marshal."

"Then how does he know the British are planning anything?

Have you not heard the reports that British reinforcements are moving southward to assist the Americans?"

"I do not question my superior's orders, Field Marshal."

"No, I suppose you do not. Well, I do. I have wired my proposed plan to Marshal Kesselring this afternoon. We shall see if your *superior* can be persuaded that waiting to see what the British might or might not do is not the plan I would suggest. I would rather attack a disorganized enemy who flees the ground in front of us. My plan might actually give us another victory, or is that not General von Arnim's purpose here?"

Rommel didn't wait for a response, moved quickly out of the tent. He stepped across the muddy road, thought, I am sick of aides, I am sick of staff officers with no authority, men who do nothing more than repeat verbatim the ranting of their *superior* officer. What is so superior about sitting still?

Rommel ignored the happy salutes, the men calling his name, the good soldiers who waited for new orders. They know as well as I do that the enemy is in chaos. With one great push, the Allied front in Tunisia will be swept away. He thought of Kesselring, all the others, the men in Berlin who spoke of him behind his back, who plotted to pull him from power. Damn you, he thought. Damn all of you. Every plan I have offered has been near perfect, every strategy complete and unfailing. The history of this war should be like the stories of Alexander, a tale written by Homer, or Thucydides: *Do not take lightly the perils of war.* We should speak to our grandchildren of great triumphs over a noble foe, brilliant generals outdueling brilliant generals. Instead, when history tells this story, it will speak of pride and vanity, politics and subterfuge. Soldiers brought to their knees by the weakness in their own command, an army left wanting because small, frightened men denied them gasoline. Now, there is opportunity once again, and once again small minds and fragile egos will thwart us.

But not yet.

FEBRUARY 18, 1943

They rode northward into Feriana, the thick, misty rain not disguising the smell of burning rubber and spent powder, black smoke rising from what remained of the American supply dumps there. Close by, the airfield at Thelepte was in German hands as well, more than two dozen American and British fighters ablaze on the tarmac.

"Could we not have prevented the destruction of the supplies?"

"It was unlikely. We gave them too much time."

"Of course we did."

Rommel tapped the driver on the shoulder, the truck slowing, pulling to the side of the road.

"Stop here. Set up a camp. I will need the radio."

The driver obeyed, the truck sliding to a stop. Rommel pulled his hat low, moved toward a grove of trees, neat rows of leafless, gnarled trunks, like so many angry old men, protesting the misery of the weather.

"Almond trees. Never seen them before."

Rommel turned toward Bayerlein. "What? How do you know?"

"The staff has been interrogating some of the local Arab officials. They asked us not to destroy their orchards. Seems they sell a lot of almonds here, ship them to Italy."

"Yes, well, we must not disturb the flow of luxuries to Herr Mussolini. I would have thought that Il Duce's minions would be concerned about securing a *victory* here. That would prevent their damned trees from getting damaged." He looked to the far side of the orchard, saw a low rock hut. "There. Let's get out of this damned rain."

Guards moved out ahead of him, men with machine guns, some moving past the hut, scanning the rolling hills beyond. One man pushed the door open, pointed his gun into silent darkness, then backed away, stood straight. Rommel moved past him, ducked low, the sharp musty odors commonplace now. The words skipped through his brain, *filth, always filth,* and he searched the darkness, nothing, no seat, no table.

"This won't do. Pitch a damned tent. I need to find out what von Arnim is doing. I must know what is happening in front of us."

He stood inside the low doorway of the shelter, waited while his men scrambled to build his makeshift headquarters. Bayerlein had brought small tins of sardines, and Rommel caught the smell now, pungent and fishy, his stomach turning, thought, that's nearly as bad as whatever the Arabs stored in this hut. He saw Bayerlein scoop a gray, oily mass from the tin, said, "Did you bring one for me?"

Bayerlein nodded, oil running down his chin, reached into a pocket, retrieved a tin, opened it, more oil on his hands now. Rommel smiled, the first time in a long while, took the tin from Bayerlein's hand. He tried not to look at the sardines, tossed the contents into his mouth, gulped down the oil and fish in one swallow. Bayerlein was watching him, returned the smile, and Rommel waited for the mass to settle, then said, "I should like someday to have a real supper, Fritz. Big fat sausages. A roast of pork. Real bread."

"Soon, sir. I'm sure of it. This war will not last much longer. The enemy is beaten."

Bayerlein opened another tin of sardines, held it toward Rommel, who shook his head.

"Yes, the enemy is beaten. But there can be no victory unless we convince them they are beaten. We are allowing them to escape. It is a catastrophic mistake. The Americans are badly wounded, but they are led by men who will certainly learn from their mistakes. We have made much about how untested they are. No longer. They are veterans now, and veterans learn how to survive, how to fight. And we have allowed them to regroup and lick their wounds and regain their fire. Here, one mistake follows another. Von Arnim is holding on to his armor, hoarding it like some old spinster counting her pfennigs. He allows his men to move slowly, orders them to be cautious, and there is only one reason. Success . . . *my* success is not in his best interests. I am quite certain that he has some show of his own he would rather pursue. His staff officer gave us the clue. The British. That would be quite a feather for him, if he drives them out of Tunisia. He can crow all over Berlin that he has avenged my defeat at El Alamein."

"Surely, sir, he would not—"

"I don't want to hear you defending him. You know very well what is being said about me. You know very well that there are officers in Berlin who are watching what happens here, waiting for my *mistake*. My grand finale."

"I do not understand that, sir. Why do they want you to fail?

Are we not fighting for one cause? Does not the Führer wish us to win?"

"I don't know what the Führer wishes. My job has always been to go where he sends me and fight the enemy in front of me. I have not concerned myself with what mattered to him, with his dreams and his grand plans. We took our tanks to the French coast, trapped the English, could have destroyed an entire army at Dunkirk. When the order came for us to halt, to sit still, I kept my doubts to myself. I watched them on the beach there, watched them climb into their ridiculous boats, watched our bombs fall on them, Göring's arrogance, that his airplanes could decide the war. We could have crushed them where they stood, but the Führer said no, and so the British escaped, and now we fight them here." Rommel paused, glanced around for listening ears, old habit. "I did not question the Führer's decision to invade Russia. Had I been ordered to go there, I would have fought as well as I fought in Libya. But it was another mistake, a disaster that may cost us this war. It makes no one proud to beg, Fritz, but I begged, I begged the Führer and his staff and Kesselring, I begged them all to see how valuable this campaign was, how important it was that we drive the British out of Egypt. I did not expect them to give me everything I asked for." He paused again. "But I did not expect to be abandoned. If we had been given a tiny fraction of what was squandered in Russia, this matter would have been decided long ago. There would have been no American landing in Algeria because we would have been far away from here. We would be feasting on the spoils of Cairo or Baghdad. We would not be eating sardines in the rain in Tunisia." He tossed the can aside, pulled his coat tighter, the chilly air driving into him. "Tell me, Fritz, what do we accomplish if we win here? What prize can we claim by driving the enemy out of Tunisia?"

"It is important to the Italians, I suppose. They are still our allies."

Rommel smiled. "Yes, our allies. We are fighting to give our allies their summer homes on the seashore, their daily supply of almonds. We are fighting to preserve Mussolini's fairy tale."

Rommel saw an aide emerge from the tent, the man moving quickly toward him.

"Sir! A message has already come from Marshal Kesselring!

He has approved your plan! However, Comando Supremo had not yet sanctioned his approval. You are ordered to wait for final approval from Comando Supremo."

Bayerlein said, "That is excellent news, sir! We can begin mobilizing the forces toward Tébessa right now! They can begin the assault by morning! Shall I issue the orders, sir?"

Rommel looked at the young aide, the man as excited as Bayerlein, and digested the message. "Kesselring is protecting himself. He approves my plan, but cannot order it to proceed. So, if I am right, he can claim that he supported me. If I am wrong, he has no share of the blame. We cannot move until Comando Supremo has given us the final authority. Prepare the orders, but do not issue them to the commanders until the final sanction has been received."

"Of course, sir."

Bayerlein was looking at him, and Rommel waited for him to move away, saw now that Bayerlein was frowning.

"What is it, Fritz?"

"Sir, forgive me, but I have never known you to defer to Comando Supremo before you begin an operation. The staff . . . with all respect, sir, we have always felt pride in how you ignore all of this foolishness. If you order it, we will move right now, regardless of what Comando Supremo says."

Rommel looked down, stared at the mud on his boots. "The world has changed, Fritz. This is not my theater any longer. It's not my stage. We require von Arnim to advance his forces with us, and he will not move without orders from above." He looked at Bayerlein now. "Make sure someone mans the communications at all times. We will wait until we hear from Rome."

He stepped out into the mud, and Bayerlein knew not to follow. Rommel walked through the grove of trees, knew that the plan was sound, that if von Arnim cooperated, the Allies would be driven completely out of Tunisia. Instead, he thought, we must wait. We must delay.

The daylight was fading, and he stopped, heard the high drone of a plane motor, a distant thump of artillery. He had grown too used to the sounds, the battle always there, some fight off in the distance, attracting no one's attention, a meaningless flicker of death under a dark and dismal sky.

FEBRUARY 19, 1943

You are to modify your plan from the proposed operation against Tébessa and deploy your attack units northward, via Kasserine and Thala, with the objective of capturing Le Kef.

Rommel stared at the aide, the paper in the young man's hand, began to feel sick, anger draining his strength. Le Kef. He put out a hand, felt for the chair, eased down slowly, said in a low voice, "This is unbelievable. This is far worse than stupidity. It is criminal."

Bayerlein was close beside him now, had heard the orders, motioned for the aide to move away, said in a low voice, "Sir, perhaps we should retire to your tent. You do not look well."

"Le Kef. We shall turn our attentions toward Le Kef. So, von Arnim has had his way. We shall attack to the north, where success will mean nothing. We have an open road to Tébessa, but we will fight through the mountain passes instead." He tried to stand, his legs weak, took a deep breath. "Von Arnim has shown us who truly has the authority. It seems that is the only success he requires."

He felt Bayerlein's hand on his shoulder, stood, moved toward the darkness, the night sky still dreary, cold and wet. He didn't want to feel the rain again, stopped at the opening of the shelter, said, "What time is it? How long until daylight?"

"It's near two o'clock, sir."

"Two? Well, then, there is time. I believe, Fritz, I should like to get some sleep."

KASSERINE PASS—FEBRUARY 20, 1943

The air was thick with smoke, a steady thunder in front of him, the roar of armor passing close beside him, a column of tanks moving toward the pass. He stood high on the seat of the truck, stared through the binoculars, strained to see, the fog and mist obliterating the mountainsides.

"Damn! We must get closer! Driver, advance, follow that panzer column!"

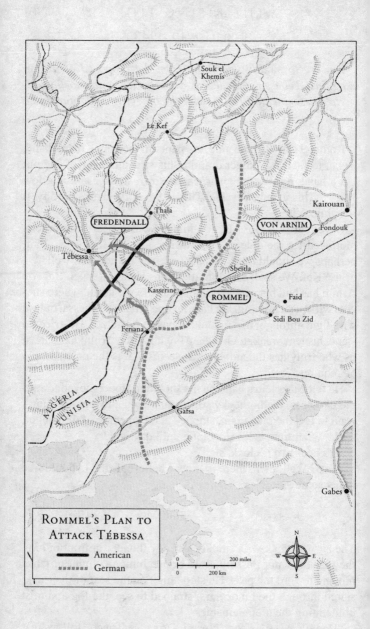

ROMMEL'S PLAN TO ATTACK TÉBESSA

— American
········ German

0 ——— 200 miles
0 ——— 200 km

N
W · E
S

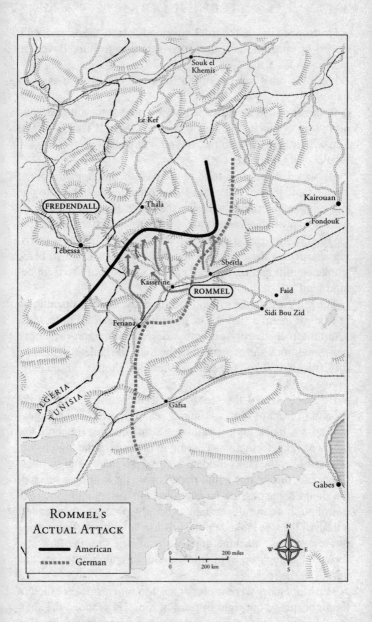

ROMMEL'S
ACTUAL ATTACK

—— American
••••••• German

| 0 | | 200 miles |
| 0 | | 200 km |

He dropped down, the truck surging forward, the air suddenly ripped by machine-gun fire, men shouting to him, Bayerlein pulling on his arm.

"Sir! We must not remain in the road! We are too easily a target!"

Rommel pulled away, turned, stared hard at his aide, shouted into the man's face, "We are all targets, General! This is a fight! You will either ride with me, or you will walk!"

"Yes, sir! Of course, sir!"

He stared ahead now, tried to see past the hulking shadow of a large tank, the heavy Panzer IV, ignored the sharp blast to one side, smoke and rock showering the truck. He felt the old fury, wanted to push the driver faster, get the truck past the armor, but the road was narrow, a sheer drop to one side, a tight hillside rising sharply on the other. He smelled the tank's exhaust, black smoke engulfing him, shouted again, "Go! Move! I'm right behind you!"

The hill crested, the ground falling away, a valley opening up in front of them, a vast sea of fire and smoke a half mile wide. The hills rose sharply on both sides, machine-gun fire above him, small rock slides peppering the road, the tanks still moving forward. He grabbed the driver's shoulder, shouted, "Stop here! I must see!"

He stood, wiped the lenses of the binoculars, scanned the ground in front of him, a hundred vehicles, most of them moving, others, black lumps, smoking, some on fire. He could see his own tanks, formations circling to one side, a flanking move, more smoke, the tanks hidden. There were sharp thumps of artillery fire, the air above him ripped open, the searing screech of the shells, some passing far overhead, others impacting the road in front of him, the closest tank suddenly tossed aside, upended, a flash of fire. He looked up the hillside, infantry darting among the rocks, more machine guns, pops of rifle fire, the flow still forward, soldiers on both sides scrambling along the cuts and gashes in the rock.

The binoculars were useless now, too much smoke, much of the fight spread out right in front of him. He scanned the shattered tanks, could easily spot the American tanks, smaller, round-topped, more compact, lighter. *Vulnerable*. His own panzers were still pushing forward, the battle drifting away, driven by the power, the great machines, the enemy swallowed by mist and smoke and fire, and the man who would not be stopped.

Kasserine Pass was the left flank of the German assault, the other wing pushing through along the road that led to Sbiba, the more northerly route that would lead to Le Kef. The attack had been slow in starting, the Germans attempting to drive straight through Kasserine Pass in a frontal assault that had simply collapsed. The Americans had put men with mortars and antitank guns in the hills high above the half-mile-wide pass, had a clear line of fire on anything that stayed on the low ground beneath them. The roadway through the pass had been mined as well, American and British engineers putting everything they had into a barrier that would slow the Germans down, to allow the Allied artillery to pound their targets. As Rommel made his way forward, he had altered the plan of attack, ordering a halt to the absurd frontal assaults, ordering German infantry to climb the hills, sweeping around the Americans. The plan had worked, American units caught by surprise on the hills, surrounded and cut off from retreat. Those who could make their escape westward found that the defensive positions west of the pass had already begun to collapse, the German armor overpowering, a wave of steel and fire that could not be stopped.

KASSERINE, TUNISIA—FEBRUARY 20, 1943

It was early, just after seven, the fights resuming all across the western side of the mountains. But the Germans had most of the higher ground, the pass itself, were gathering strength, reorganizing, assessing their losses, preparing to continue Rommel's surge along the roads beyond. In the town, Arabs offered him baskets of food, a hasty breakfast prepared by local civilians, men with toothy smiles and dirty hands. He had been polite, but had no interest in breakfast, and no patience for diplomacy. He had come to Afrika Korps headquarters to speak to Heinz Ziegler, yet another commander of an army that had too many new faces.

"What is happening at Sbiba, General?"

Ziegler ignored the maps, and Rommel thought, refreshing, a man who holds the facts in his head.

"The Twenty-first has been slowed by a stout defense, sir. The British have been meticulous with their mines and are making a strong fight. We made mistakes, sir. I have done all I can to correct them."

"I know, General. I wanted to hear that from you. I wanted to know you understood your error. We are no longer in the desert. These hills . . . we might as well be fighting in the Alps. You don't just march into the pass, you must send your men up the mountains as well."

Ziegler seemed to energize. "Yes, sir. And we have been successful, sir."

Rommel thought a moment, could not avoid the maps, moved that way, a young lieutenant stepping aside, the man who moved the pins.

"Are these the latest positions?"

"Yes, sir."

Rommel stepped closer, tried to focus on the lines, his eyes betraying him. He had suffered from poor vision for some time now, yet one more ailment, one more plague he had to endure. He stepped back, tried to hide the frustration, thought of the plan, the troop positions locked in his memory. He had held the Tenth Panzer Division in reserve, the men who had answered directly to von Arnim. But the opportunity was clear now, the way open to driving the enemy completely away. With Kasserine Pass in German hands, the route was open to Tébessa. Damn them, he thought. They do not see it. Von Arnim has no interest in success. But I will not ignore the opportunity. He can have his prize of Le Kef. I am taking Tébessa.

"General Ziegler, I believe Kasserine is our best opportunity. The Twenty-first surely has matters in hand at Sbiba, so we shall make our greatest effort right here. I will summon the Tenth to Kasserine."

"Yes, sir, I quite agree."

Rommel looked back at Ziegler, a young man who had already made his share of mistakes.

"I don't need you to agree with me, General. Just accomplish your task."

He had driven all along the frontline positions, then back toward the reserves, had watched as the Tenth Panzer Division responded to his orders. Despite the power that rolled past him, Rommel knew that something was wrong, the numbers too low. There was another noticeable absence as well, not just in numbers but in strength. The Tenth held the army's vastly critical supply of Tiger tanks, and Rommel searched for them, growing more angry along every kilometer. Von Arnim's promise to send thirty Tigers southward had never been fulfilled. But now, with the Tenth coming forward, all the Tigers should have been there, adding even more to the power of Rommel's attack. Rommel was furious, ordered his driver toward Afrika Korps headquarters again, knowing the Tenth's commander, Fritz von Broich, would already be there.

He burst through the door, saw Ziegler again, the man jumping to his feet, surprised.

"Where is von Broich?"

"Here, sir."

Rommel stared at him, von Broich emotionless, sure of himself.

"Where is the rest of your division, General?"

Von Broich did not respond, and Rommel closed the gap between them, put a finger close to the man's chest.

"Where is the rest of your division, General?"

Von Broich tried to stand tall, a display of bravado, the man quietly aware that he answered only to von Arnim.

"I was specifically ordered to advance with half my force, sir. General von Arnim is concerned that he will require the remainder along his front."

"Where are the Tigers?"

Von Broich cleared his throat, looked down, and Rommel thought, all right, here comes the lie.

"Sir, General von Arnim has requested that I communicate to you that the Panzer VI tanks are currently undergoing repair."

"Repair? *All of them?*"

Von Broich did not look at him. "I have been ordered to give you this message, sir."

Rommel felt a tightness in his chest, his fingers curling into fists. He was breathing heavily, the curses pouring through his brain. I will kill that man.

He fought against the fire, began to feel dizzy, von Broich seeming to waver in front of him. Rommel saw a chair, moved that way, steadied himself, sat slowly, said, "So, this is how I am to be regarded. We have our orders . . . *he* has *his* orders, and it matters not at all." He tried to slow his breathing, saw aides gathering, keeping a distance. "Very well. I will do what I must. We have a plan to carry out, and we shall carry it out, whether anyone beyond this headquarters cares to assist us or not."

KASSERINE PASS—FEBRUARY 21, 1943

The fighting had moved more to the west, a hard struggle across rocky hills draped by pockets of brush, dense thickets of fir trees. Rommel had pressed his people forward, fighting the hesitation and mistakes in his own command as much as his troops fought an increasingly tenacious defense from Allied artillery and antitank positions.

The truck moved downward, and he could see the river now, the Hatab, the remnants of a wrecked bridge, replaced with one by his own engineers. Tanks were moving across, black smoke rolling upriver past the tumbled wreckage of half-tracks, one long-barreled cannon shattered into pieces, embedded in the soft mud. He ordered the driver to slow, the truck rolling past a burnt-out tank, what Rommel knew now to be a Sherman, its turret tossed aside, smoke rolling up from the bowels of the crushed machine. There were trucks, four of them, what had been part of a column caught on the road, the wrecks shoved aside by his engineers. He stared at each one, men still inside, burnt black, one man in a grotesque curl around the steering wheel. Bodies were scattered all across the mud, draped across blasted trees in the patches of wood, helmets and bits of men and uniforms and weapons in every low place, the mud barely disguising the fight that had rolled over the uneven ground. The troops had met face-to-face here, and Rommel could see it now, men from both sides, black bloody stains, bayonets on broken rifles, more trucks, a jeep, its wheels bent out, like some toy crushed under a massive foot. Along the riverbank were more bodies, a neat row, pulled out of the mud by men who could not simply pass by and do nothing. The truck rolled over the makeshift bridge and Rommel did not look down, did not care about the uniforms the men wore, did not look into the face of death. The thought skipped through his mind—which of us left the greater number of dead at this place?—but he pushed it away, thought, it makes no difference. Someone else will deal with that, will do the arithmetic, the paperwork. His attention was drawn forward, a wide clearing beyond the bridge, a vast sea of destruction, blasted tanks, half-tracks, trucks attached to artillery pieces. He saw now that much of the equipment was undamaged, some of it half-buried in mud-filled ditches, crews abandoning their vehicles to escape on foot. There were more cannon, unhitched, pointing east, ready for the fight, but the artillerymen were long gone, leaving behind stacks of boxes, unused shells. He saw trucks full of gear, boxes, ammunition of every sort, crates of magazines for small arms, and more, all the equipment necessary to build a campsite, tents, cookstoves, crates of tinned food.

There were hard blasts to one side, thunderous explosions falling in unison along the hillside behind him. His driver turned, looked back at him, and Rommel pointed forward, shook his head. We're not turning back, not now. His truck rolled farther out through the open ground, and he stared across the field, saw more undamaged trucks, a half-track sitting by itself, the front wheels bent and shredded by a mine. He had to see more, put his hand on the driver's shoulder, the truck slowing, stopping. He did not raise the binoculars, had nothing to observe, the heavy mist and smoke swallowing the trees in front of him, where the fight still poured over men on both sides. He stood still for a moment, felt Bayerlein beside him, knew there were questions, why they had stopped, why *here*. Rommel stayed silent, felt the hard weight of what he was seeing. It was unending, an ocean of American steel, every truck fueled and equipped, a silent army, missing only the men who had pulled away, who did not yet have the heart to stand and make a fight

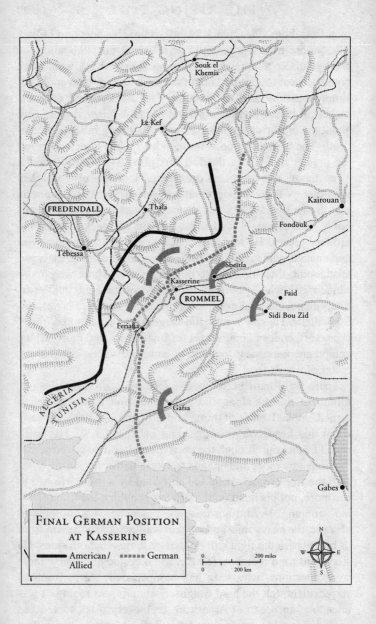

Souk el
Khemis

Le Kef

FREDENDALL

Thala

Kairouan

Fondouk

Tébessa

Sbeitla

Kasserine

ROMMEL

Faid

Sidi Bou Zid

Feriana

ALGERIA
TUNISIA

Gafsa

Gabes

FINAL GERMAN POSITION
AT KASSERINE

—— American/   ∗∗∗∗∗∗ German
      Allied

0   200 miles

0   200 km

N
W   E
S

against Rommel's powerful machine. But they will, he thought. They will learn and adapt, and they will come again. They are children with too many toys, but after this fight, they will have grown, and they will have learned, and they will bring their machines and their equipment back into the fight, new trucks and new tanks and new airplanes. He thought of Hitler's description, *mongrel race*. What does that matter here?

NEAR THALA, TUNISIA—FEBRUARY 22, 1943

He had driven away from the fighting, had seen enough of it for himself, what the commanders had been relaying to him since first light. Despite the enormous success at Kasserine, the pathways to Tébessa and Le Kef were now strongly fortified, massive numbers of artillery pieces targeting any German armor that attempted to push through the Allied defense. On both fronts, the German push had been stopped, the Allied resistance growing stronger, helped by the increasing support from the north, British artillery and fighting men who added to the American barrier.

The truck rolled into the open ground in front of the block building, the headquarters for the Twenty-first Panzer, more trucks already there. Kesselring was waiting for him.

"I would like to suggest to the Führer that you be officially named army group commander for all of Africa. Your performance here has certainly silenced anyone's criticism of you."

Rommel let out a breath, drank from a bent tin cup, warm water cutting through the dust in his throat. Kesselring was smiling at him, and Rommel had seen that too many times, felt no warmth from the man. He glanced now at Westphal, the young man accompanying Kesselring to the meeting. He had wanted to embrace his former aide, still felt enormous affection for the young colonel, had followed the young man's progress as a field commander. Westphal was not smiling at all, had greeted him with a scowl of concern, something Rommel also recalled.

"So, now I am to be rewarded for my efforts? I am no longer thought of as a *defeatist*?"

"I never thought of you that way. There has been misfortune, frustration. Regardless, you deserve this command, and I know the Führer will see it that way. Even the Italians will agree."

Rommel stared into the dingy water, thought, so no one knows of this *promotion* yet, not the Führer, not the Italians.

"My apologies, Albert, but there is little left to command here."

"Of course there is! We have earned a brilliant victory here! And even if the enemy does not withdraw completely, our bridgehead position in Tunisia is more than merely sound. It is impregnable! We need a man in command who is impregnable himself."

Rommel set the cup aside, looked again at Westphal, thought, *he* doesn't believe I am impregnable. For good reason.

"I regret that I must decline the honor of your offer. I am certain that General von Arnim has the Führer's full confidence. The strength of our Tunisian position is a credit to his leadership."

Kesselring moved toward a chair, sat, rubbed a hand on his chin. There was silence for a long minute, then Kesselring said, "I would hope you would reconsider. But no matter. Have you given the order to withdraw?"

"Yes. There is no purpose to be served by holding our current position either here or west of Kasserine. The enemy will continue to build his strength, and we have used up all we can put into this fight."

Kesselring pounded a fist on his knee, looked at him, the strange ever-present smile.

"There will be more opportunities, Erwin. The Americans are not a worthy foe."

Rommel did not have the energy for a debate with Kesselring's fantasies. He looked again at Westphal, the young man staring down. He will say nothing, Rommel thought. But he knows, more than anyone. He wanted to say the words to Westphal, but not now, not in front of Kesselring. Whether or not we can still win this fight, I am not well enough to be in command.

FEBRUARY 23, 1943

They had disengaged the enemy defenses all along the positions west and north of Kasserine, retreating southward, away from Le

Kef. He stayed close to the columns, the big armor rumbling past, men staring blankly past him, only a few cheers now from an army that understood it was moving the wrong way. He was surprised to see sunshine, the first blue sky in many days, no heavy clouds in any direction. He stared up, felt warmth on his face, a wisp of dust rolling over him, what would only grow worse as the mud dried. He waited, stared into the blue, watched the small puffs of clouds drifting past, tried to hear beyond the sound of the tanks, knew it would come, that with the good weather, the planes could fly again. He stared for a long while, and then he saw them, a V formation, very high, like so many tiny geese. He caught flickers of sunlight, the sun's reflection off a dozen windshields, knew the bombs were coming, the deadly blasts finding his men and his tanks on the roadways, disrupting the retreat. He tapped the driver, the silent order, *speed up,* the truck moving east, taking him back toward Mareth, toward the enemy he still had to confront. Along the Mareth line, the German and Italian troops who had not gone to Kasserine were building and strengthening their own works, while farther to the south, the British Eighth Army was strengthening as well, Montgomery's men pressing forward impatiently, while their commander pondered whether it was the right time to finally launch his attack.

24. EISENHOWER

"I'm not certain we should be rolling forward with an offensive, Ike. Not yet."

Eisenhower leaned back in the chair, stared out the window, caught a glimpse of planes, thought, big ones, B-17s most likely. Thank God for good weather. Keep up the pressure.

Fredendall sat across from him, and Eisenhower could hear him shifting in the chair, the man edgy, uncomfortable. Eisenhower had not called him here to talk about strategy. Eisenhower tried to say something, struggled with his words, hated this part of his job more than any other.

Fredendall said, "We can strengthen the passes even more. No chance the Huns will have their day again. Learned the lesson, for sure, Ike. Damned valuable lesson."

"Damned costly one."

Fredendall didn't respond, and Eisenhower faced him now, saw the face of a man who knows when bad news is coming his way.

"You're a fine administrator, Lloyd, a fine commander. Lord knows we need good people kicking some butts stateside, getting our boys prepared to come over here. Hasn't been that good so far, too many of us getting off the ships without a hint what the hell we're supposed to do. We've had to spend too much time training them right here, and that can't continue. It's too dangerous, keeps too many people tied up when we need them at the front. But you damned well can't make an attack with green troops. No substitute for combat experience of course, but dammit, our people have a lot of catching up to do. The British are grousing pretty heavy about how we fell apart. That won't do. Won't do at all."

Eisenhower looked down, avoided Fredendall's sadness, thought, he knows. Of course he knows. Get to the damned point. You're chattering at him like a parrot.

"I want you to accept a new position, Lloyd. I want you to spearhead the training effort back home. No one better for the job. What do you say?"

Fredendall seemed frozen for a long moment, his expression unchanging. "When, Ike? How soon?"

"Soon. We have to push forward the offensive immediately. Rommel's whipped, and Monty's about to bust him good. We've got an opportunity here, and we've got to take advantage of it. Can't give the Germans time to refit, rebuild their strength. That was my biggest mistake, Lloyd. I took too damned long to get our people into Tunisia. Took it for granted that the Germans would move as slowly as we did. Dumb, stupid mistake. No more of that. There were other mistakes too. For one, we paid too much attention to bad intelligence. Most of that was a British problem, but we followed lockstep right behind them. The Brits are doing everything they can to straighten that out. But we can't lay all the blame on them. Our biggest problem was green troops, green officers. That's why you're so valuable back home. You've got the experience now, you know what we need to be teaching our boys."

The words hung in the air, and Fredendall sagged in the chair. After a long moment, he said, "You didn't say when, Ike."

"You'll be getting written orders in a day or so. Can't waste time."

Eisenhower had nothing left to say, didn't want any more of this, was relieved to see Fredendall stand up.

Eisenhower said, "Go on back to your command post, clean up whatever staff matters you have to. You can take some of your people with you, if you want. Likely, they won't fit in too well once you're gone. You know how that goes, Lloyd. I'll consider some recommendations, but I suspect they should all be reassigned."

Fredendall nodded again, silent now, moved away slowly, stood at the door for a moment, his back to Eisenhower. There was another awkward silence, Eisenhower wanting him to move on, to leave, get this awful moment behind them.

Fredendall said, "Who is replacing me?"

Eisenhower saw the redness in his eyes, all the man's brash loudness, his mouthy cursing wiped away by the utter sadness of this moment. Eisenhower didn't want to respond, knew it could not help soften the blow, that Fredendall should simply be gone. He shook his head, a silent no. "Rather not go into that right now. Touchy matter. You understand."

The silence came again, Fredendall not seeming to understand at all, and Eisenhower thought, go back to the States, dammit, accept your medals and your promotion.

"Your orders will reach you in a day or so. You better get going."

Fredendall stiffened, threw up an unnecessary salute, Eisenhower returning it. He pulled the door open, slipped through, and was gone. Eisenhower let out a breath, sat back again, closed his eyes. Damn! I hate it, purely hate it. The worst part of my job. But I had damned well get better at it. He leaned forward again, his arms on the desk. He tried to erase Fredendall's sadness, thought, he'll get over it. They'll give him his medal, greet him with big newspaper stories, treat him like the returning hero. His hometown will probably have some parade for him. I just don't want to hear about it.

He reached down, pulled out a drawer of the desk, retrieved the cable from Marshall, the approval of the new appointment. He glanced at the words, then called out, "Harry!"

Butcher was there quickly, and Eisenhower said, "Patton's at Rabat, right?"

"Yes, sir. According to him."

"We get any more news about Colonel Waters?"

Butcher shook his head. "Just guesses. The Germans haven't said anything about who their prisoners are. We've monitored their radio, but unless they're holding a general, they're not likely to make a fuss." He paused. "There's no report of a body."

"Thank God for that. I would assume George has handled the news with his family. I haven't met his daughter. I'd bet this has them all pretty roughed up. Keep me posted, any news at all."

"You bet, Skipper."

Eisenhower looked at the letter again. "Send George a wire. I want him at Algiers tomorrow morning. We'll fly to Maison Blanche to meet him. Have him bring his chief of staff, or whatever top aide he wants."

"Right away, sir."

Butcher was gone, and Eisenhower scanned Marshall's order again, read the words, thought, yep, this will make everybody happy. Georgie will finally stop bellyaching about sitting on his ass in Morocco. And God knows I'll hear about how we should have done it this way from the start.

MAISON BLANCHE AIRFIELD, OUTSIDE ALGIERS—
MARCH 5, 1943

They stood beside the fuselage of the B-17 that had brought Patton and his aide Brigadier General Hugh Gaffey. Eisenhower stood beside his own chief of staff, Beetle Smith, had ordered

Butcher to keep a discrete distance behind them, just close enough to hear the conversation. Eisenhower faced Patton, could see immediately that Patton was like a child at Christmas.

"You know why I wanted you here, George. This change is to happen immediately. I want you to report to Alexander as soon as possible."

Patton clapped his hands one time, rubbed them together, shook his head. "So, it's true then!"

"What's true?"

"Well, Ike, we all heard that Harold Alexander was taking command here. Didn't want to believe it, but the Brits I spoke to all said he's the one in charge or that he oughta be, anyway. I had to rip some butts for that one. Nobody's insulting my boss."

Eisenhower was annoyed, had seen too much of this attitude in Patton before. "Easy, George. Alexander's my second-in-command now. He assumed command of all ground forces in Tunisia on February nineteenth. He's in charge of planning for the rest of this campaign and will also command the invasion of Sicily. Is there some problem with that?"

Patton seemed surprised at the question. "Oh, no, not at all. I heard rumors that he . . . I thought maybe he was taking over the whole works. Thought maybe you were being . . . um . . ."

"Relieved? No, not yet. It's still my command." Eisenhower had expected this, rumors coming mainly from London, talk that Eisenhower had to take the blame for the army's poor showing. He was still annoyed, thought, Morocco isn't the other side of the moon. "You should take those cables and dispatches seriously, George. We don't send them across the wire for entertainment. The idea is to clear up rumors, not start them. In case you're not clear on what's going on, Wayne is taking over for you in Morocco. Since the Fifth Army is training there, he can handle the police work of keeping an eye on Spanish Morocco. There's still the chance the damned Germans might try to pull something on us through Spain. You're to assume command of the Second Corps, and you're now under Alexander's Eighteenth Army Group, along with the French, Anderson's First Army, and Monty's Eighth. You, Anderson, Monty, and Giraud answer directly to Alexander, who answers to me. Any confusion on that point?"

"None. I'm happy to hear it."

"Your immediate task is to rebuild and rehabilitate the Second Corps to fighting strength. We're planning a rapid push, George, a quick strike. That's why you were chosen for this job. You will work alongside the British and French in a partnership. *Equal* partners. *Cooperation,* George. You'll answer to Alexander as if his orders were coming directly from me. Your first task will be to support Monty. The British Eighth is just about set to hit Rommel at Mareth, and when they do, I want your boys on Rommel's right flank. Tie up as much German strength as you can. The Eighth will be pushing northward, right up the coast, and I want you to ease the way. And, George, unless you get specific orders, you will not advance to the coast. You are not to cut in front of Monty's line of advance."

He searched Patton's face, looked for some telltale sign of an argument, knew that Patton would bristle at being handed a supporting role. But Eisenhower had no patience for a debate.

"You don't need to prove your courage, George. Not to me, not to the British. And, listen to me, dammit. I don't want you out front hauling your own flag. I want you as a corps commander, not a casualty. When I look for you in your command post, I expect to find you there."

Patton frowned, nodded, and Eisenhower still expected the inevitable argument. But Patton stayed silent.

"Good. One more thing. I want you to be cold-blooded about removing inept officers. God knows that can be tough, and I don't enjoy it one bit. But it's a hell of a lot worse getting my ass handed to me by the enemy. I hate that more than the devil hates holy water. I don't want incompetence to cost us any more setbacks. If you find a bad apple, pull him and send him back to me. I'll deal with what should happen to him. I won't tolerate softness when it comes to someone's *feelings*. We both have friends here, George. But that can't keep us from yanking a man out of line who shouldn't be there."

Patton nodded briskly, and Eisenhower thought, yes, well, he won't have any trouble with that one.

"This campaign will tell us who our best people are, George. We'll need those people down the road. You have my fullest confidence. And so does Alexander. Get along with him,

George. Someone sticks a thorn in your waistband, talk to Alex about it first."

Patton seemed to digest that, and one name rolled through Eisenhower's brain. *Montgomery.* He studied Patton for a silent moment, thought, dammit, George, just try to get along with them.

"One question, Ike."

"What?"

"I know you want me to hang back, run the show from behind. But I have to tell you . . . if the chance comes up, and it damned well might . . . I'd like to put a pistol into Rommel's belly."

HEADQUARTERS, EIGHTEENTH ARMY GROUP,
CONSTANTINE, ALGERIA—MARCH 6, 1943

"You have no problems here, Ike. No one is complaining."

He sat across the desk from Alexander, felt the man's honesty, nothing hidden.

"Thank you, Alex. I wish that were true everywhere else."

"Armchair generals, Ike. Every war has them, and always will. Auchinleck suffered for it, and I've heard the same griping ever since I've been in Africa. But it's just talk. Those with the loudest voices are the least likely to step out into the field. You know that."

Eisenhower leaned forward, put his hands on Alexander's desk. "Maybe. But not all of the talk is coming from England. There's a lot of it coming from Anderson's people. The same stuff we've had to put up with since England. Understand, it's not the commanders. The senior people have rarely been a problem. They get how we have to work together, and everyone has been first-rate. It's the junior officers, the young ones. Give a man an officer's baton, and he starts to strut, starts to tell the world how the show ought to be run. I've tried to stamp that out when I can, but . . . we gave your people some pretty good ammunition at Kasserine."

Alexander said nothing for a long moment, shook his head. "There was nothing else you could have done. Fortunes of war. Your people were put into line where they had to be, and the enemy took advantage. Credit to Rommel. If anyone here talks out of turn about the American fighting man, they'll answer to me. I'll not tolerate that sort of thing, Ike. Not a bit."

It was an echo of Eisenhower's own orders, no tolerance for anyone in an American uniform spouting anti-British comments. He was grateful for Alexander's support, had grown more comfortable with the man every time they met.

Alexander was roughly Eisenhower's age, a thin, wiry man, a light mustache, who appeared at first glance to be a Rudyard Kipling example of the ideal British officer. But there was no aristocratic stiffness to the man, no annoying air of superiority. Eisenhower had met him at Gibraltar the year before, the two men hitting it off immediately, Eisenhower surprised to find that, unlike most of the senior brass on either side, Alexander had a considerable sense of humor. Alexander's appointment as Eisenhower's deputy had come at the Casablanca conference, and immediately eyebrows had been raised, senior officers in both armies assuming that this was a relationship that could only produce friction. General Alexander outranked Eisenhower, had already made his mark as the overall British commander in North Africa. Part of Alexander's command included Montgomery's Eighth Army, and it was entirely reasonable for Alexander to accept a great deal of credit for the crushing victory over Rommel at El Alamein. But Alexander was no strutting martinet, and after the Casablanca conference, he had accepted his role as Eisenhower's second without argument. In Washington, George Marshall had been sensitive to the issue of rank, and on February 11, Eisenhower had received his promotion to full general, which added a fourth star to his collar. Eisenhower appreciated the recognition, but understood that in part it was an American show designed to bolster Eisenhower's standing with the British he now commanded.

Eisenhower recognized that Alexander had done much to save the Allies against Rommel's blow at Kasserine. Alexander had assumed command of the combined armies on February 19, in the midst of the worst chaos of the fight. His first act had been to organize the defenses that did much to grind Rommel's forces to a halt. Alexander's efficiency made it clear that, though Eisenhower was still in charge, Alexander's role was essential.

With Alexander under Eisenhower's command, one more piece of the Allied puzzle was in Eisenhower's hands. Bernard Montgomery still answered to Alexander, but now he was ultimately responsible to Eisenhower as well.

Eisenhower studied a map on the desk in front of him. "How long do you think it will take Monty to go into action?"

Alexander smiled. "Thank you for being discreet. You will come to learn that Monty can only be pushed when he is willing to be pushed. It's not something I'm completely happy about, but we have to make allowances. He's made himself quite the hero back home. Hard to find too much fault with that. Not everyone gets along with him though. He can be a prickly sort once in a while."

Eisenhower returned the smile, one man's name planting itself in his brain: *Patton.*

Alexander continued, "We're finally making good use of the port facilities at Tripoli. Monty's getting his supplies now, and there should be little delay."

"I'm not complaining, Alex. The delays might have worked out for the best. Once Patton moves the Second Corps toward Rommel's flank, it should lighten Monty's load. I don't think the Germans can hold the Mareth line if we hit them from two sides."

"Monty won't see it that way. He'd love to push Rommel all the way to Tunis, finish the job he started at El Alamein. I've already talked to him about cooperation, and he'll understand that, once we get rolling. You can count on him to do the job. It will be up to me to make sure he gets plenty of credit for it."

Eisenhower laughed now, sat back in the chair. Alexander seemed to wait for the punch line, and Eisenhower said, "I'm sorry. This isn't funny. We've got a hell of a fight, still. And you know that I have no patience for rivalries. None of this is a damned contest. But I'm just wondering what it will be like the first time Patton and Monty find themselves on the same road. As much as I hate it, I know that the very thing that makes them so damned good will also create trouble. You might have to break up a fistfight."

Alexander laughed as well. "Or a duel."

After a moment the smiles faded, and Alexander said, "I'm

not a blind optimist, Ike. We need this offensive to work, or we could be in very serious trouble here. And, I'm not sure I agree with you about Patton and Monty. A little competition can be a good thing. You fire up the generals, it can fire up the men. And we'll need all the *fire* we can muster if we're going to push Rommel out of his lines."

Eisenhower thought of Patton, the crude boast, *a pistol in his belly.*

"We need to strike quickly. Can we make any good estimate when Monty will be ready to strike?"

"He says by the twentieth, maybe sooner."

Eisenhower stared at the map, thought, damn. Two weeks.

Alexander leaned forward on the desk. "I'll push him as much as I can, Ike. And I'll push Patton as well. The only way this campaign will work effectively is if the two armies link up. Not even Rommel can stand up to that."

Eisenhower thought a moment. "You've met my new field aide, right?"

"General Bradley? Quite so. First impression, he's a good chap. I had no problem with Truscott of course. A bit more crust to him."

"He did the job. But I'm sending Truscott back stateside. We need his type of *crusty* commander to take over the Third Division. They're in training now, but it's slow going. We need them over here as quickly as Truscott can pound them into shape."

"Ah, yes, your Third Division. The Rock of the Marne. As I recall, some of those chaps saved the day in the Great War. Put quite a feather in old Black Jack's cap."

Eisenhower was impressed, thought, well, of course, a British commander would know more history than just his own.

"Bradley works a little differently than Truscott. He doesn't say much, but when he talks, people need to shut up and listen. Might be the smartest damned general I've come across. I'm hoping he'll carry those brains to the front lines. Right now, he's to serve as my primary staff officer in the field. I don't want any guff about that, and I've given Brad written orders to put in every commander's face. You know how some of those *crusty* boys react, treat a field aide like he's some kind of spy. I can't be everyplace at once, and I need accurate information. For the time being, Omar Bradley is the man who'll gather the details."

There was a knock, and Eisenhower saw a British officer at the door. Alexander said, "Yes, Ruddy, what is it?"

The man stepped into the office, handed Alexander a paper. "Cable, sir. From General Montgomery."

"Thank you. You're dismissed. Call you if I need you."

The man spun around, stepped quickly from the office. Eisenhower watched Alexander's expression, saw a frown, thought, it's bad news.

"Another delay?"

Alexander held out the paper. "Anything but, actually. It seems that we've been wasting our time prodding Monty to make his move. Rommel's beat him to it. The Eighth Army is under attack."

25. ROMMEL

SOUTH OF TOUJANE, TUNISIA, THE MARETH LINE
MARCH 6, 1943

They had rolled forward at dawn, all the power Rommel could put into the attack. The three panzer divisions pushed forward 140 tanks, hoping to do what Rommel had done so well before. The first attack had come along the coast, directed at the British right flank. It was a noisy diversion by the Italians, artillery and light armor, another familiar tactic, to persuade Montgomery to focus his attentions there. With British strength diverted northward, the primary assault had come on the opposite end of the line, inland, the power of the panzers rolling across scrub hills and flat, hard ground, seeking to turn the British left, roll back Montgomery's forces before they could prepare. Rommel's greatest successes had come with this very move, and once more he saw opportunity, knew that the British flank was hanging in the air, protected only by miles of sandy marsh that was thought impassable, the same barrier that protected his own flank at Mareth. Rommel's best hope was that Montgomery was not yet organized, his defenses not yet complete. He had seen firsthand what the fourteen-hundred-mile march from El Alamein had done to his army, and Rommel forced himself to believe that Montgomery's sluggishness meant that the great march had been far more grueling for the pursuers than for the men pursued. The Germans had recovered well, mostly because their supply line had become so much shorter. With Hitler suddenly focused on preserving this part of Africa as a great German stronghold, the supplies and reinforcements continued to roll through the ports and airfields of Tunisia, now only a short distance in Rommel's rear. Rommel knew that if there was opportunity at all, it had to come soon, before Montgomery felt he was strong enough to go on the offensive. Even as the British pulled into position below the Mareth line, Rommel had convinced himself that whether or not the British army rested and refit, Montgomery would continue to dawdle, to position and reposition his troops until conditions were perfect in the British commander's mind. Here, at Mareth, Rommel had an opening, a chance to shatter the British resolve. When the tanks rolled forward, Rommel expected they would surge right through a confused and disorganized British camp. Rommel embraced and embellished the plan in his own mind, had convinced the Italians and his own officers that their day had come again. Even Comando Supremo approved the attack, convinced by the enthusiasm of their own man at Mareth, Giovanni Messe, who fully accepted Rommel's reasoning.

From the tall hill just behind the Mareth line, Rommel had watched the sun rise, had stood tall with his binoculars, watching the wave of armor pour southward, to swarm and outflank the British lines around the village of Médenine. He kept the radio truck close by, expected the reports to come in quickly, held a hard grip on his belief that the attack would drive the surprised British flank away in complete disorder, and that the British artillery and tank gunners would not have prepared for such an audacious move.

*   *   *

The morning mist had been swept away by the rising sun, the air now thick with drifting clouds of dust.

"We will move forward. I must see. Have we heard anything?"

"No, sir. The radio has been silent."

Rommel waited impatiently for the driver, the man struggling to start the truck, the engine coming to life with a raspy cough. Rommel wanted to shove the man aside, drive himself, his brain stirring in a hot fever, his eyes blurred, hot frustration pouring through him. Move forward, damn you!

His sickness had come again, worse than he could recall, hard pains in his throat, the ache in his side. He had seen the way the staff looked at him, their distress barely disguised, and he had gone to a mirror, had seen for himself that the sores on his face and neck had grown much worse. It had always been a problem in the desert, what Rommel had believed was behind them now, the torment of so many weeks in the flat, deathly heat of Libya. The early spring in Tunisia was a pleasant time, the rains finally ceasing, a coolness in the morning that inspired the green to return. The land seemed alive in Tunisia, the flatlands nearer the coast draped by wheat fields and orchards. The men had welcomed the change in climate, the entire army growing more healthy. For a while Rommel had felt it as well, energized by the successes around Kasserine. But on the retreat back to Mareth, the sickness had swallowed him, the familiar misery of sleeplessness, the churning in his gut, the tormenting pains, the itching irritation of the open sores. He had done all he could to push it aside, fought to work through his own misery, clearing his mind for the planning that must happen for the strike against Montgomery to succeed. He relied heavily on support from Bayerlein, and even the Italian, Messe, his alleged successor, had not argued, had not drained Rommel of the energy he needed to launch this attack.

The truck carried him down into a narrow valley, thick brush flecked with concrete bunkers, the good work of the engineers. They drove up again, a short hill, reached the crest, and Rommel could hear the fight, sharp thumps, a thick cloud of dirt and dust, shouted, "Go! Do not stop here! We can get closer!"

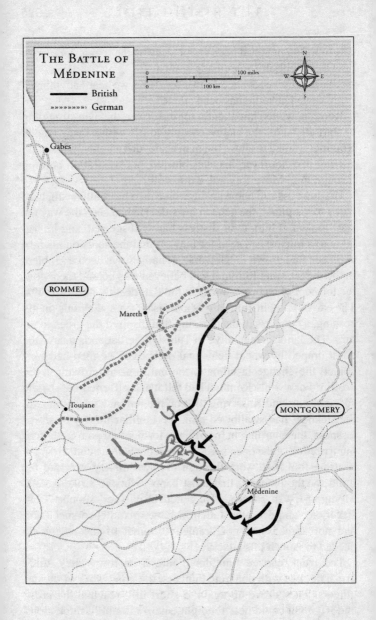

The truck moved again, the aides now watching him, and he ignored them, gripped the binoculars tightly, stared forward. There were flashes of light, and his heart surged in his chest, yes, good! We are close! The sounds rolled over them, the truck winding through a dusty cut between two short hills, then in the open again, another rise. He saw a tank now, a dense plume of black smoke, the smells engulfing him, sickening, and he closed his eyes, shouted again, "Keep going! Move forward!"

There were more tanks on both sides of the road, more black smoke, fire. The truck moved past quickly, past a scattered mass of black shapes, faceless, broken men. He would not see them, wanted to shout again, his voice choked by the smoke, hot, grinding ash in his throat. The truck swerved, the driver fighting for control, the smoke clearing, the road straightening, the man saying something to him, fear in the man's voice. Rommel ignored him, still stared to the front, the truck climbing another short rise. The road wound to one side, then fell away, and Rommel saw more tanks, a wide formation, more smoke and fire, grabbed the driver's shoulder.

"Stop!"

The truck slid to a halt, and Rommel steadied himself on the seat back, stood, raised the binoculars, thought, yes, now we shall see. He focused on a low ridgeline, beyond the tanks, scanned, saw flashes, the ground all out in front of him alive with punches of fire, thunderous blasts, screams in the air, shells streaking overhead. The blasts shook the truck, aides jumping out, seeking cover in a ditch, and Rommel ignored them, wouldn't see fear in his own men. He scanned the ridge, expected to see his tanks rolling up and over, deadly fire, a great wave shattering the enemy's position. But the tanks were not moving, the fire coming at them in a steady rumble, blasts in the dirt and brush all across the ground in front of him, tanks, his tanks, broken and battered, some pulling back, drawing closer to him. The ridgelines spread out on both sides, every nook, every low place, holding a gun barrel or a tank, heavy fire meeting his attack with perfect precision. He did not count, had no need to, could tell from the sound and the destruction that the British had far more power than Rommel expected. He lowered the binoculars, didn't need them now. What he couldn't see in the field, he saw in his mind. The British had dug in hard along the ridgelines, heavy formations of artillery and tanks. His mind opened for a brief moment, the sickness held away, the sickness that had driven him to this desperate assault. He understood now, why he had pushed this fight, why he had assumed Montgomery to be weak and disorganized. It was all the energy he had left, holding a fragile grip on the dream that the Desert Fox would make his great triumphant return, that the enemy would be driven away. He closed his eyes, fought to breathe through the smoke, ignored the voices of his men, the aides calling out for him to take cover, to take himself out of danger. The strength was gone now, the grip loosening, and he sat, felt the truck moving, the men leaping in, the driver waiting for his order. He looked at the man, saw the young, dirty face, wide blue eyes, terrified. He put a hand on the man's arm, said nothing. He looked out past the windshield, the picture complete, the disaster growing, and Rommel wanted to shout, turn his men to the front, push them harder, drive them as he had always done, lead them himself, the truck rolling forward right into the guns, oblivious to the fire, the danger, the death of his army.

He felt the truck jerk, jolted from below, shellfire coming closer. Tanks began to roll past him now, his tanks, beaten men seeking cover in the rocky hills, in clumps of brush, anyplace the power of the British guns could not find them. For many it was too late, the open ground littered with heaps of broken machines, their crews scrambling to safety, or simply falling away, cut down by machine-gun fire. He knew it now, one calm voice in his head, clarity, knew that the tanks that still fought faced well-sited guns, perfectly arranged tanks, and that the attack was simply coming apart all around him. He turned toward the aide beside him, the man staring into his eyes, deep concern, said, "The radio . . . give the order to cease the attack. Make every effort to hold the captured territory."

The aides responded, one man moving quickly toward the radio truck behind them. Rommel heard the sound of a plane, looked up, saw a squadron of dive-bombers, thought, Junkers, yes! He felt a burst of hope, a streak of light through the thick fog in his brain, yes! Hit them, drive them back. He heard the familiar scream, the planes making their dive, saw a red flash, one plane suddenly coming apart, then another, a burst of fire, streaks of antiaircraft fire engulfing them all.

After one day's fighting, the attack had been broken off completely. Along the ridgelines around Médenine, Montgomery had prepared for the possibility of a flank attack by Rommel by carefully positioning several hundred tanks, artillery pieces, and antitank guns and had prepared the ground with extensive minefields. By the end of the day on March 6, the Afrika Korps had lost more than a third of its armor. The British did not lose a single tank.

BENI ZELTEN, TUNISIA—MARCH 7, 1943

Despite the overall failure of the Kasserine battles to achieve anything more than temporary success, Rommel had been named commander of the entire Tunisian theater. The combined forces had been named Army Group Rommel, a gesture of sentiment powered by Kesselring's insistence, the man's fantasy playing out through official channels. The gesture meant little to Rommel, beyond a pathetic attempt to fortify the dream that past glories could somehow ignite a victory. Von Arnim had made no real objection, at least not that Rommel had heard, but von Arnim had gone about his business in the north as though Rommel's authority meant very little. In late February, von Arnim had attacked the British positions north of Kasserine, seesaw fights that had produced nothing but casualties for both sides. Now, with the failure of Rommel's plan against Montgomery, it was clear that Kesselring's fantasies and Berlin's delusions had to be struck down. Rommel had ordered both Messe and von Arnim to produce assessments of their situation, troop strength, what they faced in their enemy, what the realistic chance was that the Tunisian front could withstand the inevitable assaults from the Allies, who now held every advantage on both the western and southern fronts.

To Rommel's surprise, both von Arnim and Messe complied without debate, and though Rommel expected rose-colored appraisals, especially from von Arnim, he was surprised to see that neither man had any illusions about his situation. The assessments from both commanders mirrored what Rommel had already concluded. The only way for the Germans to hold on to their bridgehead in Tunisia would be for the two wings of the army to pull together, withdrawing their lines to the northeast corner of Tunisia, where they could rely on the deep-water ports of Bizerte and Tunis, and the stout ridgelines and mountainous terrain inland from Enfidaville. As it was, they were facing overwhelming power from both Allied armies, power that was increasing every day.

Rommel recommended an immediate withdrawal from his Mareth position, linking Messe's forces with von Arnim's along a line that ran inland, westward, from Enfidaville, curling northward to meet the coast west of Bizerte. The new position would considerably condense the German lines, offering what Rommel believed was the faintest hope that Tunisia might still be held. He sent the recommendation to Kesselring, requesting in the most urgent terms that Hitler consider the plan, a plan that would be the only salvation for the German and Italian troops.

"The Führer feels that you are grossly underestimating your own fighting strength. His staff has prepared these notes for you, reminding you in some detail what manpower you have in your command. It disturbs me to present this to you."

Rommel took the paper from Kesselring's hand, saw lists of regiments, units arranged by number.

"See it for yourself, Erwin. The Führer is most insistent that you not rely on your old habits. There is great concern that you are allowing your own failures to cloud your judgment about the capability of this army."

"Yes, so I am a defeatist. I have heard that before." Rommel read the papers, saw the numbers, the careful attention to mathematics. He moved to a table, sat, the numbers filling his brain, a meaningless exercise. "Very impressive. Does the Führer have any plan to equip all of these units with the armor and weaponry they are supposed to have? Or do we simply pretend that they are at full strength?" He tossed the paper on the desk, put his arms on the table. "An army on paper. Is that what I am expected to fight with? All these regiments . . . does anyone in

Berlin have any notion how a war is fought?" Rommel slapped his hand on the table.

"The Italians believe this nonsense as well, I'm certain. They give me a regiment, and because it is a *regiment,* they expect that their soldiers can therefore stand up to an Allied regiment. Give me ten, and we are equal to ten of the enemy. What of *supplies*? What of *weapons*? I have armored divisions who field a fourth of what they should have, and those tanks that run are barely operational. I have artillery batteries that have no artillery, some with worn-out guns and no crews! But on *paper* we are strong! I assure you, Albert, the Allies suffer no such illusions. They suffer no shortages, no depletion of their ranks. They do not hide behind lists and pretend that they are invincible, just because their leader claims it!"

Kesselring crossed his arms against his chest. "I will not hear any more of this! The Führer has long been concerned about you, your health, your frame of mind. Defeatism? Yes! Everyone in Berlin speaks of you this way! I have been your champion, I have kept you in the field when many in Berlin, and many more in Rome, said to pull you out."

Rommel felt a rising wave of disgust, thought, oh, certainly, you are my champion when it suits you. When I give you victories. He sat back in the chair, had no energy for a fight with Kesselring, the man seeming to tower over him. His eyes clouded, and he blinked, rubbed them with a rough hand. He tried to take a breath, the tightness in his throat choking it away, and he put a hand on his neck, rubbed, could not push away the pain. Damn! How much of this can I stand!

"Are you all right?"

He ignored Kesselring, bent over, his head down on the desk, fought to breathe, the pains rolling through him, too much, too familiar. Just leave, damn you. Leave me alone.

"Erwin, I will summon the doctor. This cannot continue."

Rommel pulled himself up, took a painful breath, his throat loosening. He looked at the papers, the Führer's reply to his report, felt a great weight in his chest. "The doctor cannot help me. But you are correct. This cannot continue. I should see the Führer myself, speak to him. There is no chance for us here unless he can be made to understand what is happening here."

Kesselring put a hand on his chin, rubbed, stared down. "Do you really believe he will listen?"

Rommel saw sadness on the man's face, couldn't help but feel it himself. He looked Kesselring in the eye, had always tried to face the man with pure honesty. But Kesselring glanced away, and Rommel could feel the gap opening up, the distance between them growing, a commander and his unruly, unrepentant subordinate. Rommel tried to stand, the weakness in his legs holding him down, and he understood now, yes, this is how it will end. He looked toward the window, felt the soft breeze, the dry, cool air, the smells he had grown used to, the sounds of his army, machines and men, moving away from him, all of it, falling from his hands, beyond his reach.

HITLER'S HEADQUARTERS, UKRAINE, SOVIET UNION— MARCH 10, 1943

The mood at Hitler's eastern headquarters gave Rommel a clear sign that all the talk about the Führer's obsession with Russia was completely accurate. The staff huddled in glum silence, the dispatchers and telephone operators held their conversations in hushed voices, and when Rommel was ushered into Hitler's private office, he was surprised Hitler was alone.

"Why are you not in Africa?"

Rommel waited for more, the furious outburst, Hitler's usual response to things that were not exactly as they ought to be. But there was only silence, Hitler staring off toward a closed window, the curtain drawn, nothing to see. Rommel didn't know what to do, no groveling aides directing him to sit, no one flittering around Hitler, guarding him from the unpleasantness of the facts.

"I have come because I am concerned that you have not been accurately informed of our situation in Tunisia."

Hitler turned, looked at him, and Rommel saw the man's eyes, heavy and black, the face worn, expressionless, none of the usual fire.

"Tunisia? We should have no concern for Tunisia. Matters there will work themselves out. We will prevail. I must face far more difficult challenges right here. Have you heard the news about Stalingrad?"

"Yes, sir. Of course. Terrible tragedy."

"It is my fault. I put my army in the hands of traitors and office boys. We needed men, fighters, and instead we crumble in the face of an inferior enemy. It has become a disaster, a ruinous catastrophe. Because of the incompetence and corruption among my generals, the Russians are allowed to grow stronger every day. They are helped by the Americans, enormous convoys of shipping passing through our sea-lanes with barely a hint of our grand and glorious U-boat screen. The U-boat command has been useless, completely ineffective at stopping the shipping, and so, one race of savages helps another."

Rommel had nothing to say, felt a strange barrier, as though Hitler were speaking to someone else, anyone, even himself.

"They try to stand in my way, every step is blocked. Weak men who will not allow me to fulfill our destiny. They have betrayed the German people. I am surrounded by those who dwell only on failure. There is great danger in that. Defeatism causes one to make wrong conclusions. Pessimism leads to mistakes!" Hitler looked toward him again. "I asked you why you are not in Africa."

Rommel felt weak, his legs giving out, looked toward a chair. "Might I be allowed to sit?"

Hitler waved his hand, turned away, stared again at the closed window. Rommel moved toward the chair, sat heavily.

Hitler said, "You do not look well. I have heard of your sickness. You should take leave."

"There has been no time, Mein Führer. Please, I must tell you . . . I must offer a suggestion. If we do not withdraw and consolidate our defenses in Tunisia, we cannot survive there. And that is but a temporary measure. The Allies are gaining strength, and . . . it is only a matter of time before we are driven out of Africa altogether."

Hitler looked at him, and Rommel saw the flash of black fire, waited for the explosion, but Hitler turned away again. "Nonsense. You have become an annoying pessimist. How did that happen? You were the best field commander I had. If I had sent you to Russia, we would be in Moscow now. Or perhaps not.

Perhaps you would have grown despondent there as well. Is it not enough that you are celebrated as a great hero? The people adore you, they speak your name with reverence. Why can I not depend on you to *fight*?"

"I will fight. But I do not relish throwing my army away in a lost pursuit. Forgive me, Mein Führer, but there is no good fight to be had in Africa. Allow me to move my command to Italy, to withdraw the good troops we have in Tunisia. We can preserve our armor, our best fighting troops. We can make a new stand, hold the Allies away from southern Europe until they recognize the superiority of our position. They will exhaust themselves against our resolve. I promise you . . . I pledge to you that I will keep the enemy out of southern Europe. It may be our best chance to hold on to all this army has gained."

"Italy? You wish me to retreat to *Italy*? That would be unacceptable to our allies in Rome. And it is unacceptable to me. There is no need to withdraw from Tunisia. You make excuses . . . you have squandered all that we have provided to you, and now you would dare to suggest that we should run away? We have suffered greatly in Stalingrad, and no one there is running away!"

Rommel felt the man's anger now, knew there was no argument to be made, thought, there is no one left at Stalingrad to run anywhere. Hitler rose from the chair, paced slowly.

"I will not hear talk of abandoning Africa. It is the sickness in you, this disease that has taken your resolve. You must recover. Go again to Semmering, to the hospital. There are good doctors there. Take some time to regain your health. Don't come to me with any more talk of Tunisia. That is no longer your concern."

Rommel felt the punch of Hitler's words. Of course. Now it is official.

"Please, I wish to resume my command. If I return to Tunisia, I can organize the best kind of defense."

"I am sick of hearing about defense. You will report to Semmering immediately. I want you fit for your next campaign. When you have regained your spirit, report to my headquarters to begin planning the new offensive."

Rommel felt a spark, watched as Hitler moved more quickly, the pacing more deliberate. "New offensive?"

Hitler stopped, spun toward him, clenched his fists, shook them in the air. "Yes! We will soon launch a full-scale strike against Casablanca. We shall drive the Americans into the ocean! I want you to lead the assault, and you must be in good health. Do you understand? Do not return to me until you are prepared to defeat the enemy!"

The plane rolled forward, gaining speed, pressing him into the seat, and he turned away from the window, stared ahead, tried to embrace the pleasant days he was facing, the quiet of the hospital, the care of the doctors, all the fluttering about from so many nurses in their white gowns. He held tightly to the hope that the illnesses would fade, that rest and recuperation would make all the difference, would bring him back, give him the fire once more. But far to the south, he knew that his men waited in dirt tombs, helpless to hold back the tide that was coming, the strike from the great beast that swarmed around them on two sides. I should be there, he thought. No matter what any of them say, Kesselring, von Arnim, or even Hitler. That is my army and they need me with them. I should not be resting in a soft bed while the *Panzerarmee* struggles to survive.

The plane made a sharp dip, the air rough, churning, and he couldn't avoid the weakness, the queasy turn in his stomach. He let out a breath, wanted to look at his watch, knew it was a long time yet, thought, I must endure this. I will be there in due time. He tried to fill his mind with Lucy's image, knew she would be waiting for him at Semmering, the strong woman with the soft heart, who only wanted to care for him, who cared so much for all of it, who would listen and understand all he had to say. He thought of the letter he had written, days before:

If only I had what one needs to make war here . . .

He had referred to the dismal supply lines, the *tools,* but he knew she would see it differently, would know he was talking about himself, the strength in his back, the resolve in his own mind. He thought of Hitler, the awful meetings. No matter how our fortunes may have turned, there can be no victory, no end to this that will not destroy our country. We are led by a madman.

26. PATTON

The sirens blared, a half dozen armored trucks leading the way, the caravan rolling up the ragged, dusty road. They passed the various checkpoints, the carefully placed barriers that Fredendall had used to secure his safety, pushed past the startled guards, the sounds of the sirens announcing with perfect clarity that the Second Corps had a new commander. Patton's promotion to lieutenant general was not yet official, and so he had adhered to protocol, his command car bearing only the two stars of his current rank. But there was no mistaking whose car it was. The stars themselves were an adornment far more pronounced than what the staff officers at Djebel Kouif were accustomed to seeing, large and silver, backed by an oversize red plate positioned squarely below the car's grill. Patton stood tall, his steel helmet clamped down hard, two stars again, stamped into the steel above his scowling brow, his jaw set hard, no smile, no casual greeting to the men who stood by and saluted gamely as he passed.

Fredendall was still there, tending to details of his own, gathering his personal effects, whatever need he had to conclude his affairs in his own way, to shake the hands of those on his staff who were remaining in Tunisia. As Patton stormed into the command center, the contrast between the two men was graphic and startling, and the men who manned the phones, who handled the paperwork for the Second Corps, were quick to understand that the changes to the corps would be far more profound than a new nameplate on the commander's desk.

*   *   *

"Where is General Fredendall? I expected him to meet me."

The aide seemed to quiver, held his salute. "Sir, the general is still at breakfast." The man pointed to one side, out past the door, then let his arm drop, still held the salute.

"Breakfast? It is ten o'clock! Tomorrow morning, breakfast will commence at dawn, and no officer will be served after six thirty. Enlisted men may eat afterward, and the kitchen will cease to serve food at seven thirty. Is that understood?"

The man still held the salute. "Certainly, sir. I shall have the mess sergeants informed."

"Is there a reason why you cannot inform them yourself? It is my job to delegate. It is yours to get the job done. Your hand frozen to your forehead?"

The man snapped his arm down to his side. "No, sir."

"And what the hell do you call that?"

"I'm sorry, what, sir?"

"That uniform. You on leave, soldier? This some sort of vacation for you?"

The man seemed confused, and Patton pointed to the collar, open, a glimpse of undershirt. "Where the hell is your necktie, Lieutenant!" Patton glanced around the room, the others standing, every man wide-eyed. "Where the hell are all your neckties? Every damned one of you is out of uniform. I will not tolerate that. I don't see a single helmet. I was told that a war is happening out here. Has no one told *you*?"

The lieutenant said, "Sir, General Fredendall—"

"To hell with General Fredendall, soldier! There is no such man, do you hear me?"

"Sir? He's having breakfast—"

Patton leaned close to the young man's face, startled him into silence. "General Fredendall is no longer your commanding officer! Or did no one inform you of that?"

"Yes, sir. We were informed, sir."

Patton was fully energized now, looked closely at each man, the room utterly silent, even the radios quiet, the equipment itself waiting for his next command.

"There will be changes here, gentlemen. Immediate changes. In short order, this corps will engage the enemy. I intend that we destroy him, and we will not accomplish that unless every one of you operates in accordance with my way of doing things. General Eisenhower did not put me here because he wanted business as usual. *Your* business as usual was an embarrassment to this army, and an embarrassment to my country! There will be no further embarrassments!" He looked hard at the young lieutenant, his voice now in full bloom, a hard, high-pitched shout. *"Now, where the hell is my office?"*

As word of the fights that swirled around Kasserine rolled into Morocco, Patton's boredom had grown far worse than tedious. A fight was going on, a real fight against an enemy who was capable of winning, who might destroy everything that Operation Torch had accomplished. Throughout the landings, as his men had punched their way through difficult barriers all across the western landing zones, it had never occurred to him that the Americans might actually lose. But with rumbles coming to him about the ponderous decision making, the inept tactics at Kasserine, he had begun to realize his greatest frustration yet: the entire mission in Africa could become a dangerous failure, and he might have nothing to say about it.

His lack of discretion had caused him problems from the earliest days of his career, every commander he served under wrestling with Patton's mouth. Patton's outspokenness and independent behavior had caused problems as far back as the First World War, and his friendship with Black Jack Pershing had likely allowed Patton's career to survive many bouts with superior officers who seemed to him to be too obtuse or too inflexible to comprehend Patton's clear perception of his own role in the army, especially an army at war. He could never grasp why generals insisted he stay at the rear of his troops. Now, that same warning had come from Eisenhower, and Patton quietly chafed at that, knew too much of history, of men like Stonewall Jackson, had never believed any soldier could be inspired from behind. He had learned much from Rommel, had marveled at the German's instinct for putting himself at the most crucial point of attack. Patton hated the notion that in modern warfare, a general's place was in some remote command post, reading reports, issuing orders by radio to men who might be far too involved in their own survival to pay attention to any radio.

Patton believed without doubt that Eisenhower's command
had come about only because the English liked him and accepted him to be the proper figurehead that would fill the difficult role of bridging the two armies, a voice for both American
and British concerns. Patton bristled at that, still believed that
the British had every intention of running the show, and that any
victory would become their own, at the expense of the Americans. One by one, Patton had watched as the senior American
generals seemed to be shoved aside, to make way for an Allied
force dominated by British commanders. Every branch of the
service was run by the British now, what Patton saw as an out-
rageously blatant conspiracy.

He had little affection for Wayne Clark and had privately
seethed when Clark had been given command of the Fifth
Army, no matter that Clark outranked him. But it was no surprise to Patton that Clark had been sent to Morocco as well,
stuck in the backwater of the war, while men like Alexander and
Anderson controlled operations in Tunisia. If Eisenhower
wanted Clark to stay put and keep an eye on some meaningless
threat from German-friendly Spanish Morocco, that was fine
with Patton.

His meeting with Fredendall had been brief and cordial, and
Patton had not addressed any of the changes that would follow
the man's departure. Fredendall was clearly a defeated man,
wore a shroud of gloom, something Patton had expected. But
Patton had admired the man's deportment, no outbursts, no
grousing, accepting Patton's occupation of his headquarters
with dignity, offering to help the transition in any way Patton
found useful. Patton had been polite and gracious, would not
add salt to the man's wounds, and by the next morning Fredendall was gone.

NEAR TÉBESSA, TUNISIA—MARCH 10, 1943

He had ridden forward with Omar Bradley, realized with some
annoyance that Bradley seemed to be watching him, studying
his performance. After a long silence, Bradley said, "It's my job,
you know."

Patton turned toward the side, stared out the car's window. "I don't need Ike coddling me, and I don't need a damned spy in my headquarters. He wants a job done, he should let me do it. You going to tell him every damned thing I say, give him a report on every butt I chew out?"

"I'm not a schoolmaster, George. You're being a little too unreasonable. Ike has sent me out here to observe as much as I can. If there's a problem, he needs to know, so it can be fixed. You know full well there are problems out here. We can't afford another Kasserine."

Patton sniffed, stared out toward a muddy field, tanks parked in uneven rows. He couldn't really feel anger toward Bradley, knew the man's exceptional reputation, why Ike had chosen him for the job. Bradley gave every hint of that key instinct that made an officer a good fighting man, a man who could handle himself in the worst crisis. Patton felt that even as they rode quietly through the American positions, visited the camps and command posts. Bradley had something intangible that Patton rarely saw in anyone of high rank. Marshall was an exception, others, such as Ernie Harmon and Jimmy Doolittle, Charles Ryder, and Terry Allen. Patton had felt it for his son-in-law as well, John Waters, the young man still missing in action. They each carried some special *thing* that commanded respect, and Patton had been surprised to find it in Bradley, the fact that Bradley seemed destined for some role on Eisenhower's staff.

"You don't belong on Ike's staff. You should be in the field."

"I belong where Ike wants me to be. The rest . . . if there's something else for me to do, I'll accept that when the time comes."

Patton continued to stare out. "Look at this miserable place. Perfect for a war. Blast everything to hell, and no one will care. You ever see so much damned rain? This whole place is like hell. Everywhere you look, there's ruins, like damned skeletons sticking in the sand. Roman, mostly, but God knows who else. All those stone pillars, busted columns. Looks like shipwrecks. We just better make damned sure the same thing doesn't happen to us." He saw trucks lined in a row, a cluster of men, felt a stab of fury. "Oh, hell. Driver! Stop the car! Hit the siren! Wake those bastards up!"

The car was slowing, and he pushed open the heavy steel door, stepped out with the car still moving, the blast of the siren propelling him forward.

"Who's in charge here?" He saw the officer, a captain, the men all standing back, some staring past him toward the source of the high-pitched siren. "You know me?"

The captain glanced toward the car, then to the stars on Patton's helmet. "No, General. But, welcome to the maintenance battalion."

"Welcome, hell. Where's your helmet? Where are their helmets?" He turned to the men, more gathering behind them. He saw some men in wool caps, every shape of hat. "Every one of you! Snatch that beanie off your head!" He glanced behind him, his aides easing up close, Bradley with them, turned to the soldiers again. "Hand them over!"

The men looked at each other, uncertain, the officer starting to speak, and Patton felt the man's protest coming, didn't want to hear it. He raised a hand, silenced the man. "This is your first offense, Captain. Next time, it costs you a fifty-dollar fine. Your men will pay twenty-five. I want to see regulation uniforms on every man in this corps! Every man!"

"Yes, sir. I understand, sir. May I ask . . . does this apply to the men working on the trucks?"

"Damned right, Captain! They're soldiers, aren't they?" Patton stood stiffly, put his hands behind his back, waited. The hats were coming off, the men unsure what to do next, and Patton had no patience now. "Were my orders not understood? Hand those beanies forward and present them to my aide. They are not regulation, and I am confiscating them."

The collection of hats gathered in one man's arms, and he stepped forward, held out the bundle. Patton's aide took them, returned to the car.

Patton said, "Helmets and neckties, gentlemen, every damned day. And I want to see some precise salutes from every one of you. The damned British laugh at us for our casual salutes. No more! Your training was not just how to handle a rifle or turn a wrench. You were taught how to salute, and I expect you to remember that. Now, back to work! We have a job to do, and the whole damned United States of America is counting on men like you to get it done."

The men snapped to attention, tossed up perfect salutes.

"Yes, that's right. Get used to it."

Patton returned their salute, spun around, moved back to the car. The aide was waiting, and Patton motioned to him, the man opening the trunk. Patton watched as the hats were tossed in, adding to the growing pile, and he smiled, looked at Bradley, felt the stir of accomplishment.

"You see, Brad? This is what we have to do. I won't have the Second Corps remembered for their pile of beanies."

"But, George, fining them so much money for their uniforms?"

Patton was surprised by Bradley's question, thought, wonderful, already he's making a list for Ike to gripe at me about. Schoolmaster indeed.

"Listen to me, Brad. This is my corps and I'll run it in the best way I know how. I could spend every hour of this inspection tour yelling my lungs out, and it would work for only so long. Hell, I'd run out of breath. But hit them in the pocketbook! Hah! You don't have to say another word. And they'll damned well remember it."

They climbed into the car, the armored trucks moving out in front, machine guns trained forward, lookouts scanning the thick, gray sky for enemy planes. They rode for a long mile, the rains coming hard again, Patton scanning the countryside, heavy mist clouding his view. He went over the command list in his head, three divisions of infantry, the First, the Ninth, the Thirty-fourth, plus the First Armored. Good men, all of them. Four strong divisions. Just let us go, Ike. Let me give them another crack at Rommel. They'll *stuff* all that bellyaching from here to Washington.

Patton spent long hours with Bradley, going over the commands of each of his divisions, the best talents of the men in charge. There was little time for lengthy planning, rehearsal exercises, and less time for Patton to test the abilities of various officers for the key jobs in the command structure of the Second Corps. To the south, Montgomery was gearing up for his major push into the Mareth line, and Patton's role had been defined even before he took command, in plans drawn up by Eisenhower and Alexander not long after Rommel had pulled away from Kasserine.

Throughout their discussions, Bradley's grasp of the necessary strategies continued to impress Patton, a quiet confidence and firm hold on sound tactics, something Patton had not yet seen in too many of his senior officers. With Bradley staying mostly in Patton's headquarters, filling his role as Eisenhower's pipeline, Patton realized that there should be an opportunity for Bradley's talents to be used for far more practical purposes. Patton's next call to Eisenhower was simple and direct. If Bradley was to spend most of his time occupying space in Patton's headquarters, he should have something better to do. Patton wanted Bradley for himself. To Patton's surprise, Eisenhower consented. However, the assignment had been no real surprise to Bradley since, unknown to Patton, he and Eisenhower had already discussed such a move. Though Bradley would occasionally issue reports directly to Eisenhower, make visits to Algiers for personal meetings, he would do so as the Second Corps's number two man. At the very least, Bradley would gain experience, learn the valuable lessons firsthand from the inevitable combat situations the Second Corps was soon to face. And Eisenhower was aware that Bradley would bring a quiet ray of calm and reason through the often tumultuous world of George Patton.

DJEBEL KOUIF, TUNISIA—MARCH 13, 1943

"Ike says I should find something useful for you to do every day, if that's possible. I'm not talking too much out of turn there. He says you'll probably tell me that yourself."

Patton walked slowly, kept pace with Alexander's methodical stride. "He's right. I'm ready to go. We're all ready to go. And if it's up to me, we'll keep going until we give Rommel a wet ass in the Mediterranean."

Alexander laughed, and Patton eyed him discreetly, thought, he's as British as they come. And yet . . . not. Curious. Alexander stopped, and Patton saw him staring out across the dirt road, saw an Arab man hoisting a water jug up onto the shoulder of a small woman. Alexander made a grunting sound, and Patton said, "Arab chivalry."

"Perhaps you and I should go over there and jolly well kick his ass."

Patton stared at Alexander for a long moment, saw no smile, thought, my God, he might be serious.

Alexander began to walk again. "Or, perhaps not. Might not play well in the newspapers, eh?"

Patton laughed, was surprised by Alexander, had not expected the man to be anything more than an arrogant snob. He kept pace again. "Ike would enjoy unraveling that one, I'm sure. He's already convinced I'm going to wake up one morning and start shelling Anderson's headquarters."

Alexander seemed surprised himself now. "Good gracious, man, why on earth would you do that?"

Patton's mind filled with replies, none of them worth the price he might pay for expressing them. "I promise, not in this war. Ike worries too much. Just his job, I suppose. My job is to put my foot in people's backsides, so they'll do the same to the Krauts."

Alexander thought a moment. "Your promotion . . . I assume you received my congratulations. Bloody well appropriate."

"Yes, thank you. Your General McCreery sent a very nice note. I'd heard a lot of talk about it, and frankly, I expected it before now. It's a dream I've had, since I was a boy. I used to play army, run all over hell and gone with a wooden rifle, calling myself *Lieutenant General Patton*. At West Point, I told a few fellows I'd make it one day. Nobody doubted it. Well, not me, anyway."

Alexander was watching him, and Patton realized he was listening carefully to every word. "That all right with you? If a man feels like he deserves something, it should be all right if he expects it."

Alexander laughed now. "No argument here, old chap. Ike says your promotion is well earned. And of course, if you're to command a corps, three stars is the appropriate rank for an American in your position."

"Four is better."

Alexander seemed to study him again, serious now. "You'll get it too. I'd make a wager, if I could. Trouble is, nobody would pay up. I might have a thing or two to say about the promotion. Never know, of course."

They walked down a short hill, past Arab women gathered at a muddy water hole, piles of white cloth spread out on fat rocks. It was unusual for a senior commander to simply take a stroll, out beyond the confines of the headquarters. Alexander had made it clear that he relied as much on private chats as he did on grand staff meetings, spoke more frankly than any other British officer Patton had met. Patton didn't trust it at first, couldn't help wondering if Alexander was doing what so many of the other Brits seemed to do, gather influence, find ways to push the Americans to the back row of the war. He knew Eisenhower didn't agree with that, thought, all right, Ike, I'll do it your way. He had accepted Eisenhower's order, that no one could openly criticize anyone by his nationality. It was one thing to criticize a man for being a son of a bitch. But you had better not call him a *British* son of a bitch.

But there was nothing disagreeable about Alexander at all, and Patton had been impressed with the man's record in the First World War, something Patton could share with pride. Both men had been decorated, and both had suffered wounds in combat. To Patton, that put them firmly on equal ground.

They walked in silence for a long moment, and Patton felt the question rising in his mind, the last detail of the plans he had already memorized, the one thing Alexander had not yet told him.

"Are we still a go for the sixteenth?"

"Likely. Sorry to be so vague about it. It's this damnable weather. The plan is in place, has been since before you got here. You know that, of course. You've met with all your commanders?"

"Yep. Good men, I think. Still some proving to do. Terry Allen's probably the best of the four."

"Yes, well, Ike agrees. Your plans call for his First Division to lead the way into Gafsa."

Patton had studied the plans, the maps, understood exactly what he was expected to do. And he wasn't happy about it. "You honestly expect that if my boys kick the Krauts off the Eastern Dorsale, they're going to listen to an order to stop?"

"Yes, I do. So does Ike."

Patton swallowed his protest, and Alexander said, "Monty's got his people in line, ready to go. But he can't make his jump-off until your people accomplish their mission. Your part of this operation is essential. You have to drive the Germans out of the hills and push the attack toward their flank. They'll have to respond to you by pulling strength out of their main line. They can't allow you to hover about in their left and rear and not send some pretty strong forces your way to answer the threat. That's all Monty needs to make the breakthrough and drive the enemy back up the coast." Alexander paused, looked him hard in the eye. "If you try to push your men east of the Eastern Dorsale, if you try to make for the coast to cut off the enemy's retreat, you know what can happen. You'll be spread out on a dangerous line across flat, open ground, vulnerable as hell on your flank. We don't know what the Germans have left in their bag at Mareth, not completely anyway. This is not Monty's operation, but it is laid out so that Monty makes the hardest thrust. Surely you understand why."

Patton knew the word, *experience,* hated it, hated that Montgomery had been successful against Rommel, while the Americans had made such a poor showing at Kasserine. There was no argument Patton could make, he had to accept the grinding truth that Montgomery's forces were better prepared to launch the strongest part of the offensive. But he hated it anyway.

On March 16, Patton's men pushed south and east, drove the Italian outposts away from Gafsa with barely a fight. The other prongs of the Second Corps moved along parallel routes, the First Armored eventually driving up toward the passes along the Eastern Dorsale. The attack spread across the entire front where, a month before, Rommel's attack had so devastated the Americans. In a few short days, Patton occupied most of the ground that Rommel's troops had now abandoned, the crossroads and villages falling into American hands. From Sbiba and Fondouk in the north, down through Kasserine and Sidi Bou Zid, to Sbeïtla and Gafsa, the Second Corps pressed hard against growing

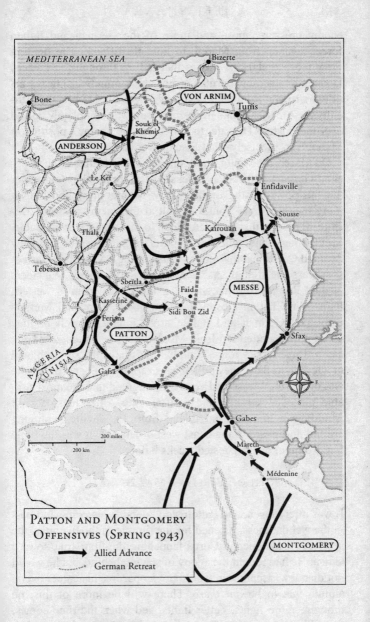

MEDITERRANEAN SEA

Bizerte

Bone

VON ARNIM

Tunis

Souk el Khemis

ANDERSON

Le Kef

Enfidaville

Sousse

Thala

Kairouan

Tébessa

Sbeïtla

Faid

MESSE

Kasserine

Sidi Bou Zid

Feriana

PATTON

Sfax

ALGERIA

TUNISIA

Gafsa

Gabes

Mareth

0   200 miles

Médenine

0   200 km

MONTGOMERY

N
W   E
S

PATTON AND MONTGOMERY
OFFENSIVES (SPRING 1943)

➡ Allied Advance
⇢ German Retreat

enemy pressure, more and more of the German and Italian forces sent up from Mareth to hold them back. The fighting grew more brutal, the passes that led up through the Eastern Dorsale manned by German armor, thick minefields, heavy artillery stripped from their positions at Mareth. Despite the difficulty the Americans had in pushing their way completely up and over the Eastern Dorsale, the effect on the enemy's position at Mareth was precisely what Eisenhower had hoped for.

On March 20, Montgomery opened his own attack, the weakened German and Italian defenses at Mareth collapsing under the full power of the Eighth Army. Montgomery had thrown more than a simple frontal assault at the enemy position. Despite all reports that the sand marsh to the west was impassable, Montgomery had relied on reports from scouts of his New Zealand Corps that the spongy mush of the dry lakebed was not so impassable after all. As the attack began, the New Zealanders pushed through the marsh and stunned the enemy's western flank. With Patton closing in from above, Giovanni Messe's combined German and Italian army fought as well as they could, turning attention from Montgomery to Patton, and back again. But Messe's forces simply didn't have the strength, and in a few short days, they pulled back rapidly to the north. By the end of March, Messe and von Arnim agreed that the most suitable place to retrench and confront the Allies' next assault would be a line that led inland from Enfidaville, wrapping around northward to the coast west of Bizerte. It was the same line Rommel had suggested weeks before.

SOUTH OF TÉBESSA—MARCH 16, 1943

It was after eleven, and Patton stood outside his command post in the wet darkness, listened for the rumble of the big guns, the artillery of his Second Corps launching the first strike toward Gafsa. He had fought the agony of staying behind, but he would not disobey Eisenhower, would not jeopardize his career over a simple lust to be *out there*. There will be more of this, he thought, more fights, better fights, and when the time comes, they'll have to put me where I want to be. He heard it now, low thunder, the flashes of fire hidden by the dismal weather. He stood quietly for a long moment, absorbed the sounds, thought, nothing else for me to do, not now. It's all happening the way it was planned, and tomorrow, I will find out what kind of men we have.

He moved back into the blockhouse, low lamplight, his cot in a closet-sized room in the rear. The aides stood when he came in, and he waved them off. "Nothing else to do now. Get some rest. But make sure the telephone operators are on the job all damned night."

He sat on the bed, pushed the door closed, his knees nearly touching the wall in front of him. His foot kicked the soft pack beside the bed, and he reached down, felt for the small, thick book, his diary, pulled it out, drew his pen from his shirt pocket. He lay back on the bed, thought a moment, knew that somewhere some radio stations across the Atlantic were already reporting the start of the assault. It was customary now, the Allied censors releasing just enough details to inform both the American and the British people that a new operation was under way, a healthy shot to civilian morale. Somewhere, he thought, some damned idiot is in some studio telling his audience that I'm right out there, at the head of the line, leading the way, sitting up high on the first tank. Damn him. Damn all of them. It's where I should be.

He stared at the blank page, fingered the pen for a moment, then wrote:

Well, the battle is on. I'm taking off my shoes to go to bed.

27. EISENHOWER

"Sir, this message was just received from General Montgomery. Not sure what it means."

Eisenhower took the paper from Butcher's hand.

Personal. Montgomery to Eisenhower. Entered Sfax 8:30 this morning. Please send Fortress.

Eisenhower read the words again, tried to make sense of the riddle. "Well, he's in Sfax. That's excellent news. He said he'd get there pretty quick and was pretty definite about it. Have to hand it to him."

"But . . . the 'Fortress'? What's he mean, sir?"

"Hell if I know. Get Beetle in here."

Butcher moved away, and Eisenhower tossed the paper on the growing pile on his desk. The reports had flowed in every hour, news both good and bad. The fighting had been severe, especially in the American sector, as much from the terrain as the tenacity of the enemy. But Patton had been noisy about the performance of his men, and it was no surprise of course, but his noise had been directed in hot words toward the First Armored in particular, General Ward's command. True to form, Patton had focused most of his ire on Ward himself, finding fault with what Patton interpreted as the armored commander's caution. Eisenhower had been concerned by that, had to believe there was something concrete in Patton's complaints. Eisenhower knew that if Patton had one expertise, it was pushing tanks into battle, and if Ward was drawing that kind of hostility from Patton, it might be something Eisenhower would have to address himself. He could not fault Patton for singling out anyone for a good lashing. Eisenhower had forced himself to look past old friendships, old affiliations from West Point. He knew the history lessons, had read enough of George Washington and Robert E. Lee to know that inept generals produced catastrophic problems, and no matter how loyal a subordinate might claim to be, a good commander could not hesitate to remove an inept general. I wonder, he thought, if the problem there was more about Fredendall than Ward. Fredendall seemed too eager to make enemies. Well, that might describe Patton too. But Patton expects excellence, his own, first of all. Then he expects it from you, makes specific demands, and if you don't live up to them, you'll hear about it. And so will I. It could be that Ward isn't performing in the tight situations like we need him to. Damn! I can't ignore that.

"Sir?"

Eisenhower saw Beetle Smith at the door, Butcher right behind him, and pointed to the note from Montgomery. "You know anything about this? Monty's asking for a Fortress."

Smith dropped his head. "Oh, hell. Forgot about that."

"About *what*?"

"Um . . . seems when I met with Monty a month or so ago, we were talking about his objectives, about his timetable for advancing up the coast. He's a bit of a boaster, sir. Well, you know that, of course. Toots his own horn a bit too loudly, if you ask me. He insisted he would be at Sfax by April 15. I challenged him on that, and we made a bet. I told him that if he made it when he said, you'd give him a B-17 and an American crew."

"You what?"

Smith flinched, the short man backing away a step. "I'm terribly sorry, sir. It was indiscreet of me. We were joshing a bit. I never thought he'd actually . . . expect payment."

"Well, apparently he does. Dammit, Beetle, what the hell were you thinking? I've had enough damned trouble convincing these generals that they should be working together, without rewarding one of them with his own damned B-17! You realize what kind of precedent this sets? Patton or Clark or Anderson, they get their mission accomplished, they'll be lining up for party favors! Are we supposed to toss out gifts to everyone who does his job? Jesus, Beetle! A B-17?"

"I didn't think he'd take it seriously, Ike. I'm sorry."

Eisenhower pushed himself down into the chair, rubbed a hand hard across his forehead. Butcher eased closer, stood beside Beetle, said, "Just tell Monty to go to hell, Skipper."

Eisenhower looked up, couldn't help but notice the contrast between the two men, different-color uniforms, Butcher a full head taller than Smith, thought, Tweedledee and Tweedledum. No, that's not fair. I couldn't run this place without either of them.

"No, Harry, we can't do that. You know damned well that Monty . . . well, dammit, Monty's got a big mouth. If it gets out that I've reneged on a bet with him . . ." Eisenhower paused. "All right, Beetle. You dug this hole. Now get us out of it. Call Spaatz at the air headquarters at Constantine. Tell him we need a B-17. We're assigning it to Monty's command. If Spaatz needs answers, tell him to call me. But he better not call me, Beetle. Explain this so that he understands the mess you've gotten me in and put it to bed."

"Right away, Ike. Very sorry."

"Go!"

Both men left the office, and Eisenhower leaned back in the chair, tried to clear his head. You wanted command, so you've got command. Whether it's relieving good officers or passing out B-17s. He laughed now, couldn't help it, imagined Montgomery crowing to his officers, giving them rides in his own private Flying Fortress. A small door opened in his brain, a question. What if Monty hadn't made it to Sfax? What would I have won? Wouldn't matter. No prize could make up for Monty falling down out there. We don't need any more disasters. So, enjoy your damned plane. If that makes you a little more enthusiastic about killing Germans, then it's for a good cause. We still have a long road.

EIGHTEENTH ARMY GROUP HEADQUARTERS,
CONSTANTINE, ALGERIA—APRIL 13, 1943

"General Ward has been relieved. General Patton has requested, and I have agreed, that he be replaced by General Harmon. General Patton has a great deal of confidence in Harmon, says he's the first man he'd want in a tank."

Eisenhower scanned the official order, looked at Alexander now, said, "I agree. Harmon *is* a tank. Tough nut. Perfect subordinate for George. Damned shame about Ward though. I thought he'd do the job."

"You can't always predict, Ike. It's not always the man who stands tall in his dress uniform who can climb the hill in front of his men. I've had to spoon out a bit of some hot lather myself. It's just . . . command."

The soothing tone of Alexander's words stuck in Eisenhower's brain, festered there, and he thought, I don't need a lecture. "I'm not happy with some of the things going on up here."

Alexander put his chin in his hand, nodded. "I understand that."

Eisenhower tried to hold his temper, had begun to understand the one flaw in Alexander's style. Alexander was undoubtedly a consummate soldier and understood tactics and strategy as well as anyone in the Allied camp. But Alexander often let the reins drop too loosely on some of his officers, handed too much responsibility to his staff. As much as Eisenhower had worked to secure harmony between the Americans and their British counterparts, he had been stunned to hear of the indiscreet spouting off from one of Alexander's corps commanders, a hint that Alexander simply didn't know what his senior officers were feeling.

"What are you going to do about John Crocker?"

"Yes, Sir John. Fine chap, sociable sort. Given to speaking to the press. Not always in our best interests, I'm afraid."

"Best interests? He publicly claims that the American troops are not combat worthy! I've seen the reports. You know as well as I do that the attack plans for Fondouk were difficult at best. The only American units available to him had minimal training, had not worked together as a unit at all, and had spent most of their time here guarding the communications depots. Crocker throws them right into the line and expects them to punch the Krauts out of their defenses. Hell, it was a difficult assignment for anyone, and only after things fell apart did Crocker send in his own . . . *your* people. Even the British troops there couldn't finish the job. The Germans were able to pull back. The whole thing was a mess, and dammit, Alex, that's the one thing we've worked too hard to overcome! Crocker was in charge of the operation, and it didn't go well, and the first thing he does is shoot his mouth off to the newspapers!"

Eisenhower was shouting, watched for Alexander's reaction, had rarely raised his voice in the Englishman's presence.

Alexander didn't flinch. "You're quite right, of course. Unwise. I'll speak to him at once."

Eisenhower forced himself to calm down, was surprised that Alexander was so matter-of-fact. "Good. Dammit, Alex, we have to keep a lid on this bickering. There's too much at stake."

"Agreed. In that light, have you given final approval to my plan? Should put your boys in a favorable light, considering all that's been said."

It was the real reason for Eisenhower's visit. Montgomery's push from the south had backed the Germans into hard defensive positions in severely mountainous terrain near the Tunisian east coast, a formidable obstacle for the Eighth Army. With Montgomery bogged down, it would be up to the Allied forces to the west to punch holes in the German perimeter, with one of the first goals being the capture of the crucial port of Bizerte. Alexander's strategy had positioned Anderson's First Army as the left hook, to attack eastward, parallel to the northern coastline. As the noose tightened around the German-held territory, the maps showed a clear picture of what Alexander's plan would mean. With Montgomery in the south and Anderson in the west, the narrowing front effectively squeezed the American Second Corps right out of the picture. The plan did not sit well with Eisenhower and had inspired a profane explosion from George Patton. In response, Alexander wisely modified his plan, to allow two of the four American divisions, half of the Second Corps, to move up to the north, to become the far left flank of the operation. Eisenhower knew it was not enough.

"I believe you've had some conversations with my naval aide, Lieutenant Commander Butcher."

"Quite so, yes. Amiable chap."

"Harry just got back from a three-week jaunt to the States, took care of some personal business and did some things for me. I guess you could call them official errands. His report gives me a pretty clear picture what's going on at home, and it's something we have to consider here. There is a great deal of . . ." Eisenhower paused. "Damn, I hate to use the word, but it is what it is. Competition. We're fighting a war on two fronts, and Doug MacArthur is pretty good at making himself known to the newspapers and the Congress."

"Competing for attention? Seems rather trivial in a war, wouldn't you say?"

"Well, there's that. But it's more substantial. Supplies, equipment, resources. We've been pretty good about supplying your people with top-of-the-line weapons, and now, we're doing the same for ourselves. But there is sentiment in the States to focus less on Hitler and more on the Japanese."

Eisenhower paused again, tried to form the words. Alexander seemed patient, waited, and after a moment, Eisenhower said, "When word of what happened at Dieppe hit the papers back home, there was hell to pay. Congress, newspapers, every damned voice on the radio, started telling the American people that, good God, we're beat. No need for American boys to die against Hitler's impregnable defense. It's hopeless. That surprised the hell out of me, but there it was. Made recruitment a real problem and turned a bunch of congressmen into pacifists, which made life pretty tough for Roosevelt. Now, with the Germans so close to being whipped here, the American people are being fed something entirely different, entirely the opposite. Hell, Marshall tells me that Roosevelt is as bad about it as anyone else. The public has this attitude now that the war here is nearly over, Hitler's done, so start up the parades. Pull everybody out of here and haul all the resources to the Pacific to help MacArthur. We can't explain every move we make to every damned reporter, and so, they just figure it out on their own, make their guesses, and dump all their *information* on the American public. I had a hell of a time trying to explain to Marshall, who had a hell of a time explaining to Roosevelt, why we stopped Patton on the Eastern Dorsale and didn't let him go all the way to the coast. All the damned armchair generals, and even Roosevelt, were asking out loud, what the hell was wrong with us? Why didn't we let Patton end the war? It's so damned convenient for civilians five thousand miles from here to look at a map and draw straight lines and assume everything falls into neat little packages." Eisenhower stopped, saw Alexander watching him, a slight smile on the man's face. "Well, hell, you don't need to hear this from me. You've been through this already."

"Quite so. I've had a few run-ins with the prime minister. You want to know about civilian interference, talk to Claude Auchinleck. Cost him his career."

"Well, it damned near cost me mine. All this Darlan business . . . my brother Milton tells me that there were papers calling me a fascist, that since I supported some Vichy jackass, I'm in bed with Hitler! Thank God for Marshall. He took the heat, kept me out of the grip of some pretty thickheaded congressmen. It's politics, plain and simple. Roosevelt has his enemies, and they look for any noose to hang him with. He doesn't need me tossing them the rope. We need to win this thing, win it the right way and win it quick, or that's exactly what I'll be doing."

Alexander still listened patiently, and Eisenhower was grateful, his rant exhausted. "Sorry, Alex, but I'm not just bellyaching. There's a point to all this. Your plan to divide up the Second Corps and keep half those boys out of the fight isn't going to fly back home. And, frankly, Alex, it doesn't fly with me. It's not just the politics. These boys have earned some spoils, and I can't let the British troops get all the headlines. I hear from Patton that some of his people are pretty miffed about this whole Crocker business. They know they got walloped at Kasserine, and they aim to make up for that. They've earned that chance, and I intend to give it to them. I want the Second Corps kept together and moved up to the north, to go at Bizerte. It'll be a hell of a logistics operation, moving so many men across Anderson's rear, but we'll do it. And once this thing kicks off, no one in the British army will be shooting their mouth off about how much *gut* the American soldier has."

Alexander smiled again, surprising him. "We can make it work, Ike. It *will* work. Has to. I don't want to hear any more rubbish out of London than you do from Washington."

He had expected more protest from Alexander, realized now why he liked the man. "Well, good, glad you agree. I'd whole lot rather be putting my eyes toward Tunis and Bizerte than looking over my damned shoulder."

"One thing, Ike. The planners have a pretty good handle on what we have to do to kick off the next campaign. I know you're going to get pressure from the States on this, and we better be ready to move quickly. I don't believe we'd be jumping the gun if we keep our eyes focused *beyond* Tunis."

Eisenhower nodded, thought a moment, the name rolling through his mind, the code name for the invasion of Sicily, Operation Husky. "You still think Monty's the man?"

"Without question. He can be difficult, but there's no one else I'd want for the job. And I assume you still want—"

"Patton. Yep. I don't see any reason to change those arrangements."

"They should make a hell of a team, Ike. We shouldn't wait too much longer to get their people into training."

"I'm not sure about the *team* part of it. But George knows what we need him to do. One problem I have right now is that pulling him out this quick might hurt morale in the Second Corps. You change commanders in short order, they assume he's taking the blame for their screwups. I want to keep this as quiet as we can for now. No need to tell the newspapers what's going on, and I sure as hell don't want the enemy to know anything about Patton being pulled out of line. Monty needs to stay where he is for now, until the job is done. You agree?"

"Definitely. He knows he's needed for Husky, so it will drive him to get his men into Tunis as quick as he can. He's already told me . . . well . . ."

"He's told you what?"

"Well, damn, Ike, you know Monty. Talks sometimes when he should be listening. He said he'd be willing to take one hundred percent casualties to get the job done. I'm just glad no reporters were around. How do you think that would play in the London papers?"

Eisenhower rubbed a hand on the back of his neck, thought of Patton. Yep, they'll make a team all right. "Let's just get them rolling toward Sicily. Get them in front of the enemy where all those words can be put into action."

"When is Patton officially being replaced? Straightaway?"

"Effective April fifteenth. I need to give briefings to everyone involved, but I don't see a problem. George will head back to Casablanca immediately and start gearing up for Husky. He's been poking me for a more *important* command as long as he's been over here. Damn him, he wants some headlines, and he knows he's not going to get them in Tunisia. I trust you to handle Monty. And the best way to manage George is, first of all, keep him out of a tank."

On April 15, Patton's staff quietly withdrew from their headquarters encampments and made their way westward, to begin the final planning for Operation Husky. Command of the Second Corps fell on the one man both Patton and Eisenhower considered right for the job: Omar Bradley.

Over the next several days, the Germans were sealed into a tight strong line, the last perimeter where they could protect the crucial port cities and still maintain the stout defenses along the mountainous terrain that confronted the tightening ring of Allied forces. With Bradley in command, the Second Corps completed a masterful maneuver, slipping out of their lines and moving north, sweeping quickly and efficiently behind the position of Anderson's First Army. As the Allies' position grew stronger, reports reached Eisenhower that German reinforcements had been attempting to cross the Mediterranean, armadas of transport planes and troopships moving toward both major ports. But the Mediterranean and the sky above it were now dominated by Allied warships and aircraft, and the cost to the Germans was horrific. Entire convoys were either sunk or sent limping back to Italy, while above them, the diminishing numbers of Luftwaffe fighters were unable to protect their sluggish transport planes from being shot out of the sky. With the spring weather improving, the Allied commanders accepted that they were as strong as they were going to be, that the time had come to break the enemy's last hold on Tunisia.

One more piece of intelligence, one report, brought everyone in the Allied headquarters to stark attention. Throughout the campaign, from the worst days of Kasserine through Patton's energetic drive in support of Montgomery, to the pressure that had now pinned the Germans into northeastern Tunisia, every Allied soldier had felt the urgency of whom they were facing. In every fight, the

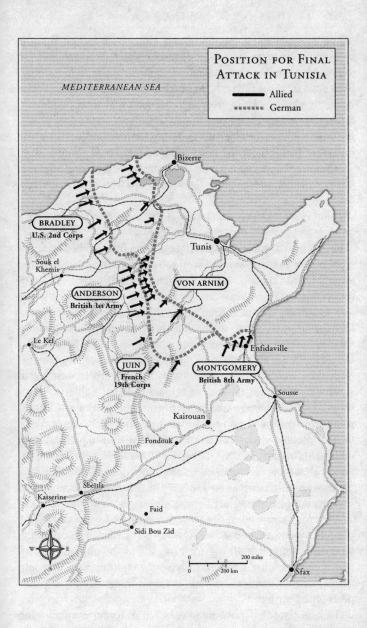

POSITION FOR FINAL
ATTACK IN TUNISIA

———— Allied
******* German

MEDITERRANEAN SEA

Bizerte

BRADLEY
U.S. 2nd Corps

Tunis

Souk el
Khemis

ANDERSON
British 1st Army

VON ARNIM

Le Kef

Enfidaville

JUIN
French 19th Corps

MONTGOMERY
British 8th Army

Sousse

Kairouan

Fondouk

Sbeïtla

Kasserine

Faïd

Sidi Bou Zid

0   200 miles

0   200 km

N
W   E
S

Sfax

name Rommel had inspired the men, either from fear or from the determination to whip Germany's most respected commander. On April 23, Eisenhower received confirmed reports that Rommel was gone, had not in fact been in Africa for several weeks. While some, especially Patton, reacted to the news with disappointment, others, including Eisenhower himself, understood the greater significance. For unexplained reasons, the Germans had lost their best man. No matter how the news affected the Allied commanders, Eisenhower knew that it would have a far more profound effect on the sinking confidence of the German troops who stood in his way.

NEAR HILL 609, NORTHERN TUNISIA—APRIL 30, 1943

They rode in a small caravan of jeeps, one fifty-caliber bringing up the rear. Eisenhower had seen too much of the great armored parades, felt no need now to surround himself with a full company of good men every time he needed to move cross-country. It had already caused difficulties, a ridiculous procession, causing transport trucks to wait at key intersections, causing attention to his presence in every camp he passed. With Eisenhower spending more time close to the front, it also became dangerous, such a cluster of vehicles likely to draw artillery fire or to present a fat target for the occasional German fighter or dive-bomber. The decision had caused grumbling among his staff, but Eisenhower had no time for anyone's motherly concerns.

The meetings and briefings had filled long days and kept sleep to a minimum, but it was far different now from the tedious chat-fests he had once endured in Algiers. The visits now dealt with communication and supply, the proper placement of troops, the best use of artillery, coordinating with the air command. And more often now the conversations were one-sided, Eisenhower the listener, while Bradley or one of his division commanders laid it all out for him. It was the ultimate luxury for a commanding general, to have the right men in the right place, sure of themselves and confident in the troops who followed their orders.

He had gone that morning to see Charles Ryder, commanding the Thirty-fourth Division, the men who would hold the center of the American position. But Ryder had been farther forward, checking on his own advance command post, and with the attack imminent Eisenhower wouldn't take the extra time just to stare over Ryder's shoulder. On the left, the Ninth Division, under Manton Eddy, stood close to the coastline, while to Ryder's right, the First, the Big Red One, under Terry Allen, was already pushing into broken and difficult ground where the Germans were making a sharp fight. In front of the Thirty-fourth stood a bald, rocky hill, a mile wide, what the maps called Hill 609. The Germans were dug in all along the hill, heavy artillery positions anchored into deep ravines, hidden by rock outcroppings. From their position up top, the German artillery observers could direct a precise pounding of the First Division's flank, and Bradley had quickly seen the urgency of pushing the enemy off that hill. The job belonged to Ryder and the Thirty-fourth.

The line of jeeps rolled to a stop, and Eisenhower could see smoke in bursts, flecks of fire. All along the route he had driven through vast formations of armor, tanks and half-tracks, the power of the First Armored Division, the big machines waiting for the infantry to clear the hills, push the German guns away from the roadways, giving the tanks an open route to cut hard into the enemy's rear. To the south, British armor waited as well, a massive fist. Alexander had pulled strength from Montgomery's positions, some of the Eighth Army's forces drawn around to the west, adding to the force of the left-handed blow.

"That's Hill 609, sir. Right there."

"Hard to miss."

Eisenhower stared at the massive rocky mound, thought, it looks like something you'd see in Arizona, for God's sake. No wonder the Krauts are up there. He stepped forward, stood near the far side of the ridge, the ground falling away in a sharp-sloping drop. The binoculars were in his hand, but he ignored them, stared at the vast open country, undulating, choppy ground, small clusters of trees. Beyond was a mile or more of wide-open grasslands, a rolling prairie, little cover for infantry. But the infantry was there, and he could clearly see the spreading wave of men and machines that rolled out, trucks and jeeps, foot soldiers pushing hard into thickets of short trees that spread out from the base of the tall, rocky hill.

There were bursts from artillery much closer to him, thin streaks of fire in a low arc, aimed at the big hill, a rippling blanket of smoke now enveloping the crest, the shells falling all along the wide peak. He felt a surge in his chest, yes, by God, those are *our* guns. Good shooting. After a few seconds the thunder reached him, a solid rumble, then scattered thumps, more flashes spreading across a stretch of open ground at the base of the hill. He raised the glasses now, stared at the dark specks, clusters of men, swarming up and over rocks, some disappearing into the cover of the trees, cuts in the rocks, nearly everyone moving forward. There was motion along the base of the hill itself now, another patch of open ground, and he fought to see, knew that would be the worst place, the last open stretch without cover. His heart was thundering, and he scanned the smoke, so much of the hillside hidden, the fight moving with the men, his army and the enemy slowly joining into one mass.

Above him, there were loud roars from a formation of planes, and he glanced up, didn't have to see, knew it would be the fighters, heavy with ammunition, men focused on the hill, as he was, seeking out the enemy. They rolled past, spreading out, wide attack formations, but the roars didn't stop, more planes, a continuous wave. High above them, the bombers rolled forward as well, but they did not focus on Hill 609, were going much deeper, punching great gaps in the roadways that fed the German troops. Some went farther still, pouring their bombs into the crowded harbors, blanketing the cities, the communication centers and supply dumps. It was the key to the entire campaign, the greatest advantage the Allies enjoyed, superiority in the air. Eisenhower thought of Tedder, and the Americans who served under him, Spaatz and Doolittle. Without your good work, this could not happen. We could not hope to make this push across open ground. Surely the enemy knows that. Surely they know they cannot stand up to that kind of power from the air.

He lowered the glasses, heard voices behind him, radios, the officers going about the business of war. He looked again to Hill 609, saw his own artillery firing again, observers choosing targets, while just above, the fighters swirled down toward targets of their own. He felt a chill, thought of Patton, yes, George, I understand why you want to be out here. *Right there.* Especially now, on a day like this, when you can see it all, when you know that your army is led by good men, men who are as determined as their soldiers to drive the enemy back. And if he will not run from us, then we will drive him, and if he will not be driven, then we will kill him where he stands, and we will move past their dead and keep moving until it is over.

28. LOGAN

BIZERTE, TUNISIA
MAY 7, 1943

He stood at the wire, a crowd of men beside him, more men emerging from the ripped tents and tin shelters. They crept forward, closer, all eyes fixed on the horizon, westward, far beyond the perimeter of the camp. Outside the wire, the guards responded, coming to life, machine guns rising slowly. The Germans were as curious now as the men they guarded, and they all began to face west, absorbed by the rumble of thunder. The prisoners ignored them, numb to the threat, fixed their gaze on a rolling cloud of haze and smoke. Logan saw it clearly, a thick, gray fog, rising slowly, pushed forward by the unmistakable sounds of artillery. From the blockhouse just outside the wire, German officers began to appear, drawn by the sounds, one man, older, ordering the guards to stay alert. They responded, moved closer to the wire, guns up, some with rifles, fixed bayonets. Out to the west the sky was growing dark with the smoke of a rugged battle. The war was getting closer.

Logan struggled against the weakness in his legs, a deep, open sore just above his ankle, the lingering price for his forced march. He wanted to grab the wire, hold himself up, but it was instinct now, a lesson deep inside his brain: *no one grabbed the wire.* It had happened too often, men suddenly running into the wire, as though they had forgotten it was there. After so many weeks in the punishing filth, some had simply gone mad, desperate men who began to call out, to scream, crying, rushing to the wire toward some place in their mind they desperately needed to be. Logan had watched it too many times, the sick mostly, small wounds like his, grown worse in the filth, infections poisoning the brain. Some didn't run at all, simply fell to the ground, a final breath, calling out to someone, a woman usually, the name cutting into each man who heard the cry, names Logan could hear in his dreams, Helen . . . Doris . . . Lola . . . and worst of all, *Mama.*

The wire enclosure was a temporary encampment, designed to hold the men only until there was space for them on the empty transport ships. The Germans had been matter-of-fact about it, one officer in particular, a young major who spoke precise English, standing outside the wire making long, arrogant speeches. Logan had listened with curiosity, wondering if the officer was telling the truth, if the prisoners were actually going to be moved to prison camps in Germany. Beyond the major's smugness there was menace as well, the man insisting that if Allied submarines continued to sink the transport ships, they would only kill their own, would send these helpless prisoners to the bottom of the sea. There was no purpose to the speeches, the officer goading them, arousing something in the prisoners, something Logan now felt himself. In the tank, he had been shooting at targets, *things,* and it was easy to forget that men were behind the faceless steel, men staring through periscopes and gunsights, trying to kill him, but not *him,* just another target. But once he was captured, once he was forced to march with hundreds of suffering men, when he had seen the brutality and the ease with which the Germans ignored the cries of the wounded, Logan began to feel a low burn, something stirring, rising up in his brain from a dark, hidden place. He had drawn it from the eyes of his captors, who treated their prisoners with a vicious disregard. On the long, brutal march, the Germans had ignored the desperate and dying, the men who begged only for water, and Logan had felt the burn growing, festering inside him like the ugly sore on his leg. Behind the wire, it festered still, and the German major's arrogance, the nastiness of the man's smile, drove the feeling to a boil, a hard, black hate. As far back as Fort Knox, the big mouths were always boasting about killing Krauts and Japs, about how they *hated* the enemy. But combat changed everyone, and when the guns were firing, the ones who boasted the loudest were rarely heard from. For the first time, Logan felt he understood Captain Gregg, knew why the man stayed so quiet. Gregg had the hate, held it tightly inside, and it made him a dangerous and frightening man. Now, when the German major came to the wire, as the man poured out his bile to the prisoners, the vicious smile and the infuriating smugness, Logan couldn't control the burn, and for the first time in his life Logan felt the urgent need to kill a man, to jump up and over the wire, to claw his way through the guards and their bayonets, to grab the man by the neck, to drive his thumbs into the man's throat and squeeze until blood poured over his fingers. As the days passed and the mud dried away, Logan found himself at the wire, waiting, hoping that the major would come, one more time, would stoke the fire, would keep the hate alive and twisting inside him. He was beginning to enjoy it.

For the first few weeks the rains had kept them huddled low in their shelters, crowded together beneath sheets of rusty tin, strips and patches of canvas, whatever the Germans seemed willing to toss over the wire. The ground was mud of course, a thick blue ooze, coating every man's feet and legs, and the faces of those men who had fallen, whose legs would no longer hold them. It was routine, the stronger men helping as best they could, keeping the wounds clean, as clean as the mud would allow. But some of the fallen could not rise at all, their final breath choked away by the wounds and the sickness, lifeless forms that the strong could only drag toward the wire. The guards would come then, but not often enough, the Germans reacting in their own time, pulling the bodies away to some place no one wanted to think about. For the first few days, Logan had done what many had done, had tried to clean his wound and himself by standing out in the rain. It had seemed to work for him, but there was a price, the rain stripping away the ragged cloth of his uniform, dissolving and rotting what remained of his boots. For the others, the weaker men, the chilling cold caused more problems than it cured. Even under the makeshift shelters the sicker men succumbed to uncontrollable bouts of shivering, blue-lipped men who could not be kept warm. The Germans tossed in blankets, soiled and worn, but with the rain, the wool stayed stinking and wet. Even with the painful sore on his leg, Logan knew he was one of the lucky ones, and after so many days of soaking-wet misery, he stopped worrying about being clean. When there was no reason to be at the wire, he huddled in chilled agony alongside the men under the makeshift shelters.

When the rains stopped, the shroud of death seemed to draw away, offer relief to the weak and damaged men. As the sun finally appeared, they emerged from their shelters like so many frightened animals, desperate for warmth. The mud began to dry, and the energy returned, the men welcoming the sunshine with grateful thanks, quiet prayers, some staring blindly at blue sky and white clouds, the sunshine offering some symbol of hope.

With the dryness came the need to open up the infested shelters, and Logan had worked with several others, the men who had somehow kept their strength, pulling the shelters apart, tearing back the rotten canvas, bringing the sun into the dark places, drying the ground and the wet filth that surrounded the men who were too sick to move. Even the guards welcomed the sun, seemed more willing to do their own jobs. From the beginning the prisoners had been fed from great metal buckets, hauled on wheeled carts. But with the endless rain, the guards more often chose to stay dry, and if the prisoners were not fed, it only meant that when the food did come again, there would be fewer men to hold a plate. Logan had welcomed the food, no matter what it might be, no one complaining, and only the men who were too sick to eat stayed away. It was mostly a soft, white mush, usually cold, each man given a scoop that flowed out on his rusted tin plate, spilling onto filthy hands. The mush triggered something strange in him, his weakened mind grasping at a memory, trips out beyond the city, places like Dade City and Brooksville. The road trips had been adventures to a young boy, and his father always stopped at one country diner, where women with a deep southern drawl heaped a child's plate with fried bacon, dark, spicy gravy poured over creamy cornmeal mush, what they called grits. But he couldn't hold the memories for long, the pleasant times sucked away by the aching hunger, or worse, buried under so many ladles of whatever he was forced to eat now, the resemblance to grits dissolving in the sickening horror of dead rodents, mice mostly, fished out of the buckets by laughing guards.

When the Germans brought the buckets, the guards had taunted the men, what Logan assumed were insults, the German soldiers calling the Americans something that sounded like *koos koos*. Logan assumed it was German for "stupid," *cuckoo*, but then, as new prisoners arrived, there had been an American officer, the man staying only a few days before the Germans took him away, but long enough to tell Logan that *koos koos* was in fact what they were eating.

The officers who came into the camps stayed only long enough to catch the attention of the guards and their commanders. The German officers seemed to welcome their American counterparts with far too much graciousness to suit the enlisted prisoners, but for the American officers, it was a blessing. They had often come into camp as badly mangled as their men, and for them the Germans brought doctors and ambulances, carried the officers to some distant place, what Logan could only guess was a hospital. Word had spread that many of the officers had been taken away altogether, that despite the German major's promise that they would all cross the Mediterranean, only the officers had actually gone.

As the wire enclosure grew more cramped, others were pulled out of the ranks as well, enlisted men, the guards reading from confiscated dog tags, calling out names, the men who could respond drifting forward. When the guards took those men away, they seemed to simply disappear, days at a time, and Logan did not understand that, his weakened mind wrapping around the mystery, the dramatic fantasy that those men might be spies, making their reports, betraying the Americans they had served beside. But the missing men had friends, men who reacted with fists to any suggestion that the missing prisoners were anything but good soldiers. Logan had begun to believe that they might just be chosen at random, and the lurid fantasy filled him that he might be next, hauled away to some kind of dark torture chamber, his imagination giving way to the ridiculous, something from a bad horror movie. But the concern was real enough, and he had searched his mind for scraps of information, if there was anything the Germans might want from him, any piece of intelligence he should die to protect.

But then, the missing men began to return, battered and bloody, and if they survived at all, they spoke of interrogation and torture that was real, and very graphic. Those who could speak at all told of a different kind of German soldier, a different kind of brutality. Logan began to notice now that each time a prisoner was taken away, there were men in black uniforms, what the guards called Gestapo, eyeing the prisoners from a distance, lurking back behind the guard shacks. The interrogations had little to do with battle plans or communication, with any details the Germans could possibly find useful. And then, they all realized that there was nothing random about the men at all. In every case, they had names like Epstein and Bromberg, and soon everyone understood that the Gestapo had come only for the men who were Jewish.

For several weeks now, the prisoners seemed to come in waves, the wire enclosure more crowded, and almost no one held hope that they would ever leave this place. The German major still spoke to them, still poured out his speech in grand gestures, glorious pronouncements, but there was no mention now of the transport ships, and no one but the officers were led away for good. Most of the captured officers were young, frontline men, many of them lieutenants. But along the march, Logan's first grueling climb up and over the passes east of Sidi Bou Zid, there had been older men as well, and a few younger officers of high rank. Logan recalled it still, the fog not erasing the stark memory of one man in particular. As the wounded fell out, one of the American officers had taken charge, had taken a dangerous chance by moving back and forth along the line, helping the men to their feet, shouting at the Germans to keep away, cursing them to provide water. Logan had watched the man through his own choking thirst, the burning pain in his eyes and lungs, had expected the gunshot that would end this foolish bravado. But

the Germans had surprised him, had backed away, seemed to respect the man's rank. Soon, other prisoners had risen to the officer's challenge, the German guards finally allowing the
Americans to help each other. Logan had tried to help as well,
and he'd glimpsed the man's torn shirt, saw the oak leaf, realized the officer was a lieutenant colonel. When they first
reached the camps, the officer had seemed to take charge, angrily demanding that the guards treat the wounded, that food
and water be quickly provided. But the protests changed nothing, and soon the German major had come, ordering the guards
to pull the American officers out of the mass of prisoners, pointing out this one man in particular. As the man was called out, he
had slipped close beside Logan, grabbing his arm, a hard, urgent whisper, words that brought Logan out of his fog. The officer told him that if Logan survived, if he was ever returned to
the American lines, someone might ask about this one lieutenant colonel, would want to know what had happened to him.
The agony in Logan's throat kept him silent, the man's words
filling Logan more with sadness than surprise. For all the officer's good efforts, Logan now thought the man insane, delusional, his mind having given way to the brutality of the march.
The man said his name was Waters, and Logan was too shocked
and too exhausted to laugh when the man told him he was
George Patton's son-in-law.

Beyond the camp, the city of Bizerte spread like a pink-white
jewel, the beauty marred now by the shattered buildings, daily
bomb runs by formations of planes too high to identify. The
camp was positioned with a distant view of the harbor, a distraction for men whose minds had nothing else to focus on. Logan
had watched the ships, constantly in motion, had listened for the
planes, bombing runs growing more frequent. Several times
each day now the air above them seemed filled with planes,
faint specks of bombs dropping into the harbor, plumes of water
peppering the ships. Then would come the great black blast, fire
and smoke, a direct hit, the prisoners responding with as much
of a cheer as they could make, but not enough to draw the anger
of the guards. The planes had come twice that morning, at first
light, and again just after the guards had brought the food buck-

ets. The guards had watched with them, one plane swooping low, streaking fire, a black, smoky trail, the plane tumbling into the harbor. Then it was the guards who had cheered, the prisoners cursing, waiting for revenge. It came quickly, a sudden flash out beyond the harbor itself, a ship on the horizon, a burst of white light, then great columns of black smoke. The guard closest to Logan had said the word *petrol,* and Logan understood. Yes, a fuel tanker, on its way into the harbor. Not anymore. Now it's on the bottom.

The rumble of artillery was growing louder, and the men continued to gather close to the wire, crowding behind him, one man close to him stumbling, a hand on Logan's shoulder. The guards were gathering as well, facing them, but the Germans could not avoid glancing behind them, toward the smoky horizon. There was no confrontation now, no one threatening with the bayonet, just two groups of men, held apart by a high wall of wire, both captured by the sounds of what seemed to be rolling toward them.

The air above them came alive, a hard shriek, a shell falling beyond the guardhouses, into a cluster of block buildings. More shells came down farther away, tossing debris skyward, the ground jumping under Logan's feet. The German officers began to call out orders, the guards responding, moving away quickly. They ran toward the destruction, more men gathering from the streets beyond the camp, all of them running toward the shattered buildings, flames rising out of the wreckage. The prisoners watched silently, no one reacting, and Logan's brain strained once more to pull itself out from behind so many weeks of fog. He felt his heart beating faster, looked again to the west, black, billowing clouds, the sudden impact of more shells, one enormous flash of light, fire and smoke, a deafening explosion, just inside the edge of the city. The Germans were mostly gone now, but he could hear the shouts of men, a new wave of artillery fire close by, a battery of German guns that had deployed a short distance beyond the guardhouses. Most of the incoming shells were falling on the city itself, shattering the stone walls, some falling closer, punching shallow craters in the open avenues. There was traffic on the nearest road, a fat truck, machine guns on both sides, German soldiers peering out, the truck bouncing heavily as it roared past. More trucks came, smoke from an engine, the truck limping from a flat tire, sparks trailing behind, the driver not slowing. The trucks and smaller vehicles continued to roll out of the city, some full of soldiers. Their drivers stared ahead, pushed on past the compound, the caravan disappearing down the one wide roadway that led toward the harbor.

Beside him, one man spoke, gravel in his weak voice. "By damned, they're running away."

A wave of smoke rolled over them, the sounds of the fight closer still, chatter and pops of rifles, a burst of machine-gun fire, jolting his brain, made him push forward, hands on the wire, straining to see. He knew the sound of the German machine guns, too much experience of the guards firing above them, or splattering the mud, just for effect. There were horrible times as well, when one of the prisoners had made his mad climb up the wire, the machine guns chopping him down, spraying blood on the men who had tried to hold him back. The German guns had a hard, hollow sound, but the gun he heard now was different, familiar, and he heard it again, mingling with the pops from the rifles. The machine gun was a Thompson. It was an American.

Germans were coming out of the rubble now, a steady stream along the blasted street, blackened hands and dirty uniforms, some without helmets, two men carrying a comrade by the arms, blood on the man's chest. They continued to come, some running, stumbling, one man, more blood, the man collapsing a few yards from the wire. The prisoners began to push forward again, some now climbing up on the wire, and Logan felt the energy, the awareness in all of them that the Germans no longer cared about guarding prisoners. Around him, more men began to climb the fence, and Logan felt himself pushed from behind, the energy building, one man pointing to the dead German's rifle. The fight was closer still, more of the Thompsons, too many sounds, the short blast of grenades, German machine guns responding.

Beyond the guardhouses, a truck rolled toward them, rolled into open ground close to the wire. Logan saw the machine gun, one fifty-caliber up top, a man at the gun, swinging the barrel toward the prisoners. Men poured out from the back of the truck, familiar, the guards, two more heavy machine guns brought forward, set on the ground, supported by tripods. The guards stood motionless, tense, seemed to wait for something, the Americans up on the wire still as well, a hard silence. Logan saw the major now, the man coming out from behind the truck, saw the face, the arrogance, a glimpse of hell in the man's eyes, the man Logan so desperately wanted to kill. The officer stopped a few yards from the wire, stood with his hands on his hips, looked up at the prisoners holding tight to the wire, smiled, shouted something in German, an order. The guards seemed to move in one motion, men close to the machine guns, pointed straight into the compound. Logan stepped back, instinct, men around him making low sounds, the men up on the wire still frozen. The major stepped closer now, stood out in front of his own machine guns, a few feet from the wire, still smiled at them, a small laugh, scanned the faces of the Americans, stared straight into Logan's eyes, said:

"You will die now."

He shouted another order, stepped to the side, and Logan saw the faces of the guards, the Germans all staring at them, wide-eyed fear, nervous hands. The men around Logan began to back away, but not all, some moving up close to the wire, the men up on the wire still motionless, hanging, waiting, all of them staring into the guns, staring into the faces of the enemy. Logan felt his heart racing, an icy chill, looked at the major, saw the man's smile fading, a cold, gray stare, the man pulling a pistol from his belt.

"You will die *now*."

Behind the guards, the sounds of artillery erupted again, a burst of machine-gun fire. The sounds were close, just beyond the guardhouse, and the guards reacted, some moving back to the truck, peering around. The major ignored the commotion, stared at Logan, the two men drawn together, Logan's fingers gripping the wire, the man raising the pistol. There were new shouts, the guards starting to run, one man suddenly punched down, tumbling heavily to the ground. They all ran now, disappeared into rolling smoke, and above Logan, the men on the wire began to call out, some climbing up higher, the machine guns that pointed toward them unmanned. Logan could not look away, focused only on the major, past the small black hole of the pistol, stared into the man's eyes, saw cold fire, felt his heart racing, ice in his hands, clenched hard around the wire, the growing fury, the wire bending, his arms pulling it slowly toward him. The smoke was all around them, a rolling cloud, and there were more shots, single pops, the truck abandoned now, the fight rolling toward them through the rubble. Logan kept his stare on the officer, the man doing the same, and the pistol wavered, a slight quiver in the German's hand, and suddenly the man's knees buckled, the major tumbling forward. The smoke engulfed them both, and Logan could see movement, shapes of men at the truck, men moving forward all through the smoke, swarming out in both directions, some moving into the guardhouses, the sharp blast of a grenade, shouts, a scream, more machine-gun fire. Logan stared at the major's body, saw blood on the man's back, the pistol still in his hand. He looked up, no one on the wire, the prisoners gone, and he looked back around him, saw a truck on the far side of the compound, the gate, the truck pushing slowly into the wire, ripping the tall steel posts from the ground. He saw now, the truck had a white star. They were Americans.

The wire collapsed on the truck itself, and the truck backed away, pulling the fence apart, ripping a great hole in the wire. Prisoners were cheering, pouring out of the compound, limping and battered men rushing forward. Some stopped just beyond the shredded wire, collapsing to their knees, soldiers gathering around them, more trucks now rolling close. Logan moved that way, ignored the pain in his leg, stumbled, the smoke choking him, and he passed a tin shelter, saw men crawling out, the sick, barely able to move, soldiers there now, stretchers, medics. He saw one man, lying flat, under a strip of canvas, and he dropped to one knee, leaned close, put his hand on a man's shoulder, said, "Come on! The fence is down! We can go! It's our boys!"

The words choked, tightness in his throat, and he felt tears, but the man didn't move, didn't seem to hear him. Logan felt his face, cold stiffness, and he leaned closer, the man's face gray and still, the name in his mind, Harris . . .

"Damn."

He felt a hand on his back. "Hey, Mac, you need some help? I'm a medic. How's your buddy?"

Logan pulled himself out from the shelter, sat. "He's gone. Didn't make it."

"Too bad. Lemme see that leg. Pretty nasty."

Logan said nothing, the man wrapping something on his leg, a hard sting, the leg jerking.

"Easy, Mac. I'll get you some morphine."

"No, that's okay. Just help me up. I'll be okay."

"We'll get you a stretcher. Ambulances are coming up. We'll treat that leg in the field hospital."

The man lifted him up under the arm, and Logan stood, the man pointing him toward the opening in the wire. A crowd was there, a chorus of shouting, cheers and crying, an ambulance rolling close, more men, officers. Logan moved that way, felt the pain in his leg, tried to fight the fog returning, his brain echoing the sounds of the fight, the machine guns, the thunder of the artillery. The soldiers were mingling with the prisoners, and he felt a chill, wanted to warn the men, thought, it can't be over . . . there's still a fight, be careful. Germans just over there . . .

He stumbled again, his hands on the ground, pain in his leg, the jolt waking him, clearing his brain. He pulled himself up, moved toward the gaping hole in the fence, looked toward the rubble beyond the camp, the guardhouses, windows punched out, more smoke. The fog drained out of him, and the sounds faded, distant and harmless. He saw a column of Germans emerging from the rubble, their hands clamped tightly on their heads, prisoners, guarded by filthy, jubilant Americans. He limped forward, pressed his way through the men at the wire, felt hands on him, words flowing past him, couldn't speak, tears blinding him. He moved out past the enclosure, walked back along the wire. On the road, trucks were in motion, foot soldiers still advancing, scattered gunfire in the distance, more smoke, burning buildings, sickening stench. He ignored it all, moved along the wire, saw it now, the gray heap, the bloody stain. He stood over the man, tried to make a fist, to feel the anger again, to open that dark and dangerous place, to bathe himself in the hard, black hatred. But it wasn't there, his fist weakening, the stirring of anger growing still. He leaned down, pulled the pistol from the German's hand, looked at it for a long moment, raised it high over his head, pulled the trigger. The gun jumped, a hard crack, and he pulled the trigger again and again, fired the gun until it was empty. Men were shouting at him, moving up close behind him, nervous, an officer, and he turned, saw a lieutenant, a flash of anger.

"What the hell . . . ?"

"It's okay, sir. He's entitled."

"I'll take care of him, sir. Had to be pretty rough for these guys. I got him."

One man came close, held out a hand. "Here, grab my arm."

Logan shook his head slowly, looked down at the German major. "I'm okay. Just had to do . . . something."

The lieutenant moved away, and the others lingered for a moment. He felt the concern, the smiles, looked at the dirty faces and rough beards, saw men like him, men who had found their targets, who had fought the enemy and driven him away.

He put the pistol in his belt and began to walk toward the ambulance.

29. EISENHOWER

As the Americans sealed their hold on Bizerte, the British drove hard to capture Tunis. The German defenders, surprised by the power of Alexander's left-hook tactic, and crushed under the weight of Allied air bombardments, could not hold back the overwhelming wave of infantry and armor. By May 13, German resistance along the entire front collapsed. Except for scattered pockets and sporadic fighting, the battle for Tunisia was over.

The German and Italian soldiers who had been swept out of the cities were pressed north and east, to the final sanctuary, the Bon Peninsula, a thirty-mile-wide spit of land that jutted into the Mediterranean. It offered the only possible avenue of escape; if the troops could be evacuated onto boats and transport planes, the Axis might salvage a substantial part of their army, as the British had done at Dunkirk. But along the rocky beaches, there was no armada, no great mass of rescue vessels. Offshore, the waters were under the heavy guns of the British navy, and in the air, British and American fighters had virtually eliminated the Luftwaffe's ability to accomplish any kind of rescue. Instead of making a mass exodus out of Tunisia, the German and Italian armies trapped on the Bon Peninsula had no choice but to surrender. The Allies captured a quarter of a million prisoners.

One final prize remained, and Eisenhower received the news the evening of May 13, confirmation that General Hans Juergen von Arnim had been captured along with his men. Eisenhower's staff had been jubilant, as though one man's capture meant as much as the defeat of the armies von Arnim commanded. Everyone hoped that the two men would come face-to-face, a moment for the cameras. The staff insisted that a meeting with von Arnim would fit so neatly into the chronicle of this war, two leaders, shaking hands perhaps, honorable gentlemen to the last. The idea appalled him.

TUNIS—MAY 20, 1943

It was after four in the morning, the skies over the harbor opening up, soft light rising behind the mountains on the far side of the wide bay. He stood at the window of the old hotel, stared into cool, dry air, felt the soft breeze, tugged at his jacket. He leaned out, looked down toward the streets below him, still hidden by the darkness, no sound, no movement he could see. He wanted to be there, outside, stroll along the wide street, walk down to the wharves, hear the water, watch the sunrise. Not a good idea, he thought. The MPs are patrolling, keeping a sharp eye for anyone moving around. It would be a little hard to explain why the commanding general was wandering the streets at four in the morning. Assuming they even asked at all. They might just shoot me.

He had given up trying to sleep, had suffered the same ail-

ment for several days now. It wasn't just the anxiety of the fight
that kept him awake, the silent hours waiting for reports from
front-line commanders. It was more from the incessant cables
and messages, the pressure coming from the Joint Chiefs in
both Washington and London. For weeks now, Eisenhower had
been urged to look beyond Tunisia, to focus his energies on the
planning for the next great campaign, the invasion of Sicily. It
was good strategy certainly, not allowing the enemy to regroup,
to hit a vital air and supply center before the Germans could
compensate for their inevitable defeat in North Africa. Eisenhower accepted that the combined Allied forces should press
ever forward, without delay. Already the maps of Tunisia had
come down, maps of Sicily in their place, reports of troop
strengths and equipment deliveries flowing across Eisenhower's
desk. Patton and Montgomery both knew what their new roles
would be, and there had already been plenty of friction between
the two men, the inevitable clash of powerful personalities,
whose personal visions of the future didn't include anyone else
sharing their spotlight.

Throughout late April and early May, Marshall prodded him
to focus on Sicily, but Eisenhower couldn't just pull himself
away from Africa, couldn't pretend that men weren't still dying
in a fight that had already lasted far longer than he knew it
should have. The mistakes had been many and glaring, and
Eisenhower knew they could not be repeated. The entire Allied
command structure had been tweaked and rearranged, lessons
learned from the errors of strategies and the mistakes of the
men who carried them out, all those things that simply hadn't
worked. He knew he was hard on the men who didn't measure
up, but no harder than he had been on himself. In the long dark
hours he pondered that, *his* mistakes.

There had been a strange and welcome inevitability to what
had happened over the past few weeks. Even as Bradley and Anderson and Montgomery drove their armies into stout enemy
defenses, their confidence fed his own, and for the first time he
allowed himself to feel a comfortable certainty that in Tunisia,
the machine was functioning, that the right men were in the
right place, and there would be no more failures. For the first
time in two years of the African campaign, it was clear that the

Germans were beaten. The myth of Hitler's invincibility had been shattered, first at Stalingrad, and then here, in the rocky hills of Tunisia. The British still spoke boisterously of Montgomery's great trumpet-blowing triumph at El Alamein, and Eisenhower would not take anything away from the accomplishment. But El Alamein did not end the war in Africa, it just moved it out of Egypt and brought it closer to the Americans. No matter Monty's bluster, every Allied general knew that once the Germans reached Tunisia, Rommel could still have turned the tide, punched a deep hole in Monty's celebration.

His mind drifted back to Kasserine. It could all have collapsed, every plan, every hope. He caught himself glancing at the maps, studying the red lines of Rommel's advance, pushing westward, the last deadly opportunity for Rommel to drive a spear that could have plunged the Germans right into Algiers. But then, it was done, the Germans halting their attacks, and just like that, the threat was gone. Something had certainly happened to Rommel, something no one in the Allied headquarters could explain. Eisenhower didn't care about speculation, had no interest in theories. What mattered was that Rommel had simply gone, and with him any notion that the Germans were unbeatable.

So, now they want me to shake hands with von Arnim and smile for the cameras and pretend we share respect, that we admire each other's grit and courage. Two good soldiers coming together as though we respect our accomplishments, we *appreciate* the struggle. He was baffled that his staff, the other commanders, thought such a thing was a good idea. He saw nothing *gentlemanly* in von Arnim, nor in Rommel, nor in any of them. The Germans had made this war, he thought. They started it and they made it what it has become, and millions of people have died. It is not about a boundary dispute, about land or treasure or politics. It is one man's quest to conquer the whole damned world. How utterly absurd that is, something from a bad novel. The whole notion of a gentlemen's war, that damned British thing, saluting noble warriors. There is nothing noble about von Arnim. He is simply a tool. If he had defeated us here, he would be Hitler's darling, a great hero, one more piece of Hitler's dream. Shake hands with him? The son of a bitch should be hanged.

He felt his heart beating, leaned out the window again, took a long breath of cool air. Damn this. You don't need to fight this damned campaign all over again. We've won. *Victory.* Hell, there's a parade today. What a stupid idea.

The energy behind the celebration had come from the French, and Eisenhower had far better things to do than spend hours in a reviewing stand, while exhausted soldiers marched past him. But it was unavoidable, and he had surrendered to protocol, had even invited Patton to come, the man always a crowd pleaser. But he had no illusions; this entire spectacle was about French power, a show for the locals, the Arabs and displaced Italians, a clear signal that this land was again in French hands. After all, he thought, the Americans and the British won't be here that much longer. Giraud knows that it is important that their *citizens* see an impressive show of power. It's important for him as well. De Gaulle is already making noises that he expects to come here and be welcomed as the conquering hero. Jackass. Giraud outranks him by three stars and proved himself under fire. De Gaulle sits in London and makes pronouncements that France is winning the war, and so his cause is triumphant. He had heard reports that de Gaulle was demanding that French soldiers sign a loyalty oath to him alone, and Eisenhower knew it could cause trouble, not only in France but in the Allies' own backyard. A civil war in Algeria, he thought. That's what could come of this. Politicians and their pride. One more reason to get the hell out of here and go to Sicily.

He moved away from the window, stood motionless in the dark, thought of rousing Butcher out of bed. No, let him sleep. And, I'll bet he is sleeping too. All of them. Basking in the glow. There was a fair amount of alcohol flowing around here last night. No harm done, I suppose. Let them have their party. They sure as hell earned it. The whole world is telling them so. Telling *me* so. I should read all of those notes again. For crying out loud, you ought to be thankful someone's paying attention. What the hell is wrong with me? I can't sleep, I can't enjoy one hearty congratulation, I can't read a single damned letter without this hard knot in my chest.

The letters had flowed in, from London and Washington, from every theater of the war, even a congratulatory letter from the Russian chief of staff. The headquarters had been festive, pats on the back rattling around like so much applause, the other headquarters, Alexander, Bradley, Montgomery, all the rest, certainly the same way. Word had already been received that Marshall was coming from Washington, that Churchill would probably visit as well. It was to be expected of course, and Eisenhower had tried to keep his mind away from all that pomp and official planning.

He saw a light in the harbor, watched for a moment, realized it was a reflection off a ship's tower. The sun was creeping just above the rim of the far hills, the harbor a ripple of activity, ships moving silently, the wharves coming to life. *Victory.* He tried to hold the word in his mind, to feel what so many of the men around him found so easy to accept. He thought of Marshall, well, all right. Come on, have your look around, pass out the congratulations, give out the medals. And then sit down with me and remind me not to get comfortable. There were footsteps in the hall, someone trying to step quietly. He moved to the door, pulled it open, saw the blue uniform.

Butcher stood straight, surprised, and Eisenhower said, "No need to sneak around, Harry. I've been up for hours. Same damned thing. I go to bed, sleep for an hour, then wide-awake."

"Anything I can do to help, Skipper?"

"Yeah. Find a way to end this damned war."

ALGIERS—MAY 29, 1943

It was a parade of a different sort, confined to conference rooms and dining halls, Churchill, General Marshall, and a mass of senior commanders and staff officers. It was entirely reasonable that with the battles in Tunisia now past, Churchill would make a visit. Eisenhower was fully aware that since the beginnings of the North African campaign, Churchill had played a crucial role in the Allied success, a chess game of sorts, the prime minister making his moves by shifting or removing British commanders, putting what he saw as the best man in the best place to get the job done. Despite grumbling from some of the field commanders that Churchill had meddled too deeply in the operations of the British army, the success of the campaign took the starch out of the critics. Now, it was perfectly appropriate for Churchill to visit the scene, to walk the bloody fields, strut admiringly among the soldiers. Along the way, if someone wished to lay credit at his feet, so be it.

Eisenhower knew that his days would not be his own, as long as Churchill and Marshall were close by. He couldn't help thinking of Patton, the man's disdain for armchair officers. Eisenhower knew that the visits were self-serving, the Brits and Americans still sizing each other up, comparing their influence, each one measuring his own place in the success of the North African campaign.

All eyes were on Churchill.

"I am well aware that there is sentiment in the United States that our emphasis be placed on an invasion of France. My position on this is clear. Our first priority must be to eliminate the Italians. They are teetering as we speak, and should Italy bow out of this war, Hitler's position on the European continent shall be weakened considerably."

Eisenhower glanced at Marshall, saw a hint of a frown.

Churchill didn't wait for comment, continued, "When Sicily falls, our immediate goal should be the defeat of those Axis armies in Italy. Any attack on the Italian mainland will only hasten the desire of the Italian people to remove the shackles put upon them by Mussolini. I have always maintained that Italy is the highway that will lead us straight into the heart of Hitler's fortress. I believe that still. The Russians believe it as well. They are most insistent that we move against Germany as quickly as possible. There are expectations that Hitler is planning another monumental offensive against our Allies to the east, and Premier Stalin is anxious that we remove some of that pressure from his beleaguered armies."

There were nods, all of them from the British commanders. Eisenhower scanned the faces, the men who had done such good work in Africa. Across from him was Tedder, the air commander, Admiral Cunningham beside him, Alexander at the far end of the table. Eisenhower expected some response from

Marshall, but the American chief of staff said nothing, and Eisenhower felt the awkwardness of the silence.

After a moment, Eisenhower said, "I understand your wish to end this war by the best means possible. But before committing myself to an attack on the Italian mainland, I must first take all possible measures to ensure our success in Sicily."

Churchill rolled his cigar in his fingers, looked at Marshall, studied him, then looked at Eisenhower, said, "Certainly, General. Without Sicily in our bag, a conquest of Italy is just a dream. Do what you must. What is your next step, if I may ask?"

Eisenhower pondered the strangeness of Churchill's question. *If you may ask?* It was suddenly clear to him, all the talk that had come from the States, the reports from Butcher and Beetle Smith, both men surveying the attitudes, testing the waters in Washington. For all of Eisenhower's efforts at uniting the two allies, the testiness and divisiveness was there still, an ongoing contest of wills. He knew that Roosevelt had sent Marshall to Africa to push forward the American priority of a cross-Channel invasion of France. But Churchill's priorities had been clear for more than a year, and around the conference table the British officers, who still followed Eisenhower's orders, were obviously in agreement with their prime minister. Eisenhower felt the spotlight falling on him, knew that Marshall would absorb and examine his every word, wondering if Eisenhower's priorities were consistent with his superiors' in Washington.

He took a long breath, said, "Our first goal is the elimination of the enemy's air bases and U-boat service facilities on the island of Pantelleria. That island lies directly along the path from Tunis to Sicily, and if we do not eliminate the enemy's presence there, our assault on Sicily could be greatly compromised. I know you are all aware of the details, but for the prime minister's benefit, and so that any questions might be answered right here and now, I would like to offer the plan of attack on Sicily as agreed upon by the combined chiefs. The assault will be made by two wings, comprising the Fifteenth Army Group, commanded by General Alexander. The easterly wing will consist of the British Eighth Army and will be commanded by General Montgomery. The westerly wing has been designated the American Seventh Army and will be commanded by General Patton."

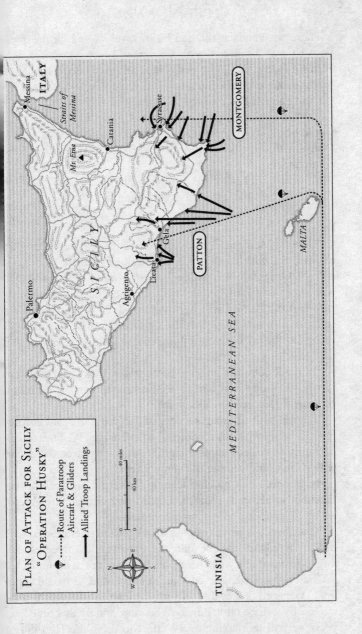

PLAN OF ATTACK FOR SICILY
"OPERATION HUSKY"

┈┈▶ Route of Paratroop
   Aircraft & Gliders
──▶ Allied Troop Landings

ITALY

Messina

Straits of Messina

Catania

Mt. Etna

S I C I L Y

Palermo

Agrigento

Licata

Gela

Syracuse

MONTGOMERY

PATTON

MEDITERRANEAN SEA

MALTA

TUNISIA

0   40 miles
0   40 km

There were nods again, and Eisenhower waited for the questions. It was his decision alone, agreed to by Alexander, that Patton's forces should be designated an *army* and so would be on the same level of command as Montgomery's. It was inconvenient enough that most of the American senior officers were outranked by their British counterparts. Eisenhower knew there would be plenty of personality clashes as it was without having to deal with some issue of rank between the two temperamental commanders.

Churchill held his cigar firmly in his teeth, said, "Seventh Army, eh? Good idea, that. Level playing field."

Eisenhower let out a breath. *Thank God.* At least George will be happy.

"General Montgomery's overall objective will be the capture of Messina, which will place the Strait of Messina under our control. General Patton will move first toward Palermo and then will sweep eastward, to link the two armies together. We anticipate that the Italians will fight vigorously to defend their own soil. We also anticipate that the German High Command will recognize the importance of this island to their own security and will offer us a stout resistance."

Churchill pointed a finger at Eisenhower, spoke past the cigar. "I would bloody well like to see another quarter of a million prisoners! Damned fine job, that."

"I agree. Our ultimate success will come if we can accomplish in Sicily what we accomplished in Tunisia. We have an opportunity to destroy another significant enemy stronghold, and with it, a sizable number of enemy forces."

He paused, saw Churchill leaning forward, waiting for more. Eisenhower glanced at Marshall again, no reaction, thought, so, it's up to *me* to say something about Italy.

"Once Sicily is secure, we must look toward operations on the Italian mainland, and beyond, to our overall strategies that might best end this war." It was his best attempt at diplomacy.

Churchill smiled, ignored Marshall now, said, "I would anticipate, General, that events will move along in a sprightly fashion. Sicily will be ours, Italy will be ours, and by this time next year, we will be making every effort to drive the Hun out of France. Well done." Churchill paused, the room silent, then turned in his chair, looked behind him, said, "Now, where the hell is the brandy?"

The details of ground operations had been turned over completely to Alexander, and Eisenhower appreciated that for a while anyway, he would not have to be involved with anyone's controversy about which division should take what piece of ground. The spitting matches between Patton and Montgomery had settled into more subdued arm-wrestling contests, arguments over air support and the distribution of naval supply ships. But the men in charge of those decisions were making progress, parceling out the support both invasion forces would need to keep either from bogging down. Once the officers were focusing on the enemy and not on each other, the machine was beginning to operate efficiently again. There were difficulties of course, from personality clashes to logistics to shortages of every imaginable kind. But the controversies had passed beyond his hands, were being handled by the men who understood that this was, after all, a joint effort.

It had surprised everyone, the invitation coming from the British that George Marshall accompany Churchill on the prime minister's tour of the various Tunisian battlegrounds. The invitation seemed sincere enough, neither man holding any antipathy toward the other, and Eisenhower understood that Churchill's gesture was designed to communicate that fact to both sides. The newspapers had long portrayed Churchill as a stubborn bulldog, a description Eisenhower had no reason to fault. But Churchill was perfectly aware that Germany would not be defeated unless the Americans were as committed to their plans as he was.

JUNE 8, 1943

They called Pantelleria the Gibraltar of the Sicilian Strait, but it was more of a rock pile than an impregnable mountain fortress. The island was the larger of two garrisons that posed continuous problems for any Allied sea traffic that sailed through the narrow stretch of the Mediterranean between Tunisia and Sicily. The Italians had long used both Pantelleria and the smaller island of

Lampedusa as military outposts, and the Germans had made considerable use of the larger island as a staging area for bombing runs into North Africa. It lay seventy miles southwest of the Sicilian coast, and if any invasion was to be pushed ashore on the south coast of Sicily, enemy activity on both islands had to be silenced.

Pantelleria was protected by fortified shore batteries that could devastate any landing force, and the British infantry commanders who received the assignment had expressed considerable skepticism that any landing could be made without terrible cost. The argument boiled over into yet another controversy, but there was no time for argument, the capture of the islands a high priority. Eisenhower finally laid out his own plan. The first strikes would come from the air and the sea, intensive bombardment from a massive wave of British bombers, supplemented by an assault from British destroyers, cruisers, and light patrol boats. The plan was designed to minimize casualties among the landing parties, using long-distance firepower to damage or destroy the enemy's ability to defend the island. Once the naval and air forces had done what they could to silence the shore batteries, the infantry would then push ashore.

After a daylong bombardment of the island, the shore batteries ceased any kind of effective response, and the order was given for the final phase of the assault. As the ground troops prepared for their landing, Eisenhower received word in Algiers that the enemy's defenses at Pantelleria had not merely been silenced, they had been obliterated. Before the first British soldier could step ashore, the entire garrison, eleven thousand Italians, offered their surrender. The effect on the Italian garrison at Lampedusa was immediate, and that island fell with even less of a fight. By mid-June, the door to Sicily had been pushed wide-open.

PART THREE

We shall not fail or falter; we shall not weaken or tire. Neither the sudden shock of battle, nor the long-drawn trials of vigilance and exertion will wear us down. Give us the tools, and we will finish the job.

WINSTON CHURCHILL

I'm sick of people telling me to "have a good jump." A good jump is one that doesn't kill you.

SERGEANT JESSE ADAMS
505TH PARACHUTE INFANTRY REGIMENT

30. ADAMS

There was no talking, and no reason to. The loud groan from the twin motors of the C-47 filled them all, two rows of men facing one another in the darkness, pressed tightly in their hard seats, each man buried under the weight of his gear. The only light came from the cockpit, faint red specks, the instruments on the dash. Through the cabin, there were scattered specks as well, the brief glow from a half dozen cigarettes.

Adams guessed at the time, thought, nine, probably. Sun's been down maybe an hour. So, we've been up here for half that. Should be soon. Why in hell do they have to make these training jumps so far out into nowhere? We could do this five minutes from the airfield. The whole damned country is a drop zone.

There was a small burst of red, the jump light coming on above him, and the men knew the routine, pulled themselves to their feet. Adams moved close to the open doorway, squatted down, one knee close to the edge of the doorway, shouted to them above the wind and the roar of the motors, "Stand up! Hook up!"

The men obeyed, perfect rhythm, attaching static wires to the cable above them, the wires that would automatically pull the parachutes from the canvas packs on their backs.

"Check equipment!"

It was the essential order, each man examining his own equipment first, checking for open pockets, loose gear. Then, each one checked the back of the man in front of him, those things a man couldn't see for himself, buckles fastened, no snags or tears, nothing coming loose from anyone's pack. Adams knew that the darkness made no difference, the men having gone through this routine so often in training that they could feel their way.

"Sound off!"

The man closest to him shouted out, "Eighteen! Okay!"

Then the man behind him followed. "Seventeen! Okay!"

He listened for each one, no hesitation, the count going down to one.

There was a pause now, each man's eyes focused on the red light. He felt the soft flutter in his stomach, the plane's motors slowing, the C-47 dropping, the pilot leveling off at the correct altitude. He looked out the doorway, saw flickering sparks from the motor, and below, nothing, deep blackness, thought, a thousand feet, no more than that. Suddenly the red light changed to green, a soft glow on eighteen faces. Adams edged closer to the side of the door, still on his knee, braced himself with one hand, tapped the first man on the leg, shouted, "Go!"

The man was out and away, and the others stepped forward, the same routine, filing past him. He kept them spaced just so, a second apart, then the hard tap on each man's leg. The green light above him gave him all the light he needed, allowed him to see their hands, right now the only thing that mattered. Each man followed the training, grabbed the outside of the door frame, pulling himself into the empty darkness, dropping into space. If a man put his hands up on the inside of the plane, it was the first sign that he wouldn't jump. Even if a man hesitated, with his hands outside he could be prodded from behind. Adams had seen it so often, that one frozen second, the rational part of a man's brain screaming at him to step back, safe inside the plane. Most of the men who hesitated still made their jumps, but there was always the chance, especially now, especially in the blind darkness, that the training would simply go away, all the weeks of jump school, all the jumps over the rugged Georgia countryside forgotten by a man who was suddenly paralyzed by fear. If he couldn't be moved out quickly, it was Adams's job to prod him, a hard command into the man's ear. If that didn't work, if a man simply wouldn't go, Adams had to jerk him out of the way. Anyone who held up the line could hurt the entire *stick,* cause them to become separated on the ground. And in the dark, separation could be a disaster.

But there was no hesitation now, Adams keeping them in perfect rhythm, waiting for the last man, the dark shape now past him in one quick motion, disappearing into the darkness, falling silently away from the plane. It was his turn now, and he stood, did not hesitate, put his hands on the outside of the plane, pulled himself into black space.

The jumpmasters didn't hook a static line; his parachute was the same as what the pilots used, smaller, a rip cord now tight in his grip. The wind pulled at him, shaking him, a hard quiver from the heavy lumps of weight in his pockets. He fought to keep himself upright, listened to the fading sound of the plane's motors, didn't count seconds, had long forgotten that simplistic bit of training. By now it was instinct, and in the darkness, when the ground could not be seen, he had to rely on the pilots, on their ability to read an altimeter, to level off steady at a thousand feet. Without a parachute, a man would drop that far in eight seconds, and there was no time to think. He yanked hard on the rip cord, the chute exploding off his back, braced himself, a brief pause, his body suddenly jerked hard, the straps beneath his groin digging in, the parachute above him billowing wide, slowing his fall. He grabbed the risers beside his head, the guidelines that attached him to the chute. It was the most entertaining part of his training, learning to guide the chute, to twist and dip by pulling on the risers, slipping them toward a target on the ground, or a better landing place. But there was no landing place now, no target he could see, just moonlight and bits of stars, the sky straight above him hidden by the chute, the ground below him a dark blank canvas. He caught the reflection from the moonlight on chutes below him, ignored that, flexed his feet and knees, prepared for the impact. There would be no time to think about it, no time to recite lessons. It was instinct in all of them now, to hit the ground and roll, to spin off the energy of the fall as much as possible.

He felt it, more instinct, the smell and feel of the ground coming at him, pointed his toes, legs together, pulled his arms in tight, and now he hit, tumbled quickly to one side, a hard, jarring thump, his body rolling over, a tangle of cords, his own

equipment rattling and bouncing him along the hard ground. He
fought to stop, his feet digging in, arms still locked tight. He
stopped, felt no breeze, *thank God,* nothing to grab the chute
and drag him painfully across ground he still couldn't see. His
mind counted one full second, his own routine, a quick check
for damage, an inventory of his pains. There was always pain,
an ankle, a knee, and he tested, nothing broken, put his hands
out, felt rocks, soft dirt. He pushed himself up to his knees,
grabbed for the buckles, unhooked the straps, slipped the harness off his shoulders, stood. His steps were slow and careful,
boots probing for rocks. The moon was soft and yellow, low on
the horizon, and he could see enough to tell that the ground was
a flat plain, small, dark shapes around him, more rocks. The
chute behind him was silent, no rustling to block out sounds,
and he moved back toward it, rolled the straps carefully in his
arms, kept rolling, folding the chute, gathering it into a neat
pile. It was another routine, from their first jump at Fort Benning, every man responsible for his own chute, from checking
the lines and the threaded seams to packing it before each jump.
For now, they would continue the pattern, haul their chutes and
walk to the target area, trucks waiting to take them back to
Oujda.

He held the chute in a neat pile, then froze, stood in silence,
listened hard for any sounds, heard them now, idiotic cheers,
and then, one man screaming. He heard a truck engine closing
on him, slowing, and a spotlight cut the darkness in front of
him, blinding him. He closed his eyes, faced down, opened
them slowly, stared at the ground, stumbled on a rock, fought to
see his feet, the fat bulges in his pant legs, all the tools, the ammunition, grenades, every piece of the hundred pounds of
equipment each man had carried. Men were calling out, the
truck moving close to the jump zone. He shaded his eyes,
thought, dammit, this isn't a county fair. Turn that son of a bitch
off. The truck engine cut off now, silence again, only the sounds
of men, and he listened for new sounds, airplanes, the caution
passed on to every squad. There was always the chance of
bombers, Germans on the way to Casablanca. The spotlight was
too convenient a target for them, and so he knew the light would

not stay on for long. It's been too long already, he thought. A lantern would work just fine. What else is there to see out here?

The spotlight moved, scanned the open ground away from him, easing the blindness, *thank you,* and he saw men carrying their chutes, coming toward the truck, some limping. The single scream was silenced, medics doing their job, and he searched the lit ground, thought, who was it? Holman? Hates jumping at night, all he talks about. Serve him right if he busted a leg. I don't need griping.

He moved toward the truck, could see a jeep out to one side, a heavy machine gun on top, another jeep close beside it. There was a bullhorn now, the voice thunderous, the voice of the regiment's commander, Jim Gavin.

"Pick it up! Let's go! This isn't Georgia!"

Adams reached the truck, saw the stretcher bearers coming across the open ground toward him, carrying a crumpled mess of a man, white bandages in a large lump on the man's knee, blood on his face.

Adams moved that way. "Who is it?"

The medic glanced at his stripes. "Cornwell, Sarge. Bad leg. Nasty. Cracked his egg on a rock too."

Adams turned away, would deal with Cornwell later. Damn. Good man too. He looked out past the lit area, more spotlights in the distance, more jump zones, hundreds of men gathering up, some as broken as the man on the stretcher. Adams walked out into the open ground, saw men still coming in, began to count, his mental list. The bullhorn came again, behind him.

"Gather your men, Sergeant. Let's go! We're not on a damned picnic!"

Adams froze at the sound, turned, searching, fought the spotlight again. But he knew the voice, had not been surprised that Gavin would already be in his jeep, would be the first to reach the truck, would go all along the jump zone until every man had been accounted for. Gavin had made the same blind jump, preparing himself the same way he was preparing his men, something Gavin had done through every part of their training. To some, he was the *old man,* the name attributed to every commanding officer in every unit of the army. But Gavin was only thirty-six, and already a full bird colonel. It was a mark of respect and recognition, different from the loyalty and dedication he got from the men of the 505th. The respect came from above as well, from the Eighty-second Airborne's commander, Matthew Ridgway, and as far as Adams knew, from the high brass as well. Adams agreed with every man in the regiment: if Ike himself didn't pin those birds on Gavin's shoulders, he should have.

Adams ripped a salute. "Yes, sir! I'm checking off the names now, sir! Looks like a clean jump. One casualty in my stick."

He saw Captain Scofield now, the company commander, moving up toward Gavin's jeep. Scofield said something to Gavin, then called out toward Adams, "Keep it moving, Sergeant!"

Adams saluted again, knew that Scofield's command was as much for Gavin as it was for the men. Scofield was a far more cordial man than the colonel, a Texan who had been with the airborne units as long as anyone in the company. Adams moved back out away from the officers, watched his men coming forward, hustling quickly toward the truck. His mind was working now, counting, seventeen still walking, only one badly hurt. Thank God. He knew Gavin would watch him, just long enough to see the job done, making his own note of the casualties. Adams heard the jeep kick into motion, the colonel moving on, leaving the company in Captain Scofield's hands. Scofield was close to him now, stood silently, and Adams knew it was all part of the test, one more jump, one more bit of experience, the officers knowing far more than their men about just what it was they were training for.

Adams shouted out, "Let's move! The trucks won't wait for you! Unless you want to walk back to base, pull your ass up here!"

They didn't need his prodding, were coming forward on their own, some men jogging, another piece of their training. Nearly everything they had done at Fort Benning had been accompanied by running, from calisthenics to meals to latrine breaks. It was simply a part of them now, even in this absurdly miserable stretch of desert. They didn't need him shouting at them, his threats meaningless, and he didn't care, had yelled at these men and many more like them for months. It had been drilled into him from the officers that the sergeant ruled by intimidation, and whether Adams thought the exercise a little ridiculous, he had obeyed. Throughout the training, he had yelled at them and cursed them at Fort Benning, at Fort Bragg, on the trains to Camp Edwards in Massachusetts. When they boarded the troopship, the *Monterrey,* he yelled again, and in early May, when they debarked at Casablanca, Sergeant Adams was the first man who told them to move their butts into Africa. But yelling alone didn't carry much of a threat anymore, not to the men who had made it through airborne training. He had learned that lesson himself, that well-trained soldiers are quick to spot a noncom or an officer who is more voice than muscle. Adams had made certain that his authority carried some meaning, that he was tough enough to do anything that he would demand of them. He took the lesson from Gavin, and now, in the desert wasteland that spread out along the Moroccan-Algerian border, Gavin's grip on his own authority, the lessons and the discipline, had far greater meaning. They were no longer jumping off towers, no longer weeding out the weak links, no longer showing off for local dignitaries who came to exhibitions at Benning and Bragg. They were in Africa for a reason, and all that shouting by the sergeants no longer mattered. The jumps had a new meaning, a grim seriousness, and if the men cursed or feared the darkness, there was meaning to that as well. Each man had boarded the C-47s fully loaded with every tool of war, every piece of equipment. Despite a thousand rumors, they had no idea what their mission was to be, where and when they would jump when the enemy might be waiting. And if they were making training jumps at night, it wasn't some officer's brainless need to damage good men. Every man knew, without Adams yelling it into his face, that one day soon, when they boarded the C-47s, it would most likely be nighttime, and it would be the real thing.

The paratroop regiments had been created in the spring and summer of 1942, and from the arrival of the first volunteers, the men who endured the training at Fort Benning, Georgia, absorbed the pride and displayed a swagger that said they were America's elite soldiers. The pride was earned, since nothing in army boot camp could have prepared them for the kind of rigorous physical experience the paratroop commanders put them through. The training seemed to border on brutality, and a sizable percentage of the men who volunteered for the duty were incapable of completing the regimen. There was no condemnation for the ones who quit. They simply went away, transferred back to the units they had come from, or other places where they might be better equipped to serve. But those who completed the training, who made their required jumps, were instantly part of something unique. Not only were they among the most physically fit men in the army, but they did something no other soldier, sailor, or Marine had ever done before: they jumped out of airplanes.

Colonel Jim Gavin led his men by example, jumping with them still, suffering through the injuries that were a natural result of a man's body colliding unnaturally with all forms of hard ground. The other officers did the same, Scofield of course, and the battalion commander, Lieutenant Colonel Art Gorham. The officers' willingness to endure the same punishment as their men had proven their worth and had given them the kind of respect no one earns by rank alone.

Jesse Adams had been with the 505th from the beginning, had slugged his way up the short ladder to the rank of sergeant. Adams was a short, trunklike man, wide shoulders and a strong back. He had a misleading smile, seemed at first glance to be overly friendly, charming, a man to offer a quick slap on the back. But the officers had seen something else, a streak of iron, Adams demonstrating a surprising lack of fear about leaping out of aircraft. It was something the sergeants had to have, an icy hardness that would put them above the men they trained beside, something that commanded instinctive respect and unthinking obedience. It didn't hurt if his men believed that Sergeant Adams was a little crazy. He enjoyed the discipline, turning soft men into hard fighters, but had never particularly enjoyed the way the army expected him to enforce it on his men. Like so many sergeants in every army that had ever taken the field, yelling into scared faces was part of the job, education by repetitive browbeating. But in the planes, when a man stood in the open doorway and faced the wind and the terror of falling,

Adams knew that shouts and curses served no purpose at all. You couldn't shout a man into bravery, you could only shame him. He didn't want men following him into combat only because they were too ashamed to be anywhere else.

Adams had come into the army just after Pearl Harbor, joining the great wave of recruits who answered the urgency of the country's call. He came from a family of hunters and so was perfectly comfortable shooting a rifle, and like most, he expected to join the infantry. With so much attention being focused on the threats from the Japanese, he also expected, like most, to go to the Pacific. As he slogged his way through basic training, his strong body grew stronger, and rather than complain about the physical requirements, he attacked the courses and exercises, and grew stronger still. After long weeks of being shaped from recruits into soldiers, the men were brought together in an old hangar, sat down to hear the words of a captain, an officer no one had seen before. The captain spoke in somber tones, as though sharing a secret, that if a man considered himself the best, the army needed him in a new place. When the captain began to speak of airplanes, the soldiers perked up, but then, he spoke of parachutes, and the officer was met with mumbling curses and low laughter. But Adams didn't laugh. From his first day in army boots, he had wanted to prove to someone, anyone, that he was the best. Best *what* didn't matter, best man, best soldier, best fighter. He was already the strongest, most athletic man in his company, and if the army wanted him to prove it by jumping out of airplanes, Adams wouldn't just ignore the opportunity. Several men from the company put their signature on the captain's sign-up sheet. Adams had been the first in line.

His great-grandfather had moved the family out of the Carolinas after the Civil War, had settled the deep Southwest, and Adams spent his earliest years in southwestern New Mexico, the rugged desert country west of the Rio Grande. His father worked the copper mines, had been matter-of-fact about soldiers, considered them fodder for someone else's machine, had talked in loud boasts about the noble life as a miner, hard men producing hard metal. Jesse heard it all through his childhood, that there was value in his father's work that Jesse might never achieve himself. His father lectured him, dismissing the boy's own dreams, dismissing talk of big cities and careers. Jesse gave up trying to convince his father of anything at all, could not fight the long-winded speeches, how the mines created the backbone that gave America its industrial power.

After so many years, his father's words had numbed him, but the images did not, and as he grew older, he saw more of the reality of the miner's life. Each evening they walked from the stark, rocky hills, toward the rows of small houses, exhausted, dirty men, struggling to find the will to make that same walk the next day. He watched his father as well, held on to the image of the man coming toward him across the dreary, open ground in front of the small house. Once in a while, the boy would see a smile, but more often his father would ignore him, passing by, his face frozen with glum despair, his thoughts far off in some distant place. Jesse would know there would be no conversation, nothing about Jesse's arithmetic test, no chance his father would toss the baseball. The only pride he saw came from the man's bragging, and Jesse began to understand that the exaggeration was some kind of tonic for the man. If there was any romance to his father's life in the mine, there was none at home. At least once a week, when the supper plates were in the sink, the shouting would start, broiling fights that seemed to tear the house apart. The shouting always began with his father, but his mother would not shy away, would answer the challenge, their voices escalating into a screaming hell that would exhaust itself long after Jesse and his younger brother had tried to go to bed. The next day, the routine would begin again, his father gone early, the two boys eating a silent breakfast, prepared by a woman whose exhausted affection was preserved only for her children.

Jesse had a bond with his younger brother even now, Clayton surprising everyone by joining the Marines. Clayton was somewhere in the Pacific, and once Jesse had boarded the ship for Africa, he knew there would be no letters. As boys they'd shared the experience of parents who seemed only to despise each other, but as he grew older, Jesse began to hear about other families, dirty secrets spilling out from teenage boys who no longer feared what their fathers could do. The streets would often echo with furious fights, and Jesse always assumed it was just like the horrible endurance matches he and Clayton hid from in their room. But the other boys told stories that were far worse, drunken brutality, terrifying violence, visits from the sheriff. Jesse realized the blessing in all his parents' shouting. His father never hit his mother, never hit any of them. The fights weren't about brutality or violence. It was one man frustrated with his own life, grappling with a woman's unwillingness to accept that she would never have *joy,* that neither of them had any reason to look in a mirror and smile.

Jesse was twenty when the war started, twenty-one when he went to his parents' house for the last time. He stood outside the screen door with a bus ticket and a mangled suitcase, had planned it so he did not have to see his father at all, the man already making it clear that his boys had turned out far more useless than even he had predicted. But his mother surprised him, surprised both of her boys with tearful thankfulness that they would leave this place, would not end up in the mines.

Clayton was already gone, had barely waited for his eighteenth birthday. Jesse had stayed closer, protective, had worked for a small construction company owned by the big mine. The work was meaningless, but it gave him a place of his own, and the long hours gave him a strong back. When he finally left, to make the long walk to the bus depot, his mother was watching him from behind the rusty screen door. There were few words, no tears, just a final wish from her, surprising him. They were simple words, filled with her own kind of emotion, a strange and urgent desperation.

"Be a hero."

The truck rolled slowly, lurched and swerved, the men cursing. Adams was close beside Scofield, had not been surprised that the captain would choose to ride in the big truck, instead of one of the available jeeps. The truck bounced again, more curses, and Scofield said, "You can all just shut the hell up. The driver's dodging holes in the road. You rather he slam straight into them? We break an axle, we'll all be walking home."

"Sir . . ."

Adams looked toward shapes in the darkness, the voice, knew it was Fulton, the young New Englander. Scofield said, "What is it, soldier?"

"We gonna get back to camp soon, sir? I got the trots. Don't think I can make it much farther, sir."

"You'll hold it until I tell you to drop your pants, soldier!"

After a silent pause, Fulton said, "I'll try, sir."

Adams could hear Scofield's breathing, simmering anger, and Scofield said, "Son of a *bitch*. That's all we need. One more for the doctor."

Adams knew the captain's anger wasn't directed at Fulton. It was everyone's shared agony, so many men suffering from intestinal problems that made any long journey a potential hell for the man himself and anyone near him. It was a common ailment, the camps in the desert infested with flies, flies in their food, flies dead in any uncovered water. The inevitable result was dysentery. Once the 505th had built their camps at Oujda, the usual training had been replaced by the necessity to stay healthy, but the army could not prevent a spreading wave of sickness. Keeping vermin out of their food was one problem, and it was essential that the men drink enormous amounts of water. But dead flies or not, the local well water was especially foul and had to be treated with lots of chlorine. It was just one more bit of misery for men who pitched their tents in a treeless frying pan of desert, who still had no idea why they were in Africa and no hint of what their mission would be.

OUJDA, MOROCCO—JUNE 15, 1943

They continued to train, mostly daylight jumps, Gavin and his officers doing as much as they could to keep the regiment fit and ready. But the camp at Oujda offered no comforts, no recreation, nothing but sunburn, flies, and choking dust. As more and more of the men fell ill, training missions became useless, too many men simply unable to participate.

Adams sat low in his slit trench, the only cool spot he could find, tried to think of the right words for the letter. The sun was baking his brain, and even the cool earth on either side of him was suffocating. He stared at the scrap of dirty paper, the only words a scribble from his pencil:

Dear Mom,

Not a damned thing to tell you about. Yep, that oughta be a good letter. Make her feel her boy is doing his bit. Brag to the neighbors. Hey, Jesse doesn't have the trots! Damned near the only man in the company! The town'll throw her a parade.

He crumpled the paper in his rough hand, then thought better of it, cursed to himself, too valuable. Keep it for later. He straightened it out again, slipped it into a pants pocket, the pencil as well, pulled himself to his feet. The camp was on a chalky plain, tents lined up in neat rows, wide dirt avenues between them. Beside each tent was a narrow trench, the only protection they had if the Germans decided to make them a bombing target. He looked up, bright blue sky, squinted, a thin crust of dry sand digging into his face. No Germans today. They got better things to do than risk coming out here. And with the kind of shape we're in, we're not worth the bombs.

"Sergeant!"

He turned, saw two officers moving toward him, Scofield, and another man, a major, Gavin's aide. Heads popped up around him, men huddled in the dusty shade of their own trenches, curious, the officers passing quickly by them. Adams pulled himself up to flat ground, stood straight, saluted, Scofield returning it.

"Orders have come in, Sergeant. Dawn tomorrow we're moving out. Pass the word, get the gear stowed, get your squad ready. We'll board trucks, first . . ." He stopped, had given Adams all the information Adams needed to know. "That's all for now."

The men began to climb up, gathering slowly, the two officers moving on. Adams liked Scofield immensely, the Texan who seemed to fit perfectly into Colonel Gavin's system, young and fit, a man in his late twenties who bore no resemblance to the wet-eared *ninety-day wonders.*

"We leaving, Sarge?"

"What's that about, Sarge?"

Adams ran a hand over his filthy shirt, looked past the men, scanned the tent city that had been their home.

"Kiss the ground good-bye, boys. We're moving out."

More men were gathering, questions, where, what the officers had told him. Adams pushed past them, stood in front of his tent.

"Tomorrow at dawn. Be ready or get left behind. All I know is, we're pulling out of *here*. Wherever we're going, it's gotta be paradise. No place can be worse than this."

31. EISENHOWER

ALGIERS
JULY 1, 1943

He had been making the rounds, visiting the various division commanders, the Americans who would lead Patton's invasion force. Bradley's Second Corps now consisted of the First Division, veterans of the Tunisian campaign, along with the Third and Forty-fifth Divisions, men who had spent most of the Tunisian campaign training for what would follow. The armor accompanying Patton would be his former command, the Second Armored Division, who, since they'd fought their way ashore in Morocco, had mostly been confined to training and security duty around Casablanca. The British commanders were firmly in the hands of Montgomery, and Alexander had done as much as could be expected in coordinating the two wings of the attack. Most of the controversies had been settled, the pressure of the impending attack finally outweighing local concerns.

On both fronts, the first strike would be made by airborne troops, Montgomery's wing led by British paratroopers and a vast armada of troop-carrying gliders. Patton's wing would be led by the men from the Eighty-second Airborne Division, paratroopers only, the 505th Regiment, with the 504th set to follow by a day or more. Eisenhower had studied every map, every unit's command roster, had shaken the hand and looked into the eye of every man whose job it was to lead their soldiers into a fight that by all measures might be the greatest struggle the Allies had yet confronted.

Around his headquarters, there was plenty of speculation, idle talk, men only able to guess what would happen once the troops reached the beaches. Some were outright dismissive of the Italians, assuming that the superior equipment of the Allies would easily prevail. Others, including Eisenhower, weren't so sure that the Italians would simply collapse. For the first time, they were fighting on their own soil, defending their homeland. With every handshake in every headquarters, he had heard confidence, was grateful for the grit and backbone of men like Terry Allen, and the Third Division's Lucian Truscott, the Forty-fifth's Troy Middleton, Second Armored's new commander Hugh Gaffey. There was inexperience of course, none but Allen's Big Red One having yet faced German and Italian resistance. But Eisenhower had to believe that Patton's faith in Bradley and his confidence in the division commanders were well-founded. If anyone could smell out weakness, it was George Patton.

The one string of doubt that ran through the entire operation was the use of the airborne. The Allies had never launched a large-scale airborne assault, and the one time they had relied on airborne troops at all, the night landings in Algeria, the results had been dismal. Eisenhower knew that the 509th's experiences in Operation Torch were a dangerous experiment and could have been a far more costly one. Eisenhower had his doubts then, the same doubts he had now. In London, when the final decisions had been made for Operation Torch, Wayne Clark had convinced Eisenhower to give the go-ahead to send the 509th to capture the two airfields near Oran. Clark had become a champion for the paratroopers, the most enthusiastic among Eisenhower's senior officers. But Clark would not be at Sicily, and neither Patton nor Montgomery were wholly convinced that paratroopers would accomplish their mission, especially since they were to be dropped at night, behind enemy positions, onto completely unfamiliar ground. In theory, the paratroopers served two purposes, capturing a vital target before the enemy could prepare, and rattling the enemy by surprising them with a powerful armed force that suddenly appeared where no one was supposed to be. But during Operation Torch, weather, poor coordination, and bad luck had combined to scatter the men of the 509th across a vast stretch of North Africa, and only a small number had actually accomplished anything close to their mission. Now, Operation Husky called for a massive airdrop of thousands of men, who would be expected to capture vital enemy strongholds, hold down key intersections, and generally disrupt the enemy's ability to launch an effective defense. If the paratroopers of the 505th were as scattered and confused as the 509th had been in North Africa, their jump might be suicidal. Eisenhower gave his approval with gut-churning reluctance.

Even as the warships were moving into range of their targets onshore, and the landing craft were poised to expel their men onto the beaches; even as the paratroopers were loaded and stuffed into the bellies of the C-47s—the final decision lay in Eisenhower's hand. If he felt that conditions had changed, or some critical error had been made, the power was his to pull the plug. The enormous machine could simply be ordered to . . . stop.

The men had chosen their seats, one man hanging a large map on the hooks fastened to the wide, empty wall. The map showed western Russia, red lines, circles, symbols that were all too familiar. The briefings on the fighting in Russia came not from information gleaned from Soviet sources, but from British intelligence, and such innocuous sources as reporters who wrote for *Stars and Stripes*. It was one ongoing mystery, that as much as Russia was committed to the defeat of Hitler's army, as much as Stalin begged and browbeat the Allied leaders to draw German forces away from his battle lines, the Soviets simply wouldn't provide any substantial information about what was happening there. Eisenhower had to wonder at that, as much as he wondered at the amazing behavior of the French. No matter that we're all on the same side. No one trusts anyone else.

The man at the map raised a pointer, and in front of Eisenhower a man spoke.

"As you can see, sir, we're projecting a setback for the Germans along this line—"

"Sir!"

Eisenhower looked past the assembled officers, saw Beetle Smith at the door.

"Sir! Sorry to interrupt. Something very important has arrived."

Eisenhower saw the envelope now, the heavy wax seal, the bold black letters, already knew what was written.

Supreme Allied Commander—Eyes Only

Eisenhower stood. "I'm sorry, gentlemen, but this will have to wait. You are dismissed."

The officers were quickly gone, and Smith stood in the doorway, said, "There'll be no visitors, sir. Call when it's all clear."

"Fine, Beetle. Thanks."

The door closed and Eisenhower stared at the envelope, slid a finger under the wax. There were several reports, typewritten pages, one signature at the bottom of each page: Alan Brooke, the British chief of staff, Churchill's closest adviser, and one of the few men who had authority over Eisenhower himself. He read slowly, carefully, absorbed the details, felt a chill, sweat on his forehead. Good God. This could be . . . well, a bloody damned disaster.

He put the papers back into the envelope, looked toward the small fireplace. The papers would be destroyed, no chance that anyone outside his own office would ever seen them. No, not yet, he thought. He ran the names through his mind, the only men in the entire theater who could know what the reports contained. Air Marshal Tedder was on Malta, and he knew that Admiral Cunningham was at sea. That leaves only one, he thought. And dammit, he needs to know this right now.

He opened a drawer beside him, dropped the envelope inside, looked toward the closed door.

"Beetle!"

He waited for the footsteps, the door pushing open.

"Call Alexander. I need him here *now*!"

It was called Enigma, the encoding machine the Germans had relied on to scramble their vital communications since before the war. Throughout every major campaign, Hitler's generals and intelligence officers had transmitted their messages using the Enigma codes. From Russia to France to the U-boats in the Atlantic, from Norway to North Africa, German orders and messages of the highest priority were sent by the encoding device that German intelligence believed was simply unbreakable. They were wrong.

The work had been done primarily by Polish mathematicians, aided by French intelligence agents, and in early 1940, the astonishing results had been conveyed to the British. One by one, the Enigma codes were being broken. As the Germans revised their codes, an enormous number of cipher experts were monitoring the German transmissions, revising their own decoding of the German communications. The work was being done now at Bletchley Park, a compound of offices surrounding a stately mansion, some fifty miles northwest of London. The actual work performed in the compound was one of the most closely guarded secrets of the entire war and had been given the name Ultra, shorthand for "ultrasecret." Ultra was so well guarded that only a handful of senior commanders knew of its existence, and fewer still knew that the German codes had been laid wide-open for the Allied command to read.

Alexander read the reports, Eisenhower watching him, waiting for the change of expression.

"Good God, man. Is this certain?"

"Seems pretty clear to me."

Alexander scanned the papers again. "It's gratifying that the Germans have swallowed our deceptions. This mentions the buildup of defenses in Sardinia and Crete. Cunningham's flotilla is doing all they can to be noticed, showing every sign they're heading for the eastern Mediterranean. Looks like the Nazis have noticed that. Good work, there. Could pull some Luftwaffe people off in that direction, take some of the pressure off."

"Dammit, Alex, I'm not concerned about Sardinia and Greece. The Germans have moved two panzer divisions across the Strait of Messina, including the Hermann Göring Division. That's a hell of a lot of armor. Read it again. Kesselring's report to Berlin spells out the disposition of the German defenses throughout this whole theater."

Alexander stared at the papers. "I don't understand that. Why would he do that? And why now? Obviously, by the way he's moving his troops around, he's convinced Sicily is our target. But why in blazes would he send so much detail to Hitler? He's listed every unit he's placed on Sicily, every reserve unit on Sardinia, all of it, spelled out with perfect clarity."

Eisenhower thought a moment. "He's covering his ass. Hitler hasn't ever given the Mediterranean the attention he should have. Now, he's probably not giving Sicily a second thought. Berlin knows we're coming, but they don't know exactly where, and I bet there's a hell of an argument about it. We'd have good reasons to hit them at Sardinia or Greece, and somebody's probably convinced we're going into southern France. Hitler doesn't want to hear all that; he's still looking at Russia."

"But why would Kesselring—"

"He thinks we're coming to Sicily, and he wants everyone to know about it. If he's wrong, no one will really care. If he's right, he's a hero. Especially if he puts two panzer divisions up our ass."

Alexander stared at the papers, handed them slowly to Eisenhower. "What do we do about it?"

"Not a damned thing. You know that. We can't suddenly change our troop deployments because of this report. We can't tell Patton or Monty they're marching into two panzer divisions. Any hint gets out that we've been reading their mail, *any* hint, and the Germans will scrap Enigma altogether. We get one staff officer captured with some scrap of paper that mentions Ultra, any hint that we know about those panzers, and Bletchley Park might as well shut down."

Alexander was silent, both men understanding the gravity of what Eisenhower was saying.

"You're right, Ike. All of it. I suppose we could try to add to the infantry's antitank capabilities."

"With what? We've got bazookas that have never been tested in battle, handed to men who've never fired one. Heavy artillery can't be brought ashore until the infantry has secured the beachheads. If two hundred Tiger tanks suddenly pop up on those sand hills, no infantry's going anywhere. Damn this!"

"What of the paratroopers, Ike?"

The word punched him in the gut. "Dammit. We can't say anything to the Airborne. Nothing. Not a damned word."

"Could be a bloody mess."

Eisenhower sat back in the chair, looked past Alexander, felt the hard twist in his stomach, too many times now. "Nothing we can do about it, Alex. Right now, we're still a *go* on the tenth, and that's all there is to it."

"Not necessarily, Ike. We're a go only if you say so. We might be sending our people into something they can't get out of. How do you explain that later on?"

Eisenhower was growing annoyed now, didn't want these kinds of questions from a subordinate. Every senior commander who knew this extraordinary secret had already faced his own moral dilemma, none any more than Churchill himself. Churchill had known in advance of at least one bombing raid against a specific British city during the Luftwaffe's brutal campaign against British civilians. But no warning had been issued, no one prepared to expect the attack. Eisenhower had never discussed this sort of thing with Churchill, but now he was facing the same kind of awful dilemma. And, like Churchill, Eisenhower could say nothing at all, could give no warning to his troops, could offer no hint that would betray the vital secret.

"There is nothing we can do, Alex. I'm under the same orders you are. Roosevelt, Churchill, Marshall, Brooke, every one of them is holding this secret inside him, and every one of us knows that people have died because we couldn't mention it. But I have to believe that breaking those codes will eventually win us the war."

"No matter how many men we lose in the process?"

Eisenhower rubbed his hands together, fought to keep his temper. "I'm not going to debate morality with you, dammit. This is a war, not a cricket match. We didn't start this, and if we lose this thing, we'll be worrying about a lot more than our moral compass. You have your orders. Right now, Operation Husky is a go for July tenth. Do you understand that?"

"I quite understand, Ike. However, I will allow myself a brief prayer for those paratroopers."

MALTA—JULY 9, 1943

It was close to midnight, the moon lighting the land around him, rolling grasslands, and out to the southwest, the vast open sea. Far out in the darkness lay the coast of Tunisia, the massive airfield at Kairouan, the starting point for 264 C-47 transport planes. He stared at the black sea, the dancing flickers of light, the moonlight broken by the boiling rage of the water, whipped high by the hard wind. He looked up now, no sound but the wind. He had hoped to hear the motors, that the sounds might guide his eye to one or more of the formations as they passed overhead, Malta serving as one of their navigation points. The air people had told him to look for flickers of white light, the reflection of moonlight off the planes, the only visible sign of the first great wave of the assault.

He thought of the message from Marshall, the unmistakable urgency of a man too nervous to wait for Eisenhower's own cable.

Is the attack on or off?

The message had come several hours before the deadline, and Eisenhower had not yet been prepared to respond, could only wait in raw agony at Cunningham's headquarters, staring at wind machines, the British sailors making their estimates, predicting the unpredictable. Eisenhower had simply stayed out of the way, letting the weather specialists do their job, reports called out to Cunningham, their jargon, *force four,* and then, *force five.* He didn't know the precise meaning, how that translated to miles per hour, but outside, after hours watching the rapidly spinning wind machines, standing upright against the hard gale, Eisenhower knew they could be in serious trouble.

He kept Marshall's cable in his pocket, would wait until the last possible minute, knew that once the order was given, there would be no turning back. There had been some encouraging reports from the navy southeast of Sicily, that since Montgomery's landing zones were mostly on the leeward side of the island, the landing craft there could push ashore without difficulty. But along the southern coast, the waves were pounding the rocks, deep swells rolling the ships and the landing craft,

Patton's troops huddled in what Eisenhower could only guess was a growing plague of seasickness.

After long hours with Cunningham, Eisenhower was running out of time. There was some encouragement at least, the weather specialists predicting that by midnight the wind would die down considerably. It was the one piece of news on which everything turned. With one hour to go before the planes left Kairouan, Eisenhower radioed Marshall. The attack was on.

He tried to see his watch, too dark, stared up again, ignored the men behind him, staff officers, watching as he was, searching for some glimpse of the planes. He had stopped thinking about the ships at all, knew that Patton would do what had to be done. Even if there was a delay along the south coast, Montgomery could get his people ashore, which would draw enemy resistance that way, taking considerable pressure off the American landing zones. It will work, he thought. One hundred sixty thousand men. I don't care how many tanks they have, we have good people and, dammit, we're simply better than they are. There is no other way to look at it. What the hell are the Germans fighting for? What *cause* is so damned important? When it comes down to guts, you have to believe that you're dying for something worthwhile. Dying for a man like Hitler is not worthwhile.

It was a futile pep talk, and the words drained from his mind, replaced by the one image he had fought against, unavoidable. Weeks earlier, he had spent long hours discussing and analyzing this operation with the Eighty-second Airborne's commander, Matthew Ridgway, and Ridgway's subordinate Jim Gavin, the man who would lead the paratroopers in their jump. Eisenhower had learned a great deal more about paratroop operations than he had ever known before, and Ridgway's words were digging at him now. *Fifteen miles per hour.* That was the limit, the maximum wind speed that Ridgway insisted would allow a safe jump. He closed his eyes now, felt the buffeting wind on his back, thought, it's a hell of a lot more than that now. It shouldn't be. It's midnight, for God's sakes, and this hasn't let up. *Force five.* Does Ridgway know that? Gavin? They have to, it's their job. They have to know what they're being asked to do.

There was a voice behind him, arms in the air, pointing. He looked up, saw it now, the glimmer, more reflections, a string of planes. He forced himself to watch them, tried to say a prayer, ask something, what? Protect them? He pushed it away, no, you cannot do that. You cannot think of the men, what might happen. They are one part of the whole, and the whole is what matters. It is *all* that matters.

He stared up, the wind rocking him again, harder still.

32. ADAMS

OVER THE MEDITERRANEAN
JULY 9, 1943, MIDNIGHT

Thirty-five miles per hour.

Adams had been close to the cluster of officers, heard the grim reports, Gavin's simple response: "What the hell do you expect me to do about it now?"

As they gathered at the planes, the men had been fully loaded, pockets and pouches bulging and heavy. More equipment was hanging from the C-47s themselves, mortars and heavy machine guns wrapped in canvas bundles, hooked beneath the wings. Adams had struggled to keep the dust out of his eyes, trying not to think what the strong winds could mean to the paratroopers. After checking his own equipment, he had moved to each man in the stick, silent coaching, every man stuffed and wrapped with every conceivable tool and weapon he had been trained to carry. A few men had tried to talk, spending their nervousness in chatter, mostly to themselves. But there had been none of the joking, the teases, no one had been playful. For so many months they had tormented their bodies and tested their courage, and Adams felt the strength of that, knew they all felt it, that there was a kind of power in them that made them better soldiers than anyone they would face, maybe anyone else in the world. As the time grew closer, the sounds had been few, the men around him buckling up and cinching the straps, hoisting the chutes onto their backs, counting their grenades and their ammunition clips, checking every piece of gear in every pocket, and then, checking it again.

They had climbed aboard the C-47 after dark, close to eight thirty, the briefings from the officers locked in their minds. It was a three-and-a-half-hour flight, nearly all of it over water, and so each man had his Mae West strapped on as well, one more encumbrance. No one had complained.

The C-47 would carry a stick of eighteen paratroopers plus the two pilots up front, whose job it was to negotiate the route laid out on the maps. They would fly at a low altitude, keeping close to the water until they reached the coastline. The C-47s were to follow a circuitous route around the massive invasion fleet, avoiding friendly fire from overanxious antiaircraft gunners on the Allied ships. But the briefings had dealt more with the paratroopers themselves, the location of the drop zones, what they would find there, and what they were supposed to do about it. The drop zones were several miles inland, east and north of the coastal town of Gela, directly north of the Acate River. There were specific targets, one crucial intersection of roads that led away from the coast, designated Objective Y, which was guarded by a heavy concentration of pillboxes and gun emplacements. To the northwest of the drop zones was a hill named Piano Lupo, which commanded a view of the Gela airfield. If all went according to plan, the vital routes the enemy could use to confront the amphibious landings would be closed off, and once captured, the Gela airfield could be used immediately to ferry in supplies and reinforcements. Once the Y was cleared, the routes inland would be open for the two infantry divisions, the First and the Forty-fifth, the men who would make their landings on the beaches closest to the 505th's drop zones. The first part of the mission might be the most difficult, finding the drop zones in moonlight, in the teeth of what continued to be gale-force winds.

Adams didn't know how many planes had taken off from the various fields around Kairouan, but he knew the men, knew that thirty-four hundred paratroopers had gone aloft in the skies around him, every one with the same job, the same information, and every one carried the same piece of paper, the final message passed out to them from Colonel Gavin.

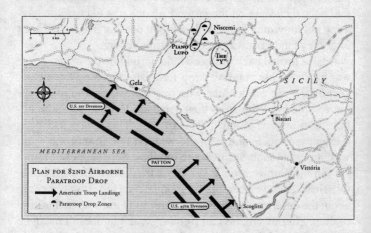

Soldiers of the 505th Combat Team

Tonight you embark upon a combat mission for which our people and the free people of the world have been waiting for two years.

You will spearhead the landing of an American force upon the island of Sicily. Every preparation has been made to eliminate the element of chance. You have been given the means to do the job and you are backed by the largest assemblage of air power in the world's history.

The eyes of the world are upon you. The hopes and prayers of every American go with you. . . .

Adams sat up front, closest to the pilots, would be the last man out of the plane. At the rear sat Ed Scofield, the captain wrapped and buried under his own bundle of equipment and tools, squeezed into place against the man beside him. Scofield sat closest to the open jump door and, when the time came, when the green light flashed, would be the first man to jump.

The plane dipped, tilting to one side, the pilot pulling it

straight again, groans from the men. They were used to bounces and air pockets, but this was different, a violence in the sky around them that grabbed the plane like a child's toy, tossing it from side to side. Adams had tried to sleep, strong advice passed along from Gavin. Captain Scofield had reminded them that once they were on the ground, no one was likely to do anything but move and fight. With daylight coming five or six hours after they landed, it was going to be a long day.

Adams leaned back, his head held upright by the chute. There was no sleep, his mind working furiously, watching the others, keeping an eye on the men who might weaken, who might require some extra jolt from their sergeant. He didn't want to believe that anyone would fall apart now. These men had been through too much, and even the weakest link in this one chain was strong enough to finish the job they were supposed to do. He ran the names through his mind, tried to predict. McBride, O'Brien? They've been pretty good lately. Hell, I was bitching about the desert as much as they were, and I grew up in this kind of crap. Fulton? No, he's all right. A weak gut doesn't mean he isn't a good soldier. Adams sat back again, took a deep breath, felt the calmness of the cool air. It was the one blessing, a hard chill, the jolting turmoil of the flight eased by the coolness around them. There was no worse combination for airsickness than rough air and heat, and they had suffered through plenty of both over Fort Benning. But now, even in the chill, Adams had watched his men carefully, looked for the telltale signs, hands covering mouths, men suddenly lurching over, sickening smells that would infect the rest of them. There had been a few, but only a few, early, some men succumbing within the first hour of flight. But that was sickness of a different kind, the gut-churning fear, the first time any of these men would actually face the enemy. Adams knew that each man held to his own thoughts, some praying, others reciting the letters they had left behind, *I might not return . . .* , others simply staring into their fear, doing all they could to hold away the terrifying fantasies of what was waiting for them on the ground. When the smells of sickness had drifted through the plane, they all knew that some were better at it than others.

He had left his own letters, one for his mother of course. That one was easy, full of sentiment and soft confidence, all the things she would expect to read, that any mother would want to read. But then he had written to his brother, surprising himself, the words flowing out in a rapid stream, things he would never say to anyone else, things he knew the censors might have some problem with. He didn't yet know what kind of experiences his brother had seen, what it was really like for a Marine in the Pacific, whether Clayton had actually faced the Japanese, whether he had been wounded, whether he was even alive. No, Adams thought, the army would tell me that. They're supposed to anyway. But, who the hell knows what those jungles are like, islands in the middle of nowhere. Clayton may never get the damned letter. But, I had to write it. Had to tell someone. I'll bet he'd do the same. Maybe already has. He thought of Gavin, the assembly one morning, months ago now. *Any man tells you he's not afraid going into combat, the first thing you do is shake his hand. Then, you call him a liar.* There had been protest after that, the mouthy boys making their speeches about all the things they'd do to the Nazis. But Adams knew in some instinctive place that Gavin was right, that when the time came, when the jumps would land them right into an enemy's camp, or right beside a ten-gun pillbox, well, damned right I'll be afraid. And that's . . . right now.

He leaned forward, saw Scofield at the rear of the plane, staring down through the jump door. There had been a wager, some of the men wondering what the captain would do when he jumped. It had become customary now that as every man jumped, he yelled out "Geronimo." The custom was cloudy in origin, some claiming to have started the ritual themselves. Adams was convinced that it had started with a movie the men had watched at Fort Benning. It was a forgettable story, some typical Hollywood version of cowboys and Indians, except for one climactic moment, when the famed Indian chief called out his own name as he purposely rode to his death over a cliff. Only the most gullible believed that the real Geronimo had done such a thing, but the men had decided it made for a dramatic way to depart a plane. The officers mostly ignored the ritual, but Captain Scofield was closer to his men than some of the others, had commented that he might just take up that call himself.

Adams had his doubts. It was one thing to emulate some famous Indian when your supposed death leap was over a jump
zone in Georgia. It was quite another for an officer to imitate a
lusty embrace of certain death when the jump might be exactly
that.

He tried to see his watch, too dark, knew they had been aloft
now for hours. *George Marshall.* He shook his head. *George
Marshall.* Someone's idea of a joke, maybe. But we'll remember it. Damned well better.

It was the call sign; once they were on the ground in the dark,
no one could know if the first man he contacted was friend or
enemy. The entire jump team had been given the code words,
the one-word greeting: *George;* and the response: *Marshall.*
They could have come up with something better, he thought.
How about *Rita Hayworth*? Well, maybe not. Even the Krauts
might answer to that one. He scanned the men closest to him,
leaned forward again, looked down the rows of men facing each
other, no one moving. At the rear of the plane Scofield suddenly
rose to his feet, surprising him, the captain moving forward, the
men pulling in feet and legs, making way. Adams felt a jolt of
concern, waited for Scofield to move close, said, "What's up,
Captain?"

Scofield ignored him, moved into the cockpit, his voice just
reaching Adams over the drone of the motors.

"You want to tell me where the hell we are?"

Adams felt a stab of cold curiosity, leaned forward, stared out
the small window across from him. There was nothing to see,
moonlight reflecting on black water sliding by only a few hundred feet below them. He twisted around, looked behind him,
the window close by his own head, saw a speck of light, low on
the horizon. And now, a streak of white lights, rising up, and another, his brain kicking into gear. *Antiaircraft fire.*

Scofield was still in the cockpit, passing words back and forth
with the pilots, and Adams stared at the lines of tracer bullets,
more of them, closer now. The plane rocked suddenly, a white
flash in his eyes, loud curses beside him, the men coming to life.

"What the hell?"

"We hit?"

"What is it, Sarge? What's going on?"

Adams called out, "Shut the hell up! It's ground fire. We're getting close. Keep calm. Nothing we can do about it."

He stared out the small window again, heard Scofield, a hard shout: "Turn this son of a bitch around!"

The plane dipped to one side, a hard banking turn, more streaks of white light, a heavy rumble, the plane bouncing, another bright flash. Scofield stayed in the cockpit, and Adams felt himself rising up, straining under the weight of his gear, but he could not just sit. He eased up behind Scofield, said, "What's going on, sir? We okay?"

Scofield turned to him now, looked past him, eyed the men. "All right, there's no secrets now. You men need to know that our pilots are not sure where the hell we are. You see those tracers? That ground fire?"

"Yes, sir."

"That's supposed to be on the right side! The coastline is supposed to be *that way* . . . north of us. But that fire is on the left! The jackasses flying this plane can't find their asses with broomsticks! Sit down, Sergeant! We'll sort this out if I have to toss these idiots into the ocean and fly this thing myself!"

Adams obeyed, felt a new kind of fear, realized Scofield was as angry as Adams had ever seen him. He looked again through the window behind him, the coastline gone now, the plane still rocking from the gusting wind, another hard bounce. He heard Scofield again.

"There! Follow that beach! You see those ships out there? Those are ours! Stay the hell away from them. There's ack-ack up ahead, aim for it. That has to be the enemy. If they're shooting, it means our planes are passing through there. Keep your heading west!"

Adams watched the men, saw faces all looking forward, tense, silent men, the only voice the captain's. There were more flashes now, to the right side, and suddenly there was a chattering sound, like the rattle of so many pellets against the aluminum skin of the plane. The men were moving about now, twisting toward the windows behind them, useless with so much encumbrance.

Adams said, "Sit still! That's only shrapnel, spent ack-ack. If we get hit by something heavy, we won't have time to worry about it. Every one of you, grab hold of your straps, keep your arms in tight! We gotta be getting close."

Scofield was still talking to the pilots, said, "There! A lake! It's on the maps. Turn north."

The captain backed away from the cockpit, looked down at Adams. "I think we're okay. Landing zone coming up." Scofield began to move back through the plane, made his way slowly past the men. "Hang on, boys. There's a few planes still out there with us, and we're about to move over land. There's bound to be a reception for us."

The plane bounced hard again, the wings rolling to one side. Adams sat back, knew there was nothing to see now, no reason to do anything but sit and wait. The plane began to climb, gaining altitude, hard rocking of the wings. The plane jumped again, another flash of light, men reacting, the reflex, sharp cries. There was a new sound, another rattle, different, like a spray of small rocks. Shrapnel again, he thought. We're flying right through the stuff. He looked toward the cockpit, the pilots focused forward, holding the plane as steady as possible, still climbing, long streams of white tracers rising up in front of them. The plane dipped again, a hard turn to the right, Adams's stomach trying to catch up, more bumps, the plane leveling out again.

The red light suddenly blinked on, startling him, the others reacting with a mixture of shouts and grunts.

Scofield stood, called out, "Hook up! Check equipment!"

The men rose, struggling under the weight of their gear, moved into line, each one hooking his static line to the overhead cable. Adams did the same, couldn't see the doorway now, ran his hands over his belts and pockets, did the same for the man in front of him. He heard a voice, low, could barely hear the words. It was Scofield again.

"God bless you boys."

Adams leaned to the side, could see Scofield at the door, staring out, waiting. No one spoke now, no sound but the dull roar of the plane motors, the rush of wind, flickers and flashes of light in all directions, streams of machine-gun fire like small fountains on all sides of them. He felt his heart racing, cold in his fingers, stared past the man in front of him, every man frozen, all eyes on the red light. His legs quivered, and he closed his eyes, tried to fill the black, empty space, some image, some memory, his brother. But there was nothing there, nothing in his mind but the red light, and he opened his eyes, stared at the light, angry at the light, holding them there, keeping them in this deadly box, this tin coffin. Damn you!

And then, it was green.

The word burst out from the rear of the plane, rolling forward, cutting through them, pulling them toward the door, the final cry from Scofield:

"Geronimo!"

Adams lay still, his heart pounding hard, sorted through the pains, held tightly to the straps, pulled the parachute toward him, flattening it, slow, steady rhythm. He stayed on his back, could see streaks of white fire, the rattle of machine guns, no direction, no aim. They were everywhere. The parachute was flat now, and he slipped out of the harness, rolled away, pulled the Thompson from the straps behind his back, felt the pockets, the heavy bulges, ammo clips, grenades, everything still where it was supposed to be. He rolled over to one side, eased a clip into the machine gun, pulled the bolt back, slow and easy, the *click* making him flinch. The gun was loaded now, ready, the power of that rolling through him. Thank God. At least I can fight somebody.

He rolled over to his back again, stared up, stars, the moon low on the horizon, sinking, the white streaks fewer now. He saw tree limbs, silhouetted to one side of him, thought, *woods*. All right, that's a good place to be. He rolled over to his knees, raised himself up, tried to see anything, kept himself motionless, an animal, listening for prey, for any movement, the only sound the quick, hard thumps in his ears, his own heart. The machine guns rattled on, but farther away now, much farther, no danger, and he looked toward the black woods, gripped the Thompson in his hand, touched the cloth bag of grenades again, began to move.

The ground was grassy, and he was moving downhill, slow and steady, soft steps, eyes sharp, nothing to see, black trees, brush, and now, a low wall. He stopped, squatted, peeked up over the wall, good cover, good place to sit. He listened again, no sounds, felt a sudden burst of fear, anger at himself, where the hell is everybody? He wanted to call out, what? Something . . . hell, the call sign. *George.* No, not yet. Krauts could be anywhere. Machine guns.

He looked up, searched the sky, saw the Big Dipper, the edge of the "cup" pointing to the North Star. It was procedure that once they were on the ground, the last man in the stick would move in the opposite direction the plane had flown, the best way to find the others. And when we jumped, he thought, we were flying north. He leaned against the wall, tried to calm himself, slow his breathing. Good wall. Thick rock. Dammit, can't stay here. Scofield, where the hell is Scofield? South of here, for sure. We couldn't be that far apart. Where the hell is everybody else? There were too many planes, have to be guys all over the damned place. Somebody's gotta be hurt, there's always somebody hurt. But, keep quiet, no screaming, not now, not here.

He heard sounds now, a motor, stared toward the noise, saw a glimpse of motion, reflection, a truck. The truck moved slowly past, no more than fifty yards away, no lights, low voices. He gripped the Thompson, froze, perfect stillness, good cover against the rock. Don't go shooting at anything. There could be a hundred more. They're just looking around. They know we're out here. No searchlight, thank God. They think we don't hear them? He was breathing heavily still, closed his eyes, clamped his arms close in tight, slow, easy. Just . . . find somebody.

The truck was gone now, silence, more gunfire, far in the distance, voices, behind him, beyond the wall. He froze again, the voices silent, now one man, foreign, meaningless words, soft-spoken, a whisper. Adams felt ice in his gut, sweating hands holding the Thompson, the grenades beneath him, unreachable. Damn! There were footsteps, close behind the wall, one man laughing, low, soft, another voice, angry, silencing the man. Adams stared at his own legs, realized one was extended, the wall barely three feet high, his boot reflecting moonlight, like some bright, glistening light on the dark ground. Dammit! Dammit! The footsteps still moved, past him now, moving away, and now another voice, beyond the wall, from the trees.

"George!"

The men at the wall stopped, silence, and Adams tried to see them in his mind, staring at the strange sound, pointing, silent commands. Adams was pulsing with anger, thought, no you jackass. You stupid . . . who the hell . . . what the hell is the matter with you? Don't just call out! The footsteps moved away quickly, the rustle of grass, the men away from the wall, and Adams pulled his leg in close, one long, slow breath, pulled himself to his knees, raised up, peered over the wall. There was nothing, black woods, moonlight on gnarled trees. He could see the path now, where the men had been, a wide track on the far side of the wall, a cart path. He waited, listened, nothing, pulled himself up, stepped high, swung his legs over the wall, on the other side now. He dropped down again, strained to hear, the voice again.

"George!"

He felt his insides turning over, no, no, damn you, and now another cry, the same voice.

"Hey!"

And then the short, high scream.

He stared at the sounds, the voices coming again, calling out, foreign words, shadows emerging, four men, coming onto the cart path, moonlight on rifles, helmets, the men a few yards away, moving off. He pointed the Thompson, thought, a quick burst, take them all. But there was another truck now, on the road beyond the wall, coming fast, and he pulled the machine gun back close to his chest. No, don't be stupid. You'd have a hundred of these bastards on you in no time.

He stayed low, moved away from the wall, slipped into the tall grass, then past, the ground hard and flat. The trees were around him, a low limb punching his helmet. Damn! He ducked, dropped to one knee, moonlight broken by the thick clusters of branches, realized, an orchard, rows of trees. He moved farther in, to where the sounds had been, soft steps, the Thompson pointed forward, saw a bright mass, moonlight on a parachute, the chute draped across the top of a tangled tree. He moved closer, could see the dark mass beneath it, the man hanging a few feet above the ground, silent, still, and Adams was there, put a hand on the man's boots, felt cold wetness, the hard smell of blood and urine, the smell of death.

He backed away, turned toward the road. I can find them, the bastards. The sons of bitches! He was helpless!

"George!"

It was a hard whisper, behind him, and Adams froze, stood silently, his mind wrapping around the sound, the meaning. He felt a rush of energy, tried to speak, dry crust in his throat, the word coming out in a hoarse croak.

"Marshall!"

The man came toward him, another, and Adams felt his breathing again, cold turns in his stomach. Thank God!

"Private Fulton . . . Company A."

"O'Brien—"

"It's Adams. Shut up, you jackasses."

"Sarge! Oh, hell, Sarge!"

The whispers were growing louder, and Adams pulled Fulton by the shirt, a low, urgent growl:

"Shut up! Enemy all over the place!"

O'Brien moved to the dead man. "We heard him, Sarge. We got here too late to help him. Kraut bastards."

Adams pulled them both to the ground, whispered, "Guineas, probably. Shouldn't be many Krauts here. Let's cut him down, then move south. We should find some more guys. We gotta find the captain."

Adams reached into a pants pocket, pulled out his small switchblade, the same knife they all carried, for the single purpose of cutting the straps in case you found yourself hung up in a tree. It was one more piece of the training, but Adams knew it was false comfort, since if you came down in a tree, you might be too torn up to do much of anything about it. The straps were cut, the man lowered, and Adams leaned low, pulled the man's helmet away.

"Oh, Christ. It's McBride."

The others were low beside Adams, and Fulton said, "We gotta bury him."

"Not now we don't. We know where he's at. We'll come back for him. We have to move south, and right now!"

He couldn't let them hesitate, no emotion, not now, not with so much still to be done. They were three men out of three thousand, and they were lost in the enemy's backyard. Adams moved away, the others close behind him, made his way ducking low through the trees, keeping close to the edge of the orchard. He looked to the sky again, the North Star. In the stark clarity of the New Mexico skies, he had spent nights learning the stars, scanning for meteors, naming the constellations. Now, they were his guide, and for now it was the only guide they would need.

He had five men behind him, the squad fanning out slightly, easing through patches of thick brush, more walls, low boundaries that seemed to divide open grassy fields and orchards. The moon was gone, the last orange glow below the horizon, but his eyes had grown sharp, absorbing the features of the ground, landmarks sticking in his brain, shadows that had meaning.

The machine-gun fire had come again, mostly distant, several directions, no way to tell if anyone was actually in an organized fight. As they moved southward, the orchards had ended, and he kept the men close beside a wide drainage ditch, one man dropping down low, testing, confirming the depth, a soft bottom of mud and water. On the near side of the ditch, the ground rose up, a wide hillside flecked with dark patches. Adams gathered the men in close, whispered through heavy breaths.

"Let's head up to the higher ground. Maybe we can see a village, some kind of reference point. Keep low. Don't make a silhouette!"

They fanned out again, and he heard one man grunt, stumbling, the ground rocky and hard. He cursed to himself, but there was nothing to say, no one needing a reminder that the enemy could be anywhere around them. He focused on one large cluster of bushes, led them that way, thought, cover at least, maybe there'll be something to see. It would be nice to know where the hell everybody is.

He was breathing heavily, reached the brush, a thick mass of thorny bushes, the men pulling up close to him. He jerked at his canteen, shook it, still nearly full, took a short drink.

"What now, Sarge?"

"Let's keep moving. We're not doing a damned bit of good here. Go toward the crest, but stop just short. Let's take a look around."

"George!"

They froze, heads darting around, each man trying to locate the voice.

"George, you morons."

Adams smiled, breathless relief, knew the voice. "Marshall, sir."

It was Captain Scofield.

The brush in front of them was alive with movement now, and Adams saw Scofield slipping toward him, others emerging from the brush. He realized close to a dozen men were on the hillside, the brush offering them perfect cover. They said nothing, small grunts, Scofield moving close, and he put a hand on Adams's shoulder, a low whisper.

"Six of you? That's it?"

"All we've seen, sir. They killed McBride."

"They killed several, Sergeant, and we've got several more badly busted up. We made an aid station back in a drainage ditch, base of this hill."

"We saw the ditch, sir."

"If you'd have kept going, you'd have walked right into them. We saw you coming up the hill, let you get close enough so we could tell who the hell you were. I heard you talking. Eyeties don't speak English." Scofield stopped, looked back toward the crest of the hill. "Enemy machine guns are anchored along the next ridge, four or five hundred yards north. Several pillboxes, looks like. Maybe a house too. Trucks coming and going. They were shooting at shadows for a while, but somebody in charge probably shut 'em up. Eyeties, most likely. Krauts would have come out here looking for us. Eyeties would rather stay put. We got fifteen men now. Two mortar carriers, one bazooka. That's enough to get something done. I'm not going to just sit here and wait for daylight. We're supposed to engage the enemy, and he's right out there. I'd rather do it in the dark."

Scofield dropped low, flicked a match, a brief flash of light, covered by his hand.

"Three a.m. You take the right point, I'll take the left."

Scofield moved away, Adams absorbing the orders, so matter-of-fact. He stood upright, felt the quiver in his legs, scanned the hillside. To one side, Scofield was gathering the men, more low whispers. Adams felt a strange calm, could feel that Scofield was in complete control, the simple mission, *get something done*. Well, hell, what else we doing out here? He stood still for a long moment, stared up at the crest of the hill, and his brain began to work now, the questions, how many men are out there, how many machine guns? Guess it doesn't matter. No way to find out until we give them something to shoot at. Fifteen men. He looked down at the Thompson, touched the bolt, the gun still ready, unfired, no targets yet. He was impatient now, moved out to the right, still below the crest, watched Scofield, the man giving him a quick wave, pointing out to the left. Adams waited for the men to fall into position, and he felt suddenly ridiculous, childlike, fifteen men, an *army,* like so many kids in a backyard playing war. The chill was all through him now, and there was no laughter, the absurd image washed away by the fear, a flash of pure terror in his brain, spreading out through him, the annoying quiver in his legs again. He gripped the Thompson hard in his hands, fought it, the terrified voice in his brain, the urge to do anything but advance on a cluster of machine guns. There was another voice, the hard steel, months of training, cursing him, shaming him. Grab hold of it, mister! Follow the man in charge.

The men began to creep forward, Scofield leading them up and then out to the left, around the crest, keeping them low. Adams knew his role, waited for the last man to fall into line. He was doing what he had done in the desert, what he had done in the planes, keeping the men together, bringing up the rear, no stragglers, no one hanging back. The voices were quiet now. There was nowhere else to go but forward.

The fight erupted right in front of him, enemy lookouts picking up movement and sounds in the darkness. Scofield was still on the left, the men lying flat in clusters of low brush. The ground fell away behind them, narrow cuts in the rocky hillside, a gentle slope that led straight up to the pillboxes. Adams slid upward into a shallow gap, tried to raise the Thompson, the rocks too tight around him, his mind working, damn, nothing to shoot at anyway. I can crawl farther up.

Behind him he heard a hollow punch, the sound of a mortar, and he flattened out, knew to wait, the shell arcing overhead. It came down now, a sharp blast, and he raised his head, tried to see, what? Fire? Nothing else, just darkness, the enemy machine guns spraying the rocks again. The punch came again, the wait, the new blast, and Scofield was calling out, pushing the mortar crews to continue their fire.

Along the rocks beside him, men were creeping forward, pops and flashes of rifle fire, and Adams shouted out, "Cease fire! No targets! Save your ammo!" He heard motion in the rocks below him, realized he could actually see, faint light, shapes, thought, *dawn*. He saw a man slipping along, searching, looking up at him, Scofield.

The captain crawled up the hillside, was close now, said, "I'm going forward, taking one man for cover. We can't just sit here, and they're too strong for us to have a damned shoot-out. There will sure as hell be reinforcements coming up. Everybody in this country has heard this fight. We can't wait! Give me two minutes to get into position, then throw out some covering fire. Try not to shoot my ass!"

Adams said nothing, watched as Scofield slid back down the hill, crouching through the low brush. He looked to the side, faces watching him, said in a low voice, "On my command, shoot like hell. Then lay low. They'll answer."

He tried to see Scofield, the man hidden by the scrub, felt his own impatience, the Thompson itching his hands. The daylight was increasing, and he could see his hands, black with dirt, realized now, dried blood, McBride's blood. Enough of this. We can't accomplish a damned thing pinned down here. Two minutes. Hell, I lost my damned watch.

"Give it to 'em! Now!"

The men rose up, carbines and submachine guns ripping fire toward the enemy strongholds. The response came now, and Adams slumped down in his cover, the air and the rocks above him shattered by machine-gun fire, dirt and debris spraying him. He waited for a pause in the fire, rose up again, saw the shape of the closest pillbox, aimed, emptied the clip of the Thompson, the men following his lead. He dropped low again, waited, the machine guns splitting the air above him, another spray of rocks and dirt. He curled his fingers around the machine gun, saw smoke from the barrel, felt the heat of the steel.

The clip, he thought. He reached down, felt his pocket, pulled out another, stabbed it into the gun, jerked the bolt. The fire had stopped again, men searching for targets in the low light, and he eased himself slowly up, could see it all, up beyond the hill, a row of pillboxes, like fat concrete haystacks, gathered around a house. There was a burst of fire, rocks splattering against his helmet, and he slumped low again, damn! Stupid! Stay down! He saw others watching him now, men all along the hillside, familiar faces, Fulton, yes, this time I'm the moron, not you. We'll laugh about that later. The firing from the pillboxes had stopped again, and he thought of Scofield. Well, where the hell are you? Adams was sweating, furious, the Thompson pulled tight against his chest, the barrel against his cheek. Dammit! Where the hell did he go? He get himself killed?

There was a quiet pause, voices in the pillboxes, his face close to the ground, dirt and small rocks, can't stay here in daylight, this brush isn't much cover. He looked out to the right, knew he was the end of the line, but there was no cover out that way, the sloping ground bare, small dots of brush. They can't surround us that way. Unless they send a pile of men out there. He thought of Scofield's word, *reinforcements*. Yep. There could be. Here I am, Mr. One-Man Flank. Dammit, Captain, what are we supposed to do now?

There was a sharp blast, shouts from the pillboxes, short pops of rifle fire. The enemy machine gun began again, ripping the air above him, and Adams heard another sharp punching blast, the gun silent. He raised himself out of the cut in the ground, knew the sound, said aloud, "Grenades!"

There was another blast, another grenade, a flash of light at the house, smoke pouring from windows, more pops of rifle fire. There was shouting now, English, *Scofield,* and Adams responded, crawled up out of his cover, saw smoke pouring from the slits in one pillbox, felt a burst inside him, yelled out, "Let's go! Advance!"

He scrambled up the soft dirt, the men coming up behind him, a brief burst of machine-gun fire, then silence, more smoke, men screaming, loud cries, a surge of motion from the house. Adams dropped to one knee, the Thompson pointed forward, men drawing up beside him, spreading to the side, some up to the house itself, low against the flat stone. Scofield was there, close by the house, shouting at them, waving.

"Go! Inside! Prisoners!"

Adams ran forward, was at the house, smoke still pouring from a window, men calling out, foreign words, no firing now. He eased along the wall, more of his men gathering, soldiers emerging from the pillboxes, strange uniforms, hands and handkerchiefs in the air. It was over.

They had captured fifty prisoners, with more than a dozen heavy machine guns and an extraordinary supply of ammunition. Adams had to believe that Scofield was right about enemy reinforcements, that the small squad of paratroopers could not simply sit tight and wait for the enemy to pour fire on them. The prisoners were an inconvenience, certainly, but they would come along, could serve one useful purpose: haul their own machine guns, the heavy ammo boxes. They could be guarded by a few of the Thompsons, men who would bring up the rear, keeping the prisoners together, move them along, all of them pressing toward the ultimate goal, the place on the crumpled map in Scofield's jacket: Objective Y. The incredible haul of heavy machine guns was only one surprise. The second came from the prisoners themselves. They were not all Italians. Among the men were a dozen Germans, men who gave their unit as the Hermann Göring Panzer Division. They were front-line observers, the forwardmost eyes of an enemy that no one expected to see. Adams had heard the briefings, that they might find some German engineers or technicians, advisers to the Italian commands. But their prisoners told a different story. The enemy would certainly be reinforced, and when those reinforcements came forward, they might be driving tanks.

They had ninety men now, had found a cluster of headquarters personnel and scattered paratroopers, a squad of antitank fighters, bazooka carriers, all of them completely separated from their own commands. They had also found Lieutenant Colonel Art Gorham, the battalion commander, the man known throughout the Eighty-second Airborne as *Hard Nose*. With the daylight came a clear view of the lay of the land, and the satisfying conclusion that Adams and Scofield had indeed landed close to their drop zone. Their blind advance had taken them directly across the wide, hilly prominence of Piano Lupo, exactly where they were supposed to be. With Gorham now in command, the paratroopers spread out across the dismal open scrub, climbing still, assuming that once they reached the vantage point where Objective Y could be observed, they would find the rest of the 505th, or at least enough men that the assault on the enemy stronghold could be done with the power necessary to accomplish the mission.

"No one. Not a damned soul. Three thousand men couldn't just disappear." Scofield lowered the binoculars, handed them to Adams. "Here. Look for yourself. Unless I'm blind, there's not a man to be seen. You'd figure we could see somebody lying low, small groups maybe. There's shooting to the east, but way the hell off. That could be some of our guys."

Adams raised the binoculars, scanned the brush, rolling, uneven ground, nearly treeless. He saw the road, a white, dusty ribbon, an intersection, and along one side a row of low, fat concrete mushrooms.

"Pillboxes. Out there, in those hills above the road. More than a dozen of 'em."

"Sixteen. The colonel says this is it. Objective Y. The maps describe it pretty well. This is what we're supposed to hit."

Adams lowered the glasses. "With what?"

Scofield rolled over onto his back, slid down the hill, Adams following, heard no response to his question. Colonel Gorham was waiting for them, said, "Pretty clear what we have to do. We can set up the mortars in that low ground to the left, some deeper hills there. The rest of us can spread out along whatever cover we can find. We have to use the land, get as close as we can, let the mortars bust 'em up a bit. We make enough noise, it might draw some of our own men out of hiding, let them find us."

Adams looked down the wide hillside, saw the prisoners guarded by a dozen paratroopers. The Italians had seemed almost eager to surrender, officers as well as their men, the few Germans more sullen. But there was no defiance even from them, no anger, all of them seeming to be exhausted by the war, accepting captivity with quiet stoicism. He watched them for a moment, the questions rising inside him. How many battles? Where? Africa? Russia? Or maybe they've been here the whole time. But it's been a while. None of them look like recruits. It would be nice to get rid of them, not lose those men to guard duty. We need all the Thompsons we can get.

He looked toward the paratroopers now, the men lying flat, some helmets covering faces, others with canteens and ration tins, the first chance any of them had had to eat. Most of them still showed traces of the face-black, the foul-smelling ash that Gavin had ordered them to use for camouflage. It was thought best to cover their white faces in the moonlight, but now, in full daylight, the men simply looked filthy. Gorham and Scofield continued their discussion, and Adams felt his own hunger, pulled a tin of crackers from his pocket, said in a low voice, "We look like a bunch of damned savages."

Gorham stopped talking, looked at him, pointed a finger into Adams's face. "Damned right, Sergeant. That's an asset. General Ridgway said that the Eyeties have been told we're nothing but escaped convicts and Indian scalp hunters. We might as well look the part. Could scare them enough to just give up this fight. Propaganda works both ways."

"Yes, sir."

Adams crushed the dry crackers in his mouth, thought, yeah, and it could also convince them to fight like hell to keep us from capturing them. He washed the dry mush down his throat with the last swig from his canteen.

Gorham moved down the hill toward the men, and Scofield followed, motioned to Adams to follow. The men began to gather, responding to the colonel, and Gorham waited for them to close in, said in a low voice:

"It's time to go. Our objective is beyond these hills here, two thousand yards or so. We have no way of knowing what's waiting for us, so just shoot hell out of anybody who doesn't look like us, and don't stop moving forward. There's a good spot for the mortars about halfway there, and we can make it pretty hot for whoever's in those bunkers." He paused. "We could wait a while longer, try to gather up some more men. But I don't know any more than you do, and all I know is a whole bunch of para-troopers landed God-knows-where, and they're not where we expected them to be. But *we're* here, the enemy's over there, and we still have our objective." He pointed south. "The beaches are that way, and we've got a hell of a lot of infantry coming ashore. This intersection in front of us joins two roads that feed out of two key towns north of here, where the enemy is supposed to be waiting in force. Once they know where our landing zones are, they'll be hauling everything they've got this way. We have to take this intersection, and then, hold on to it. We throw up a roadblock, we can slow the enemy enough to give the infantry time to establish and fortify their footholds. If we give way, if the enemy shoves past us, those boys on the beach could be in a world of trouble. That's why we can't just sit and wait and try to find more of our people. We have to make a go with what we have. And you're it."

Adams scanned the faces, saw men looking at each other, their own silent head count. Yep. Ninety men. Geronimo.

The mortars began to drop their shells, finding the range, bursts of white smoke billowing up and around the concrete pillboxes. The men pressed forward, some of them hauling the captured machine guns, metal cartridge boxes, larger than anything the paratroopers carried themselves. With all the firepower the small force could muster, Gorham's men pushed toward the in-tersection, pressing through low gullies and dips in the sloping hillsides. As the men drew closer, they were surprised by an enormous explosion, the air above them ripped wide by a heavy artillery shell. It was long-range fire from at least one naval ship, and whether the navy had any idea if their shelling was ef-fective, to the ninety paratroopers who expected to storm the pillboxes, it produced an astonishing result. Gorham reacted quickly, relying on the enemy inside the pillboxes to be as surprised by the naval artillery as he was. The plan was risky, Captain Scofield coaching one German prisoner who spoke En-glish, giving the man an ultimatum to carry into the concrete strongholds. Scofield's ultimatum promised that unless the Ital-ians surrendered, he would direct the naval gunfire to destroy every pillbox and kill every man who held his ground. Whether or not the German noticed that Scofield had no radio at all, he did as he was told. The ultimatum worked. In only minutes, the Italians poured from the bunkers, hands raised. Objective Y, the important intersection guarded by a network of heavily fortified and heavily armed defenses, surrendered completely before any of their officers discovered just how few men confronted them, and how powerless the Americans were to call in any kind of fire from the navy.

33. ADAMS

NORTHEAST OF GELA, SICILY, OBJECTIVE Y
JULY 10, 1943

"Range?"

Scofield knelt on the crest of the ridge, stared hard through the binoculars. "Four thousand yards. Plenty of dust. Could be armor. Has to be."

Gorham rubbed a hand on his face, looked at Adams. "Spread 'em out on both sides of the road, low cover. Put the heavy machine guns on the flank. Everybody stays down. Until we know what's coming, how much strength, we don't want to tip our hand."

Scofield motioned with his arm. "Colonel, vehicles coming. One small truck, two motorcycles. They're out in front, leading the way."

Gorham crawled up beside Scofield, stared through his own binoculars. "Coming pretty quick." Gorham turned toward Adams. "Get moving, Sergeant. Flank the road, keep everybody quiet. We should eliminate that advance party, but not until they're right on us. I'll stay right here, good vantage point. Nobody shoots until I signal. You'll hear me shout."

"Yes, sir."

Adams moved away, crossed the road quickly. The men were spread out along the near side of a ridge, protected by low, thick brush. He moved up the rise toward them, faces all watching him, and he stopped, dropped to his knees, held the Thompson sideways, motioned downward, *stay low*. He crawled up to the nearest man, saw it was Ashcroft, the small, thin man lying in a shallow foxhole, fresh dirt, kicked out by the man's boots. *Good, do what you can to make some cover.* He looked toward the others, silent stares, called out, a harsh whisper:

"Pass it on! Nobody shoots until you hear the command, or until you hear *me* shoot! You got that? Show me a yes!"

The closest men waved to him, a thumbs-up, the word spreading along the ridge, more waves, and Adams watched them all, dirty faces, carbines and submachine guns pointed forward. Behind him, six men came up, carrying three of the heavy Italian machine guns, and Adams waved them out to the side, watched as they hauled the guns up the hill. Four more men came now, two more of the captured guns, the men sweating under the load of the heavy steel ammo boxes. Adams waved them to the side as well, a harsh whisper, "That way! Spread out on the flank!"

He stayed on his knees, moved up the ridge, pushed past a thick bush, long thorns, a small snake darting away. The sweat was in his eyes now, the heat rising up from the hard ground beneath him, the grit finding its way into his boots, inside his shirt. *Damn, what kind of place is this? I thought it would be good to get out of New Mexico. Hell, I brought it with me.*

He eased up to the crest, could see the road to his left, only fifty yards away, white and chalky, the dust cloud on the horizon closer, drifting off to the east. There was sound now, engines, and he froze, stared out to the low ridge in front of him, the road leading up and over the crest. The sounds were distinct, the rough growl of the motorcycles, and he settled low, peered through the thickets of brush, slid the Thompson up beside him, pressed the butt of the stock into his shoulder. They appeared now, the motorcycles rolling up over the rise, a quarter mile, the truck close behind, four men. His heart was racing, and he blinked through the sweat, eyed the iron sights on the Thompson, aimed at the man on the second motorcycle, more of the training. Plenty of men would be aiming at the first man.

They rolled closer, oblivious, and he saw the truck clearly, the black cross, the distinctive helmets. *Germans*. His hands tightened on the machine gun, his finger dancing just off the trigger, his eyes on the targets, long, slow breaths. He fought through the pounding in his ears, watched them come closer, a hundred yards, closer still, his mind listening for the word, the single short command.

"Fire!"

Adams squeezed the trigger, a burst of fire from the Thompson, the man on the motorcycle collapsing, a heap of wreckage. The ridge erupted around him, sharp bursts, pops, and the truck swerved to the side, stopped, two men spilling out, crumpled, the others pushing hands in the air, cries.

"Kamerad!"

He saw Scofield in the road, the captain running quickly toward the Germans, two more prisoners, Scofield pulling them quickly back behind the ridge. The dust cloud was boiling up over the wide hills in front of him, a mile, maybe less, and he heard Gorham, close behind him, surprising him.

"Good shooting, men! Get ready! We're not done yet!"

Gorham slid up beside him, had the binoculars, stood above the brush, stared out.

"Trucks, and a few tanks. Some Kraut officer glassing me, staring back at me. Maybe I should wave."

Adams pushed himself up to his knees, close beside Gorham, who said, "They've stopped. They're trying to figure out what to do. They have no idea what they've run into."

Adams blew dirt off the bolt of the Thompson, looked along the ridge, the men still huddled low, waiting. "That's gonna change pretty quick, sir."

Gorham moved quickly back down the hill, called out, "Captain! Bring the bazooka team up here!"

Adams watched them come, four men, hauling two of the strange metal tubes, a box of rocketlike shells. He had never fired a bazooka, wasn't sure just what you were supposed to do with it.

Gorham motioned to the ridgeline. "Find a good spot out there, to the flank. Might be the best chance we have. Don't bother to shoot at any tank that's pointing at you, won't do a bit of good. You got that?"

The men seemed to understand, and Adams looked back at Gorham, thought, don't shoot at a tank who's about to blow you to hell? Sounds to me like bad advice. But he's the officer. Gorham was up beside him again, stood out in the open, glassing toward the Germans.

"They're still not moving. Somebody over there smells a trap. Wait . . . oh, hell." He backed down the hill again. "Same orders! No one fires until I give the command! Stay low!"

Adams stared out, thought, what the hell is he talking about? He straightened up slowly, his line of sight rising, the dust cloud gone. They were no more than a half mile away, the road lined with black machines, heavy trucks, tanks with long-barreled cannon, behind, trucks hauling artillery pieces. The column stretched back around far curves in the road, more tanks, good God. The whole damned German army. Now he saw the movement, spreading out along both sides of the road, *men,* on foot, thick lines dispersing, a slow-spreading stain. The cold came again, and he dropped back down, looked for Gorham, the colonel on the far side of the road, moving among the men on the far flank, giving them the same instructions. He looked down his own ridgeline, saw the men staring at him, curious, some of them peering up over the brush.

"We're gonna do it one more time! Pass the word! No one shoots until I do! We got infantry coming at us! Pass the word!"

The routine repeated, the men acknowledging, and he rose up slowly again, glanced toward his flank, the heavy machine guns well hidden. There was movement on the low ridge to the front, the wave of men coming forward, black figures, still too far away. He settled down into the brush again, thought, all right, stay low. They still don't know where we are. *What* we are. His mind wrapped around the coldness in his chest, a question in his mind. They have no idea what's up here, so they send their foot soldiers to find out? A half dozen tanks could wipe us out in ten minutes, and they send . . . men. He peered carefully through the brush, could see the line of soldiers clearly, still advancing, guns held low, pointing forward. They closed the gap quickly, stepped through the brush, and he scanned the line, faceless, gray uniforms, thought, two hundred of them, no, closer to three. A full company. They're just . . . coming. What the hell is the matter with these people?

There was a sound along the ridge, nervous chatter, low voices, and he glared to the side, made a hard hissing sound, punched the air beside him with a fist, the word spreading quickly, the men quieting. He peered out through the brush again, saw faces, two hundred yards, the Germans still walking forward, spread out on both sides of the road. They came at a steady pace, began moving up the low ridge, still kicking through the stiff brush, one hundred yards, faces staring blankly. He saw eyes now, raw fear, terror on frozen faces, silent death, long seconds, the word coming from behind him, punching his brain.

"Fire!"

He squeezed the trigger of the Thompson, sprayed the line of men, his men on the ridge pouring out fire again. The line of Germans seemed to collapse, men tumbling forward, some spinning to the side, sharp cries, screams, some dropping down, shooting back. Farther out on the ridge, the heavy machine guns punched the air, sheets of fire, streaks of white light ripping into the Germans, shredding the brush, chopping the ground. He saw men raising their arms, trying to surrender, but the fire was too hot, hard fingers gripping heavy triggers, and in a short minute the German soldiers were simply gone.

The voices came now, movement in the low brush, men crawling away, shouts from their sergeants. Adams felt his hands shaking, stared at the twisted forms of men, some rising up, trying to run away, pops of rifle fire, and he heard the order now, Gorham.

"Cease fire! Hold your position!"

Adams rose to his knees, saw German soldiers in full flight, the survivors, terrified men, disappearing over the far ridge. The ground close to the ridgeline was speckled with dead and wounded men, movement, desperate cries. Gorham was beside him again, Scofield as well, the others on the ridge rising up, looking out as he was.

"We got a man hit, sir!"

Gorham responded, something about a medical bag, and Adams ignored him, ignored the men around him, stared at the bodies, then beyond, past the far ridge, the road, the German tanks, an officer, somewhere, one man's decision to hold back the tanks, to send his men to spring this bloody trap. He thought of Gorham's words, the propaganda, *American savages*. The anger boiled inside him, the Thompson gripped hard in his hands, the hot steel close to his chest, smoke still curling out of the barrel. I will find that German officer. I will show him what a savage can do.

The prisoners were becoming too many to handle, and the wounded paratroopers couldn't be adequately cared for, the wounded Germans not at all. Of the ninety men now under Colonel Gorham, by a miserable twist of chance there was only one medic. Each paratrooper had his own emergency medical kit, a bandage, some sulfa, one small syringe of morphine. The training had taught them how to apply it to a wounded comrade, and most of the men accepted that readily, none wanting to believe he might have to administer any of it to himself.

Gorham had no choice but to lighten the load, march the prisoners to the south, toward the landing zones, guarded by the least number of men the job would require. There seemed to be little chance that the Italians in particular would attempt to escape. As their numbers grew, the reality of their situation seemed to settle over them, and many were smiling and talkative, jovial men who seemed entirely pleased to be out of the war and under the care of the Americans. But moving so many prisoners across wide-open ground was a dangerous job, since anyone observing a column of enemy soldiers might decide to drop artillery fire on them. The navy had already demonstrated an uncanny ability to put heavy shellfire precisely where it would do the best work.

Gorham kept them spread out on either side of the road, the column of German armor still silent, Gorham and Scofield both staring through field glasses, Adams close by, waiting for orders. He kept his eyes on the wounded German soldiers, men who still had rifles, some men trying to crawl, other just calling out, soft cries, piercing wails.

Along the ridge, the Americans were responding, one man calling out, "Sir! Can't we do something?"

Gorham lowered the glasses. "No, soldier. We don't have the medical supplies, and we can't show ourselves. We're well in range of those Kraut guns, and we don't need any casualties of our own. Just hold your position."

Scofield still held his binoculars. "What are they going to do? They have to know we don't have any artillery."

Gorham shook his head. "Like hell. Some German colonel over there smells a rat, thinks we're laying an ambush. Probably figures we're not tipping our hand, and he's not about to make a mistake. If I was in his shoes, I'd send those tanks out on our flanks, sweep around, test for heavy guns. Sure as hell, he's thinking about it."

The ground in front of the ridge suddenly burst into fire, rocks and dirt blowing over them, both officers tumbling back, Adams's face sprayed full of dirt. He rolled backward, down the ridge, heard men shouting, held his helmet tight on his head, tried to see. Gorham and Scofield were dragging themselves down the hill, Scofield moving closer to Adams, a hard hand gripping Adams's shirt, pulling him downhill.

"You okay?"

Adams blew dirt from his mouth, blinked through the sand in his eyes. "What the hell? What happened?"

The blast came again, farther down the ridgeline, and Gorham began to shout now, "Stay low! Behind the ridge!"

There was another sharp blast, across the road, the hillside tossed up in a cloud of brush and debris, and Scofield said, "Artillery!"

Adams wiped his eyes, his ears ringing, and he saw men scrambling back down the ridge, behind the crest, better protection. There was another burst, back behind them, the shell overshooting them. Adams felt Scofield pulling him, the two men now at the base of the ridge, Scofield jerking him hard to the ground.

"Dammit, Captain, I'm okay!"

"Shut up! Stay low!"

The dust was thick around them, a hot breeze, and Gorham

was up, moving away, shouting to the men, pulling them all back from the ridge.

"Eighty-eights! Have to be! You don't hear 'em coming. Just the damned impact. No arc, just a flat line of fire. We should be okay behind the hill."

Adams was confused, thought, flat line? Never heard an artillery shell that didn't make a sound in the air first, let you know it was coming.

There was another blast, more dirt raining down on them, the men lying flat, and Gorham was back, said to Scofield, "We have to pull back! They keep us pinned down, they can send more infantry up here, and we won't know it until they're right in front of us. This ridge is no place to hole up from those eighty-eights. I'll go to the left flank, pull those men back. Captain, do the same here. Pull back to that high ground on the right, looks like a half mile or so."

Scofield was up quickly, said to Adams, "Go to the flank, get the machine-gun and bazooka crews out first! Don't screw around! The Krauts could roll those tanks right over this hill in about five minutes' time!"

Adams was up now, moving quickly, ignored the men, the questions. He moved toward the far end of the ridge, saw the bazooka crews in motion already, the machine gunners watching him from their positions along the ridge.

"Let's go! Pull out!"

The machine gunners dragged their guns back, the men hoisting them up on shoulders, two men per gun, making their way down through the brush. He saw the last gun, the two men struggling, and he cursed, pushed up the hill, said, "Move it! What the hell's the problem?"

The men had the gun now, and he saw that one of them was Fulton, the thin, wiry man, the gun barrel on his shoulder now.

"Good! Get going! That high ground . . . there!"

The blast came again, the shell punching through the crest of the hill above him. The force knocked him flat, his chest empty of air, gasping, choking through the dirt. He rolled downhill, tried to stand, saw the machine gun, broken, twisted metal, a man's boot, a piece of a shovel. His mind pulled him away, no, nothing you can do, and he looked for the second man, saw him now, his body spread out in the brush, Fulton, the face upturned, the helmet gone. Adams felt his knees shake, couldn't escape it, dropped down, oh Jesus, oh bloody Jesus. He saw men running, moving back, away from the artillery fire, the orders in his head, Scofield's command, *no screwing around*. He fought for his breaths, still felt the hard blow in his chest, checked the Thompson, jerked the bolt, a fresh cartridge, the gun ready again. There was another blast, back toward the road, where he had been before, and he ignored it, moved away with his men.

The sound of the tanks was clear and distinct, and Adams could feel the rumble of steel deep in his gut. The men huddled low again, another ridgeline, not much higher than the last, fewer of them now, wounded men dragged back into a low area, a deep cut in the hillside, blessed shade.

There was no shelling now, the Germans in motion, their officer finally making a decision, the column of armor pushing forward. Adams listened to the sounds, heard what they all heard, the tread of the tanks rolling on the hard-packed road, hidden only by the dust clouds and the lay of the land. He had not seen Gorham in a while, assumed him to be down on the flank, some preparation to defend the line from that direction. Adams lowered his head, touched the rim of his helmet on the Thompson. Hell of a mess, Jesse. I always thought it was the Marines who had it tough. How the hell we going to get out of this? Where the hell is everybody else? *"Hell."* He repeated the word out loud. Pretty well describes this. Not for Fulton though. Damn! He tried not to see the man's face, Donnie Fulton, the man with the weak stomach. That shell. It must have come straight through the ground, clipped right into those guys. The other guy . . . who the hell was it? Won't know until this is over, who's missing. Pieces scattered all over Sicily.

Scofield was behind him, said, "Listen up! There's tanks heading out on our left flank. I'm taking three bazooka crews out that way, see if we can do some good. Sergeant, you come with me. The rest of you stay tucked in here. Pull out only when ordered. You got that? We still have a job to do, and right now, it's slowing the enemy down. You remember what the colonel said. We're a roadblock. So, block the damned road. We don't know what's happening at the beaches, but we have to give the infantry every minute we can. Any man leaves this spot, I'll shoot him myself. Let's go, Sergeant."

Adams followed him, saw the bazooka carriers now, six men, one for each tube, one for each box of shells. They moved in silence, Scofield leading the way, Adams bringing up the rear. The dirt was softer here, and Adams heard the thick brush cracking under his boots. The heat was draining him, sweat in his eyes again, and he wiped his face on his shirt, rough grit on his skin. They dropped into a gully, dry white sand, softer still, the men struggling with the heavy boxes. Scofield pushed on, the gully narrowing, thick brush at the end, tall bushes. He stopped, held up his hand, and Adams heard the tanks, farther out, Scofield pushing up into the brush, staring out.

"Four hundred yards. They're spread out, heading to our left. They're trying to get behind our position." He turned. "You boys done this before?"

Most of them shook their heads. One man holding a bazooka said, "Only in training, sir. I was pretty good at busting up the old pickup trucks."

"Shooters, what's your names?"

"Gilhooly, sir."

"Darwin, sir."

"Feeney, sir."

Scofield looked at Adams. "Well, we're going to make veterans here, Sergeant. Can't say I know a damned thing about a bazooka, but this looks like a good spot for an ambush. Spread out, find a good place to shoot. Get comfortable. Sergeant, you move out on the left flank. I'm betting these boys can knock out one of those tanks on the first shot, and you and I might get a tank crew to shoot at."

Adams looked at the six faces, all young, scared men. The sounds of the tanks were closer now, and Scofield said, "Get in position. Pick a target, aim low on the turret. Hell they taught you that much, didn't they?"

"Yes, sir."

Adams flattened out against the side of the gully, dug his boots into the soft sand, pushed himself up, was surprised to see a tank rolling close, a hundred yards, black belching smoke,

black cross on the turret. There was another behind it, four more
to one side. He stared, felt the rumble of the tank engines all
through him, the ground shaking as they rolled closer to the
gully. His mind froze, his eyes staring at the long gun, short
stumps of machine guns pointing out in every direction. He focused on the closest tank, eighty yards, closer, slowing, turning
to avoid the gully. His hand gripped the Thompson, his mind
screaming at him, useless damned weapon. The tank was within
fifty yards now, Scofield's voice again, hard urgency.

"Anytime now. Anytime *now*."

The bazooka closest to Adams fired, startling him, the shell
erupting at the base of the tank's turret, smoke and fire. The
other two fired now, a direct hit on the second tank, more fire,
thick smoke drifting over both machines. Adams stared,
amazed, my God, it worked. The tanks were motionless, coils of
smoke erupting from the hatches, men screaming, smoke drifting across the open ground, hiding the other tanks. Adams
pointed the Thompson, searched for targets, nothing, no movement, the sounds again, the other tanks still coming. There was
machine-gun fire now, the air ripped above him, the men ducking down, tank engines in a loud roar, closer, moving around the
gully.

Scofield shouted, "Pull back! Stay in the gully, stay low!"

The men moved in one motion, Adams in the lead, and he
looked back, saw the young men moving quickly, driven by the
pure terror, the enormous machines rolling alongside the gully,
past them, in front of them now. Adams stopped, saw the closest
tank, the turret swinging around, a voice behind him.

"Get down!"

He was pushed from behind, his face in the soft sand, a loud
explosion above him, a bazooka firing, Scofield pulling him up.

"Let's go! Keep moving!"

Adams ignored the sand in his eyes, ran, stayed in the low,
soft ground, the sounds of men behind him, tank engines,
machine-gun fire. The gully flattened out, and he stopped,
searched frantically for cover, some low place, the ridgelines familiar, gentle slopes.

Scofield was past him now. "This way! Get over that hill!"

There was a thunderous blast, the ground rising under

Adams's feet, tossing him up, rolling him. He tried to see, motion, a man running, another, and he followed, staggered, pain in his leg, his side, stumbled up the hill, machine-gun fire chopping the ground behind him. He was over the crest now, saw Scofield, another man, sliding down. Adams looked back, one man running hard, machine-gun fire, the man collapsing, the bazooka still in his hand, bouncing on the ground. Adams fired the Thompson, useless rage, the tank turning toward him. He dropped down the hill, protection, Scofield calling to him, "Move! Let's go!"

His legs were rubber, his heart ripping his chest, Scofield in front of him, pointing.

"There!"

Adams followed, the two men dropping into a cut in the hillside, the third man there quickly. Adams looked at the man, one of the ammo carriers, no ammo, no bazooka, Scofield shouting into his face, "What happened to the others? Did you see them hit?"

The man was frozen, stared at Scofield with wild animal eyes, and Adams said, "I saw one man go down, Darwin I think. Didn't see the others. We can't stay here, sir."

"The hell we can't. Those tanks aren't going to waste fuel chasing us all damned day. They're behind our flank, and there's not a whole hell of a lot we can do about it without a weapon. We have to find a way back to the colonel, get everybody pulled back toward the beach. I know what he said, but we can't hold the tanks back. We've done the best we could. Unless we get the hell out of here, we're just going to end up as prisoners. You ready to be captured?"

"Not today, sir."

"Where are the tanks? Let's see what direction—"

There was a high ripping sound, louder, the roar of a freight train, and now the impact came, the ground shuddering beneath them. Adams ducked low, and Scofield said, "What the hell?"

It came again, another thunderous blast, out beyond the ridge, the three men shrouded in dust, the stink of explosives. Adams held himself tight against the ground, waited, another shell, the same impact, the ground shaking him. Scofield crawled up beside him, peered out, then dropped quickly down, covering his head.

"Artillery fire! Big stuff!"

Adams tried to hear the tanks, to hear anything else, his ears a fog of deafness, another shell impacting, farther away, two more, Scofield suddenly slapping him.

"Coming from the south! The navy! It's naval fire!"

The third man was down below them, grabbed Adams's boot, pointed out behind them, beyond the ridge.

"Sir! Infantry!"

Adams turned, the Thompson coming up, saw a dozen men, crawling forward, one man with a radio, the wire whip in the air above him.

Scofield said in a low voice, "Easy, boys. Those look like the good guys."

Adams slid down, followed Scofield out of the crevice, saw Scofield raise his arms, thought, yep, damned good idea. He held the Thompson up high, waited for the young private, followed the man into the open. The shelling had stopped, the air thick with the smells, gunpowder and gasoline, black smoke rising up from beyond the ridge. Scofield kept his own Thompson in the air, and the soldiers began to rise, calling out, the ringing deafness in Adams's ears clearing just enough, voices reaching him, the man with the radio, another beside him, an officer.

"Awfully close. Sorry. Couldn't be helped. Those panzers were about to cause your people some serious trouble. Looks like we chased them away for now."

Adams lowered his gun, blinked through the crust and filth in his eyes, saw smiling faces, another man calling out, "Hey Lieutenant, they don't seem glad to see us."

The officer saluted Scofield. "Frank Griffin, sir. Sixteenth Infantry Regiment. Colonel Crawford's boys."

Scofield returned the salute, and Adams saw now, the shoulder patch, every man. The young private had been right. They were infantry. It was the Big Red One.

34. ADAMS

As the fighting quieted with the end of the daylight, Gorham's paratroopers were attached to the Sixteenth Infantry, men who filled the hillsides around them, holding the ground just north of Piano Lupo, what they knew now as Hill 41, waiting, as the paratroopers waited, to see if the German armor would come yet again. With nightfall, the confusion on both sides had been complete and stifling. Gorham's men could still not locate any more of the 505th, had no way of knowing that when the jumps had been made, the C-47s had been scattered by the gale across a front sixty miles wide, some coming down as far away as the British zones to the east. But there had been benefit to the chaos, and though few of the paratroopers had found more than a few of their own, the small squads of men had vigorously attacked whatever enemy positions they could find. Telegraph poles and phone lines had been cut, rear-echelon outposts assaulted, German and Italian troops encamped miles from the front lines suddenly set upon by what the enemy supposed were tribes of war-painted maniacs. With so much scattered confusion, the interruptions in the communications between front line and rear headquarters posts gave rise to fantastic rumors. Eventually, word filtered back to the highest levels of the Italian command, estimates that more than a hundred thousand Americans had come out of the sky.

For Gorham's paratroopers, the day ended very near where it had begun, the men still holding to the ground that protected the beachheads, where American infantry, artillery, and armor

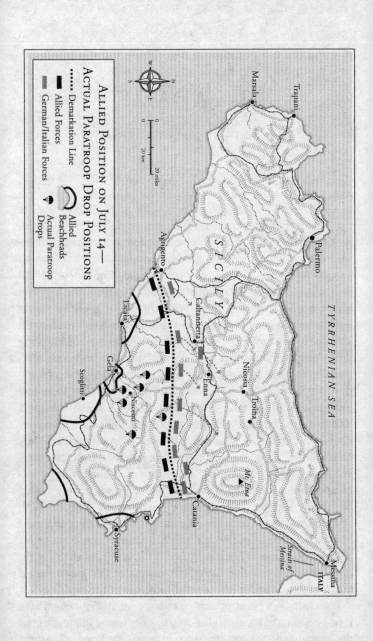

ALLIED POSITION ON JULY 14 —
ACTUAL PARATROOP DROP POSITIONS

Demarcation Line
Allied Forces
German/Italian Forces
Allied Beachheads
Actual Paratroop Drops

N W E S

0   20 miles
0   20 km

SICILY

TYRRHENIAN SEA

Marsala
Trapani
Palermo
Agrigento
Caltanissetta
Enna
Nicosia
Troina
Mt. Etna
Catania
Licata
Gela
Scoglitti
Niscemi
Syracuse
Messina
ITALY
Straits of Messina

continued to come ashore, strengthening and securing what was still a vulnerable position.

Adams drank the last gulp from his tin cup, cold, bitter coffee, twisting his tongue. In the darkness around him, men worked, digging in, some taking time to eat or just lie flat and sleep. Colonel Gorham had kept Adams close by, using him as a liaison to the infantry that added to their strength. Throughout the early evening, Adams's job had been to help move the infantry into position, working alongside young, untested lieutenants, men who regarded the paratroopers as grizzled veterans, the men who had faced the enemy and survived. No matter that the experience that so inspired the admiration of the slick-faced infantry officers had come in only one full day of combat.

Adams didn't know where Scofield had gone, but there was work to be done all along the perimeter, men energized by the sounds coming across the rolling hills around them, German armor gathering, waiting, as they waited, for the first hint of daylight. For now, Adams's work was done, and he had returned to Gorham, had time to tend to his own foxhole, his own meal, to prepare himself once more for the enemy, which even now was using the cover of darkness to edge closer to the American position.

"What's your name, Sergeant?"

"Adams, sir."

"I know. Your first name."

"Jesse, sir."

"Good work today, Jesse. Damned fine work. Some of these your men?"

"Yes, sir. Several. I found most of our stick. We jumped with Captain Scofield."

Gorham put a piece of dry bread in his mouth, and Adams searched his pockets for another piece of his dinner, found a tin of the instant coffee, poured it into his cup, black glue now in the bottom of his cup. He felt for his canteen, nearly empty again, had done what many of the men had done, filling it from a small stream at the base of the hill. He poured the water into the cup, swirled it with a dirty finger, poured it down his throat, his throat clenching tight, a struggle to keep it down.

Gorham seemed to hear his grunt. "Vile stuff. Nasty. I'd settle for a glass of Italian wine about now. I'm sure the Krauts
have their share."

"Yes, sir. We'll find some."

Adams looked out over the hillside, nothing to see, darkness
hiding the men. There could be no fires, nothing to draw enemy
observers, the men huddling low in makeshift foxholes. He
pulled his jacket tighter, had not expected the harsh chill, the
darkness bringing a blanket of cold across the open scrub.

Gorham made a crunching sound with his teeth. "Damn. This
stuff must be left over from San Juan Hill. Remind me,
Sergeant, we get back to where somebody important might be,
put in a requisition for some decent rations."

"Yes, sir."

Adams saw Gorham looking at him, couldn't see the man's
expression.

"Don't talk much, do you, Sergeant?"

Adams chose his words carefully. "I haven't spent a lot of
time talking to senior officers, sir. But when I did, I always
thought it best to do more listening."

"Me too. You ever been in a powwow with a half dozen generals? Well, no, probably not. It's a little like that coffee you just
drank. Hard to swallow."

Adams was surprised by Gorham's openness, had heard much
of the man's nickname, Hard Nose. Gorham had a reputation for
gruff discipline, little tolerance for anyone who simply didn't
measure up. It wasn't supposed to be that way, not from a senior
officer anyway. The army had seemed to insist that anyone who
couldn't endure paratroop training not be ridiculed for it. There
were plenty of good soldiers outside the paratroop regiments,
including men that Adams knew were on the hillside around
them now, men of the Big Red One who could handle themselves against the enemy as well as anyone. But Gorham was
said to have no hesitation to break a man with words, if that man
was not making the grade. Adams had no problem with that,
thought that the army should be training the paratroopers to be
something special, an elite force, what most of them accepted as
their role anyway. From their uniforms, boots, insignia, they
were different from the infantry, and every man in the Eighty-

second Airborne considered himself a superior soldier. Whether or not the army wanted them to brag about it, Adams didn't really care. Apparently, neither did Gorham.

Adams felt the weariness crawling over him, searched the ground, soft dirt, good place for a shallow dug-out bed. He rolled his pack over, pulled the shovel out.

Gorham said, "You mind if I use that when you're done? Mine seems to have disappeared."

"I'll dig a hole for you, sir. Where would you like it?"

Gorham laughed. "So, you don't think lieutenant colonels should work for themselves? Or maybe you think I forgot how to dig a hole in the ground? You get done there, give me the damned shovel."

Adams held it out. "You first, sir."

Gorham laughed again. "Dig your own, Sergeant. I can wait."

In the darkness there seemed to be something in Gorham's voice, something Adams hadn't noticed before. Youth.

"Excuse me, sir. You a West Pointer?"

"Yep. Class of 1938."

"You get a late start, sir?"

"Is that your way of asking me how old I am, Sergeant? I'm twenty-eight. Same as Captain Scofield, I think. You?"

"Twenty-one, sir. Didn't mean to be personal."

"Stuff that. Any man who gives you orders that might get you killed, you have a right to know who the hell he is. I'm from Brooklyn, New York, originally. Grew up in Ohio. My wife is at Bragg right now. I have a son, six months old. Might get to see him again before he goes to college. You married?"

Adams choked on the question. "Good God, no, sir. I mean . . . sorry, sir, never had the opportunity. Not too many available girls where I come from. They either marry right out of high school, or, the smart ones, they just leave. Men too. Copper country, New Mexico. Not a place likely to attract anyone looking for West Pointers."

"Why you decide to jump out of airplanes?"

"I like it, sir. Pay's good. They made me a sergeant pretty quick, said there'd be more to do than yell at grunts on latrine duty." He paused. "They were right."

"You know much about the history of the paratroopers? Interesting stuff. Think about it, Sergeant. Imagine the first fellow that said, gee, today I'm going way the hell up in a hot-air balloon and then jump out. Maybe I won't die."

Adams worked the shovel, the foxhole deepening, tried to form the image. "Pretty impressive. Took some guts. How'd he even know what a parachute would do, if it would work at all?"

"He tested it. Frenchman named Blanchard, back in 1785. Being the good Frenchman, though, he didn't do the test on himself. Decided to try it first with a dog. He actually tossed the poor little bastard out of a hot-air balloon. It worked too. The dog hit the ground and apparently made it okay. Then he took off running and nobody ever saw him again. Can't say I blame him."

Adams stopped digging, looked at Gorham, tried to see the man's face, thought, is he full of crap or just a good storyteller?

"Excuse me, sir, but how did the French fellow know how to build a parachute? Just guess at the design?"

"You're a skeptic, Sergeant. But it's all true. The design came from Leonardo da Vinci, and somewhere, those drawings can still be seen. He sketched a triangular-shaped cone, wrote all about how it would actually work, given his careful calculations. Of course, da Vinci could claim anything he wanted. He didn't have a hot-air balloon or anything else to make a real test. If somebody had showed up with an airplane, da Vinci might have decided to recheck his numbers."

"If he was so damned smart, he would have come up with the dog idea. Could have tossed it right off a church steeple."

"You're right. Good idea. Guess that's why you made a sergeant."

Adams dug again, Gorham eating something from his ration tins, and Adams stopped, stepped one foot down in the hole, measured the depth to a second hole beside it.

"There you go, sir."

"What do you mean? You dug a hole for me?"

"You were eating, and I had the shovel in my hands. Was no trouble at all, sir. I figured you'd probably expect an enlisted man to do it anyway."

Gorham laughed again. "That's why they made me a lieutenant colonel."

Hill 41—July 11, 1943

The armor rolled toward them at first light, heavy steel on rough roads, spreading out in open country, tank commanders seeking their own avenues into the vulnerability of the American positions. The infantry had done as the paratroopers beside them, dug in to shallow protection, but the German tanks had continued to use the darkness to spread out in wide formations, ready to drive hard into and around the flanks of the Americans, with little the men in their cover could do to stop them.

Adams heard the first blast, hard thunder on the hill behind him, a direct hit on a narrow trench. The cries came quickly, wounded men, and then, new sounds, rolling over them, artillery, the shells cutting the air from behind, from the south, his mind wrapping around the thought, *friendly fire.*

The shelling grew louder, dropping close to the men, and Adams hugged the ground beneath him, hands gripping dirt, the impacts bouncing him. Men were calling out all around him, their voices extinguished by the roar of shellfire. His brain screamed at him, curses at men far behind him, what the hell are you doing? You're hitting your own people! He knew there were radiomen with the infantry, thought, damn them! Someone call back there, surely some idiot observer can see where the shells are falling! All they're shooting at is tanks, and we're right in the middle of them!

The artillery fire began to move away, blanketing the ground to one side, gunners seeking targets from the formations of moving tanks. He let out a breath, the artillery fire slowing, yes, some officer just reamed out a spotter. I find you, I'll thank you. The sounds of tanks were all around him now, punches of fire down the hill in front of him, the roar from heavy engines, clanking steel growing louder. He rose up, a quick look, saw the tanks moving in all directions, no formations at all, single machines, turrets spinning, guns firing, targets close, point-blank impact. Their machine guns were firing as well, each tank an arsenal of its own, men in the trenches helpless, the artillery still bouncing dirt and rock close to the tanks, but not close enough. Gorham peered up beside him now, shouted something, and Adams saw a man scrambling low, rolling toward them, a captain, young, too young. The man said something to Gorham, and Adams saw the shoulder patch, infantry, the man pointing back along the ridge.

Gorham nodded, waved the man away, shouted to Adams, "Gather up anyone you can! Head to the highest ground, or any good cover! The tanks are moving around behind us! We're about to be surrounded!"

Gorham was up and gone now, and Adams crawled from his cover, a quick glance at the Thompson, dirt in the magazine, a sharp breath, jerked the bolt, clearing a fresh shell. He scanned the shallow foxholes, a pattern of pockmarks in the low brush, saw men firing weapons, useless exercise, one man heaving a grenade, more futility, the impact only adding to the smoke. He kept low, ran down the ridge, shouted, anyone, men looking at him, some understanding, pulling out, moving away quickly. Men were emerging from the cover in small waves now, no orders, just leaving, the infantry, green men, too much fire, too close to an enemy none of them had faced before. He dropped into a foxhole, shouted to anyone who might be close by, "Pull out! Retreat to the hilltop!"

No one responded, the ground in front of him empty, the men gone already. The sound of steel was close, the roar of a single engine, black smoke, and one tank rolled up from the low ground, suddenly in front of him, fifty yards, easing along the hill, the turret turning slowly, searching, scattered fire from the machine guns. He raised the Thompson, reflex, pulled it back down, stared at the tank, much larger than what he had seen the day before, thought, good God, that's a Tiger. Has to be.

The tank's big gun fired, a long tongue of flame, thick smoke, the shell streaking right over him, a quick blast farther up the hill. He felt for the grenades, one bulging pocket, all he had left, thought, what the hell do I do? Climb up on the damned thing? The tank turned toward him, the treads ripping the ground, rolling up the hill, a surge of power, a thick cloud of smoke. The machine guns were firing again, and he ducked low, the ground shaking. He raised his head, the tank only yards away, no place to go, and he dropped, flattened himself in the shallow hole, the sounds of the tank deafening, darkness, a great steel monster, rolling over him, loud-screaming terror in his brain. The tank kept moving, slow seconds, the ground flattening around him, more smoke.

And then it was past.

He sat up, stared at the tank, sweat and mud in his clothes, dirt in his eyes, his heart racing. The tank continued up the hill, the big gun firing again, the shell ripping a flaming hole in a cluster of brush. He reached for the grenades, his hands shaking, no, don't be a jackass! It's too damned big! More tanks were in the distance, one turning his way, following its companion into the fight, the first tank rolling right toward the men Gorham had pulled away, the cover worthless, nothing to hold back the Tiger. Adams shouted aloud, wordless fury, crawled up out of the hole, moved low along the deep scars in the earth, the path of the huge tank. He saw men running again, emerging from cover, a mad scramble back over the ridge, machine-gun fire on the far side, tanks there as well, Gorham's word punching him: *surrounded*. Can't just sit here! We need bazookas! Where? He was frantic now, pulled himself up the hill, the machine-gun fire everywhere, pops of rifle fire, the infantry's futile defense. The Tiger was gone, over the crest of the hill, and he ran up that way, his hands on the grenades. Dammit! Get close to him! You had your best chance!

The hilltop was bathed in gray smoke, a putrid fog, chaos below him, fire and tanks and running men. The men were moving off in one direction, deep-cut ground, another hill, difficult for tanks. Yes! That way! There were men around him now, shattered and bloody, some movement, the wounded, no sounds but the awful roar of the tanks, the thunder and rattle of the guns. He moved down the hill, saw men scrambling up the ragged ground, one man with a bazooka, emerging from the brush, moving into open ground, the man dropping to one knee, the bazooka on his shoulder. It was Gorham.

The tank's gun erupted, punching the air, a blast of fire, smoke, the barrel aimed directly at Gorham. Adams felt his gut turn, ice in his legs, dropped to his knees, the smoke clearing. Gorham was lying flat, the bazooka twisted and bent, the tank moving on, more targets. Adams fired the Thompson, sparks on the tank, was running now, slid down beside Gorham, ripped, smoking earth, a deep gash in the man's forehead, a thick flow of blood. Other men were there now, an officer, a medical bag, and the ground erupted again, a blast close behind them, another shell, the man tossed aside, rolling over on him, Adams pushed flat on his back. He tried to move, the man on his chest, crushing, the sounds a hollow bell in his ears. There were more men, and he felt hands, wiped at blood on his face, the body above him pulled away, the sounds coming again, words, *medic*. They were working on Gorham, but Adams knew the look, the stare, lifeless, the bazooka still hooked in the man's hand, and Adams would not see it now, could not watch Gorham's death, closed his eyes, pulled the Thompson in close to his chest, lay back on the ground. He blinked hard, wiped the dirt from his eyes, began the old ritual, searching for pains, for anything broken. Then he rolled over, pushed himself to his feet, and followed the men back into the cover.

The fight lasted most of the rest of the day, German armor pressing hard toward the beachheads, the paratroopers and infantry powerless to hold them back. But Gorham's efforts, and the success of the first day's actions, had delayed the advance of the German armor by a full twenty-four hours. With the luxury of that much time, the landings along the center of the American zone had proceeded virtually unmolested. Despite the powerful advance of the panzers, the landing zones on the southern beaches were now firmly under American control. As the landings progressed, the tanks and artillery were finally brought to the sand dunes, radiomen, observers, aided by spotter airplanes, directing communication with the gunners on board the warships. By the time German armor came within range of the beachheads, the fight had become a duel, not between German tanks and American infantry, but between the panzers and American tanks and artillery. Confronted by the additional power of the British navy's big guns, the Germans could not sustain their attack, and by nightfall, the German commanders had no choice but to pull away, salvaging what armor they could save, and to accept that their efforts to prevent the American landings had failed.

To the east, Colonel Gavin had found himself far beyond where he was supposed to be, had come down closer to the

Forty-fifth Division's landing zone. But Gavin had done as Gorham had done, gathered what few men he could find, making the best fight he could make. Gavin accomplished his own unplanned objectives, a difficult series of fights that gave the Americans there precious time to secure their position. Along every beach, in every zone from the British landings on Sicily's eastern coast, to the Third Infantry Division's landing in the westernmost zone near Licata, progress was being made, the enemy resistance wilting, unable to stand up to the strength of the invasion.

By all measures, the paratroop drops had been a dismal failure, the thirty-four hundred men scattered well beyond the primary drop zones, some of the C-47s and their human cargo blown as far as the British positions to the east. But at Piano Lupo, the goals had been met, the objectives captured, an enormously powerful force of the enemy held away. The death of Lieutenant Colonel Arthur Gorham could not overshadow his accomplishments. Though his orders had specified that he attack his objectives with a full combat battalion, he had accomplished extraordinary success with less than a hundred men.

35. PATTON

During the original planning sessions for Operation Husky, Eisenhower had approved Patton's authority to call in more manpower at certain points along the beachheads, as Patton saw fit. With the hold on the beaches close to Gela still fragile, Patton believed he should add strength to the troops that were struggling to drive the panzers away, and so, early on July 11, Patton had made a call to Matthew Ridgway, commanding the Eighty-second Airborne. Ridgway had been prepared for Patton's order, that the Eighty-second send a second wave of paratroopers to make a drop around the Ferella Airfield, west of

Gela, adding considerably to the strength of the ground troops who might still be under a serious threat from German armor.

On July 9, only one section of the 504th Regiment had made the first jump with the 505th, but most, some two thousand men, had stayed behind. As the desperate fighting rolled over the hills of southern Sicily, the men of the 504th milled about at the airfields around Kairouan, wondering if they were destined to remain behind in Tunisia, sitting idly while the rest of the Eighty-second Airborne earned a glorious reputation in Sicily. But by late morning on July 11, Ridgway had passed along Patton's instructions to his officers, and once those orders reached the paratroopers, their mood changed from gloom to raucous enthusiasm. By dusk, the equipment had been loaded, the men strapped into the chutes. Near eight o'clock, with darkness drifting over the fields, 144 C-47 transports took to the sky. The pilots had been instructed to fly the same circuitous routes that many of them had flown two nights earlier, but the winds had calmed, and despite the darkness navigation was thought to be far less complicated for this second jump. But there was one adjustment to the routes the pilots had flown through the horrific gale of July 9. With so many navy ships anchored just offshore from the Sicilian beaches, it was thought to be far safer for the lumbering C-47s to fly the last thirty-five-mile leg of the mission more to the north, just over the land itself, avoiding nervous antiaircraft gunners on board the ships, who had already endured numerous assaults from enemy planes.

During the first jump on July 9, the C-47s had drawn ground fire from the beaches themselves, scattered gun emplacements, manned mostly by Italian troops who had no real idea what was happening around them, who had no reason to expect that the drone of airplane motors above them heralded the start of an enormous invasion. But this time, those same beaches were held by weary American and British troops, with antiaircraft guns of their own, who knew exactly what the enemy could do, who had been bombed and strafed by German planes both night and day since the landings began.

Patton knew there was a potential for serious mistakes, and orders had gone out to every one of his primary subordinates, to Bradley and the division commanders, passed down to the officers who held tight rein on the discipline of their gunners. The orders were plain and direct, details of the 504th's mission, when and where the C-47s were coming. The final caution was given to gunners on both land and on sea, that antiaircraft batteries had to be certain of their targets before firing.

Throughout the day and the early evening on July 11, well before the men of the 504th took to the air, German planes had continued to attack, the Allied antiaircraft gunners responding with weary intensity. By ten thirty that night, those gunners were anticipating another long night of assaults, itching for another chance to knock the enemy planes out of the sky. As the drone from the C-47s drew louder, the orders from the ground commanders became meaningless, the officers unable to control the nervous intensity of the men at the guns. When the planes began to pass, it began with one man, his discipline giving way, sweating hands on a steel trigger. No officer could control what the man saw in his mind, glimmers of moonlight from planes flying closely overhead, his mind replaying the image of so many dive-bombers, the black crosses, too many near misses, the ground quaking beneath him too many times. When the man pulled his trigger, the reaction was predictable and tragic. From the batteries along the sand dunes, to the gunnery stations on the nearby ships, the single streak of fire ripped the taut nerves of every man at every gun. Within seconds, the sky was alive with a storm of red tracers.

In the planes, the helpless paratroopers knew it was friendly fire, lessons from training. The enemy's tracers were white, Allied fire was red. With only sluggish maneuverability, the C-47s couldn't avoid the devastating effects of the fire. Some simply came apart, exploding in midair, a *victory* for the gunners, which only stoked their manic enthusiasm. Some of the planes were disabled, the pilots steering helplessly toward the shallow waters, a desperate attempt to save their men and themselves. Survivors struggled from the wreckage, only to be machine-gunned by soldiers on the beach, the men who watched the show proud of the deadly accuracy of their gunners. Some of the pilots simply panicked, illuminating the green jump light prematurely, the paratroopers obeying, anxious to escape, some not reaching land at all, men drowned by the weight of their gear. The lucky ones made it through, and those pilots at the tail end of the caravan, who recognized what was happening, turned away, either moving inland quickly or turning back altogether, to find their way once more to the safety of Tunisia.

Though a good many aircraft completed their run to the target, most were damaged, some barely able to stay in the air. Twenty-three aircraft were destroyed altogether, some still occupied by the helpless men of the 504th. Many more paratroopers died as a result of their jumps, some never to be found.

HMS <u>MONROVIA</u>, PATTON'S HEADQUARTERS, NEAR GELA, SICILY—JULY 12, 1943

From the first minutes of Eisenhower's arrival, Patton knew that the visit was to be a dressing down. But Eisenhower's fury wasn't reserved just for Patton, and Patton understood that no matter how much blame was assigned to anyone below him, the responsibility for any disaster lay firmly on the shoulders of the commanding officer. For now, Patton could do nothing but listen, absorbing Eisenhower's wrath, building wrath of his own, shaping and harnessing his temper, hoping that he would find out himself what had gone so terribly wrong. Despite the good work of the troops along the beaches, the efforts of so many good men who had done so much, the entire operation now had a bitter taste, a pall cast over it by an outrageous act of stupidity. The word was repeated by Eisenhower, *tragedy,* and Patton could only nod, allow Ike to complete the tirade, the man redfaced, pacing the cabin. But Patton was growing more annoyed, did not care to be dressed down by anyone, not even Eisenhower.

"Dammit, Ike, we sent out word to everyone, told every commander in every zone that the planes were coming! What the hell else was I supposed to do?"

"I don't want to hear that, George. This is your command, and it was your responsibility to make sure that your people knew when those C-47s were coming over. What do you think is going to happen back home when the newspapers hear of this? What do you think Marshall will say, or the president? What do they tell the parents of those boys? 'Sorry, but we made a mistake. Nobody's to blame.' I won't accept that, George! And neither will the American people!"

Patton turned away, walked to one corner of the cabin, turned back, faced him. I have enough problems, he thought. I don't need a full-blown war with Ike.

Eisenhower said, "Start an investigation, George. Talk to the navy people. The British had a hand in this too."

"Of course the British had a hand in it. I'm glad you see that. I know you have to jump on my ass. Fine, I can take that. But there's a few other asses who need jumping on too." He saw a deep frown on Eisenhower's face, dammit, shut up! Don't stir this pot again. "Sorry. That's not the point, of course. Look, Ike, I've already sent inquiries to the navy, to every ground commander. So far, no one is saying anything. No twenty-year-old is going to step up and tell his commanding officer that he fired the first shot. You want me to start relieving people? All right I will. I'll send every damned lieutenant home. Will that satisfy the president?"

"Knock it off, George. I'm not looking to hang some kid because he made a mistake. But this happened because that kid wasn't prepared for it. That's his commander's mistake, and if his commander wasn't prepared, it's your mistake. If you want to run the big show, George, you have to accept responsibility for it. There's no such thing as *nobody's responsible*. I'm quite sure that we may never know how this started. But we have to finish it, and not just by burying paratroopers. For one thing, we will make damned sure this never happens again!"

Patton stiffened. "You can be certain of that."

Eisenhower paced slowly, and Patton could hear artillery in the distance. Eisenhower stopped, listened, the thunder growing, different, not cannon, hard thumps: bombs.

"I thought we cleared the skies. The enemy still hitting us from the air?"

Patton shrugged. "Scattered attacks. There are thirty airfields on this island. We'll get to 'em soon enough. Gotta admire those Nazi pilots. They know they probably won't make it back to their bases before the Spitfires knock them out."

"The only enemy I admire is one who surrenders, George."

Patton frowned, turned away again. He couldn't let Eisenhower know how he felt, but he had no interest in hearing bluster from a man who had never stood up to enemy fire. It was too common, the men at the top, big noise about forcing the enemy to do this and that. Try it sometime, Ike. Then tell me how to make them surrender.

Eisenhower seemed to ignore his scowl, moved to a small wooden chair, sat, glanced out the porthole.

"I had serious problems with the whole plan for this airborne assault, George. Clark, Ridgway . . . I let them convince me. Not sure I would do it again."

Patton moved closer in front of him. "I can't agree, Ike. Those boys opened the door. Damned Krauts had a hell of a lot more armor here than our boys expected. We might not have made it if those Tiger tanks had been waiting for us right at the beach."

"Maybe. But I understand the paratroopers were scattered all over hell. We're lucky we didn't lose the whole lot of them."

Patton tightened the grip on his words, took a slow breath. "I disagree again. It worked to our advantage. They raised hell behind the enemy lines in far more places than we had intended them to. Allen's people tell me they were responsible for holding up the panzers for hours, if not all damned day. There're some medals to be handed out, Ike. Lots of them. From the reports I've seen so far, they came down over a sixty-mile area. Sure, you can describe that as *scattered to hell*. I describe it as putting good men in more places than the enemy can handle."

Eisenhower shook his head. "But if that *sixty miles* had been farther inland, or to the west, they'd have been stumbling around in the middle of nowhere, with no enemy in sight. It would have been a wasted effort. We'll take a hard look at this, when this is over."

Patton clenched his jaw, said slowly, "Whatever you say, Ike."

There was a silent moment, and Patton rocked back on his bootheels, hands clasped behind his back, thought, leave, dammit. I have work to do.

Eisenhower said, "Did Alex tell you he wants to meet with you? Both you and Monty, once we're in a more secure position. Monty's front seems pretty tight, the port of Syracuse is under our control. The enemy there is backing away toward the big hills to his north. You know what you have to do here. Keep the enemy moving backward, keep those panzers off our front lines. We're stepping up the air attacks, tracking down those tanks wherever we can find them. That should keep them on the run. I understand the Italians are surrendering in boatloads."

"Yes, sir, they are. That will continue. If we push hard enough."

"No one's stopping you, George."

Patton said nothing, waited for more.

Eisenhower stood, adjusted his jacket. "I'm off, then. I'd like to go ashore, see some of the positions along the beach before I head back to HQ. I understand the Canadians did some exceptional work east of here. I'd like to offer them a congratulations, help their morale if possible. I think some of their people back home assume we don't give them enough credit."

"Good idea."

Eisenhower was at the cabin door now, glanced toward the maps, hanging low on one wall.

"Nice work, George. Let's wrap this up, capture the whole lot of them."

"Already planning on it."

Eisenhower ducked through the doorway, and Patton let out a long breath, felt a pain in his chest, like some giant fist holding him upright. The cabin was both his office and his stateroom, and he moved into the small bedroom, sat on the narrow bed. He thought of the tragedy, the loss of so many paratroopers, the stupidity of that. It was the darkness, pure and simple. Why the hell couldn't we just send them in broad daylight and guard the hell out of them with Spitfires? Who is making these decisions? It had gnawed at him for months now, the control the British seemed to have over Eisenhower. He thought of Eisenhower's shoes, the first thing he'd noticed when the man had arrived. Brown suede shoes, just like something a British field marshal would wear. Dammit, Ike, you're becoming more *British* than they are. Keep everyone happy, don't make any decision until it is talked to death. This won't last, can't last. They'll use you up, spit you out when they're done with you, and the rest of us will find out what they've been planning all along. This war isn't about Hitler, it's about England. We're here because the English want us here, but dammit, Ike, when this is over, you'll see how little use they have for us.

One thing I have to admire, he thought. I'm still here. Ike could have yanked me for this paratroop mess, and he didn't, at least not yet. I probably owe him for that. But they'll find something, sooner or later.

He stood, moved out into the main cabin, stared at the maps, heard voices outside, British crewmen moving past. He peered through the porthole, ships spread out along the shore, movement everywhere, the landings still ongoing, supplies and equipment moving ashore in a steady flow. I need to be off this ship, he thought. Pretty soon, we should be able to move the command center to Gela, or someplace close, set up a permanent HQ. I'll get flack about that, I'll bet. The British will want me here as long as they can convince Ike this is where I should be. Damned ship is like a prison. Can't take a pee without some limey writing it down.

GELA, SICILY—JULY 14, 1943

He looked at the basket in the staff officer's hands. "Champagne . . . and what's that? Cheese?"

"Yes, sir, that's all we could find."

Patton grunted, looked around the huge room, towering ceiling, ornate paintings spread all along the alabaster walls, marble trim, the floor marble as well.

"What a waste. All this artwork in such a rathole. The whole place looks like this?"

"Yes, sir. Some local official lived here. Gone now. The place was empty. We cleaned it up a bit."

"Clean it up a bit more. But it'll do. Bedrooms upstairs?"

"Yes, sir. Linens were still on the beds. Not the cleanest place."

Patton stepped past the man, hands on his hips. "I brought my bedroll. I'll use that. Not too fond of bedbugs. Give word to the staff, set the place up, get it done quickly. For now anyway, this is home."

"One of the rooms overlooks the courtyard, sir. Should I stow your gear there?"

"Fine. We need an office, a conference room. There something like that upstairs?"

"Yes, sir. Four bedrooms. One is quite large, private. I'll set it up right away, sir."

The man set the basket down on the heavy dining table, was quickly gone. Patton moved to the table, felt a rumble in his stomach, picked up a round ball of cheese, wrapped in a loose cloth net, held it close to his nose. The smell was overpowering, an image of dirty socks, and he set it on the table, turned away, thought, what kind of people could live like this? Divine beauty on the ceiling, filth in their cupboards. No wonder they can't fight worth a damn. Not one of those Eyeties has ever eaten a steak.

The aides came in now, boxes of papers, the radio set, men moving quickly, his chief of staff directing them. The men moved past the table, and Patton could see glances at the champagne, hunger in their eyes. Oh, hell, he thought. This can't be much worse than rations. When in Rome . . . he smiled, thought, yep, that's a good one. When in Sicily, do as the Sicilians do. Well, maybe not. Pretty nasty bunch. He stepped to the table, picked up the ball of cheese, avoided smelling it, pulled out a small pocketknife. The knife blade cut easily through the cloth netting, and he sliced a wedge from the ball, slid it off the knife blade into his mouth. He tried to hold his breath, the cheese soft, melting quickly, sliding down his throat. The smell vanished with the flavor, and he was surprised, thought, damn, that's pretty tasty. He sliced another wedge, stared up, studied the painting above him, a Madonna and child, fat cherubic angels. How old, he wondered, how long has that thing been up there? Thousand years, five hundred? You'd think they'd fight to keep us out of here. But, then they should have fought to keep the Germans out first. Now, we have to do it for them.

The house rapidly became his headquarters, guards outside, curious townspeople passing by. He watched them from the window of his bedroom, studying the town, the people, wondering about snipers, the nagging caution from his staff. Even from that distance he could feel the same kind of wretchedness he had too often seen in North Africa. He had as little regard for the Sicilians as he did for the Arabs, gave no thought to the *liberation* of the people who clogged the roads with donkeys and pushcarts, the annoying inconvenience to the movement of his armor. But there were problems here that the Arabs had seemed to avoid, hunger for one, the granaries empty, consumed by the needs of the war. The harvest season was approaching, some of the wide fields actually cultivated, ripening wheat, but Patton had seen few able-bodied men, thought, of course not, they're all out there, in those hills, wondering if they should shoot at us first or are they better off shooting at the Germans next to them. They'll find out soon enough.

Below his window, the courtyard itself was little more than a barnyard, goats and chickens darting about, protected from the people by a stout stone wall, the irony of that not lost on him. I should just turn the livestock loose, let the damned people get some meat in their cook pots. No, probably not a good idea. We don't need to waste time managing a riot.

He backed away from the window, could hear the movement of the staff, the business of his army filling the large house. He was still hungry, thought again of the odd cheese, could smell it on his fingers still, realized he could smell it in the walls of the house. Don't even think about that, he thought. If it tastes good, it doesn't much matter what the hell they made it with.

He moved out into the short corridor, toward the stairway, an aide flattening against the wall, allowing him to pass. He glanced at the man's necktie, the perfect knot, tight on the man's collar, said, "Good! Keep it up. That will win us this damned war."

"Yes, sir."

His boots clicked down the marble stairway, and he aimed for the dining table, still spread with unopened champagne bottles, more of the cheese, several different kinds. It would be his lunch, the only thing his staff had come up with, thought, if I could have just one hot dog. Just *one*.

He heard voices, pushed back from the dining table, saw a British officer at the door, familiar, one of Alexander's aides.

The man saluted. "Sir! General Alexander has arrived.

Should he meet with you here, or do you have a more suitable location?"

Patton slid a slice of cheese into his mouth, thought, wonderful. He's interrupting my lunch. Just jolly.

"Come in, Major. There's a conference room upstairs, the maps are on the wall, good place to talk and have some privacy. Or *privvasee*."

The man ignored his mockery of the accent, stood to one side, and Alexander was there now, tall, lean, the man examining the grandeur of the room.

"Quite nice, I do say. This your headquarters, General?"

"For now. Care to go upstairs? We can talk in private. Or do you have some other reason for being here?"

Alexander moved past him. "Yes, upstairs." He turned, motioned to his aides, three men passing by, climbing the stairs, officers Patton had dealt with before, one man holding a rolled map beneath his arm. Alexander called after them, "Do see if you can locate a comfortable chair hereabouts. These roads have given me a bit of a backache."

"We'll find something, sir."

Patton motioned toward the stairway. "After you, sir."

Alexander began to climb, and Patton stopped, slipped back toward the table, grabbed the ball of cheese, stuck it under his arm, followed Alexander up the stairs.

"It's Monty's idea. He's run into a bit more resistance than he had estimated. The enemy is backed up in the hills north of Syracuse, putting up a pretty stiff front. He suggests making a swing to his left, here, using this road, 124, through Caltagirone, then pushing up through Enna, clearing away any resistance there, then pressing the enemy from the west. Done this sort of thing before, you know, the old left hook. Quite effective."

Patton felt a jump in his stomach, was already holding tight to his words. He studied the map, put his finger on the small town, said, "Monty's plan puts him directly in our line of advance. Bradley's people are moving up that way right now. It is our objective to use that road as a main artery for our advance through the mountains."

"Yes, I realize that, of course. But Monty is most insistent, says he can wrap this whole thing up in short order, once he circles around the Huns who are dug in below Mount Etna. The enemy has made it something of a rough go at Catania, and Monty is afraid he'll bog down. Messina is the ultimate goal of course, and with some speed, we can hit the enemy before they can withdraw and strengthen their position there. The best way for Monty to accomplish that is to flank Mount Etna from the west and bypass the strongest enemy positions."

"That was my intention all along."

"Ah, yes, well, Monty suggests that your people move out more to the west, thus securing his flank. There is still quite a threat out that way, of course."

Patton felt his throat tightening, the words squeezing through. "His flank? The Seventh Army will serve to protect Monty's flank?"

"Well, yes. Since the Eighth Army is positioned closest to Messina, it is perfectly obvious that they would push toward the goal of taking the port and shutting down the enemy's ability to escape."

"Except there's a big damned mountain in the way."

"Mount Etna, certainly. The Huns are making good use of the natural defenses thereabouts. As I said, Monty's having a rough go pushing north. This was his plan, and I must say, it made sense to me. Once he sidesteps Mount Etna to the west, the Huns could be in a serious bind, trapped with their backs to the wall, so to speak."

"Especially if we're protecting his flank."

"Your people will of course deal with enemy forces to the west. Those mountains in the island's center should prove somewhat difficult, but Monty should manage with his people. Veterans, you know. Seen much worse, certainly. Your people can handle the open ground to the west, should find much easier going."

Patton could see discomfort on Alexander's face, weakness in the man's resolve. Monty's plan. Of course this is Monty's plan. This was Monty's plan when he joined the army. He doesn't just want Messina, he wants Alex's job. And Ike's. And Winston Churchill's.

"Does *Monty* have a plan on how I am to reposition Bradley's two divisions? The Forty-fifth is definitely planning on using that same road. Enna was their next major objective." His brain was churning, heat on his face, his hands clenched tight, and he fought to hold the words inside him, thought, maybe the Seventh Army should just go back to the beach and take a damned holiday.

"I would leave that up to you, of course. But haste is required. Monty's already put his plan into motion. Could cause a logistical problem if his people start mingling with yours."

"*He's already in motion?*"

Patton stared at the map, ignored the details, red fire in his brain. It's a good thing Monty bothered to tell Alexander what he was doing. Probably an afterthought.

Patton backed away from the map, tried to silence the fury in his brain. The room was quiet for a long moment, the other men standing frozen, silent.

Patton cleared his thoughts. "Well, then, I should talk to Bradley right away, fill him in. May I assume that my men are free to attack the enemy as we find them?"

Alexander seemed relieved at Patton's question. "Oh, why certainly. As Monty pushes north to Enna, your people should move with him, lockstep as it were. The Hun is showing every intention of withdrawing toward Messina, but there are still stout pockets of resistance. Some of those hills west of Enna are a bit rough, could offer the enemy some good defensive positions."

"I've studied the topography."

"Oh, well, yes, of course you have."

Patton saw the entire operation in his mind, the ego of one man, a lusty fantasy. Yep, that's exactly what Monty has in mind. Drive the main body of the enemy back toward Messina, capture the glorious trophy of the city and destroy the enemy. And we will sit on the sidelines and be his audience. He thought of Eisenhower. Did you approve this? Do you even know about it? And if you don't, it makes little difference. This is Monty's war, after all.

He studied the map again, his eyes clearing, focusing on details, the western part of the island, his mind sifting through plans, the alternatives. He pointed now to the southern coast-line.

"There. Would you permit us to advance westward to that port, Agrigento? Since we're going to move out on that flank, it makes sense to eliminate any threat behind us."

Alexander seemed to welcome the suggestion. "Oh, by all means. Good thought, that one. It is important that we clean things up as we go, secure the countryside, pacify the citizens."

Patton looked at Alexander, the man's sunburned skin, the mustache, the genteel bearing, the perfect British commander. Ike can only wish for that, he thought, all that *breeding*.

"Very good. I must ask if I may be dismissed from this meeting, sir. I should see General Bradley immediately, give him the details of Monty's plan. We can't have our people getting in Monty's way."

"George! Are they serious?"

"The directive comes straight from Army Group, Brad, from Alexander's mouth. You have to shift the Forty-fifth Division from the Enna road. Monty is going to use that to flank Mount Etna and drive the enemy into Messina."

Bradley stared at him, mouth open. "George . . . what the hell is going on? We're within artillery range of the road now. We could probably take Enna in two days."

Patton turned, glanced at the aides. "Leave us for a while, gentlemen."

Patton waited for the door to close, chewed on the cigar in his mouth, a cloud of smoke drifting up around him. The tobacco tasted bitter, harsh, and he set the cigar down on the edge of the table, said nothing.

Bradley spoke again. "George! This will play hell with both the Forty-fifth and the First! The entire advance will stop! Both Allen and Middleton will scream bloody hell! What the hell—"

Patton held his hands up, had expected the explosion from Bradley. "Orders, Brad."

"Does Ike know about this . . . well, hell, of course he does."

"I'm not sure of that at all. This is Monty's decision."

"*Monty's* decision?"

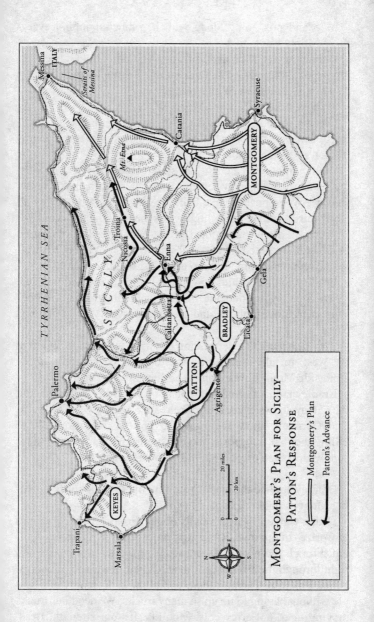

MONTGOMERY'S PLAN FOR SICILY—
PATTON'S RESPONSE

→ Montgomery's Plan
→ Patton's Advance

"Alexander is going along with it, rubber-stamping everything Monty wants to do."

Bradley seemed stunned, and Patton couldn't hold it back any longer, had struggled with the heat in his brain long enough.

"Orders, Brad! We follow orders!"

"Whose orders, George? Monty's?"

"Seems so. The commander of Army Group himself is willing to concede authority to Monty. Seems like Ike is too. Guess we don't have any choice."

Bradley moved to a chair, sat, stared at the darkness outside, his hands hanging between his legs. "It doesn't make sense, George. We're pushing like hell, the enemy is falling away all along our front. We're hauling in prisoners by the thousand."

"Yep. All along our front. But not Monty's. He's run into a brick wall on the coast, and that's a pill he's not about to swallow. Won't make him look too good in London either."

Bradley looked at him now, tilted his head, seemed puzzled. "Why aren't you bouncing off the walls about this, George? This is blatant stupidity, and I've never seen you so damned calm."

"We've been given permission by Army Group to push out to the west, to take Agrigento, and to push your people north, alongside Monty's west flank. That's what we're going to do."

Bradley stood, moved to the map on the wall. "All right. But the enemy shows every sign of retreating back toward Messina. The Germans know they have to protect the straits. We're killing their air transports, and the straits are their best hope for supply, and even escape, should it come to that."

"Yep."

Bradley studied the map. "You want me to push north, guarding Monty's flank, against . . . what?"

"I don't give a beaver's balls about Monty's flank. I want a few prizes of our own. Right now, most of our supplies are coming through the port at Syracuse. We have to haul everything right through the British positions. Ridiculous waste of energy. I want Palermo. The port there will allow us to supply our people without having to tie up so many trucks. We need our trucks moving men, not army cots. Mobility. It's our strength, Brad. The British take weeks to get a single soldier on his feet. We need to get somewhere, we damned well get there. Monty hasn't changed. Every move he makes is calculated, planned down to the last detail. Alex is concerned Monty will get bogged down. Hell, he already is! If we advance like I know we can, Army Group won't have any choice but to let us go forward. There is no way Alex can order us to hold up our advance and stop kicking the enemy's ass just because Monty is taking his time. Even Ike won't stand for that."

"What are you figuring, George? You have a plan?"

"I want Palermo, and I want to cut that coast road up north."

"Do we have orders to go that far?"

"You do your job, and I'll get the orders. We move faster than Monty, make better progress, then Alex will have to agree to turning us loose. I want Palermo, I want the ports on the west coast, and I want you to push north with all the muscle you've got. Let Monty bust his nose against those damned mountains. Every time he gets punched in the teeth, he takes a step back, makes a new plan, talks about it, examines it, and when he's in the mood, he takes another step forward."

"I don't understand, George. You want Monty to fail?"

"Hell, no. We're *allies*. I just want him to do what he always does, what they all do. It's just their *way*, Brad."

Bradley looked at him, a long silent pause.

Patton picked up a paper, held it out. "I intend to create an additional corps, under Geoff Keyes, as a temporary command. The Third Division, the Second Armored, the Eighty-second Airborne, and maybe one regiment of the Ninth. He'll move along the west coast, take the smaller ports, Agrigento, Marsala, Trapani, then drive toward Palermo from the south. With the First and the Forty-fifth, you should push north and kick the enemy the hell out of your way."

Bradley studied the map. "So, I'll be protecting Monty's flank."

Patton ignored the map, picked up the cigar again, moved to the window. He felt a rush of energy, thought of Alexander, the vague orders, the weakness, British generals running away with their own plans. Fine, we can all go to that party.

He turned back toward Bradley, took a short draw from the cigar, fought the sharp bitterness. "Oh, by all means, you will protect Monty's flank. You will protect his flank until you reach the north coast. And then, you will protect it all the way to Messina."

By July 16, Bradley had successfully maneuvered and redeployed his divisions westward, to allow Montgomery to take control of the roadway that would give the British Eighth Army a route of advance toward the western approaches to Mount Etna. Once the Americans were in their new position, Bradley wasted no time and drove his Second Corps northward, through the gut of Sicily's central mountains. Though Middleton's Forty-fifth Division could only make use of one primary roadway, Bradley's men did not hesitate, and the enemy could not stand up to the power of the American advance. On July 18, Bradley captured a key intersection, the town of Caltanissetta.

To Bradley's east, the Canadian Division, part of Montgomery's forces, confronted a strong German resistance south of the city of Enna, the town that stood in the way of the British left-hook move toward Mount Etna. Instead of feeding good troops into a slaughter, the Canadian commander shifted his troops to the right, attempting to bypass the town altogether. The move exposed the right flank of Bradley's First Division, which could have caused serious consequences had the Germans recognized the opportunity and had they been inclined to advance out of their defenses to attack Bradley. Instead of pulling troops away to protect the vulnerable flank, the First Division, under Terry Allen, simply drove into Enna itself, attacking the Germans from both the south and west. The surprised Germans hastily gave way. Though the Canadians responded with embarrassed gratitude for Bradley's assistance, in Montgomery's headquarters the victory at Enna was fed to the British news media in a way that surprised no one in the American camp. With the Americans already planning their next move, to continue their push north of the town, the BBC trumpeted the conquest, claiming that Enna had of course been captured by Montgomery's British troops.

Patton had long ago tried to ignore that kind of absurdity and issued his own congratulations to Bradley and the men in his command. But Patton did not dwell on the details of Bradley's successes. He had confidence that, in the drive northward, Bradley had matters well in hand. Patton himself was more interested in the western arm of his advance, the ports along the coast that would give him far more efficient supply depots for his army. On July 22, with the Second Armored leading the charge, the vanguard of Patton's army rolled into Palermo.

In the east, Montgomery continued to struggle, facing the bulk of the German forces that continued to back toward Messina. While Montgomery bumped methodically into heavy German defenses, Patton's rapid sweep had eliminated the enemy from all of western Sicily and put every coastal town on that half of the island in American hands. The same day that Patton's tanks rolled into Palermo, Bradley's troops completed their northward push, weary American infantry surprised to be staring north into the blue waters of the Tyrrhenian Sea. Unless Alexander could be convinced that the British needed more than just a guard on their flank, the Americans had gone as far as they could go.

36. PATTON

PALERMO, SICILY
JULY 23, 1943

Palermo was a large city, larger than Patton had expected, and showed a surprising amount of destruction, buildings bombed and shattered by Allied raids from weeks earlier. The port itself was clogged with wreckage, and American engineers were quickly at work clearing the vital waterways. The shattered city was one cost of the war, but Patton saw past that, saw that even though Palermo was said to have been a thriving port, it was one more place blanketed by filth. Though Patton had been surprised by the amount of rubble, the wretched condition of the ragged and underfed civilians was no surprise to him at all.

He had first come into the city late at night, so late that Keyes and the other senior officers were asleep in their newly captured beds. By the next morning, his presence in the city was made known, Patton enjoying the high visibility, knowing that it would magnify the impact of what the Americans had accomplished. He responded as he always responded, took the opportunity to move among the men, to congratulate them merely by his appearance in their ranks.

His jeep had rolled alongside a caravan of trucks, traffic drawing to a stop frequently, the roadways packed with vehicles that worked to avoid the rubble and the clusters of Sicilians who rolled their carts once more into the city that had finally been rescued from the war. Patton waited patiently behind a canvas-covered deuce-and-a-half, the two-and-a-half-ton truck that had become the workhouse of the army. The truck pulled aside now, tilting precariously above a steep drop-off, the driver suddenly aware of the jeep behind him, a glimpse in the mirror of the three stars displayed prominently on the front grill, a three-starred flag as well fluttering beside the hood.

The aide drove the jeep past the truck, and Patton saw the truck driver saluting him, a wide, beaming smile, Patton acknowledging with a quick nod.

In one respect, the city of Palermo was no different from many of the smaller towns the Americans had occupied. In each village and small port, Patton rode through his men with the kind of pomp they expected of him, standing tall in the well-marked jeep, the steel helmet polished, the legendary pistols at his belt. They saluted and cheered him, as they did now, and he saluted back, the cheers growing louder still. These were his most glorious moments, so far away from the stuffiness of the conference rooms, all those careful conversations, the delicate toes of men you dare not step on, men who had never known what it was like to feel *this*, the ride among the tank crews and truck drivers and artillerymen.

The jeep rolled into an intersection, the grand palace to one side, his new headquarters, one more piece of extraordinary grandeur coated in centuries of grime and disrepair. Soldiers were everywhere, gathering as the jeep rolled to a stop, and he stood upright, stared at them, no smile, the stern face of the man who controlled the power they carried inside them. The streets were a trampled mess of color, flowers, crushed by the boots of these conquerors. The civilians had reacted to the soldiers with an amazing outpouring of affection, tearful cheers. And so many flowers. There were civilians now as well, the people who gathered wherever the soldiers gathered. They emerged from small, shattered homes, makeshift shelters, anxious, ragged people gathering along the side streets. He looked beyond the helmets of the men who cheered him, saw old Sicilian men easing forward, holding boxes of . . . what? Anything they could trade for cigarettes, he thought, fruit maybe, trinkets, junk of one kind or another.

It surprised many of the commanders that the Sicilians would so rapidly transform themselves from unbridled hostility to unfettered affection, a newfound loyalty to the cause of these American troops who marched through their towns. Even the snipers had disappeared, Patton wondering if their rifles were still lodged in secret nooks on a hundred rooftops, while they tested the staying power of these newly arrived warriors, the men who had vanquished the evil Germans. He scanned the civilians, thought, no young men here of course. They're either in our POW compounds, or they were pulled out of here a while ago. Surely the Krauts knew that these people would be far more eager to return to their homes than to fight and die for the damned Nazis. They probably scattered the Sicilians all over Italy, or put them on Sardinia, and right now every damned one of those Eyeties is hoping we'll drop a few thousand paratroopers on them too. Give it time.

SYRACUSE AIRPORT, SICILY—JULY 25, 1943

He made the trip in a C-47, two British Spitfires guarding against any potential intrusion from German fighters. But the Luftwaffe had seemed to virtually disappear, Patton curious about that, wondering if Kesselring was already moving men and equipment off the shrinking battlegrounds of Sicily. With no Germans to fear, he had passed the time by staring out the small windows, ignoring the rolling, desolate ground beneath him, focusing instead on the imposing cone of Mount Etna, always visible, glimmers of snow on the peak that stood two miles above the surrounding plains. It was one unique piece of beauty in a land that Patton already despised, his mood not helped by the journey he was taking now. He wanted it to end quickly, wanted to return to Palermo, but it was the formality of command, and if he expected anything positive for his army, he had to play by the rules.

He didn't have time to become impatient, the flight barely an hour, the C-47 dropping down quickly to the airfield. The plane bounced once, rolled to a stop, and Patton saw officers, a small crowd, and behind them, rows of British fighters on the tarmac, crews in motion around them. He stepped from the plane, the officers moving toward him, British and unsmiling. There was one American uniform, Beetle Smith, a surprise.

Smith held out a hand. "Good to see you, General! Ike wanted me to participate, if you don't mind. We're trying to coordinate the navy transports still, figure out what your command might need. I thought this was a good opportunity to meet with Monty's naval coordinator, and the G-4, General Miller."

Patton forced a smile, didn't care for Smith, the short, round man Patton's perfect image of a deskbound soldier. "Glad you're here, Beetle. You can tell Ike about the fireworks."

Smith stopped smiling, said in a low voice, "Something I should know? Another problem with Monty?"

Patton held up his hand, saw the British officers watching him. One man came closer, pointed to a wide hangar. "General, I'm Colonel Grayling. Welcome to Syracuse. The meeting will take place over there, inside. A table has been set up, maps posted. We've kept it well protected of course."

Patton moved that way, following the man's directions, thought, protected from what? Me?

He had never enjoyed the official meetings with Alexander, but this one had weight, the focus on what lay ahead, no time to jawbone about which army had made the greatest gains. It was a moot point to him anyhow. Patton knew that he had made good mileage with Alexander by his army's extraordinary drive across western Sicily. The Americans were already making use

of the western ports, especially Palermo, relieving congestion at
the British bases on this end of the island. Alexander would certainly have no criticisms, and Patton expected to hear a good
bit of congratulations. It would be entirely appropriate. But
Alexander wasn't to be the only senior officer at the meeting.

Patton saw it now, a long, black car, the windows up, stopping
just outside the hangar. An aide emerged from the passenger
seat, moved quickly to the rear door, pulled it open, stepped
back with perfect stiffness. There was a pause, and Patton
walked briskly, left Smith and the British officers to catch up.
He did not want to seem late, would not be the last man on the
scene. The car door remained open, no movement, and Patton
was there now, stopped, gathered himself, realized Montgomery
was simply watching him, waiting for the perfect moment to
emerge from the car.

"Ah, General Patton! Jolly good of you to come! Quite a
row in these parts, wouldn't you say? Outstanding work, outstanding!"

Montgomery held out a hand, and Patton took the hand, said
nothing, Montgomery withdrawing it quickly. There was an
awkward pause, Patton examining the odd black beret Montgomery wore, too big for his head, had always wanted to know
why he wore it at all.

Montgomery said, "I shan't waste our time, General. Captain
Bailey, retrieve the map, please."

The young officer responded, ducked into the car. Behind Patton, the British officers were gathering around, and the colonel,
Grayling, said, "Sirs, if you will follow me this way. General
Alexander has not yet arrived. We have a meeting place set up
for you inside. Refreshments all around, a bit of lunch."

Montgomery's aide emerged from the car with a rolled-up
map, and Montgomery said, "Unnecessary. We shall discuss
these matters right here. No time for trivialities. Captain, spread
the map out on the auto."

The aide obeyed, unrolling the map on the car's hood, Montgomery moving close, his fingers running across the map. Patton moved up beside him, had not yet spoken to the man.

Montgomery said, "Here. You see this line, General. I have
drawn a demarcation boundary, separating our commands.

Thought it might clarify things a bit. As you can see, the Hun is anchored quite firmly in the vicinity of Catania. He is using the treacherous terrain around Mount Etna to his full advantage. I am quite pleased that he is completely bottled up where he is. It allows us considerable flexibility with regard to Messina. Don't you agree?"

"I agree that Messina must be our immediate target. My men are in position to move east with all speed."

"Ah, yes, hoping you would say that! You have a plan, then?"

Patton was cautious, had not expected anyone at this meeting to *ask* him anything, especially not Montgomery. He leaned closer to the map, pointed.

"Yes. The coast road out to the east of Palermo is under our control, and once we are in position, we can use that to the greatest effect. In addition, there is this . . . parallel road, some twenty miles inland, passing through Nicosia and Troina. I anticipate that within a week's time, my men can make good use of both routes to strike the enemy before he can solidify his defenses. When successful, we can drive the enemy all the way back to the Messina peninsula, trapping him there. I have planned on several amphibious operations along the northern coast, to land forces back behind various German positions. This should cause considerable havoc in their ranks and might possibly grab us a considerable store of prisoners. Naturally, I hope to gain Alex's approval for this."

"Ah, excellent. Yes, by all means. That's the plan then."

Patton stood up straight, glanced at the men gathered behind them, saw nods, approval.

"Should we not allow Alex to give *his* approval?"

Montgomery laughed now, surprising him. "Ah, dear boy, that is not the issue here. Alex will give this a go, no question about that. I just wanted to be sure that you and I were fighting the same war, eh? Nothing complicated here. By all means, your Seventh Army will take those two roads, with your men deployed as you see fit. I will push up from below, drive around both flanks of Mount Etna. Should give the bloody Huns a headache. They're already looking backward, so to speak. Eye on the prize, and all."

Patton felt a tingle on the back of his neck, thought, what

prize are we talking about? He was feeling uneasy, cautious, had not expected any cooperation from Montgomery. He pointed to the eastern tip of the island. "If the enemy retreats as we expect him to, I will continue the amphibious assaults. Certainly, once he accepts that he is defeated, the enemy will attempt to use the straits to escape. For this operation to be completely successful, we cannot allow that."

"Ah, not to worry, dear boy! The Royal Air Force is all over that one! Should the Hun elude our grasp, he will quite simply be boxed in at Messina, nowhere to go. Should be a duck shoot for our flyboys. What the bombers don't get, the navy will, quite sure of that. Our job, you and me, is to see that Jerry stays put long enough for us to destroy him completely! Hitting him from two sides like this . . . excellent! Short work, certainly! We should have this entire island in our pocket in a month's time!"

A month? Patton absorbed the words, thought, he actually believes that. Well, of course. With all his *planning,* he can't do anything quickly. But a month is a damned eternity.

On the runway behind them, planes had been moving in steady procession, fighters mostly, the unending sorties against German positions to the north. One plane landed alone now, larger, a different sound, a flock of fighter escorts following behind, passing overhead.

Behind Patton, a man called out, "Sir! General Alexander has arrived!"

Patton watched the plane, taxiing close now, the engines shutting down. The officers drifted toward the aircraft, preparing their customary greetings, Patton moving with them. He looked back toward the car, saw Montgomery still there, studying the map, the young captain to one side, holding the map in place. Well, he thought, I suppose Monty speaks with Alex often enough he doesn't need formality. Or courtesy.

The door opened, and Alexander stepped down from the plane, short, clipped words for the officers, saw Patton, said, "Welcome, General. Glad you're here. We're getting close, you know. Tough road still, but with the job your people have done, the enemy has to know he is beaten. Just a matter of time, I suspect."

Yep, Patton thought. A month.

Alexander focused on Montgomery now, said, "Ah, Monty! Office in the field, I see."

"Alex."

Patton moved up beside the car, his eye on Alexander. He saw a hard frown, unusual, a tenseness to the man, thought, he's looking for more from Monty. And he's not getting it.

Alexander said, "We have some sort of strategy in mind, Monty? I should like to hear it."

"Not to worry, Alex. George and I have ironed it all out. Quite simple, really, perfect precision. The Hun's all but in the bag."

Patton stood silently, watched as Alexander crossed his arms, rocked slowly, the frown settling into a hard scowl. "Monty, I should like to hear your plan, if it's all right with you."

Montgomery shrugged. "We've been over the details. George sees things the same way I do. I expect no difficulties—"

"*Tell me your plan.*"

It was the first time Patton had heard Alexander raise his voice, cold silence now holding them all still.

Montgomery seemed to pause, his voice low, calm. "Certainly, Alex."

Montgomery spoke for long minutes, others joining in, the men around them offering information, filling in details, Smith contributing as well. The details did not change the overall plan, Patton realizing that his every suggestion had been accepted without argument, which was more than simply unusual. As the discussion continued, Patton mostly watched and listened, could clearly see Alexander's anger. He felt suddenly giddy, was now overjoyed that Beetle Smith was there to witness this scene, to pass the word on to Eisenhower. Patton had rarely been the innocent bystander, the one man in the crowd who wasn't the source of the friction.

After long minutes in the sun beside Montgomery's car, after the details had been sketched and analyzed, Alexander silenced them all, looked at Patton. "What of it, General? This seems like a plan that offers the Americans an opportunity to share the spoils, so to speak. Ike has been most insistent about that, as have you. Is this acceptable to you?"

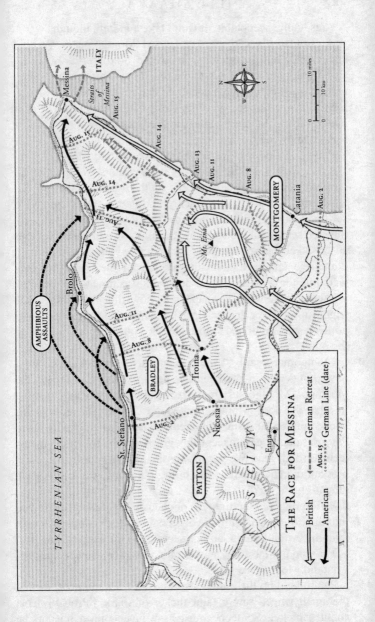

THE RACE FOR MESSINA

British
American

German Retreat
German Line (date)

"Yes. Quite acceptable. It won't take a month, though."

Alexander glanced quickly toward Montgomery. "A bold statement, George. Victory favors the bold, certainly. But I won't hold you to it. I must note one thing. This level of cooperation must certainly demonstrate that my command, that Fifteenth Army Group, is completely Allied in mind. I favor neither army. Ike has been assured of this many times. I hope this satisfies you on that point."

Patton nodded slowly. "It certainly seems that way."

"Very well. I will return to my headquarters. You gentlemen have my perfect confidence. Let's get the job done, shall we?"

Alexander moved away quickly, and Patton was surprised to see him board his plane. Alexander's staff was surprised as well, the men scrambling to catch up, the pilots still in the cockpit, as surprised as their passengers. Patton looked out toward his own plane, the crew seated in the shadow of the wing, the men watching for his signal, the order that it was time to go. But Patton wasn't sure what was happening now, thought of lunch, the suggestion offered by the British colonel. He turned to Montgomery, who motioned to his aide, the young captain rolling up the map.

Montgomery said, "I told you not to worry! Alex knows I have things well in hand here. As he said, it's up to us to get the job done." Montgomery moved around the car, the aide rushing to open the door. Montgomery stopped now, reached into his pocket, pulled out a small cigarette lighter. He held it out toward Patton, said, "Please accept this gift, George. Token of my esteem, and all that. We get to Messina, I'll have a formal celebration, dinner, whatnot. You bring this along, we'll light each other's cigars, eh?"

Patton fingered the lighter, watched as Montgomery climbed into the car. Around him, the officers were dispersing, each man with his own job to do, no one seeming to think about lunch.

The car pulled away, and Smith was there now, said, "So, what did Monty give you?"

Patton held up the lighter, examined it for a moment, flicked the small wheel, saw a faint flicker of spark. "Probably cost about a nickel. Someone must have given him a box of the damned things."

Smith said nothing, and Patton began to walk now, moving across the tarmac, Smith calling out, "I'll tell Ike about this. All of it. We're behind you, George."

Patton raised a hand, a brief wave, moved toward the plane, his mind on the maps, the two roads that led to Messina, Montgomery's boast, his plan for a dinner, lighting each other's cigar. Where will we do that, Monty? In my headquarters or yours? I guess that might depend on who gets to Messina first.

37. KESSELRING

ROME
JULY 25, 1943

It was late, the city darkened by rumors of Allied bombing raids. It had been a struggle to convince anyone in the Italian government that the city was under threat, but Kesselring had heard too many radio intercepts and too many intelligence reports, had to believe that the Allies were giving strong consideration to violating the informal agreements that Rome should be spared. It is our fault, he thought. We have put this place at risk. It is one thing to man the nearby airfields and ring the city with troop encampments, but now . . . the war has come too close. This city could become a battlefield. Would we bomb it if *they* were here? He shook his head, knew the answer to that already.

He stared into the darkened streets, saw cars with headlights, a direct violation of the blackout order. It had been that way since the lights had gone out, so many of the Italians still oblivious to the war. He marveled at that, thought, they are a unique race, so enraptured by their history that they are incapable of seeing the present. We are so different from that. So much of the Führer's strength comes from using the past as a tool, inspiring Germany against those who have struck her down, who would keep her down still. It is an imperfect strategy, of course. So often, Hitler has chosen to look away from things as they are, dreaming of a world as he wishes it to be. That is a luxury a soldier does not have.

He backed away from the window, pulled the black shroud over the tall glass, moved to his desk, lit the small lamp. Who is right, after all? A soldier cannot think on that either. We do not weigh the value of our cause, we simply fight to preserve it. We might certainly be fighting now just to preserve ourselves. He reached for the bottle of brandy, pulled the cork, held the bottle to his nose, breathed in the sharp, flowery warmth. The small glass snifter sat empty on the desk, and he poured a small amount from the bottle, thought, not too much. I don't need any headaches in the morning. He turned toward the curtain, thought, a warm night, no breeze. I should take a walk. I should truly enjoy that. No, it's foolishness to think of that. Far too late. Much to do tomorrow. There is always much to do. I must see the reports, I must know what the enemy is doing. I should send for Hube, meet with him face-to-face. We are fortunate to have such a man in Sicily, a man I can depend on. He thought of Rommel, had once felt the same way about him. Rommel is in the Führer's lap now, and it must be killing him.

Rommel had spent six weeks in the luxury of Semmering, recovering from his illness, and Hitler had patiently waited for his return, still regarded the Desert Fox with a biased affection that boiled the blood of the senior German staff. For some weeks Rommel had stayed close to Hitler, serving as an adviser, in reality, a man with nothing to do. But then, German intelligence had become convinced that the Allies would attempt an invasion of Greece, to drive a wedge west of the beleaguered German army that was still embroiled in a massive campaign against the Russians. Rommel had been chosen to lead the forces that would presumably confront the Allies when they came ashore in Salonika, the Greek peninsula that jutted into the Aegean Sea, the most logical place for such a landing.

Rommel is there now, he thought, pulling men together for an invasion that even Rommel knows will never come. No matter, he will do the job. He will live out the perverted joke, poring over intelligence reports from men who still believe the invasion of Sicily is a feint. There are still men in Berlin who believe the Allies have so many resources, they can mount operations anywhere they choose. Kesselring smiled through his gloom, thought of Hitler. Ah, but none of that matters to you as much as holding Rommel close to you, so you can keep one hand on his shoulder. Greece is better than Africa. The Führer knows what I know, that Rommel cannot always be trusted to do what we wish him to do. And if he were not in Greece, then he would be here. What would he do in Sicily? How would he deal with Montgomery this time? We will never know the answer to that. The Italians will not have him. It is my security, the one thing that keeps me in good graces with all those nattering generals in Berlin. No one else can get along with the Italians.

He sniffed the brandy, swirled it in the glass, took a small sip. How much longer will that matter? How much longer will the Italians allow us to fight this war on their soil? Despite what Mussolini tells his ministers, the Italian army is crumbling, falling apart, and that will only get worse. The only force holding the enemy back in Sicily is German. Hans Hube is the best we have right now, perhaps even better than Rommel. We can no longer dream of driving the enemy into the sea. There is no victory to be had in Sicily, there is only survival. Rommel understood that in Tunisia, tried so hard to convince all of us to withdraw and save the army. But Berlin would not yet hear that kind of talk, and Rommel was too noisy about it, paraded his cause with heavy boots, was never a diplomat about anything. He believed he was fighting the war himself, that if it was not Rommel's way, it was failure. It didn't matter that he might be right. He made enemies.

Kesselring shook his head. He has one friend though. I do not understand why Hitler loves him so. If I had disobeyed so many orders, I would have been shot.

He finished the brandy, thought, they will come. There will be bombs in this place, and the Italians will be outraged. The Führer must believe that will help us, inflame the Italians to be better fighters, to drive the Allies off their soil. He shook his head, moved toward the lamp. No, it will only make them quit. These people are not the British. They do not have that kind of resolve, will not watch their country destroyed and vow to fight on.

He paused at the lamp, was not yet ready for the dark, thought, so many errors, so many disastrous errors of judgment and strategy and planning. We are supposed to learn from our mistakes, but there can be no lessons when the mistakes never end.

There was a soft knock at the door, and Kesselring said, "Yes. Enter."

The door swung open, and he saw Westphal, Rommel's former aide, now Kesselring's chief of staff.

"Sir, my apologies. But it is most urgent!"

Kesselring tilted his head, his ear trained to hear the sound of bombs, but there was only silence. "What has happened?"

"Word has come from the palace, sir, directly from the king himself. Herr Mussolini has been deposed by the Fascist Grand Council. He has been placed under arrest."

Kesselring leaned against the desk, felt the air leave him. "But I spoke to him yesterday. He was fully confident in their loyalty. There was no hint that anything was wrong."

Westphal said nothing.

Kesselring stood straight again. "Just like that? Tonight? Without warning?"

There was no answer to his question, and he stared past Westphal, tried to shuffle through the names and faces, all the men who would scramble to the top, the fights that were bound to erupt. Who had remained loyal to Mussolini, and who had betrayed him? It has to matter. Who is in command now? He thought of the king, the fragile old man, Victor Emmanuel. It had been a tenuous relationship between the monarchy and Mussolini, and though Mussolini had taken the power, he had wisely left the king to his throne, knowing that the Italian people loved the old man and respected his influence.

"Send word to the king. I must meet with him as soon as possible. This changes our situation considerably."

"Right away, sir! Heil Hitler!"

Westphal was gone, and Kesselring felt the warmth from the brandy, reached for the bottle again, pulled the cork, said aloud, "Yes. This changes our situation considerably."

*   *   *

General Hans Hube was a veteran of the First World War, had lost his right arm at Verdun, but unlike so many who carried horrific wounds, he had lost none of his spirit for the fight, had continued what was now a lengthy career in the army. Hube had served well at the Russian front, surviving the disaster of Stalingrad, while catching Hitler's eye as one of the premier fighting generals in the German army. Now, he commanded the German forces in Sicily and, in that theater, was subordinate only to Kesselring. Hube had gained the command not by his own ambitions, but by a strong recommendation from Rommel, who had convinced Hitler that Hube was the right man to turn the tide against the power of the Allied invasion. Kesselring gave little credence to Rommel's reasons for supporting Hube, had even wondered if Rommel had suggested Hube for the command because he thought Hube would fail. Kesselring could not avoid speculating that Rommel's separation from the front lines was more painful to him than the illness he had carried home from the desert. If Rommel truly missed life among the tanks, Kesselring had to believe that Rommel might be tempted to engineer a disaster, just so Rommel could ride south and save the day. But any doubts Kesselring had about Hube had been put to rest. In the two weeks since Hube's arrival, Kesselring had seen none of Rommel's defeatism and rebellious independence. Even better, Hube seemed completely free of the delusional fantasizing that surrounded Hitler and his staff. Hube understood exactly what was happening in Sicily, what his role was, and he was going about the job with perfect efficiency.

ROME—JULY 28, 1943

"I have met with King Victor Emmanuel. Fortunately, he and I have always had a cordial relationship. The king informs me that Pietro Badoglio is now the head of the government and has assumed command of all Italian armed forces."

Hube said, "Can we trust him?"

Kesselring shrugged. "He is the king. He insists he is our ally still and will remain so, and that Badoglio will continue to cooperate with us."

"Do you believe him?"

Kesselring smiled. "It matters little what I believe. It matters that we continue to do our jobs. I am quite certain that the Führer is devoting a great deal of energy to the reappraisal of our relationship with our ally. However, until I am notified otherwise, my role here has not changed. Neither has yours."

"Certainly, sir."

Kesselring said nothing for a long moment, Hube content to wait for whatever came next.

"You are a patient man, Hans. I have not enjoyed such luxury in the past."

"I don't know what you refer to, sir."

"Never mind. I am being indiscreet. Tell me about *your* Italians."

Hube seemed to energize, the subject turning to his own concerns. "I do not feel there has been any significant change. Since my arrival, I have been somewhat careful not to place any serious reliance upon General Guzzoni, and I have not considered the Italian army to be an asset to my planning. I have no plans to deploy them in any area requiring great skill or sacrifice. In any position where there is danger of a significant enemy assault, our own people have been used."

Kesselring smiled again, thought, *I have heard this sort of thing before.* "What of the officers?"

Hube shook his head. "The Italian officers do not seem affected by the arrest of Mussolini, but of course, that may change. As you know, some of the senior commanders known to be especially loyal to Mussolini have been replaced. Those changes are the concern of General Guzzoni. They are of no consequence to me."

Kesselring tapped his fingers on the desk, thought a moment. "I wish you to continue with your overall strategy of gradual withdrawal. But you should know that once we are out of Sicily, all of Italy might become a hostile area. No orders have come to me from Berlin, and I suspect it is because I am seen as a friend to the Italians. But already there is troop movement to the north, and I have received reports that our forces are strengthening the mountain passes along the Austrian border. Despite what the king tells me, I do not believe the Italian government is long for this war. It is in the air here, in every hushed conversation. The alliance between our country and Italy was made possible by the Führer's friendship with Mussolini, and now that Mussolini is gone, I have seen indications from the Italian politicians that our troops are being seen more as an army of occupation. I am quite certain that the Führer will not allow Italy to slip away, but I fear they already have." Kesselring paused. "I am far more concerned with preserving German troops and equipment than I am in holding on to Sicily."

"Yes, sir, I have understood that from the beginning."

"The Führer certainly understands that a war of attrition will eventually cost us more than anything we might gain. There is far more value to us in delaying any efforts the Allies might make toward occupying Italy. Any such move would likely drive the Italians out of this war and might possibly cause them to change their allegiances altogether. I have no doubt that it was always the enemy's intention to use Sicily as a launching ground for an assault on the Italian mainland. Churchill speaks of it openly, and I do not believe he is clever enough to offer that as some sort of ruse. The catastrophe that occurred in Tunisia must not be repeated on Sicily. Your forces are needed for the next campaign, and I will not lose you to an Allied prison camp. To that end, you will employ a precise plan of withdrawal and maintain the port of Messina as your primary point of evacuation. It must be done carefully and with severe penalty to the enemy. The success of this evacuation will rely on your ability to make the enemy pay dearly for what he will believe are his successes. I am confident that Montgomery will oblige us, as he did in Africa. He is a methodical man, slow to take advantage of opportunity. That will be extremely helpful to you. I do not know this man Patton. He could be far more dangerous, and you must teach him to use caution as well."

"Sir, there is risk that the evacuation itself could be disastrous. The Allied naval and air power—"

"There are advantages the enemy cannot counter, General. The straits are too narrow for warships to maneuver effectively. The crossings can be made at night and, with only two miles to span, can be accomplished quickly. I will order every available antiaircraft and flak battery transferred to the Messina area. We will employ them on both sides of the straits. Any Allied planes seeking to interrupt our plans will be met with a wall of fire such as they have never seen before."

"Sir, do we intend to evacuate the Italian troops as well?"

Kesselring thought for a long moment. "Your priority is to preserve those troops who are best equipped and most willing to continue this fight."

Hube stared at him, sharp eyes. "We will accomplish our mission, Field Marshal. And the enemy will pay with blood for every step he takes."

Only days after Mussolini's ouster, German troops began to behave as the Italians feared they would, much more as an army of occupation than friendly forces protecting an ally. In the north, along the Alpine mountain passes, German troops were growing in number, troops that Kesselring knew might become an invasion force, ordered to drive south to grab vital supply arteries and key defensive positions all over Italy. To no one's surprise, especially Kesselring's, Erwin Rommel was ordered away from his post in Greece and placed at the head of the new German command, Army Group B, with his headquarters in Munich. Kesselring knew that Rommel was now looking over his shoulder and, with Hitler's backing, might have ambitions to take command over the entire theater. But Kesselring still had Sicily in front of him and had to focus on his primary objective, to ensure that those German troops on Sicily would be able to fight again, a fight that Kesselring continued to believe would embrace the Italian mainland.

38. PATTON

The jeep carried them past heaps of white rubble, the remains of an old church, a sight Patton was accustomed to now. He could tell that Eisenhower was absorbing the scene, seemed visibly upset by the destruction of such an ancient place.

"I suppose it was necessary."

Patton stared ahead, past the helmet of the driver, tasted the dust from the scout car that rode out in front of them, thought, I had nothing to do with this. Blame the air force.

They rode out onto a hill, a point of high ground overlooking the harbor. Patton knew the spot, had driven up here more than once, enjoyed watching the engineers at work on the waterfront, the men who had cleared so much wreckage, opening the deep passageways for the supply ships, the port already up and functioning. The driver slowed the jeep, and Patton tapped his shoulder.

"Here. This is good."

The jeep stopped, the scout car in front turning abruptly, sliding to a halt. Behind them more jeeps gathered, one truck with a large machine gun. They were men of the Fifteenth Regiment, the unit that Eisenhower himself had once commanded. As word of Eisenhower's visit had filtered through the senior commanders, the men of the Fifteenth had requested they be allowed to provide an escort, a salute to their former commander, what Eisenhower described as an honor guard. Patton thought the escort was ridiculous, a holiday for soldiers who had better things to do. There is nothing in this city that requires so much security, he thought. But he could not object, knew better than to protest any show Eisenhower wanted to make.

Patton was up and out of the jeep, stepped to the edge of the rocky escarpment, his hands at his sides, resting on the butts of his pistols. He waited for Eisenhower, coming up beside him now, and Patton said nothing, knew the view would inspire a reaction.

"Marvelous, George. Truly marvelous. I heard the place was a royal mess."

"The engineers. Credit where it's due."

He could hear Eisenhower's breathing, strange silence, thought, he wants to tell me something. It has to be bad news. I've seen this before, Ike fighting for the right way to say something.

After a long pause Eisenhower said, "I've heard you intend to relieve Terry Allen. You certain about that?"

"Yep. The First has done everything we've asked of it, but every road has an end. Allen has pretty clearly overdone himself. He's been in the middle of this war since Oran, and he's earned a break. We need some fresh energy at the top."

"Teddy too?"

"Teddy too."

Teddy Roosevelt, Jr., was President Theodore Roosevelt's son, had served the Big Red One as Allen's second-in-command. During the weeks leading up to the invasion of Sicily, the First Division had become something of a disciplinary problem, the generals not living up to Patton's expectations of how a combat division should be managed. Just prior to their embarkation for Sicily there had been a complete breakdown of authority, the division engaging in a binge of looting and destruction in Algiers that neither Allen nor Roosevelt had seemed able or willing to prevent. Once in Sicily, the men of the Big Red One had performed reasonably well against the enemy, but had never seemed to recapture the powerful spirit of their best days in North Africa.

Patton expected an argument, knew that Teddy Roosevelt had powerful friends in Washington.

"It's your decision, George. Do what's best. I'll clear it with Marshall."

Patton said nothing, thought, well, that's a surprise. Ike's letting me run my own show.

After a moment, Eisenhower said, "Monty's already planning for the next operation. I know he has his hands full right now, but he has to look ahead. We all do. We're going into Italy as soon as the landing craft can be assembled, and that includes those craft assigned to you."

"I only have a couple dozen. The navy's been pretty damned stingy with those things."

"Make do with what you can get, George. Everybody's stretched pretty thin as it is. You still intend on launching those amphibious operations?"

"Damned right. If we come in on the beaches behind the Kraut lines, it should make the infantry's job a hell of a lot easier. Any confusion we can cause the enemy, the better off we are. Or don't you agree?"

"It's your operation, George."

"It would be a hell of a lot better if I had fifty or sixty landing craft."

Eisenhower said nothing, and Patton knew he had made his point. No need to upset the navy, he thought. Cunningham can't be bothered with any details that would only help the Americans.

Eisenhower said, "The landings around Naples will be Wayne's operation, you know. The Fifth Army has been training for that for a while now. Monty expects to hit the enemy directly across from Messina, push straight up the toe of the boot. With Wayne pinching in from the north, any German forces in southern Italy will be cut off. We might just roll up Italy like a rug."

Patton took a long breath, said nothing. He had expected Clark to get some sort of plum command, thought, of course, once we chew our way through the Krauts here, Wayne will get to *roll up* Italy. Clark's gotta be doing a dance in Casablanca. He's been sitting on his ass for too long, chomping at the bit. But Monty? He can't drive those soldiers into another campaign so soon. Not without a break.

"Do you think Monty will be ready for another large-scale operation so soon, Ike? His people are getting pretty beat-up."

"So are yours. We have to punch hard while the enemy is

vulnerable. Everyone's behind this, especially Churchill. But obviously we can't make any moves until things are secure here. I have high expectations for you, George. Everyone does. We need to have this situation wrapped up quickly."

Patton swallowed the word *everyone*. Does that include the British?

"We'll get it done, Ike. Everything's in place. We have a hell of a one-two punch out there. The Forty-fifth is pushing on the coast, the First is inland. Bradley is ready to put the Third in behind the Forty-fifth. I'm sure Middleton's boys will need a break, and the Third can take over for them. The Ninth is preparing to ship over through the port here, to add manpower to the First. If we need to, we can pull the First out of line altogether, led Eddy's boys have a crack. The Krauts can't stand up to that much strength. We're giving them hell, Ike. And we're not going to stop until we're standing in the middle of Messina."

"Excellent, George. This will make a name for us, this campaign. The president is hanging on every report, Marshall too. But it's more than official. There were too many people on both sides of the Atlantic who thought we were a paper tiger. The damned BBC acts like we don't even exist, keeps feeding the British people all sorts of nonsense about Monty. I'm really sick of that."

Patton was surprised, looked at Eisenhower, saw anger on the man's face.

Eisenhower said, "Nothing I can do about it, that's the problem. Churchill is a huge thorn, you know. He keeps making announcements to parliament, to his newspapers, gives out all sorts of details about the victories we're winning here. He's feeding the press the names of towns we've supposedly captured, places that are still held by the enemy. Sure, we'll capture them sooner or later. But he can't wait for facts. He loves the limelight, being the bearer of good news. The Brits need that, I suppose. Those people have suffered as much in this war as they did in the last one. But, dammit, I wish they'd rein it in a bit."

"I know one thing we can do about it, Ike. We take those towns, we grab the Kraut prisoners, we stick a few American flags in front of those BBC idiots, and they might have a tough time claiming that the British are winning every damned fight."

"Careful, George. The BBC is my problem. But you're right on one count. Get the job done quickly. Show everyone, not just the BBC, that our boys are doing their part. This is an Allied front, one army. I still won't tolerate any kind of bickering nationalism out here, and I'll do everything to keep it out of the papers back home. But in the end, it's up to you to drive this train. I'd like to see your name in the paper as much as Monty's."

Patton smiled, had not felt much affection for Eisenhower in a long time, realized now, Ike's walking a tightrope, serving too many masters. *The best way to put my name in the paper is to put our boys in downtown Messina before anyone else. Even the BBC can't ignore* that.

From Bradley's left flank on the north coast to Montgomery's position to the east, the attacks pushed forward against German positions that fought back with more tenacity than even Patton expected. Despite the difficulty of the rough ground, the men of the First and Forty-fifth divisions shoved hard against their enemy, driving across deep valleys and rugged hills, confronting shattered roadways and blown bridges. In the east, Montgomery struggled as well, still faced German forces clinging tightly to the rugged defenses around Mount Etna. Casualties mounted on both sides, but Bradley's forces continued their push, and one by one, the coastal villages, Cefalù and San Stefano, Brolo and Falcone, fell into American hands. Inland, across some of the most difficult terrain the Americans had yet seen, the stubborn resistance of the German defenders finally gave way, and the mountain towns of Nicosia and Troina fell into Bradley's hands. To the east, after a long week of difficult fights, the German defenses near Catania began to withdraw, Montgomery finally pushing up on both flanks of the great mountain barrier. As the Germans withdrew, their front lines began to contract, the soldiers protecting a front that grew more narrow with every backward step. Despite the horrific bloodying inflicted by every Allied assault, General Hube was accomplishing exactly what Kesselring had hoped. With less ground to defend, the Germans began maneuvering troops out of their frontline position, shifting them to the evacuation points around Messina.

Many of the Italian regiments continued to fall apart, mass surrenders that poured refugees into the American lines. But not all the Italians were happy to lay down their rifles. As the Germans executed their carefully controlled withdrawal, many Italians went with them, still willing to fight to hold back the Allied advance. Veteran Italian commanders were well aware that if they delayed, if they kept their people out on the front lines, that what had happened in North Africa might happen in Sicily as well. More than once Rommel had made only token efforts to rescue the slow-moving Italian infantry. This time, the Italians who still had the spirit for a fight had no plans to be left behind, to be sacrificed only so the Germans could make good a rapid escape. As the German lines contracted, the Italian commanders were pulling their people in a rapid retreat into Messina. On August 3, the first Italians to reach the straits made good their crossing onto the mainland. The great evacuation had begun.

NEAR CERAMI, SICILY—AUGUST 10, 1943

The men stood aside, allowed the jeep to pass. Patton watched them, saw the salutes, men calling out, exhausted smiles. He wanted to stop, to speak to them, wanted to encourage them, snap them by the collars, put the fire into their steps. Just give me a little more, he thought. Dammit, we are getting there, and if it were up to me, we'd have ended this fight by now. He had grown impatient with Bradley, with all the commanders, had churned himself into a tornado against the navy, the men who seemed to delay and argue over every operation. The amphibious assaults had not been as effective as he had hoped, the Germans often pulling back before the men could make their landings. Others had been victimized by German bombers, the precious landing craft destroyed or damaged before the men could even begin the operation. Old ladies, he thought. And not just the navy. All of them. Infantry commanders who would rather sit on their asses than fight.

The BBC had continued their absurdly biased reporting, Patton learning that London was being told the Americans were spending most of their time eating grapes and enjoying the beaches, while the valiant British soldiers bloodied themselves in a vicious fight around Mount Etna. He needed little inspiration as it was to find fault with his own officers, to believe that Bradley and his division commanders could be driving the Germans back toward Messina at a far faster pace. Now, the British people were being told that the Americans were having a jolly time of this war, at the expense of their own gallant lads. One BBC reporter, just one, he thought. Bring that son of a bitch to me and let him walk through these hospitals, let him haul his arrogance over these hillsides. I'll show him a holiday on the beach.

Patton had made it part of his routine to stop at the field hospitals, had gone to special lengths to arrange the presentation of Purple Hearts to the wounded, a special treat for him, and certainly, from the astonished surprise he had seen on the faces of so many wounded men, receiving their medal from him meant a great deal to the men as well. The hospitals were distinctly unpleasant places, and more than once he had paused beside the bed of a gravely wounded man, could tell by the reaction of the doctors that the man had no chance of survival. It bothered Patton more than he would admit, bothered him now. The images would not leave him, one man missing the top of his head, brains shielded by layers of white gauze, the doctors shaking their heads. There were many others, cavernous gaps in chests, men clinging to life by a thread of desperation. I cannot look at them, he thought, not like that. Not one at a time. No commander can afford to do that, to see his men as . . . *men*, with wives and mothers.

There had been an unpleasantness of a different kind, that image hard to erase as well. The man's name had stuck with him, Kuhl, no injury except he wasn't *feeling well*, the man claiming that he simply couldn't take it. Take what? Looking out for your buddies? Fighting the enemy? Patton had reacted to the man with blind rage, had screamed at him, ordered him out of the hospital. When the man did not respond, Patton had picked him up by the scruff of the neck and tossed him out of the place himself. It had caused a scene at the hospital, infuriating the doctors, but Patton had ignored them, rode away confident that at least *one* coward had been set straight. I'd do it again too, he thought. No room for that in my army, none at all. It's a disease, pure and simple. One bad man infects a whole platoon, one platoon a whole company. Battles have been lost for less. But not in my army. Not while men in those same hospitals lie in their beds fighting to survive.

The jeep passed by a deep, rocky chasm, men working below, shovels and pickaxes, shoring up the road. He glanced up at a bare hillside, men hauling equipment, artillery pieces rolling forward. He washed the memory of the one shirker out of his mind, focused on the wounded. They do so enjoy my visits, and, dammit, it's my job. This army suffers too much from hesitation, from officers who would rather delay than push forward. Every damned officer I have should spend some time in his own field hospitals, see what happens to his men because he delays the fight by a day or a week. It was an obscene word to him, and he spit it out, said in a low voice, "*Hesitation.*"

I will not have anyone here compare us to Montgomery, he thought. No one will ever call me *cautious*. If I have to kick some well-dressed asses at headquarters, I will make my point. I intend to be in Messina before the British, and if it costs the lives of soldiers to accomplish that, well, that's the price of war. But it will cost far more lives if we sit on our dead asses and *chew* about it.

He blew through a cloud of dust, a truck pulling to the side in front of him, the driver waving him past. His own driver pushed the jeep precariously to the edge of the narrow roadway, men in front of him jumping down, clearing the way, still waving, calling his name. He did not respond, was too close to them, to the faces, the sharp eyes, thought, they are the tools of war, and my job is to use them like tools of war. That's what victory is about.

The jeep rolled out of the gorge, crested a hill, more men in a column on the road, trucks in a large park, white tents, topped by a large red cross. He saw the sign now, *93rd Evac Hospital.*

"Stop here!"

His driver obeyed, the jeep turning in, men in white smocks gathering.

"Sir!"

"Welcome, sir."

He motioned to them, a brief wave, moved toward the largest tent, caught the smell, blood and disinfectant, took a deep breath, held it for a moment, moved into the tent.

More than a dozen men were in a row, blood on bandages, heads and chests wrapped in white, bare legs, one man's foot gone, his shortened leg ending in a clump of white gauze. Some of them were asleep, or unconscious, and he would not think of that, looked away from the wounds, searched for the smiles. They came now, low voices, and he felt the familiar tightness in his throat, spoke to each man, useless words, felt helpless, weak. He moved slowly past each bed, touched one man's leg, heard, "Bless you, sir."

"No, bless you, soldier." He stopped, looked back along the row of men, wanted to say it aloud, the words choked away. Bless all of you.

He turned, moved toward the end of the row, saw one man sitting upright, no bandage, the uniform intact, the man holding his knees tight to his chest, his helmet pulled low. Patton was curious, moved close to the man, said in a low voice, "What's wrong with you, soldier? You wounded?"

The young man looked up at him, tears on his face, white, pale skin. "It's my nerves."

The man began to cry aloud, heavy sobs, and Patton felt something turn inside him, thought, good God, *another one*! He stepped back, bent low, stared into the man's face.

"What did you say?"

"It's my nerves. I can't stand the shelling."

Patton felt a punch in his chest, a searing bolt of heat. *"Your nerves! Hell, you're just a goddamned coward, you yellow son of a bitch!"*

The man was still crying, the awful sobs cutting through Patton, piercing him, the anger rolling to his fists. He stepped close to the man, his brain screaming, stop that! Stop crying! He pulled his hand back, the heat driving his anger, the burning in his chest, raw fury, the man's tear-soaked face, the awful sobbing. He brought his hand down in a quick motion, slapped the young man, knocking him sideways, shouted again.

"Shut up that goddamned crying! I won't have these brave

men here who have been shot at seeing a yellow bastard sitting here crying!"

He stepped back, saw the man pulling himself upright, more sobs, unstoppable, the man's red eyes staring at him. But the man did not stop crying, and Patton leapt at him, swung his hand down hard again, the man's helmet knocked away, the soldier bareheaded now, sobbing louder. Patton backed away again, realized men had gathered, the doctors, the wounded men all staring at him. He fought to calm himself, turned, saw a white-coated officer, said, "Don't you coddle this yellow bastard! There's nothing the matter with him. I won't have the hospitals cluttered up with these sons of bitches who haven't got the guts to fight!"

He looked at the soldier again, sitting upright again, red-faced, the sobs growing quiet.

"You're going back to the front lines, and you may get shot and killed, but you're going to fight! If you don't, I'll stand you up against a wall and have a firing squad kill you on purpose!"

The man began to cry again, voices behind Patton growing, the room hot, swirling, stinking air. Patton felt his stomach turn, could not escape the sound of the man's sobs, the fury coming back, fire in his brain. He reached down, his hands wrapping around the butt of his pistol, the gun pulling loose from the holster.

"I ought to shoot you myself, you goddamned whimpering coward!"

The man was staring at the pistol, and Patton held it out, tried to point it toward the man's face, felt the men around him, moving closer, his own hands shaking now. He glanced to the side, saw faces, men and women, doctors, soldiers, nurses, a crowd, staring, wide-eyed shock. The pistol was heavy in his hands, and he looked down, the fury pushed aside by dark horror. The gun slid back into the holster, and Patton backed away, turned toward the opening of the wide tent, looked at the officer again, cold hate in the man's face. Patton tried to bring the anger out again, how dare you show disrespect . . . but the man did not move, kept his eye focused on him, unflinching. Patton turned away now, moved to the opening, the blessed air, forced the words, shouted again.

"Send that yellow son of a bitch to the front lines!"

He was outside now, more people gathering, his driver standing by the jeep, waiting, obedient, and Patton climbed into the jeep, said, "I just saved a boy's soul, if he has one. Let's go. Bradley will wonder where the hell I am."

The driver complied, the jeep moving quickly, the crowd of people behind him emerging from the hospital tent, watching him drive away.

SOUTH OF MESSINA—AUGUST 17, 1943

The sun was rising, the barren hills empty of life, the chill in the night air already warming. The men made their way slowly, stepping across large rocks, piles of dirt and concrete, hands out, the men helping one another across the treacherous ground. Above them, the bridge had been blasted into rubble, the roadway simply gone. They were used to it now, these British commando units who had worked feverishly alongside their engineers, pressing forward as the Germans withdrew, threading their way across deep valleys, repairing or clearing the roads so the rest of Montgomery's army could continue the northward push. It was too common, so many of the roads simply narrow cuts carved into hillsides, the Germans detonating the rock above, burying them under tons of debris. The deep gullies and crevices were a greater challenge still, the destruction of the bridges delaying the vehicles. The engineers had used every tool in their arsenal, every trick, pulleys and winches, levers and cables, bridging the chasms, creating roadbeds where none existed.

The commandos left the ravine, crawled up onto flat ground, stared north, waiting now as a single jeep was pulled through the ravine behind them. With one great gasping effort, more men rolled the jeep up onto the road, the grateful commandos making way for their senior officer, the man slipping into the driver's seat, others piling on, the engine firing, the jeep making the final dash, the two-mile push into the city.

His name was Jack Churchill, a lieutenant colonel commanding the Second British Commandos. As he drove toward the city, he held the reconnaissance reports in his mind, the

observers telling him what he had seen himself. There had been
a sudden lack of enemy fire, artillery batteries growing silent,
infantry in the rocks no longer picking targets among his men.
The reports told him what any officer could see, that the Germans had pulled away into the city. But the commandos knew
more than that, knew by the silence that the Germans were not
manning their defenses, that the city itself was not rumbling
with the activity they had expected. Night after night, the air
force planes had made their runs, blindly pouring their
bombloads on targets they may or may not have hit. For nearly
two weeks navy patrol boats had crept close to the port, quick
snatches of information, confirming massive movement in and
out of the port. But the bombardment he had expected had never
seemed to come. Now, the roadways into the city were scattered
with broken machines, the debris of war, hillsides speckled with
dark spatters, what was left of artillery pieces and the crews
who'd manned them.

It had been a mystery to him, the reports coming forward to
one lieutenant colonel not detailed enough to tell him exactly
what was happening. It was his job to find out, after all, to press
forward with his men, to confront any stronghold where the
enemy might still be waiting. As he drove the jeep, he thought
of the city, the dreaded inevitability of house-to-house fighting,
snipers and hidden artillery. But if the Germans had pulled back
even farther, the mystery deepened. He knew the maps, knew
that beyond the city there was little room to maneuver, little
ground to offer the Germans any serious protection. There was
only one possibility, that the sketchy reports of the ongoing
evacuation of Sicily by German and Italians forces had to be accurate. If the enemy was gone, had somehow managed to escape the clutches of Montgomery's army, the officer knew there
would be hell to pay, that loud voices at headquarters would
want explanations. But none of that was his problem, not now,
not on this gray morning, not with the plump, ripe cherry of a
city straight in front of him. It was a moment he had not expected, an honor falling upon him by chance. His commandos
had done excellent work, the enemy responding to so many
sharp fights by backing away. He smiled, pressed the accelerator closer to the floorboard, the jeep responding, thought, yes, if

the enemy is gone, truly gone, then we will have the prize. We will capture this city. *I* will capture this city.

They rolled past small, white buildings, taller buildings beyond, the black water of the straits spreading out to the east. He pulled the jeep around a tight curve, slowed, the road opening into a wide street, flat-topped houses, and now . . . people.

They stood beside the road, some waving, some just silent, watching this strange, new army roll into their city. But it was hardly an army at all, just a few men on one jeep, and Churchill ignored that, thought only of the prize, the city of Messina. He saw a wide square, slowed, more people, flowers, loud voices, and he moved slowly, crept into the square, saw a crowd of people on the far side. He stopped the jeep, his men rolling off, rifles held ready, the crowd parting slowly. Churchill pushed through the faces, all civilians, held a carbine, poked it through more of the crowd, women, the crowd opening, uniforms, a cluster of men sitting on the steps of a small church.

"Well, good morning!"

Churchill lowered the carbine, knew the uniforms, the men calling out to him again, "Good morning! You'd be British, right? Welcome to our town!"

Churchill glanced at his own men, felt their energy draining away, low curses, the carbines going up on their shoulders. He stepped forward, saw an officer, a young lieutenant, hold out his hand. If it wasn't to be his moment, his conquest, it was a victory after all. The men were Americans. Patton had won the race.

39. EISENHOWER

" ' I am attaching a report which is shocking in its allegations against your personal conduct. I hope you can assure me that none of them is true; but the detailed circumstances communicated to me lead to the belief that some ground for the charges must exist. I am well aware of the necessity for hardness and toughness on the battlefield. I clearly understand that firm and drastic measures are at times necessary in order to secure the desired objectives. But this does not excuse brutality, abuse of the sick, nor exhibition of uncontrollable temper in front of subordinates . . .' "

Eisenhower stopped, looked at the secretary, the pencil poised for the next words. He saw wide-eyed surprise in the man's eyes, said, "Don't say a word, Sergeant. Give me a minute."

He stood, paced slowly, felt sweat in his shirt, put a hand up on the wall, stretched the aching muscles in his shoulder. Damn you, George. Damn you to hell.

He moved back to the desk, ignored the sergeant, weighed the words, fought for the right phrase. So what do I do now? Rip the man's stars off his shoulder? How often has he done this sort of thing already? If not for the indignation of one army doctor, I might not know about this at all. Bradley probably knows, and God knows who else. Kept their damned mouths shut, and I can't punish anybody for that. But I should. Hell, the reporters know about it already. Damned doctors aren't soldiers, they don't care who hears their gripes. Thank God the press boys listen to me, or Patton's name would be all over every newspaper in the States: the general who slaps his sick soldiers.

He looked toward the map on the wall, Sicily and Italy, red marks showing the new operation, what they called Avalanche. For long weeks, the army and navy planners had struggled to find the most effective way to capture the port at Naples, had debated the least dangerous strategy for striking and possibly capturing the massive airfields at Rome and Foggia. He saw Patton in his mind, thought, I don't need your stupidity right now, George. Is this the price I have to pay? You win a campaign, and you give me a reason to sack you, all in the same week. I wanted your name in the newspapers, but not for this, not for being a jackass. He looked at the sergeant, the man still waiting, pencil point on the paper.

"All right, Sergeant. Let's go on. 'In the two cases cited in the attached report, it is not my present intention to institute a formal investigation. Moreover, it is acutely distressing to me to have such charges as these made against you at the very moment when an American army under your leadership has attained a success of which I am extremely proud.' "

He stopped again. There could be hell to pay for this. If I don't make some kind of stink publicly, I could be accused of covering up the charges. George's head won't be the only one going on the block. Dammit! What do I do with you now, George? Where can I put you where you can still do some good? Slapping men in a hospital. Someone else would court-martial you. Someone else might be right. But I need you, George. This army . . . *every* army needs someone who spits in the enemy's eye, who kicks a few asses. But it can't be like this. A man can't lose control of himself.

He looked at the sergeant, moved toward the chair, eased down slowly. There were sharp pains in his back, spreading out from the incurable pain in his shoulder. The sergeant was watching him and Eisenhower said, "Hell of a thing, isn't it?"

The man nodded slowly. "Yes, sir."

"Toughest letter I've ever had to write. You better be damned good about keeping your mouth shut."

He regretted the words, had no reason to doubt the man's ability to keep a secret.

"Yes, sir, I understand. I'd have a tough time with this too. Is it all true, sir? Did General Patton really do this?"

Eisenhower leaned back in the chair, wiped a warm hand across his forehead. "Afraid so. The doctor's report is pretty explicit. He claims a dozen or more witnesses. The press people came to me as well. George really put his foot in it."

The sergeant still watched him, questions on the man's face.

"You're wondering if I'll relieve him, right?"

"It's not my place to ask, sir."

"I need to hear George's side of this. Hopefully, I can convince him to issue a personal apology, to the specific soldiers, and to his command. If it was up to me, that would be it. We'd file this away and never think about it again. Problem is, it might not be up to me." He searched the man's face, the sergeant looking down, a tight frown, the man shaking his head. "What is it?"

"Just wondering, sir, how his men will take this. His soldiers, I mean. I can't speak for anyone else, but if my commanding general did such a thing to one of my buddies, I wouldn't feel too friendly toward him, if you know what I mean, sir."

"I know what you mean. But, dammit, sergeant, he *wins*. He doesn't make excuses, he doesn't find reasons why he should sit still, he's not cautious. He knows what his men can do, and he puts them in the place they need to be. There are very few people in this theater of the war who can think like he does, who can get the results he does. That means something, Sergeant, and no matter if this blows up in my face, and no matter if the damned newspapers get this on their front page, we have to have men like Patton on the front lines. I just wish . . ." He stopped, had said too much already, thought, you don't need to bury this man in your bellyaching. "I just wish I could do my job, and everyone else could do theirs."

The intrigue in Rome was increasing daily. With the fall of Mussolini, the Italian government was in shambles. Eisenhower had expected there to be infighting, that surely there would be a number of Italian officials still loyal to Hitler, men who would do all they could to maintain some kind of control, to convince Hitler that Italy was still an ally. He scanned the reports, the Ultra intercepts, London quickly passing to him any dispatches offering some word on how the Germans were responding to the chaos.

He sat at the desk, read the latest dispatch, thought, if the Germans believe the Italians are going to quit this war, there could be blood everywhere. They might start bombing Italian cities, a show of strength, just to intimidate whoever's calling the shots there. Will the king allow his people to be massacred? Would Hitler kill civilians just to punish them? Stupid question. He already has. At the very least, the Germans will be testing loyalties, finding out which Italians can still be trusted. How many will that be? How many of them will be more interested in preserving their palaces than in getting the Krauts out of their country? How many of them are willing to fight a bloody battle to make their point? Any civil war would be a one-sided affair, surely. If the Germans had help from a good percentage of the Italian army, they could crush anyone who spoke against them. Unless we were there to help them. Will they ask us? Tricky situation there, certainly. With Mussolini out of the way, is there anyone in the Italian government with guts enough to risk turning on the Germans? They'd have to be damned discreet about it. How much effort will Hitler make to hold on? Would he risk killing the king?

The planners of Avalanche had speculated that the Germans might simply pull away, shift their troops north of Rome, allowing the Allied landings to move in unopposed. Wishful thinking, he thought. The Germans can't simply hand us those airfields, can't offer us a perfect launching ground for our bombers. We can already reach German cities from bases in England. This would give us so many more options. The long-range bombers might even be able to reach the Russian positions, or come close enough to raise hell with the Kraut supply lines there. That would sure as hell make Stalin happy. No, Hitler won't make it that easy. He may have an Italian mess on his hands, but he won't just hand us the country. So how long will it take until someone in Rome contacts us, asking for help? Someone in the Italian hierarchy must surely see the opportunity here, that the smart move would be to pull Italy out of the alliance with Hitler.

He thought of Palermo, his visit to Patton. The city had been utterly destroyed by Allied bombing, too many military targets to ignore, targets whose destruction brought down far more of the city than anyone would have wanted. Dammit, it's war. The Vatican begs us not to bomb Rome, and so, the Germans use it as a staging area. How long can we put up with that? Or will the Germans fight us for every inch of every street, use the Colosseum as a tank park, the Roman Forum as an ammo dump? What happens then? Just like Palermo, do we obliterate the city? Surely that's incentive enough for the Italians to want out of this war. But they will need our help.

Word had come first by way of Lisbon, Portugal, brought by the hand of General Giuseppe Castellano, who claimed to be a representative of Marshal Badoglio himself. Castellano carried documents of introduction from the British minister to the Vatican, documents that seemed to verify the man was authorized to speak for the Italian government. Castellano's proposal was simple and direct. If the Allies were to land troops onto the Italian mainland, the Italian government would respond by issuing an order of surrender and would immediately join with the Allied cause by taking up arms against the Germans.

It was excellent news. But Eisenhower had no power to respond officially, could only forward the inquiry to the Allied governments. After a long day of tense anticipation, Eisenhower received permission to respond to Castellano in definite terms. The Allies would only accept unconditional surrender. It would also be expected that the senior officers in the Italian army would influence their men to do whatever they could to cooperate with Allied operations. Though Eisenhower didn't expect the Italians to suddenly start firefights with the Germans camped alongside them, the Allies insisted that the Italians make strenuous efforts to sabotage their infrastructure, including bridges, roadways, and airfields, as well as attacking or capturing any sources of local supply that the Germans used to sustain their men in the field.

As Castellano waited in Lisbon for some official response, Eisenhower received authorization to send two of his own people to deal with him. Logically enough, he chose his chief intelligence officer, Brigadier General Ken Strong, as well as his own chief of staff, Beetle Smith.

ALGIERS—AUGUST 20, 1943

"You look pretty whipped, Beetle."

Smith had sunk low in the chair, his round body sagging into the dark leather.

"I don't know about all this spy business, Ike. There's something about looking over your shoulder for Gestapo agents that doesn't have appeal. I'd liked to have spent more time in Lisbon. Seems like a nice place."

Eisenhower was already impatient. "This wasn't a vacation. Tell me what happened."

Smith took a deep breath. "Castellano hates the Krauts, no confusion about that. The Italians are insisting they be allowed to stand side by side with us as a fully recognized ally. He claims the Italian army is ready to change sides at a moment's notice and start shooting Germans."

"I'm not authorized to offer him anything like that. London and Washington have made their position clear. We don't even know who's behind this offer in the first place, who Castellano speaks for, how many of their people will actually go along with it. It takes guts to do something like this with a hundred thousand Germans in your backyard. They can't just call themselves our allies until we know what that means. My orders authorize me to secure their promise that they will serve us as collaborators. Did you say that?"

"My exact words. I emphasized that to him. Not sure he recognized the difference between a collaborator and an ally. Not sure I do either. I think he expects that if he promises they won't shoot at us, we're supposed to do the same thing. I explained to him it wasn't that simple, that the precise definition of *surrender* is one of those things that ministers and diplomats deal with. It seems that he's a soldier first and doesn't care about nuances, specific terms of treaties. But one thing's clear. He's sure as hell an Italian. He spoke long and hard about Italian honor, how important it was, how they had to preserve it for their grandchildren. In the next breath, he's talking about how eager they are to change their loyalties, and how perfectly cunning they were in arranging Mussolini's removal. Honor seems to be defined as whatever works at the time. Reminds me of the French."

"He tell you where Mussolini is now, where they're holding him?"

Smith laughed. "Nope, not a hint. I think he knows too. He says Hitler would love to know that as well, Gestapo agents all over the place, trying to find clues where the king squirreled him away. Castellano's scared of the Germans, for sure, figures they'll shoot him on the spot if they find out he's involved in this."

Eisenhower sipped from his coffee cup, felt a low burn in his stomach. He glanced at his watch, after midnight. "You have to be pretty exhausted. I've been spending every damned minute with the staff and the planners, going over all the logistics of Avalanche. Wayne will be here in a day or so, getting his final instructions. Monty and Alexander are ready to go, but it's not likely that Monty's part of the operation will be as tough. If we're lucky . . ." He paused, hated the word. "If all goes according to plan, we'll have Naples in the bag pretty quick. Ought to make Churchill happy as hell. Monty's chewing at his reins waiting to cross the straits. You know how he gets. Keeps telling me he'll just roll right up the toe. That's the kind of talk Churchill will expect to hear. Monty might be right. From everything we've seen, the Germans have already pulled a good ways away from the Strait of Messina."

Eisenhower finished the coffee, saw a deep yawn spreading across Smith's face.

"Excuse me, Ike. Long damned day. Oh, one more thing. I guess this is pretty important. Castellano was eager to show off everything he knew about the German positions, troops strengths, all of that. Laid it out in pretty good detail."

Eisenhower sat up straight. "Yes, that would be considered important. Jesus, Beetle, you just think of that?"

"Sorry, Ike. I've got it all written down."

Smith reached into a pocket, pulled out a small roll of paper. "General Strong has the larger copy. I jotted it down for myself in case we got split up, or something . . . bad happened."

Eisenhower took the paper, unrolled it, sat back in the chair, felt the heat in his stomach again. "Is this accurate? Well, hell, how would you know?"

Beetle seemed to ignore the insult. "Castellano was pretty exact, Ike. He wanted to give us something to show us how sincere they were, and how high up the ladder he really was. He knew we had doubts about him, whether his word amounted to anything."

Eisenhower pulled himself out of the chair, scanned the paper again. *Fifteen German divisions.* He moved toward the telephone, picked up the receiver, held the phone in his hand, his mind growing blank, the weariness overtaking him. *No, not now. They need sleep too. Nothing will change by morning. Clark has to know about this, though. All of them.*

He turned toward Smith. "You realize what this means?"

"Not really."

"It means that there are a hell of lot more Germans in Italy than we figured. It means that our little victory in Sicily didn't accomplish nearly what it could have. We let them go, Beetle. We let the enemy escape. Patton and Montgomery got so caught up in their damned race, so damned concerned with who had the biggest bulge in his pants . . . they lost sight of their real objective. We spent so much energy capturing a *place,* like it was some game of capture the flag. Tunisia was a victory, an honest, crushing victory. But Sicily . . . dammit, Beetle, we didn't win a damned thing there. We let the enemy get away. We let them haul away their guns and their tanks and most of their people, and now, those people have been reinforced. I didn't really think Hitler would spend so much energy on Italy. But we've heard that Rommel has taken command there, and sure as hell, Hitler wouldn't have put him there if he didn't expect a fight. But *this* . . . unless Castellano is handing us phony information, the Krauts are holding tight. Hitler's playing wait and see. This says Kesselring is still in Rome. He wouldn't be there if he didn't have an army to command, if he didn't expect something to happen. Dammit!"

Eisenhower slid the paper into his pocket, moved toward the door. "Avalanche . . . everything's in place, Beetle. We're set to begin this thing in two weeks. Unless we delay the whole operation, it's just too late to make any serious changes." He paused.

"I really hoped they would be gone. I just thought that maybe we could march into Naples and then Rome, grab the whole country without a serious fight."

CARTHAGE, NEAR TUNIS, TUNISIA—AUGUST 23, 1943

Eisenhower had created an advanced headquarters at Carthage, to be nearer the Italian operations, but also to draw closer to the various headquarters of the heads of each branch of the service. It had become obvious throughout the Sicilian campaign that having the senior commanders spread all over the Mediterranean only added to the spiderweb of complications that already infected every large-scale operation.

Montgomery had never wavered from his own plan, to launch his invasion force from Sicily directly across the Strait of Messina, driving up the toe of Italy. Every dispatch, every piece of intelligence, had seemed to show that the Germans had pulled away, that Montgomery would likely face only local opposition, most of that from Italian units who would easily be encouraged to surrender. Once established on the mainland, Montgomery could broaden his attacks to drive a wedge toward the ports of Taranto and then Bari, on Italy's east coast. With support from Cunningham's warships, it was unlikely the Germans could hold Montgomery back, especially from any place that was attacked from both land and sea. But the second prong of the plan troubled Eisenhower and drew concern from most of the others. It was realistic to describe Montgomery's attack as a strong diversion, whether Montgomery cared for that description or not. Clark's Fifth Army was to be the stronger attack, would land the larger force at the Gulf of Salerno. Clark's first goal would be to establish a secure beachhead, and then, the primarily American force would drive north and east to capture the port of Naples. Though intelligence showed no major concentrations of enemy troops close to Clark's landing zones, there were a great many shore batteries, defensive works spread along any place that the Allies could use for their landings. What caused concern were reports that the troops who manned those batteries had recently been changed, from Italian to German. With so much maneuvering in the Allied bases, so much preparation that enemy intelligence agents might certainly observe, Eisenhower had to assume that such a change in personnel was not simply a product of chance. If the Allied planners considered the Gulf of Salerno to be the most logical place for the Americans to go ashore, it seemed apparent now that Kesselring agreed.

The lunch had been boisterous, Montgomery in usual form, the others staking claim to their own interests. The men were mostly gone now, Alexander and Tedder boarding the planes that would take them to their headquarters, Cunningham traveling by car to the nearby port of Tunis. Most of the staff officers were gone as well, Eisenhower's intelligence and planning officers retreating to their offices, every man feeling the weight of what lay in front of him.

With the luncheon drawing to a close, Eisenhower had seen the unspoken question on Clark's face, had welcomed the chance to speak to Clark alone.

"I've missed having you in my office, Wayne. There have been a few times when I needed a bomb of honesty dropped on someone's bellyaching."

Clark stretched his long frame, settled into a chair. "A lot has happened since Gibraltar, Ike. It's only been nine months, and I feel like the whole world has changed. I wish I had been more a part of it."

"All things in time, Wayne. You were exactly where we needed you. Nobody's better at putting an army together, cutting through all the administrative bull. I needed you to get your people organized and get them trained. We got our asses kicked in Tunisia because we weren't ready. It's different now. We're ready, and that's because of you."

"Thanks. Hell of a thing."

"What?"

"I feel like I'm standing in a beehive. It's one thing to run these meetings when you're in charge, when you can tell some jackass to shut the hell up. But here . . . so much of the heat is directed right at me. Everybody's got his idea how I should handle this, everybody's got some reason why their plan is better than everyone else's."

Eisenhower saw something on Clark's face he had never seen before. *Uncertainty.* "You'll do fine, Wayne. We're a hell of an army now. Nobody's a recruit anymore. We're all veterans."

"You. Not me. Not Walker and Dawley."

"Jesus, Wayne. Knock it off. You've got good men under you, and plenty of veterans right beside them. You think I'd have put you in this spot if I thought you weren't the right man to handle it?"

Clark looked down, nodded. "Just nervous as hell, Ike. It's one thing to draw it up on paper . . ."

"Everybody's behind you, Wayne: Marshall, everybody in London. Hell, Churchill's doing a jig that we picked you for this job. This is his baby, this whole damned campaign. When he heard I wanted you, he was like a kid at Christmas. From the time we landed in North Africa, every good man in this command has gotten his chance to do something big. This is yours. This operation will shorten the war and give us options we don't have now. We take Italy out of the war, then we can finally . . . *finally* put our attention on the cross-Channel operation. Even Churchill concedes that. We've gone along with most everything they wanted us to do here, every damned operation since we've been here has been pushed by the British. They're actually starting to talk about France again, and this time it's not an argument. Churchill and Brooke both insist we begin moving people to England, start a buildup there, start training people for operations next spring. Marshall's beside himself, Wayne. He's been pushing for us to hit France for two years, but until now, he was shouting at a brick wall. But no more. With Italy right in our hands, the British are opening the door. It's exciting as hell, Wayne!"

Clark nodded. "Good news, Ike. Great news. We know who's going to be in charge?"

"Not yet. Time will tell. Maybe a Brit. Doesn't matter now. What matters is that you give the enemy a bloody nose in Italy and keep punching him until he gives up. You hit the Germans hard, take Naples, and the Italians will line up right alongside you. The Krauts will know they can't stand up to that much pressure, and in a few months . . . hell a few weeks, you'll be the biggest damned hero in this army!"

Eisenhower stopped, felt uneasy now, didn't enjoy cheerleading, had never been one to spout out predictions. It nagged at him, the strange gloom from Clark. Not even the Ultra intercepts could tell him what Kesselring might have up his sleeve, what the Germans really intended to do, how they would react to the Allied landings. And Rommel, sitting up north in the Italian Alps, waiting . . . for what? But I don't need to see this, he thought. I don't need Clark to be wavering.

Clark seemed to read him, the strong link between them still unbroken. "We'll do it, Ike. *I'll* do it. You're right. We've got good people."

"Damned right."

Clark tilted his head, looked at Eisenhower, a change in his mood. "How's George? I haven't talked to him in a while, not since . . . the problem."

Eisenhower sat back in the chair. "So far, it's not a problem. He accepts that what he did was stupid and knows damned well that it could have cost him his career. He sent the appropriate letter to Marshall, owning up to it all, and I made damned sure he apologized to the kid he slapped. That had to be tough as hell. *Humble* isn't something he excels at. So far, we've kept it quiet. The press boys could make a hell of a stink with this, but they haven't. They know how important George is to this army. I never thought I'd be thanking a bunch of reporters for having good sense." Eisenhower paused. "If I know George, he's going nuts waiting for something else to do. Not much I can do about that, not right now. Bob Hope was here, and I made damned sure he took his show to Palermo. He had Frances Langford with him, that gorgeous singer. I'm pretty sure that took George's mind off anything else."

Eisenhower stopped, saw no change in Clark's expression. He realized now, Clark's interest in Patton was simply good manners. Or maybe just curiosity. He knew that Clark and Patton had little affection for each other, the difference being that Clark did a better job of hiding it. Clark's command of Avalanche would have been a sharp stick in Patton's side, an attitude Eisenhower was used to now. He wants every damned command on every battlefield. Not now, George, not with your own self-made mess hanging over your head. It's time to just sit still for a while.

CARTHAGE—AUGUST 29, 1943

Eisenhower watched the plane, a wide circle, the pilot bringing it down smoothly, none of the gut-punching drops that had been so necessary on the short airstrips, or anywhere the enemy might be close enough to position antiaircraft fire. It was the same throughout all of North Africa and Sicily now, the entire region a secure Allied base, troops and equipment continuing to roll in from transport ships and cargo planes. Every port held by the Allies had become a hive of activity, freshly trained recruits adding to the strength of the veterans, new, more modern tanks, better artillery pieces, much of it destined for Italy, for the beachheads that Clark and Montgomery were certain to secure. In the wide Atlantic, the deadly cat-and-mouse games with the U-boats had become increasingly one-sided, British and American destroyers, dive-bombers, and torpedo planes taking an enormous toll on the German submarines. As the quantity and effectiveness of the U-boats dropped dramatically, massive convoys from America were passing through once-dangerous waters virtually unmolested. Though many of those ships continued to funnel through the Strait of Gibraltar, adding to the power at Eisenhower's command, many more were reaching ports in the British Isles, a buildup geared toward an entirely new operation.

While Eisenhower welcomed the British enthusiasm for the cross-Channel invasion of France, he had begun to feel concern that the British were too confident that the fight in Italy would be brief, the outcome a foregone conclusion. That energy was driven primarily by Churchill, his boisterous pronouncements inspiring the same enthusiasm from Cunningham, Alexander, and Montgomery. From Gibraltar to Cairo, British officers and their civilian ministers were drinking celebratory toasts, certain that the final thrust into Italy would rip the underbelly away from Hitler's Fortress Europa.

Eisenhower was grateful for the enthusiasm he was receiving from Marshall, enthusiasm of a different sort. The Americans who had so loudly pressed for the invasion of France were finally going to get their way. The British had opened the door wide to the American desire to drive a hard blow into northwestern France. Eisenhower's attentions were still squarely focused on Clark's efforts at Salerno, but already, orders were coming to him to begin the transfer of American units to England, to begin serious training for the invasion of the French coast, expected to take place the following spring.

The operation was now called Overlord, and British and American planners were deep into the details, fashioning a plan that would obliterate any memory of the failure of the Dieppe raid. The invasion had to be designed to drive a powerful force across the beaches of France, to secure beachheads and strongholds with enough power that Hitler would have no choice but to respond by weakening his forces in Russia, and anywhere else the Nazi war machine had secured footholds.

Eisenhower's authority only included the Mediterranean theater, and he knew that with planning for the new campaign already under way, he would be asked to make hard choices, to send some of his best people away, the men who would assume new responsibilities with Overlord.

He faced one of those choices now, watched as the single plane touched down, could only wait patiently as the pilot taxied toward the tarmac. In a few seconds the motors were shut down, the props slowing, and quickly the door at the tail of the plane opened. Eisenhower moved that way, his aides gathering a short distance behind. He saw a face, a young officer, unfamiliar, the man stepping down quickly, a sharp salute. Eisenhower returned it, waited, saw another face, older, the uniform perfect, the three stars on the man's shoulder catching the sunlight. The promotion to lieutenant general had come only weeks before, no one questioning, no jealousy, none of the intrigue and backbiting that suggested a man had not earned the rank. Eisenhower couldn't help but smile, returned the man's salute. It was Omar Bradley.

They walked along the shore, and Eisenhower stared out to the open water, one British destroyer at anchor. It was Cunningham's precaution, that with Eisenhower's advance headquarters at the seaside town, there was always danger from a surprise attack by German dive-bombers or commandos, the Luftwaffe still launching the occasional raid.

"I don't believe this, Ike. How can this be?"

"Believe it. Marshall has already approved your transfer."

Bradley walked in silence, and Eisenhower was surprised by the man's lack of enthusiasm. "Is there something you don't understand?"

Bradley stopped, turned toward Eisenhower, put his hands on his hips. "I don't understand why Marshall or anyone else would pick me for the job."

Eisenhower could see it now, it wasn't just humility. Bradley seemed genuinely concerned.

"Brad, the job is yours, unless you can give me a damned good reason why we should pick someone else." He paused, waited, Bradley silent. "Good. You're the man for the job. As soon as you can get your ducks in a row here, you will report to General Devers in London and assume command of the First Army. You will establish headquarters at Bristol, most likely. Even though by title Jake Devers commands American forces in the European theater, make no mistake about this, Brad. I don't expect Devers to lead troops in the field. It's just not his strength. Your command will eventually spearhead our role in Overlord."

Bradley began to walk again, rubbed his hands together. "I understand. Who's replacing me at Second Corps?"

"John Lucas."

Bradley nodded, and Eisenhower could see the man's mind at work, already digesting, absorbing everything that might lie in front of him. He looked at Eisenhower now, a slight squint in his eyes.

"You're telling me I'm being promoted to army commander. That's a hell of a pat on the back. I'm not sure how to react to that. I'll give it everything I can, but, Ike . . . something doesn't feel right. How is this going to sit . . ."

"With Patton?"

"Yeah. With Patton. This ought to be his command, Ike. He outranks me. You're shoving me up the ladder right past him."

Eisenhower said nothing, kicked at the hard sand with his

boot, dislodged a round, white rock, kicked it toward the water. Bradley started to speak, and Eisenhower held up a hand.

"You know George as well as anyone. Do I have to explain it to you?"

"You mean . . . it's all about the slapping incident?"

"That's part of it. I shouldn't have to spell it out for you, Brad. This operation is going to involve some pretty intensive training, some pretty tough coordination with the Brits. Chances are Monty will be involved in a big way, and I haven't been told yet who will command the overall operation. I don't think the decision's been made. But be honest with me. Do you think George is the right man to command something this complicated?"

"I can't answer that, Ike. George is the best ass-kicker in the army."

"Well, I can. The job is yours. We don't always need ass-kickers, Brad. You know damned well that some of Patton's subordinates don't agree with his style of doing things." Eisenhower paused, wondered if Bradley would open up to him. He knew that Bradley had been concerned that Patton's infatuation with Messina might get more of Bradley's people killed than the prize was worth. "I want that honesty, Brad."

"He has his ways, Ike. Usually it works. You can't argue with success."

"To hell with that."

Bradley stopped again, stared out toward the British ship.

"All that razzle-dazzle looks good on magazine covers. But I heard it from the men, Ike, after those parades that George would lead through the troops, all those clean uniforms, the flags and sirens. It didn't always go over well. My boys were fighting the toughest enemy we've ever faced, on ground more difficult than anything in Africa. Then George would come through with his sirens blaring and expect them to cheer. They did, some of them. But not everybody. When he belted that kid . . . there were people on my own staff who wanted to see him strung up." Bradley paused, and Eisenhower could see the man searching for words. "I heard all this stuff about Rommel, how he won battles because he was out there with his men. I don't know how much of that is true, how much is German baloney. If Rommel seemed to be one of his men, if he seemed to feel what they were feeling, if he was willing to pick up a rifle or climb into a tank, sure, I can understand how that would pick his men up. But that's not what George does. If we still had plumes in our hats, he'd have the biggest one. If we rode horses, he'd have the white one. Dammit, Ike, don't misunderstand me. There may be no better tactical officer in this army than George Patton. Nobody knows how to maneuver troops under fire like he does. Audacity, Ike. That's what it is. Every army needs a Stonewall Jackson once in a while. But Jackson's uniform wasn't spotless, he didn't have a polished helmet, and if he'd carried pearl-handled pistols, he'd have fired them at the enemy once in a while." He stopped, looked down. "My apologies, Ike. I spoke too freely."

"I told you to be honest. I can't disagree with one thing you've said. But right now, George isn't your concern. I don't know how he'll respond to your transfer, but I can't worry about that now. I have my hands full right here. Marshall wants you in England, and the sooner the better. I'm already getting orders to prepare combat units to follow you there, and they need to begin training as soon as the bases are set up. You're in command up there, Brad. There's nobody in this army I'd rather see at the wheel."

40. ADAMS

They had been pulled out of Sicily on August 20, the entire Eighty-second Airborne Division reestablished around the airfields at Kairouan, Tunisia. Almost immediately, the recruits had come, the new men to fill the depleted ranks. With the new men came new training, and the jumps continued. As they had done so many times before, Adams and the other jumpmasters manned the doorways of the C-47s, coaching and prodding the unfamiliar faces, insuring that when they jumped into a combat zone, they would know that the bone-jarring landings would be no different from what they had practiced so often at Fort Benning. Of course, no amount of additional training could predict how a man might actually respond when he jumped into the middle of an enemy machine-gun nest.

Unlike their first encampment in North Africa, this time the misery and boredom did not continue for more than a few days. By early September, they were sent back to Sicily, the airbase at Licata, on the southern coast, and the men in charge began ironing out the problems that had plagued the 505th's first jump. Homing beacons and portable radio sets were old technology, but no one in the Airborne command had seemed to consider that this sort of communications was an absolute necessity in the field. After Sicily, they changed their minds, energized by the pilots, who pushed their officers to find better ways to guide them to their drop zones. The Airborne's drop into Sicily had been extraordinarily valuable, blocking the German advance, which might have saved the entire operation. But most of the Allied commanders, including Eisenhower, considered that to be a fortunate accident. No matter how effective the men of the Eighty-second had been in Sicily, their jump had been a chaotic mess. Criticism of the paratroopers had come from all directions, rumors filtering down that the Eighty-second might be disbanded, or redesignated as infantry. Like most such rumors, Adams knew that such a radical change was unlikely to happen, but with Eisenhower himself voicing serious doubts about the effectiveness of the paratroop force, the officers were taking the rumors seriously. General Ridgway responded vigorously to Eisenhower's criticisms and had ordered that steps be taken to insure that future jump missions be equipped with the tools necessary so that regiments actually landed on their designated drop zones.

At Licata, some of the men had been organized into smaller units, trained for a specific job. They were called pathfinders, paratroopers whose job would be to land twenty to thirty minutes before the main body, to set up small radio transmitters that would guide the pilots to the proper jump zones. Besides the radios, some of the pathfinders would carry a krypton light, a small beacon that emitted a single blinding flash of light visible miles away. If all that failed, the pathfinders were taught that once they heard the C-47s, they could simply light a fire in the shape of a *T,* which would clearly designate the landing zone. How exactly the pathfinders would find the correct zones themselves was not revealed to men like Adams. His faith in the pathfinders was as limited as his faith that some officer would come up with any gimmick designed to make a soldier's life simpler. His men agreed, most of them convinced that it was still up to the pilots. If the men in the cockpit got lost, there wasn't much anyone on the ground could do about it.

LICATA FIELD, SICILY—SEPTEMBER 8, 1943

He sat beneath the wing of a C-47, double-checking his pack, killing time, the men around him waiting as he was, nothing else to do until the orders came to board the planes. There was little talking, even the new men subdued, their nervous chatter held down, each man locked into his own thoughts.

He counted his ration tins, far fewer than he had carried on Sicily. Their personal gear had been pared down, blankets, toilet articles, and extra clothing reduced to a minimum, or eliminated altogether. It was one valuable lesson from the jumps in Sicily: armament had far more value in the field than personal convenience. The Sicilian countryside had offered them all the comforts a man required to survive. What they could not replace were the weapons, the grenades and explosives, parts for the heavy machine guns. At Fort Benning, the men had practiced by dropping their heavy equipment separately, in bundles attached beneath the wings of the C-47s. But Sicily was not Fort Benning, and the men had learned that stumbling around in the dark searching for lost bundles was a surefire way to attract the enemy's attention. More often the bundles were simply lost, many of them still scattered in the rough hills and thickets that spread across southern Sicily. If the men wanted use of a heavy machine gun or a bazooka, they would find a way to carry one with them.

Adams counted his grenades again, glanced up at the others, saw each man following his example. His platoon had only a few new faces, none of them yet showing him the telltale signs of becoming a weak link. They had responded well to the training, had made two night jumps around Kairouan, with no disasters. Now, they sat close to the rows of planes, trying to keep out of the way of the maintenance crews, while they waited for the officers to give them the order.

Scofield had been gone for some time, long meetings with the other officers, Adams glancing up every few seconds toward the low block building at the far end of the tarmac. He saw the captain now, others, pouring out of the building in a rush, moving quickly.

Adams's heart jumped, and he called out, "Here we go! Ready packs. Prepare to board up!"

Scofield was jogging toward them, waved his hands in the air, shouted, "Stand down! The mission's been scrapped!"

Scofield motioned to the men to gather, was clearly angry. The entire company moved close, and Scofield paced in small, quick steps, a tight circle, his arms waving like the wings of a deranged bird.

"Dammit! Second time in a week! Brass can't make up its mind what the hell to do with us! We're not going anywhere today! Giant Two has now been scratched. Just like Giant One. They make a plan, get us all fired up to go, and then some general chickens out!"

"Why, Captain?"

The voice came from behind Adams, one of the new men, Unger, the high-pitched voice of a child. Scofield looked at the young man, seemed to calm, gather himself. Adams could see that Scofield was scolding himself, thought, easy, Captain. Officers aren't supposed to gripe about generals, especially not to pimple-faced enlisted men.

"Never mind. All you need to know is we've been ordered to stand down. Colonel Gavin got the word from General Ridgway. Those orders came from higher up. The colonel didn't tell me any more than I'm going to tell you, so no questions. It's no secret anymore, so I can tell you that Giant Two was a drop on the airfields around Rome. We were supposed to land right on the fields, and the Eyeties were going to be there to help us. They had agreed to supply everything we would need to capture the landing strips and secure them against any German units in the area. They were supposed to help us out by blowing up bridges, taking out German antiaircraft batteries, and once we hit the ground, they would furnish us with a considerable amount of supplies. Apparently, General Ridgway had some concerns about this and questioned whether or not the Italians could actually deliver what they promised. It seems someone above him shared those concerns. Count your stars, gentlemen. We might have jumped right into a massacre."

Adams had crawled out from under the wing, stood, said, "So, what now, sir?"

Scofield put his hands on his hips, shook his head. "We remain on high alert. The Five-oh-five isn't the first team on this one anyway. The 504th and the 509th will take the point on any new orders. We did our part in Sicily, and so, they're figuring we can hang back as the reserve. But don't any of you think we're on vacation. They might call for us at any time. Seems like this operation is already *fumtu*. As much confusion as there's been already . . ." Scofield stopped. "Check that. Just keep yourself ready to go. Get some sleep. Eat something. We get a call from General Ridgway, we might need to be up at it pretty quickly."

Scofield moved away, and Adams slid back under the wing, gathered his gear. The others were talking, low grumbles, mostly the new men, and he ignored them, thought, don't be in such a damned hurry to get your ass shot off.

"Sarge?"

The voice was unmistakable, and he turned. "What is it, Unger?"

"The captain said this operation is *fumtu*. What the heck does that mean?"

Adams laughed. "You should already know, Private, that in this army, there's *snafu* and there's *fumtu*."

Unger stared at him, empty expression.

"You a churchman, right, Unger?"

"Yes, sir. Every Sunday."

"All right, I'll give you the clean translation. *Situation Normal All Fouled Up*. But what the captain was telling you is, this operation is *Fouled Up More Than Usual*."

*   *   *

The Fifth Army's landings at Salerno began at 3:30 a.m., September 9, four divisions, two American and two British, supplemented by American rangers and commandos. To the north, the town of Salerno fell easily into American hands, but in the center, the British forces confronted heavy resistance from German defenders in the heights above the beaches. After a long day of difficult fighting, the British finally secured their beachhead, aided considerably by firepower from the naval artillery offshore. On the right flank of the landings, the American Sixth Corps, under Ernest Dawley, pushed only into light resistance and had, by nightfall on September 9, accomplished most of its objectives. With the landings complete, General Clark had every reason to believe that Avalanche was off and running.

Kesselring's reinforcements were quickly summoned, and within hours of the landings, German panzer units were surging toward Clark's beachheads. In the center of the beachhead, the Sele River flowed into the Gulf of Salerno, and along the mouth of the river, sandbars had formed, preventing the landing craft from putting troops near the river itself. The result was a gap, several miles wide, between the British troops in the center and Dawley's corps on the right. On September 10, Dawley still believed he had the upper hand in his sector, and he chose the Thirty-sixth Division to make the hardest push inland, seeking to capture roads, hilltops, and key intersections. The Thirty-sixth had yet to be tested in battle, but with little opposition, they had made good progress and accomplished most of Dawley's objectives, extending the beachhead far inland. What Dawley did not realize was that to his left, Kesselring's panzers were driving toward the beach and were already beginning to fill the gap. When the Germans launched their counterattacks, Dawley's men found themselves dangerously flanked and were soon virtually cut off. Along both sides of the gap, the Allied positions were now engulfed by German armor, and on the right, the green soldiers of the Thirty-sixth began to crack. Over the next three days, Clark's initial successes were erased by the German assaults, and the Allied beachheads began to crumble, panicked troops falling back toward the beaches, protected only by the umbrella of fire from the naval artillery.

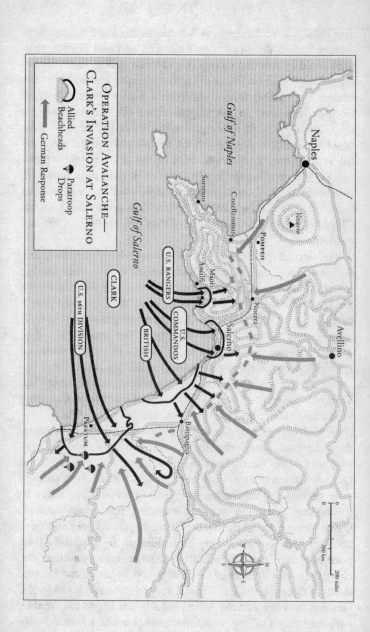

OPERATION AVALANCHE—
CLARK'S INVASION AT SALERNO

Allied
Beachheads

Paratroop
Drops

German Response

U.S. 36TH DIVISION

CLARK

U.S. RANGERS

U.S.
COMMANDOS

BRITISH

Gulf of Naples

Gulf of Salerno

Naples

Sorrento

Castellammare

Vesuvio

POMPEII

Maiori

Amalfi

Nocera

Salerno

Avellino

Battipaglia

PAESTUM

200 miles

300 km

N
W E
S

On September 13, Clark sent Matthew Ridgway a desperate plea for assistance, and Ridgway responded immediately. That night, Colonel Reuben Tucker's 504th Parachute Infantry Regiment made the Eighty-second Airborne's first drop into Italy, a desperate attempt to fill the wide gap in the Allied lines and bolster the battered Thirty-sixth Division. The following day, the 509th, under Colonel Edson Raff received orders to jump as well. The 509th had been the first wave of Operation Torch, had begun the Allied invasion of North Africa by being dropped haphazardly across two hundred miles of desert. Throughout the Sicilian campaign, the men of the 509th had impatiently stewed in North Africa, while the 504th and 505th did the work. Now, Clark ordered the 509th to make the Airborne's most dangerous jump. They would attempt to secure a critical crossroads near the village of Avellino, far inland, and far into enemy territory, to prevent any more German reinforcements from reaching the already reeling Allied troops. If the 509th was to survive at all, they would have to hold on until someone from Clark's Fifth Army reached their position. If the Germans succeeded in driving Clark's forces back into the sea, the 509th would simply be swallowed up.

On September 14, the men of Jim Gavin's 505th stayed close to the planes, wondering if they would be used at all. By midafternoon the questions were answered. Gavin learned they were not to be held back as reserves after all.

LICATA AIRFIELD—SEPTEMBER 14, 1943

They had camped among the olive groves, broad fields of ancient trees. Except for the wings of the C-47s, the olive trees were the only shade within reach, the only place a man could rest without baking in the sun.

Adams had slept, lying on his back, his helmet on his face, sweat soaking his clothes, a soft breeze cooling him. He was awake now, stretched his legs, raised the helmet slightly, glanced at his watch. Three o'clock, he thought. If something's gonna happen, it better happen quick. He heard voices, the sound of a man choking. There was laughter, and Adams knew the routine, pulled the helmet away, blinked through the sunlight. He saw Unger, the young man on his knees, red-faced, spitting furiously, scratching at his belt, trying to grab his canteen. Adams slammed the helmet on his head, rolled to one side, pushed himself to his feet. He was already angry, slapped at the dirt on his pant legs, had gone through this routine too many times.

"Which one of you jackasses told him to eat the olives?" The men close to him were veterans, every one trying his best to hold back the smile. "None of you willing to admit it? Fine, tell you what. Since this is your idea of fun, why don't we all eat one? Millions of the damned things, just reach up and grab one! Come on! We deserve a treat!"

They were watching him now, and he had no patience, knew they were wondering if he was serious. He plucked an olive from a branch above him, hard and black, held it up.

"They sell these things, you know. Ship 'em all over the damned world. Your mamas probably used them to cook with, right? Well, chow down, boys! No reason to let the new men get all the fun!"

He saw one man step forward, head down. It was Newley, the loudmouth from Chicago. "It was me, Sarge. Nobody else."

Adams wasn't surprised, had seen Newley victimize more than one recruit. "You hungry, Newley? Have an olive. Grab a handful."

"I didn't mean nothing, Sarge. Just playing."

Adams felt the heat now, sunshine ripping through the branches of the old trees. "This is the Airborne, Private. You stopped *playing* when you stepped through the gates at Fort Benning. You notice how many of those C-47s took off last night?"

He saw nods from the men around him, and Newley said, "Yeah, Sarge."

"That was the Five-oh-four. You think those boys are *playing* today? Tell you what, Newley. Next time we climb in a C-47, Unger's sitting right next to you. I want you jumping right in front of him. You know why? Because I want you to think about what Unger had to accomplish to be here. I want you to think about what *Airborne* means, what you mean to one another out there in the dark. You come down in a briar patch or break your damned leg in a ditch, Unger might be the man who saves your ass. Or, he might not. He might not hear you call out. He might think about what a bastard you are and go the other way. Would you want him to do that, Private Newley?"

"No, Sarge."

"Then give Unger your canteen. Help him get that crap out of his mouth. And, Unger!"

Unger was still spitting, his face twisted, the words coming out in a croak. "Yes, Sarge?"

"Next time somebody tells you to eat something . . . make sure *he* eats it first! You were briefed about this in North Africa: olives have to be cured before they're edible. Pay attention next time. I have no room in this squad for a dumb son of a bitch."

"Yes, Sarge."

Newley was beside Unger now, others as well, the joke over. There had always been the jokesters, the tricks played on the recruits. It was good sport at Fort Benning, rituals that every unit had gone through. But Adams had no spirit for it now, no energy for anyone's idiotic meanness. He moved out of the olive grove, stared across to the airfield, thought, save all that, boys. Especially the new ones. They haven't seen it yet, haven't watched a man come apart in a burst of fire, haven't scraped a dead man's blood from their fingernails. I know why the veterans do this stuff. They need something to laugh at, and there's nothing funny out here. There's nothing funny about what happened to McBride and Fulton. And Colonel Gorham. He looked back, the men going about their routine now, some lying flat, helmets covering faces. He couldn't stay angry with any of them, not even the ones he just didn't like. We're one unit, one damned dangerous weapon, and we're better at this than anyone else in the world. You want to be a bastard, be a bastard to the enemy.

There had been little sleep the night before, the veterans kept awake by the drone of the C-47s, four dozen planes, stuffed with the men of the 504th. There was a strange emptiness to that, watching another regiment lift away, while you lay comfortable on your blanket. They probably felt the same way about us, he thought, watching us take off at Kairouan. None of them had had any idea what the hell we were gonna do on Sicily, how many of us wouldn't come back. And then they flew into hell on earth, shot to pieces by our own guys. Rabid stupidity. Hell of a way to die. That wouldn't sit well with Mama.

He heard a vehicle, stepped out away from the grove, saw the dust cloud following the jeep. It rolled closer, stopped, and he saw Scofield, was surprised to see Colonel Gavin. Adams straightened, reflex, saluted, the officers moving toward him.

Scofield said, "Sergeant Adams, see to your platoon. We've gotten our orders. We jump tonight."

Gavin walked past him, moved into the trees, the men responding, short, clipped greetings.

"Sir!"

"Colonel!"

Adams watched Gavin move through the men, the colonel seeming to inspect them, grading them.

After a moment, Gavin said, "How many of you jumped here in July?"

Adams held up his hand, saw the others, more than forty out of the fifty men in the platoon.

"Good. Damned good. General Clark's boys are in a hell of a pickle over on that beach. They're counting on us to hold the line against the enemy. The Five-oh-four's had a rough go of it today, but we'll be dropping right beside them. By tomorrow morning, the Krauts are in for a surprise."

He turned toward the jeep, stopped. "You boys have cause to use the bazookas last time out?"

Adams said, "Yes, sir. Some of us were at Piano Lupo, sir."

Gavin looked at him. "I know where you were, Sergeant. You fire a bazooka yourself?"

"No, sir. But the captain and I were with a couple antitank crews. They took out a pair of panzers before . . . they got hit."

Gavin seemed to recognize him, studied him for a moment. "You were with Colonel Gorham."

"Yes, sir."

Gavin turned toward the others. "Hell of a thing. We could use a lot more men like Art Gorham." Gavin motioned toward Scofield now. "Captain, read the men that bulletin we just got."

"Yes, sir. Right here. 'From War Department G-2. Intelligence has gathered information indicating that the bazooka now in use by our troops is inadequate to penetrate the frontal armor of the German Tiger tank.' "

Gavin looked at Adams. "Quite a revelation, eh, Sergeant? Army Intelligence has speculated that if you want to destroy the enemy armor, you shouldn't do it from in front."

"Yes, sir. I was informed of that, sir."

"When?"

"At Piano Lupo, sir. Two months ago. The antitank crews knew to hit them from the flank."

Gavin looked at him, hard eyes, seemed to measure him. Adams straightened, thought, all right, shut up. He doesn't need to hear what a smart mouth you have.

Gavin held the stare for a long moment, then turned away, said, "Next, they'll be telling us that they think C-47s might be too slow to avoid antiaircraft fire. Whole offices full of these geniuses who actually think they're soldiers. All right, get ready to roll, gentlemen. We have a job to do. Captain, let's get moving."

Gavin and Scofield climbed into the jeep, moved away quickly, more jeeps appearing, officers moving out among their troops. Adams bent low, gathered his knapsack, knelt down, tightened the laces on his boots. He tapped the empty pockets on his baggy pants, knew that the ammo and grenades were already being spread out near the planes. He glanced at Unger, thought, he can't be eighteen. Sixteen, if that. Forged his papers, sure as hell. He doesn't even shave yet.

"Unger!"

"Yeah, Sarge?"

"You know what a Kraut is?"

"Yeah, Sarge."

"What are you going to do when you see one?"

"I'm gonna blow him to heck, Sarge."

Adams glanced at the others, saw the smiles. Yep. War is heck.

The flight was smooth, none of the gut-twisting turbulence of their first flight to Sicily. Adams could see the beach, hints of white caught by the moonlight, a wide spit of land, what the maps showed to be a long peninsula. The drop zone was just beyond, the officers assuring the men that the pathfinders would be there first, lighting the way with a fiery signal, a *T* that would easily be visible to any pilot in the area. Adams leaned back against his parachute, thought, if I was a Kraut artilleryman and I saw a damned fire lit with enemy planes overhead, I'm guessing that fire would make a pretty easy target. Who the hell thought that was a good idea? He looked down the row across from him, saw Gavin, couldn't see his eyes, wondered if he was sleeping. He hadn't expected to be in Gavin's stick, had boarded the plane expecting to see Scofield, the usual routine. But Scofield was behind them, the next plane in the formation, and Adams was curious about that, wondered if it was simply luck, or if there was some reason why Gavin had boarded his plane.

He had begun to feel more than simple respect for Gavin, more than the sergeant's allegiance to a commanding officer. The senior brass always had some sort of strange aura, much of it manufactured by the officers themselves, the men who portrayed themselves as something larger-than-life. The soldiers had little use for that, learned quickly to measure a man by what he could do under fire, not how good he looked on the parade ground. Adams had sensed none of that with Colonel Gorham, certainly, the man's death seeming to affect everyone, including Gavin. Adams wished he had known Gorham more than a couple of days, had to wonder about any man who would give his own life trying to duel with a tank. Adams sensed the same about Gavin, the aura of a different kind, authority and respect inspired by a man who seemed to know what it was to stare at the point of a bayonet. Gavin was far too young to have fought in the first war, had none of that vacant stare that Adams had seen in the old veterans. There had always been officers who tried to act like the soldiers they commanded, a counterfeit act to show that they were a buddy. That rarely worked, most of the soldiers not interested in being *pals* with any officer. No matter how much the men griped about officers, when the fight started, every soldier wanted a man *in charge,* a loud voice to cut through the deadly confusion. The noise from the loudmouths, the men like Private Newley, couldn't cover up every man's silent fear. It wasn't just the enemy, the bullets. Every man carried that sliver of doubt, wondered if he had the guts, if he might run, if he would get his own men killed because he fell apart.

That was the officer's job, to rip that doubt away, to pull the men away from their own thoughts and send them forward as a single weapon, a perfect fist. Not every lieutenant could be an inspiration. But Adams felt that strange ingredient in Gavin, as he had for Scofield. It was instinctive, perfect confidence that if they jumped into a bloody awful mess, Gavin was the man you wanted giving the orders, the man who could keep you alive.

The plane began to lose altitude, and he snapped awake, stared at the dark place near the open doorway. After a long moment, the red light erupted, the men reacting with a sharp motion, low grunts. The flight had been shorter than most expected, nothing like the tortuous route they had taken to Sicily. They stood immediately, and Adams hooked his chute to the wire overhead, went through the routine once more. Gavin was at the door, would be the first man out, and Adams stood three men away from him, saw the colonel staring out, heard a loud curse.

"Nothing! Damn them!"

Gavin glanced toward the front of the plane, toward the pilots, and Adams watched him, the man's face bathed in red light, hard fury, Gavin's hand slapping the edge of the doorway. Adams felt a chill, thought, something's wrong. Are we lost? Not again! Can't anybody get this right? What the hell we supposed to do . . .

The light turned green.

Gavin was quickly gone, the men following close behind. Adams did not hesitate, put his hands outside on the plane's skin, tucked his chin tight, faced forward, was out, falling, wind pulling him. He braced himself, the chute pulled open, the straps now jerking him from below. He could see the first chutes below him, drifting slowly, and he stared at the ground, tried to see shapes, saw nothing, black emptiness. He searched frantically, any sign of what they were jumping toward, brush or trees, deadly obstacles. Gavin's curse was still in his mind, a flicker of fear, and suddenly a bright light was beneath him, a strange orange light, the shape of a *T. Fire*. He blinked away the light, was blinded now, braced himself again, knew it was close, the last seconds, tightened his knees together, his toes down, thought of the pathfinders below, lighting the fire, idiots, too late to do them any good, the pilots finding the zone anyway. Damn. Good job.

By morning, Gavin's twenty-one hundred men had formed a line alongside the men of the 504th, adding considerable strength to the American position, and sealing a major portion of the gap that threatened the entire front. Though the Germans pushed forward once more, their commanders realized that their greatest opportunity had passed, that the Americans would not simply be driven into the sea. Rather than continue a costly assault, the Germans began to pull away, strengthening their positions to the north and east.

In the south, Montgomery's troops had advanced up the "toe" of Italy with virtually no opposition, and British forces had landed at the "arch" and "heel" of the boot as well. The Germans responded as expected, Kesselring showing that he did not want a broad confrontation with the Eighth Army. Instead, the Germans gathered their strength, spreading troops across the Italian peninsula along natural defensive terrain, making good use of the rivers and mountain ranges. Though Clark's Operation Avalanche had finally succeeded, the risk had been extraordinary, the contest far too close for Eisenhower to accept. Blame immediately fell on Ernest Dawley, who had relied too heavily on his untested troops. Dawley's misfortune was that he shared the same enthusiastic confidence of many American commanders. To Eisenhower's dismay, Dawley's assumption that his troops could sweep aside anything they encountered had nearly resulted in an Allied catastrophe. Within days after the victory at Salerno, Ernest Dawley was relieved of his command.

As the Allies expanded their strongholds along the coast, the 505th was shifted toward the Italian town of Amalfi, marched out to the high ground that overlooked the Sorrento Peninsula, which gave the paratroopers an astounding panoramic view of the city of Naples. For two weeks, the Allied troops had numerous firefights, each side testing the other's strength, but the Germans continued to pull away just enough to avoid a full-scale confrontation. As Gavin's men pressed forward, they were attached to a British mechanized unit, allowing them greater mobility as they shifted positions to meet the enemy's movements. With Naples as the ultimate goal, Gavin had finally been ordered to move his men off the heights, the paratroopers expecting to battle their way into the city. On the morning of October 1, after a brief stand, German resistance simply melted away. Jim Gavin and the men of the 505th marched into Naples virtually without a fight.

The Allied forces continued their pressure against the Germans, and the 505th advanced out to the east of the city, support for British and American infantry units who continued to seek some way to outmaneuver the German defenses. But Kesselring's withdrawal had been carefully organized, the Germans giving ground reluctantly, allowing them time to fortify a strong defensive position in their rear. Clark's forces continued their slow progress along the coast, and Montgomery's troops were surging northward in the center and along the east coast of the Italian boot. But Kesselring's plan had now become apparent. The Germans had anchored themselves in the rugged terrain along the Volturno River, and farther east, German infantry and panzer units had made effective use of the gift the rugged Apennine Mountains provided them. Any major confrontation now would come at a place of Kesselring's choosing.

NAPLES—OCTOBER 5, 1943

The order had come from Captain Scofield, the men sent off the road to rest in a grove of lemon trees. Adams was surrounded by them now, twisted, gnarled branches, protected by enormous thorns. They were similar to the olive trees, ancient and twisted, but the fruit was strange, enormous yellow globes that looked more like melons. He had already suffered through the stupidity of the experiments, so many of the men obsessed with tasting this absurdly freakish fruit, no resemblance to anyone's idea of what a normal lemon should look like. As Adams expected, the lemons were bitter and stunningly sour, the men quickly convinced that no Italian could possibly know what good lemonade was supposed to taste like.

He looked for a place to rest his back, avoided the thorns beside him, laid the Thompson across his legs. He saw Scofield up on the road, the captain spotting him, turning toward him. Scofield sat, pulled out a tin of crackers, held it out toward Adams.

"No, thank you, sir. I had a tin of stew."

"Better than these, that's for certain."

Scofield drank from his canteen, and Adams waited, sensed there was something more to the captain's choice of where to sit.

"We have new orders, sir?"

Scofield lowered the canteen, looked at him, then away, pointed to the white road. "Romans built these roads, you know. Probably cultivated lemons in this same field. Lot of history in this place. Every time we blow some building to hell, I wonder how long it had been there. Same way on Sicily. The Romans built these roads to move their troops, keep control of their empire. We're marching in their footsteps, Sergeant. Somehow I think they'd appreciate that."

"Yes, sir. I suppose they would."

"Even the tanks don't tear them up. Some of our road builders back home could take some lessons."

"Yes, sir."

Scofield poked at the crackers. "I'm going to hate to lose you, Sergeant. Nobody gets these boys into shape like you do."

Adams sat up straight. "Lose me where?"

Scofield ate another cracker, and Adams saw a brief smile.

"What's going on, sir?"

Scofield tossed the empty tin aside, unscrewed the top from his canteen. He took another drink, replaced the lid, and Adams could see he was enjoying himself.

"Sir . . ."

"Sergeant Adams, Colonel Gavin has been relieved of duty with the Five-oh-five."

"What?"

"Relax, Sergeant. General Ridgway has recommended him for promotion to brigadier general. He's to become Ridgway's second-in-command of the entire division."

"Damn! We're losing the colonel?" Adams was suddenly angry, held his words, saw the slight smile on Scofield's face. "I don't get it, sir. This is terrible news. I mean, it's good for the colonel, but nobody is going to be happy about this."

The jeep came past now, slid to a halt, and Adams saw the driver searching the faces.

Scofield stood, waved. "Here!"

The driver climbed out, moved into the grove. "Captain, I'm looking for—"

"Yes, I know, Corporal. This is Sergeant Adams."

The corporal was older, surprisingly, the face of a veteran. He scanned Adams, appraising, a slight frown. "Sergeant, I've been ordered to fetch you, bring you to Colonel Gavin's command post." He stood back, held out a hand. "After you, Sergeant."

Adams was baffled, looked at Scofield, at the faces of the men gathering, as curious as he was. Adams was growing nervous now. "What's going on, Captain?"

"Orders, Sergeant. Go with the corporal."

Adams stood, hoisted the Thompson onto his shoulder. He looked toward the men, no smiles, one low voice.

"The sarge in trouble? What's he done?"

Scofield held out a hand, and Adams hesitated, realized what the captain was doing. He took the man's hand, felt a hard grip, a firm handshake, and Scofield said, "You take care of yourself, Sergeant."

Adams felt a wave of cold spreading through him, his mind forming a protest, no, I'm not going anywhere.

"You sending me home, sir? Why?"

"Home? Hell no, Sergeant. You've still got some work to do."

505TH PARACHUTE INFANTRY REGIMENT,
MOBILE COMMAND POST—OCTOBER 5, 1943

"Sit down, Sergeant."

Adams obeyed, the chill still rolling through him, his hands shaking. He said nothing, watched as Gavin spoke to an aide, the man disappearing out the door. Gavin turned toward him now, and Adams was squirming, felt uncomfortable, thought, you should be standing up. Nobody sits in front of a damned general.

Gavin pointed to him. "Cigarette?"

"No, sir. Thank you."

"You're from the Southwest, right?"

"New Mexico, sir."

"Beautiful country. Wide-open spaces. Good place to grow up."

"Yes, sir."

"What you aiming to do when you get back home? You ranch? Farm?"

"It's mining country, sir. I may not go back, exactly."

"Mining? Can't blame you. I grew up in Pennsylvania, coal country. Couldn't get out of there fast enough. Looks like I found my spot. Expect I'll be in the army the rest of my life. You consider that?"

"No, sir. I should, I guess, sir. Not sure what I want to do."

Adams was swimming in questions, thought, what does he care? What the hell have I done? Gavin moved to a small table, and Adams looked around now, realized there were curtains on the windows, someone's home. Of course, you idiot. They wouldn't just build a house for us to use. Some Italian probably bitching like hell.

He focused again. "Sir? Begging your pardon, but I don't know what I'm doing here."

"You need to know that, Sergeant? You need all the answers?"

He realized now, there was meaning to the question. "No, sir. Absolutely not, sir."

"Good. Because you're not getting the answers just yet. You're here because I sent for you. I'm being pulled out of here. You hear about that?"

"Yes, sir. Captain Scofield said you were being promoted. Congratulations, sir."

"Stuff that crap. I screamed like hell when General Ridgway told me that. No, that's not quite right. You don't scream anything to Ridgway. But . . . turns out this promotion's not such a bad thing. There's more to it than just a rank. I'm pulling out of Italy. I can't talk about it in detail, but I've been given a new assignment, to be part of the planning for a new operation. And I'm taking you with me."

"*Me?* Excuse me, sir—"

"It's not open to discussion, Sergeant. I know all about you. I know how you handle the men, how you handle yourself under pressure. I told Ridgway that I thought it was wrong to take good combat soldiers out of combat, that we should be using men like you—and me—where we do the most good. That kind of argument doesn't wash in the army. As I said, this is all about the planning of a new operation. I need the best men with me, and you're one of them."

"Thank you, sir. I still don't get it. What kind of operation? Where are we going?"

"I told you, no questions. You got your gear?"

"Yes, sir. Right outside."

"You can leave your Thompson, your grenades. They'll find a good home. You won't be needing any of that for a while."

NOVEMBER 18, 1943

His uniform was clean, his hair cut, and he still wasn't sure if this were some sort of bizarre nightmare. He missed the Five-oh-five, Scofield, Unger, the rest of them, but there was no time for bellyaching. Gavin seemed to understand, and in between the long hours of work, Gavin had spoken to him of the missions and the memories. Adams had come to understand that Gavin had every intention of jumping out of airplanes again, that no matter this new duty, the new responsibility, all the administrative work, Gavin was no different from him. There was one difference, of course. Gavin was a brigadier general, and Adams had been impressed to learn that the promotion had made Jim Gavin the youngest general in the American army.

Within a few weeks, the secrets began to be revealed, Gavin passing along the first details of what Adams and Gavin's other staffers were about to begin. There were no dates, no specifics as to troop movements, targets, who or where the enemy might be. But every day the urgency seemed to grow, unmistakable preparations for Gavin to finally embark to the new headquarters of this new assignment.

With only days to go, Adams finally received word. He was going to England.

The flight had been agonizingly long, stops in Algiers and Marrakech. On the last leg, they had flown all night, the men stretched out on the floor of the heavy transport plane, seeking whatever sleep the frigid air would allow.

Adams had been awake for several hours now, far too nervous to sleep, sat on a bundle of mail, stared out the window of the crowded transport, had watched the sun rising over a far-distant coastline. He glanced at his watch, nearly noon. Well, maybe not here. Eleven, maybe. God knows. I should pay more attention to maps.

He looked down, the wing just in front of him, two of the plane's four big engines easing off slightly, the plane beginning to drop. A solid layer of clouds was below, the plane settling into the foggy whiteness, nothing to see. He stared downward, waited, thought, how bad can the weather be? Bad I guess. Always heard that, rains all the time.

The clouds were suddenly gone, the plane emerging beneath the soft gray layer. Land was beneath them, thick carpets of green, dotted by small towns. He pressed his face close to the frigid glass, studied the countryside, so different from the bleak landscapes of North Africa and Sicily. The plane continued to drop, and he felt his stomach tighten, the air in the plane still sharp and cold, not as cold as the ice in his chest. He was more nervous now than he had ever been on the C-47s, and even after weeks in Gavin's office, he still had the nagging fear, the uncertainty about what he was expected to do. It was still too strange, too different, the men around him too calm, and he thought, I'm not like them. What the hell am I doing here? I'm just a sergeant. I yell at idiot recruits and I jump out of airplanes. He thought of Gavin, several rows in front of him, thought, why do they need someone like you? Are we some important part of this new operation? Well, yeah, dammit, or we wouldn't be here. I have to write Mama. Nope, not yet. Can't tell her a damned thing. She wouldn't get it anyway. How the hell am I supposed to be a hero in England?

He looked out toward the green again, saw the airfield, knew it was Prestwick, Scotland. He looked toward Gavin again, thought, you promised me we'd jump again. If you're gonna take me away from my platoon, if I have to be on your staff for a while, all right. But when this Overlord happens, you better damned well send me out there toting a parachute.

AFTERWORD

Throughout November and December, Allied forces continue to push northward up the boot of Italy. Besides eliminating Italy from the war, and possibly gaining the use of Italian troops and equipment against the Germans, the invasion of Italy is also designed to tie down and possibly destroy a significant number of German troops, troops who might otherwise be available to resist the eventual invasion of France. The strategy works, but not in the way the Allies hope. German troops are indeed tied down, but there is no quick victory for the Allies. Instead of rapid success, Clark's Fifth Army confronts a stubborn enemy, and German forces put up a far more vigorous fight than expected. Predictions of the rapid capture of Rome are proven woefully optimistic. The city does not fall into Allied hands until June 4, 1944, two days before the launch of Operation Overlord. General Mark "Wayne" Clark is faulted for what seems to many to be his plodding advances and ineffective tactics, but credit must be given to the German commander, Albert Kesselring, and the tenacity of the men in his command, whose efficient use of Italy's natural defenses insures that the Allies suffer a far more costly and time-consuming struggle in Italy than anyone expects.

As planners in London and Washington focus greater attention toward the invasion of France, resources that could aid Clark's army in Italy are gradually stripped away. The command structure begins to change as well, particularly with the British. Though Harold Alexander remains in overall command of the ground forces in Italy, his primary subordinate, Bernard Montgomery, is ordered to London, joining Omar Bradley as one of the two principal ground commanders for Operation Overlord. But throughout the fall of 1943, there is still a vacuum at the top of the Overlord command. Word reaches Eisenhower that a consensus is building that the American chief of staff, George C. Marshall, is being touted as the best choice for the command. To Eisenhower's enormous disappointment, he learns that he and Marshall will, in effect, reverse roles. Once Marshall goes to England, Eisenhower will return to Washington and occupy Marshall's chair, becoming the chief of staff and the liaison between the War Department and Congress. Eisenhower has no enthusiasm for the job.

In late November 1943, President Franklin D. Roosevelt meets with Winston Churchill in Cairo. Though the meetings are geared toward discussions of strategies regarding Russia, the Middle East, and the Mediterranean theaters, Eisenhower learns that the decision to name Marshall to overall command of Overlord is not yet set in stone. Roosevelt tells him, "It is dangerous to monkey with a winning team." Less than one week later, Eisenhower receives a cable from Marshall, which eliminates all rumors. On December 10, 1943, Dwight D. Eisenhower is named supreme commander of the Allied Expeditionary Force, and effective January 1, 1944, he assumes command of Operation Overlord. Despite his uneasiness over Clark's progress in Italy, Eisenhower welcomes his new responsibility, and on New Year's Day 1944 he leaves North Africa.

Despite the ongoing struggles in Italy, vicious fights yet to be waged at Anzio and Monte Cassino, the Allies now put their greatest energy toward the invasion of France, which the planners have tentatively scheduled for May 1944. Allied commanders and their civilian leaders agree that if the war in Europe is to end, if Hitler is to be defeated, Operation Overlord cannot fail. On January 13, after a brief visit to the United States, Eisenhower reestablishes his headquarters in London and thus will begin the greatest buildup of troops and military equipment in history.

ERWIN ROMMEL

With Allied progress in Italy stymied by Kesselring's stout defenses, Rommel sits idly at Lake Garda in northern Italy with virtually nothing to do. Though Rommel expects Hitler to name him overall commander of the entire Italian theater, such a move would place Rommel over the head of his former superior Kesselring. Hitler and his staff, satisfied that Kesselring is handling his forces with admirable skill, ignore Rommel's wishes. Frustrated as always with inactivity, Rommel welcomes a new assignment, but feels he is once more being placed in a backwater of the war. On November 21, 1943, his Army Group B is ordered to relocate to France, and he moves his headquarters to a small town south of Paris. He is now under the command of sixty-eight-year-old Karl von Rundstedt, one of Germany's most capable and respected commanders. Rommel effectively becomes the unofficial inspector general of Germany's defenses along the west coast of France, known as Hitler's Atlantic Wall. Predictably, Rommel's aggressive personality clashes with that of the aging von Rundstedt, who, along with Hitler, dismisses predictions of an Allied invasion of the French coast.

GEORGE PATTON

To the dismay of the entire Allied command, Patton's "slapping incident" becomes public knowledge in the United States, when the event is revealed in detail by newspaper columnist Drew Pearson. The outcry is immediate and damning, especially from Roosevelt's enemies in Congress, and enormous effort is made in the War Department and in Eisenhower's command to deflect the well-publicized outrage, which could certainly end Patton's career. Patton accepts fully the responsibility for the tidal wave of negative sentiment, and in a series of well-documented appearances, he apologizes publicly to his troops. His contrition does much to blunt the calls for his dismissal, as does the unwavering support from both Marshall and Eisenhower, who understand Patton's value as a commander of troops in the field.

As Mark Clark's Fifth Army churns its way through Italy, Patton remains frustrated by what he sees as incompetence from yet another Allied commander. He believes with perfect certainty that the Italian campaign should have been his to lead.

As men and equipment are stripped away from the Mediterranean theater, Patton's Seventh Army is nearly denuded of troops. By the end of November, the Eighty-second Airborne and the Forty-fifth Infantry divisions are transferred to England, as part of the Overlord buildup. Faced with command over a nonexistent army, on November 17, 1943, he tells his diary,

I have seldom passed a more miserable day. From commanding 240,000 men, I now have less than five thousand.

On November 25, his mood reaches its darkest hour.

Thanksgiving Day. I had nothing to be thankful for, so I did not give thanks.

Despite Patton's gloom, both Eisenhower and Marshall know that Patton will not simply remain in Sicily. Though Eisenhower tells Marshall that Patton "thinks only in terms of attack" and that Patton's need for "showmanship" can prove costly, both men agree that Patton must have a significant role in Operation Overlord.

On January 25, 1944, after receiving his new orders, Patton gratefully departs for London. He is not yet fully aware that his new position will place him under the command of his former subordinate Omar Bradley.

JACK LOGAN

After his rescue from the prison camp in Bizerte, Tunisia, Logan spends more than a month on an American hospital ship in the Mediterranean, suffering from the wound on his leg, which stubbornly refuses to heal. Once he is released, he is transferred back to the tank center at Fort Knox, Kentucky. Promoted to sergeant, he serves as a trainer to new recruits and witnesses the army's intense campaign to modernize and improve tank design.

Logan makes considerable effort to determine what became of his crewmates after the tank battle at Sbeïtla, but neither their physical remains nor any record of their capture is ever found, and all the men, including Captain Roy Gregg, are permanently listed as missing in action. Though he intends to return to Tunisia, always believing that some documentation can be found, he never makes the journey. It is a cross he bears for the rest of his life.

With the war's conclusion, he is discharged from the army and returns to his family home in St. Petersburg, Florida. He serves that city briefly as a police officer, but cannot ignore his love of the waters that surround his home. In 1955 he buys a fishing boat and becomes a commercial fisherman, a career that sustains him until his death in 2004 at age eighty-six. Though friends know he served in the war, he almost never speaks of his experiences, refers to himself simply as "a veteran." He claims never to have married, but his funeral is attended by several elderly women, who offer no explanation for their presence.

HAROLD ALEXANDER

He remains in overall command of the Allied forces in Italy until the capture of Rome, in June 1944. Promoted to field marshal, he is named supreme Allied commander in the Mediterranean in December 1944 and occupies that post until the end of the war. He is the senior Allied commander to receive Germany's final surrender in Italy, in April 1945.

After the war, Alexander becomes the last British governor-general of Canada, and in 1952 he is granted the title of First Earl of Tunis. He retires from government service in 1954, after a dismal turn as Churchill's minister of defense.

He pens his memoirs, a book widely dismissed as inaccurate and self-serving, and yet remains a popular public figure in England until his death in 1969, at age seventy-eight. Always regarded as an extremely capable administrator, his career is nonetheless marked by criticism of his inability to confront and control those subordinates whose personalities dominate his own. Most notable among these is Bernard Montgomery.

CLAUDE AUCHINLECK

One of Britain's most capable commanders, Auchinleck never receives credit for the groundwork laid in North Africa, which provided much of the foundation for Montgomery's enormous victory over Rommel at El Alamein. Betrayed often by the hes-

itation or outright incompetence of his subordinates, Auchinleck is blamed by Churchill for the loss of Tobruk, and he accepts the responsibility for the failures of his command with
predictable dignity. Often ignored is that both his replacement,
Harold Alexander, and his primary subordinate, Bernard Montgomery, adopt the identical strategy that Auchinleck had already proposed to confront Rommel.

In a gesture designed to save face for Auchinleck, Churchill
offers him command of British forces in Persia, but Auchinleck
refuses, and after nearly twelve months of inactivity, he is
named commander in chief of Allied forces in India, a post he
had previously held. He serves there under Lord Louis Mountbatten, who commands the entire South East Asia Theater. The
two men clash repeatedly, and after the war, their conflicts continue, primarily over differences in the handling of the boiling
political turmoil in India. Ultimately, Mountbatten prevails, and
in 1947, at Mountbatten's insistence, Auchinleck resigns his
command.

Never one to champion his own accomplishments, he returns
to London to life as a private citizen, becomes active in various
civil causes, including the London Federation of Boys' Clubs.
He displays surprising talent as an artist, and despite intense
commercial interest in his paintings, he never pursues his art as
anything more than a hobby. He dismisses his own talents and
claims that interest in his paintings comes about only because
"you don't expect field marshals to paint."

In 1967, Auchinleck surprises his friends by moving to Marrakech, Morocco, which he believes will offer him, at eighty-
two, a climate more suitable to his ailments, though he remains
in excellent health. He dies there in 1981, at age ninety-six.

ANDREW CUNNINGHAM

Once the Italian government negotiates its surrender with
Eisenhower, the Italian navy accepts the terms as well, and in
September 1943 the fleet escapes potential capture by the Germans by fleeing to the British base at Malta. Credited with that
success, the aging Admiral Cunningham has the final word in
engineering Allied control of the Mediterranean Sea.

In October 1943, after nearly forty years' service in that theater, Cunningham is named first sea lord, the highest-ranking naval office in the British military. He serves as Churchill's chief naval adviser throughout the remainder of the war, though he often clashes with the fiery prime minister, who as a former sea lord himself often intrudes into Cunningham's areas of responsibility.

He resigns the position in 1946, believing his service to the Crown is over. He is not quite correct; in 1950 he is appointed lord high commissioner to the General Assembly of the Church of Scotland.

In the mid-1950s, he writes his memoirs, an extremely popular account of his life at sea. Widely regarded as one of Britain's most accomplished and able seamen, he dies in London in 1963, at age eighty. He is, of course, buried at sea.

ALBERT KESSELRING

The man known derisively as Smiling Al continues to prove that his optimism over the capabilities of his troops is completely warranted. Though Kesselring's strategy in Italy contradicts what both Hitler and Rommel consider the wisest use of troops, Kesselring proves that Hitler's decision to stand by him is of enormous benefit to the German cause. Throughout the Normandy invasion, Kesselring remains in Italy, and in mid-1944, after the fall of Rome, he continues to withdraw German forces northward with bloody stubbornness.

In March 1945, Kesselring replaces Karl von Rundstedt as Hitler's highest-ranking field commander in Western Europe. As Germany collapses under the weight of Allied and Russian armies, Kesselring, alongside Admiral Karl Dönitz, maintains command of the last-gasp efforts of German forces. He is captured in May 1945 and charged by a British court with war crimes against Italian civilians, but is spared execution, instead receives a sentence of life in prison. His health begins to fail, and since he is never linked to the atrocities committed by the Nazis, the British release him from prison in 1952. Shortly after, he completes his memoirs, which are published a year later. He dies in 1960, in Bad Nauheim, Germany, at age seventy-five.

MARK "WAYNE" CLARK

Often blamed for prolonging the war in Italy by his plodding and ineffective operations, Clark is nonetheless praised by Eisenhower and Marshall as one of the Americans' most capable commanders. Though the capture of Rome seems to be a logical and successful conclusion to the Italian campaign, Clark insists on pursuing the German forces northward and thus insures that the costly fight will continue into 1945.

In December 1944 he replaces Harold Alexander as commander of the Fifteenth Army Group, and in March 1945 while still battling German forces in northern Italy, he is promoted to full general. At age forty-eight, he is the youngest four-star general in the American army.

After Germany's surrender, Clark commands American troops in Austria, where his no-nonsense diplomatic style puts him in constant conflict with his Soviet counterparts. In 1946, he transfers to London, where he continues to haggle over issues related to Austrian sovereignty and the Allies' efforts to deal with the collapse of that country's economy.

In 1947, he returns to the United States, settles in San Francisco as the commander of the American Sixth Army. He is nominated by President Truman as the first U.S. ambassador to the Vatican, but there are boisterous objections. The Italian campaign had resulted in the destruction of many Italian landmarks, including the complete obliteration of the monastery at Monte Cassino, which presumably, Clark had ordered. Whether or not he can be held culpable, the protests by Catholics in both the United States and Italy force Truman to withdraw the appointment.

In 1950, his memoirs are published, which provide a no-holds-barred examination of his life as a soldier, though of course he justifies his actions in every instance, a lightly veiled reaction to his many critics.

Two years later, Clark is named UN supreme commander in Korea, replacing General Matthew Ridgway. Clark oversees the peace talks at Panmunjom and succeeds both militarily and diplomatically in breaking the deadlock, which ultimately brings that war to a conclusion.

In 1954, Clark is named president of the Citadel, in Charleston, South Carolina, a position he occupies until 1965. He remains active after his retirement, serving as a popular and well-respected president emeritus of that institution. He dies in Charleston in 1984, at age eighty-seven, and is buried at the Citadel.

ROBERT MURPHY

The man responsible for much of the political labor between the Americans and the French in North Africa is rarely given credit for what he accomplishes in that post. Eisenhower recognizes that Murphy's efforts allow a far more peaceful occupation of Morocco and Algeria than the army could have accomplished with force alone. Murphy is faulted by some in the State Department for being a champion of both Henri Giraud and Jean Darlan and is often dismissed by his peers in the diplomatic community, especially the British, who consider him only to be Eisenhower's minion. It is an unfair criticism.

He continues to assist Eisenhower with the diplomatic delicacy required in North Africa and, in late 1943, is instrumental in engineering the surrender of Italy.

As Charles de Gaulle gains influence in North Africa, Murphy requests a transfer to another post, a gracious admission that he simply cannot handle de Gaulle.

After the war, Murphy assists Eisenhower once more, this time by helping to establish an Allied administrative government in occupied Germany. In 1952, he becomes U.S. ambassador to Japan, the first man to hold that post after the conclusion of the war. But Washington recalls him a year later, the State Department recognizing that his skills can be used to assist in the growth of the fledgling United Nations.

He retires in 1959, turns down an appointment as ambassador to Germany, believes that the energy required for diplomatic tap dancing is best found in younger men. He publishes his memoirs in 1964 and occasionally serves as a diplomatic adviser to

Presidents Kennedy, Johnson, and Nixon. Murphy enjoys a comfortable retirement in New York City and dies in 1978 at age eighty-four.

PAUL TIBBETS

The pilot of the B-17 *Red Gremlin,* who so often flies Eisenhower and Clark through the treacherous skies between London and the Mediterranean, does not remain in that theater of the war past 1943. Though Tibbets has proven to be an accomplished bomber pilot in numerous combat missions over Europe and North Africa, he receives a radically different assignment. Promoted to colonel, he is transferred to Wendover Field in Utah, where Tibbets begins to train as a pilot in the far-larger B-29 bombers. In spring 1945, Tibbets is transferred to the island of Tinian, in the western Pacific. He participates in several bombing runs on the Japanese mainland, and on August 6, 1945, he is the primary officer on one mission that will change history. He pilots the B-29 *Enola Gay,* which drops the atomic bomb on Hiroshima.

AND,

GENERAL DWIGHT D. EISENHOWER; GENERAL OMAR BRADLEY; SERGEANT JESSE ADAMS; CAPTAIN EDWIN SCOFIELD; GENERAL JAMES GAVIN; GENERAL BERNARD MONTGOMERY.

These men, as well as Patton, Rommel, and many others, will combine to create the most vivid historical event in the twentieth century. In June 1944, the world will wait breathlessly as the Allies launch the largest and most powerful military invasion in history. But that's a story all its own.

Read on for a sneak peek of

THE STEEL WAVE

JEFF SHAARA

The air underwater was foul and wet, five men pulling against the thinning oxygen. He sat erect, his back painfully pressed against a coil of wire, part of the electrical system of the craft. She was an X-5 class midget submarine, designed to deliver a magnetic mine or similar explosive device, something to be attached to the bottom of an enemy ship. They were stealthy, of course, no blip on anyone's radar screen, so the British navy had used them on raids all along the coastline, from Norway to the Mediterranean, usually with enormous risk to both the subs and their small crews. But tonight the sub was not armed, and where explosives had once been stored she now carried three passengers and their equipment.

He tried to stretch his back—no room—and twisted his shoulders instead, working out the kinks. The air was growing worse, thin and acrid, bitter smells of oil and wet cloth. There were no dry places in the small sub, every surface had a slick coating of oily grease or water, mostly condensation. The engine made a low hum, deadened by the steel of the bulkhead, the sub lurching slowly from side to side, held now by long low waves that rolled silently toward the beaches.

"Suit up, lads."

The voice was low, a croak from the lieutenant. He knew the order was coming, yanked hard at his small duffel bag, and retrieved it from the tight gap beneath his feet. Inside were all the tools he would need for the mission. The first priority was unrolling the tight spool of the rubber suit, a single piece, zipped open down the front. There was little room to stand, and he fought to slide the thin rubber over his legs, working his feet downward, pushing. He slid the suit beneath his bottom, pushed his arms into the narrow sleeves, freed his fingers, gave one loud grunt, and pulled the suit up over his shoulders. The others were grunting as he was, straining in the tight space, backs and arms bent low, each man forcing himself into his taut suit. He tried to relax, leaning back against the bulkhead, and took a breath, sour air filling his mouth, took another, felt his chest heave in a futile gasp. He was sweating, worse inside the suit, and the air was growing fouler still. No matter how the air cleaners strained, they were not designed to handle the nervous breathing of five men.

He leaned forward again, pulled the zipper tight against his neck, then tugged at the headpiece, sliding it over his ears, snug, only his face revealed. He reached again into the bag, found a small tube of grease, black and oily, squeezed a thick stream onto his fingers, and rubbed it on his face, coating any part that would reflect moonlight. The duffel was nearly empty now, but he found his knife, his only weapon, and strapped it to his leg, tight and secure, then went into the bag again for a small bundle, a cloth pouch attached to a thin belt, and slid it around his waist. The man beside him gave him a nudge with his elbow.

"All set here. You all right, Dundee?"

"Yep. You tight in? Ready?"

The man slapped his hands on Dundee's leg. "Ready as I'll ever be."

Dundee leaned forward, looked past, and said to the third man, "Lieutenant? You set, then?"

The lieutenant scanned both men. Dundee could see his face sweating, a dull wet mask, lit by the yellow glow from the sub's instrument panel. Then the officer began to smear his face with the black grease.

"Don't concern yourselves with me. My job is to worry about you. And right now I'm ready to get this little show moving."

From the main control seat, the sub's commander turned around toward them.

"We'll be on the surface in half a minute. On my command, Mr. Higgins will open the hatch, and out you go. Make it quick. I'll not chance there's some Jerry lookout who's good at his job. This tub won't take pleasantly to incoming fire, and the sooner I can drop us out of sight, the better I like it." He looked at his watch. "Orders say two hours. I'll wait for three if I have to, but that's it. I'm not about to sit out here and wait for the damned sun to come up. Sitting ducks, all of us. You got that?"

The lieutenant pointed at his own watch. "I know my orders, Captain. We'll be back in two hours. Don't go off sightseeing. You've got a periscope—keep an eye in it. I don't plan to tread water any more than I have to."

"I know my tub, Lieutenant. And we're lucky tonight. The surface is pretty smooth right now. A dicky bird swims within a hundred yards of me, I'll spot her. You just do the swimming; I'll see you."

Swimming. Dundee swallowed the word silently. Most of the commando operations were launched from surface crafts, LCNs, small and rugged navigation boats. The LCNs slipped in close to shore, depositing their commandos in folbots, folding canvas boats, flimsy canoes the men would paddle hard to the beach. But there was too much tide and too much current along this stretch of the French coastline, and a folbot might swamp and drown the men before they could even reach the shore. It was a painful lesson; several men had been lost already in earlier operations. Besides being a danger to her crew, a folbot had to be hidden from German patrols, patrols that were growing vigilant. And so, tonight, they would swim.

The captain turned toward his instruments and pulled a lever, the sub tilting upward, the bow rising. Dundee pushed his hands into the narrow metal seat, his back leaning hard against the tight coils, and tried to distract himself, thought suddenly of the captain's boast. What the hell is a dicky bird? The sub swayed, rolling to one side, then upright again, and Dundee's stomach rolled, the stink in the air filling his head with a dull pain, now growing worse. He heard the splashing of water against the bulkheads; the sub was level again, and the captain's lone crewman stood, his hands pressed upward against the narrow hatch, and stared forward toward his captain.

"On your order, sir."

"Steady, Higgins. Not quite on the deck. Wait for it."

They sat quietly, feeling the low hum of the engine and, now, silence, the captain shutting down the engine. Dundee took a long breath, tried to ignore the sickening smell, his head pounding, a quiver in his hands. He shook his head, thought, All right, Henry, hold on to yourself. They taught you this. It's all about lack of oxygen. We'll be out of this damned can in a few—

"Now, Higgins."

The crewman pulled hard on a round crank: The hatch was suddenly open, cold air filling the cabin, a splash of water. The lieutenant stood, hunched over by the overhead close above him, moved toward the hatch, slapped the captain on the shoulder, said nothing. Dundee waited for the man beside him, Henley, up and moving, the well-rehearsed routine, Dundee close behind him. The air was cold and delicious; a blast against Dundee's face and the headache had vanished. He pressed forward, following the other two toward the blessed opening, watched the lieutenant pull himself up through the hatch, now just his legs and then gone. Henley followed quickly, up and out of the way, and Dundee grabbed the edges of the hatch and pulled himself up, his head clear of the dismal space. He was outside now, in cold darkness, and he pulled his knees up between his arms, thrust out his feet, sat on the edge of the hatchway, the deck of the sub narrow and flat. The water was black and silent, long low swells. Now came the splashes, the other two already swimming, the lieutenant leading the way, long strokes of his arms, already distancing himself from the sub, Henley trailing behind him. Dundee looked out that way, saw the shoreline, a vast shadow against the night sky. The sub suddenly rocked, caught by a swell, and Dundee released his hands, slid down, let the motion of the sub push him away, pressed his feet against the steel hull, and gave one sharp push, his arms and legs working the water, the training taking over. He moved with precise rhythm, his face bathed by the cold. He was a strong swimmer, essential for this job, slicing quickly through the water, lifted by more swells, the cold gone now, the strength returning, the power taking over: so many miles of swimming and running, months of lifting and climbing, all condensed into these long moments.

His brain kept count of the number of strokes, an exercise that might have no meaning at all. But in the dark, they would make this swim again, and if the captain was wrong, if the waves picked up or the surface became choppy, at least the men could swim out to within yards of where they had left the sub. It had always seemed to be a foolish gamble, but here, in the black water, it might be the only chance they had to be picked up again.

His brain ticked past three hundred strokes, and he paused, raised his head, scanned the shoreline, fought for a glimpse of the others, but there was nothing to see, dull blackness, new sounds in his ears, surf, gentle waves rolling forward. He swam again, pushed out sharp breaths, felt aching in his arms, his legs growing stiff, his chest heaving with each breath. Something rose up in front of him, a thin black shape, a man, standing and then dropping down again, crouched low, one hand pointed toward him, a signal, more of the training. *Stand up.*

Dundee eased his legs downward, his feet stopping on hard sand. He was breathing heavily, felt giddy, stupid, thought of the lieutenant, the man's face invisible in the darkness, laughing at him. Every time, he thought, every damned swimming drill, so many times before. Every officer had teased him about it: Dundee, the man who swims until the sand bumps his chin. He knew what the lieutenant was thinking, had heard it too many times. Yes, you can stop swimming, you idiot. It's three feet deep.

The three men moved close together, and Dundee stared at the beach, a wide stretch of flat sand, saw a fence row, posts, odd, his brain trying to understand. Fences? The lieutenant moved away, low in the water, crawling, moving up onto the sand, seeming to ignore the others, and Dundee followed, feeling his way with his hands. They were clear of the shallow surf, and the lieutenant kept himself low, began to run, heavy deliberate steps. There were no orders now, the training so familiar, and the others followed automatically. Dundee felt the sand hard beneath his feet, his footsteps echoing in small thumps, shallow puddles. He passed one of the fence posts, glanced up, saw it tilting outward, toward the open water, a small round hat on top. He understood from the briefings, drawings they had seen. They're not fence posts. It's low tide, and they're shore obstacles. And the hat on top? It's a mine.

The sand began to slope upward, the men climbing, the sand softer, beyond the high-water line, and Dundee kept running, felt the strength in his legs, his breaths heavy and sharp. The lieutenant stopped and knelt low, ducking behind a long low mound of rocks, something else from the briefings, another landmark. Then he pulled a small bundle from the pouch around his own waist, and Dundee understood. It was the tape, the fluorescent stringer that would guide their return, the only way they would ever find their way back to this point on the beach. Dundee watched him unroll it and anchor one end in the sand with a small metal spike. The lieutenant seemed to pause. All three men were breathing heavily, and Dundee heard a whisper.

"Time to go to work, gents. Welcome to Omaha Beach."

They were one squad of the Combined Operations Assault Pilotage Party, a mouthful of description for the men who were sent ashore to find out just what the Allies might be facing on the beaches that had been designated for Operation Overlord. The training had begun months before at the enormous facility at Achnacarry, Scotland. Nearly every commando unit in the British army had received training at Achnacarry, and the Americans had gone as well, Darby's Rangers, men who had already been through the bloodiest days of the fights in the Mediterranean. Many of the commandos had been designated to make armed raids, landing in

fleets of rubber rafts, attacking the enemy's seaside installa-
tions, ammo and supply dumps. Some of the raids were
launched against various ports, other midget submarines
slipping into the harbors to target German ships. Few of the
raids had been terribly successful, and many of the Royal
Navy's higher-ups considered the midget subs a dangerous
waste of machines and good men. The X-5 class midgets had
no defenses and could barely escape the enemy's spotter
planes and fast-moving E-boats, but in the dark the subs
could bring their commandos close to the shore, close
enough for the folbots and, tonight, close enough for the men
to swim.

Their mission was absurdly simple: Gather samples of the
sand and rock on Omaha Beach. The beach itself was cut by
four draws, deep ravines, passageways that led inland, dividing the high bluff into sections that the mapmakers had designated by various code names. But those ravines interested
not just the infantry commanders but the engineers as well.
Over the centuries, streams and floodwater had flowed into
the sea, and with it had come tons of silt. If that silt was too
soft to support the weight of trucks, tanks, and other armored
vehicles, an amphibious landing on Omaha Beach simply
wouldn't work. The entire motorized portion of the invasion
would grind to a halt, embedded in a mire that would make
them stationary targets for the German artillery above.

The engineers had another concern as well, so more commandos had gone ashore on other nights with other objectives. Behind the bluffs, around the seaside villages of
Colleville-sur-Mer and Saint-Laurent-sur-Mer, the land was
rich in history, a countryside once occupied by the Romans.
But the Romans had left a mystery and, possibly, a deadly
problem. The land along the Normandy coastline had often
been used to farm and gather peat, thick layers of sod used
for fuel and building material. The question had to be answered: Had the two-thousand-year-old peat bogs
become vast pits of soft mud? For now, though, that wasn't
Dundee's problem. His problem was keeping up with his
lieutenant.

On this night, Dundee's mission had much more to do with

engineering than combat, the men armed only with their knives, since any weapons fire was certain suicide. On the bluffs high above what the planners had named Omaha Beach, German gun emplacements, artillery pillboxes, and machine-gun nests covered the open sands below in what would certainly be interlocking fields of fire. Among the various outposts, German infantry had also been positioned, the Allied aerial reconnaissance showing miles of trench works. Any lookout who heard movement on the beach would know to fire a star shell or a Very light, which would bathe the beach in the glow of man-made sunshine for deadly seconds. As much as Dundee felt the itch to have his pistol handy, tonight there could be no firefight. Just do the job and then find that precious line of tape and make your way back into the surf, all the while praying the midget sub's captain could find you in the black water.

They moved across the sand in total silence, even the gentle surf too far away. Dundee knew the timetable, the tide expected to rise well before dawn, but to a level he found hard to believe. The training taught them that the tide here rose eight feet or more, and in a few short hours, the flat plain of hard sand they had run across would be completely submerged. The high tide would provide a fatal disguise, submerging the posts, the steel girders and wooden poles capped by the mines. As the tide came in, the distance they had to swim would lengthen by hundreds of yards. But it would be far worse to make that swim over and around the hidden obstacles. There was danger enough from the enemy lookouts, without risking a single kick of the leg that could blow you to pieces.

He followed the shadows, the lieutenant leading the way, Henley between them. The ground above them seemed to fall away, a deep cut opening up in the hillside, a wide draw: their objective. Dundee was counting to himself, more training, each step forward ticking off how far they had come, and as the lieutenant stopped, Dundee's mind locked on the number of steps: *Two hundred eighty-six.*

They remained still. Dundee, staring at the dark form in front of him, thought, What is it? I don't hear anything. Sure as hell nobody out here tonight. We in the right place? Looks like the draw we're supposed to find, for sure.

And then he heard the voices.

The men moved along the rocky ledge, a few feet above the commandos, the sounds of footsteps on loose rock. Dundee took a long breath, put a hand slowly down, slid it along his leg, and touched the small leather strap that clamped around his knife. The men above them moved closer, low voices, now one man talking aloud, clear and sharp, the words bursting into Dundee's brain. He didn't know much German, only what the training had taught him: the right questions to ask if he was captured, the right responses to give. The loud German began to laugh, right above them, more steady footsteps, moving past. Dundee wrapped his fingers around the knife, stared ahead, fought the aching need to look up: *No, keep your face down.* He held his breathing in, soft and low, his brain focused on the sounds above and the feel of the knife in his hand. *Where the hell is my pistol?*

The Germans were past them now, the talk continuing, and now one voice rang out from above.

"Hauptmann Schlieben!"

The men stopped, one man close by responding to the call, more words flowing down from high up on the hill. Dundee listened to the words, his brain screaming at his own ignorance: Dammit, teach us German next time! What they hell are they saying? The Germans began to move quickly, away from the rocky wall, climbing, moving into the draw, their footsteps fading. And then they were gone.

He felt himself sag, released the grip on the knife, saw the lieutenant turn and sit down slowly in the sand; audible breathing. Dundee wanted to say something about his pistol: Who the hell thought of that? Send us in here without a bloody firearm? He knew the answer, of course. We're not here to kill Germans. And, we're expendable, after all. Part of the stinking job.

The lieutenant began to move again, pulled himself up,

grabbed Henley by the shoulder, pushed him away. Dundee knew the message: The time had come for the men to spread out, go to work. He felt for the pouch at his waist, the small zipper, felt inside, the cloth sack he was supposed to fill. Henley was scampering silently up the ravine, staying close to the left side. Dundee waited, and the lieutenant reached back, touched his shoulder. All right, sir. I got it.

He felt his way silently over the small rocky ledge, hard flat ground above it. He pushed out to the right, focusing on that side of the draw, his brain still counting steps. Won't get lost now. Those rocks behind me are what matters, just so I can find that damned tape. He thought of the Germans, moving up this same direction: Bloody swell, that is. One of them stops to drain a kidney, and I'll run right up his fanny. Of course, if they went this way, it means there's no booby traps, no mines. Keep a good thought, mate.

He glanced to the left, tried to see Henley, fought the urge—Nope, stay on course. He knows what to do. The ground was softer under his feet, and he stayed low, his knees beginning to ache, thought of crawling. Slowly, mate. It's here, don't break your damned neck. His eyes probed the dark, the lightness of the sand, and he saw now the wide yawning ditch, what the reconnaissance maps had shown to be a tank trap, a wide trench dug along the mouth of the ravine. He probed with his foot, slid down the side of the ditch, the bottom hard and wet, and climbed quickly up the other side, a spray of sand in his eyes. Dammit! He was up again, past the tank trap, and his brain began to count the steps, methodical, a steady rhythm, the orders matching the cadence of his steps.

Find . . . some . . . damned . . . rocks . . . small . . . ones. The count continued, the steps slowing, the hill growing more steep, his brain clicking off numbers: *One hundred.* He paused and took a long low breath. One hell of a mission: finding something for the engineers to play with. You'd think, if this place was full of rocks, that's all they'd want to know. Hell, you could see them from a damned plane. He thought of the briefing the night before, the colonel, those two engineers.

"We have to know what kind of rocks are on this beach, what kind of ground we will have to deal with in these draws."

So here I am. Bloody hell.

He saw movement out in the open center of the draw and froze, a cold shiver in his chest. The shape was hunched low, as he was, and he thought, It's the lieutenant, you stupid idiot. He's got the happy job after all, waltz right up the wide open middle of this damned ravine and scoop up a pail of dirt. Dundee moved forward again, his brain still counting: *Two hundred.* All right, time to do the job.

He pulled the cloth bag from the pouch, settled down on his knees, ran his hand across the ground. He felt a rock, smaller than his palm, let out a breath. Good, that's one. Eleven more, and we can go home. He stuffed the rock into the bag and reached out again, his hand sliding over the rough dirt. Another rock? No, hell, too large. Keep looking, mate. He crawled to his right, closer to the high wall of the draw, felt soft dirt with his hands. All right, now we're getting into it. He felt another rock, the size of an egg: Perfect, stick that one away. The ground was still soft, and his fingers pushed through, probing, and now he felt something hard, thought, No, too big . . . and then he froze. His brain snapped into focus, his breathing stopped. It wasn't a rock at all. It was steel and curved, buried slightly beneath the soft dirt. He knew the shape, had drilled and studied, and on one terrible day during training he had watched one blow off a man's legs. It was a land mine.

He pulled his hand away, felt his fingers twitching, his heart pouding. That's why the ground is so damned soft, you bloody moron. You're in a minefield. He looked to the side, saw no one, no motion, thought, *Two hundred steps.* That was the drill, where I'm supposed to be, and that's where I am. No one said anything about a minefield. But those damned Jerries came up here. . . . Well, hell, they knew the trail, even in the dark. Something about land mines makes you pay attention to that sort of thing. He backed away now, retraced his knee prints. The ground was harder, and he let out a breath, closed his eyes, thought, The lieutenant won't mind if I just . . . take a bit of a break. He felt the cold again, a breeze on his face, clenched his fist around the top of the cloth bag. A dozen. All right, mate, keep looking.

The bag began to fill, and Dundee raised up, searching, saw the shadow of the lieutenant again, the man huddled low, watching him. He began to back slowly down the flat draw, his mind locked on the number of rocks in the bag, and now his hand gripped one more, perfect and round. Bloody hell. That's twelve. He slipped silently toward the lieutenant, saw the man's hand come up, Yes, all right then. Slow it down. He thought of the timetable, how long has it been? Well, that's his job. Mine's done.

He was beside the officer now, heard the soft whisper.

"Bag full?"

"Yes, sir."

"Let's go, back down to the rocky ledge. Henley might be there already."

Dundee followed the lieutenant, both men crouched low, soft steps. They slipped down into the tank trap, then up again, and he could see the rock ledge, lining the shore, remembered the lecture, some geologist, so many years of pounding surf, the ocean spitting out these small bits, pressing them up on the sand. The lieutenant went over the ledge, dropped down, still silent, waited, Dundee doing the same. He felt his breathing again, relief, the bag of rocks heavy at his waist. Bloody engineers. Ought to keep one for myself, a souvenir.

Above them, up in the draw, there was a sudden flash of blinding light, the sharp echo of a blast. He looked up, over the rocks, saw nothing, heard a tumble of rocks, the low voice of the lieutenant.

"Land mine. Henley. *Son of a bitch.*"

And now, loud voices, up high, straight above them. Dundee felt a hard hand on his arm, steel grip, low voice:

"Go! Now!"

The lieutenant was up and moving, and Dundee followed, jelly in his legs, quick steps, realized he could see the tape. He stared down, ran in step with the lieutenant, his brain taking over, counting, one hundred, but the thoughts were swept

away now, no need to count, the tape visible even in darkness, some toy invented by some engineer, the stupid joke
from training: *Your line of bread crumbs.* His chest was
burning, hard breathing, and now there were shots, blasts of
machine-gun fire, arcing lights streaking over the beach. He
wanted to stop, to lie behind the cover of the rocky ledge, but
the lieutenant kept moving, and Dundee knew to follow,
could not forget the training. *Never stop.* The streaks of
tracer fire popped close overhead, a shattering of rock behind him, fire well out in front of them. His brain screamed
at him, They don't know where we are! Firing blind! Thank
God! The lieutenant suddenly turned, ran toward the water,
and Dundee saw now, the tape had ended. He followed, felt
the soft sand, gluelike on his feet, slowing him down. Behind
him, at the draw, men were calling out, the rattle of machine
guns filling the darkness, more tracers arcing into the open
water. The lieutenant was leaving him behind, a faster run-
ner, and Dundee focused on the man's back, lit by the tracers,
the sand harder, splashes of water. The water was up to his
knees now, and still they ran, louder splashes, water in his
face, the beach behind him suddenly bright with daylight,
the pop of a star shell. The lieutenant dove down, was gone,
and Dundee took a hard breath, couldn't hold it, gasped for
air, tried again, filled his lungs, felt the water at his waist. He
dove as well, streaks of light past his head, pops and splashes
of machine-gun fire, zips in the water. He could hear nothing
but his own swimming, gasped for breath, rolling over in the
water, a quick glance back, the flare extinguished. His feet
couldn't touch the bottom, and he began to swim again, his
arms and legs leaden, searing pain. He had forgotten to
count, vicious anger in his brain, stupid orders, useless. He
pushed himself through the water, ignored the burning, Find
the rhythm, one arm, turn, the other, steady kick. He couldn't
hear the machine guns, the sky black again, his shoulders on
fire, numbness in his legs, a quick look up, straight away
from the beach, Yes, keep going. Thank God for swimming.
No damned folbot, not tonight. We'd be staring at bayonets,
or worse.

He kept swimming, peered up every few seconds, felt

himself rise up on a swell, scanned the smooth surface, no sign of the lieutenant, dammit! What the hell do I do, swim to Dover? He looked back toward the beach again, saw a searchlight, the sound of a truck, Yep, you go right ahead, search that whole damned beach. He let his legs drop, treading water, thought of Henley, the man's big laugh, always a slap of the hand on your back. Swim, you idiot. He turned in the water, began to kick again, the motion steady, thought now of the submarine, where the hell are you? And now he heard a quick shout, raised his head up, a huge hulking mass. Oh, God! Thank God! He gulped a bellyful of salt water, pushed himself that way, his legs useless now, no strength at all, and there was a hand, grabbing his, pulling him clear of the water, the submarine already moving, submerging, and he dropped down, inside, the hatch closing above him.

He gasped for air, felt a lurch, the submarine rolling to one side, the captain at the controls, no words, the crewman close to Dundee, looking at his face.

"We ha'nt seen your mate! You sure he's not coming? Captain, ought'n we wait for him?"

"Can't do it, Mr. Higgins. All hell's opening up on that beach. They'll spot us in a flash."

Dundee realized now the lieutenant was lying on the narrow deck beside him. The officer rolled over, said, "No. Get moving. Henley's gone."

Dundee tried to sit, the sub tilting, rolling him forward, and he reached out, felt the lieutenant grab his hand.

"Thought you were gonna swim straight home, Dundee. You passed me like a damned fish."

He looked at the lieutenant's face, saw the man's head go down. Dundee, still gasping, spit salt water. "A land mine. There were minefields. It had to be. Henley . . ."

"Yeah. Never knew what hit him, most likely. A blessing in that. We were damned lucky to get out of there." The lieutenant looked down toward his own belt, raised the pouch. "Mission accomplished. Got what we came for. They'll test this sand, see what it can hold."

Dundee nodded slowly, tried to see Henley's face, gone

now, as though he never existed. The word came to him again, the word they all understood: *expendable.* He put his hand on his waist, felt for the pouch, the rocks. He pulled the pouch around in front of him, unfastened the strap, held it up. Mission accomplished. Those bloody engineers had better make some use of this. We lost a good man . . . for a bag of rocks.